Tom Bradby is a novelist, screenwriter and journalist. As a broadcaster, he is best known as the current Anchor of ITV's *News at Ten*.

He has been with ITN for almost thirty years and was successively Ireland Correspondent, Political Correspondent, Asia Correspondent (during which time he was shot and seriously injured whilst covering a riot in Jakarta), Royal Correspondent, UK Editor and Political Editor, before being made the Anchor of *News at Ten* in 2015.

Of his six previous novels, *The Master of Rain* was shortlisted for the Crime Writers Association Steel Dagger for Thriller of the Year, and both *The White Russian* and *The God of Chaos* for the CWA Historical Crime Novel of the Year. He adapted his first novel, *Shadow Dancer*, into a film directed by Oscar winner James Marsh.

www.penguin.co.uk

Praise for *SECRET SERVICE*:

'Teems with twists and the denouement is imaginative and unexpected.' *The Times*

'A gripping thriller.' *Sunday Times*

'Enthralling and fast-moving . . . packed with details of modern tradecraft in the twilight world of spooks, against a background of politics at its most Machiavellian, it is the stuff headlines are made of.' *Daily Mail*

'An excellent thriller straight out of today's headlines . . . a fast, riveting yarn.' *The Sun*

'Cracking, uber-topical spy thriller . . . Bradby deftly works in current fears of Moscow infiltrating our institutions amid a plot full of twists and turns.' *Financial Times*

'A strong dose of international politics with an all-too-plausible premise.' Jonathan Freedland, *Observer*

Praise for Tom Bradby:

SHADOW DANCER

'Quite exceptional . . . a taut, compelling story of love and torn loyalties.' *Daily Telegraph*

'A remarkable first novel . . . Bradby handles the tension with skill to produce a gripping tale.' *The Times*

THE SLEEP OF THE DEAD

'Elegant, spooky and a compulsive page-turner.' *Daily Mail*

'A race-against-the-clock thriller and a complex psychological drama.' *Irish Independent*

THE MASTER OF RAIN

'Rich, dark, atmospheric, this fine novel captures time and place perfectly. A great crime story that ends up in a place you won't predict.' Lee Child

'Nigh on impossible to put down . . . This intelligent thriller brings Shanghai to life as *Gorky Park* did for Moscow.' *Time Out*

THE WHITE RUSSIAN

'Unfailingly evocative . . . Reminiscent of *Gorky Park*.' *The Times*

'Intrigue of the highest order . . . sad, atmospheric and richly entertaining.' *Washington Post*

THE GOD OF CHAOS

'Bradby has the talent of a reporter but the heart of a storyteller.' *Daily Mail*

'The kind of historical fiction that may send you back to the real history books to learn more.' *Washington Post*

BLOOD MONEY

'The smoky romantic notion of speakeasies and Irish beat cops . . . is captured beautifully by Bradby's love of minute detail.' *News of the World*

'This feisty, pacey thriller by TV news reporter turned writer Tom Bradby has it all – nervy gangsters, crooked politicians, gutsy cops and a sexy moll. It is also blessed with excellent timing . . . A top-notch piece of crime writing.' Press Association

Also by Tom Bradby

Shadow Dancer
The Sleep of the Dead
The God of Chaos
The Master of Rain
The White Russian
Blood Money

Secret Service

and

Double Agent

Tom Bradby

CORGI BOOKS

TRANSWORLD PUBLISHERS
Penguin Random House, One Embassy Gardens,
8 Viaduct Gardens, London SW11 7BW
www.penguin.co.uk

Transworld is part of the Penguin Random House group of companies
whose addresses can be found at global.penguinrandomhouse.com

Secret Service first published in Great Britain in 2019 by Bantam Press
an imprint of Transworld Publishers
Corgi edition published 2019

Double Agent first published in Great Britain in 2020 by Bantam Press
an imprint of Transworld Publishers
Corgi edition published 2020

This Corgi edition of *Secret Service* and *Double Agent* published 2021

A CIP catalogue record for this book
is available from the British Library.

ISBN
9780552178969

Typeset by Jouve (UK), Milton Keynes.
Printed and bound in Great Britain by Clays Ltd, Elcograf S.p.A.

The authorized representative in the EEA is Penguin Random House Ireland,
Morrison Chambers, 32 Nassau Street, Dublin D02 YH68.

Secret Service

Tom Bradby

CORGI BOOKS

To Claudia, Jack, Louisa and Sam

Prologue

KATE HENDERSON GAZED through the windscreen at the steady drizzle and tried to hold back her increasingly familiar sense of dread. 'Stop it, Rav.' Her deputy was rhythmically tapping the steering-wheel, as he always did when he was bored or nervous or both.

'You're in a shit mood today,' he said.

'Thanks. That'll definitely help.'

The radio burst into life at the same time as the street in front of them.

'She's bolted,' a voice announced over the static, as Lena Savic raced past them, a vivid dash of colour in the drab London day.

'Fuck,' Rav muttered. He and Kate each grabbed a door handle and sprang out of the car.

Lena wove her way through the Kingston lunchtime shoppers with the deftness of an international rugby fly half, her long blonde ponytail swinging. Kate followed her along the pavement while Rav ran down the middle of the road, shouting at her to stop.

Lena darted left into a yard at the rear of a dry cleaner's. She scrambled onto the lid of a refuse bin, bounced up to the top of the wall behind it and crashed down onto the neighbouring corrugated-iron roof.

Kate followed her. She almost slipped off the coping that topped the wall, but regained her balance and jumped clear of the roof onto the tarmac. She rolled once, straightened, and followed as Rav blocked the only exit.

Lena realized she was trapped, spun around to face them, like a cornered wildcat, then ducked into the gloom of a bicycle workshop. She charged up an iron staircase but the windows there were barred. She had propelled herself deeper into the trap.

She came back down the stairs with a bike chain in her hand as a tall, close-cropped mechanic in an oil-stained boiler-suit emerged from a side office. 'What the fuck—'

'Stay where you are!' Rav yelled at him.

Up close now, Kate could see the girl's piercing blue eyes and high cheekbones. Her mouth was twisted in a defiant snarl that revealed a set of gleaming white teeth, at least two of which were broken or chipped. A childish, crudely drawn cross was tattooed on one forearm. The expression of the cartoon *femme fatale* that rippled across the other bore more than a passing resemblance to her own.

'Put it down, Lena,' Kate said.

'Who are you?'

'You need to come with us.'

'Who are you? How do you know my name?'

'Put down the chain.'

'Put it down!' The echoing command came from a uniformed police constable, who had appeared at her shoulder.

Lena lunged, swinging the chain so fiercely that Kate felt the rush of air on her cheek as she side-stepped to avoid it.

'Put it down, Lena,' Kate said again. 'Or this is going to get much, much worse for you.'

'I've done nothing wrong.'

The constable nodded at his companion and closed in on her.

Kate stepped back and watched Lena struggle, a wiry five foot five, full of rage, spitting and biting as she tried to fight them off.

She was exactly what they needed.

An hour later, Kate leant against the glass of the one-way mirror in the local police station as she watched the two female detectives at work. They emerged after a few moments, closing the door carefully behind them.

'She's all yours, ma'am,' the older of the two said.

Kate nodded. 'Thank you.'

At seventeen, Lena was barely two years older than Kate's own daughter and the contrast was haunting. The terrible circumstances of her birth and upbringing shone through the anger in those blue eyes. She was staring straight ahead through the glass. She knew she was being watched, and dared her tormentors to do their worst.

Kate left her shoulder bag where it lay and slipped into the room. She placed a slim folder on the table between them and sat down. 'Good afternoon. My name is Sarah Johnston.'

Lena stared at her.

'You still claim you don't know how the bracelets got into your bag?'

'How did you know my name?'

'I'll come to that in a moment. How did the bracelets get into your bag?'

'*He* put them there.'

'Who is *he*?'

'I told them!' She gestured at the policewomen's point of departure. 'The store detective. He came over and asked if I would go out for a drink with him. I said no. Then he arrested me, took me to the stock room and said he would only let me go if I gave him a blow-job.' Her English was good, her accent only faint. She was a bright girl, who had evidently learnt fast. 'So who are you? How did you know my name?'

Kate picked up the remote control, gestured at the screen on the wall and pressed play. They both watched the footage, which clearly showed the security officer inspecting her bag and lifting out three gold bracelets. 'And yet there they are.'

'He planted them!'

'So you say.'

'He was harassing me. He must have slipped them into—'

'I know he did,' Kate said. 'I told him to.' She opened the folder. 'You're here illegally, Lena. You do understand that we'll have to send you home?'

Lena shook her head slowly.

Kate pushed a freeze frame from a CCTV camera across the table. 'Recognize this?' It showed Lena, in a short skirt and knee-high leather boots, on a street with a man in a leather jacket. 'Milos Bravic, one of Europe's most notorious sex traffickers. A monster, as I hardly need tell you. I can only imagine the courage and guile required to escape his clutches and recreate yourself as the clean-cut au pair from Clapham.' Kate handed Lena a shot of her walking into Clapham Junction station in blue jeans and a crisp white shirt, her tattoos carefully hidden.

'Who *are* you?'

Kate spread three Belgrade police photographs in front of her, and glanced through the accompanying statements as if she was acquainting herself with them for the first time. 'You insisted that those bruises to your face, neck, upper body and breasts were the result of falling off the bunk bed you shared with your sister.'

Lena closed her eyes. And Kate caught a glimpse of the wounded child within.

'We know your stepfather beat you, Lena. But what else did he do to you?' Kate turned the page. 'Here's the X-ray of your sister's skull from the hospital on Kralja Milutina last weekend. This time, he managed to keep his handiwork away from police scrutiny.'

Lena didn't lift her gaze from the floor.

'Look at it, Lena. Your sister is home alone, except for your mother and your stepfather. And you know what that means.'

Slowly Lena shook her head. 'You are not a policewoman.'

'No, I'm not.' Kate glanced at the photograph. 'My daughter is the same age as Maja. She even looks a little like her.' It was a line Kate might have used anyway, but it also happened to be disconcertingly true. 'I know what I would be feeling if he'd done that to her.'

Lena looked up at her. 'Who are you?'

'I'm with the British Secret Intelligence Service.'

'What do you want?'

'You.'

'Why?'

'You sold yourself to the sex traffickers to get here, then

managed to escape their clutches. You're clearly a remarkable young woman and I need your help.'

'How could *I* possibly help *you*?'

'We have a job for you. It's simple, straightforward and not unpleasant. If you were prepared to do it, I'd help you in return.'

'How?'

'We would allow you to stay in this country. We could arrange for your sister to come and join you. We'd pay you enough to tide you both over for a while and enable you to get somewhere to live.'

'How much?'

'Enough.'

'And we could both stay here?'

Kate saw something like hope spark in her eyes, despite the air of brittle cynicism that was her first line of defence against the only world she'd ever known. She nodded.

'For ever?'

'If you wanted to.'

'We would have . . . passports?'

'That's a complicated process, but in time . . . We always look after our own.'

'Why me?'

'The job requires a young au pair or nanny who speaks Russian. It needs someone with courage, which you clearly have in abundance.'

'Many people speak Russian.'

'We need someone who is not Russian but comes from a country that Moscow would view as being within its sphere of influence. It's a job that requires tenacity, toughness and intelligence. You would be perfect.'

Lena stared at her. 'What would I have to do?'

'The same kind of work you've been doing in London for the last few weeks.' Kate reached for the folder and extracted a final photograph. 'This is the *Empress*. She'll be cruising the Mediterranean this autumn. The owner's son and his wife need an au pair for their three-year-old son.'

Lena gazed at the massive, gleaming super-yacht. 'And what would I have to do for *you*?'

'Once in a while, we'd want to talk about what you might have seen, who came, who went. That's all.'

'I'd be a spy?'

'Just eyes and ears.'

'Who is the owner?'

'He used to be the head of Russia's Secret Service.'

'So I would be listening to him?'

'Yes. And some of his friends.'

'A suicide mission.'

'No,' Kate said. 'You'd be employed by a reputable Western agency. The worst that could happen is that you'd be summarily dismissed and thrown off at the next port.' She waited.

'They'd kill me—'

'You'd be fired. There would be angry words, but no

more. The owner belongs to that small group of oligarchs who are still able to store most of their money in the West and haven't been impacted by sanctions. We have, of course, deliberately chosen to keep it that way. He couldn't afford the scandal that would erupt if anything happened to you somewhere other than his own backyard.' She treated Lena to a warm, motherly smile. 'A few weeks in the sun and your life will be truly your own.'

'The Russians do what they want, wherever they want. There. Here. They don't care. Everyone knows that. Milos and all those other bastards in Belgrade – they all answer to the big bosses back in Moscow. Serbia is just a playground for them. So they do what they like.'

'Not the ones who keep their money where we can find it.'

There was a very long silence. Eventually Lena said, 'I can't do it.'

'I'm very sorry to hear that,' Kate said, 'but not as sorry, I think, as your sister will be.'

A single tear rolled down Lena's cheek. She brushed it away, clearly furious with herself for betraying weakness. 'The Russians kill whoever they want to kill. All over the world. Here in England, at home in Belgrade. Everybody knows that.'

Kate leant forward again and laid a hand on Lena's forearm. 'Maja really does look like my daughter, Lena. I know that's the kind of thing someone in my position would say, but it's true. My girl is sleeping safely in her bed just a few miles from here. I'd do anything to protect her. If you look into my eyes, you'll see that. *Anything.*' Kate gave her a gentle squeeze. 'You've had to become the mother neither of you had. And that's not fair. I'm guessing your plan is to go back and rescue her when you can. So, now you have a choice. Go home and let that monster do what he will with you both, always supposing you can escape the clutches of Milos and his traffickers. Or do what I ask, and save not just yourself but Maja too.'

Kate slid the picture of Lena's sister closer to her. 'Take a look at what he did to her last week, then tell me you want me to leave.'

Lena recoiled, and Kate gripped her wrist. 'You can do this, Lena.'

'No . . . *no.* I can't do this. The Russians kill everyone . . .'

'They won't need to, if you let your stepfather do it first. We can move your sister beyond his reach. Starting today. The moment you say yes to me, we can start looking for ways of getting her over here, ways of helping her.'

Kate allowed the silence to lengthen between them. When Lena looked up again, she adopted an expression of regret. 'If you don't take this offer, you'll leave me no choice. You'll be going back there. To him, to this, and to the mother who did nothing whatsoever to help you. Maja won't stand a chance.' She paused. 'I'll give you a few minutes to think about it.'

She stood up, went to the door and left the room.

Rav was leaning against the far side of the glass. 'Well?'

'She'll need a moment or two. But she's our girl all right.'

Rav turned and stared at the crumpled figure in the interview room. 'You can be a ruthless bitch. You know that, don't you?'

1

KATE PLACED THE mug of heavily sweetened tea carefully on Stuart's side of the bed. 'Morning, Rocky.'

Her husband was splayed across the mattress, snoring loudly. He reeked of alcohol and cigarette smoke, and the black eye he had achieved the night before was darkening nicely. He groaned in acknowledgement and she opened the curtains to let in the dawn.

'Jesus . . .' he said.

'Not exactly. I do a passing impression of Mother Teresa, though – rather too often for my liking. You need to get up.'

'What time is it?'

'Six thirty.'

'Fucking hell.'

'As you will no doubt recall, it's the school's National Costume Day. Gus will kill you if you put him in a kilt. And so will I.'

'What about Fi?'

'She's going as a Swede.'

Stuart pushed himself up onto his elbows. 'Why?'

'Because she's fifteen.'

'What does going as a Swede involve?'

'I don't know because she won't tell me. And I'm not sure I want to know. You definitely won't.'

'Great.' He sipped his tea and looked at her overnight bag by the door. 'Where are you going?'

'I'm worried you really are getting Alzheimer's.'

'No, wait, I do know . . . Of course I do. You told me. I'm sorry. Vienna.'

'Almost. Istanbul.'

Stuart looked at his watch. 'I have a conference call at eight thirty.'

'Then you'll have to delay it.'

He rubbed his stubbled cheek. 'Right, right.'

Kate moved back to the bed and sat beside him. 'Was there anything left of the goalpost?'

He looked confused.

She pointed at his eye. 'When you got home at dead of night, you kindly woke me up to tell me you'd collided with a goalpost.'

'Oh, shit, yes . . . Sorry. No. It was in a terrible state.'

'Do you think it might be time to acknowledge you're too old for this game?'

'It would be fine if all the other bastards weren't so young.'

She touched his hand. 'I have to go. I'll sort Nelson out, then you're on your own.'

'When will you be back?'

Kate got up and went to grab her bag. 'You should know better than to ask.'

'How about a goodbye kiss?'

'No. Because (a) you absolutely stink, and (b) you don't mean just a kiss.'

'You are an incurable romantic.'

Kate made it to the door before she relented. She came back and gave him a kiss that she allowed to linger. 'You are my one true love . . .'

'Stay a moment . . .'

'No!' She pulled herself free of his octopus arms.

Stuart groaned again, in frustration this time, and turned over.

Kate went downstairs. She put her phone back on charge, then wiped the island clean in the pathological way she always did when she was leaving or returning home. She took down Nelson's lead, clipped it to his collar and pulled him to the front door. Once upon a time any trip to the park would have sent their white and tan Beagle into raptures, but he was ageing now, fat, lazy and grumpy. He lingered on the pavement and only advanced when tugged hard. His collar kept slipping over his head. 'Come on, you old codger,' she said. 'I really don't have time for it today.'

She crossed the road and coaxed him through the park and up towards the river. The sunlight filtered through the trees and sparkled on the water. Nelson had perked up a bit – perhaps it was the weather. His belly almost brushed the ground as he went. Kate insisted it was just his fur, but Gus had taken to googling 'animal fat farms'. The dog had been with them almost since Fiona was born and Kate could see he was approaching the end of the line. 'All right, then. Don't say I didn't warn you.'

She started back. Nelson never needed a lead on the return journey because it meant the end of his morning torture and the strong possibility of food. When they got home, he slumped into his palatial basket in the corner of the kitchen. Kate put his breakfast in front of him, but he didn't stir. He gazed at her mournfully from beneath eyelids that drooped with age. She knelt down to stroke his head. 'You're almost done in, aren't you, old chap?'

Kate cleaned the island one last time, then picked up her bag and headed for the door. Anton was this morning's driver, and he was her favourite because he didn't like to talk beyond their exchange of greetings.

'Would you like the radio, ma'am?' he murmured.

'No, thank you.' As if there wasn't enough to be depressed about already. Kate rested her cheek on the window, relishing the cool of the glass. She wished she could share Stuart's easy and uncomplicated relationship with sleep. But then, while he knew about her mother, of course, and her slow and terrible decline, he didn't know that Fiona wanted to dress as a Swede so that she could look like a porn star and thus, in her mind, increase her chances of getting together with the inappropriate boy in the sixth form. And he couldn't know about Operation Sigma, which was about to unfold in Istanbul and had deprived her of any lingering chance of a good night's rest.

She'd got clearance for it on a series of half-truths, but it represented a huge amount of work and expense. She had to make it pay. And she had to make its pay-off look like a lucky break.

The *ping* of Rav's incoming WhatsApp message interrupted her thoughts. *All set. See you when you land.*

True to his word, Rav was waiting for her in Arrivals, with an umbrella. A savage electrical storm was raging over the city.

'You brought the weather,' he said, as she climbed into the car. 'And it's messing with the signal.' He handed her his phone. The pictures on it streamed live but not fluidly from their camera on top of the Hotel Kempinski.

Kate watched a black Mercedes pull up in the centre of

the screen. Three young women got out and trotted on high heels towards a motor launch bobbing beside the quay. 'How many does he get through?' she asked.

'They're the third lot since we arrived. He appeared to be having some kind of party last night – old men and a lot of young women. He must be keeping Viagra in business.'

'Is Mikhail there?'

'Not yet. He's landed, but went straight to the embassy. Katya checked into the Kempinski with their kid.'

'What time is Lena's interview?'

'Six. We arranged the meet for between four and five, so you'll be in position in good time.' Rav tapped the driver's shoulder. 'Let's go.'

'You've briefed the teams?'

He smiled. 'Don't worry. It's all good.'

'I do worry, Rav. I always worry. That's my job.'

'Well, if you worried less you'd sleep more, and we'd all be the better for it.'

She touched his arm and he gripped her hand in return. As far as a chief and her deputy could be, they were close friends. Rav was quiet, laconic and intense. The son of two Pakistani doctors, he'd only come out in his mid-twenties and had yet to tell them he was gay and living with his partner, Zac. But, then, no one kept secrets like members of the Secret Service.

'We should go straight there,' he said.

'Where are we set up?'

'Four Seasons. Not far from the Kempinski. We have a team on the roof with a good line of sight to the stern of the yacht.'

Kate looked again at the video stream on Rav's phone. The *Empress* was a sleek multi-storey gin palace with a helicopter pad, a shining beacon of ostentation in the grey afternoon. But even at a hundred and fifty million plus, it had made hardly a dent in Igor Borodin's fortune. Kate's Russia Desk estimated his total net worth at around sixty billion – roughly half the sum accumulated by the Russian president, whom they had assessed to be, by some distance, the richest man in the world.

A former head of the SVR, Russia's Foreign Intelligence Service, Borodin had been a close friend of the president from their KGB days, and they were the principal shareholders – via proxies – in Keftal, which sold the lion's share of the Motherland's oil and natural resources on the world market. Nobody *had* to trade through Keftal, of course, but few wished to contemplate the consequences of trying to go a different route.

Igor's only son, Mikhail, and his new young wife, Katya, had rubbed shoulders with the cream of the British public-school system – at Eton and Downe House respectively – in order to get to know the landscape they intended to dominate or destroy.

Another incoming WhatsApp message prompted her to pull out her own phone.

Stuart: *Had massive argument with Fi over her costume. Is she completely insane?*

She responded: *No. As I said, she's fifteen.*

Stuart often complained he didn't get to spend enough time with his teenage daughter, so now was his chance. Good luck to him.

Their SUV pulled up and they stepped out into a sudden burst of afternoon sunshine. The hot, humid air ramped up the claustrophobic atmosphere of the tightly packed streets. They headed for the entrance to the Grand Bazaar. Kate pulled a scarf from her pocket and wrapped it around her head as they passed a group of women, wearing *niqab*s, walking with a young boy in a clean white T-shirt. As if to emphasize the international flavour of the city at the crossroads of two continents, two old Turkish men sat by a stall selling sweet pastries in front of a Chinese restaurant painted a deep red, with lanterns that swayed in the warm breeze.

Kate's stomach tightened. 'Are the teams out already?'

'No. We told them to spend the day sunbathing and getting drunk on raki.'

'Very funny. You gave them the picture but nothing more?'

'Nothing more, as you said.'

Kate led the way into the covered bazaar. She had a profound affection for Istanbul's easy secularity. Women in headscarves mixed with scantily clad tourists as they moved between tiny stores selling silver teapots and hookah pipes, rugs, Turkish delight, chessboards and handbags. They passed a café where old men sat smoking and watching the world sweep by.

She glanced over her shoulder.

'Relax,' Rav said. 'We're clean.'

That's all very well, but we've missed the signs before, Kate wanted to say. She turned right and swung through a doorway at the end of an alley.

Julie's wide smile and auburn hair lit the money-changer's gloomy interior. She'd become an indispensable part of the team. 'All set.' She draped a scarf over her head and departed.

Kate took her seat behind the desk, positioned so that she could see out of the window while remaining almost invisible to the outside world. She picked up a set of worry beads and flicked them over and over her fingers as she thought of the succession of shops, cafés and houses she'd sat in at times like this. Vladivostok, Riga, Kabul, Lahore, Riyadh, Beirut, Cairo – the list was long, but the sensation in the pit of her stomach never changed.

A sitting duck once more.

She'd been cornered only once, in Lahore, and ended up having to fight her way out. An al-Qaeda double had arrived at the rendezvous with two gunmen. All three were dead before they'd managed to fire a single shot. She owed her life that day to the speed of Rav's reactions. For a slight man, he packed one hell of a punch, with a gun in his hand and without.

'So how was the legendary dinner?' she asked, in an attempt to distract herself.

'Grim.'

'Urgh.' She turned to face him. 'What happened?'

'The boy, David, doesn't speak to me. And I wish his sisters wouldn't. It's like they've taken a course in how to lace every sentence with enough poison to wound, but not quite enough to justify a reprimand.'

Rav's partner, Zac, had left his wife and children to be with him. None of them had taken it well.

'It *will* get better.'

'So you keep saying.'

'You have to keep trying.'

'What – until they're fifty?'

'Teenagers are teenagers. If it's any consolation, it's not much easier when they're your own.'

'Well, it couldn't be any fucking worse. They're just bloody rude. And don't start lecturing me again on how tough it is for them. It's not my fault their father's gay.'

'For an emotionally intelligent man, you can sometimes be a right pillock.'

Rav was staring at his phone. 'She's en route.'

Kate glanced at her watch. 'Early.'

'She's clear.'

'Sure?'

'Sure.'

Kate tapped the worry beads against her leg. And, sooner than expected, Lena was in front of her.

'I'd like to change a hundred dollars.'

'Of course.' Kate fished the package out of her handbag. 'Remember what we said?'

Lena didn't answer.

'There's no rush. Just see how freely you can move around the yacht. We'll be keeping an eye on you. You should activate the microphone and plant it where they're most likely to exchange confidential information. Remember to look as if you've dropped something. We don't know where the security cameras are hidden.'

Lena had turned the colour of icing sugar.

Kate pushed the small brown package across the desk, but the girl didn't take it.

'I need some air . . .' Lena raised a hand to her forehead and was a couple of paces outside the door when her knees folded.

Kate leapt to her feet. 'Rav!'

He was already in the alley. Together, they gathered her up and carried her back into the shop, where she shook them off, bent double and vomited.

Kate crouched beside her. 'It's okay,' she whispered. 'It's okay.'

Lena was sobbing, in great, lurching gasps.

'Calm down,' Kate said. 'It's all right. Really . . .'

'I can't . . . I can't do it.'

'Just wait a moment—'

'What if they catch me?'

'We've been through that. They won't.'

'But what if they *do*? I can't stop thinking about it.'

Kate took a handkerchief from her bag. She held Lena tight, straightened her and wiped the remnants of vomit from her mouth. 'Just breathe, breathe deeply,' she said, 'and get a grip on yourself.'

Lena did as she was told and her panic gradually subsided.

'I'm here. And you trust me, right?'

Lena nodded uncertainly.

'We've talked about the risk. In the worst case, you could expect an hour or two of shouting. Our relationship with the Turkish security services is good. The Russians simply wouldn't risk anything more than throwing you back onto the quay.'

'But if they—'

Kate took Lena's chin in her hand and fixed her with a steady gaze. 'Believe me, Lena. Please. I have your back.'

Lena tugged anxiously at her ponytail.

'Forget about us,' Kate said. 'Think only of the part you must play. Have you ever been on a yacht like that?'

She shook her head.

Kate smiled. 'I'd love to have a nose around. It looks bloody amazing.'

Lena managed to smile back. 'Why don't *you* do it, then?'

'Tempting . . . but, sadly, they know all too well who I am.' Kate touched her arm. 'Come on, enjoy it. It'll be something to tell your grandchildren about.'

'Who says I want grandchildren?'

'That's more like it.'

Lena took a deep breath and picked up the small brown package. She looked up at Kate once more. 'I do trust you,' she said. 'You remind me of my grandmother.'

'I'm not sure that's a compliment.'

'She is very young.'

'With respect, she can't be *that* young.'

'She is a good woman.'

'And she would be proud of you.'

Lena started for the door.

'Next time I see you, we'll work out a plan. There's no pressure. You're there to look around, no more.'

'If I get the job.'

'You *will* get the job.'

Lena turned and the door snapped shut behind her. Kate watched as she passed the window. She didn't look back.

2

JULIE WAS WAITING in Reception at the Four Seasons. 'We might have something interesting.'

She took them up to their suite on the tenth floor, where Danny, their unit technician, juggled a bank of screens. It was a spectacular room in tasteful beige and mahogany with floor-to-ceiling windows that afforded a stunning view of the Bosphorus. Julie was back in place, sitting beside Danny. She pointed to the man on the left of the screen.

'Mikhail,' Kate said. The young Russian was sitting alone on the terrace by the hotel pool, drinking coffee and smoking.

'Now rewind,' Julie said.

Danny maximized the recorded feed from the left-hand side of the screen, rewound about an hour's worth and played the video again. Mikhail walked out onto the terrace in the corner of the shot, and paused to speak to someone at a table by the entrance.

'There,' Julie said.

Danny froze the frame. Kate peered closer.

He highlighted the man's face, then expanded it.

'Sasha Rigin.' Kate straightened. 'Keep going.'

Danny let the playback continue. Mikhail moved on to his own table, unfolded a copy of the *International Herald Tribune* and lit a cigarette. 'He hasn't moved since.' Danny returned to the live feed. Mikhail now appeared to be staring out across the water.

'What the hell would the head of their London Desk be doing in Istanbul?' Rav asked.

'Meeting an asset?' Julie said.

Kate didn't answer. She went to stand by the window and looked down at the choppy waters of the Bosphorus. The wind had got up since they'd arrived. Then she sat on the bed. 'I'd relax,' she said, speaking almost to herself. 'I think it's going to be a long night.'

She turned and focused on the screen. This was the strangest and perhaps most tiring phase of the job. Nothing of any interest took place for very long periods, yet loss of concentration risked missing something significant.

Just after seven, Mikhail, his wife and their young son walked out of the Kempinski, with Lena at their side. 'Looks like she got the job,' Julie said.

Kate allowed herself a smile of satisfaction.

The little boy was already holding Lena's hand as they climbed down the steps into the launch, and kept holding it as they headed out to the *Empress*, clambered aboard and disappeared below deck.

The team ordered room service. Kate had a Caprese salad and water. Rav had pizza. He always had pizza, wherever they were in the world. It was a miracle he was so thin. 'You think it's a coincidence Sasha Rigin is here in the hotel?' he asked.

'No,' Kate said. 'Sasha Rigin doesn't do coincidences.'

'You think we should put a team in there to watch him?'

'No. I don't want to risk it. We just need to be patient.'

At ten, Mikhail's son was spotted sprinting along the top deck with Lena in pursuit. Kate nodded at Rav. It had been his idea to encourage Lena to play hide-and-seek with the child – or any other game that would allow a young nanny to poke around parts of the yacht that might normally have been barred to her.

After that, there was nothing more of any note. At midnight, Kate stood up. 'Okay, let's take shifts. I'm happy to do the first.'

'I'm all right,' Danny said. 'I've had a few weeks' R and R. I'll call you if anything happens.'

'You sure you don't want us to put a tail on Rigin?' Rav asked. 'We might be missing a trick.'

'I'm sure. But let's get a signal in place by dawn.'

Rav frowned. 'Isn't it a bit soon for that? I mean, she's only just climbed aboard. It might spook her.'

'Rigin's presence here really is no accident. I think we're in the right place at the right time, and need to move quickly.'

Rav shrugged. 'You're the boss.'

Kate slipped out to her bedroom next door to the suite. There was no message from Stuart – perhaps he'd navigated around their daughter's desire to dress as a Swedish porn star instead of pressing the nuclear button. But as Kate turned out the light, home was far from her mind. It was always the same when you had someone out there: the sense of responsibility, of vulnerability, was like a shadow over every waking and sleeping moment.

She was awake long before dawn.

The first thing she did was check with Danny that the signal was out. The team had done its work and ensured a red T-shirt was clearly visible through an open window of the sixth-floor room they occupied at the Kempinski.

Kate breakfasted with Danny, who insisted again that he didn't need sleep. She poured herself a coffee. Soon Julie joined her. She sat down, lit up and offered Kate her Marlboros.

Kate grimaced. 'Not before breakfast.'

Julie held up the cigarette. 'This *is* my breakfast.'

'That's what my dad used to say.'

'Mine too.'

'How's he bearing up?'

'Fine, considering. I sent him back up to Doncaster when I knew I was coming out here.' Julie took a deep drag and funnelled the smoke upwards. 'I told him about your mum.' Julie's mother, like Kate's, had destroyed her family with an ill-judged affair.

'I'm not convinced that would have helped.'

'He doesn't want to open the door to the possibility that she isn't the woman he still tells himself she is.'

Kate sighed. 'I should have warned you about that. It's the only thing I ever really argued with my father about. Have you called your mother?'

'No.'

'I know I should probably shut up about it, but I still think it's better to grasp the nettle.'

'I've thought about it. And I'll never speak to her again as long as I live.'

Kate looked at her young protégée. At times there was an unsettling intensity to her.

Rav joined them. He took a cigarette from Julie's packet without asking. 'I'll do tomorrow night,' he said.

'Did you sleep?' Kate asked.

'Course not. You?'

Kate shook her head.

After a while, they went back to join Danny at the screen. The *Empress* seemed deserted.

At one o'clock, Kate and Rav walked towards the rendezvous near Taksim Square. They dodged the rackety trams and crowds of shoppers on Istiklal Avenue and chose a café with chairs and tables scattered along the edge of the road. Rav ordered coffee with a hookah and opened a copy of the *Financial Times.* They watched the flow of pedestrians for a few minutes, then Kate got up and crossed the street to the Turkish baths.

She paid her entry fee and was directed down a murky corridor to a small glass-and-wood cubicle. She undressed, wrapped herself in a towel and slipped on a pair of ungainly wooden clogs. She clip-clopped down to the central bath area, where the afternoon sun filtered through slats high in the domed ceiling and cast ridged shadows across the cool stone floor.

Kate allowed herself to be washed in hot water, scrubbed and soaped. After about twenty minutes, a young Turkish woman made her way quietly towards her. Zehra was a friend of the owner, and, more importantly, the eldest daughter of Yusuf, who had been the Service's Istanbul station manager since the 1970s. *'As salaam alaikum,'* she said.

'Wa alaikum salaam.' Kate smiled. 'It's so good to see you, my friend.'

'You too.'

'Your father is well?'

'Convinced he'll live for ever.' She smiled. 'Which is rather touching in a man of our profession.'

'He's done all right so far. I rather fell in love with him when we were checking out that Russian translator.' Kate had worked with Yusuf and Zehra on one of her first operations in the Service, an attempt to assess the reliability of a young Russian KGB translator who had offered her services to the British Embassy in Istanbul during the chaotic period after the collapse of Communism. Turncoats were there for the taking, but few in London saw the need to spare the time and expense. Kate had completed the original assessment and passed the girl on to Ian but, as far as she knew, nothing had ever come of it.

'I warned Ian about her,' Zehra said. 'I didn't trust her.'

Kate frowned. 'What do you mean, you "warned Ian"?'

'She smelt of trouble.'

'But I thought he passed on her.'

'I don't think so. But I don't expect she did him much good.'

Kate was still frowning as Zehra turned away. The secrets of the field were best not shared with London, even with an officer you liked and trusted.

'I'm here if you need me,' Zehra said. 'I've seen Rav. We're well covered.' She wandered back down the corridor.

Half an hour later Lena appeared, head up, shoulders back. She was shown to the rear of the marble partition, where Kate was waiting. 'I have time,' Lena said. 'An hour's break every day. They say I can go wherever I want.' Her eyes were bright. 'It is just like you said. Mikhail and Katya are really nice. Alexei is a sweet boy. They are very generous, and say I must not overwork.'

'Did they *encourage* you to leave the yacht?'

'Encourage? They say I can come and go as I want.'

'What about Igor?'

'He doesn't say much. Mikhail and Katya switch between Russian and English because they want Alexei to be familiar with both languages, but Mikhail's father only talks in Russian and is mostly on the phone.'

'Where does he take his calls?'

'He normally leaves us and goes along the deck to an office – he called it the boardroom. He came to eat dinner with us last night, but was only there for a few minutes. Every time he sat down, he took another call and had to go away again.'

'Have you been in the room?'

'No.' A haunted look replaced the excitement in her eyes.

Kate leant forward. 'Lena, I need you to get inside that room.'

'I can't.'

'Listen to me. I think we're on to something here. I saw you chasing Alexei around the decks yesterday. That was clever. You've set up your right to roam. Did he enjoy it?'

'Yes. Very much.'

'Well, now I want you to wait until Igor is off the yacht, or preoccupied with something else. Then suggest another game of hide-and-seek. It doesn't matter where you think Alexei is. All you have to do is go into that room, call his name, crouch down, as if you're looking for him, and fasten the activated microphone beneath the best piece of furniture.'

'I can't do it.'

Kate clasped her wrists. 'You can. You told me that Mikhail and Katya are nice.'

'But not the father. The father is not the same. He frightens me.'

'You'll be doing nothing wrong, Lena. You didn't know that room was out of bounds. You *do not* know that. You'll just be having fun with his grandson . . .'

Lena was smiling now. 'You are a crazy woman. Why does it matter so much?'

'Trust me. It does.'

'Is Maja safe?'

'She will be very soon.'

'If I do it, will that be enough?'

'I really hope so, yes.'

'All right. I cannot promise, but I will try.'

Kate patted Lena's arm, then stood up. 'Enjoy your bath.'

She rejoined Rav at the café to update him. He folded his newspaper and got to his feet. 'You ever worry that it's all going too well?' he said.

'Like I said, I always worry.'

3

JULIE WAS WAITING for them in the hotel's ornate lobby. She held back until the lift doors had shut. 'Guess who just made a special guest appearance?'

'I don't know. God, maybe?'

'Better than that. The Holy fucking Trinity. Markov, Barentsev and Vasily himself.'

'You sure?'

'They're drinking cocktails by the pool.'

They strode out of the lift and into the top-floor suite. Danny greeted them with a megawatt smile and gestured at the biggest of the screens, where three burly Russians, jackets off and ties loosened on the hotel terrace, raised their glasses to the backdrop of the Bosphorus: Markov, head of Directorate S, responsible for agents abroad; Barentsev, head of Operations; and Vasily Durov, the all-powerful chief of Russia's Foreign Intelligence Service, the SVR.

'Fuck . . .' Kate breathed. 'Full house.' She couldn't quite believe her luck.

'Too good to be true?' Rav said.

Kate continued to stare at the screen. He had a point. 'So Igor's been busy. They're all his people.'

Another man came into the frame and shook the hands of those around the table. 'Rigin again . . .'

'So, why would Rigin be here with the big boys?' Julie asked.

'My money says not just for happy hour,' Rav said. He turned to Kate. 'If we get anything, you're going to look like a genius.'

'That's because I *am* a genius, Rav. And we'd better bloody get something or you're all fired.' She sat back. The op had started as a fishing expedition. Now it was something else. Rav had ordered food and a bottle of wine, but she picked at the pizza and avoided the wine.

Half an hour later, the four Russians stood, slung their jackets over their shoulders, sauntered to the edge of the quay and boarded the launch. Igor emerged onto the bridge wing and watched them power towards the *Empress*. The microphone was activated and the tension in the suite ratcheted up several more notches as they saw Lena and her young charge racing around the lower deck and disappearing inside.

Igor greeted his guests with bear hugs, and ushered them below. Kate realized she was chewing her fingernails. Rav grabbed Julie's cigarettes, lit up and went to stand by the window.

The yacht was a blaze of light, but there was no sign of anyone on deck and the microphone fed them only static. Kate could stand it no longer. 'I'm going to the gym. Call me straight away if you get anything.'

She was halfway down the corridor to her room when she heard Rav behind her. 'You going to level with me?' he asked.

'About what?'

'Everything.'

'Such as?'

'C'mon, Kate.'

Kate shook her head, though she knew what was coming.

'You insisted Igor was still more active than we knew so, all right, I bought the operation. Just. Maybe it'd be worth all the time, effort and expense, not to mention Lena risking her scrawny neck. But it looks like you're going to win the lottery here. And that's a bit too much of a coincidence to be credible.'

'You mean *we're* going to win the lottery.'

'We know each other far too well for this, Kate.'

She still didn't answer.

'I backed your hunch. And so did the top floor. But I don't buy that this was just a coincidence, and neither will they. You knew they were going to be here. How?'

She gazed at him steadily.

'Are you going to deny it?'

'Let's just get on with it, shall we?'

'It's one thing keeping it from me, but if anyone on the top floor thinks you have an undeclared source of intelligence, they'll go crazy.'

Kate went back to her room, relieved to have got away without giving Rav a straight answer. She went down to the gym and pounded the running machine for longer than she'd intended. She showered and returned to the suite where the surveillance equipment was set up. Danny shook his head to indicate nothing had changed.

Shortly before midnight, a black Mercedes van pulled up outside the hotel foyer. Half a dozen women spilt out and were shepherded through Reception to the quay beyond the pool. Rav peered at them as they waited for the motor launch. 'Bet they don't come cheap,' he said.

They picked up something on the microphone feed shortly after one in the morning. Danny leant forward and adjusted the volume dial. They heard a girl laugh, then giggle and moan encouragingly. Before long, she was panting as unconvincingly as her male companion was grunting loudly.

'Fuck's sake.' Julie groaned. '*Please* tell me Igor hasn't just invited them there for a sex party.'

'Hookers are part of Igor's hospitality shtick.' Kate lowered the volume. 'But I very much doubt that's Vasily getting his rocks off in the boardroom.'

'Top deck,' Rav said.

Danny maximized the close-up of the yacht's stern. The three most powerful men in Russia's Foreign Intelligence Service had gathered there, with Vasily at the centre – but they weren't drunk enough to have forgotten their own standard operating procedures. They kept their backs to the shore.

'Lower deck,' Rav said.

Danny pulled up the screen and closed in on Igor's son, Mikhail, leaning against the rail next to a blonde hooker.

'Go on,' Kate said.

Danny enlarged the screen and peered closer. Lip-reading was one of his many skills. 'She's asking questions in English. Where does he spend his time? All over the place, he says. Mainly Moscow, these days, but he travels a lot in Europe. He's . . . expecting to spend a few weeks on his father's yacht. Paying homage, he jokes . . .

'She doesn't seem to know whether to laugh. Where is his favourite place? Zermatt. He loves skiing. She loves skiing, too. She once spent a winter in . . . somewhere . . . didn't catch it . . . Oh, Cortina. She also loves Venice. But for the fucking, not the skiing. She asks . . . Oh, okay, what would he like to do to her? He can do anything. Anything he likes. He's not answering. He seems shy, she says, but she likes to make sure her clients have lived out their most extreme fantasies, so she's happy to do anything he wants. She's—'

'We can see what she's doing, Danny,' Kate said.

'She's asking if he'd like some Viagra. She has her own supply. He says, yes, that would be good.'

'So would being heterosexual, maybe,' Rav said.

'It makes it harder, longer, better, she says. Her English is a bit stilted. I can't quite make . . . Well, she's trying to arouse him, whispering something . . .'

'Is his wife still aboard?' Julie asked.

'Yes,' Kate said. 'But Igor makes it very clear that fucking hookers regularly is a fundamental duty of manhood, and a prerequisite for membership of the Mafia class. He thinks his son and daughter-in-law are dangerously Westernized already, so this is his way of reminding them of the chauvinistic imperatives of Russian power politics. Mikhail won't dare to refuse. Katya won't dare to object.'

The hooker led the apparently unwilling Mikhail inside. The three men on the upper deck had also vanished.

'You should go to bed,' Rav told Kate. 'This could take days.'

'With those guys on board? Are you kidding? They're here for a reason.'

They heard the door to the boardroom open and close, then voices. They listened in silence. Even with the level of technical wizardry the Service could deploy, the microphone's performance had been heavily compromised by its size, so the conversation came and went. To begin with, they seemed to be talking about Moscow Centre's internal politics.

'Who is Kyril?' Kate whispered.

'Not sure,' Rav muttered. 'GRU, maybe.' Moscow's military intelligence arm had a substantial foreign operation of its own. The tension between the two organizations was notorious.

Igor was talking now. He offered the men cigars and disappeared to the far end of the room, frustratingly out of earshot for a minute or more.

When he came back, Vasily, whose voice was familiar to them all, said, 'Now is our moment.' He was speaking in Russian, which all of Kate's team spoke fluently. They leant closer to the speaker on the desk.

'What makes you so sure?' Igor asked.

'The Prime Minister has prostate cancer. He will resign this week.'

They could hear Igor lighting the cigars. 'Who stands in our way?'

'The woman in Education, perhaps. But there will be other candidates, of course.'

'Viper can help.'

'Yes. We will have to wait and see. But we won't need to for long. Viper says—'

Somebody must have moved a chair or table, because there was a screech that had them all covering their ears and the voices became much fainter. Danny tried to work his magic with the dials, but to no avail.

'Fuck,' Kate said. She leant further forward. 'Turn it up.'

Danny kept trying. 'I think it's been damaged. This is maximum volume.'

They leant even closer, but hearing anything was next to impossible.

'It's on record,' he said. 'I'll see what I can get with some enhancement.'

Kate moved to the window. Rav and Julie lit up. Rav offered Kate his cigarette and she took a few puffs. 'If the PM was sick,' Julie said, 'wouldn't we know?'

'I've not heard a whisper,' Rav said.

'But let's assume for a moment they know something we don't,' Kate said. 'They were implying they would have a dog in any leadership fight. So who's their guy?'

'How do we know it's a guy?' Julie said.

'And how do we know that "Who stands in our way?" refers to their candidate,' Rav asked, 'and not someone – or something – else entirely?'

Kate took another drag of his cigarette. '"Who stands in our way?" And "There will be other candidates . . ." They absolutely must have their own horse in the race. And, given their enthusiasm for interfering with the democratic process, it would be more of a surprise if they *weren't* trying to pull some stunt. If they've tried it in other countries, why not in the UK? Some of our politicians probably come cheaper than others elsewhere.'

'And who the hell is Viper?' Julie asked.

'"Viper can help".' Kate shook her head. 'It could be anyone – a politician, someone in Whitehall, a newspaper editor.'

Rav trod his stub into the stone floor of the suite, then picked it up and put it into the ashtray. 'Ian's going to love this. It'll bring out all his inner machismo.'

'The foreign secretary has to be prime suspect,' Julie said. 'He served in Kosovo with the Paras. The Russians were all over that place like a rash.'

'That's a bit of a leap,' Kate said. 'And probably wise not to rush into pointing the finger at our nominal superior.'

'We can hardly ignore him,' Rav said. 'Every piece of speculative crap in the last five years puts him on the list of leadership front runners.'

'I'm not saying we should,' Kate said.

'Has Stuart heard any whispers? It looks like his boss is in the clear,' Rav said. 'Unless, of course, they're already fucking us about.'

'A lot of people in the party want someone from the next

generation,' Julie said, 'so Imogen could easily be in the frame. But the field is actually pretty wide.'

'Right,' Kate said. 'Julie, you stay here and keep an eye on Lena. Rav and I will get the first flight back in the morning. Well done, everybody. They may still be talking about this operation in fifty years' time.'

She turned at the door. 'Especially if we crash and burn.'

4

IT WAS ALMOST four in the afternoon by the time Kate reached the space-age bubbles that controlled entry to Vauxhall Cross. Rav had gone home for a change of clothes, so she rode the lift to the fifth floor alone.

The office occupied by C, the head of the Secret Intelligence Service – currently Sir Alan Brabazon, a tall, good-looking man, who'd made his name in his dealings with Russia and the former Soviet Union – was not quite as magnificent as his wood-panelled executive dining room on the top floor, but it still boasted a spectacular view of the Thames and the Houses of Parliament, their stonework gold in the occasional shaft of sunlight.

Sir Alan's desk stood in the middle of the room with two open laptops – one internal, one external – at the ready, but he ushered Kate and her boss, Ian Granger, head of Europe and Russia, to the soft seating area in the far corner. Unless he had bad news for you, he served coffee and biscuits, which Ian could never resist.

Ian was lean and wiry – tales of his Iron Man triumphs were legendary for their tedium – with wavy blond hair he allowed to curl over the nape of his neck, like a 1970s rock star. He was clever, and couldn't resist letting everyone know it. He also had a tendency to state the blindingly obvious as if it were biblical revelation. Kate had just about found a way to cooperate with him until Sir Alan had named her as one of his potential successors the previous summer. Their relationship had since been plunged into the deep freeze.

'I think we have to be realistic,' Ian said. 'Don't you, Alan?' Ian's version of being realistic was to agree that someone else must have made a mistake. He tugged at his cuffs. He had once made a point of telling everyone in the office that he had his suits, shirts and shoes handmade on Savile Row. It had been his way of auditioning for entry to the inner sanctum of the establishment. He'd dropped the references since diversity had become the management's watchword, and begun stressing his state-school credentials instead. He hadn't lost his taste for the clothes, though.

C displayed quality tailoring with a great deal less effort

and more pleasing effect than his colleague. He picked up Kate's file, raised his tortoiseshell-framed glasses and cast his eye once more over the transcript. 'Realistic, Ian?' he said. 'In what way, precisely?' His stillness was unnerving, and even Ian was not immune to it.

'Well, we start with a basic credibility problem. Are we really being asked to believe that three of the most powerful men in Russia's intelligence hierarchy – arguably the three most powerful – suddenly turned up on a yacht in the Bosphorus to discuss these vital and sensitive matters at a time when we just happened to have an intelligence operation in place?'

Sir Alan's gaze was steady. Silence was another of his weapons, and he used it now.

'It's a classic misinformation ploy,' Ian said. 'They're hoping to spark up a witch-hunt among our political elite for whoever is their "dog in the fight", as Kate puts it, and a mole-hunt across Whitehall and beyond for this rather colourfully named agent "Viper". They must be laughing their heads off in Moscow Centre already. And they'll split their sides if they get a whiff of the possibility that we might be taking it seriously.'

Kate's cheeks reddened. She hadn't expected Ian's assault to be quite so obvious.

'Fair comment, perhaps.' C lowered his spectacles and gave Kate his undivided attention. 'What do you think?'

'Perfectly fair,' she said, 'but not entirely reliable.'

'Let's roll with it for a minute,' C went on. 'The clear implication here is that in a potential leadership contest – and I'll come back to the premise in a minute – our foremost adversary will have a candidate.' He was still looking at Kate.

She nodded again.

'Who?' he asked.

'We've looked at it all ways,' she said, 'and, honestly, your guess is as good as mine right now. Some backbench MPs say they want one of the new generation, but in a lightning-strike contest, I think it'd be difficult to imagine someone more or less unknown to the public becoming a serious candidate. Which means it probably has to be a current member of the cabinet, and Vasily would be aware of that. So, to be talking about this seriously, their man – or woman – must already be close to the top of the tree.'

'Well, we can rule out Imogen Conrad at Education, since they helpfully – but perhaps too helpfully – identify her as the principal barrier.' C twirled his glasses and gazed, apparently absently, at the Houses of Parliament. 'So I guess that leaves Simon Wishart at Defence, the chancellor, and our very own foreign secretary.'

'Meg Simpson would be an outside bet, though the NHS strikes might have done for her.'

C rose to his feet and moved to the window, as if seeking inspiration from the home of British democracy. 'I've known the foreign secretary for a very long time, and it's no secret that I'm not his biggest fan. But it's a bit of a stretch to perceive him as a potential agent of a foreign power.'

'Unless they've found a pressure point . . .'

'Hmm. He's never made any great virtue of marital fidelity, so it's equally hard to imagine that some video of him with even a roomful of hookers might cause him any sleepless nights.'

'Given everything, we should stick this recording in the bloody bin where it belongs,' Ian said, almost under his breath.

'What do you mean, "given everything"?' Kate said.

'It's just another Russian conjuring trick. They love these things.'

C turned from the window and walked back. 'What Ian means is that we've been caught out before and, no doubt, will be again. But I'm afraid we need to take each case on its merits. That has to be the golden rule. They want us to let each drop of invective and every tissue of lies poison the well. Then they *would* have achieved their aim.'

'How have we been caught out before?'

'Ian ran the Russia House before you, and I did before him. So we've all been on the receiving end of the Kremlin's fantasy factory's output.'

'Should we talk to MI5?' Kate asked.

'Of course not!' Ian almost choked on his coffee.

'It's a bit early for that,' Sir Alan said, more smoothly. 'I may not have long to go in this chair, but I think even I have to be sensitive to the fact that James Ryan is the foreign secretary and thus our direct superior. As luck – if it is luck – would have it, we've been offered an easy means of testing this. According to the transcript, the prime minister is going to resign this week. I've heard not a whisper that he's unwell, let alone that he has cancer. If that proves to be correct, we'll need to take it all seriously. If not, we can come back to it. Agreed?'

Kate nodded. Ian followed suit reluctantly.

'I'll say this for the Russians,' C said, 'they certainly conspire to keep life interesting.'

Kate followed Ian to the lifts. He hit the call button as if it was an explosive device and waited with a disproportionate degree of impatience.

'Have we come across something like this before?' Kate asked. 'It would be helpful to know.'

'No,' he said. 'Not that I can think of. I mean . . . not specifically like this.'

The doors slid open and they got in. 'If there *has* been anything similar, then I guess—'

'As you should know, Kate, it's the first rule of the Desk to assume that everything you get fed by the Russians is manufactured. Start there, and you can't go far wrong.' He hit the wrong floor button, cursed and tried again. The doors closed.

'While we're on the subject of manufacturing, did you take up that translator I checked out in Istanbul? Irina?' Kate asked. 'I've been meaning to ask.'

'No.' He gave a sigh of what might have been exasperation. 'Why?'

'Just wondered. I met our Turkish connection in a bathhouse and remembered the last time I'd been there.'

'Jesus,' Ian said. 'She was a nobody, with zero prospects. And that was a lifetime ago.'

'Of course. It's all flooding back now.'

The doors opened. They got out and turned their separate ways.

'Have a good evening,' Kate said.

Ian didn't bother to reply.

She walked down to her small corner office overlooking Vauxhall station. Rav was scrutinizing an aerial photograph of the foreign secretary's home in Hampshire on his laptop screen. 'He's got a very big house for a man who has only ever really been an army officer and an MP.'

Kate smiled. 'As you never tire of telling me, the ruling classes have deep reservoirs of inherited cash, so that doesn't prove anything.' She signed the stack of expenses forms on her desk and put them in the out-tray for Maddy to process.

Later, when she called home, Stuart answered. 'I'm coming,' she said.

'Exciting. How was your trip?'

'Very good.'

'Did you get what you were looking for?'

'More than.' She ended the call and stood. 'See you tomorrow, Ravindra. Sir Alan wants us to leave it for now.'

He carried on tapping away.

'You did hear me, didn't you? C said to park it for now. It sounded like an order.'

'I heard you.'

'Sometimes you bear a striking resemblance to my son.'

'Have a nice evening.'

'Is Zac at home?'

'He's with his parents.' Rav looked up. 'In Scotland.'

'Well, don't stay here all night.'

Kate swapped her heels for trainers and retrieved her coat. 'Funnily enough, Stuart and I are having dinner with Imogen Conrad and her husband tonight.'

Rav swung around. 'Are you going to ask her about the PM's health?'

'I don't see any harm in saying I've heard a rumour, do you?'

He raised his palms. 'Could have come from anywhere.'

Kate thought about this. 'You're right. See you tomorrow.'

'I can hardly wait.'

She always walked home, rain or shine. It wasn't the capital's most scenic route, but provided time for reflection. She thought about what Ian had said. The Russians loved misinformation almost as much as they loved agents of influence and raw intelligence from inside government departments. But she had been extremely careful, right from the start, about how and when details of the Istanbul operation were disseminated.

Ian knew that Igor and Mikhail were the intended targets, and had signed off on the cost, but he hadn't known – or asked to know – how they had planned to get a microphone inside the yacht. The security teams setting up and manning the equipment and sweeping the approach to the money-changer's cubby-hole in the bazaar had been told no more than they needed to know. Danny had had no idea of what they were up to until he'd done his techie stuff that night. Only she, Rav and Julie knew all the details, including Lena's identity. It was inconceivable to her that either of her close colleagues could be compromised. And if the operation was secure, how could the SVR have believed they were planting misinformation via that microphone?

And the final possibility: that the man who'd let her know that the cream of Russia's intelligence hierarchy would be meeting on Igor's yacht had done so only to manipulate and deceive her . . .

No. She'd thought of that. Night and day. And continued to dismiss it.

It was not possible.

He would never lie to her.

It had started raining again so Kate ran the last hundred

yards to her front door. The mood in the house matched the weather outside. Gus was at the kitchen table, shackled to his Facebook feed on the iPad they'd bought him for Christmas. He had his headphones on to shield him from the yelling match taking place upstairs. Kate removed them. 'What *is* going on?' she asked.

'What do you *think* is going on?'

'Well, I've just come in from several days' rather complicated and demanding work and while I am, by common consent, a genius, I'm not blessed with second sight. So how about you just tell me?'

'They're having an argument.'

'You don't say. About what?'

'Guess.'

'Your father wouldn't let her go out until she'd finished her homework.'

'That was the last straw. But they've been at it since you left.'

Kate kissed her son's head and wrapped an arm around his chest. 'Hello, Mum, how lovely to have you back.'

He grunted.

'How was your trip? Oh, it was fine, thank you, Gus. It went rather well, actually.'

Now he was smiling at her. 'You were away?'

'Cheeky,' she said.

He gestured upstairs in the direction of the shouting. 'We missed you.'

Kate took off her raincoat and hung it in the hall, then came back, kissed Nelson, and lay down for a moment beside him.

Gus wrinkled his nose. 'I thought you told us not to kiss anyone until we knew where they'd been.'

'You're right,' she said. 'He does bloody stink.'

'He's old,' Gus said. 'You'll smell that bad when you're his age.'

'Nice.'

'Granny does. Which reminds me, the care home called.'

'How long ago?'

'Twenty minutes.' He scratched his head theatrically with his stylus. 'Or maybe yesterday.'

'What did they say?'

'Not much. They asked you to call back. Not urgent.'

Kate picked herself up and went to join the skirmish on the landing.

Stuart just looked at her. '*Now*,' he said.

'*No!*' Fiona's response wasn't discernibly muffled by the door that separated them.

'It was *not* a request!'

'Go away! I hate you!'

He held up an imaginary white flag and eased past Kate. 'All yours.'

'Welcome back, my darling,' Kate said, as he disappeared downstairs. 'How was your trip? Oh, actually, it went really well.'

But Stuart was long gone.

She moved to the bathroom door and knocked. 'Hon, it's me.' She waited. 'Fi, it's me. Mum.'

'Actually, I have a pretty good idea who "me" is.'

'Can you open up?'

'Why?'

'For starters, because I haven't seen you for a few days. And because I love you and missed you terribly.'

'That I doubt.'

'All right, but the loving-you bit is true. And because you've clearly had an argument with Dad and, honestly, he looks a bit cross, which probably means you're even crosser, and because I'm tired and would like to progress to a cup of tea without too much more time elapsing.'

Kate waited again. No one had warned her about the titanic reserves of patience one required to deal with teenagers. The door was eventually unlocked. A few moments later, it opened. Kate took a step forward.

'*Don't* come any closer!'

Fiona sat on the edge of the bath, her eyes puffy. Kate sat down beside her. 'So . . . I'm guessing Dad wouldn't let you go out tonight.'

'He's a total jerk.'

'Well, he can be, but we've all been there. I suspect he was concerned about your homework.'

'I'll do my homework! I always do my homework!'

Kate drew her daughter gently but firmly towards

her and hugged her. 'I assume you wanted to go and see him.'

Fiona didn't answer.

'You won't believe me, but he'll like you more for not jumping every time he calls.'

'You know literally nothing.'

'True.' Kate stood. 'But I have to go to the home now and see Granny.'

'Is she all right?' The concern in her daughter's voice was instant and genuine and reminded Kate – not for the first time – that the children reacted to her mother with an affection she'd never managed. There had to be an explanation for their desire to excuse the older woman's many faults, but she couldn't conjure one up.

'I'm pretty sure the dementia is here to stay. Aside from that, I should think so.' She paused. 'A cup of tea can be very soothing. Will you join me?'

'I'll come down in a minute.'

Kate took that as a 'no'. She kissed her daughter once more and returned to the kitchen.

Stuart already had the kettle on. It was as close as he got to telepathy. 'What is *wrong* with her?'

'It's a long story.'

'I'd like to hear it. I've never met anyone more irrational and unreasonable in my entire life. And that includes you.' He smiled, came over and kissed her tenderly. 'I'm sorry, my love. How was your trip?'

'It was – potentially – incredibly successful.'

'Can you say why?'

'Not really. But we'll see.'

Kate and Stuart sat at the table for another half-hour, grappling with the infinite mysteries of his favourite subject: logistics. They took in the school run, a weekend he was trying to plan in Norfolk, Christmas and what to do with her mother (hope she's dead), and an invitation he wanted to accept to a five-a-side football tournament in Bristol.

Kate countered by asking whether he'd booked the villa in Greece for half-term, as agreed. He hadn't.

After that, she left again, taking Gus's silence with her.

As she closed the door, Stuart fired two parting shots. 'Don't be late,' he said, since she was a notoriously poor timekeeper at home, which was odd for a woman whose workplace measured it in life and death, and 'Have fun,' which was obviously heavily ironic. Fun was one thing she was absolutely guaranteed not to have down the road with her sick mother.

The phone call turned out to have been about an unpaid bill, which she might have guessed. The home was a genteel establishment for elderly residents who liked to consider themselves a cut above the rest. It suited her mother down to the ground.

When she could finally delay the dreaded moment no longer, Kate went up to the eleventh floor. Lucy sat by the window in her room, staring out over the treetops in the park. A carer was clearing away the evening meal.

As she pulled up a seat, her mother turned to her. 'Hello, love,' she said. It was so long since she had recognized her daughter at all – let alone at first sight – that Kate had to suppress a tear.

'Hi, Mum.'

'How lovely to see you.'

Kate tried to smile. 'I'm sorry, I've been away for work.'

'You're always *so* busy.'

'I know. I'm sorry.'

'The children came. It was charming to see them. Gus is going to be a very big boy. He's like a gangly giant already.'

'He's growing fast. It's hard work keeping him in clothes.'

'I don't know why Fiona has to dress like that. What's wrong with her?'

'She's a teenager, Mum. You may remember having one yourself.'

Lucy smiled. 'Well, yes, I do. You used to wear those awful lurid trousers and went out with a boy who had a pierced ear.'

'Pete Carter, the trainee anarchist.'

'Stuart was with them.'

The first hint of the minefield. 'Well, yes. He would have brought them. He's their father.'

'Hardly said a word. Cat got his tongue?'

'He's been very busy too. And we don't have a cat.'

'You want to watch him. I've told you that before. He's a nice enough man, but I don't trust—'

'Let's not go there, Mum, all right?' Kate was not in a mood to take lessons in trustworthiness from her mother, and she had long since decided that Lucy's basic issue with Stuart was that he was too much like Kate's father. Which, in her own eyes, was his shining virtue.

Lucy shifted uncomfortably in her seat. 'Oooh. Would you mind getting me my pills? They're next door.'

Kate went through to her mother's bedroom, and took a couple of very deep breaths. The pills were on the lurid pink and gold bedside table her mother had always treasured, but something else had stopped Kate in her tracks: the photograph of her father smiling on a Cornish beach, which had once taken pride of place beneath the lamp, had been replaced by one of a man with a pencil moustache and striped swimming trunks.

Kate sat for a moment on the bed, in an attempt to contain her fury. Then she picked up the pills and went back to her mother.

'What's wrong?' Lucy asked. 'You look like you've seen a ghost.'

'Perhaps I have.'

5

'OH, DON'T BE SO silly.' Lucy took two large white tablets out of their blister pack and gulped them down with a glass of water. Kate hoped they might choke her.

'You've replaced the picture of Dad with one of David Underpants.'

As her mother met her gaze, Kate realized she knew precisely what she was doing. Nothing about this moment was lost in the mists of memory. There was no shame, no regret. It occurred to Kate that the bedside mission might have had nothing to do with the urgent need for medication.

'Don't be a prig, Kate. It doesn't suit you.'

'Where's the photo of Dad?'

'Oh, I don't know. Somewhere.'

Kate stared at her mother. Even now, after all the water that had flowed under the bridge, the old bitch's capacity to wound took her breath away.

'Honestly, where's the harm in it?' Lucy threw up her arms extravagantly. 'They're both dead, for God's sake. And I will be soon!'

Not soon enough, Kate thought. 'I don't know how to answer that,' she said eventually. 'Apart from noting that you were married to one of them – my *father* – for fifty years, and the other destroyed our family life.'

'That's your opinion.'

'It's absolutely everyone's opinion.'

'Oh, well,' Lucy said. 'Why does it matter *now*?'

Kate took a deep breath. 'I can't believe you have the gall to ask that. To you, clearly, *incredibly,* it doesn't. But it might have occurred to you that it could possibly matter to me. Just a *bit*.'

The corner of Lucy's mouth began to twist in the way it always did when she was thwarted. 'You were nowhere near as much the apple of your father's eye as you like to think, you know. And he was never the man you imagined. So you might want to get him down off that pedestal and see him as—'

'I don't need any instruction on how to view my father, thank you. Neither do I want your demonic version of how he felt about me. And as for David bloody Underpants, I—'

'I don't know why you insist on calling him that.'

'Because he was a ridiculous figure, a testament to your towering misjudgement. And why you think I would ever give a shit what you of all people think of Stuart, I can't imagine.'

Lucy sighed. 'You were *such* a disappointment to your father. To both of us. We so wanted to have a boy. Then everything would have been different.'

On other occasions, duty – she possessed her father's stoicism, and drew inspiration from his relentless good humour – had forced Kate to sit there and soak up the bile, but not today. 'I'm going now,' she said. 'Call me if you're dying.' She reached the door. 'And I might come back to say goodbye.'

Kate burst out of the home. The wind and rain tugged at her hair as she charged through Battersea Park towards the river. She wanted to scream her rage at the night sky. It had been Stuart's idea to move her mother there, in the fond belief that having work, home and filial duty within walking distance of one another would reduce the burden on her, but having Lucy so close had achieved precisely the opposite. It was a dark cloud in the morning and a thunderhead at night. Not to visit meant guilt. Visiting meant hurt. How did people end up like that?

David Johnson and his wife Emma had been their oldest and best family friends. Their daughter Helen had been more or less a sister to Kate, and young Neil the brother she had never had. They'd gone on holiday together every summer, to the same bungalow by the same Cornish beach. Even now, Kate could see David in his unprepossessingly snug swimming trunks as they played tennis in the garden or cricket on the beach.

And then one day the friendship and the laughter had come to a sudden end. There were no more Sunday lunches and neither of Kate's parents talked about the impending summer holidays. Worse, when Kate had plucked up the courage to call, Helen had taken the phone from her brother and said simply that they couldn't be friends any more.

It took several weeks for her father to get round to a partial explanation of what had happened, sufficient to allow logic and her imagination to fill in the rest. Her mother had been having an affair with David Johnson, perhaps for many years. His wife had now decreed that the two families were never to speak again. And they never did.

A year or two later, Kate had urged her father to leave her mother, and the worst of it all was that she had thought less of him when he wouldn't, or perhaps couldn't. His dependency – weakness, even, she sometimes had to admit – had fuelled her mother's cruelty.

Kate reached the river wall and looked down into the dark, swirling water. She had always suspected her mother of continuing to see her lover over the years, and her extravagant reaction to David's untimely death long before her husband's had more or less confirmed her suspicions.

Kate blamed the rain for dampening her cheeks. What kind of wife and mother fucks her husband's best friend? And what part of that woman had lodged itself genetically in her daughter?

If Kate could have run away from the reality of her upbringing at that moment, she would have done so, but she had long since known there was no escape. The shame followed her like a shadow. She walked home and put her arms around Stuart – who was leaning against the cooker, staring at his phone intently.

'Is it Christmas?' He looked at her. 'What happened?'

'Lucidity, that's what. She recognized me straight away. I can't remember the last time that happened.'

'And? What did she say?'

'Not much. But quite enough. She's thrown out the picture of Dad by her bedside and replaced him with David Underpants.'

'So you had an exchange of pleasantries.'

'Indeed.'

'Oh, shit.' Stuart hugged her. 'That's the last time you do that. From now on I'll go, once a week, and if she tries anything on with me, she's going to get it with both barrels. I'll chop her up and bury her under the back patio. And the picture of that weirdo in his very tight trunks can join her.'

Kate put her hand to his chest. 'It's a nice idea, and you're positively heroic. But she's *my* mother.'

'That is a matter of opinion.' He glanced at his watch. 'I

was going to point out that you are very slightly late, but under the circumstances I'll let it go. However, in the nicest possible way, you do need to get into the shower.'

Kate followed Stuart upstairs, her hand resting between his still quite finely honed shoulder blades. She loved her husband for many of the same reasons she'd adored her father. He was funny, generous and kind. He had an insatiable curiosity about the world, and a lively mind. 'My dreamboat,' she said.

'They still handing out the wacky-baccy at the home?'

Kate had a bath, not a shower, and took her time. She could tell that Stuart was torn between hurrying her because they were going to be late, and relaxing her to the point where she might feel like rolling around before they left. She dried herself slowly and shook out her hair.

'We really need to get going,' he said. 'But do you want to fool around for a bit first?'

'Do you mind if we save it for the weekend? It's been a punishing few days.'

He came over and kissed her. 'Of course not. But it'd better be good.'

She began to dress. 'What happened with Fi?'

Stuart sat on the bed. 'She wanted to go out. I said that was fine, but I wanted to see her essay on the Tudors before she went. She said she *would* do it, but in her own fucking time and . . . Well, you can imagine the rest.'

'You did the right thing. Frankly, anything to keep her away from Jedhead.'

'I don't think that's your most brilliant domestic strategy.'

'You haven't met him.'

'She's fifteen, not five.'

'You just wait.'

'Still, I don't think we can start trying to control who she sees. That never ends well.'

Kate inserted a pair of earrings and they went downstairs. Stuart was filling Nelson's water bowl when the doorbell sounded. Kate answered it.

'Good evening, Mrs Henderson.'

'Hello, Jed.'

Of course he was called Jed. He was six feet tall with enough hair gel to keep a toiletries company in business for a year.

'How are you?'

'I'm very well, thank you, Mrs Henderson.'

His polite and sincere smile seemed at odds with the tattoo wrapped around his neck, and the numerous piercings. Ashamed of herself, Kate tried to smile back. 'Can I help you?'

'Is Fi around?'

'I'm here!'

Fiona came down the stairs at speed, barely dressed and waving a sheet of paper. 'There,' she said, shoving it at Stuart as he came to join Kate at the door. 'The Tudors. An illuminated manuscript.'

'That must explain the ink splotches. But where exactly do you think you're going?'

'Out!'

'Wait!'

Kate turned back to the tattooed youth. 'Jed, I'm very sorry, but would you mind holding on a moment?'

She closed the door and faced her daughter again.

'You said I could go out if I finished my essay,' Fiona told Stuart. 'And, look, I *have* finished it.'

'I did not say you *could* go out if you finished it. I merely said you couldn't because you hadn't.'

'What's that? Russian?'

'You're not going out with him,' Kate said.

Fiona swung back towards her mother. 'I'm not going out? Or I'm not going out *with him*?'

'The distinction is academic. Because you are not going out, full stop.'

'Why not?'

'At this point, honestly? Because I say you're not.'

'And that's, like, an argument?'

'Kate . . .' Stuart said.

'She's not leaving this house, Stuart, and that's—'

'I can't spend the rest of my life wrapped in cotton wool,' Fiona said.

'Let her go for an hour,' Stuart said. 'And no more.'

Kate hated it when Stuart did this, but continued to face her daughter. 'I'm not trying to wrap you in cotton wool.'

'Yes, you are. You always do. You come home and treat us like porcelain dolls. Well, he's not the Russians and he's not the Chinese and he's not ISIS. He's a really nice seventeen-year-old boy.'

'He's nearly eighteen, and you are only just fifteen.'

'And you are two years younger than Dad. That's how it's supposed to be!'

Stuart took hold of Kate's arm. 'Let her go for an hour.'

Kate shrugged him off and stepped back. She went to get her coat, trying without success to hide her rage. She heard Stuart open the door, give the boy strict instructions on when to return his daughter and scold Fiona for the incredibly sloppy presentation of her essay. 'You'll have to do it again when you get back.'

All Kate heard after that was 'Thanks, Dad,' and the front door banging.

Stuart was waiting for her in the hall.

'I hate it when you undermine me.'

'You were being unreasonable and you know it. You can't protect her from poor judgement, and you'll make her choices worse if you try. Besides, he seemed like quite a polite lad to me.'

'I shan't let it go because you did undermine me.'

'I steered us both to a more reasonable course of action that will reduce the chances of her running away to Gretna Green with him. Or the nearest tattoo parlour . . .'

6

STUART PILOTED HER swiftly out of the house and took her hand in the Uber. She wanted to push him away but knew she couldn't justify her irritation. Fiona was right: she *was* too protective.

They bowled into the restaurant with profuse apologies to Imogen and Harry.

'I don't know why you bother saying sorry,' Harry said. 'You're always late.'

'It's Jed's fault.'

'Of course it is . . . Who the hell is Jed?'

'You may well ask. It's a story for the third bottle.'

Harry wasn't much to look at – his nose was flat and

wide and he'd long since lost his once-flowing locks – but Imogen was very pretty, with dark hair cut in a neat bob, long lashes and startling green eyes. Kate had met her about seven years ago, when Imogen had first been appointed as a junior minister in the Foreign & Commonwealth Office and Stuart had been her private secretary. She had moved on to Health and eventually into the cabinet as the secretary of state for Culture, Media and Sport. She'd graduated to Education a year ago in the last reshuffle, and had asked Stuart to join her.

Since their children were young and the badlands still some distance away, Harry and Imogen were always hungry for tales from Planet Teenager. Stuart got a great deal of mileage out of Fiona's love-struck angst and the appearance of the tattooed Jed on their doorstep.

Kate didn't say much. Her attention drifted back to Lena on the super-yacht. She wondered what she was doing. Only the progression of the conversation to politics and the security of the prime minister's position brought her back. Imogen was in full flow, hiding her ambition none too convincingly behind protestations of loyalty as much now, in private, as she did in public. With a small majority and a lot of self-generated errors, the prime minister's fate was a matter of almost constant debate.

'How long do you think he's really going to stay on?' Kate asked.

'Out by Christmas, we said, then Easter. But he's still

there. I think the basic truth is that our beloved foreign secretary will never force the issue because he's not as confident as he pretends to be that he would win.'

'I thought the PM looked bone tired the other day,' Stuart said. 'Maybe his wife will force him to quit.'

'When do they ever do that?' Harry asked. He was on his third gin and tonic already, and had taken to tugging his corduroy jacket as tightly as possible over his belly, a nervous gesture that gave away a preoccupation with his swelling girth. Imogen had already shot him a few warning glances, though she herself had had a couple of glasses of red wine.

'You haven't heard any rumours about his health?' Kate asked.

Imogen frowned. 'Why do you ask?'

'Something I picked up. Crossed wires, probably.'

'Well, you would know.'

'Maybe, maybe not.'

'What's supposed to be wrong with him?'

'There were just rumours he might not be in the best of health. I wondered if you'd heard them.'

'No, but—'

Their waitress passed the table and Imogen stuck out her hand so far it almost blocked her progress. 'Could we have that bottle of red wine sometime in the next decade? I've asked a couple of times already.'

The waitress stammered an apology. Harry stared uncomfortably into his glass as she departed.

Imogen locked her sights on Kate again. 'I mean specifically. What did you hear?'

'That he hadn't been well.'

'In what way?'

Kate shrugged. 'No more than that.'

'I mean flu or fatigue – or something more serious?'

'I honestly don't know any more.'

'C'mon, Kate. You know everything.'

'Leave it, love,' Harry said. 'It's probably one of those things Kate can't talk about, and we shouldn't press her.' He winked at Kate. 'However much we might want to.'

The waitress came back with the second bottle of red wine. She seemed nervous – Imogen did that to people – and a slightly clumsy twist of the bottle after filling her glass left a couple of spots on the frilly cuff of Imogen's shirt.

'For God's *sake*!' she exploded.

'I'm so sorry,' the waitress spluttered, her gaze transfixed on the two red dots on the cream material as if they were blood. 'I'll get a cloth . . . some salt maybe . . .'

'No!' Imogen barked. 'This is a McQueen, for fuck's sake.'

The waitress brought a salt shaker from the neighbouring table and Imogen snatched it away from her, then insisted on seeing the manager and explaining loudly that it was a *designer* shirt. He looked as confused by the significance of this as Stuart might have been, but promised to pay for it to be expertly cleaned or replaced. He said he wouldn't charge them for the evening's wine.

Harry made one attempt to intervene, but was swiftly silenced and reduced to staring into his drink. Stuart offered his boss discreet support, tut-tutting once or twice, then adding, 'Hopeless,' and 'Ridiculous,' for good measure. Kate couldn't think of any other situation in which Stuart would have behaved like that: he hated rudeness. But when Imogen shone her light on people, she could do no wrong.

After the drama had played out, Stuart and Imogen were drawn back to work chat, which left Kate wondering whether Imogen had behaved so oddly because she really didn't know about the PM's illness, or because she did. Perhaps it was just her driving ambition, which was aroused at the slightest scent of a rival's blood in the water. But Kate had a strong sense that Imogen would be a very good liar.

And good liars made good spies.

Kate closed her eyes. It was the curse of the case officer to be able to see every possibility in the most nuanced detail.

Kate and Harry listened to their spouses half-heartedly, chipping in about holiday plans and kitchen extensions until, after the main course, Stuart excused himself. Kate noticed he took his phone – the digital detox agreed the month before was going well then – and returned ashen-faced.

'Fuck me, Kate, sounds like you were spot on. The PM is

about to make an emergency statement. Robert Peston tweeted that he thinks he's going to resign.' Stuart handed Kate his phone and she passed it around the group. There was a stupefied silence.

'At almost ten o'clock at night?' Imogen said.

'Somebody must have been about to break the story,' Stuart said.

'I think he's got cancer,' Kate murmured. She looked at Imogen. 'That was the rumour.'

'You *do* know everything,' Imogen gushed, but Kate thought her expression was more guarded than impressed.

They paid quickly and hurried to Harry and Imogen's, only two streets away. On the television screen, Robert Peston was standing in front of a podium outside Number Ten Downing Street. The prime minister had been hoping to go on for some time, he said, but a sharp deterioration in his condition had forced a snap decision.

No sooner had he said that than the prime minister emerged from the iconic front door. His tall and beautiful wife stood beside him. They held hands for a moment before he began. 'I'm sorry to bring you here at this late hour,' he said, 'but news I received earlier today has forced my hand.

'I was diagnosed with prostate cancer three weeks ago. I had hoped that it could be effectively treated, and that I would be able to carry on with my work more or less uninterrupted, happy to be cared for by the brilliant staff of the best healthcare system in the world. However, though hope is by no means lost, the news I received today was less encouraging.

'I thought about taking a break from the business of government for a short period but . . .' he looked across to the media scrum that had been quickly assembled before him '. . . after talking it over with my staff and my family this evening, it was evident to me that this is not practicable. The country can never have a part-time prime minister, for whatever reason, and I would be letting you all down if I were to attempt it.

'I'm sorry again to have brought you here so late, but I was warned rumours might start to circulate and I wanted you to hear this from me. It has been a great privilege to serve my country, by which, of course, I mean all of you. I hope I will be able to do so again in some capacity, but for now, from this office at least, it is goodbye.'

He took his wife's hand once more. Tears were running down her cheeks. He waved to the cameras and led her back inside.

'Shit,' Stuart said.

'Oscar-winning,' Harry said.

Stuart turned to Imogen. 'Are you going to stand? You have to! James will be on the phone already.'

Imogen looked shell-shocked, which was more or less how Kate felt. She glanced at an incoming message from Rav. *Bingo,* it said, with an excitement she couldn't match.

She disappeared to the loo, closed the door and sat, elbows on her knees, while she messaged back: *Now what do we do?*

His response arrived via WhatsApp. *Focus on who runs. Investigate (the foreign secretary first, but the rest too, INCLUDING Imogen). Return to source operation and see what more we can get. And let's not forget 'Viper'. Why might he/she be in a position to help? PS Your call, but think we'll have to bring in 5. I know Pete Gibbs. Smart.*

Kate put the phone into her pocket. Pete Gibbs headed up a highly secret unit at the heart of MI5, tasked with investigating all attempts to infiltrate British public life. Rav was probably right, but Kate intrinsically disliked widening the circle of knowledge. No matter how tight the procedures and how careful the intentions, it would become harder to shield the original source of the intelligence. She had promised Lena she wouldn't put her at risk, and she had every intention of sticking to that pledge, even if she hadn't yet stepped in to shield the girl's sister.

In the taxi home, Stuart was pretty high on the night's events. 'She'll win.'

'She'll run him close, but she won't win.'

'She's young, she's telegenic, she's smart. Take a look at the polls. The fall-off in support for the government amid the under-thirties has been calamitous, and she's the only one who stands a chance of winning them another election.'

'She's all of those things, but they won't endear her to the party rank and file.'

'Well, I think you're wrong, wrong, wrong.'

'We'll see.'

By the time they got home Gus was asleep, but Fiona was still poring over her computer. 'I heard the news,' she said, when Kate looked in. 'Poor guy.'

'Somehow we never expect someone in such a position of power to be struck down by something so ordinary.'

'It sounded like he's about to die.'

'It did rather, didn't it?'

'His wife was crying a river. What's he like?'

'Decent enough. When push comes to shove, the sort of man you want to have in a job like that.' Kate moved over to kiss her daughter.

'I was back on time,' Fiona said defensively.

'I'm sure.'

'He's not the boy you think he is.'

Kate sat on the bed. 'He's just much older than you, love.'

'You mean he has loads of ink and piercings.'

'I don't want to have another argument. I just urge you to be careful and go very slowly.'

'You mean about sex?'

'Sex with him would be rape, so that is not a good idea.'

'Of course it wouldn't be rape!'

'Statutory rape. You're a long way from sixteen. He would go to jail, which is not something either of you would be happy about.'

'No one would know.'

Kate took Fiona's hand. 'I'm not trying to imprison you. I'm just trying to look out for your best interests. I'm not going to discuss sex because you're too young for that. If you're still going out with him in a year's time, perhaps it's something we can talk about. If he waits that long, maybe he *is* the boy you think he is.'

Fiona pulled her hand away. 'You have no idea how out of touch you are.'

'I have to be in work early, so I may not see you in the morning. Have a good day.'

Kate went to take off her make-up, then brushed her teeth and climbed into bed. Stuart would normally be snoring by now, but he was wide awake. 'You can't beat a bit of political intrigue,' he said.

'Hmm.'

'And it would be quite exciting if our friend became the most powerful woman in the country.'

'You're forgetting the Queen.'

'I'm serious.'

'It would be complicated, that's for sure.'

'Do you think she'd ask me to go with her?'

'I imagine so.' Kate leant over and kissed his cheek. 'Just make sure you don't spill anything on her *designer* shirt.' She rolled over. 'Now go to sleep.'

He did, but she didn't.

At least, not for long.

At two in the morning, she was woken by a vivid dream in which she discovered Lena's mutilated body in a wood, signs of torture clearly visible on her face and neck, arms and breasts.

Kate sat up with a familiar feeling of panic in her chest. She got up, her body covered with sweat. She went to the window, drew back the curtain and looked down into the street. It was deserted. She breathed in deeply and exhaled slowly, as the psychotherapist had taught her, and after a while the panic began to subside. She went downstairs, made herself a cup of tea and sat on a stool alongside the kitchen island to drink it.

With a start she realized that Stuart was behind her. She swung around.

'What is it?' His voice was creased with worry.

'Oh, same old.'

'Work or home?'

'We have someone out there, a young girl I recruited, not much older than Fiona. Our daughter is risking her virtue, but that girl is risking her neck – and the lack of balance was getting to me.'

'I often think you have everything under control, but . . .'

Kate sighed. 'Maybe it's what happened in Lahore with Rav – or my mother, I don't know. But the dread in the pit of my stomach is always the same.'

'Have you seen your counsellor recently?'

'Not for a few months. I thought it was getting better.'

'You're the most conscientious and careful woman I know so I'm totally sure you're doing everything you can for the girl you have out there.'

'I hope so, but she's there because of me. That's hard to get out of your head in the middle of the night.'

Stuart sighed. 'We've talked about this. I know it's an important job and you're very good at it, but we agreed it's not worth damaging your health. You have to be able to leave it locked inside that fortress. You can't bring it home, and leave part of yourself behind. That's not a good deal.' He kissed the top of her head. 'If I can help, call me.' He walked to the stairs.

'You do help, my love. It's not really the work but the sense of vulnerability that I can't help bringing home,' she said. 'No brothers, no sisters, no father, no mother to speak of. Work is intellectual stimulation, God is a fantasy. In the balance sheet of my life at dead of night, it's you, Gus and Fiona in the plus column. That's it. Nothing else. Whatever may trigger it, it's the fear of losing you all that brings on the dread.'

'But we're not going anywhere.'

'How do we know what Fate will decree? My love for all of you is paralysing at times. If I didn't know about the threats out there, I wouldn't be so gripped by the need to man the barricades. But I do.'

'I understand. Of course I do. But in the morning, I'll still emerge from the duvet looking like a demented wild boar, as you have been known to suggest, Fiona will still be a hormonal teenager – though hopefully over her Swedish-porn-star phase – and Gus will still struggle to utter five words before breakfast. Normal transmission will continue. And we'll live for the day, not for all time. Because that is what we all have to do.'

'But in the middle of the night, I fear the threat rather than revel in the joy.'

'You can't protect us from life. And you'll squeeze the humanity out of us if you try.'

'I don't want to protect you from *life*—'

'You are not your mother, Kate. You're not going to do what she did, and our family will not go the way of your own. Keep your anxiety locked away with her and with your work. Back here, you simply need to have faith in us.'

She smiled at him. 'I know. I'll be up in a minute.'

'You're a nutter,' he said, and disappeared back to bed.

7

THE FOLLOWING MORNING, the meeting with C was early enough to take place in his dining room on the top floor of MI6 Headquarters in Vauxhall. Kate rode the lift up and gave her overcoat to Beddows, the butler, who ushered her wordlessly into a cosy room with a dramatic view of Big Ben. If it was designed to convince guests that this was where real power rested at the heart of London's inner-most establishment, it could not have done a more successful job. Even the carpet seemed thicker than any-where else in the building.

Sir Alan and Ian were already eating bacon and scram-bled eggs. Rav was pushing some fruit and yoghurt around his plate. He never ate breakfast and rarely lunch. He was the archetypal night owl.

Beddows poured Kate some coffee. Sir Alan was already in full flow, and Rav was the beneficiary. 'I see no reason to waste time drawing up a huge list of potential runners and riders for the leadership. We can assume that if one of them is a Russian agent, he or she will stand. So as each candidate declares they list themselves as a potential suspect. We can safely predict the foreign secretary will put himself forward, so you should begin your investigations there today. The same, too, I think, with Imogen Conrad. Since they effectively represent each wing of the party, they may end up as the only candidates.'

'I still think we should wait and see if we can get some corroboration,' Ian said. 'If there's any kind of leak, it'll be hugely—'

'We can't wait. And there won't be a leak.'

'We *know* the Russians. What if this *is* just another—'

'We're damned if we do and damned if we don't. I'm well aware of that. But for now the greater danger is inaction.' Sir Alan was glaring at him.

Kate caught Rav's eye.

'We're not talking about a thin stream of intelligence from a single agent,' Sir Alan went on. 'We're discussing a conversation involving the most senior officials in the SVR that we can all listen to and form a judgement on. We'd look ridiculous if it emerged we'd just sat on it.'

'Rav suggested we bring in Pete Gibbs from Five,' Kate said.

Ian responded like a scalded cat: 'Out of the question.'

'I understand your reluctance,' Kate said, aware that Rav was still deploying his best poker face, 'but are we not under an obligation to inform them?'

'Yes,' C said. 'And indeed we will, in due course. But for now I want to keep the knowledge we have within this building. It's our intelligence. We own it and we need to take care of it.'

'Imogen Conrad stays on my list,' Kate said, still trying to distance herself from the glimpse of egocentric volatility she had been treated to the previous evening.

'Agreed. We should remain open to all possibilities. If Istanbul is an attempt to wrong-foot us, then it's conceivable that she *is* their woman and the foreign secretary their enemy. More prosaically, we may need to provide evidence ourselves some day that we conducted our investigations in an even-handed manner from the receipt of that first intelligence.'

'Any no-go areas?'

'Run the slide rule over everything. Finances, relationships, sex lives. Conduct yourselves exactly as if you were assessing the vulnerability of a foreign agent to an approach. We can simply pass it off as routine positive vetting, brought forward as a result of this contest.'

'But don't get bloody caught doing it, all the same,' Ian said.

'That might be difficult.'

'I'm sure you'll manage, Kate,' Ian said. 'We all know how resourceful you can be.'

'There is one other thing,' C said, glossing over Ian's waspishness. He tapped the file. 'Viper can help, they said. So who is Viper?'

No one answered.

'If he or she exists, we must confront the possibility that they have a desk inside this building.'

Kate glanced at Ian, who was staring out of the window.

'And, if somewhere else, then in what way can he or she "help"?'

'Could be anyone,' Ian said. 'In Number Ten, Whitehall, a journalist . . .'

'Let's start with the most senior civil servants around the secretary of state for Education and the foreign secretary,' Sir Alan instructed. 'Talk to GCHQ. Start with the basics: lifestyle, phone records, travel history. See if you can spot anyone or anything that sticks out. And I want you to go back to the source *here*.' He was pointing at the file.

'In what sense?' Kate asked.

'The only way they could be pissing us around is if they saw us coming. And if you were as tight with your procedures as I would expect you to be, that should have been more or less impossible. So let's not give up on the source of it. Your agent is still in place. Let's plant other devices. Let's see what else she can tell us.' He tapped the file. 'Looking through the transcripts again this morning, I think we should resume our focus on the son, Mikhail. If he's gay, he'll be finding an . . . outlet somewhere, even if it's not in Russia.'

Kate glanced at her phone. 'A message from Julie. The yacht disappeared overnight.'

'Then let's track it – and be there when it reappears.' He flipped the file shut and nodded to them, their audience over.

'Bang goes our quiet autumn,' Ian said, as they waited for the lift.

Kate raised an eyebrow. 'I hadn't figured you as a season-of-mists-and-mellow-fruitfulness fan.'

'You're going to need more help. Who would you like me to bring in?'

'Ops teams later, of course, but we should start off by trying to do it ourselves.'

'Excellent.' He adopted his habitual expression of messianic zeal. 'You're not alone on this, Kate.'

She glanced at Rav and tried not to laugh. Ian had never taken to her deputy, whom he had made a habit of ignoring. They rode the lift down in silence. When they reached their floor, Ian turned away without another word.

'What's he hiding?' Rav asked, when Ian was out of earshot.

'You might have to ask his tailor.' She grinned. 'He's at his most disconcerting when he starts trying to be helpful.'

'No, I mean specifically. He said, "We know the Russians, but what if this *is just another* . . ." Then Sir Alan cut him off. So, just another what?'

'He said something similar the other day. I didn't read too much into it. We know how Moscow works. They may well be misleading us.'

'No, no. That isn't what I'm saying. He and Sir Alan were looking at each other and they were talking about something specific they were aware of but we weren't.'

'If that's the case, I'm still not.'

They reached their office and the telltale signs of Rav's vigil: a McDonald's bag in the bin, half a dozen styrofoam coffee cups.

'Did you go home at all?' Kate asked.

'No.'

'What did you find?'

'All kinds of interesting things. If you get me a coffee, I'll give you a presentation.'

'You don't need another coffee, but it's a deal. Just give me a second to log on.' Kate stepped into her own small glass-walled office. As she sat at her desk, there was a knock on the partition door.

'Do you have a moment?'

Kate turned at the sound of Sir Alan's mellifluous tones. 'Yes, of course.'

He closed the door behind him. 'It seems like only yesterday I sat here, enjoying the same uplifting view of Vauxhall station.'

'You must miss it terribly.'

'Promotion does have its drawbacks.' C leant back against the filing cabinet. 'I didn't want to say anything in front of Ian but I'm not naive enough to believe that the intelligence gathered from Istanbul was solely down to luck.'

Kate didn't answer.

'Kate, I know every agent, every source we have in your neck of the woods. And since you started this job – my old job – I have noticed the occasional gem of information, whose origin I cannot completely fathom, creeping into the reports crossing my desk. Somebody tipped you off that one or more of those men were going to be on that yacht, didn't they?'

Kate stared pointedly out of the window.

'Clandestine sources are beguiling, but dangerous. They allow us to be manipulated and misled, with potentially serious consequences.'

'Is that what Ian was alluding to?'

'Yes.'

'It would be helpful to know how we were misled.'

'In an operation that began very much like this.'

'That doesn't tell me anything remotely useful.'

'It's a matter that is now closed on the orders of our

political masters. But it's the oldest story in our profession. You think you're buying gold, only to find you've paid a lot of money for highly coloured glass. But back to the present. I'd like to know if the impetus for this operation came from a source you haven't declared.'

She looked at him, sifting her options. 'Yes, it did.'

'Who was he – or, indeed, she?'

'I gave him my word I wouldn't say.'

'That wasn't what I'd call a request, Kate.'

'Well, I'm sorry. I can't tell you. I won't break my word – for you, or anyone else.'

'How very noble of you.' C switched off the light in his eyes. 'So where does that leave us? Perhaps we should be looking for someone you met during your time at Cambridge. Most probably on your year in Russia. Since then, he or she will have risen to a position of some importance in the Russian intelligence community – or perhaps their foreign service – and your contact is . . . episodic. Getting warmer?'

He waited out her silence. What a cool customer he was.

'You're a clever and ambitious woman, Kate. If I looked in your vetting file, I guess I'd find the name I'm looking for somewhere down the list of declared contacts from your Russian sojourn. I don't think you'd have been foolish enough to omit all mention of a contact of this . . . significance.'

'You probably could, but I still can't say.'

'I'd respectfully suggest that you're adopting an unnecessarily inflexible position.'

'Perhaps. But I think you'd do the same. It's one of the many reasons why I've always admired you. It comes down to a basic principle: you either trust my judgement or you don't.'

'Alas, in the real world, it's not as simple as that.'

'I'm not trying to challenge your authority. You're a very large part of the reason I'm still slaving away down here day after day. As I said, I gave my word.'

'Is it possible you were set up?'

'No.'

'How can you be so sure?'

'Instinct.'

'A sometimes mercurial guide, if I may say so.'

She turned to face him. 'You're right. He's someone I got to know when I was studying in St Petersburg, long before any of this.'

'A lover?'

She hesitated a moment too long. 'No.'

'You should tell me, if so.'

'No,' she said emphatically. 'Someone who might have been in other circumstances. I'd met Stuart by then.' She paused. 'I'd heard nothing from him for years until he turned up in London.'

'Possibly not by accident.'

'I've thought about that, of course, but I met him at an

American Embassy reception about three years ago and we chatted for a few minutes. I heard nothing more until this time last year when I had an anonymous letter in the post. It said we should watch Igor closely as he moved around Europe. We already were, as you well know. And then I got another letter a month ago.'

'Saying what?'

'Just tipping me off about a meeting of senior intelligence officers on Igor's yacht on the Bosphorus. We already had an operation in mind. We'd been planning to try to find a way to get close to Mikhail, so I just brought it forward.'

C remained impassive, except for a faint ripple of the jaw muscles. 'Very well. There are things *you* don't know. Vasily is not as powerful as he once was inside Moscow Centre. There are those who believe that his attempts to interfere with the democratic politics of the West are a distraction, which might prove costly. They're trying to persuade the Russian president he should concentrate only on the country's direct sphere of influence, and leave the West to unravel by itself. So perhaps you've been used. And perhaps you haven't.' Finally, he smiled. 'We all like to think our relationships are special. But let's not forget Moscow plays a very long game. From now on, I want to know everything, Kate. No secrets.'

'Of course.'

'I'm glad we understand one another.' He opened the door. 'Good luck.'

He shared his smile with Rav, who slipped in as soon as C had rounded the corner.

Kate forestalled Rav's question. 'He wanted to remind me of the almost inestimable size of the can of fucking worms we've just opened. Now I really will get your coffee. Wait here.'

Kate went down to the kitchen and closed the door. She could feel the heat in her cheeks. She punched the machine. Rav joined her before it had spewed out the second latte.

'You're so incredibly impatient,' she said.

'You'll already know point one of the briefing I was about to give you.'

'I don't. But I feel sure you're about to enlighten me.'

'I've been putting our foreign secretary under the microscope.'

'All night?'

'All night. And there is a great deal I have to tell you. But page one, paragraph one, *point one*: guess who was at school with him.'

'Sir Alan. It's not a secret.'

Rav was not remotely deflated. 'I bet you don't know this: they were in the *same house, in the same year*.'

Kate frowned. 'You're right. I didn't know that.'

'It's your highly over-privileged world. How many boys is that?'

'It's not my world, Rav.'

'You went to private school.'

'I went to a small Quaker school where you were expelled if you failed to get straight As and where the playing fields had been sold off to build a block of flats. It wasn't Eton.'

'Eton doesn't accept girls.'

'Don't be pedantic.'

'Okay, but how many do you reckon?'

'In a year in a house? I don't know . . . twelve, thirteen, fourteen?'

'He gives the impression he doesn't think much of the man he calls our "nominal" superior, doesn't he?'

'Well, yes, though he's reasonably discreet about it. And I don't see why it matters that much.'

'But it's *interesting*, right? You know how the establishment likes to stick together? It excludes you just as much as it does me, and you went to Cambridge.'

She thought about it for a moment. 'Yes. It is interesting.'

8

BACK IN KATE'S office, Rav pulled up a chair and deposited his pile of notes on her coffee table. He flipped around the three files in front of him so that the one marked 'Conrad' was on top. 'I'm going to start with your friend Imogen, if you don't mind, because although there's less to report, in some ways it's more interesting.'

She waited.

'Her finances look commensurate with her role and her husband's job with Oxfam: one house, which you know about, in London, and no sign of any other wealth. She gets a hell of a lot of abuse online, I mean really disgusting stuff – rape threats, the works.'

'She's a woman in public life and has made the mistake of being pretty.'

'Well, the internet is not a flawless intelligence resource, but I can't see any rumours of extra-marital affairs or anything else that might be used against her. However, her record on Russia is a bit odd.'

'What sort of odd?'

'When she became a minister, she was very voluble, particularly about the murder of Alexander Litvinenko, which had happened a few years before she joined the Foreign & Commonwealth Office. She took a very tough line, demanding stiffer sanctions and actually getting them imposed on a wider section of the president's inner circle. In 2012, she was invited by the Foreign Affairs Select Committee to accompany MPs on a fact-finding mission to Moscow, St Petersburg and, of all places, Ekaterinburg, Ipatiev House—'

'Where Tsar Nicholas and his family were assassinated. And?'

'And she's barely spoken publicly about Russia since.'

'2012 . . . She must have got promoted to Culture, Media and Sport around then.'

'Later that year.'

'So her silence on that subject is hardly surprising.'

'Maybe.' He was flicking through to the end of the file. 'But on most of her other favourite subjects – human rights in China, Tibet, Saudi – she has continued to be quite frequently and widely quoted. At a conference fringe event last year. At a discussion on shaping the modern world at the Chalke Valley History Festival a few months ago. On Russia, however, even with the Salisbury nerve-agent attack and everything that followed, nothing.'

'Have you got a list of who accompanied her on that Russian trip?'

He fished it out and handed it over. 'Interesting or not?'

'The trouble is, once you start looking for things that might seem extraordinary, then graduate to the curious absence of the ordinary, that way madness lies.'

Rav flipped open the second file. 'Okay, our illustrious foreign secretary, James Ryan, of whom the reverse appears to be true. Leaving aside the moments when he's had to be critical – such as the attack on Salisbury, for example – he's said incredibly little about Russia, which is intriguing, given that he's been foreign secretary for half a decade. He's filled acres and acres of newsprint on the US, Europe, Saudi, Yemen, Israel, Syria, ISIS, the Middle East in general, China, North Korea, Japan – but Russia only rarely, and he's been only mildly critical, even of its role in Syria.

'Before Salisbury, he was on record as saying, "At least the Russian president knows what he wants." And in general, he's the least hawkish of the cabinet, perhaps surprising, given his time in the military. He has never been in favour of pursuing and confiscating the assets of the London-based oligarchs. And the Foreign & Commonwealth Office has been kind enough to remove sanctions and travel restrictions on eight more members of the president's immediate circle – to "improve relations" with the Motherland.'

'Cosy? Or merely pragmatic?' Kate mused.

'I've looked into the possibility of some kind of *kompromat* on the foreign secretary and I'm with C on this. His reputation as a shagger is so Olympian that even if they had footage of him in bed with any number of women – or men, or even goats, for that matter – they'd have no real hold over him.'

'You never know what really goes on behind the scenes in a marriage, though. Perhaps Sophie chooses not to believe the rumours, but would find the evidence utterly devastating.'

'She seems to have learnt to live with the fact that he has at least one love-child.'

'Is *said* to have a love-child.'

'Have you seen the pictures?'

'No.'

Rav pushed across a printout: a young boy holding a woman's hand in a playground. To say he was the image of James Ryan was understating the likeness between them.

'Hmm. I see what you mean. All the same, wives, husbands – partners – can always blind themselves to what appears obvious to everyone else.'

'Not sure I agree, but let's park it for now. His financial

status is puzzling. He left school at eighteen and joined the military. Only made it to major before quitting, and after a very short spell in business, he became an MP. Yet he has a house in Chelsea, that pile in Hampshire I showed you, a cottage in Cornwall and sends all three of his children to public schools, whose fees for each child are now almost forty grand a year.'

'The privileged among us mostly pay for their children's education through inheritance. It's what keeps the class system afloat.'

'Not in this case.'

'Go on.'

'His dad was also an army officer. He died two years ago, leaving everything he had to his wife. She lives in a cottage near Basingstoke and holidays in James's Cornish shepherd's hut. Sophie's father was RAF and her mother was a nurse and they're both dead. The mother left an estate valued at just over half a million three years ago.'

'That's not nothing.'

'Enough to pay the school bills, possibly, but not the rest of it. She also has a sister.'

Kate glanced over the relevant paperwork. 'What next?'

'Follow the money. I'll look into what he did after leaving the army. We should also try to speak to people who knew him at school and in the military, particularly, I would say, during his time in Kosovo. Can I at least ask Five for his vetting file?'

'No.'

'That will make everything harder.'

'You heard what Sir Alan said.'

'Fair enough.' Rav reached for the last file. 'Viper. Potential suspects.'

The names were listed under just two headings: *Imogen Conrad* and *James Ryan*. Stuart made an early appearance.

'Sorry,' Rav said.

'For what?'

'If there's ever a review, we're both going to look stupid if we leave him out.'

'Of course,' Kate said. 'Perhaps I'll discover he has a secret gambling habit. It might explain how all our money seems to vanish into thin air.'

'I don't think I'd want someone in my team investigating Zac.'

'Then you should have more faith.' Kate handed back the dossiers and eyed the McDonald's wrapper. 'Not good,' she said. 'But the coffee is probably worse. If you insist on being here all night, you're going to have to cut down or you'll be dead before you're forty.'

He gave her an unwitting glimpse of unutterable sadness. 'I'll be dead long before I'm forty.'

'That's an extreme and frankly stupid thing to say.'

'Trust me. I will be.'

'Don't talk like that, Rav.' Kate looked into his eyes and saw the vulnerability he worked so hard to hide. Rav had always felt unloved and unworthy in his parents' estimation, which left him prone to often crippling depression. It was a reminder that she was not alone in her unresolved demons.

Rav slipped out and closed the door behind him.

Kate tapped her keyboard and opened the Records entry portal. Zehra's response to her question about the translator she'd assessed in Istanbul still nagged at her. If the recruitment *had* gone ahead, why had Ian lied about it? She typed in her own name and staff code and entered *Irina Demidova* in the search bar. A few seconds later, she was rewarded with *No items found*.

Maddy knocked and entered. 'Morning. I hear Istanbul went well.'

'Yes, it did. We're going to be very, very busy.'

'That'll make a nice change.'

Maddy was in her early forties, tidy, steady, married and childless. She was one of those women who could be annoyingly pedantic – pedestrian, even – over detail, but would always have your back. She was also a world-class gossip, which had its uses in that building. 'You might want to come and watch,' Maddy said. 'He's out of the blocks already.'

Kate joined Rav in front of the TV screen on the far wall. As an apparently impromptu press conference was being set up outside the Foreign & Commonwealth Office in King Charles Street, Kate passed Maddy the list of MPs on the Moscow trip. 'Can you get me in to see one of these champions of the people this morning? Angela White might be favourite – she's been around a while and is quite vociferously anti the Russian president.'

Kate checked that she was not about to sit on anything, then perched on the edge of Julie's desk. It was bare, save for the picture of her brother, Jason, who'd been killed on the top deck of a bus during the 7/7 London bombings. She'd always said she was there to play a meaningful part in the war on terror but, bright as she was, plenty of department heads gave her a wide berth. She'd been to places not many others had experienced, even in a building like this, which set her apart.

A suave, dark-haired man emerged onto the street and approached the microphones. Rav picked up the remote and pumped up the volume. James Ryan paused for a moment, glancing about him. 'Thank you very much for turning out at such short notice. I'm sure you were all as shocked as I was last night to hear what the prime minister had to say. His service to our country has been exemplary and we hope and pray he will be successfully through his treatment and back to front-line politics in no more than a heartbeat. We know he's in the hands of the best health-care professionals anywhere in the world today.'

'Why do they all say that?' Rav asked. 'It isn't true, and they don't mean it.'

'The prime minister's legacy is a great one,' Ryan

continued. 'He's led this country with an energy and optimism that are the envy of other world leaders. A golden future awaits us as a proud, independent, free-trading nation, developing new and exciting relationships with countries across the globe.'

He surveyed his audience.

'Was he the original model for Action Man?' Kate whispered.

'If it's him against Imogen Conrad,' Rav said, 'it'll be the best-looking political contest in British history.'

'He's too smooth for me,' Maddy said. 'I wouldn't trust him to put out my rubbish.'

'None of us would choose to be here today . . .' the foreign secretary went on.

'You fucking would,' Rav whispered.

'. . . but I have never denied that, if the moment were to arise, I would aspire to lead our great party and our wonderful country. Such sad circumstances serve to remind us that in adversity there is always opportunity – and today the question before you is, who can give this country the bold and optimistic leadership it needs?

'I count myself truly fortunate to have had so many calls of support from colleagues, urging me to run. And so this morning I announce with considerable pride that I will be putting my name forward. I'm sure an open, exciting and vigorous contest awaits us. May the best man – or woman – win! Thank you!'

As the assembled reporters shouted questions, the foreign secretary turned smartly and re-entered his domain.

Maddy put down her phone. 'Angela White can see you now, if you have time. They'll come down and get you from Reception at Portcullis House.' She followed Kate into her office. 'Any expenses from Istanbul?'

'Somewhere. I'll put them on your desk.' Kate picked up her coat, then hesitated. 'Maddy, you know I don't like to ask about your stint with Ian . . .'

'I've never understood why you insist on being so scrupulous. He wouldn't.'

'I don't want to put you in an awkward position.'

'You mean like I was the whole bloody time I worked for him?'

Kate smiled. 'All right. Do you recall him recruiting a woman called Irina Demidova? I assessed her in Istanbul. Originally a relatively lowly secretary in the KGB, but she may have progressed beyond that. Ian told me yesterday that he never moved forward with her, but I'm not so sure.'

'I don't, but that doesn't mean much. If he told me it was Wednesday, I'd still check a calendar.'

'But if she *had* gone on the payroll, it would have been down to you to process it through Finance?'

'Probably, unless she was one of the little secrets he liked to keep.'

'If she *had* gone on the payroll, Finance would still have a record, right? I mean, if the management committee wants to take someone off the books, they can remove them from the central system, but there's no procedure for taking it out of the accounts?'

Maddy closed the door quietly behind her. 'That's a pretty big question. What's going on?'

'I have to keep everything tight for now and I'm not sure this is relevant anyway.'

Maddy shrugged. 'I really don't know. You'd have to talk to Rose.'

'I thought you might say that.'

Kate walked down the back stairs to the Operations Room on the floor below. Maddy's visceral dislike of Ian was partly explained by his attempt to get her sacked for incompetence, as a result, she said, of her having refused his advances. Only the fact that she had once worked for Sir Alan had saved her.

Danny's colleague Hamid was staring at a set of screens in the far corner of the Ops Room. 'Morning,' Kate said. 'You look knackered.'

He manipulated the mouse on the pad in front of him and pulled up a satellite feed displaying the progress of Igor's yacht. 'Headed for Greece, at a guess, but not in any particular hurry.' He moved to the screen on the right. 'There was something we missed, though.' He fast-forwarded through the stream of video from the top of the

Kempinski. 'Danny went through the pictures from the very small hours . . . And here we are. Four thirty in the morning . . .'

A group of men were getting onto the launch, speeding in to the shore, offloading on the quay, then walking towards the hotel. At the head of the group, which included Vasily and his colleagues from the Russian Intelligence Service, was Igor.

'They got into two separate Mercedes, drove to the airport and took off in a private jet bound for Moscow.'

'No sign of Mikhail, his wife and son or the au pair disembarking?'

He shook his head. 'As far as we can tell, they're still on board.'

'Will you tell me as soon as they get within reach of a dock?'

'Sure. Danny's packing up in Istanbul and heading home. Is that all right?'

'Yes, but I'll want him to turn straight round and head out to wherever they make landfall.'

'I'll give him the good news.'

Kate took the lift to the ground floor. Rose's office was only just far enough above the exterior walkway to afford its incumbents a view of the river. 'They put us here,' her aunt had once told her, 'because they'd be only too delighted if someone planted a bomb on the wall and the whole Finance team got blown to smithereens.'

Rose's secretary had poorly dyed blonde hair and a lurid green cardigan with bright brass buttons pulled tightly across her chest. Jane was originally from Poland in the days when it had laboured under Communist rule and looked like she'd never left. Her manner was pure Iron Curtain too, and it was a mystery why Rose was so loyal to her. 'She's in a meeting,' Jane announced, as Kate approached, allowing herself a rare moment of delight.

'No problem. Will you tell her I dropped by?' Kate glanced at the frames on Rose's desk, which included photographs of her husband and beloved dog Stanley, Kate and her father, arm in arm on the Ridgeway, just above Rose's home.

Rose Trewen was Kate's father's sister, and the principal reason Kate had joined the Service. She was also as close to a mother as Kate had ever enjoyed, though the depth of their emotional connection was not something either tended to advertise at work.

'Can I help you with something?' Jane asked.

'Don't worry. It can wait.' Kate turned away, then thought better of it. 'Actually, could you do a system search? We're doing some internal vetting.'

'I am sure Rose would want us to help.' Jane's accent was still strong enough to make that sound like a threat.

'Could you check whether we've ever made any payments to an Irina Demidova?'

Jane turned to her monitor, tapped away for a few

moments, then went very still. 'You will have to speak to Rose about that,' she said.

'Oh . . . of course. I'll come back later.'

Kate emerged from Security into a close afternoon. Banks of dark cloud brooded over Vauxhall station, threatening to explode at any minute. She thought about the expression on Jane's face when her screen had sent her a message she clearly hadn't expected.

It seemed obvious that Ian *had* recruited Irina Demidova. So why was he so evasive at the mention of her name?

9

KATE CLEARED SECURITY into Parliament at Portcullis House with unexpected speed. The fig trees on the other side of the barrier seemed to reach up to the great glass roof, but she had little time to admire them.

The woman who came to meet her was tall and slightly forbidding. She tucked a strand of long, grey-streaked hair behind her ear as if rebuking it for an act of momentary disobedience. 'Angela White,' she said. 'I was passing through from the House, so I thought I'd take you up myself.' She swiped Kate through the glass security portal and gestured at the light and airy piazza beyond. 'I'm guessing you've been here often enough.'

'Not really.'

'You were admiring the fig trees. Quite right too. They cost our loyal taxpayer four hundred thousand pounds. Oh, the glory of the Blair years. Those were the days!' She broke into an unexpected smile and gestured at the coffee shop. 'Would you like to come up to the office or stay down here?'

'Probably best to have a little peace and quiet.'

'I assumed as much. Let's go up.'

Angela led Kate up to a small but well-appointed suite on the third floor, which overlooked Big Ben and a slice of the river. She smiled again. 'You have no idea of the native cunning required to get an office like this.'

'With a view like that, I might have been tempted to indulge in a little light skulduggery myself.'

'Tea?'

'Coffee, if it's on offer.'

Angela motioned to her smaller, more intimate chamber with an even more spectacular perspective of Big Ben. Kate sat on the sofa by the window, as invited. 'The chimes must be deafening.'

'Oddly, you get used to them, to the point when you look out for the strike of the hour as a signal to go and do something, and somehow always miss it.'

'It's a hell of a place.'

'It is, but I try not to let it go to my head. My seat isn't exactly a marginal, but it wouldn't take much of a turn in the tide . . .'

'You've been here a while, though.'

'Seventeen years. It only feels like five lifetimes so far.'

Angela's assistant brought in a tray of tea, coffee and biscuits. They were silent for a moment as they helped themselves and settled back in their seats.

'Have you ever wanted to be a minister?' Kate asked.

'No. An MP is what I am, and what I shall remain. That's partly to do with the children – we have three, all grown up now – but also because I think one has to choose early on in here between ambition and principle, and I found it too hard to win my seat to readily let go of the things that really matter, which perhaps sounds a bit priggish. I try not to stand on my principles too often, which is harder than it might appear . . .' She sipped her tea. 'Sorry. I imagine you didn't come all the way here to discuss my less than impressive career.'

'I can't help feeling that choosing integrity over office is pretty impressive.'

'Kind of you to say so.'

Kate put down her cup. 'I know you must be busy, so I'll get to the point. My office was probably rather vague—'

' "Opaque" is a word that springs to mind.'

'I can't stress strongly enough the sensitivity of what I'm about to discuss. Which is a roundabout way of saying that after listening to what you've just told me, I'm going to speak more openly than perhaps I would otherwise.'

'That sounds . . . dangerous.'

'I've kept up to speed on much of what you've said at the Foreign Affairs Committee hearings, and you seem to have a very dark view of modern Russia.'

'Are you suggesting I'm wrong? After the nerve-agent attack in Salisbury, I thought it was generally accepted—'

'My God, you're not wrong. It's a gangster regime and the Russian president is the nemesis of everything we hold dear. In his view, a great modern Russia requires a corrupt, weak and supine West. He is the most serious and well-organized enemy of Western civilization.'

'Go on.'

'Oh, I could be here for hours. He's everywhere. He's trying to provoke war with Georgia via the breakaway republics in an attempt to deter NATO from admitting it to membership. He's funding and equipping right-wing paramilitary groups in Latvia, Estonia, Lithuania and even Slovakia. Look closely on the satellite pictures into some of the camps these groups are building in the middle of the countryside and you'll see armoured cars and stashes of semi-automatic weapons. What would they need those for? A long while back you alerted the committee to the Russian president's attempts to undermine the operation of Western democracy and since then, of course, it has exploded into the public consciousness in America and everywhere else. But it isn't just the false social-media accounts and the hacked emails, the leaking and assistance given to candidates of dubious views who once might not have had a cat's chance of high office.'

Angela was listening intently now.

'They're doing much more than that. We know that they're trying to bribe, bully or blackmail leading figures within these walls. What could be more satisfying than having Western leaders as your agents of influence? Which brings me to the current leadership election. We're trying, very carefully, to check out the main candidates, so I'd be grateful if you didn't read anything significant into the choice of individual I'm here to discuss.'

Angela's gaze was now hawk-like. 'Isn't that MI5's job?'

'Yes. But in this particular case, because of the nature of the original intelligence, we need to pursue things ourselves, at least initially. If we find evidence that it's correct, Five will be fully briefed.'

'Okay.' Angela visibly relaxed. 'I'll try to keep my trap shut.'

'About seven years ago, you went on a trip to Russia with Imogen Conrad. At that point, she was a junior minister in the Foreign & Commonwealth Office.'

'I did, yes.'

'Was there anything about her conduct on the trip that struck you as odd or worthy of note? Anyone she saw, anything she said?'

'That's a rather open-ended question, if I may say so.'

'True. But I think you know what I'm driving at.'

'All right. I'll tell you what I really think of Imogen Conrad, in the privacy of this room. She's what you might call a man's woman, at her brightest and most vivacious when there's a man around she wants to impress. She *is* attractive – what men would call sexy – and she knows it. I think she likes to feel she has the men around her exactly where she wants them. She is, consequently, not someone who finds women – particularly jobsworth backbench MPs – of much interest. So, mostly, I find myself somewhat impervious to her no doubt considerable charm.'

'How did that particularly manifest itself in Russia?'

'To be brutally honest, she didn't seem especially interested in the place or its issues, which struck me as curious for a young minister early on in her brief. And less than sensible, given that her colleagues on the trip – mostly women, unusually, in this instance – might one day play a role in her future, as now seems about to be the case.'

'So she didn't speak to you?'

'She didn't speak to anyone very much. She had various flunkeys with her, all men, at least one of whom she appeared very friendly with indeed.'

'Which one?'

'Oh, I can't remember. Some Scottish fellow.'

Kate suddenly found herself concentrating very hard on the floor. 'Did he have a name?'

'I suppose he must have done.'

'Someone from her private office?'

'Probably. He seemed to be with her all the time.'

'What did he look like?'

'I really can't . . .' Angela leant forward. 'Are you all right?'

'Yes. Fine. Sorry, just a little warm.' Kate composed herself. 'Do you think she was having an affair with this man?'

'I really don't know. I didn't consider it my business. But . . .' She tilted her head to one side. She was still looking intently at Kate. 'On the last night we were taken to the ballet at the Mariinsky and they slipped away the moment the official part of the evening was over. I saw them coming in together later that night. They looked . . . Well, I don't quite know how to put it. I think you understand what I'm getting at.'

'And if something had happened between them, the Russians might well have been aware of it?'

'We were all warned to be careful. I'd be amazed if she and her team weren't given a similar briefing.'

Kate could feel the colour in her cheeks now. She stood, too quickly. The remnants of her coffee spilt across the low table and onto the floor. 'Oh, God! I'm *so* sorry.'

Angela whisked some tissues out of a box on her desk and began to mop up. 'Don't worry about it.' Kate stood awkwardly by the door as she deposited the soaked tissues in the bin. 'There, no harm done.'

'Thank you for your help. And your time.'

'Was there . . . anything else?'

'Yes. No.'

'Well, it was a pleasure to meet you.'

'Likewise.' Kate realized she was still glued to the threshold. 'There is one other thing. A long shot . . . I don't suppose you kept a list of who was on that trip by any chance?'

'I very much doubt it, but I'll let you know if we can dig it out.'

Angela insisted on taking her back downstairs. Stuart's incoming message made Kate struggle to engage in further small-talk. She and Angela shook hands slightly awkwardly at Security, and she tipped out into the spitting rain on the Embankment, then returned to her phone screen.

She's standing! High excitement here! Official statement later this afternoon.

Kate crossed Westminster Bridge, head bowed against the gusting wind. She wanted to avoid the office, so slipped into Waterloo station to hide in the upstairs Pret a Manger. She ordered a coffee and sat looking down over the departure boards.

She closed her eyes.

No, no, *no* . . .

She knew nothing. There was no evidence of anything.

Imogen must have had more than one Scottish adviser. And, if Angela had unwittingly been talking about Stuart, there was no evidence of an affair. They got on well. She knew that. They were friends. Stuart hated the ballet, so a couple of mates hurrying away from a cultural evening with a dowdy group of MPs would have been no big deal.

She opened her eyes again and scanned the cluster of passengers waiting for their train to appear. 'You can pick a destination,' her father had once told her, 'but you can never predict the journey.' He'd been talking about his marriage, an oblique answer to an oblique question, since they never spoke directly of her mother's infidelity and the pain it had inflicted on him.

The years had not dulled the shame of her mother's affair, the burning sense of injustice on her father's behalf, and Kate's humiliation at being the daughter of a woman who could behave in such a way.

She thought about what Stuart had told her only the night before. 'You can't protect us from life. And you'll squeeze the humanity out of us if you try.' What had he meant by that?

She had spent so long worrying about not becoming her mother that she had never really considered the possibility that Stuart might turn into his father. Alec Henderson had run out on three marriages in quick succession. Stuart had somehow retained a cordial relationship with him throughout, and never been more than mildly censorious of his father's inability to keep his trousers zipped.

Kate selected a sandwich and a compact beetroot-coloured drink brimming with good health. Half an hour later, she had wrestled herself back into some kind of equilibrium.

*

'How did you get on?' Rav asked, when she walked back into the office.

'Something and nothing, as my granny used to say. Maddy, can you find me a list of everyone on that FO Russia trip, not just the MPs?'

'I'll call the Foreign Office now.'

Rav followed her. 'I've started with his schooldays. Found a guy who sounds dull, provincial and tediously reliable. Rupert Grant. Same house, same year.'

'Good.'

'Believe it or not, he still lives close by. So much for devotion to the Empire. It's about two hours on the train. You want to go now?'

Kate looked at the clock on the wall. 'No. I have to be home in reasonable time tonight. Let's do it first thing tomorrow.'

'Okay. I'll focus on his time in the army and in business before he became an MP.'

'We should take a careful look at trips to Russia as well. More lists for Maddy. She'll love that.'

Kate nudged the door shut with her foot as Rav went back to his desk. The pain behind her eyes was blinding now. She reached into her drawer, knocked back four ibuprofen and stared blankly at her computer screen, then pulled herself together and logged on.

If Imogen Conrad was her subject, she needed to treat her like any other. She googled her name and began to read about her friend as if she was a stranger. She hadn't got much further than an article in her constituency newspaper when Maddy put her head around the door. 'She's standing.'

Kate joined the others in front of the screen as Imogen and her team approached the bank of microphones. 'Do you ever wish we could wind back time,' Kate asked, 'and scrub what we think we know from our minds?'

'Not really,' Rav said. 'It's going to put us all through the wringer – but that's nothing new, and if we end up nailing some bent politician, then few things would give me greater satisfaction.'

'Good afternoon.' Imogen was now at the microphones. She looked uncharacteristically nervous. 'Thank you very much for turning out at such short notice. As you know, there is a vacancy at the head of my great party. But before I talk about the hole in our lives that needs to be filled, can I first pay tribute to the prime minister for all he has done for us and, more importantly, for our country? There have been many tributes already. And rightly so. There will, no doubt, be many more. Some will be less genuine than others, but I dare to believe that anyone who knows anything at all about life here at Westminster will be aware that my admiration for him is genuine and heartfelt. I am very, very sorry to see him go.'

She paused for a moment, surveying the massed ranks of commentators assembled in front of her. 'However, we must now look to the future. We must look closely at how we as a party can best continue to serve the interests of this great and diverse nation. The question I ask myself is no different from the one you must be asking: who is best placed to take forward the prime minister's vision of a country at ease with itself and with the modern world, a nation determined to make the best of the opportunities that now present themselves?

'I have been overwhelmed – slightly stunned, in fact – by the number of hugely encouraging calls I have already received today from colleagues, some of whom you see with me now, and from my very supportive constituents. I have been persuaded, therefore, that I should indeed put my hat into the ring. I am here to announce my candidacy for the leadership.'

Imogen allowed herself a modest smile at the flurry of dutiful applause from the MPs – largely men, Kate noted – behind her. She was hitting her stride.

'I will set out my vision for our country in more detail in due course, but I want to flag one issue today, which I believe stands out over and above all others. It has been the privilege of my life to serve as the secretary of state for Education. As we now make our way in the wider world, it is imperative that we have a workforce educated to the highest possible standards. Without it, we will simply not be able to compete and thrive. A previous prime minister once listed his priorities as "Education, education,

education." Whatever one may think of his legacy, I would like you to know that I am *deadly* serious. I have already tried to improve standards in the state sector and force private schools to do more to help local state schools, but I intend to go much, much further. And that cannot be achieved without a significant – perhaps a *very* significant – reallocation of resources.'

She smiled again. 'The fine detail is for another day. For now, I thank my colleagues for their support, my constituents for their trust, and I thank you all for coming.'

Imogen turned to accept another burst of applause from the phalanx of party faithful, and walked away from the microphone.

'Class act,' Rav said. 'She's going to give him a run for his money, and he's a fool if he doesn't know it.'

Maddy was at her shoulder. 'The list you asked for.'

Kate took the sheet of paper, walked back into her office and closed the door. As a minister, Imogen's name headed the page, and was followed by those of the officials who had travelled with her: *Stuart Henderson, private office; Alastair Macintosh, special adviser; Callum Rennie, Foreign & Commonwealth Office press office.*

Her suspicions and uncertainties closed in on her, like a winter's night, and it took her a considerable amount of time and willpower to beat them back. Of course her husband was noticeably Scottish, but she was pretty sure Alastair, the special adviser, spoke with a broad Glaswegian lilt. And for all she knew, Callum Rennie might be a kilt-wearing, skean-dhu-waving Highland reeler too.

Kate returned to her screen and continued her trawl. For someone who was now a serious prospect as future leader of her country, Imogen had made very few waves. She was interrupted by another of Stuart's increasingly overexcited messages: *She's going to promise to double – DOUBLE – the education budget. That will create a few waves!!! Just working out where the money is going to come from. Xxx*

Kate switched her phone to silent and tried to concentrate on Imogen's life, work and finances. After a relatively futile hour or two, punctuated by increasingly graphic images of a variety of unwelcome stains spreading across Imogen's McQueen, she gave up, changed her shoes, and headed for the lifts.

Maddy managed to catch her before she headed out into the night. 'I forgot to say – Rose came looking for you. She said she had to leave early today, but will be in tomorrow. Do you want me to fix a time?'

'Oh. No, don't worry. I don't think . . . It's not important now. I'll bend her ear next time we bump into each other.'

Maddy's normally imperturbable brow creased. 'Are you all right, Kate?'

'I'm fine. Yes, fine. Why?'

'You don't look quite yourself.'

'No, really. I'm just a bit tired. I need to get home.'

10

WHEN SHE GOT back Stuart was still out. 'He's at Imogen's,' Fiona said. 'Busy planning to take over the world.'

Kate took off her coat, trainers and socks. She padded across the cold floor in bare feet. 'Where's Gus?'

'How on earth would I know?'

'Sisterly concern, perhaps.'

'I have no idea what that even is.' Fiona headed for the stairs.

'Did you feed Nelson?'

'Er, no. Sorry . . .' And then she was gone.

Nelson eyed Kate dolefully.

'Believe me, I know just how you feel, old chap.' She

loved her children more than life itself, but the gap between the affection they professed for the family's pet and the care they were prepared to offer him never failed to irritate her. She crouched down and eyeballed him again. His tail wagged with dim enthusiasm. 'So, are *you* pleased to see me, at least?'

He rolled onto his back. 'You're really just hungry for love, aren't you?' She scratched his belly for a while. 'Join the club.'

She stayed by his basket longer than she'd intended, then got up, filled his bowl and put it in front of him. He didn't move for a while, but as she walked away to make herself a cup of tea, he forced himself upright and picked at his dinner.

Ten minutes later the door slammed open and shut and Gus blew in.

'What's wrong?' Like all teenagers, he had broadcast his mood at twenty paces.

He clenched his teeth and then his fists. 'Why do you *always* ask what's *wrong*?'

Kate stared at the ceiling and said a silent prayer. She followed him upstairs. Before she could ask anything else, he said, 'I got dropped.'

'From what?'

She instantly regretted asking. Of course she knew from what.

'The A team!'

'No! Did Mr Wilson give you a reason?'

'He didn't say a thing. Just put the list up on the board. Without my name on it. At the beginning of term, he said he might make me captain. And now I've been bloody dropped!'

'Perhaps—'

'Perhaps nothing. He said I was his guy, the one the rest of the team looked up to. And now he's chucked me on the scrapheap!'

Kate moved into his room and leant against his chest of drawers. It was a source of irritation to her – and near apoplexy to Stuart – that the teachers in the school they were bankrupting themselves to pay for frequently didn't seem to feel the need to communicate in any meaningful way with the children in their care. At least, not where the things they actually minded about were concerned.

'I don't want to discuss it,' Gus said.

'Who did they pick instead?'

'Adams.'

'Bizarre.'

'What would you know?'

'Dad says he thinks you're one of the best players in the school, not just the team. He was saying the other day he thought you might make it into one of the club academies.'

'Dad thinks I'm going to play for Scotland. He doesn't know *anything*.'

Kate could see the hurt in her son's eyes, but couldn't think of anything to say that might help. She kissed him and withdrew quietly, wishing Stuart was there. His predictable anger at the decision might at least help convince their son he was the victim of a genuine injustice rather than simply not good enough.

She knocked on Fiona's door and slipped into the room. Her daughter sat cross-legged on her bed, bent over her laptop.

'How was your day?' Kate asked.

'Fine.'

'What did you get up to?'

'Not much.'

'How were lessons?'

'Fine.'

Kate knelt and started to pick up her daughter's discarded clothes, fold them, and pile them neatly on the chair.

Fiona didn't look up. 'Please leave those where they are.'

'I'm just trying to—'

'No, Mum. You're just trying. End of.'

Kate stopped, mid-fold. 'That's not massively polite.'

'It's my room.'

'And it's my house.' Kate carried on folding, wondering how, try as hard as she might, she always sounded like her own blindingly unreasonable mother at such times.

'*Our* house, actually,' Fiona said. 'After all, Dad pays half the mortgage, doesn't he?'

'I'm really not going to have this argument again.' Kate finished her self-appointed task and rose to her feet. 'Is it my imagination or are you in a rather more bullish mood today?'

'I have no idea what's in your imagination, Mum.'

'Has something happened?'

'No.'

'What's going on with Jed?'

Fiona shrugged. Her eyes were still fixed on the screen, but she wasn't concentrating on whatever it contained now. A worrying sign.

'What does a shrug mean?'

'If I tell you, you'll only freak out. So I'm not going to tell you.'

'Please promise me that you haven't—'

'We're *going out*.'

Kate sat down on the bed.

Fiona raised her palm. 'I don't want to talk about it.'

'Well, I do.'

'There's absolutely nothing to say.'

'I'm going to need you to promise me that you won't, under any circumstances, take things further than—'

'Than what? A coy glance? The occasional swoon? It really isn't your problem.'

'You're fifteen. If you were to . . . make a mistake—'

'I'd get an abortion. It's no big deal.'

Kate bit her lip. Her daughter knew how to push every

one of her buttons and did so with a precision she found enraging. 'As I've said to you before, I know you better than anyone else does. And I know that beneath that teenage exterior lies a sensitive, loving and caring young woman. You'd find having an abortion a seismic experience. You'd carry it with you for the rest of your life.'

'Not everyone is you, Mum.'

'And not everyone is you, either. Maybe to some of your friends it's no big deal. But I promise you, my darling, it *would* be for you.'

Fiona was still avoiding her gaze, but Kate knew her daughter well enough to be sure that she had got through to her. 'Just go slow, that's all I ask. And I wouldn't tell Dad you and Jed are definitely going out.'

Fiona finally looked her in the eye. 'He's a lot more reasonable than you are.'

'What's that supposed to mean?'

'He's not intent on protecting my purity until I'm an old maid.'

Kate stared at the raging bag of hormones and insecurities beside her. 'Let's leave it there before we both say something we might regret.'

She closed the door behind her and went downstairs. Sometimes being the only adult in the room, in the whole house, was too exhausting for words. She made a cup of tea and started to plan supper. This is not a chore, she told herself. This is therapy.

She scanned the shelf for inspiration. Her cookbook selection was a series of foreign missions, but without the endless waiting and life-threatening confrontations. She messaged Stuart to find out when he might be back and got a swift reply: *Eating at Imogen's. Big crew here. Come over when you're done.*

Dinner was like a party at an undertaker's. She got half a dozen words out of Gus and only a few more from Fiona. She had to tell both of them several times to put away their phones, and in the end simply left them to it. 'Perhaps you would be so kind as to do the washing-up,' she said. 'I'm going to spend some quality time with your father.'

She didn't get a response to that either.

It was a balmy night and Kate decided to walk. The route took her past her mother's place and she looked up at her window to see if the light was on. It wasn't. She tried to push away the dark cloud that seemed to wrap itself around her. The worst of it was that she understood why her mother was the woman she was. Abandoned as a baby in Galway, she had spent the first four years of her life in a convent before being adopted by an austere Catholic family in Limerick. It was hardly surprising that she had little understanding of how to give or receive affection.

Kate ended up so lost in thought that she wandered past Imogen's house, despite the very obvious presence of two photographers and three journalists outside it, and had to double back. They didn't pay her much attention as she rang the bell and was ushered in without question or introduction by a young woman she'd never met.

Kate offered her hand. 'I'm Stuart's wife.'

Her greeting was left hanging in the hallway with the discarded coats as the girl's hurriedly retreating back screamed, *I'm busy with very important stuff*, which reminded Kate of how much she detested the breed of apparatchik that managed to attach itself to politicians on the rise.

The sitting room was full of people, perhaps twenty in all. Most were on their smartphones. Kate recognized quite a few ministers and MPs. Stuart sat on the sofa, next to Imogen, poring over a vital strategic document. The intensity of his concentration suggested that he might have forgotten that the two of them weren't in the process of discovering a cure for cancer.

Kate waited, suddenly awkward and unsure. Eventually Imogen's young special adviser materialized and greeted her. He was called Ben, or possibly Steve. They had come and gone with bewildering speed over the years. 'Stuart!' he shouted, pointing at Kate.

Stuart raised a hand, hauled himself to his feet, came over and treated her to a perfunctory kiss. His eyes were wide with excitement. 'We have sixty guaranteed names, with twenty more actively leaning in our direction.'

'Active leaning. That's my favourite kind.'

'We don't think James Ryan has any more – and we have a hunch the new intake of younger MPs is coming our way.'

'Has anyone else declared?'

'No – and the smart money says they aren't going to. Support for Imogen and James is sufficiently strong and evenly split for any other contender to seem like an also-ran from the start. They're all trying to bolster their future careers by hitching their wagons to one or the other – and an awful lot of them are still playing hard to get, to maximize their price.'

'But Imogen won't win when it goes to party members, will she?'

'Conventional wisdom says no, but I'm not so sure. Her message on education is striking a chord and I think people are tired of talking about our place in the world and the great free-trade opportunities that seem mostly a mirage. They want someone to focus on everyday issues. Plus she has bags more charisma.'

Either his tone or the look of pure joy on his face meant Kate couldn't stop herself asking, 'Do you think you should be here?'

The air momentarily left his balloon. 'What do you mean?'

'You're a civil servant.'

'I'm helping out as a friend.'

'All the same . . . there are a lot of politicians here.'

'There are indeed. And they're all on the team.' He leant closer. 'Honestly, you can be a bit of a killjoy sometimes.' He gave her a peck on the forehead. 'Go home, if you want to keep your distance. I'll be back in a bit.'

He returned to his seat beside Imogen, who looked up, caught sight of Kate, waved and pulled a face – *Oh, God, what have I got myself into?* – then returned to the sheet of paper in front of her. Stuart did not glance up again.

Kate waited a few moments more, ill at ease, then walked home. She felt a bit stupid in a way she couldn't quite articulate, or perhaps didn't want to.

Gus was appealingly meek when she kissed him goodnight, and he hugged her tight when she said that she was sure his father was right: he was very good and would win through in the end. He even listened when she delivered a short speech about adversity making one stronger. She quoted Jonny Wilkinson as an example of someone who'd had setbacks but gone on to conquer the world. It was no more than guesswork, but she rather liked the sound of it – and so, apparently, did he.

Even Fiona was in a more malleable mood. 'I'm sorry I shouted at you,' she said, 'but it is *my* life.'

Kate got in a bit of a speech there, too, about the value of people who love you and have your back. Much to her surprise, Fiona said, 'You never had that, did you?'

She pulled the duvet up to her daughter's neck and kissed her forehead, as she had done so often when Fiona was a little girl. 'Granny has many strengths,' she said, as outrageous a lie as she'd told all day, 'but thank you for thinking of me.'

She retreated to the bathroom to remove her make-up and brush her teeth, then read for a while, although she was still finding it strangely difficult to concentrate. She turned out the bedside light, but couldn't sleep. She tossed and turned. She picked up her book again, but without much success.

It was one in the morning before Stuart crept in, as quiet as a herd of elephants. 'Good God, are you still awake?'

'Just . . . reading.'

'Why didn't you go to sleep?'

'I don't know. I suppose I was waiting for you.'

'Why?'

'God knows.' She attempted a grin. 'Sometimes it's nice to chat. How's it going?'

'Much as I said earlier.'

'You really think she's going to win?'

'I do, which will be fucking amazing. There's every chance I'll be right there at the heart of it.'

'That would be . . . great.'

'You didn't sound like you thought so earlier.' Stuart was naked except for his boxers and socks. He almost fell over as he tried to take off the socks. He was more pissed than she'd thought.

'Put it down to the spy in me. I always feel uncomfortable in a roomful of politicians.'

Stuart made his way uncertainly into the bathroom and noisily brushed his teeth. Sometimes she thought a separate bathroom was the key to lasting happiness.

He tumbled onto the bed, fiddled with the light switch and stifled a belch.

'Aren't you going to kiss me goodnight?'

He did, then immediately turned his back on her.

'Have you spoken to your father recently?' Kate asked.

'No. Why?'

'Just wondered. Is he still with Suzy?'

'Of course.' Stuart faced her again. 'Why do you ask?'

'You said they were arguing a lot, that's all. And he has a habit of moving on.'

'He's been with Suzy for twenty years. Your point being?'

'I don't have a point. We haven't seen them for a bit.'

'You always have a point.' Stuart sat up. 'So come on, what is it?'

Kate felt cornered, which she hadn't anticipated. 'I'm sorry. I don't know what I'm saying, really. I sometimes feel stupid. Out there in the real world, people spend their lives shitting on their nearest and dearest . . .'

'What on earth are you talking about?'

'You say I'm not my mother. But why am I so obsessed with what she did? I mean, my father forgave her – and is anyone faithful for a lifetime anyway? Why do I—'

'Stop it, Kate. And to answer your questions: (a) yes, they are. And (b) it wasn't only your father your mother hurt, but you. Yes, people do behave badly to their nearest and dearest and, yes, I know, it's your job to be up to your neck in it – and sometimes well beyond. I understand why you stand guard over our family with such ferocity. I know you want something in this world of shit to be true and honest. But we're all well aware of that, believe it or not, and we're good for it. So do us all a favour and leave your work where it belongs. Home is another country. We care for each other here. It's a place to relax. Now get some sodding rest. You'll be a lot less likely to start at the wrong shadows.' He turned over once more and was asleep in seconds.

Which was more than could be said for his wife. Kate lay there, staring up at the ceiling, long into the night. When she finally drifted off, it was not for long. She woke up bathed in sweat, despite the chill in the room. The image that had loomed at her from her dreams was Lena drowning in an unusually murky and turbulent stretch of the otherwise clear blue waters of the Mediterranean Sea. She went to the window and peered out as the first harbingers of dawn crept through the deserted streets.

11

KATE DECIDED NOT to catch the train to the West Country. She had no desire to share their findings, or even their gossip, with a carriage full of eavesdroppers on the return journey. She got up, took Nelson out and left a note telling Stuart she'd taken the car.

In her eagerness to leave the kitchen, she knocked his iPad off the work surface. She cursed silently as she knelt and plucked it off the stone floor. And more loudly when she saw the crack in the top right-hand corner of the screen. Her husband was very particular about his possessions, especially those of an electronic persuasion. She toyed with the idea of leaving an apologetic Post-it note, but decided it would be better to confess later, face to face.

She parked in front of Rav's house and tapped out a WhatsApp message. *Am outside. No hurry.*

He was with her in less than five minutes.

'Wow. That was quick.'

'Not sleeping much.'

'Me neither.'

Kate pulled away and started winding through the west London traffic.

'Music?' Rav asked.

'Why don't you dazzle me with your conversation?'

'It's too early for dazzling. How was your evening?'

'I spent a lot of time channelling that book you gave me on how to deal with extremely awkward teenagers. And that was just when I was with Stuart.'

'Did it work?'

'It stopped me committing murder, so in that sense, yes, it did. He was at Imogen's, planning their takeover of the world.'

'Is that wise of him?'

'I'm not sure it is. But I got an earful when I suggested he might want to think about it. How about you?'

'Zac's still with his parents, so I was just meandering about.'

'When's he back?'

'He didn't say.'

'How are his parents?'

'You mean physically, mentally, spiritually – or with me?'

'I guess mostly the latter.'

'I haven't seen them since we went up there for Easter. I've spoken on the phone to his father a few times. I find him a lot easier than the mother. But, well, it is what it is. It's one thing your son leaving his wife and three children, but it's a bit of a twist in the tail when it turns out he's gay as well. I think they want to come to terms with it, but I'm not sure they ever will.' Rav turned to her. 'Did you get anything on Imogen yesterday?'

For a moment, Kate toyed with the idea of keeping the information to herself. But she withheld nothing professionally from Rav, and not much personally either. 'The MP I saw was very measured, sensible and credible. She obviously doesn't like Imogen much. She said they didn't see a lot of her on the Russia trip because she appeared to be quite wrapped up with one of her male advisers.'

'Which one?'

'She wasn't sure. I think it was a young guy who was her special adviser at the time, but I'm going to have to check that out.'

'Have you talked to Stuart about it?'

'No. He was on the trip, so if it comes to it, I will. But it'll be hard to do it without giving some hint of what I'm after, so I'm going to hold off for now.' She glanced at him. 'How about you? By the look of you, I'd say you'd been up half the night. And it's becoming a habit.'

'Lots of interesting circumstantial stuff. You won't be surprised to hear that our man in King Charles Street was the liaison officer with the Russians in Kosovo. He had a young Montenegrin interpreter whose *Like* button he'd have wanted to press, judging by her social-media profile, even if she had the good sense to resist him. I'm trying to locate someone who served with him there. And I'm still circling the money and the security business he set up after he left the army.'

They chatted a little more, then drifted into silence. Rav slept. He'd always been good at napping. She was hungry and needed coffee, so pulled off the dual carriageway to stop at a Little Chef. In the event, she dragged him in for breakfast, possibly because it summoned appealing memories of the trips she had made with her father and sometimes her aunt Rose to see their parents in Fowey. Her mother rarely accompanied them. She'd had little affection for her parents-in-law, and they'd made no attempt to hide the fact that the feeling was mutual.

It was almost lunchtime before they reached Sherborne. They lost their way a few times around the abbey and ended up having to park by the station, then retraced their route past an attractive public garden, still bursting with colour in the autumn sunshine, to the bottom of the high street. Rupert Grant's estate agency was three shops in from the corner.

Grant stooped slightly, perhaps from a lifetime of apology for being so tall – six feet three or more. He was greying at the temples, and had the laconic, charming smile of a man now at ease with himself. He greeted them as if this was the most exciting thing to have happened to him for a while, and took them upstairs to his office.

Coffee poured, biscuits distributed and niceties exchanged, Rav cleared his throat for the business at hand. 'Mr Grant, I hope you'll excuse me for saying this, given that we've so rudely imposed ourselves on you, but it is imperative that you do not disclose our conversation to anyone. Is that all right?'

'A matter of national security?'

'I'm sorry if that sounds overly dramatic, but in essence, yes.'

'I find it difficult to imagine what I could possibly reveal in this charming rural backwater that might shake the establishment to its core, unless it stems from my time in Hong Kong, but go ahead. You certainly have my word that what is said in this room will stay in it.'

'What did you do in Hong Kong?' Kate asked.

'I was based there for fifteen years. Commercial property. This is the family business. We only came back when my father died.'

'Our questions relate to two of your former school friends,' Rav said.

'So are you MI5 or MI6?'

'The Secret Intelligence Service, MI6.'

'Sir Alan is your *direct* superior?'

'He is,' Kate said.

'And my old sparring partner, the Right Honourable James Ryan, also has a degree of influence over your destiny . . .'

She nodded. 'Two reasons why this whole situation is potentially extremely awkward. But we should stress that the focus of our enquiries is not our boss.'

'Well, that's certainly livened up my day. Carry on, do.'

'I'm afraid we can't tell you precisely what we're investigating,' Rav said, 'but rest assured that it's entirely routine in the context of modern intelligence operations, and no accusation or suspicion is implied or intended.'

'We're just trying to build up a picture of the kind of man the foreign secretary is,' Kate added. 'From those who have known him best.'

'I haven't seen him for more than three decades.'

'But you spent five years in very close proximity when you were at school. I imagine you got a pretty good handle on him.'

Rupert Grant thought about this. He sipped his coffee and appeared to lose himself for a moment in another world. 'I'm not so sure, to be honest. It was a very long time ago. A different life. And I wouldn't say it brought out the best in any of us.'

Rav was about to jump in but Kate raised her hand. They waited. If she had learnt one thing from Sir Alan, it was the value of silence.

'I can tell you what I remember, but I'm really not sure how it could be of the remotest use.'

'We'd be grateful.'

He picked up a shortbread biscuit, tapped it on his plate, then put it down again. 'First, it was a pretty rough environment. We were hunkered down just along the road there, almost overlooking the games pitches. A rather forbidding pebble-dashed building, no longer a boarding-house. It would have benefited from modernization, as the particulars might have put it.

'The housemaster was a good man, but remote, and the place was run almost entirely by the boys, which, if you have any knowledge of the public-school system, is another way of saying it was more *Lord of the Flies* than *Goodbye, Mr Chips*. In retrospect, it seems to me rather like prison. Except that there wasn't much homosexuality, as is commonly supposed. In fact, the atmosphere was pretty homophobic. The few chaps who were probably gay had a very rough time indeed.

'Sherborne was a rugby-playing school, so much of its life was conducted as if it were an extension of the games field.'

Rupert sipped his coffee again, perhaps because he

couldn't quite bring himself to look them in the eye. 'There were several baptisms of fire. When we arrived, there was a boy in the year above whose favourite trick was to lurk in the changing room, on top of the lockers, and urinate on our heads as we threw on our kit.'

'Charming,' Rav said.

'Not our future foreign secretary, I should probably add. But, as I said, it was a bit of a zoo at times, and I don't think it brought out the best in any of us. Frankly, I found the whole thing terrifying. In fact, I barely spoke for that first year. But over time, I found my voice, and my place, and I ended up really enjoying it – loving it, even – because the camaraderie was akin to what I imagine you might experience in war or any extreme environment where men are pushed together.'

'So how did the two of them cope?' Kate asked. 'Rumour has it they didn't much like each other.'

Rupert frowned. 'Who told you that?'

'It's just the impression we've got.'

'Then someone is trying to throw you off the scent. They were best friends. We began life in dormitories and we spent our rugby-free waking hours outside of lessons in what was known as the day room – essentially lots of desks lined up in a row. In the second year, we graduated to a study, which in due course we were allowed to sleep in as well. As far as I recall, Alan and James shared one until we were given single rooms in our final year.'

'I guess that would end up sealing a friendship,' Rav said. 'Or make you the best of enemies.'

Rupert looked from one to the other as if they were hard of hearing. 'They weren't just friends, they were inseparable. Most of the rest of us switched roommates periodically. They stuck together, through thick and thin.'

'Are you suggesting that there was something more than—'

'Good God, no. They were both heterosexual, James rampantly so. I think they just got along. They had the same sense of humour, the same slight detachment from the life of the school. I think their response to the madness of the first year was to join forces and, after that, saw no reason to open up much to anyone else.'

'Slight detachment, you say . . . Could you elaborate?'

Rupert shook his head. 'It's quite difficult to explain. It was such an odd environment. James and Alan were the unofficial leaders of our year all the way through. They *were* the establishment, if you like. Well, Alan was. He was head of house and so on. James was a maverick, uncontrollable in some ways. Always smoking, endlessly up at the girls' school, mostly in the middle of the night. It was a miracle he wasn't expelled – though that might have been because Alan usually covered his back.'

'So they were the gamekeepers *and* the poachers,' Rav said. 'How did that work?'

'They knew how to play the system. And when caught

between a rock and a hard place, they were able to come out with the most bare-faced lies, never turning a hair. We were all rather envious. I'm not in the least surprised that James went on to become a politician and Alan rose to the top of an organization like MI6. It was what they were destined for. You could say, I suppose, that it was what our school life – or their experience of it – trained them for.'

'You paint quite a picture,' Kate said, 'both vividly illuminating and more than a little confusing. What did you *personally* think of them? Did you like them? Did you trust them?'

Rupert didn't answer immediately. The striking of the abbey clock seemed to prompt him to do so. 'No,' he said. 'I didn't like them. People are often rude about public-school boys and girls, which I understand. We have a terrible habit of hanging together as a tribe, which can be intimidating, even if we don't intend it to be. And it's no accident. It is an extraordinary experience, not good always, but certainly unique.

'Back then, we spent five years in a tumble-dryer lined with sandpaper. Some people were destroyed by it. Some were just numbed. Some simply lost their rough edges. The Jameses and Alans of this world worked out how to insulate themselves from the harsher elements of the environment, sometimes at the cost of their companions.

'One consequence was that beneath our often unattractively pompous exterior, we developed quite a high level of social skill, and not just of the cocktail-party variety. Most of us are now rather good at navigating our way around conflict and pouring oil on troubled waters. All of which is a very long-winded way of saying that we learnt how to get along.

'So, if you asked James what he'd thought of me then, supposing for a moment that he could remember, he would probably say, "He was a good man." And, yes, we had a laugh and rubbed along fine. On the day we left, we parted with a warm handshake and a genuine smile. But I haven't seen him since, and there's probably a reason for that. I thought him just . . . well . . . immoral, on a very basic level, really intensely unprincipled.

'He had a good brain and was brilliant in an argument. We'd stay up late at night in the dormitory, even as very young boys, arguing about everything under the sun – it was a surprisingly stimulating environment – but he would change his position on a whim, then argue as if it were his most deeply held conviction, even if it was the polar opposite of what he'd defended to the hilt the previous night. We used to say to ourselves, "It's just James," but there was something quite disturbing about it.'

'Did that manifest itself in how he treated people?' Kate asked.

'Not in how he treated us. I certainly wouldn't have relied on him, but he wasn't mean or unpleasant. He was quite good to the juniors and even stepped in to defend one or two when they were being given a hard time. I'd go so far as to say that the house was better run when he and Alan were in charge than it was before and possibly after.'

'If not "us",' Kate said, 'then who?'

'I found his treatment of women pretty distasteful. He was a good-looking guy. A lot of the girls carried a torch for him . . . Perhaps I needed to get out more.'

'Or perhaps you had a point.'

'What about Sir Alan?' Rav asked.

Rupert repeated his shortbread ritual. He could not be accused, Kate thought, of glibness. 'Alan was different. I'm not sure I liked him much more, though. He was a stickler for the rules, particularly when it came to the lower forms. He was unyielding, strict even, though never with James. He was capable of great charm, but I found that the closer you got to him, the less warmth he exuded. He was quite Machiavellian – which is uncomfortable in a teenager. Again, he wasn't someone I would have chosen to go to war with.'

'Why not?' Rav leant forward. 'I mean precisely.'

'James would have given a rousing speech on the eve of battle. But you wouldn't trust him not to desert, or to sell your rations to a black-marketeer, or even defect to the enemy, if he thought it would be more profitable. Alan wouldn't have hesitated to send you out on a mission he knew to be suicidal, if that was what the orders said. And he'd do it with a glint in his eye.'

12

THEY GOT A bite to eat in a delicatessen on the road that led past the abbey and began the return journey in silence. The sun was bright on the honey sandstone of the terraced houses along the way, so the journey felt like a slow departure from a bucolic idyll. 'He was very thoughtful, insightful and articulate,' Rav said, as they passed the turning to Warminster, 'but I can't help wishing we hadn't come.'

'Don't be so feeble.'

'Well, let's recap. He told us that the foreign secretary is an unprincipled bastard, who could easily have sold himself or his granny to a foreign power, and that our own superior was his best friend, despite vigorous attempts to claim otherwise.'

'Wasn't it you who suggested we should just treat this like any other case?'

'That was when I wasn't thinking about it properly.'

'Well, man up.'

Rav stared out of the window as they approached Stonehenge. 'Thanks. I appreciate the pep talk.'

'We have no evidence of anything yet. It was a moderately compelling but ultimately insubstantial portrait of the pair as young men. I'm not sure anyone I was at school with would have said anything much more positive about me.'

'You were the class swot. There's nothing wrong with that.'

'At school, there's everything wrong with it.'

'I thought you said that was the point of your school.'

'It didn't make it popular.'

'Well, anyway, did you miss the bit where I reminded you that our hitherto trusted leader was best mates with one of our potential traitors, yet goes to great lengths to indicate the polar opposite? Don't you find yourself wondering why he does that?'

'All right, Rav. I get it. Now calm down.'

He didn't, though. And neither did she.

The Ops Room updated them on the *Empress* as soon as they got back to the office. Kate, Danny and Rav studied the satellite footage of Igor's super-yacht arriving at the port of Gavrio on the Greek island of Andros, and watched Mikhail and his wife wander along to an ice-cream shop on the quayside with Lena and their son in tow.

'Why Gavrio?' Rav said. 'Not really Mikhail's kind of town, is it? Looks like a port that time forgot . . .'

'It's a stop-off point for the Piraeus–Mykonos ferry,' Danny said. 'Maybe he's planning a day trip.'

Julie had just landed at Heathrow from Istanbul, so Kate immediately rerouted her to Athens, and booked herself and Rav on the first flight out the following morning. She messaged Stuart to say she'd be late home, and left Rav to handle the operational paperwork while she ordered up another mic from the technical team, then took a closer look at Gavrio.

When she was finally ready to go home and pack, Sir Alan popped his head around her door. 'Athens-bound?'

'Yes.' She glanced not too pointedly at the wall clock. It was past nine. 'First thing.'

'Good call. Have you briefed Ian?'

'I was going to email him in the morning.'

'Don't worry. I'll talk to him.'

She was momentarily surprised by his sudden interest in a routine operation and wondered how he'd found out about it so quickly. Perhaps he had come via the Ops Room.

He advanced towards her desk and placed a photograph

in front of her. Kate found herself staring at a grainy surveillance shot of a man climbing into a car on what looked like a London street. She felt her cheeks redden again, not just because of the sudden clash between principle and ambition.

'I believe his name is Sergei Malinsky,' C said. 'But you won't need me to tell you that.'

'I don't mean to be impertinent, but I haven't changed my mind. I made my position clear.'

'Are you saying you don't trust me, Kate?'

'I have trouble trusting anyone.'

'Join the club. A handicap, perhaps. Or possibly an advantage.'

'Time alone will tell.'

'You won't be taking my place, nor should you be, if you don't learn to put the interests of your country and, indeed, of this organization before your own. I don't know what this guy is to you – friend, lover, performing seal – and I don't care. Your files make it pretty clear – to me, at least – that he's your undeclared source. So why would you fail to ID him when you'd already listed him as a previous contact in your vetting?'

She met his penetrating gaze but did not answer.

'The most benign interpretation is that he wanted to be off the books and, in deference to whatever relationship you had – or have – with him, you felt duty-bound to respect that. Correct?'

Kate watched the minute hand on the clock pass the quarter.

'I'm trying to help you here, Kate. It might be a good idea if you contributed to that admirable objective.'

'I will, if you can tell me why you're pushing this to breaking point.'

'Because you and I need to be able to talk honestly. And not simply about this.'

He waited, but she still wasn't going to budge.

'Let me tell you what's at stake, both professionally and personally,' he said. 'Your intelligence suggests that our superior, the foreign secretary, or one of his rivals for the premiership, is an enemy asset, assisted by another agent somewhere in Whitehall, perhaps inside this building. That leaves two possibilities: either we're being subjected to a calculated campaign of misinformation, or it's true. Either way, the threat to our organization and, indeed, our democracy, is of the severest possible kind. Do you agree?'

'Yes, I do.'

'Then let me tell you what is at stake personally. I don't shout about it much, but I have known the foreign secretary for a very long time. The fact that we were at school together is a matter of public record, though for obvious reasons I tend not to highlight our close proximity – or that we were friends, good friends.

'In recent years, our relationship has soured. Like most politicians, he favours the kind of expediency that I find . . .

discomfiting. And if he discovers that we're investigating him as a possible traitor, he'll flay us alive. All of us. Do you understand that?'

'Yes, sir. I do.'

'Less of the "sir", if you don't mind. I simply cannot hope to plot a course through this area of turbulence unless I have all relevant information. And Sergei Malinsky is a piece I lack.'

Kate looked at the photograph again.

'Perhaps I need to remind you that it's often wise to go back to basics if you're to have any chance of assessing motive and reliability. It's perfectly possible that they found out about the prime minister through some other channel, and saw a chance to embarrass us. I think your man Sergei was where it began. So I need to know what he's up to. Who does he really work for? Where do his loyalties really lie?'

Sir Alan ran a manicured index finger down the length of his cheek. 'I'm not trying to catch you out, Kate. You do know that, don't you? The question here is whether or not we're a team.'

'Whoever he may or may not be, I don't know who he works for. All I can say is that his information has proved one hundred per cent accurate so far.'

'All right. I'll back off. But I will say this. Whoever your . . . contact may be, you need to find a way to activate him, and reassess his motives for giving you this information. And I want to know about that meeting. I *need* to know about that meeting. Is that understood?'

'Yes.'

The index finger moved from his chin to the picture of Sergei. 'A piece of friendly advice. Admitting something of this nature only when forced to, even though it was inevitable that I – or someone else – would find out in the end, is not . . . sensible. It speaks of some kind of flaw you might want to think about.' He paused. 'Good luck in Greece.'

On his way out, Sir Alan seemed hardly to notice Rav, still hunched over his desk. Kate closed the door behind him, went to the window and looked down at the people scurrying in and out of Vauxhall station in the rain. She could still feel the colour in her cheeks.

Kate had first met Sergei on a wintry afternoon in January 1992. The Soviet Union had been falling apart and she'd taken a break from her lonely studies in central St Petersburg to catch the train to Tsarskoe Selo fifty minutes outside the old Russian capital to spend the afternoon looking around the Alexander Palace, the unprepossessing yellow stucco building that had been home to the last Tsar of Russia and his family.

Sergei had been a volunteer at the palace and offered to show her around the dowdy, poorly kept rooms that the Romanovs had occupied. He'd claimed he wanted to practise his English. She'd insisted he endure her still shaky

Russian. They turned out to share an obsession with the life and times of Tsar Nicholas II, Emperor of All Russia, one of the most infuriating and tragic figures in world history: a good, kind, devoted husband and father, who was as stubborn and foolish a leader as had ever lived. His wilful inflexibility had perhaps lost his country the chance to take its place gradually in the democratic landscape, and had pitched it instead into a nightmarish experiment from which it had still to emerge.

Sergei was the son of an elderly couple who lived on Vasilevsky Island, close by the old stock exchange. His father was the caretaker at the Ice Palace, home of the SKA St Petersburg ice-hockey team, and Sergei had ended their tour of the last tsar's rooms with an offer to join him at a game that evening.

Later she had spent many hours wondering if it was only loneliness that had prevented her refusing. That evening, they hardly watched the game. They talked about politics with enormous passion. Sergei's maternal grandfather had been an important figure in the Leningrad Communist Party and had fallen victim to one of the very last of Stalin's purges, so his family had had even more reason than most to be happy at the demise of the old regime. Sergei's enthusiasm and excitement at the prospect of a new and democratic society emerging from the rubble of the old Soviet Union was utterly infectious, but he was unnerved by the chaos and feared that old Russia herself – the great steppes that he maintained had barely changed in a century, a place to which he held a romantic, almost mystical attachment – would end up a poor and backward nation rather than the first-world country he believed it should be.

Afterwards he'd taken her to a basement bar just off the Nevsky Prospekt that had become a favourite haunt of student radicals. He introduced her to some of his friends, but somehow it was always his bright eyes in the centre of her vision. They drank beer and vodka shots, and she could hardly stand when she tipped out onto the snowy streets in the crisp hours of the early morning.

He walked her home to her seedy digs on the top floor of a run-down building at Podolskaya. He hooked his arm through her own, but made no attempt to kiss her. Kate was conscious of a faint twinge of regret at his reticence in the few seconds between when her head hit the pillow and she passed out, fully clothed.

In the sober light of dawn, she remembered she hadn't even told him that she had a boyfriend – and not just any man: Stuart.

After that, he called every evening. She didn't answer for almost a week, but was caught out when she thought it was her father. He said he would be round in ten minutes. She went out for a long walk by the Neva. When she got back, he was still waiting, sitting on the step of her tenement in his thin leather jacket.

'You're a fucking idiot,' she said.

'I know you have a boyfriend,' he said, 'but I am happy just to be your friend.'

She'd wanted so badly to renew his acquaintance that she'd let that line go and invited him up for a cup of coffee. After that, they were inseparable.

Sergei's parents had welcomed Kate, their son's English 'friend', into their lives, and for a while she had felt almost part of the family. By the time the summer came, she was spending weekends at their primitive wooden dacha on the Gulf of Finland – which Sergei's mother's family had somehow managed to hold on to after the execution of her father – and everyone assumed they were lovers.

And that was very, very nearly true. When she thought of him even now, she could still feel a twinge of the ache that had gnawed away at her that summer. She'd certainly lusted after him: with his dark stubble, blue eyes and steady gaze, he was nothing if not handsome. But it was worse than that. He had a droll, laconic sense of humour and made her laugh, more than anyone before or since. More even than Stuart. Slowly, inexorably, she had come to accept that she loved him.

Lucy, predictably enough, had told her to go ahead and roll in the hay with Sergei. 'The Russians must have more hay than they know what to do with,' she'd said. 'And you only live once.'

But she wasn't her mother. And since she was already

committed to Stuart, that summer had been about proving it. It was the last time she'd ever asked her mother's advice, and on the plane home, she had pushed Sergei forcefully from her mind – right up until the moment she'd bumped into him at the reception at the US ambassador's London residence.

He hadn't changed much. His languid lopsided smile was as ready as it had ever been. A wife and mother now, she'd felt no more than a pleasant hint of the old glow, and they had reminisced happily for half an hour about their time in St Petersburg and the turns life had taken since. He had joined the foreign service, he said, and been posted to Hanoi, then Washington, between long periods chained to a desk in Moscow. He'd never married. 'Your fault,' he'd told her, with an easy laugh. 'You broke my heart.'

Kate had considered the encounter no more than a pleasant interlude until the letters had started arriving. There had been four in total, written in his unmistakable flowing hand and accompanied by a clear instruction to burn upon reading. The first two had been full of relatively inconsequential information, but the third had directed her towards a chain of secret companies controlled via a Swiss lawyer by two of the Russian president's closest friends. And then the tip-off that Igor's super-yacht was a meeting place for the power brokers of Russia's intelligence elite in early autumn each year – a place to meet up, plot and gossip, away from the eyes and ears of Moscow Centre.

She might well have set up the operation anyway, or something like it – Igor and Mikhail had long been targets – but she had to admit it was doubtful she would have pushed it through so hard and so fast without Sergei's impetus.

All of which left her with Sir Alan's questions: why had he done this? What *were* his motives?

The truth was she trusted him, as absurd as that would sound were she to articulate it anywhere beyond the confines of her own head. Lovers they might not have been in the physical sense, but she *knew* every fibre of him. He'd done it *for her.*

And it had worked. Without the knowledge of the prime minister's condition, she would undoubtedly have put it under Ian's heading of misinformation, but how else could the Russians have known such an intimate secret were it not for a source – or sources – close to the heart of the British establishment?

Kate stayed in her office until close to midnight, and left with a strict instruction to Rav that he should stay no longer, which she knew he would ignore.

In the lobby, she caught sight of a familiar figure. 'Rose . . .'

Her aunt turned. 'Kate, my dear . . .'

'You're here late.'

'C wanted something. And what he wants, he gets.'

'He's just been on my case, too.'

'Yes . . . I don't know what's going on. Something's got to him.' She clasped Kate's hand. 'How are things on the top floor?'

'Ian bats his little-boy-lost eyes at our political masters and everyone else has to watch their backs. Alan will prevail, but it's like watching a tired old lion trying to keep the pack's most ravenous cub at bay. Ian makes no attempt to hide how much he wants it, these days.'

'But he won't get it. He's cut too many corners, and that will come back to haunt him.' Rose's smile lit her penetrating blue eyes and handsome features. 'But, most important of all, how are *you*?'

'Oh, fine.' It occurred to Kate as she said it that she had no idea whether that was true. 'I think.'

'Jane mentioned you were looking for me.'

'Oh, yes. It wasn't urgent. Something that didn't quite chime from way back. If I gave you a name, I wondered if you'd be able to check if someone was ever on the books.'

'I think the most honest answer is that it depends.' Rose looked towards the entrance. Kate had the sense that her aunt knew exactly what she was talking about, even if she was pretending that she didn't.

'I'll pop down at some point.'

'Of course. Any time.'

As they made their way towards the security portals, Kate tried to convince herself that her aunt was not being deliberately evasive.

'Stuart called me this afternoon,' Rose said quietly.

'Oh, yes? What about?'

'Your mother.'

'One of our favourite subjects at the moment.'

'He's right, you know.' Rose touched Kate's shoulder. 'You're not your mother and you never will be. You need to see her for what she is: a difficult and damaged woman, who deserves our pity, not our anger.'

'I'm her daughter. I can change what I think, perhaps, but what I feel is a different matter. I suspect pity is out of reach.'

'Well, I'm here for you if you need me.' Rose took Kate in her arms and, for a moment, in the warmth of her embrace, Kate found herself close to tears. 'Come down to us for a weekend,' Rose said. 'I haven't seen the children for far too long.'

'The way they're behaving, you won't want to.'

'They're great kids and charm itself with us. So you must be doing something right.' Rose kissed her niece and strode out into the night.

Stuart was sitting on the edge of their bed, hunched over his iPad. She was at his shoulder before he noticed her, and he almost jumped out of his skin. 'Christ,' he gasped. 'Don't *do* that!'

'Don't do what?'

'That spy shit. Save it for the day job.'

Kate was taken aback. He looked startled. Guilty, even.

He clicked off the iPad and put it on his chair. 'Sorry,' he said. 'You gave me a shock.'

'Why did I give you a shock?'

'I didn't hear you come in.'

'You look like someone caught in the act of emailing his mistress.'

'Oh, for God's sake.' He got up and went into the bathroom. 'I should be so lucky. Where have you been?'

'I have to go away in the morning.'

He came out again, toothbrush in hand, foaming at the mouth. 'Why?'

'Sir Alan thought I deserved an all-expenses-paid holiday.'

'Very funny.'

'Work.'

'What kind of work?'

'An op.'

'Where?'

'Greece.'

'Thanks for telling me.'

'I just did.'

Stuart went back into the bathroom and completed his nightly regime more noisily than he needed to. It didn't take a genius to spot that he was spoiling for a fight when he returned. Kate knew she had overplayed her hand.

'When did you find out you were going to Athens?'

'I didn't say I was going to Athens.'

'Well, through Athens, I assume. Don't split hairs.'

Suddenly overwhelmed by tiredness, she dropped her bag on the chair and sank on to the bed. 'I'm sorry,' she said. 'I should have called. We have something quite big going on, and new intelligence came through earlier this evening.'

'You can't go.'

'I don't have a choice.'

'You can't. Whether or not you approve of what I'm up to, the next few days are critical for Imogen's campaign. I can drop the kids at school in the morning and probably pick them up, but I can't be tied to the house in the evenings.'

'Fi will keep an eye on Gus for a few hours.'

'Who's going to feed them?'

Kate gave a sigh of exasperation. 'You knew it was going to be like this, Stuart. We talked it all through. You agreed to—'

'I agreed to do my level best to support you.'

'Look, maybe I could delay my departure to the second flight tomorrow, so I can take them to school . . .'

Stuart circled around her. It was not a good sign. 'Is this to do with national security or your own personal ambition?'

'I'm going to pretend you didn't say that.'

'All right, then. It's standard Service advice that one's

closest relative can be briefed on some detail of one's activity in order to share its burden. Or words to that effect. That's the deal, isn't it? So what the fuck are you doing in Greece that can't be done the week after next?'

'Investigating a serious and credible attempt to undermine British democracy during this leadership election.'

'What the hell is that supposed to mean?'

'We bugged a boat and overheard some major Russian intelligence officials cooking up something horrifying.'

'About what?'

'A significant attempt to undermine and corrupt our democracy.'

'Come off it, Kate. We're doing a pretty good job of undermining our so-called democracy all by ourselves. Which is why I'm doing what I'm doing, by the way. A few spotty wankers in Vladivostok posting crap on Twitter is hardly a global conspiracy.'

'You're right. But the possibility that one of the candidates for the leadership is a Russian spy isn't so easily dismissed.'

'Which one?'

'We don't know. Yet. That's what we're trying to work out.'

For the first time she could remember, Stuart seemed not to know how to respond. He got into bed and turned over.

'When did you buy a new iPad?' Kate asked.

'What are you talking about?'

'I'm really sorry – I knocked yours on to the kitchen floor this morning and cracked the glass. But you've got a new one.'

There was a momentary silence. 'The office swapped it.'

'I didn't know it was an office one. I wouldn't have worried so much.'

'I asked them to fix it. They loaned me another in the meantime.'

'Christ, some government departments are freer with their cash than others.'

'Go to sleep, Kate.' He switched off the light.

She had little choice but to swallow her resentment and get undressed in the dark. She went to the bathroom and took a long, hard look at herself in the mirror. Then she switched off the light and sat on the toilet to try to calm down.

Stuart could be a grumpy git on occasion, but he had a point. She should have called him earlier. His willingness to hold the fort at short notice, at random moments, was more remarkable than perhaps it should have been.

She went back into their room, got into bed and tried to sleep, without success. The iPad loomed. Had his department really supplied a new one at the drop of a hat? That wasn't her experience of government procurement. And why had he been so startled when she'd appeared at his shoulder?

She tossed and turned and tried to think about other things, but the doubt kept nagging. She retrieved Stuart's new iPad from beneath his sweater, left him snoring, and took it down to the kitchen. She said hello to Nelson and made herself a cup of herbal tea.

Pretty much anyone could have cracked Stuart's passcode, since he only ever remembered his own birthday. He'd never have made any kind of spy.

Once in, she glanced through his emails and texts. Weirdly, months of archived texts appeared, and not just those sent through iMessage, but nothing of any interest. She accessed his WhatsApp exchanges with Imogen and scrolled down and down. Nothing to set the alarm bells ringing there either. Just endless discussions about MPs and ministers who might or might not be joining the cause, policy ideas, media enquiries, the procedural tedium that one would expect of a professional relationship between a politician and a trusted aide.

Kate went back upstairs, replaced the iPad and slipped into bed. This time, finally, she slept.

13

THE JOURNEY TO Andros was longer than she'd bargained for. They flew into Athens International, hired a car and drove to Rafina, a sleepy port just south of the capital. They shared beer, pitta and Greek salad in a taverna on the quay and sunned themselves at the water's edge as they waited for the ferry. When it arrived, the port burst into life with the organized chaos that is the hallmark of so much of Greek life. They waited their turn at the back of a long queue. 'Do you think the fact we have a ticket for this ferry will make any difference?' Rav asked.

'No.'

They got on, just when it looked as if they might not,

and Kate was preparing to argue the toss with the men waving cars and lorries forward. They locked the car and went to catch the sun on the upper deck. As the ferry cast off and steamed away, Kate watched the mainland dwindle into the distance, lost for a while in pleasant memories of a childhood holiday when her father, Aunt Rose and her husband had taken Kate away without her mother. She couldn't remember which island they'd visited, the memory little more than an imprint of sound, scent and colour, with a rare feeling of happiness and contentment.

Rav came over and insisted on briefing Kate on his trawl through the company accounts of James Ryan's security business. It had managed to rack up losses of almost a quarter of a million pounds in three years on a very modest turnover, before it was wound up. He'd then acted as a consultant for a while before entering politics. It begged a number of questions, not least who had bankrolled the venture.

It was more than two hours before the ferry cruised in towards its destination. Andros was a big island, more rough and rugged than its prettier cousins with sparse rocky hills, but the whitewashed cottages in the port of Gavrio were as attractive as any. The ferry steamed into a sweeping turn, past the fishing boats bobbing against the harbour wall, then backed onto the jetty. Kate marvelled at the efficiency of the seamen this time as they lowered the ramp and had the cars rolling off within seconds. They went downstairs to discover they were holding up a line so got in swiftly and disembarked.

Julie was waiting for them on the main road ashore. 'You're burnt,' she said. 'It's still hotter than you think.' She slid into the rear of the hire car and directed Rav, who was driving, to the end of Gavrio's main street.

It was a tiny town, full of small shops and stalls, and cafés with white sofas where tourists watched the chaos along the main street as if it was the most interesting thing that had happened all afternoon, which perhaps it was. Julie directed them and they wove through the speeding mopeds, then drove over the hill to their hotel on the beach at the far side of the town.

'It's not exactly the Bel-Air.' Julie wasn't kidding: the reception area was like a set from the seventies classic *Saturday Night Fever*, with a ceiling that hoped to be mistaken for a distant galaxy.

They all had rooms along the poolside, and sat out for drinks and dinner on the terrace. Danny had already set up, and the surveillance team was billeted in a bed-and-breakfast halfway down the main street, ready to start work the next morning.

'What have they been doing on the yacht?' Kate asked.

'It seems very quiet. They've been ashore once – you probably saw the pictures – but went straight back onboard once they'd bought ice-creams. We've seen Lena and the little boy on the deck a couple of times today, but there's been no sign of Mikhail and his wife.'

'Any idea why they're here?'

'None, really, apart from the obvious. It's not the most popular destination for foreign tourists, which may be why Athenians love the place. A load of them have holiday homes here. It's pretty, in its own way, so if you were planning a tour of the Cyclades, it would be no hardship to stop here for a day or two.'

'How far is it to Mykonos?'

'A couple of hours, I guess. I'd have to check.'

'Perhaps Mikhail intends to head there by himself. Is it still the gay capital of the Med?'

Rav remained staring into the still waters of the pool.

'Ground Control to Major Rav. That question was beamed in your direction.'

'Oh, Christ, I don't know. It's not really my scene. I think things have moved on a bit, but I imagine it's the kind of place you might get some action if that was what you were looking for.'

'Can you ask the surveillance team to be ready to infiltrate and wire a room at short notice?'

Julie nodded. 'Are we looking for the same kind of play?'

A young couple had wandered in, holding hands, and settled at the far end of the terrace. Kate pulled her chair forward and turned her back to them. Rav and Julie leant in. 'We'll give Lena another bug, but the boardroom isn't likely to yield much while Igor's in Moscow. So Mikhail's our target. We know he loves England. I think there has to be some doubt as to the depth of his loyalty to modern Russia, and he certainly isn't going to want his father to find out how he likes to entertain himself on his nights off.'

'You think it's possible Igor doesn't know?' Rav asked.

'Who goes digging around for uncomfortable truths about their own loved ones?'

'Psychopaths, like Igor.'

'So here's our challenge. Even if we pick something up on the mic, Ian and the others will dismiss it as deliberately planted. If the foreign secretary wins this contest and makes it into Number Ten, our investigation is going to get even more difficult, or perhaps impossible. We need something more tangible, and we need it quickly. If we can corner him, Mikhail may be able to ID the agent of influence, and Viper. That would give us enough to open a formal investigation.'

Julie didn't look convinced.

'What is it?' Kate asked.

'Just worried about tomorrow, that's all.'

'Why?'

'We're proceeding on the assumption that the Russians are in blissful ignorance. What happens if Viper has already alerted them to our investigation, and they're on the lookout? The moment we meet up with Lena, they'll know how we came by our intelligence.'

'How could they know?' Rav asked.

But they were all well enough aware of the answer to that. If Viper was inside the Service, rather than somewhere else in Whitehall, it was possible they knew the truth already.

Kate swirled the ice in her gin and tonic. 'We'll be as careful as we possibly can be. Lena's safety is our first priority, of course. But some days we just have to roll the dice.'

'We could wait,' Julie said. 'Sit back and watch.'

'That's not necessarily going to make any difference.'

When Rav disappeared to bed, Julie didn't follow suit. Kate sensed she wanted to talk. 'Are you all right?'

Julie finished her vodka and lime. 'Not really.'

'Anything I can do to help?'

'It's Jason's birthday.' She covered her eyes. 'I'm *so* sorry. I had to tell somebody. And that somebody, inevitably, was going to be you.'

'How old would he have been?'

'Twenty-six. I've been thinking today what I've thought on this day every year since – if we hadn't argued that morning, if I hadn't shouted at him and he hadn't skipped school . . .'

'Then everything would have been different. Of course. But you were just a young girl, and you had to be a mother to your little brother. You didn't have a choice. And I know that's one of the reasons you can't forgive your own mother, and I know I should stop trying to persuade you to give it a go. But *every* tragic accident is dogged by a haunting amalgam of what-ifs and if-onlys . . .' She gazed at the dregs in her own glass, aware that her voice was becoming slightly slurred, and that she wasn't completely sure how many times they'd re-ordered. 'Anyway, in a hundred years, we'll all be dead. So in the great sweep of human history, whether you live long or short doesn't matter that much.'

Julie took a moment apparently to reflect upon this nugget of timeless wisdom. 'I'm not sure that helps, to be honest.'

'I have a doctor friend who told me the other day that the number of genes we have is actually statistically small. So another way of looking at it is that we get reconstituted – remade, if you like – fairly frequently anyway. Next time, perhaps he'll live long enough to be a boring old fart. Then you'll be sorry.'

'Are you telling me you believe in reincarnation?'

'In a way I am, yes. I don't believe in God – there are too many, all with competing theories about life, the universe and everything – but I try to take some comfort in the idea that there probably is an answer we haven't yet found. And in the meantime reincarnation makes about as much sense as anything else. Have you spoken to your dad?'

'Yes. He wasn't in great shape. He never is today. He thinks if their marriage hadn't fallen apart, Jason and I wouldn't have argued in the first place.'

'And what about your mum?'

Julie shrugged.

'Despite what I just said, dare I suggest, not for the first time, that this might be the moment to—'

'I've tried.' Julie snapped the cocktail stick she had been toying with. 'She destroyed us. And she doesn't regret it.'

Julie was close to her father, who, like Kate's, still carried a torch for his adulterous wife and had never remarried. Julie had blocked her mother out of her life until the previous January when, partly at Kate's encouragement, she had agreed to a meeting in a pub, providing the joiner her mother had run off with years before was not present. Her mother had appeared to be as good as her word – until the joiner had turned up for an apparently spontaneous 'hello' as they ordered coffee.

An incredibly acrimonious argument had followed, and Julie had walked out, vowing never to speak to her mother again. Kate thought she was unlikely to relent. But from her own experience she knew that rejecting a parent entirely in such circumstances was perhaps an act of self-harm.

When the waiter next approached, Julie shook her head at his offer of another drink, but Kate sensed she still wanted company. 'Are there ever times,' Julie said, 'when what we do keeps you awake at night?'

'I'd like to say it gets better over the years, but I can't. What's getting to you?'

'Lena, mostly. That any mistake we make is likely to be

fatal for her. And what we learnt in Istanbul. I feel its weight more than perhaps I should.'

'Well, you're not alone. We're right at the cutting edge. But isn't that why we got into the business in the first place?'

'I suppose so.' She smiled ruefully. 'Sometimes, when I have to cancel yet another date, I wonder.'

'You have time on your side, not to mention brains and beauty. It's a rather fabulous combination.'

Julie conjured up another smile, but this one was tinged with sadness. 'I love working for you. I don't know that I'd want to stay if you moved on.'

'Why not?'

'Ian gives me the creeps, and some of the other senior men aren't much better. And . . . well, you know how it is. I can manage the pressures and the anxieties that fuck me up in the middle of the night because I believe in you. And I trust you. So there we have it.'

Kate took her hand. 'There are plenty of people like us. And though I won't say that Ian or even Sir Alan exudes much warmth, you'd be surprised at what they're capable of when the chips are down. We're all on the same team, whatever might obscure that in the day-to-day.'

Not long after, Kate said goodnight and went to her room. She lay down, hoping that the combination of too much gin and the slowly rotating ceiling fan might help her drift off. Instead, they made her feel dizzy. She grabbed a bottle of mineral water and sat by the sliding glass door that led out to the pool, looking up at the sky.

There was something different about Julie, these days. She couldn't quite put her finger on it. A softness, an uncertainty, a vulnerability? Hints of all those things, though none quite fitted. Maybe the vodka had encouraged her to display the cracks in the emotional armour she'd worn since her brother's death. Kate couldn't make up her mind if that was a good thing. Or perhaps she still couldn't confront the possibility that the qualities of an attractive human being were likely to prove fatal to a spy.

She tried to think through tomorrow's operation, but her mind was dragged back to Stuart and the iPad.

She began to wonder if she had imagined knocking it off the counter. When you lack sleep, your brain can do that to you. She circled the issue for a while, without achieving clarity and building a mountain of self-doubt. Why was she suddenly suspicious of Stuart? She hadn't doubted him before – not in all the years they'd been together. In fact she'd probably given him more substantial grounds for suspicion than he had ever provided for her. If the wish really was father to the deed, she was on the thinnest of ice – because she had wanted to sleep with Sergei in that dacha.

Sergei Malinsky.

'I believe his name is Sergei Malinsky,' C had whispered in her ear. 'But you won't need me to tell you that.'

Ever since Sir Alan had come to her office, she'd been thinking about how to handle his laser-like insight into her source. He must have gone through every one of her positive vetting files and worked through every individual she had ever listed, cross-referencing, then eliminating each until he had found Sergei. It was tempting to bury her head in the sand and hope it went away, but that was not realistic. And Sir Alan had every right to question the motives of her original source. Given what was at stake, she probably needed to rekindle her connection with Sergei.

The first step, at least, would be easy. This year's soirée was in less than a week's time, and the unanswered invitation from the US ambassador was in her bag. What followed would be increasingly fraught with risk – and not just that of being caught in the vortex of East–West power politics.

Kate closed the glass door and crawled back into bed. She concentrated on slowing her breathing. She needed sleep.

14

IT CAME EVENTUALLY but, as ever now, not enough. She got up at dawn and strode along the rugged coastline until she reached the succession of beaches that stretched away to the south. She commandeered a sun-lounger and stared out to sea for a while, then walked back to the hotel for breakfast – fruit, Greek yoghurt and honey. She was installed in Danny's room with a cup of coffee before eight.

One of the cameras the surveillance team had installed was focused on the yacht, the others on the street by the quay, which was still empty, save for a scattering of early-morning shoppers. Kate sat and watched nothing much happening. It was going to be a long day.

'You know what?' she said, to no one in particular. 'I think I need to take a look around.'

Julie agreed to come with her on the recce – there was no sign of Rav yet – and they retraced the route they'd driven the previous day, back down the hill to the harbour. Gavrio was a world away from the teeming labyrinthine alleys of Istanbul, so they began at the part closest to the sea, settling at a table outside an ice-cream shop at the far end of the quay.

A host of small boats busied themselves in the lee of Igor's super-yacht, which looked as if it had been teleported from another galaxy. Kate scanned their immediate surroundings, then went to the back of the building and checked out the toilets.

Julie glanced up when she emerged into the sunlight.

Kate gestured at the ice-cream shop. 'It's certainly far enough from the yacht and there's a good view of the approaches. But let's go for a wander.'

Kate led the way towards the far end of the harbour wall, to a street of cafés and bars with seating areas that offered glimpses of the boats without being in clear view of the people aboard them. They doubled back behind the main street, where shops selling food, clothes and beach kit were interspersed with the odd travel agent and car-hire firm. The cobbled alleys were still largely deserted.

Kate was sweating by the time she got back to Danny's room at the hotel. 'Where's Rav?'

Danny didn't move from his screens. 'Haven't seen him.'

'Go and wake him, would you?' she said to Julie. She poured herself another coffee. Her third.

Julie reappeared without Rav and raised both palms, but they were diverted by Danny: 'We're in business.'

They joined him in time to see Mikhail usher Lena, his wife and son onto the motor-launch. The door squeaked open again and Kate shot it a sideways glance.

'Sorry,' Rav said sheepishly. 'Needed to clear my head.'

They watched Mikhail's group clamber onto the quay and lost sight of them periodically as they drifted from shop to shop, then picked them up again as they settled in a café at the far end of the strip.

'How do you want to play this?' Julie asked.

'Let's sit tight.'

The family ordered coffee, pastries and ice-creams with apparent relish, but Lena only picked at hers. They didn't need Danny's close-up to see that she was very, very nervous.

Kate felt her phone throb in her pocket. *Meg Simpson from Health is standing. Complicates it a bit for us.*

Another message followed a few moments later: *We'll have to have a run-off with MPs now, before going to party members. Should still win through, but it'll be close. First debate on Sky News tomorrow night. Heavy preps tonight. When u home?*

'On the move,' Rav said.

Kate shoved the phone back into her pocket as Mikhail

threw a wad of euros onto the table and put his arm around Katya's shoulders. They leant into each other affectionately as they sauntered away.

'You sure you're right about his orientation?' Rav asked.

'Totally.'

'You think they have an . . . arrangement?' Julie asked.

'He wouldn't be the first gay man in history to be living a lie.'

The group appeared to be in no hurry to get back into the launch. Mikhail and Katya boarded first, then Lena handed down their son, but stayed where she was. The three waved to her as they pulled away.

'Let's take the car,' Kate said. To Danny, she added, 'Tell Ralph I want a clean sweep of the town.' She unfolded her sunglasses, slipped in her earpiece, taped the microphone to her neck, draped a scarf over her head against the sun and hooked a shopping basket over her shoulder.

They drove down the hill and swung the car around just in front of the ice-cream shop. Kate waited, listening to the sound of static in her ear.

The seconds crawled by. She watched a child with her parents throwing a tantrum over ice-cream.

And then the relief of hearing the stentorian Scottish brogue of Ralph, the head of their surveillance team on Andros: 'All clear.'

Kate climbed out of the car and strolled along the sea front. She began to fill her bag from the mouth-watering display at a grocery stall by an intersection on the way to the quay, from which she could see in four directions without appearing to be paying undue attention to anything other than the largest tomatoes she'd ever set eyes on.

She spotted Lena emerging from the pharmacy sixty metres away. She paid the stall's proprietor and strolled in her direction, slowing momentarily as their paths crossed. 'The ice-cream parlour,' she murmured. 'Paradeisos. Just back from the quay.' She went into the pharmacy, bought a packet of Nurofen and glanced across the harbour. There was no sign of anyone on the deck of the *Empress*. Mikhail and Katya must have gone below.

Lena was seated inside the entrance of Paradeisos, tucking into a bowlful of something smothered with cherry sauce. Kate ordered a frappuccino and sat at the neighbouring table. She sipped her coffee while Lena looked steadily out at the sea. When she had finished, she went to the toilet. About thirty seconds later, Lena tapped on the door. Kate eased her in and turned the lock.

'There's nothing much,' Lena said. 'They're really nice people. They never talk about Russia or politics or his work, only about Alexei and holidays and food and where they will go skiing this winter and they also ask a lot about me and my family and—'

'Take a breath,' Kate said. 'It's all right. We have time.'

'Two minutes, you said before. Never more than two minutes.'

'Do you know where they're going next?'

'No.'

'Do you know where Igor's gone?'

'Moscow, they said.'

'How long for?'

'They didn't say.'

'Where does Mikhail go when he receives a call about work?'

'I don't know . . .' She thought about it. 'I guess in that boardroom place. Yes, he goes there sometimes.'

Kate took another tiny microphone from her pocket. 'What you did last time was brilliant. But these bugs are quite fragile, and can be easily disturbed.'

Lena stared at the device.

'Just do exactly what you did last time. Before Igor gets back.' She slipped it into Lena's pocket.

Lena stayed where she was, her back against the door, barring Kate's exit. 'I still get scared sometimes. So scared I can't breathe.'

Kate reached for her hand. 'You're doing really, really well. The most difficult bit is over. Once Mikhail leaves the yacht, we'll take you out. But for now, I just want you to keep an eye on him and Katya . . .' Kate tried to release her, but Lena clung to her.

'You should go now, Lena.'

'Have I truly done well?'

'Better than you can possibly imagine.'

'I am frightened.' She gripped Kate's hand more tightly. Her gaze was imploring.

'You're a star. We won't ever forget what you've done for us.'

'Is Maja safe?'

'Yes. We have her under surveillance. We can't intervene until we lift you out. In case Igor's people are watching.'

'Something good can come of this, can't it?'

'It can, Lena. It really can.' Kate gently prised her hand free and kissed the girl's forehead. 'Go now. Be safe.'

By the time she had retrieved her groceries and emerged onto the quay, Lena was already stepping into the launch. She watched the water churn beneath the outboard as it powered back to the *Empress*.

Kate walked up the hill to join the others. 'Anything?'

'Not a ripple,' Danny said. 'Ralph and the guys are still out there.'

'So the town is definitely clean?'

Danny shrugged. 'As far as we can tell.'

Kate sat on the sofa in Danny's room and exhaled slowly.

'Did she have anything?' Rav asked.

'Only that Mikhail and Katya have been very nice to her. I've given her the new mic.'

Danny stayed where he was while they went for lunch on the terrace. Kate called Stuart several times, but he didn't pick up. He messaged at teatime: *Sorry frantic day will call later. Hope all going well. Everything under control here. Xxx*

In the early evening, Kate left the room to try Stuart again, but the line went to voicemail. Julie grabbed her before she could press redial. 'She's on the launch.'

'Shit.' Kate hurriedly followed her.

Back in Danny's room, they all took their usual positions. Lena stood alone in the bow of the launch as it closed on the quay. Once alongside, she stepped off and ducked under the awning of the nearest café.

Kate took a series of slow breaths. This didn't feel right. 'Where is she going?'

The other three were watching her closely now, waiting for a decision. If Kate put Ralph and the surveillance team on her tail and the Russians were watching, it risked exposing her.

And yet . . .

It had been clean all day. Why would they be testing her now?

'Any sign of her?' Kate asked. You could feel the tension crackling in the room now. They could all see the screens. Lena had disappeared.

'Do it,' Kate said. 'But tell them to keep their distance. Maximum discretion.'

Danny spoke into the microphone on the desk, then fiddled with his laptop and maximized the feed from a camera listed as Bravo Four. The screen was suddenly filled with the image of a lone figure disappearing rapidly down an alleyway in the gathering darkness. It was just about possible to make out that it was Lena.

'Where the fuck is she going?' Kate asked. 'Come on, Lena, don't do this to me.'

'Look.' Danny pointed at the neighbouring monitor. Igor's yacht was now making a tight arc as it headed towards the harbour mouth.

'Something's wrong here,' Kate said. 'Where the fuck are you going, Lena?'

They turned back to the Bravo Four feed, but the guy carrying it had stopped dead. 'She went into that door on the right,' Danny said. 'The one at the end.'

Kate's heart was thumping. 'Get someone around the back!'

On the largest of the screens, the *Empress* was now steaming towards the spot where the sun had almost sunk into the sea.

Danny brought up another feed: Bravo One. 'Back door,' he confirmed.

'Sure?'

He was studying a map of the town. 'Yup. Has to be.'

There was no sign of life in either shot. No lights, no people passing.

'For fuck's sake,' Kate said. 'Go in.' She started towards the door. 'Go in hard, both sides.'

As Danny gave the instruction to the team on the ground, Kate sprinted towards the hotel entrance, Rav and Julie half a pace behind her. At the bottom of the slope, they swung into the cobbled alley leading off the quayside. Rav had fired up Google Maps on his phone: he was trying to look at the screen and run at the same time.

It took them less than a minute to locate the house. It wasn't difficult: the front door was hanging off its hinges. The surveillance team were already combing through the place. 'Where is she?' Kate asked Ralph, a slight five feet ten of Scottish skin and bone whose appearance belied his strength and agility.

'No sign of anyone.'

Kate doubled back. 'Spread out,' she told Rav and Julie, then called over her shoulder, 'All of you.'

She hurried up to a nearby square, where a handful of tourists were eating in the lee of a church. She turned left at the top of the hill and began to work her way back down towards the water sweeping everything in the arc of her vision, one way and then the other. She could not afford to lose Lena. She was not going to lose her.

She was in deep shadow now. A solitary street lamp flickered uncertainly ahead of her. She spotted Rav beside a battered white Fiat that looked as if it had been recently abandoned, its rear doors and boot thrown open.

The shutters of a nearby apartment block banged in the wind. Kate moved towards it. She held up a hand when they were a couple of metres short of the entrance. She and Rav stopped in their tracks.

Kate pushed open the door with infinite care and stepped inside. A hint of movement and the glint of gun-metal at the periphery of her vision prompted the response that had been second nature since her training at Fort Monckton all those years ago. Her swiftly raised hand sent the silenced round up the stairwell. She grasped the barrel and reversed it against her assailant's wrist until she was able to rip the pistol – a Sig Sauer P226, complete with suppressor – from his grasp. She fired twice into his groin and was about to give his knees the same treatment as he went down when a fist cannoned into the back of her hand and launched the weapon into the shadows.

The second man had a blade, and she slammed herself into the wall only just in time to avoid his thrust.

She and Rav backed away, then darted up the stairs. It was virtually impossible to disarm a trained killer with a knife, and neither of them was about to try.

Rav wrenched a fire extinguisher out of its wall bracket as they arrived on the landing, and sent a chunk of plaster tumbling down the way they had come. They turned and stood their ground. It was pitch black, except for a sliver of moonlight, so they had to rely upon the sixth sense that had saved them from a bullet in the head moments before.

Kate strained her ears for the slightest sound above the distant howl of the wind.

They waited.

It was two against one, but the odds were still with him. Kate and Rav needed him to commit, to make the first move.

The air molecules in the stairwell were momentarily re-arranged as the knifeman lunged forward. Rav blocked him with the fire extinguisher and Kate swung behind him, wrapping her right arm around his neck.

He knew exactly what she was doing and tried to reverse the blade and thrust it towards her, but she'd planted her elbow between his shoulder blades and was beginning to close down his carotid artery.

Rav feinted at his chest and brought the canister down on his wrist, but the man had been swiping at thin air by then, confused as to whom he should have been targeting. His weapon skittered across the floor, and five seconds later, he dropped like water.

They stood over him, breathing hard. Rav felt for the pulse in the man's neck, but they both knew it was a formality. She heard him run his hands through every pocket, sensed rather than saw the shake of his head, then followed him down to the ground floor to retrieve the pistol.

As he stepped back towards the shaft of moonlight that was forcing its way between the leading edge of the door and its frame, she saw that something was troubling him. He stopped and seemed to sniff the air for a potential attacker. Kate froze as the shaft suddenly widened and a third man burst into the hallway, weapon raised, muzzle in the aim, with her as its prime target. But Rav had already raised the Sig, and double-tapped the intruder, centre mass, before the man's eyes had adjusted to the darkness.

They stepped back into the shadows and listened. 'You mustn't keep saving my worthless neck,' she muttered eventually. 'It's getting embarrassing.'

'No, it's not,' he whispered. 'It's the only way I know right now of persuading myself I'm not completely useless.'

Kate selected the torch app on her phone and they circled the building. If Lena had ever been there, Kate had to acknowledge that she wasn't now. She sat down on the stairs. 'Now what?'

Rav shook his head.

'Kidnap, murder?'

'I don't know.'

'We'll have to talk to Athens.'

Rav pointed at the corpses. 'They'll go mental.'

Kate stood. 'Let's go.'

When they got back to the hotel, she called the MI6 station chief in Athens. He sounded miffed not to have been told of the operation and said the Greeks would be furious when they discovered it was being conducted on their soil without their knowledge. But Kate was the ranking officer and she cut him dead. 'We need to find her,' she said. 'So please just do it.'

They found Julie again on the quay. 'You've cut your face,' she said.

'They were waiting for us.'

Julie glanced at the blood on Rav's right hand. 'Yours?'

He shrugged. 'Possibly. Possibly not.'

'Where are they now?'

'In a stairwell. Do you have anything?'

She shook her head, trying, Kate thought, to keep last night's demons away. 'She's vanished. Like a ghost.'

'She can't have vanished!' Kate insisted.

'Ralph and the team have been over every inch of the town and of the house. They must have bundled her into a car by the back door before we could get the camera there.'

'Talk to GCHQ and the CIA. See if there was any satellite cover.'

Kate and Rav retreated to Danny's ops room and reviewed the footage from the main cameras in forensic detail, then the feeds from each member of the surveillance team. They all told the same story. Lena appeared on the deck of the *Empress*. She did not look distressed or concerned. She climbed down onto the launch and came ashore. She walked towards the awning of a café, then disappeared. No more than sixty seconds later, they picked up her receding figure in the darkened alley, heading towards that doorway.

And then nothing.

They reran the alley sequence again and again.

Lena's hair. Lena's clothes. Lena's shoulder bag. Lena's walk.

But they only ever saw her from the back. It would take painstaking motion-capture analysis to be sure it was her.

Kate glanced at her watch. It was almost eleven o'clock. About four hours since Lena had climbed aboard that launch. Her phone rang. It was the Athens station chief. 'The Greeks are raging. It's going to take me a few hours to calm them down enough to help.'

'We don't have a few hours.'

'I'm doing my best, Kate.' He was called Nick and they'd met once, at an unarmed-combat refresher course at Fort Monckton five years before.

She hung up. The phone rang again. This time it was Ian. She didn't answer.

'I'm going to take a shower,' Kate said. She turned to Julie. 'Would you mind dealing with the police? You can't miss the building. It's full of dead Russians. And there's a white Fiat Punto outside with its doors open.'

'Always supposing they *were* Russians,' Rav said. 'They didn't say anything, even when we got up close and personal. And they were sterile.'

'Couldn't you *smell* them?' Kate said. 'They were Russian all right.'

Kate didn't get into the shower immediately, though she badly needed to wash off the blood and the unmistakable odour of failure. Maybe if she just sat on the bed for a while she could persuade herself that Lena had found another great place for ice-cream, then nipped back for a fun evening with those nice people on board the *Empress*.

She glanced at her phone. There was a missed call from Stuart, but she couldn't face getting back to him now. Besides, her hands were shaking so badly she'd probably press the wrong button. It was a long time since she'd killed a man, but it didn't get any easier.

She looked around the room, searching for distraction. Then she got up. Something wasn't right. The rug had been moved. Its edge was no longer quite parallel with the floor tiles. And the tiles were cleaner than they had been that afternoon.

Housekeeping didn't operate in the evening.

She went into the bathroom, but nothing there seemed to have been disturbed. She studiously avoided catching sight of herself in the mirror above the sink. Instead, she went back to the bedroom and pulled open the wardrobe door. There, against the wall, staring at her sightlessly, was Lena's body, naked and covered with blood.

15

AT ELEVEN O'CLOCK the next morning, Kate stood in a gloomy basement room with peeling green paint and four rickety air-conditioning units. The Greek capital's Forensic Science Centre in Antigonis Street was some distance from state-of-the-art.

If Lena looked at peace, she knew it had much to do with the sympathetic attentions of Dr Minakis and her assistant. The senior pathologist was a woman of around Kate's age, with a warmth and passion for life that Kate had learnt, perhaps counter-intuitively, to associate with those in her profession. She looked at Kate over her reading glasses. 'Nothing complicated. They drugged her.'

She pointed at the needle mark in Lena's upper right arm. 'We don't yet know what they used, but will do as soon as we have run the tests. I will let you know, of course.'

Dr Minakis lifted Lena's right wrist. 'They bound her. I don't know why. I don't think she was in a position to struggle. We have found dog hair beneath her nails, perhaps from the boot of a car. There might be something for you there.'

'We've found the car,' Kate said. In the middle of the night, the CIA had come back with the requisite satellite coverage. It showed Lena being bundled out of the back of the building they had seen her entering and into a grey Renault Espace. They had killed her in the car, then driven straight to the hotel, where two men could be seen depositing the body in Kate's room. They drove on to a beach a few miles further down the coast where a dinghy was waiting to take them to a fast boat that returned them to Athens. They boarded a private jet at the airport. It had filed a flight plan to Georgia, but had rerouted once it was close to Russian airspace.

It had all been planned with the kind of ruthless efficiency of which the Russians so often showed themselves capable.

'The rest you can see. They cut her throat. We can all be thankful that she died swiftly.'

'Thankful' wasn't the word that echoed in Kate's head. The sight of Lena's lovely young face, the clear blue eyes and unblemished complexion, was almost harder to take than the livid gash beneath her beautifully sculpted chin. She was haunted by the contrast between her own privileged daughter and this girl who had come from nothing and been forced into taking a risk she hadn't sought to try to save her sister and make something of her own life.

Forced by Kate.

It had been her call. Her idea. Her operation from the beginning. Irrespective of the findings of an inquest, she was in no doubt about who deserved the blame. She had witnessed death often enough. She had ordered it, and seen the whites of its eyes. But she knew she would never be able to wash the taste of this one out of her mouth.

She became aware that Dr Minakis had stopped talking, and was looking at her sympathetically. 'I'm sorry for your loss.'

Kate nodded, and had some difficulty swallowing. Not for the first time, she took momentary refuge in procedure. 'I'd like to know what drug they used, Doctor.' Kate gave her a card with a Foreign & Commonwealth Office cover but an email account that was routed through to her via a number of digital blind alleys.

She saw herself out. Rav and Julie were waiting on the street. 'How did you get on?' she asked.

'They're still mightily pissed off that we didn't let them know we were here,' Rav said, 'but they'll get over it. They're even more worried about the Russians than we are.'

'Have they found anything else on Andros?'

Julie had been liaising with the local police and the coast guard. 'You want me to get an Uber? We could make the afternoon flight to London.'

Kate squinted against the late-morning sun. 'Please. I'm tempted to find somewhere I can bury my head in the sand, but I need to go home and face the music.'

'Two minutes,' Julie said.

Too tired to talk, Rav and Julie shared a cigarette. Kate stepped back into the shade and leant against a wall.

'Don't stare at me like that,' Julie said.

'Like what?' Kate said.

'Like you're wondering why I look so shit.'

'There are quite a few things I can't get my head around right now, but that's not one of them.'

'Good. Because I haven't been crying. It's just the smoke.' She held up her Marlboro and managed a weak smile. 'Gets in my eyes.'

Kate insisted Rav and Julie go straight home from Heathrow, and wished she could do the same. Ian was waiting for her in his office, blinds drawn and the lights down low. He looked like thunder. 'Have a seat,' he muttered. 'Coffee? Tea?'

'Coffee might help. I haven't had a lot of sleep.'

'Suzy's gone home, so I'll get it myself.'

He vanished before she could offer to go.

Kate glanced at his books. Nearly all non-fiction, politics or history. Margaret Thatcher's memoirs. Andrew Roberts on Napoleon. Le Carré's novels occupied one entire shelf. Who did Ian think he was? George Smiley?

A framed photograph of him dressed from head to toe in Lycra and holding a bike above his head at the top of a mountain pass took pride of place on the far wall. The not-completely-spontaneous shots of the family in the Alps, on Mustique and at the Monaco Grand Prix alongside it sent a message that was rather easier to decode. His desk was covered with snaps of his wife and three teenage boys. As he never tired of reminding anyone who came within reach, he and Ella had met at Oxford. She ran her own internet retail business, now reputedly worth a fortune. Ella dutifully attended all office functions, but she looked a little wearier each time. After a throwaway comment a few years back – 'Show me *one* middle-aged couple who has sex any more' – Kate had begun to appreciate why she might turn a blind eye to her husband's many office affairs. He was spectacularly unsubtle about it, so she couldn't possibly have missed the signs.

Ian returned with her coffee. 'Two sugars,' he said. 'Thought you might need it.'

'Thank you.'

He sat on the sofa opposite her, tugging his trousers up a little above the knee – another of his annoying habits – then crossed his legs, as if this was a languid philosophy tutorial rather than the dissection of an operation that had led to the death of a girl in her charge.

She expected a barrage of questions about every twist and turn of the Andros mission, and every decision she had taken along the way, but Ian was a lot more clinical. 'We started work as soon as you called last night. Thank you for the rapidity of the heads-up, by the way. I appreciate it. I brought in a team and we began by looking at traffic through Athens airport.'

He flipped open the file on the coffee table in front of him and pushed across a selection of CCTV images from the immigration hall and photographs of five men from their own files. 'Recognize them?'

She tapped three. 'They were the guys who ambushed us in the stairwell.'

'One of their specialist wet teams,' Ian said. 'I'm afraid the Serbian girl never had a chance. And the fact that you got the better of them does you great credit.'

Kate left the pictures where they lay.

'Check out the time stamp on the CCTV grabs,' Ian said.

11.27.

'They hired a speedboat in Rafina for cash and were on your island less than an hour later.'

Kate continued to stare at the pictures. 'So they knew.'

'Someone must have alerted them that you were on your way to Andros.'

'But we didn't take the decision to go until . . . well, early evening the previous day. I'd have to go over the timeline, but—'

'Exactly.' He let that hang in the air for a moment. 'So they do have a source. And I'd hazard a guess that he or she is inside this building.'

'So Viper is real.'

'I'd say so, wouldn't you?'

Kate needed to buy time to think. She stood up, went to the window and looked out through the blinds. 'How much do you think they knew?'

'Let's take a different route. What *could* they have known? Or, more precisely, what *could* someone have told them? The surveillance team first. More of them, so more possibilities. But, so far as I'm aware, they knew nothing beforehand, except that Andros was your target. Why would they think that would be of any interest to Moscow? And why would Moscow have wanted to send a wet team – which is, after all, not without risks of its own – for some unknown operation in a European backwater?'

'Do you think they knew about Lena?'

'My guess – and it's only a guess – is no. At least, not initially. I suspect they knew that you and your team had somehow gleaned intelligence on their assets and wanted to make quite sure that your source was shut down. To put it another way, they knew the int came via you, so it was *you* they were tracking.'

'You think they'll suspect Mikhail?'

'Depends on how unreliable they reckon he is. But even if they did, they wouldn't move against him. He's Igor's son. I'm afraid that someone saw you with Lena near that quayside and drew their own conclusions.'

In despair, Kate came back and sat down.

'We all make mistakes, Kate.'

'Not like that we don't.'

'Yes, we do.'

'She was just a kid.'

Ian waited until she had composed herself. 'So who knew that you were about to get on a plane to Athens?'

'My team, obviously.'

'Anyone else in your office, apart from you, Rav, Julie and Maddy?'

'No. And even Maddy didn't know. She went home early.'

'All right. You emailed me, so I was aware. Who else?'

'Danny. And C.'

'Did you tell anyone beyond the three of us?'

'No.'

'Your husband?'

'Well, yes. I guess I did say I was going to Greece, but not to Andros.'

'That might have been enough. He knows the form, of course. But could he have let any of that slip to anyone else, however inadvertently?'

She hesitated a moment too long as she turned over the

possibility he had mentioned it to Imogen. 'No. He was brought up to speed again in the latest vetting round. He knows that *anything* I tell him or talk to him about is sacrosanct, and can't be discussed elsewhere, under any circumstances.'

Ian's eyes seemed to glint in the low light, as if he sensed her doubts. 'Did anyone in your team behave in *any* way you thought worthy of note? Did they appear uncomfortable? Did they disappear for a period, or do anything you remember thinking was odd at the time?'

Kate recalled Rav's disappearance on the morning of Lena's death. He'd be the last person on earth to betray her. So why was she even giving it a second thought? 'No,' she said.

'How much did you tell Sir Alan?'

Kate stopped in her tracks. 'What do you mean?'

'When I arrived here in the morning, he clearly knew about the operation. But I hadn't briefed him. Had you?'

Kate cast her mind back to the late-night stint before she'd left for Athens. 'No. I didn't formally brief him.'

'But did you talk to him about it?'

'Yes. He came to my office.'

'And?'

Kate shifted uncomfortably.

'Did he ask you where you were going?'

'No! He didn't need to. He seemed to know. He said, "Bound for Athens in the morning?" Something like that.'

'How did he know it was Athens?'

'He said we should move as soon as the *Empress* docked. You heard him. So I guess Danny must have told him. Why do you ask?'

Ian pursed his lips. 'Don't be naive. If you don't know where this is headed, then you should. In all likelihood, the foreign secretary is going to win the leadership contest and become prime minister. So I don't need to explain, to you, at least, that we're holding a tiger by the tail. And sooner or later, as is the way of such things, it'll turn and bite us on the bum. Then the hard-faced hatchet men across the river will launch the mother and father of all investigations.'

'I don't understand.'

'Oh yes you do. We all have to protect ourselves. And we can only do that by ensuring that our loyalty is – above all – to our country.'

Kate narrowed her eyes.

'Sir Alan is a school friend of the foreign secretary,' Ian continued. 'He will admit to it when he has to, but generally chooses not to shout about it. You know as well as I do that, when push comes to shove, children of the establishment always stick together. So all I'm saying is that we may have to answer for our conduct one day, and we need to be aware of that.'

'Are you saying C could be Viper?'

'I'm saying that *no one* here is above suspicion. Not me,

not you, not Rav, Julie or Danny. And not Sir Alan – particularly given his close connection to James Ryan.' Ian sat back. 'To begin with, to be fair to all of us, anyone in Whitehall or beyond could be Viper. But this operation changes everything. Now we know he or she is in this bloody building. So from now on I'd like any information you uncover to come direct to me, please.'

Ian stood up.

Her audience was clearly over, so she rose with him. He put a hand on her shoulder. 'You must be . . . exhausted.'

'That's one word for it.'

'C wants to see you in the morning. Go straight up as soon as you're in.'

He ushered her out and she returned to her office in a daze. She sat at her computer and stared out into the darkness.

Her phone sounded. She glanced at the readout and pressed the green button. 'Hi, love.'

'Are you back?'

'Just got to the office. Sorry, I was about to ring.'

'Could you get over here? I'm at Millbank, waiting for this debate.'

Kate frowned in confusion, her mind blank. 'What debate?'

'The first of the TV leadership debates. It's on Sky News tonight. It's meant to focus primarily on foreign affairs, so James Ryan has the upper hand and we need all the help we can get.'

Kate glanced at her watch. 'I was about to go home and see the kids.'

'They're fine. We'd appreciate a bit of assistance. Imogen's nervous. She's less confident on foreign-policy stuff.'

'All right. I'll come over.'

Given what she'd previously said about feeling uncomfortable around Imogen's campaign, Kate had to suppress her irritation at being asked to help directly. But since Stuart had provided cover for Athens with no warning, she wasn't in a strong position to object. She went out into the blustery autumn night and decided to walk along the river and over Lambeth Bridge. The lights of the Houses of Parliament shimmered on the choppy waters of the Thames.

The TV crews outside the offices of Number Four Millbank showed little interest in her. She swept through them unhindered and up to the Sky News office. She gave a fake name to the security people and was just wrestling with the absence of any ID to match it – she had left it in her desk – when Stuart appeared and talked her in.

He kissed her perfunctorily and led her down the corridor. 'I know I'm not supposed to be here,' he said, 'but she needs me.'

Imogen did indeed look nervous, drained of her usual poise and self-assurance. She was heavily made-up and muttering quietly as she scanned her notes. Neither she nor the two male aides alongside her acknowledged Kate's presence.

Stuart interrupted: 'Imogen.'

She finally looked up, smiled at Kate and came to kiss her. 'Sorry, we have a minute to sum up our vision for the country. Which is, honestly, impossible.'

'I'm sure you'll be great.'

'It's such an unnatural thing, speaking for a minute. Oh, well, what will be will be.'

She was about to go back to her papers when Stuart stepped in. 'Kate's here to help on the stuff we talked about.'

'Oh, yes,' she said absent-mindedly. 'I was going to take a tough line on Russia – strict economic measures, sanctions and so on, and a broad alliance against them, but I do think we have to be careful to avoid a march to war.'

'Given the way the Russians have been deliberately trying to undermine Western democracies,' Stuart said, 'not to mention their enthusiasm for cold-blooded murder on our streets, attempted or otherwise, I think they should be the focus of our attacks. I mean, who knows what they may be up to in this election? Look what they did in the US!'

Kate glared at him.

He carried on regardless: 'Our guys have been doing some analysis. A lot of social-media accounts heavily support the foreign secretary – more than you'd think he might merit – and an equal number say the vilest things about you, Imogen. I think we should tell it as it is. The new Cold War.'

One of the aides finally tore himself away from his phone. 'We think they're bots, like we saw in the EU referendum – fake automated accounts, set up and later deleted. Quite a few have already gone.'

Stuart was looking at Kate for some kind of reaction. 'What do you think?'

'About what?'

'Is that possible? Isn't that the kind of thing the Russians are always doing?'

Kate shrugged. 'I don't know. It's not really my area.'

Stuart's face reddened. He stared at the floor. But if the tension was there for all to see, neither Imogen nor her assistants noticed it. She was too preoccupied with her notes, and they with their phones.

'I'll leave you to it.' She didn't meet Stuart's eye. 'I'll watch in the lobby.'

She fetched herself a glass of water and sat in a corner with a clear view of the TV screen on the wall. The foreign secretary swept in, late but unfazed, even though his cohort of aides could barely conceal their panic, and she shrank back to avoid being seen. She'd never been asked to brief him, but it was increasingly on the cards, and she wasn't keen to have him feel – or, worse, know – that he'd seen her before.

He chatted cheerily to the Sky News producers and allowed himself to be led to the make-up room. He exuded charm, she thought, whatever his critics might say.

The debate began about ten minutes later.

James and Imogen both had a natural ease in front of the camera. If it had been a dating show, they would probably have hit it off immediately and rushed away for a wild weekend in Brighton, leaving Meg Simpson, pale, technocratic and dull by comparison, to stand beneath their window and complain about the noise. But about ten minutes in, James got to her.

'I think we've probably had enough of the public-school charm,' Imogen said. 'After all, it's provided us with little but uncertainty wrapped up as destiny.

'It's not that I don't care about our relationship with the European Union – in the past and the future – and our place in the world. But right now I'd prefer to be talking about the scale of our social-care challenge or the still significant size of the deficit, not to mention our national debt. I'd like to talk about our students struggling with ever-increasing fees. They can't get a well-paid job or buy a house. I'd like to talk—'

'You do believe in capitalism, don't you, Imogen?' James shot her and the invited audience his trademark megawatt smile.

'I do. Enough to want to save it.'

'And if we don't get out there and build our trade across the world, as our forefathers did, then we won't have the money to do all the things you've so thoughtfully listed. And while I admire your ambition to double – to *double* – the education budget, you have not yet begun to let us know how you plan to fund—'

'*That* is how we compete in this brave new world you and your fellow posh boys have created,' Imogen said.

She was rewarded with a ripple of applause. Imogen was coming across as younger and fresher than her fellow contestants, with ideas that hadn't been talked to death over the past few years, but Kate still found it hard to tell precisely how well she was doing.

She was certainly right about politicians failing to confront the things that really mattered. The ageing population, a health service that couldn't continue in the way it had without an enormous injection of cash, unaffordable public-sector pensions, the fact that no one had a plan to build anywhere near enough houses, or that all public-sector finance projections relied on high levels of immigration, which the government was determined to reduce.

On and on. It seemed never to change.

And that was before you got to the really intractable issues – a deeply hostile Russia, and a China that grew in power each day without taking a single tiny step towards genuine reform. Who would want to talk about that when you could fill the airwaves with irrelevant shit about our place in the world from morning to night, dreaming up deals with every country and planet this side of Mars in the fond belief that it equated in some way to trade?

It was pathetic. They were pathetic. So pathetic she couldn't take any more. Her head hurt, and filling it with more politics wasn't the cure. She decided to walk home, in the hope that it might make her feel a bit better. She set off through the night, head down, mind drifting. And by the time she got to their front door, she had more or less forgotten her irritation with her husband.

16

WHEN SHE GOT into the house, Fiona and Gus were already asleep, so Kate went straight to bed. But an hour later she was still trying to bury herself in a book when Stuart arrived back.

'Where did you get to?' he asked.

'I was tired. I didn't think you'd notice my absence.'

'What's that supposed to mean?'

'It's supposed to mean exactly what it said.'

'You want to explain to me why you've been so weird these past few days?'

'I have no idea what you're talking about.'

Stuart put his hands on his hips. 'So now we're going to

do the bit where we pretend we haven't been married for ever?'

'We might not be for very much longer if you keep salivating over Imogen twenty-four seven.'

Stuart stared at her. She could tell he was genuinely shocked, and cursed inwardly. She hadn't meant to say it.

'What the fuck are you talking about? She's one of our best friends!'

'One of *your* best friends, if we're being brutally honest.' Kate immediately regretted saying that, too.

'Is that why you were so weird when I asked for your help and advice on Russia?'

'You were inviting me to comment on something I'd told you in literally the deepest confidence – the most sensitive national secret that only five people know.'

'I was absolutely not! Everyone knows you're the local Russia expert. I was inviting you to chip in on whether you thought we might be the victims of a well-known modern intelligence warfare strategy. The use of bots and fake accounts has hardly been the deepest, most sensitive, only-five-people-know national secret during God knows how many recent elections, has it?'

His blood was up, but it wasn't just bluster. She knew she had wounded him, genuinely and unnecessarily. 'I'm sorry,' she said. 'I had an operation that went very badly wrong in Greece.' Suddenly she couldn't stop herself. 'I recruited a blameless young girl to work for us. Actually, "recruited" is too nice a way of putting it. I blackmailed her into it. And then, in the middle of an operation, she disappeared. Rav and I went looking for her and got ambushed in a stairwell and had to kill our three attackers. Back at the hotel, I had to wash the blood off and change my shirt. I found the girl in my cupboard, with her throat cut. So . . . I'm probably not in the best frame of mind.'

Stuart was dumbstruck. She watched the emotions sweep through him, anger giving way to incomprehension and then, eventually, pity. 'Oh, shit, Kate,' he said. 'I am *really* sorry.'

'No. It's my fault. I shouldn't have taken it out on you.'

He came to sit next to her and rested a hand on her leg. 'I don't know what to say. That is . . . *horrible.* Are you . . . all right?'

'Physically, yes. I'm fine. It's a long time since I had to fight my way out of a stairwell, but Rav is young, fit and very good. We're both okay.'

She looked at him. 'So, yes, you're on the money. The Russians are ruthless murdering bastards. But I can't say that in public, and especially not now.'

'What will the consequences be?'

'Of her death? For me, not good. For the Service as a whole, it depends.'

'On what?'

'Everyone is looking over their shoulder now. The

Russians knew we were coming, so someone must have told them.'

'Who?'

'That is a very good question.'

Stuart had turned his back to her. 'Yours is a brutal business. I sometimes forget that. Or maybe I try not to remember it. Politics is sweetness and light by comparison.'

'War *is* brutal. And that's what it is.'

He looked at her again. 'Do you ever worry about the damage it's doing to you?'

'All the bloody time.'

Stuart began to undress, perhaps to make what he said next appear less loaded. 'Do you think it's possible to be the warrior you need to be and the wife and mother you want to be?'

So there it was. The question Kate could not and would not ask herself, articulated clearly between them at last.

She knew what his answer was, but she couldn't get her head around it now, so she let the silence play out.

He appeared to be deep in thought. Then he said, 'The Russians definitely killed this young girl?'

'I'd better stop talking about it. We've already got down to which of us knew exactly what, when.'

Stuart went to do whatever Stuart did in front of the bathroom mirror. After a while, he came back, removed the electric toothbrush from his mouth and stopped it for a moment. 'You should see the abuse and trolling Imogen gets online. It's off the scale. James hardly has anything like it. Don't you think that's strange, given what a complete dickhead he is? I reckon they're trying to swing the election in his favour. I can't help feeling it's all connected.'

'They?'

'Your Russian pals.'

Kate closed her book and switched off the light. 'I need to sleep.'

'Will you keep me posted? It feels important.'

'Right now, we're looking at a total shutdown, even when it comes to sharing certain information with each other internally.'

Stuart went back to the bathroom to finish off, then quickly slid between the sheets next to her and spooned her, which he hadn't done for as long as she could remember. She wrapped his arms around her waist and folded them over her stomach. It felt very good to be held.

'I do love you,' he said.

She felt his breath against her neck.

'And I have some good news.'

'I can hardly wait.'

'I went to see your mother. I agreed we'd take her down to see your aunt Rose this weekend.'

Kate was too exhausted to protest. 'A whole day with my mother. My cup runneth over.'

'On the plus side, she'll be on her best behaviour – she always is when the kids are around – and we might get the chance to murder her and dispose of her body on the way back.'

'As long as you do the time, I'm up for it.'

'Okay. Let's work up a plan in the morning.'

He turned over and, seconds later, was snoring quietly.

'To answer your question,' she whispered, 'do I think it is possible to be a warrior and the wife and mother I want to be? No, I don't.'

17

SIR ALAN'S MESSAGE had said: *Early meeting at the RAC Club. How about breakfast there at 8.30?*

Kate knew that the early meeting was in fact his morning swim and, sure enough, chlorine was the aroma she detected as she kissed him in the lobby.

'Sorry to drag you over here,' he said. 'But sometimes escaping from Mission Control can be productive.' He led her to the upper atrium, with its beautiful domed ceiling, where a red vintage Ferrari had been parked on the carpet. 'I'd recount its history for you in some detail, if I had the slightest interest in motor vehicles.'

'Well, thank God you didn't drag me to an automobile club.'

His eyes sparkled. 'Indeed.'

'I thought you were a member of the Travellers?'

'I am. But it's impossible to go there without feeling . . . noticed.'

The waiter leapt to attention as they moved through into the dining room. 'Good morning, Sir Alan!' He took them, without further discussion, to a table that was carefully hidden from view and where there was no prospect of being overheard. It was exactly the kind of place you would expect a spymaster to be taking his breakfast. Sir Alan had learnt his trade in the KGB's heyday, and old habits died hard.

'How are Stuart and the kids?' he asked.

'Stuart is well. The children are teenagers.'

'Ah, yes, been there, got the scars to show for it. And so has my wallet. You'll be pleased to know they emerge as surprisingly sophisticated and likeable human beings.'

'I'll hold you to that.'

The waiter took Sir Alan's order of scrambled eggs and smoked salmon. Kate wasn't hungry, but asked for the same, and coffee.

Sir Alan leant towards her. 'I just wanted to offer you my support,' he said quietly. 'I know how it can feel when an operation goes wrong, especially one in which a young girl lies dead. But we're fighting a war, as you know, and however much we attempt to guard against it, the innocent are often casualties. There is no merit or sense in blaming yourself, and I hope you're not going down that road.'

'I'd love to take a different one entirely, but I can't.'

'Why not?'

'Because I *am* to blame.'

'Is that what Ian said?'

'No. He was quite decent about it, actually.'

'I'm sure he was. He'll be positioning himself and, no doubt, in his situation I'd be doing the same. He's already looking forward to the day when this explodes into the public domain and costs me my head.'

'I'd like it if that didn't happen.'

'So would I. In the meantime, allow me to share my vision of the future. The first bout of the leadership contest on Monday will see Imogen and James go through to the run-off vote with the party members. Ballots will go out very soon afterwards. It's even possible that one or other of them will stand down, paving the way for an immediate coronation. Although it shouldn't make any difference, we all have to consider the political reality. Once one or other is prime minister, we're going to find it difficult to continue to investigate him or her without the most solid evidence imaginable – which, let's face it, is a rare luxury in our trade. Or, to put it another way, if we don't nail this in the next few days, we may have to park it for ever, with potentially incalculable costs for our country. The clock is ticking now and we need a result fast.'

The waiter returned with a large silver jug of coffee, but knew better than to invade Sir Alan's personal space without invitation. He got the nod, poured for them both and left the jug.

Sir Alan took a sheaf of papers from an inner pocket, unfolded them and placed them on the table. 'I had GCHQ take a look at what's going on across the web. The vast majority of the most suspicious activity is swinging behind James, although they seem to be refuelling Imogen as well, to try to throw us off the scent.'

'What if that's just another part of the misinformation ploy?'

'It could be. But I think we're better off assuming they have a dog in the fight and want him to win. If they really have compromised him, their reward will be considerable.'

'If they compromised him, how did they do it? And how do we prove it?'

'I've known James Ryan long enough and well enough to be in no doubt that there is nothing in his sexual closet that would trouble him. He can't keep his flies done up and might have illegitimate offspring in every port, for all I know, but I don't think that would embarrass him unduly or surprise his wife. I'm not quite clear about the basis of their marriage, but conventional fidelity doesn't come into it.

'He's always been greedy, though. His father was a gambler and womanizer, who was periodically penniless after he left the army. James was constantly worried that he was going to be pulled out of school. I've always wondered how he manages to fund his lifestyle, and send his children to the most expensive establishments in the land without apparently breaking sweat. So, my advice is to follow the money.'

'Rav is on to it.'

'I know. I've spoken to him already this morning. Beyond that, I want you to concentrate on two things. First, Mikhail. Danny says the *Empress* is moored off the coast a little way from Andros, but as soon as it pulls in anywhere else, let's put a team on the ground. This time I don't want anyone but me to know.'

'You want to cut Ian out of the loop?'

'I'll tell him what he needs to know. In addition, I want you to keep me informed about Sergei.' His gaze was steady again, those grey-blue eyes boring into her own. 'This is the last time I'm going to ask. I understand personal loyalty, but this goes beyond that.'

'You make it sound like a test.'

'Everything is a test. Of your suitability for high office because, as you well know, this is about the integrity and security of our country. And nothing – at least nothing we do – is more important than that.'

The waiter brought their food. Kate looked at her plate. 'I'll try to make contact with . . . my source, but there's no way of hurrying it. The US Embassy reception is next week, as you know. If he doesn't turn up there, I don't know any other way of making contact without colossal risk for him.'

'You should know that Ian is also aware of Sergei's existence.'

Kate failed to hide her surprise. 'How?'

'He might be a selfish shit, but he's no fool. He asked the same questions as I did, and arrived at the same conclusion.'

'He came to talk to you about it?'

'Yes. I told him you had been lovers—'

'I didn't sleep with him. Ever.'

'That comforts me not at all. Love is infinitely more dangerous. Anyway, suffice it to say that he didn't buy it, and I'm not sure I do either.'

'Buy what?'

'That Sergei was helping you out of long-held affection. Ian suggested there were only two realistic possibilities – that Sergei was manipulating you for his own ends, or those of his masters in Moscow, whoever they may be.'

'You said there were two possibilities.'

Sir Alan gazed at her from beneath hooded eyelids. 'Or that he had recruited you a long time ago.'

'You think I'm Viper?'

He finished his scrambled egg before he answered. 'I believe the former explanation is more likely. But I prefer to keep an open mind. Either way, it would help if we could place Sergei within the system. At the moment, we're coming up blank. We have no idea what he does and are therefore struggling with motive.'

'But Ian favours the latter?'

'Yes. Though it may occur to you, as it has to me, that this might be a convenient way of diverting suspicion from himself.'

Sir Alan tilted his head in the direction of his empty plate, and her still full one. Kate gave him an apologetic smile. 'It's a terrible waste, I know. But I'll just stick with the coffee.'

Sir Alan had an appointment in Downing Street, so Kate walked on alone. As she skirted the Horse Guards end of St James's Park, she saw the prime minister's wife emerge from the rear gate and set off for a jog. She looked pale and drawn, and who could blame her?

Kate accelerated past the Foreign & Commonwealth Office as it started to rain, and jumped into a cab in Parliament Square.

When she finally got to work – it would have been quicker to crawl on all fours along Millbank – Rav was at his desk. He didn't hear her approaching.

'Morning.'

He responded as if she'd set fire to his trousers. 'Shit! You gave me a shock.'

'What's wrong?'

'Nothing.' He shook his head vigorously, but somehow

without conviction. 'C's asked me to refine the search for Viper. These are the names.' He handed her a handwritten note. Kate featured. So did Ian, Rav, Julie, Danny and C. 'So I'm in the unusual position of having to investigate every one of my superiors. Thank God I never liked you.'

'The job is the job, Rav. You'd be the first to say it – just put one foot in front of the other, and we'll see where it lands.'

'I've asked Maddy to start pulling the phone records as soon as she's in.' He sucked his enviably white teeth. 'Mine will come to you.'

'If someone inside this building is betraying us to a foreign power, I'd like to think they were smart enough to avoid giving themselves away that easily.'

'I'm pulling everything else as well.'

'Good.' But Kate could tell that wasn't what was troubling him. 'Spit it out.'

'I've got a lead on the foreign secretary's African business activities. The man is now a teacher and lives in Oxford. We should get going.'

'We will. As soon as you tell me what's on your mind.'

Rav gazed at her. 'The initial feedback on our original Viper search group.' He opened his drawer and took out a dossier. 'I've been going through it for most of the night. I can't find anything at all unusual on anyone around the foreign secretary. We've got every email they've ever written that mentions Russia, and if they *are* working for

Moscow, they've been doing a great job of hiding their true feelings for a very long time. The same is true of those around Imogen Conrad.' He cleared his throat uneasily. 'Except . . .'

'Except what?'

'I've been agonizing about this, actually. I imagined what I'd feel if this was about Zac. I wouldn't want to know. But I think you would.' He handed her a wad of papers. 'Stuart calls Imogen a lot.'

Kate's heart was pounding, but she was determined not to show it. 'So he should. He's her right-hand man.'

'The night before last, when we were in Greece, he called her at three in the morning. I tracked her phone. Half an hour later it was in your house, which I guess means she was too.'

Kate turned the pages of the call log. Rav had circled those he thought unusual or worthy of note. She found the one at three in the morning. There were several more for the hours beyond midnight. 'I'll take a look,' she said.

'I'm sorry, I—'

'It's fine, Rav. You did the right thing.'

Kate picked up the file and retreated to her office. She closed the door and wished she could bar it. She sat down and stared at the log again. After a while, her vision blurred. She could feel sweat on her palms, her forehead and at the back of her neck. She had an overwhelming urge to pick up the phone, call Stuart and yell at him.

Rav knocked and entered before she could stop him. She didn't dare turn round. 'I'm sorry,' he said again.

'For what?'

He hesitated. 'There's almost certainly an innocent explanation. I sometimes call *you* at three in the morning.'

'I understand. I'll deal with it.'

Rav didn't move. Kate turned to face him. 'I said I'd deal with it, Rav. Okay? It's absolutely not your problem. Leave it to me.'

'But that's kind of the thing. I *do* have to deal with it.'

'What do you mean?'

'Well, you *know* what I mean. Given what's at stake, it obviously isn't appropriate that you deal with it so I must. I'm going to cross everyone else off the suspect list for Viper, but I need to transfer Stuart onto the new one.'

'Rav—'

'The pattern of phone calls is . . . odd. Not suspicious or anything, but odd. At the very least, he had access to your movements in Greece, so—'

'Rav, this is my husband we're talking about.'

'I know. I get that. It's awkward, but—'

'It's a bit more than fucking awkward.'

He put up his hands. 'All right. But in all . . . well, ninety-nine per cent probability, there's nothing to it. Like I say, we regularly call each other at three in the morning. It's a matter of internal record, though, that these logs have been delivered to me. The only line of interest in them is glaringly obvious. If I hand it over to you and the case is ever subject to review for any reason, we'll both end up being hung out to dry.' Rav waited. 'I'm just covering your back, Kate. I hope you know that.'

Kate watched the grey clouds gather above Vauxhall station. 'Fine,' she said. 'You're right.' She thrust the papers back at him and turned on her computer.

'I can go to Oxford on my own,' he said.

'I'm coming to Oxford. Just indulge me for sixty seconds.'

He retreated to the door.

'And I'll need to see whatever you get on Viper, when you get it. If you don't mind.'

Kate drove to Oxford in one of the office Astras, mostly in silence. She tried to conjure up a vaguely convincing reason as to why her husband might call Imogen at three in the morning if they were not lovers. She couldn't. And that ate away at the logical, rational part of her brain until it was hard to concentrate. Eventually, Rav said, 'For the avoidance of doubt, I assume you'll check Zac's phone records as well as mine. It's your duty to do so. And *I* would. If I were you.'

Kate wasn't in a mood to answer.

'So, just to be clear, I *don't* want to know what you find. I mean, do what you have to do for work, but if there's anything else – anything at all – I don't want to know about it.'

'You're making a bit of a mountain of this, Rav.'

'No, I'm not. You seem to forget I've known you for a very long time, and I can see exactly what it's doing to you, even though, given what I know of Stuart, I should think there is almost certainly an innocent explanation. And I'm not as robust as you . . . so, I'm just telling you that I don't want to know.' He waited. 'Do you understand that?'

'I get it. There won't be anything, so let's just forget about it.'

To change the subject, Rav filled her in on their visit. The man they were going to see had worked with the foreign secretary for the brief period after he left the army. 'The *Guardian* ran a story a few years back saying Blandwick Security did some work for Mugabe and his family,' Rav said. 'James threw his lawyers at it, but the only man the *Guardian* quoted was Blandwick's in-country manager, David Snell. I don't know whether he left Zimbabwe by choice or not, but he's now a teacher at the Dragon School.'

'Quite a change of career.'

'The *Guardian* seems to have given up on the story after that. They've never written anything else.' Rav had bits of paper all over his lap. 'Blandwick was wound up after three years. Its income stream tells an intriguing story. The losses were pretty chunky. Ryan was a consultant for a few years afterwards, working mostly in Africa.'

'None of which sounds out of the ordinary for an ex-soldier.'

'Perhaps not. But just before he became an MP, he bought that house in Hampshire for £1.75 million. Two years later, he applied to build a swimming pool with an elaborate pool-house complex. And the year after that, he bought the mews house in Chelsea for £2.2 million.'

'Maybe he won the lottery.'

'The African lottery, perhaps.'

'It's hard to see what that has to do with Russia, though.'

'I agree.'

18

THE DRAGON SCHOOL was in a leafy part of north Oxford and David Snell lived in an apartment at the rear of the school.

He had the tanned, leathery skin that appeared to be the preserve of southern Africans of a certain era. 'You're late,' he said. 'I've been waiting for you.' He ushered them into a small, gloomy sitting room, where the furniture was down-at-heel, the paint grey and peeling in places. The mantelpiece was crowded with bronze trinkets and wooden carvings, but the walls were completely bare except for an old watercolour of the African bush. There were no photographs. If David Snell had a family, there was no evidence of any affection for it.

'I suppose you'll need tea.'

'No, thank you,' Rav said. 'We're fine.'

'What is it you want of me?'

'We need to ask a few questions.'

He indicated that they should sit down.

'I'm sorry to be blunt,' Rav said, rehearsing his usual spiel, 'but I'm afraid we must ask you to treat the following conversation in the strictest—'

'I know who you are, for God's sake. And I know the drill. I wasn't born yesterday. I also have a geography class to teach, so please get to the point.'

'We'd like to ask you about your work at Blandwick Security,' Kate said.

'It was a long time ago. What do you want to know?'

'How long did you work for James Ryan?'

'About two years.'

'How did you meet him?'

'He came out to Zim to look for a country manager for a new security business he said he was setting up. He had a friend who'd been in the Recces in South Africa. That's the equivalent of the SAS there—'

'Thank you. We're aware of what it was.'

'He recommended me. I met James. I worked with him for a few years. That's it.'

'What did you do?'

'Not much. He was looking for business, guarding big international firms and their premises. But, first, there weren't many doing any work in Zim, and second, insofar as there was any business, he didn't win it.'

'Did you work for Mugabe?' Rav asked.

'Everybody in Zimbabwe worked for Mugabe in those days. He had a hand in pretty much every concern in the country. We did some work briefly for a South African food-processing company, which had a subsidiary owned by one of Mugabe's relatives, but the *Guardian* story was basically bullshit.'

'Did you see much of Mr Ryan?' Kate asked.

'No. He travelled a lot, throughout Africa. Even when he was in Zim, I rarely saw him.'

'So he paid your salary,' Rav said, 'and you sat around waiting for him to call with business, which rarely materialized.'

'I rarely sit around. His was just one contract I had. We agreed it was flexible.'

'But he paid you a retainer?'

'Correct.'

'Annual?'

'Yes.'

'And he rarely asked you to do a huge amount in return?'

'Also correct.'

Kate leant forward. 'If you don't mind me saying so, Mr Snell, something about this doesn't entirely add up.'

He glared at her, but she didn't flinch.

'Which is a polite way of saying that I don't think you're

telling us the *whole* story.' She was glad he didn't have a weapon within reach. 'Look, we aren't trying to catch you out. This is just a series of routine enquiries being conducted as part of a vetting—'

'That's what you said last time.'

Kate frowned. 'What do you mean, last time?'

'You said all this when you came here before. I spilt my guts out to you and nothing came of it.'

'Mr Snell, unless I'm going prematurely senile, I can say with some confidence that I have never set eyes on you before in my life.'

'Your people.'

'Which people?'

'I don't know. I can't remember his name. Some guy asking about James bloody Ryan.'

'From the Security Service or the Secret Intelligence Service – MI5 or MI6?'

'Six.'

'Are you sure?'

'Of course I'm sure. I was in the same business back in the Rhodesian war. I served in the Central Intelligence Organization, then the Selous Scouts.'

'Can you remember their names?'

'There was just one guy. Ian something.'

'Granger?'

'Maybe.'

'What did he look like?'

'Slimy. Unreliable.'

'I mean physically.'

'Five ten, dark-haired, receding hairline, slim. Looked like the kind of guy intent on trying to recover his youth – trim and fit.'

'What did he want?'

'Exactly the same as you. Same questions. Tell me about James Ryan's business, and so on.'

'And what did you say?'

'I told him that James Ryan was an unreliable cunt and that whatever he was doing in Harare had nothing whatsoever to do with the business he hired me for.'

'Which means?'

'He was there every five minutes. It's my country, for Christ's sake, and there's no one I don't know.'

'What was he doing there?'

'Crawling so far up the Mugabe family's backsides you could have seen his head whenever they opened their mouths.'

'To what purpose?'

He looked away.

'To what purpose?' Kate repeated.

'I don't know.'

'It looks to me like you might have a pretty good idea.'

'He left his briefcase in the office one day on one of his rare visits to us. I shouldn't have looked through it, but I did.'

'Go on.'

'I realized that whatever he was doing with his time, it had precious little to do with us. And I left.'

'What was in the briefcase?'

'Nothing very much. Except business cards and letterheads with his name on from a company called Hamilton Capital Management, which I had never even heard of.'

'What did it do?' Rav asked.

'I have absolutely no idea.'

'If you had to guess?' Kate said.

'Someone had to be keeping the Mugabes afloat. The country was bankrupt and there was practically nothing left to steal. So that was an opportunity, right, for anyone who wanted to buy assets or influence. The assets went long before, so who would be interested in buying influence? The Chinese . . . Shit, I don't know. Take your pick.'

'That's a bit of a leap, if I may say so. The Mugabes still controlled the rights to the country's natural resources.'

'He wasn't a mineral engineer, let me tell you. The rumour was he was a bag-carrier. That's all I can say.'

'What do you mean, exactly?'

'Moving money and assets around for the Mugabe family and outside investors who wanted to buy influence.'

'You heard that from old friends in the CIO?' Rav asked.

'Old friends and new. Like I said, Zim is a small country.'

'And you told all this to Ian Granger?'

'If that was his name, yeah, sure I did.'

'Do you have any idea where the money came from?'

'No.'

'You mentioned the Chinese.'

'It was a guess. They were trying to buy influence and assets all over Africa at the time and still are, as far as I know. They thought it was going to provide the natural resources they'll need in the future.'

'What about the Russians?'

'The same, but for them it's more like getting back to the days of the Cold War. It's the Soviet mentality – they want every country in the world in their sphere of influence.'

'Did you ever see James Ryan with any Russians?'

'I hardly saw him, like I said.'

'But specifically . . .'

'No, I never saw him with any Russians.'

'But he was bringing large sums in and out of the country and Moscow might have been the source of the cash?'

'Might have been.'

'If you had to guess?'

'I've told you as much as I know. The cash came from somewhere, but where exactly I couldn't say.'

Kate and Rav left David Snell to his unfortunate pupils and began their journey back to London.

'What the hell was all that about?' Kate asked, as soon as they were in the car.

'Maybe Ian had an investigation and it just ran into the sand,' Rav said.

'I'll check it out when I get back.'

They were silent for a while. 'I'm sorry about earlier,' Rav said eventually.

'About what?'

'Maybe I should have dropped it. Like you said, Stuart is your husband.'

'Of course you shouldn't, for all the reasons you gave.' Kate turned to him. 'I'm not talking about this again. Stuart might turn out to be a lot of things, but I've been married to him since you were a child, and I can assure you infidelity is not his vice.'

'I envy you your certainty.'

'Are you trying to make this worse?'

'No. It's not about you. It's about me. I've met Stuart. I can see why you feel that way about him. But how can we ever really *know*? I love Zac. I think he's a genuinely solid guy. But I don't know that I trust him a hundred—'

'Let's drop it, Rav.'

'You once told me you didn't trust anyone.'

'It's just a phrase I use to shut people up. I shouldn't.'

'You said it was one of your problems, but maybe it's everyone's.'

'It's just the business we're in.'

'You said it had nothing to do with the business we're in.'

'You really shouldn't have such a good memory.'

'I sometimes wish I didn't.'

'I'm fond of you, Rav, and I think you know that, quite apart from the fact that you've saved my life on more than one occasion—'

'And vice versa.'

'—but I'm still going to kill you if you don't shut up for a while.'

Rav did as instructed. And Kate tried to think about what the schoolmaster had told them. The problem was that suspicion was not only corrosive but explosive. It could dynamite the certainties that underlay not just a marriage but a life. What possible reason could Stuart have had to call Imogen at three in the morning? And why would she immediately come to their house?

Back at Vauxhall, Kate tried to force herself to focus on something else. She logged in and searched the records for any reference to Snell. The database came up with one result but no corresponding file.

Kate called the Records Office. 'Hi, Duncan. Kate Henderson from Russia Desk. I'm trying to locate the records for a David Snell. I have a feeling he was interviewed in connection with a prior investigation. His name comes up when I do a search, but I can't find the file.'

'Let me take a look. What did you say his name was?'

'Snell. David Snell. From Zimbabwe. Ex-Rhodesian Central Intelligence.'

'Hold on a second.' Duncan put down the phone. He was gone for a few minutes. 'There was a file,' he said, when he came back, 'but it has a red flag. It's been closed.'

'By whom?'

'I'm sorry, Kate, that's above my pay grade.'

Kate was about to hang up when she tried one last throw of the dice. 'Is there a Finance reference?'

'Yes.'

'Could you give it to me?' As he spoke, she jotted the number on a piece of paper and went straight down the back stairs to Rose's office.

'I'm sorry, Kate,' Jane said, 'but she went early today. Said she was having guests for the weekend.'

'That's us, so I can't complain.'

'Oh!' Clearly Jane didn't know what to make of that.

'She'll be exhausted by Monday,' Kate said, 'so cut her some slack. My mother's coming too.'

'I'll need her to authorize any discussion on the matter you raised the other day,' Jane said defensively.

'I understand that.' She didn't, though, now she came to think of it. 'I'll talk to her. But this is about something else.'

'Oh,' Jane said again. She looked relieved, which in itself told a story.

'I just wanted to see if we have any codes for a guy called David Snell. Ex-Rhodesian CIO.'

Jane tapped her keyboard reluctantly. The ability to use the Department of Finance to reverse into the filing system was something few understood. Every trainee had to spend at least a week in every department. Most took a mental break during their time in Finance, but Kate had spotted weaknesses in the system that not even the senior management entirely understood, and which hadn't been eradicated during numerous upgrades.

'There are quite a few references to a David Snell.'

'Could you give them to me?'

The printer buzzed, then Jane handed her a sheet of paper, which she took down the corridor to the Records Office. Duncan Black had a shock of curly red hair and skin as white as alabaster. He was lost in his iPhone. He snapped to attention when he saw her badge. 'Sorry!'

'Duncan, I've just been given these codes from Finance, and I need to have the corresponding files, please.'

He didn't look convinced. He'd probably never had a request like that before. Kate gave him the warmest of smiles to discourage him from questioning her. He retreated to his screen and she heard the printer going seconds later. Duncan came back with her cover sheet and a thick wad of paper. 'We've got all these.' He pointed to the eight or nine at the top of the list. 'But this one is the most recent.'

'So . . . where is it?'

'Not there.'

'How can it not be there? It's got a direct corresponding Finance reference.'

'Like I said, it's been closed.'

'By whom?'

'I'm not supposed to say. Someone on the management committee.'

'Right.' Kate frowned, as if trying to work out what to do. 'But Rose Trewen, the head of Finance, wants it. And she's on the management—'

His cheeks began to match his hair. 'She closed it.'

Kate stared at him. It took her a few beats too many to recover. 'Ah. Okay. Thank you for your help.'

She went back to her office, which was deserted now. Maddy's desk light was still on, but the corner that Rav and Julie normally occupied was in darkness.

Kate sat at her desk and interrogated Duncan's offering. David Snell had been an occasional informer for the Service in the final days of the Rhodesian war, but there was nothing else to be gleaned.

Maddy returned and handed Kate a small stack of paperwork, kicked off her shoes and tucked her feet beneath her on the soft chair next to her desk. She was the only person who ever did this. Comfort corner, she called it.

'I can tell you have bad news for me,' Kate said.

'Complicated news.'

'Go on, then.' Kate leant back. 'I'm not sure today can get much worse.'

'Rav said I needed to start asking GCHQ for material on the new list for Viper. I've only got the phone records so far.'

'Go on.'

'It might be nothing but it did kind of leap out at me.' Maddy handed them over. 'Julie and Ian.' She pointed at the circled numbers. 'The top sheets are hers, with his number circled. The bottom sheets are the reverse.'

Kate turned the pages. Far too many for there to be any doubt. 'Jesus . . . She always claims she can't stand the sight of him.'

'The heart has its reasons.'

'I'm not sure the heart plays any role in this. And it's not a crime. They're two consenting adults. He's married, but that's his business, not ours. It shows there's no accounting for taste, but little else. Unless I'm missing something.'

Maddy pulled the face she used when she wanted Kate to question her own judgement. Mostly, her commitment to covering Kate's back was endearing, but occasionally – like now – it was annoying.

'It honestly doesn't matter,' Kate said.

'Except that Ian is *always* trying to undermine you.'

'Don't worry. Really. Whenever he gets on his Savile

Row-clad high horse, I remind myself of Stuart cornering him at the Christmas do.'

Kate had been forced to ban her husband from office parties after he'd told Ian, when playing Diversity Snakes and Ladders, that being a woman trumped state-school GCSEs every time 'so she's always going to slaughter you'.

'But now we have a mole-hunt,' Maddy said, 'during the course of which he'll be doing everything in his power to point the finger elsewhere.'

Kate took the papers and locked them into her drawer. 'I really appreciate this. Thank you. But that's where these belong for now. And where *is* Julie? I need to talk to her about Lena's sister.'

'C is on the case. She flies to Serbia tomorrow, first thing.'

'Why is C on the—'

'He said it was his moral responsibility.'

'In what way?'

Maddy shrugged. 'An agent lost on his watch.'

Kate tried to hide her irritation at being outside the loop. And the idea of Julie and Ian as lovers was bizarre. Maddy was hovering. 'Come on, Maddy, spit it out.'

She handed over yet more paper. 'Rav's phone records.' She grimaced. 'And Zac's.'

'Okay,' Kate said. 'I'll take a look.'

'It's just . . .'

'I'll take a look, Maddy.'

'Right,' Maddy said. 'Have a good weekend. I'll see you

on Monday.' She'd long since mastered the art of lowering the curtain without leaving her audience in any doubt as to her true feelings.

Once she'd gone, Kate glanced over Rav's records. Nothing of note. But as Maddy's expression had made clear, Zac's were less comforting. Zac's Scottish trip had been Rav's excuse for spending so many nights at his desk. But his partner's phone very clearly placed him at his former wife's Fulham address.

Kate shuffled them to and fro on her desk. She went and fixed herself a coffee, then came back and drank it. When she'd run out of excuses not to, she picked up her phone and dialled Rav.

'You've got the records,' he said.

'Yes.'

'So why are you calling?' There was real anger in his voice. 'I told you not to.'

'He hasn't been cheating on you.'

Rav was silent. He didn't invite her to go on, but neither did he ask her to hold back.

'He hasn't been in Scotland. He's been with his kids at the house in Fulham.'

There was a long, long silence.

'Rav?'

'I *told* you not to fucking tell me, Kate. I *begged* you. Don't you understand *anything*?' He severed the connection.

19

KATE TOOK AN extra turn around Battersea Park in the fading light. Part of her wanted to burst through the door and ask Stuart about his three a.m. phone calls. Another part wanted to give him the benefit of the doubt, and do nothing more to disturb the already troubled surface of their pond. He'd only ask her why she didn't trust him, and she couldn't blame him for that because she'd have asked exactly the same question if the shoe was on the other foot.

When she got home, Stuart already had the car more or less packed. But the washing-up had not been done, or the bins put out, and the house was still a tip. Kate sublimated her anger and frustration by tearing through it at speed.

She pulled the overstuffed bin-liner free and Stuart tried to leap to her aid as she carried it across the kitchen. 'I'll do that.'

'Just make sure the kids are ready to go,' she hissed, as she stormed past him, only to have it burst over the paving stones. Kate stared at the scattered contents for a moment, then caught sight of their neighbour watching through her sitting-room window. She didn't know whether to laugh or cry.

She scraped up the mess, almost on autopilot, until she found something stuffed into a tin of Nelson's dog food. A condom wrapper. She stared at it for a while, her rage re-ignited, then went back inside, unrolled a sheet of kitchen paper, wrapped it up and shoved it into her pocket.

When she had finished, Stuart had the good sense to avoid any further conversation. Kate gave him a wide berth and climbed the stairs. She went into the bathroom, locked the door, slumped into the Lloyd Loom chair and put her head into her hands. Her heart was thumping and her hands were shaking more than they had after their encounter with the SVR wet team.

Eventually she managed to lift her head and gaze out of the window. After the endless wind and rain, it was a beautiful autumn evening, but the clear sky mocked her instead of restoring her spirits. By sheer effort of will, she managed to quieten the tumult in her mind and body, then left the refuge of the bathroom and busied herself with her packing.

Stuart pushed open the bedroom door. 'Are you all right?'

'Why wouldn't I be?' She felt as if her facial features had been carved in stone, and his expression told her she wasn't wrong.

'You don't look . . . well.'

'I'm fine,' she muttered. 'Considering.'

'I don't think you should have gone to work today.'

She looked at him as if he was speaking a foreign language.

'You can't just shrug off what happened in Greece, Kate. I can see the impact it's had on you. No one is superhuman.'

'I'm fine.'

'No one would be fine after what you've been through.'

'Well, I am.'

He hovered uncertainly. 'There's something I need to tell you,' he said.

She couldn't remember ever seeing him so nervous.

'I have a terrible feeling you're not going to like it.'

She sat down on the bed, with her back to him. 'I suspect I already know.'

'Try not to go crazy. I can explain.'

'It had better be good.'

He came to her side of the bed, but she couldn't bring herself to look up at him.

'Jed is coming with us. For the weekend.'

'What?'

'I did say don't go crazy.'

'What do you mean, Jed's coming with us?'

'Please bear with me, Kate. I know it's not ideal, but it's actually not crazy either. The Swedish porn star and I had an argument. Actually, it was worse than that. But in the end she said the situation was really very simple – she wanted to see Jed this weekend, and would only come to Rose's house if he could join us. I offered her every argument you would have done – believe me – but you know how goddamn stubborn she can be. In the end, I thought, I'm tired, you're tired, what the fuck does it matter? It's a fight we don't need to have. I called Rose. She was fine with it. Separate bedrooms and no corridor-creeping, obviously.' He put a hand on her shoulder.

Kate shrugged it off. 'Okay.'

'Honestly? Jeez, you *have* had a bad week. I didn't think you'd agree in a month of Sundays.'

'You know she's doing this to provoke us?'

'Of course she is. But if we roll with it, she'll get tired of fighting.'

'I doubt it.'

Ten minutes later Jed arrived. He'd removed some of the metalwork from his piercings and selected a strange ethnic coat for his weekend wear. 'Th-thank you very m-much for inviting me, Mr and Mrs Henderson,' he stammered, anxiety pouring off him in waves.

'It's our pleasure, Jed,' Stuart replied, gripping his

outstretched hand while Kate was still struggling to concentrate.

Jed climbed through to the third row of seats in the back of the car, and Fiona followed. Kate's mother was less obliging when they picked her up, but obeyed, uncharacteristically meekly, when Stuart instructed her to sit next to Gus. She stared stonily ahead as they crawled along the Embankment. Gus and Fiona were on their phones and Jed stared out of the window.

'What was today like?' Stuart asked Kate.

'Difficult.'

'There's an awful lot of traffic,' Lucy said.

'Yes, there is, Mum.'

'Can't you do anything about it?'

'Her people usually clear the roads in advance,' Stuart said, 'but they're having the day off.'

'It's a disgrace. Where *is* everyone going?'

'Out of London for the weekend,' Kate said. 'Just like us.'

'Why on earth are they doing that?'

'God knows, Mum.'

Stuart started to laugh.

'So many cars. There is a *lot* of traffic.'

'I was thinking poison,' Stuart murmured. 'But I may just resort to a blunt instrument.'

'It's not funny.'

'Who is that boy?'

'Which boy, Mum?'

'The one in the back, with that awful jacket.'

Gus snorted. Like father, like son, Kate thought.

'That's Jed. He's a friend of Fiona's. We just introduced you. And it's a very nice jacket.'

'He looks simply *awful*.'

Kate swung around. 'I'm so sorry, Jed. My mother isn't very well.'

'It's fine, Mrs Henderson. Fiona told me. I understand.' He gave her a sheepish grin. 'And I worry about the jacket, some days.'

'I don't know *what* you're talking about,' Lucy said. 'There's *nothing* wrong with me.'

'I know, Mum. You're an example to us all.'

'Always have been,' Stuart said. 'Or so I've been told.'

'People in glass houses . . .' Lucy muttered. 'If you ask *me* . . .'

'Thank you for the words of wisdom, Mum, but we're not asking you.'

'Who *is* that boy?'

Kate glanced over her mother's shoulder and rolled her eyes at Jed, who suddenly, and rather delightfully, followed Gus's example.

Over the course of the next hour, the state of the traffic and the offensive nature of his jacket shared top billing in Lucy's increasingly monotonous string of complaints. Gus took cover beneath his headphones, and Fiona handed Jed one of her earpieces to share. Kate tuned in to Kenny

Rogers on Magic FM. When her mother suddenly went silent, she hardly dared breathe, but looked back as the traffic on the M40 cleared and saw that all four of their passengers had fallen asleep.

'Have you told the girl's parents?' Stuart murmured.

'Mother and stepfather. I don't think they're going to miss her. That's where the trouble started.'

'Hmm. Doesn't it always?' He risked a grin as he glanced in the rear-view mirror.

'Julie's going to Belgrade, to try to rescue her younger sister.'

'Is that wise?'

'It's the least we can do. By which I mean the least *I* can do.'

'Not everybody wants to be rescued,' Stuart said, keeping his eyes peeled for the slip road that would herald the final phase of their journey. 'Did you ever think of that?'

Kate's aunt lived with her ex-investment-banker husband in considerable style just beneath the Ridgeway in the Oxfordshire countryside. A pair of wrought-iron gates glided open as they turned off the road and closed again as they made their way along the gravel drive to where Rose and Simon were waiting at the grand entrance of their Georgian mansion.

'Bloody hell,' Stuart said. 'Is it my imagination, or does this place get bigger every time we turn our backs on it?'

After the greetings, Simon showed Kate and Stuart to the folly at the far end of the formal garden, which was done up in the luxury one might expect of the finest country-house hotel, complete with roll-top bath and a fireplace in the bedroom. 'We'll keep an eye on Lucy and the young,' he said, 'but Rose thought you two could probably use some privacy.'

At dinner, Jed was the centre of attention for the first two courses. Much to their distress, Rose and Simon had never had children of their own, and asked him the sort of questions that made Kate embarrassed by her own lack of the right kind of curiosity. He answered with scrupulous politeness and gentle wit. His parents were doctors, his father a GP and his mother a psychiatrist. 'When we got up her nose as kids, she used to hit us with textbooks.'

Stuart winked at Kate, but she was still in no mood to wink back.

Lucy stared at 'that boy' throughout the meal, as if she were about to launch another wave of invective but she held back, perhaps because she'd suddenly remembered her habitual need to cast herself in the role of Fairy Godmother in front of the grandchildren.

Simon and Stuart pitched into an animated discussion about the state of the nation over port and Stilton, then retired to the billiards table. The children went to watch TV, and Rose escorted Lucy to bed. Kate was painfully aware that she had said hardly a word during the evening, and knew her aunt had sensed something was wrong.

When she came down, Rose tore Kate away from the washing-up and made herbal tea for them both. 'What the hell?' She smiled. 'You only live once!'

They settled next door by the fire, a lovely room with low beams, antique panelling and modern Scandinavian fixtures.

'You look tired,' Rose said.

'Looks can be deceptive.' Kate sighed. 'I'm completely and utterly knackered.'

'Work, the children, or both?'

'Both, probably. But I guess my mother deserves a fair amount of the credit.'

'Jed is a nice boy.'

Kate nodded and sipped her tea.

'You don't have to tell me anything if you don't want to,' Rose said.

'It's more a question of where I should start.' Kate gazed into the fire. For a moment, she thought of telling Rose about the condom wrapper in her pocket and the suspicion that was tearing her apart, but she couldn't bring herself to articulate it. 'Don't *you* feel tired sometimes?'

'I'm not in the front line in the way you are.'

'I suppose it depends how you define the front line. I could put it down to losing someone this week, a young girl who deserved an awful lot better, and knowing beyond a shadow of a doubt that it was my fault. I could also claim it's because we're all overworked and underpaid. I might even blame it on the fact that, like every middle-aged woman, I find trying to be a mother and a wife at the same time as a warrior for truth is not as easy as we all feel the need to make it look. But I'd be able to live with that if I didn't feel we're being overwhelmed by an incoming tide that we're completely powerless to hold back.'

'I suspect that every generation has to grapple with its own version of that.'

'But in the old days, it seemed like a fair match, didn't it? We faced off against the KGB. The two intelligence services, each at the heart of their respective establishments, locked in combat, with a succession of victories and defeats. As long as we could spot their feints and sleights of hand, we could go home reasonably secure in the knowledge that our world – the safe, civilized, *free* West – would continue along its relatively well-maintained tram tracks. It isn't like that any more. They go behind us and around us and beyond us to the people and the country at large, whipping up hostility and division and dissent, their tentacles reaching down a thousand different alleyways. I don't know which front we should be most energetically defending now. And the only thing I can say for sure is that it's a battle we're losing. It's not just that they come over here and murder people right under our noses, but they get a distressingly large number of people to believe it's all a conspiracy by the *British* government. It's bloody surreal at times.'

'But that makes what we do more important than ever, doesn't it? Which at least gives our work a sense of urgency and purpose.'

'That's what I keep telling myself.' Kate looked up. 'While we're on the subject of urgency and purpose, can I ask you something about work?'

'Of course,' Rose said, but her smile was suddenly devoid of its usual warmth.

'Who decides to put a red flag on a file?'

'The management committee.' The flames danced in her eyes. 'As you well know.'

'Sorry. And, yes, I do know.' She paused. 'I was looking into something last week. I mentioned it to Jane.'

'Oh?'

Kate frowned. Rose's expression remained opaque. But it was impossible that she didn't know. 'I was asking about someone I had to assess for recruitment a long time ago.'

'And you tried Registry?'

'Yes, I did. And the file on her was closed. I tried to use Finance to reverse-engineer an enquiry, as you once taught me. I was pursuing something else today, and that led to a dead end too, with another big red flag.'

'It happens.'

'Rarely, though. At least, I thought that was the theory.

And the odd thing is, I know of no connection between those two files. So why would they both be closed? It's a bit of a coincidence, isn't it?'

Rose shrugged.

'It *had* to be by order of the management committee? There's no other way?'

'Yes. And no.'

'But you're on the management committee.'

'Not present at every meeting.'

'One of the red flags was signed by you.'

Kate had rarely witnessed the flint at Rose's core, but did so now. A reminder, perhaps, if one were needed, that you didn't get to the top of the Service without it.

Rose leant forward to throw another log onto the fire.

'You're not going to help me, are you?' Kate said.

'Of course I'm going to help. But I won't put either of us in a position we might both regret.' She turned. 'I look upon you as a daughter, you know that. And I feel a tiny bit responsible for luring you into the Service. But for those endless conversations on the way to Cornwall, you might have been safely installed at Goldman Sachs by now, earning a king's ransom.'

'Not really my style.'

'Your father always held me responsible, and he was right. So, I will *always* do my best to help you. But there's a handful of things that are more important than family, and this is one of them.'

'Is that a piece of advice?'

'Possibly.'

'To do what?'

'Tread carefully.'

'What's the connection between the two closed files?'

'That's not treading carefully.'

There was a long silence as Rose appeared to weigh up how much she should say. 'Ian,' she said eventually. 'He's the connection. But he dragged in Alan. And Alan is unlikely to forgive him for that.'

Despite the fatigue and the alcohol, Kate's brain was turning faster now. 'So that's what they meant when they talked about "another" attempt at disinformation. Ian brought in Irina, but kept her to himself. And she sold us a pup.'

'Correct.'

'What breed of pup?'

'We paid Irina a lot of money over quite a number of years. She was Ian's prized asset and he dined out on her. She seemed to be a never-ending source of quality material. And some of it was undeniably true. You know how clever the Russians are. They hooked us with lots of sprats so that we'd swallow the mackerel whole.'

'The mackerel?'

'Sorry. We're getting a bit zoological here, aren't we? The mackerel was cast-iron intelligence that the German treasury minister was a paedophile who had been caught and turned by the Russians. We had everything – internet history, emails, phone records, videos of him with a series of under-age boys . . . Hideous, of course. We went over and over it. It was totally convincing. Everything checked out.'

'Except it was all fake.'

'Every single bit of it.'

'And we'd already handed it over.'

'Worse than that. The foreign secretary had used it as leverage. So it blew up in his face in the most embarrassing way imaginable. It was a miracle no one on the German side leaked it to their press.'

The fire crackled, and sent up a small shower of sparks. 'If that was Ian's operation – if he owned it from first to last – why didn't it ruin him?'

'The second closed file gives you your answer. But I can see you no longer need it.'

'He'd been digging around in the foreign secretary's African business interests. And there was plenty there.'

'They say knowledge is power,' Rose said. 'But sometimes it's a burden, too.'

'Why is your name on the file closure?'

'I think Alan's a good man. I always have. He's been loyal to me, and I have to him. He was taken in by this when he shouldn't have been. Shutting down the Africa investigation was the price of keeping him in his job, and I thought it was worth paying. But everyone knew he was a school friend of the foreign secretary, so his name on the closure would have made him a hostage to fortune.'

'What about Ian?'

'We had no choice but to leave him where he was. He knew too much.'

'Did the Africa file trace the source of the foreign secretary's cash?'

'Not to my knowledge. Mugabe or his cronies, I assume.'

'The other day you told me Sir Alan seemed preoccupied with something. Do you know what?'

'No. He's been more than usually secretive.'

'There's something he might not want to share with you, under the circumstances,' Kate said. 'A week ago we received intelligence that suggested one of the leading candidates to replace the prime minister is working for the Russians.'

'In what capacity?'

'We don't know the what, why or how.'

'What about the who?'

'It's very likely to be the foreign secretary.'

Rose nodded, as if it made complete sense.

'The same source suggested there's a mole, probably inside Vauxhall Cross, which would explain why we lost the girl. The op appears to have been compromised from the word go.'

'So you're on a mole-hunt.'

'Yes.'

'How close do you think you are?'

'It's a small pool. Half a dozen people knew enough to put the Russians where they were at the time they were there: me, my two assistants, Danny from Ops, Ian and Sir Alan.'

'This story doesn't have a happy ending, Kate.'

20

'IS THERE ANY way I can help?'

'No. You've given me too much already.'

Rose got up and kissed her. 'As I said, you're the daughter I never had. But now you need to go to bed.' She took the empty mug from Kate's hand. 'You need to rest and recharge. Simon and I will look after the children and your mother in the morning. Why don't you and Stuart take that fabulous walk along the Ridgeway, have lunch at the White Horse? I'll send Simon to pick you up afterwards.'

'Rose . . .'

She stopped at the door. 'Yes, my love?'

'Do you ever think you can have too much knowledge?'

'In our business?' She pursed her lips. 'Not if you want to win. And you've always been very competitive. In what we laughingly call real life? Perhaps.'

Kate hadn't meant in their business, of course, but she didn't correct her aunt.

She almost collided with Jed as he emerged from the ground-floor loo. 'I'm so sorry, Mrs Henderson.'

'Night, Jed.' She headed for the door into the formal garden.

'Er, Mrs Henderson . . .'

She stopped and turned.

'I know you don't think much of me, although you were very nice about my jacket, but the thing is, I *really* like your daughter. I get that you're worried about the age issue, but I . . . I care for her. A lot.'

'I can see that, Jed. And I'm sorry if I appear unwelcoming. I have a lot on my plate right now so please don't take it personally.' She felt herself smile at him in a way she hadn't managed with anyone recently. 'Goodnight.'

The tension seeped from her shoulders as she walked through the garden. The perfectly sculpted box hedge brushed her leg and she ran a hand through an ornamental rosemary bush, snapped off a sprig, rubbed it between her fingers and raised them to her nose. The night was still but for the sound of the breeze in the treetops and the distant hum of traffic. An owl hooted as Kate gazed up at the constellations above her. She glanced about her. All was still.

She meant to wait up for Stuart, but her eyelids grew so heavy once she'd burrowed beneath the duvet that she couldn't stave off sleep a moment longer. She woke to find Stuart leaning over her with a bone china cup of tea. 'Role reversal,' he said. 'I've been given strict instructions from Rose.'

He drew back the curtains and let in the bright morning sunlight. Kate sat up and sipped her Earl Grey. The four-poster bed afforded a magnificent view of the rolling hills beyond the garden's ancient stone walls, and of the blue sky above them.

'Apparently, we're embarking upon a major expedition to the White Horse, and leaving the children to your mother's tender mercies.'

'Rose said she and Simon would look after them all.'

Stuart threw himself onto the bed. 'Well, I couldn't think of a better idea if my life depended on it. Let's get going. It's a beautiful day.'

'What time did you turn in?'

'Late.' He hauled himself up again and went to the bathroom. 'Simon's Lagavulin is invariably a mistake, so I'm going to have to blast up that hill to eradicate the traces.' He turned on the shower. 'You must have slept well. You were snoring when I came in.'

'I was *not*!'

His grin appeared around the door. 'You most certainly were.'

She showered while he dressed, and then they had a huge family breakfast. Afterwards the two of them set off, feeling only moderately guilty. The children had been more than happy to be left behind. Gus and Fiona viewed a long country walk as the least amusing of all adult tricks, and Jed was not about to contradict them.

The merest hint of cloud brushed across the sun as they climbed towards the horizon, but the sky was clear again as they drew closer to the ridge, and the green fields below them were luxuriant in the sunlight. 'On a day like this,' Stuart said, 'there's not a shadow of a doubt that Jerusalem was builded here . . .'

'Hmm,' Kate said. 'Pity about "those dark satanic mills".' Her nose was running, so she reached into the pocket of her jeans and almost took out the condom packet wrapped in its sheet of kitchen roll.

It burnt a hole in her pocket and her mind for the rest of the climb.

Stuart's phone *ping*ed and he fished it out of his Barbour.

'You need to switch it off,' she said.

'Controversial.' He smiled at her. 'But all right.'

'So?'

'So what?' he asked.

'What was the text about?'

'Ah – now who's breaking her own rule?'

'What's happening?'

'Imogen is on a media round tomorrow morning. She's

going to announce that she plans to review Trident and redirect all savings entirely to the Education budget.'

'Bloody hell. Does she mean to ditch Trident?'

'Not immediately, but that might be the outcome. She wants a nuclear deterrent, just doesn't think it has to be Trident in this day and age. On Monday she'll share a stage with three retired admirals, two generals and an air chief marshal who will all say they think she's right.'

'The press and the party will go crazy.'

'Some of the press, perhaps. The party? I'm not so sure. The idea is for a new kind of leader with new priorities and ideas for a new generation. If she looks and sounds like the future, she may well swing it.'

Kate walked on in silence. It was a bold play. She wondered what the Russians would make of it.

'You've been a bit odd this week,' Stuart said, from behind her.

'Have I?'

'You know you have.'

'I'm sorry.'

'About Imogen, I mean.' He took her arm and swung her around. 'What *is* eating you?'

'Nothing.'

'Come on, Kate. Tell me. I can't stand tiptoeing around in no man's land.'

'I just wonder if you're having an affair.'

'For God's sake . . .'

'What on earth were you doing, calling her at three in the morning?'

He gaped at her, dumbfounded. 'You're spying on *me*?'

'The Russians have someone inside our organization, for fuck's sake. Or close to one of the candidates. We had to pull your phone records along with everyone else's.'

'What do you mean?'

'A spy, a sleeper, a mole.'

'How do you know?'

'The same way we know about our foreign secretary possibly being one of theirs.'

'And you thought it was me?'

'Of course I didn't. But my team couldn't exclude you or me from the search. They'd get carpeted and sacked if it ever came to light. They pulled everyone's logs. Yours show just how much you call her. Which is fine. But I've found it difficult to explain why you might have needed to speak to her in the middle of the night.'

'That's difficult to explain, is it?'

She shook herself free. 'Of course it bloody is.'

'Even though you regularly call your team at all hours?'

'That's different.'

'Why? Because your job is more important than mine?'

'It's *different*. I was away in Greece. You were on your own with the children. You called her at three in the morning, and half an hour later, her phone was located inside our home.'

'So I must have been fucking her?'

'Were you?'

'I am not going to dignify that with an answer.'

'Don't lie to me, Stuart.'

'Jesus, Kate . . .'

She retrieved the kitchen towel, shook out the condom wrapper and handed it him. 'So explain this, why don't you.'

Stuart took the gold wrapper as if it were about to burst into flames. He stared at it for a moment. 'You're right. I did put this in the dog-food can and shove it in the bin.' He looked at her, his gaze cold as ice. 'And that is because I found it under the sitting-room sofa. Why was it there? Not because I can't wait to hump my boss the moment your back is turned but because that was where your new best friend Jed left it.

'I confronted Fiona. She admitted she'd lost her virginity to him while I was upstairs in our bedroom watching television. She begged me not to tell you. Begged me. I didn't promise not to – after the last lecture you gave me – but reckoned I'd wait for a better moment, given everything you have on your mind. And, yes, I echoed every point you apparently made to her the other day, including the legal definition of statutory rape.

'So let's move on to the phone records – not that I should have to answer your stupid questions. Someone in our department got himself arrested in Scotland for allegedly downloading child pornography. We were shitting ourselves about the news leaking first thing in the morning. You were away. She texted me. I called back. Of course, if I was shagging her, I wouldn't have *had* to call back, would I? I'd have been right there on the kitchen table with her. But that clearly never occurred to our local neighbourhood super-spy. She came over, we talked it through, she went away again. *End of.*'

Stuart was shaking with rage. Kate reached for his arm and only succeeded in tugging at his sleeve as he stepped further away.

'All right,' she said. 'I'm sorry . . . really sorry. I've been under a lot of pressure.'

'Fuck your pressure, Kate. Fuck your job. And fuck you.'

He stormed on up the hill and she let him go. He was a big, strong, athletic man and he could move at quite a pace when he wanted to. For half an hour or so, he charged ahead and she struggled to keep within fifty metres of him. When he eventually slowed, she closed in on him and this time wrapped her arm around his. 'I'm truly sorry,' she said.

He turned to her.

'Truly.' She saw his features soften, and dared to hope that the worst of his fury had blown through. 'I'm not going to try to excuse myself,' she said. 'Except to say that my love for you has always been a kind of madness.'

'It's incredibly hurtful, Kate.'

'Of course it is. But it's not really about you. After what

my mother did, I find it difficult to trust anyone. You know that.'

'Honestly – screw your mother. Jesus, seriously, let's do her in and bury her here, under the Ridgeway, and then we can move on. I'm well up for it. I don't want to live with someone who doesn't trust me to be as good as my word. It's totally debilitating, and just a bit fucking depressing . . .'

'I know, I know.' She drew him closer and kissed him.

He gripped both her arms, took half a pace back and looked into her eyes. 'I need you to be in no doubt that I would *never* betray you.' His voice cracked. 'I never have. Never even wanted to.' He smiled at her sadly. The skin around those big blue eyes crinkled in a way she had always found almost impossible to resist. 'Even though you're emotionally autistic, frequently remote and pre-occupied, you're still the one.'

'A ringing endorsement. Lucky me!'

'We love who we love. Sometimes, as you say, it's beyond reason.' He kissed her this time, the palm of his hand gently cupping the back of her head. 'On the plus side,' he said, 'you're still unbelievably sexy and have a great sense of humour.'

They held hands along the ridge, and her footsteps were lighter than they had been in a while. Until her thoughts returned to the condom wrapper.

'I suppose I should talk to Fiona,' Kate said.

'I suppose you shouldn't. I've already said everything

that needs to be said, and issued every warning that needs to be issued. Besides, we've had enough tension in the house, so just leave it.'

'I'm her mother.'

'True. And I'm her father. And parenthood, as I recall, is a shared responsibility. Even though we both know "literally nothing".' He let go of her hand, but only long enough to mime a pair of quotation marks in the brisk autumn air.

Later they walked arm in arm to the folly, peeled off their hiking gear and sat in front of the fire, which one of their hosts had lit. Still later they lay together in the roll-top bath and then Kate sat naked in the deep armchair by the fire, the relief still washing through her like a drug. Stuart caressed her with the languid ease that only long experience can muster. He massaged her feet, then ran his fingertips over her knees and the inside of her thighs, and brushed his lips across her stomach.

She rested her hands on the back of his head as his tongue darted ever lower, and arched her back, losing herself in the sheer, exhilarating pleasure of the moment in a way she would not have imagined possible only a few hours ago.

They lay in each other's arms, by the fire, occasionally glancing up at the hands of the mantelpiece clock, willing it not to march them too briskly to reality. Eventually Kate raised herself on an elbow and kissed him. 'Let's get dressed and head over for supper before people begin to wonder what we're up to.'

She had a quick shower and was humming as she got dressed. As they strolled through the garden to the main house, she stopped for a moment by the rosemary bush. She picked another sprig and raised it to his nose. 'Rosemary,' she whispered. 'For remembrance . . .'

When they arrived in the kitchen Rose was frying slivers of foie gras, as Simon eased the cork out of a bottle of chilled Muscadet. 'Ah, the young lovers,' he said easily. 'Time for something restorative, I fancy.' He poured the wine and handed Kate a glass.

'And why not indeed?' She could hear the children joshing with their grandmother in the sitting room over the burble of the radio. Even Lucy seemed caught up in the magic of the occasion.

Rose turned as Simon held out her glass, but her expression was a mixture of curiosity and alarm. 'Oh, bloody hell,' she said.

'What?'

'Imogen.' She motioned Stuart in the direction of the radio.

Puzzled, he reached across and turned up the volume.

'The Westminster Confidential website has published a tape of the minister for Education having sex with one of her aides, which appears to have been filmed in a hotel during a government-sponsored visit to the Russian capital.'

21

KATE PUT DOWN her glass, swung around and rushed out into the garden. Stuart trailed her as she sprinted across the grass and into the folly. He was beside her as she opened her laptop on their bed, firing the same question at her, again and again: *'What the hell are you doing?'*

It took her seconds to find the site and the tape. She hit play and they were suddenly watching graphic images of flesh against flesh. They froze, unable to tear their eyes from the screen.

The quality of the footage was incredible, the action as explicit as any porn film. Imogen straddled a man, whose face was out of frame, her head tipped back as she panted and writhed, her small breasts bobbing. She giggled as, eventually, she raised a shapely knee and eased herself off her lover.

The camera tracked up his glistening torso and Kate finally saw his face.

It wasn't Stuart.

It was Andy or Connor or Gregor – or somebody else entirely.

'Would you like to turn it off now and tell me what the bloody hell is going on?' Stuart's tone was icy again.

Kate closed the screen. She breathed in deeply and gave herself a moment. 'The Russians must have leaked it.'

'What do you mean?' He looked horrified.

'They want Imogen out of the race. Who is he?'

'Andy Mac.'

'Did you know they were an item?'

'Suspected. Not knew. They were pretty discreet. But, honestly, I only care how you and I behave. I don't want to be the world's moral policeman.'

'Was Andy on that now legendary Russian trip?'

'As far as I remember, yes.'

'And they were fucking each other back then?'

'No idea.' Stuart was shaking his head. 'You thought it was me,' he said.

'No.'

'That was why you dashed across here, like a scalded

cat. Even after everything we've said and done today, you still thought it was me.'

'I know what the Russians are trying to do. I think about it almost every waking moment, and most sleeping ones, too. The last few hours have been the most wonderful escape from that reality – but this just took me back with a bang.'

'For a spy, you're a shit liar. And for the record, the children and I are going to need a bit more than a few hours away from that reality.' Stuart grasped her arm and gripped it tight. 'That's it, Kate. That's the last time you doubt me. Understood?'

She nodded.

The door banged shut behind him.

Kate sat on the bed, shaking. Her phone pinged. A message from Rav: *Have you seen it?*

She WhatsApped back: *Hard to miss.*

It would be quite a turn-on if I was straight.

Then: *In fact, it's still a turn-on – she has a hell of a body and so has her stud.*

Inappropriate, Kate replied.

She lay back and stared at the gathered silk canopy of the four-poster, relief still flooding through her. Stuart annoyed she could handle, Stuart angry, even. But Stuart a liar would have killed her.

The phone sounded. 'I can't speak, Rav,' she said.

'My sources tell me she hasn't been shagging him for a while, so they've sat on this for years.'

'Have we got a trace?'

'GCHQ don't hold out much hope. It'll have arrived on a USB stick, in the post.'

'I'm here with my family, Rav. I have to go.'

'It puts her out of contention, wouldn't you agree?'

'Yes.'

'There's something else. More on Ryan's little business venture. Guess where it was incorporated?'

'British Virgin Islands?' Kate sighed. 'Belize?'

'Belize. Via a Panamanian law firm. But here's the interesting bit: GCHQ have pinned François Binot as the intermediary.'

'Christ.'

'Yup.'

Binot was a legendary Swiss lawyer who'd once worked for the International Criminal Court in The Hague, helping to compile cases against Ratko Mladić and the other butchers of Bosnia. But in the early 2000s he appeared to have switched course to represent, or at least assist, some of those he'd previously been investigating. He had quickly acquired a reputation for taking on tasks and individuals others would not contemplate and before long had found his way into the orbit of the Russian president. It was Binot who had set up the offshore companies that stored the wealth of the Russian president's closest associates. He was the president's bagman. 'How the hell would James Ryan have come across him?'

'Kosovo. Ryan served there, and the last work Binot did in The Hague was on those accused of war crimes in Kosovo. I can't prove a connection, but I'd bet you any money they met there.'

'I have to go,' Kate said. 'Let's talk in the morning.'

'I want to get on a plane to Zürich first thing, to try to get in front of Binot. Will you authorize?'

'No, Rav, I won't. I want a proper risk assessment and I'd also like a discussion about what getting in front of him is likely to achieve. Apart from alerting everyone involved as to how much we know.'

'I'll go anyway.'

'No! Stay right where you are. We'll talk about it in the morning.' She waited, but he didn't hang up. 'I'm sorry about yesterday,' she said.

He didn't reply.

'If it had been infidelity, I wouldn't have told you, but I thought you needed to know.'

'But don't you see, Kate? It *is* infidelity. Worse, even. It makes a mockery of everything we've been through together.'

'Have you spoken to him?'

'No. And I'm not going to.'

'Rav, I really think—'

'It's none of your fucking business, Kate. It wasn't your job to tell me, and I asked you not to. I don't want a lecture, and I don't want to talk about it again.'

Rav cut the call and she put her face into her hands. So much for a break from reality.

Perhaps inevitably dinner became a low-key affair. They paid the price for Lucy's earlier good humour, and Rose put her to bed early. Simon kept the conversation ticking over, mostly talking to the three kids about their lives, plans and hopes.

Fiona was particularly forthcoming, announcing that she now wanted to be a doctor, despite having little previous aptitude for or interest in science. Since the source of this newly discovered passion was obvious enough, neither Stuart nor Kate sought to puncture her balloon. Only Jed felt obliged to share the profession's drawbacks, based on his experience of his parents' lives.

Kate wondered whether her daughter's sudden volubility had something to do with the tension in the air between her and Stuart. She could tell that Rose knew something was wrong too, but she didn't want to talk about it tonight, so turned in straight after they'd finished eating. She heard Stuart come to bed hours later, reeking of whisky, and found herself thinking how strange it was that you could sense your husband's wakefulness in the dark, yet not be certain of his fidelity. She felt ashamed for doubting him.

The journey back to London began in silence, but Kate knew she could rely on her mother to make matters worse. It was just a question of when.

'Rose says you don't look after me properly,' she said.

Kate continued to stare out of the window.

'She says you don't come to see me enough.'

'She actually said she was worried that Kate was working too hard,' Stuart said, 'which is not quite the same thing.'

'Your father would be ashamed of you.'

Kate let that go, too. Her mother was like a spiteful child, who would go on prodding until she got a reaction.

'He always said you were selfish.'

Stuart kept his attention fixed on the road ahead. 'That quarry a few miles back would be a good place to hide a body.'

Kate glanced over her shoulder. Gus was sitting next to Lucy again, with his headphones in. Fiona and Jed were in the row behind, their heads together as they watched something on his phone. 'I said I wanted you to do the time,' she told him, 'but, actually, I wouldn't mind doing it myself.'

Stuart smiled and reached for her hand. They locked fingers.

'I'm so sorry,' Kate said.

'You're an idiot,' Stuart replied, 'but, thankfully, you're my idiot.'

Kate found Magic again, to discourage her mother from offering further contributions.

'Who do you think leaked the footage?' Stuart asked.

'No prizes for guessing that one.'

'How?'

'In a manner we won't be able to trace. The simplest way, probably. Put it into an envelope and sent it to the website, which is unscrupulous enough to have run it without any checks.'

'You think it could be fake?'

'No. They've used fake videos to devastating effect in the past, but you can always tell it's real when the quality is so good. The Russians like to shoot their porn in high definition.' She paused. 'How is she?'

'Devastated, needless to say. Harry has taken the kids and gone to his mother's. Would you mind popping round to see her tonight?'

'Will that help?'

'I don't think she should be alone. And I suspect she'd rather have a woman to talk to. Also, I've persuaded her not to pull out, and I think a word or two from you would help. If that wouldn't be above and beyond the call of duty.'

'I'm afraid it's now her duty to go on running. And to win, though I doubt she has any idea what she's really up against.'

'That's what I said you'd think. But she needs to hear it from the horse's mouth.'

Kate looked at him. 'I'm sorry, darling, I really am.'

'I know you are. But it's water under the bridge. Just don't bloody do it again. You are not your mother and I am not my father. And that's all there is to say.'

*

In the early evening Kate went round to Imogen's. There was a sizeable media pack outside the front door, so at first she kept her distance and messaged her. Together they devised an alternative route through the side entrance of a neighbour's garden and over the dividing wall.

'In other circumstances,' Imogen said, 'I'd find this funny.'

Moments later, Kate was inside the house and Imogen made her a cup of tea. They sat at the kitchen table. 'I know I shouldn't say this,' Imogen said, 'since, in a very literal sense, I made my bed and now have to lie in it. But I feel almost as if I've been raped.'

'That's a pretty understandable response.'

'It's bloody out there for ever now, and I have no desire to show my face in public again. I mean, what happens if my parents see it?'

'No one you care about is ever going to set eyes on it.'

'The internet is today's version of the Wild West. All the newspaper websites are running the video with the bits helpfully pixellated, while giving every reader a shortcut to the unredacted version. I mean, some porn videos are less explicit.'

'On the plus side, thank God you have such a great body.'

Imogen looked at her, clearly aghast. And, for one terrible second, Kate thought she had misjudged the moment. But then Imogen burst out laughing. And started to cry.

Kate touched her shoulder. 'I'm sorry, that was a terrible joke.'

'No, it was a good one. And if I lose sight of the funny side of this nightmare, I'll go upstairs and blow my brains out.'

Kate was tempted to give her a hug, but it wasn't her style, so she waited patiently for Imogen to gather herself.

Imogen wiped the tears defiantly from her cheek. 'Christ, what a mess,' she said.

'I hardly dare ask about Harry.'

'He walked out with the children, saying he'd see me in court. Under the circumstances, I didn't feel there was much I could do to stop him.'

'I imagine he'll be feeling pretty humiliated, apart from anything else. But we have to believe that doesn't necessarily have to be permanent, don't we?' Kate sipped her tea awkwardly, marvelling at her own hypocrisy. 'Do you mind me asking you when and where it was filmed?'

'I don't know.'

'How long did you . . . ?'

'On and off for a while.' She snorted with laughter. 'No pun intended. We did a lot of foreign trips together.'

'Were you with him at the time of your Moscow trip?'

Imogen frowned. 'Fuck knows. No, I don't think so. I'm not sure it had started by then. But . . .' she looked intensely sheepish '. . . unfortunately, I have to admit it could have been recorded in quite a number of places. I just don't remember that particular hotel.'

'Hmm. They didn't focus much on the décor, did they? There's no doubt it's you?'

'Afraid not. It's me, all right. I'd recognize those tits anywhere. I've hated them my entire life.'

'I have no doubt whatsoever that plenty of us are currently green with envy.'

Imogen smiled again. 'So, who was holding the camera?'

'Your previous hosts.'

'How can you be so sure?'

'They had the means, the method and the motive. They were on home turf. And they do it all the time.'

'What motive?'

Kate stared at the table. Tread carefully, she told herself. 'I think they'd rather James won this particular race.'

'For the leadership?'

'Yes.'

'Why?'

'They think he'd be more likely to align himself with their interests. And they've already demonstrated countless times that when they make that judgement they're not afraid to try to affect the outcome.'

'But neither of us has talked much about Russia in recent years, have we?'

'You have in the past.'

'Years ago.'

'They have long memories.'

'And that's it? They did all this because of something I said years ago?'

'I think so, yes. And that's one of the many reasons you shouldn't step down from the leadership contest.'

'I can't carry on with it, Kate.' She leant back, spread her hands. 'I just can't. I'm going to have the battle of my life trying to keep my family together. Harry isn't the world's most forgiving man, and he was only half supportive of my ambition in the first place. If I go on, I'll lose any slim chance I have of winning him back.'

'You *have* to stay in the race, Imogen.'

'Why?'

'Because it's important for the country. I'd even go as far as to say it's your duty.'

'What *aren't* you telling me?' Imogen gave her the full benefit of her unblinking almond-shaped emerald-green eyes. 'Come on, Kate, I'm at my lowest ebb here. You owe me the truth.'

'I can't.'

'Or won't?'

'Either. It doesn't matter which.'

'So you want me to throw away my husband and children but you won't tell me why?'

Kate took a couple of deep breaths. 'We think your opponent might be a Russian spy.'

'Fucking hell.' Imogen just stared at her. 'What does that mean?'

'I'm not totally convinced he has an ideological bone in

his finely hewn body, so it would mean he's been coerced or bribed into working for them.'

'Are you *sure*?'

'No, not yet. But I'm confident enough to break every rule here and tell you why you can't come out with a white flag. And I'll do my absolute best to help you.'

Imogen put her head in her hands. 'Jesus,' she said. 'What is the world coming to?'

'In a way, you should take it as a compliment. The Russians try to acquire compromising material on everyone of influence. The fact that they had something on you confirms their perception of your significance even back then. And choosing not to try to coerce you indicates that they don't believe you would bend. So they kept it up their sleeve to discredit you, if need be.'

'Diabolical,' Imogen said.

'Dirty and immoral. They always have been. Unfortunately, they're also *very* effective.'

'I'll have to think about it. I'm still . . . I just don't know if I can.'

'I'm not going to sugar-coat it. You don't have a choice.'

Imogen looked at her. 'You're a tough woman, Kate.'

'Not always a compliment.'

'From a man to a woman, it wouldn't be. But from a woman, it is. Especially a woman like me.'

'Why *especially* a woman like you?'

'Politics is a dirty word for some people, I know. Even

you, perhaps, when you're in the privacy of your own home. It's also a lonely business. And the higher you climb, the lonelier it gets. I'm not completely sure I want it that badly.'

'You once told me that, though it was a terrible cliché, you really did come into politics to make a difference to people's lives.'

'I'd never say that in public – everyone would die laughing.'

'Perhaps. But isn't it also true that the higher you climb, the more difference you can make?'

'Most people don't believe politicians are capable of altruism.'

'Maybe they don't, but I'm not most people. Any more than you are. I work in a world where the threat to us is rawest. And it's very, very real. If people like you and I don't stand up and face it, there's no telling where this story might end.'

'I'll do it if you agree to work for me.'

'That's a discussion for another time.'

'Do we have a deal?'

'I assume you'll take Stuart with you to Downing Street, and . . . look . . . I'd like to count myself as your friend. I will help. I promise you that much.'

Raised voices in the street made Imogen glance towards the front door. 'I'll think about it. I'm ambitious and I do want to make a difference – though there are probably more egotistical and less attractive motives in there as well. But I don't yet know if I want it enough to risk losing my family. Would you?'

'That,' Kate said, 'is a very good question.'

She waited. She'd done as much as she could. There was just one more question she needed to ask. 'Imogen, I'm not sure how best to ask this but . . . is there anything else?'

'Do you mean any*one* else?'

'Both, I'm afraid. Anything financial? Any other . . . affairs?'

'Affairs. Such an odd word, isn't it?' Imogen shook her head. 'No. Even for me, one really bad sin is enough.'

'So there's nothing else that could bite you on the bum?'

'Nothing I can think of.'

'No other . . .'

Imogen's brow furrowed. 'I'm not a scarlet woman, Kate. I made a mistake. Harry and I haven't had the most active of love lives these past few years, and I sought solace elsewhere. I'm ashamed of it. And now I'm paying the price.'

Kate raised her palms. 'I'm not prying. I just need to know what might be coming down the track.'

But, of course, that wasn't the whole truth. Kate walked home with a spring in her step, feeling foolish and relieved in almost equal measure.

22

WHEN KATE ARRIVED at the office shortly after dawn, Julie was already there.

'How was Belgrade?' Kate asked.

'Complicated and inconclusive. I'll explain when we have more time. Have you seen this?'

'Seen what?'

Julie pointed at her screen. 'It's just dropped on the *Guardian*'s website.' The gist of the story was instantly clear from the headline. *MI6 Investigates Foreign Secretary over Links to Russian Intelligence.*

'Fuck,' Kate said.

'C's asked you to go up.'

'Where's Rav?'

'He's in Switzerland.'

'Doing what?' Kate asked, though she knew well enough. He had gone to see the Swiss lawyer, Binot, the insubordinate bastard.

Julie looked confused. 'He said he'd told you about it.'

'Tell him to get on a plane back, and I mean yesterday. That's an order. And if he ignores it, I'll ensure he's fired before the day's out.'

Kate strode into her office, slammed the door and called Imogen's mobile. She answered almost immediately.

'Have you seen the *Guardian* website?'

'Yes. Christ, I—'

'Please tell me you're not responsible.'

'Of course I'm bloody not!'

'Imogen, it's going to save a lot of time and trouble if you're straight with me. I simply cannot afford to—'

'I haven't told a soul. I swear it. I mean, I wouldn't, of course. But I've also barely spoken to anyone since you left. My only incoming call was from my mother, and I can assure you this wasn't at the top of her list of priorities.'

'Okay. Listen. I shouldn't have told you. I'm now going to have to lie about it to my superiors, which makes me feel deeply uncomfortable. And if anyone knew I *had* told you, I'd be out.'

'I may have my idiotic moments, Kate, but I'm not a complete fool. I won't tell anyone. You have my word on it.'

'Are you going to stay in the contest?'

'The first ballot is tonight, so I have only the next hour or two to make up my mind. But I think I have to, don't I? Meg is a good woman, so she might beat him anyway—'

'She doesn't have a chance. You have to stay in. Look, I've got to go. Good luck.'

Kate placed her forehead against the cool metal interior as she rode the lift up to C's floor. She found him standing by the window in his office, but from the set of his shoulders, the view over the Thames was not uppermost in his mind. Ian was already seated, ready for her arrival.

'Close the door, please,' C said, keeping his back to them. 'And sit down.'

She pulled up an armchair next to Ian. Sir Alan still didn't turn, maintaining his distance from the pair of them. 'Kate, I'm going to ask you the question I've just put to Ian.'

He swivelled on his heel and his eyes bored into hers, like lasers. 'Did you tell *anyone* outside this building that we were investigating the foreign secretary's links with Russia?'

'No,' she said.

'Not your husband?'

'He knew about my trips to Istanbul and Athens, but he couldn't possibly have connected any of that with the foreign secretary.'

'Is it not the case that your husband works with Imogen Conrad, and that she is a family friend?'

'It is.'

'And that Mrs Conrad is the principal beneficiary of this leak, in both its nature and its timing?'

'I think she may pull out anyway, so I'm not sure that's right.'

'Have you seen her since the sex tape was released?'

'Yes. I went round there last night. She was in a very poor state.'

'And you didn't mention, even in passing, that we're investigating her principal opponent, as incredibly useful as that intelligence would have been?'

'No,' Kate said more tersely. 'I did not.'

'Very well,' he said at length. 'Ian has given me a similar assurance. And I'm right in thinking that the details of what you recorded in Istanbul are restricted to the occupants of this room, plus Rav, Julie, Maddy and Danny?'

She waited for him to continue.

'That is not a rhetorical question.'

'That's correct,' she said. 'But Maddy wouldn't have known enough to leak.'

'And the surveillance teams?'

'They'd have been aware of some details about the yacht and possibly about Lena, but no one outside the core group knew of the contents of that recording.'

'What about the people you've spoken to in the course of your investigation?' Ian asked. 'We're going to need a list.'

'Of course,' Kate said. 'But I've conducted or been present at all the interviews to date and, while it was clear in each case that we were asking about the foreign secretary, we gave no hint of the central allegation – and no one could realistically have drawn that inference from any of our questions. We were, of course, punctilious.' Kate thought about Rav in Switzerland. She had no idea whom he'd spoken to there as he closed in on François Binot and his relationship with the foreign secretary, or what he might have said. Another lie she could snare herself with.

'That will have to do, for the time being,' Sir Alan said. 'The foreign secretary wants to see all of us, right now. I then have to see the PM and our colleagues across the river to explain why, if this story is correct, we haven't called them to look into the matter, as we're obliged to do.'

C retrieved his raincoat and homburg from his hat-stand and led them down into the street as commuters continued to pour out of Vauxhall station. Kate was acutely aware of several surprised glances from junior employees among the throng before they turned east against the wind and headed towards Lambeth Bridge.

C liked to walk around London. He made a point of it. And he walked fast. Kate had almost to run to keep up. 'We're going to need to buy some time,' he said, to no one in particular. 'Don't you think?'

'Yes,' Ian said.

'Any ideas?'

'You know what I think. We're being played. Why don't we just say so?'

C didn't respond. Apparently deep in thought, he didn't speak again until they were in the foreign secretary's palatial office overlooking Horse Guards. Very nearly the size of a tennis court, with leather-bound books and red sofas, it boasted the airy grandeur of the empire builders who had once sat behind its enormous desk. The foreign secretary rose from his seat and strode towards them.

'Old friend,' he said, offering Sir Alan his hand. 'Ian, yes, we've met.'

'And this is Kate Henderson from our Russia Desk,' C said.

James Ryan shook her hand. 'The woman at the heart of the action! Very pleased to meet you.' He appeared entirely unfazed by the morning's controversy. 'Have a seat.' He ushered them towards the red leather sofas in the centre of the room and ordered coffee. 'Well, this is a rum business, and no mistake. And all from my old mate.'

'I'm sorry, James,' Sir Alan said. 'We're not going to pretend the *Guardian* story is anything but an embarrassment.'

'My comms people tell me social media is ablaze. I'm being torn limb from limb even as we speak.'

'I think it will be a momentary disembowelment.'

'Well, I should hope so. It's damned uncomfortable. What *is* going on?' He smiled at Kate. 'I suppose you'd expect me to ask that if I really were a Russian spy.'

Kate tried to smile back. In general – and long before the events of the last week – she did not find him remotely amusing.

'The original intelligence stems from an operation Kate ran in Istanbul,' Sir Alan said. 'We managed to bug a meeting between three of the most senior officers in the SVR. They discussed the prime minister's prostate cancer, before it had been made public. They went on to imply that one of the leading candidates to succeed him was what we would call an agent of influence.'

'And they claimed it was me?'

'It wasn't clear whom they were talking about. We've since been trying to assess the underlying value of the intelligence, and someone has chosen to use this against you.'

'I'm not sure I'm catching your drift.'

'We think, sir,' Ian said, leaning forward, as if taking command of the meeting, 'that we're caught up in a classic Moscow campaign of misinformation – a sophisticated sting – of the kind we know all too well.'

James Ryan glanced at Sir Alan. 'In which case, we don't seem to be learning very much from past mistakes.'

'Early days,' C said. 'And we haven't reached any conclusions yet.'

'Go on,' the foreign secretary said.

'You might ask,' Ian went on, 'how we came to be overhearing this particular conversation – between three of

Moscow's most senior intelligence officials – aboard that yacht at the exact moment the revelation was made. In fact, you might ask what they were doing on the yacht in the first place. Does it not strike you as a bit of a coincidence?'

'Now you come to mention it, yes, it does.'

'We were tipped off about that meeting.'

Ian glanced at Kate, and she felt her face redden. Whatever she had expected from this morning, it was not to find herself humiliated in front of her ministerial superior.

'I see it as a classic attempt to cause us havoc. They obviously found out about the prime minister's condition and decided to use it to plant a series of devices at the heart of our political system.'

'A *series* of devices?'

'There was also the suggestion of a mole in Whitehall, who would be able to assist their candidate,' Sir Alan said.

'What kind of mole?'

'The whole purpose of the operation,' Ian said, neatly dodging the question, 'is to have us chasing our tails, and to create chaos at the heart of our government. So far, their plan appears to be working rather well.'

'Indeed – to the point at which I'm being ripped apart on the morning of the first leadership ballot. Not an ideal situation, if you happen to be in my shoes.'

When he next looked at Sir Alan, the air of geniality had

clearly evaporated. 'And what I would like to know is what the fuck you intend to do about it.'

'If you're referring to today's story, nothing.'

The pair glared at each other. If they were seeking to hide any evidence of their friendship, they were making a good fist of it.

'What do you mean, *nothing*?'

'I would suggest that the Foreign & Commonwealth Office put out a general statement to the effect that this is, as Ian said, yet another Russian attempt to interfere in the Western democratic process. And you can add your own denials, of course.'

'That's big of you.' He leant back. 'And what about your lot?'

'We don't comment on ongoing investigations or operations. The fact is that we have intelligence and are looking into it. If we get drawn, we would have to start lying, which we never do. Better to leave us out of it.'

'But your man can brief the press that it's a load of cobblers, as Ian here suggests, designed to alter the course of the leadership election.'

'I have instructed our press liaison to say nothing.'

Ryan's expression lowered the temperature in the room by a further ten degrees. 'That's a brave stance, Alan, under the circumstances, if I may say so.' He shook his head in amazement. 'Especially given that someone in your neck of the woods obviously leaked it.'

'We don't believe that was the case.'

'How could it have been anyone else? You just told me no one else knows about it.'

Kate was watching James Ryan's face. He was trying hard to control his fury, and not succeeding.

'We think the Russians leaked the information,' Ian said smoothly. 'They gave us the intelligence, knowing we'd have to look into it. Then, after a suitable period had elapsed, they leaked that fact, knowing we'd get ourselves into further trouble if we tried to deny it. They're clever. That's no secret. And increasingly successful at exploiting the weaknesses of an open democratic system in the internet age.'

'They're bloody outrageous.'

'It's what modern espionage looks like, I'm afraid.'

'Did you know about the prime minister's illness?' Kate asked.

He peered at her, as if he was trying to recall who she was. 'Did I know what about it?'

'Were you aware he had prostate cancer?'

'No. Er, I don't think I was. No, I was not. Why?'

'We knew nothing of it. We wondered if others in the government or Whitehall might have had some inkling.'

'As far as I'm aware, only his wife and doctors knew until the day he resigned. But you'd probably have to check that. Maybe some of the staff in Downing Street? I don't know. No, I . . . No, it was a bolt from the blue for me.'

Kate thought that, for a very senior politician apparently at the height of his powers, he was making very heavy going of a pretty simple question.

Shortly afterwards they filed out. Sir Alan waited until they were halfway across the courtyard before he turned to Ian. 'You'd do us all a favour if you could be a little more adept at hiding your ambition.'

'I was trying to be helpful.'

'Then perhaps you should learn the value of keeping your mouth shut on occasion.'

Sir Alan peeled away in the direction of Downing Street. 'I'm going to tell the PM the bare minimum,' he said. 'I don't want to add to his woes, but we may need his support before this is over.'

Ian and Kate proceeded in silence towards the King Charles Street exit.

'They're pretty good at hiding their friendship, don't you think?' Ian said.

'I don't think the foreign secretary was faking his anger, if that's what you mean.'

Ian wasn't in a mood to walk back to Vauxhall, so he hailed a taxi on Whitehall. They climbed into it by the Cenotaph. As she settled into the back, Kate said, 'Has the foreign secretary ever crossed your radar before this?'

'What do you mean?'

'Have you ever had cause to give him a closer look before now?'

'No,' Ian said. He was concentrating perhaps unduly hard on Big Ben and the House of Commons through the rain-spattered window. 'Never heard a whisper of anything amiss until now, which is what makes me more than a tad suspicious of the whole business.' He smiled. 'Sorry, not what you wanted to hear in there, I know. But at least it got us out of a jam.'

'This is not a game of Moscow disinformation, Ian, and you know it.'

'That's what we always think.'

'I don't care what mistakes were made before. I know what this is. It's true, real. We have not one but two spies.'

'So you're infallible? Sometimes, Kate, your arrogance is a little wearing.'

Kate had been back at her desk for a matter of minutes, and had hardly begun quizzing Julie about giving Lena's sister Maja safe passage, when her office phone rang.

'Kate. James Ryan here.'

'Yes, Foreign Secretary.'

'James will do just fine. I need to speak to you in private. There's a coffee shop in the Tate, the one on the other side of the river from you. I'm sure you know it. Could you meet me there in ten minutes?'

'Of course.'

She hung up, then turned back to Julie. 'Where were we?' His call had interrupted her mid-sentence.

'She's still in hospital and the doc is right on side. They'll hang on to her until we can sort out her visa.'

'And the stepfather?'

'Keeping his distance.'

'Long may it last,' Kate said. 'And if it doesn't, I'll kill him myself.'

23

HER MAJESTY'S FOREIGN secretary had stationed himself in the far corner of the Tate's basement café. Kate spotted his two close-protection officers immediately, though they were discreetly enough positioned not to be broadcasting their presence.

'Thanks for coming,' James Ryan said. 'Let me get you a coffee.'

'Actually, I'm okay.'

'Come on, I'm going to have one.'

'Then an espresso would be great.'

He went to make the order himself. Kate nodded at the protection officers, who had taken a table on the opposite side of the room where they could watch the flow of people coming towards them. She settled into the chair with her back to them as Ryan returned.

'Thanks for coming at such short notice.'

'Did I have a choice?'

'Look, I'll cut straight to it. Nothing is certain in this day and age – and it might be a whole lot closer than most people expect – but I'll probably win this leadership election. Imogen is smart, charismatic, and I wouldn't climb over her to get to Meg, but she won't go down well with the rank and file. If I do make it, I'm going to have to form my own Praetorian Guard in Number Ten at the double, because we all know how events lay siege to a leader. So I'll need to have someone I can trust as head of SIS.'

Kate glanced over her shoulder, an involuntary tic when she had her back to any door, despite the presence of the protection officers.

'I'm not a perfect candidate,' he went on. 'I have a colourful past. There have been too many women, and I cut a few corners in the accumulation of my fortune, the details of which I know are lurking somewhere in your archives. You could have a go at sinking me if you wanted. But I don't think it would even dent me if the sexual indiscretions became public.'

'I'm not quite sure where all this is leading.'

'The point is, I wouldn't paint myself as a saint. And neither would anyone who knows me. But I'm no Kim Philby, and this is the second time Sir Alan and Ian Granger have landed me in it. And twice is at least once too often.'

'I know there was a slip-up a few years ago.'

'A *slip-up*? A calamitous weapons-grade fuck-up, more like, which made Her Majesty's Government in general and me in particular look like absolute arses. We were beyond lucky that the Germans had their own reasons for keeping it secret.'

'I know it was an unfortunate set of circumstances.'

He massaged his steel-blue jaw. '*How* do you know? The files were supposed to be locked and all details of the affair scrubbed from the record.'

'It's hard to erase things in the House of Secrets if you know where to look.'

'And you know where to look?'

'I do. Yes.'

'That's why I need you,' he said. 'The world affects to hate politicians, and sometimes with justification. But I'm not afraid to admit I want the top job badly. There's so much I feel I could do. I don't mind being denied it for something that's my fault, but this Russian-spy nonsense is prize bullshit.'

He leant forward. He was a handsome man and, against her most fundamental instincts, she could see how the full force of his personality might weaken a woman's defences. 'He may have been a close friend of mine, but I no longer trust Alan, or Ian. Neither their loyalty nor their competence. And this is one screw-up too many – unless, of course, they set out to destroy me, and I wouldn't put that past them. Like I said, if and when I make it into Number Ten, I'll need to surround myself with extremely competent and loyal people I can trust. And it's high time a woman was in charge. Stella and Eliza did a great job at Five, but now it's Six's turn to enter the twenty-first century.'

He was clearly expecting her to answer. 'I'm happy to serve whoever is—'

'That's too mealy-mouthed for me. I'm offering you an opportunity. Give me your loyalty and I'll make you the first female C in British history.'

Kate looked at him properly, perhaps for the first time. There was a directness to his manner – a desperation, even – that was almost appealing. 'What is it you want?'

'I'd like to be kept informed on what the fuck is going on inside your building. I'd like to know where this investigation is going. And I'd like to know it before everyone else does.'

Kate stared into the dark liquid in her cup. Whatever else, she thought, you couldn't accuse James Ryan of subterfuge. Or subtlety.

'Politics is the art of the deal, Kate. And I'm offering you one.'

'And espionage is a game of snakes and ladders. But, right now, all I can see is snakes.'

'Do you think it's remotely conceivable that I'm a Russian spy?'

'I've lost track of what is conceivable and what isn't.'

'If that's how you see it, I'll leave now. But think about what I've said. Give me your loyalty and you'll get an empire in return. I want a strong, robust Britain, capable of standing up to the likes of Russia and China. I'm led to believe you want the same. So we can be a very good team.' He offered her his hand. It seemed an odd gesture, but she took it all the same. And then he was gone.

She felt like Faustus on the walk back across Vauxhall Bridge. If politics *was* the art of the deal, then this was the opportunity of a lifetime. But if she took it, she'd never be able to look herself in the mirror again.

When she got back to the office she went straight to Julie's desk. 'Have you got hold of Rav?'

Julie shook her head.

'Keep trying, would you?'

Minutes later, Julie was at her door again. 'Your friend is about to say something.'

Imogen was facing a bank of cameras, on the front steps of her house. She raised a hand to still the barrage of shouted questions. 'Most people will be aware of the events that have engulfed my family these past twenty-four hours,' she said. 'Some may have seen the video, though even the pixellated version should come with some kind of eighteen rating.'

'Nice touch,' Maddy said. She had come to stand between Kate and Julie.

'This poses a number of extremely important questions, of course,' Imogen went on, 'starting with the ones *I* have to answer. How could I have been so stupid? How could I have treated my husband and children – the people I love most in this world – in such a selfish and careless fashion?

'Some will no doubt believe that these considerations should disqualify me from holding any kind of public office. And the way I feel today, I don't entirely blame them.'

She breathed in deeply. 'But there are other questions, arguably of more importance to the country at large. Who recorded this material? Where did they do it, and why? Who leaked the footage? And for what purpose was it released at this precise moment? I don't have the answers yet but, given what many of us have read in the *Guardian* this morning, we may have our suspicions.'

'Christ,' Kate said.

'She's bloody going for it,' Julie said. 'And, frankly, good on her.'

Kate looked at her askance.

'You're not telling me a sex tape would put the foreign secretary out of the race?' Julie said. 'It would have MPs and party members flocking to him even faster.'

'Fair point,' Maddy said.

'Many of you might, with great justification, take the

view that I should now be pulling out of the race to be leader of my party,' Imogen went on. 'I can certainly see many difficult days ahead, as I seek to persuade my family to forgive me for my *un*forgivable behaviour. I don't pretend that it's going to be easy or quick. But these are evidently *not* normal times, and I have been repeatedly told by colleagues during the course of the night that I have a *duty* now to stay in the ring. Given the public's understandable cynicism about politicians and their motives, I can see why you may be inclined to take this with a pinch of salt, but we know all too well now of the Russians' repeated attempts to interfere in our democratic process.

'I have decided therefore that I have no choice but to continue to fight what I believe to be a good fight. I will leave it to my fellow Members of Parliament to judge tonight whether I have done the right thing.'

As she turned and walked away, Kate's screen lit up. *Thank you*, it read. *You persuaded her.*

She messaged back: *What news from the front line?* She was in her office before her phone *ping*ed again. *Support still amazingly solid. Meg uninspiring and no one knows what to make of claims re James. She's still in the game.*

'A couple of sex addicts, and one a foreign spy,' Kate muttered to herself. 'What can possibly go wrong?'

She was scanning the flurry of emails from colleagues sympathizing with her predicament – or what they had inferred from the day's events – when Rav rang. Kate checked the door was closed before she answered. 'What the hell are you doing?'

'I have something,' he said.

'A very short rope. And you're going to hang yourself with it unless you give me a good explanation.'

'You remember my Cambridge mate at the *Guardian*? Did some stuff on the Panama Papers?'

'Vaguely.'

'He had a way in to the Swiss lawyer, so I offered him a trade.'

'What kind of trade?'

'He'd got to one of Binot's former secretaries in Zürich. Turns out Binot was a complete lech. This girl remembered Ryan and the offshore company they set up for him. She also recalls some very large amounts of money being transferred to him personally as well as to the company account. And you will probably guess the source. We might have him.'

'Does she have any paperwork?'

'She says she has evidence of millions of pounds being moved via Zürich from one of the Russian government's cipher accounts into Ryan's personal account in Belize.'

'Fuck.'

'My thoughts entirely.'

'How do we know this isn't the Russians playing us?'

'Because I've met her. And so has my friend from the

Guardian. She's either on the level or she's the best actress I've ever seen.'

'It seems a tiny bit convenient that we've just happened upon—'

'You say that every time I get a break into anything.'

She bridled, perhaps because there was an element of truth in it. 'And what did you trade for this information, Rav, with your friend from the *Guardian*?'

'Nothing of any consequence.'

'Have you seen their story today?'

'Yes. I mean, no. Of course I didn't bloody give him that! I'm not totally out of my mind. He's looking into one of the Russian president's friends, and the cash being ripped out of the Crimea. I gave him a small contribution. Look, I have to go. I'm meeting her again this afternoon.'

'Be careful, Rav. If she is the real deal, then—'

'Of course I'm going to be careful.'

He ended the call. Kate listened to the rain lashing against her window. Perhaps it was her imagination, but she felt as if the world was closing in on her. She went down the corridor, shut the loo door behind her and splashed water on her face. She looked at herself in the mirror. Her eyes were full of fatigue. 'You're out of your depth, my girl,' she whispered to herself.

She dabbed her face dry with a paper towel and returned to the office as James Ryan was graciously accepting the attention of the cameras and fielding questions from journalists in the rain-swept courtyard of the Foreign & Commonwealth Office. 'It's all just hokum,' he said. 'Arrant, utter nonsense – the Russians up to their usual tricks. But I say to the Russian president, it isn't clever, and it isn't sophisticated, and it isn't fooling anybody any more. We've seen it too many times before and we'd have to be absolute lunatics to fall for it.'

'Do you deny that MI6 is investigating such claims?' one reporter asked.

'I deny they're taking them seriously. I spoke to the head of SIS this morning. They look at mounds of Orwellian misinformation every day and it's their considered view that the idea that I'm linked to the Russians was leaked by the Russians themselves to discredit me, and interfere with our leadership election, as is their wont. You can draw your own conclusions from that. I'm confident that neither the party nor the country is stupid enough to fall for it.'

'So you won't stand down?'

'Of course I won't! In fact, I consider it a vaguely preposterous question, as will everyone watching.' He smiled at them and waved airily. 'I apologize for making you stand outside in this appalling weather. I blame Siberia for that too. Let the contest go on, and may the best man or woman win. I sympathize with young Imogen, by the way. There but for the grace of God . . . And that's a joke, of course!'

He turned and hurried back inside. Kate, Julie and Maddy watched him go. 'Wow,' Julie said. 'He's got some chutzpah.'

Kate sat down at her desk. Her first new email was from Dr Minakis, the Athens pathologist. Attached to it was the final autopsy report. Kate looked through it, trying not to dwell on the photographs, or the fact that they had found the microphone shoved deep into Lena's larynx.

The police report followed. There was nothing in it of any note, of course. The Andros squad had found an abandoned car, but it had been torched, so all forensic traces had been erased.

A sixth sense made Kate turn to find Sir Alan at her door.

'A minute of your time?'

'Of course.'

'We need proof, by the end of the week. Otherwise we have to shut down the investigation into both politicians and Viper, then make clear that we looked into the matter and concluded it was only the Russians pissing around again. The PM's direct order. He may be ill, possibly dying, but he still has all his faculties and, for the moment, his word remains final. He's no fan of James Ryan, it's true, but he seems reluctant to accept that any politician of his seniority is capable of such perfidy.'

'Did you tell him—'

'Naivety may be a beguiling quality in a human being, but not in a prime minister.'

'It's better than having a spy in Number Ten.'

'That's what I tried to tell him, or words to that effect.

I even asked if it was possible he might reconsider his decision and delay standing down until after his treatment is completed, but he wouldn't hear of it. I think his wife wouldn't let him. So . . . we are where we are.'

'Why Viper? I mean, Ryan and Conrad I can understand. If the foreign secretary wins, then the country needs to have faith in him, and if we can't prove it's misplaced, we should drop it. But I'm not sure why Viper should be in the same category. Isn't a potential mole inside our walls still a matter for *us*?'

'Not any more. I had to come clean about everything, and the PM's views were extremely clear.'

'How did he look?'

'As unwell as you'd expect.' Sir Alan opened the door. 'I've just come from the Ops Room. The *Empress* has docked at Mykonos. So you could do worse than start there.'

Kate followed him to the lifts.

Danny was, as ever, juggling screens, as if he was in charge of Apollo Mission Control. 'You were right about where he was heading.'

'Who's on board?'

'Just Mikhail. Katya and the kid left for the airport about an hour ago.'

'Okay, Danny, pack your bags. Take all your toys. We're going to need a second surveillance team to join the one on the ground.'

Kate spent the rest of the afternoon with Julie, mapping

out the logistics of the operation, then left early and went home to cook Fiona and Gus supper. They were both unusually talkative. Gus was in the A team once more, so his life was back on track, and she wasn't inclined to probe Fiona's happiness long enough to discover the cause. Every time she came anywhere near broaching the subject of sex, contraception and Jed, Stuart's warning rang in her ears. She didn't want another argument. With any of them.

After a shower, she took an age to choose her dress for the US ambassador's party – finally selecting the same strapless stretch-woollen Roland Mouret she'd worn last year. She adored its cinched waist and origami-style sculpted panel, and wearing a red dress to meet a Russian source at an American Embassy soirée gave her something to smile about.

She laid it on the bed and sat at her dressing-table, tying back her hair, keeping half an eye on her phone for an update from Rav. Then she applied her make-up, with infinite care. It had been an age since she'd made so much effort with her appearance.

She almost missed the *ping.*

Bingo. Got him. The documents are devastating.

Proof?

Close. Serious explaining to do. And then some.

She asked where he was and when he was due back, and got no response, then looked up to see Stuart at the door. She wondered how long he'd been standing there.

He eyed her warpaint, and the Roland Mouret. 'Going out?'

'Yes.'

'The US Embassy thing?'

She nodded.

'Will he be there?'

On her return from Russia as a student, Kate had admitted to Stuart that she'd 'developed feelings' for someone else while she'd been away, though she'd sworn on everything dear to her that her relationship had remained platonic (and she'd had to, since Stuart's rage had been terrifying). It had taken him a long time to forgive her, and even to this day, he wasn't above throwing it at her in the heat of an argument.

She'd made the mistake of telling him she'd bumped into Sergei at last year's do, and he'd spotted the crisp, embossed invitation on the kitchen worktop.

'Who?'

'Don't treat me like an idiot, Kate.'

'Never that, Stuart. Never that.'

She shrugged on the dress and turned her back to him so that he could pull up her zip. She could feel his breath on her bare shoulders and neck.

'Shouldn't I be worried when you're sneaking off to see an old lover, and looking good enough to eat?'

'You bought me this.'

'Did I? Must have been channelling Chris de Burgh.'

'And I never did . . . with Sergei. You know that.'

'But you wanted to.' He looked haunted now. 'Isn't that almost as bad?'

'No. It's not.' She turned and kissed him. 'You can't seriously be upset about something that didn't happen more than twenty-five years ago. That would be absurd.'

'Would it?'

'Yes.'

'It's funny,' Stuart said. 'I was thinking about it the other day. I have such a clear picture of that Gulf of Finland dacha – the huge open fire, the ice-hockey pictures on the wall, the low ceilings upstairs, the endless beach and the sun on the still water at first light.'

'It is a wonderful place.' She slipped on her much-loved black patent Gianvito Rossi 105 pumps – she'd had to avert her eyes from the screen of the credit-card reader when she'd tapped in her PIN – and picked up her handbag. 'But slightly odd that it has such a hold on you.'

'Why?'

'Because, as far as I know, you've never been there.'

'That's precisely my point.' The muscles bunched along his jaw. 'It occupies such a vivid place in my imagination because it continues to do so in yours. You've stopped talking about it, but I know you haven't stopped dreaming about the bloody place.'

She sighed. 'I think we've had enough jealousy for one year, don't you? If I was going to sleep with Sergei, I'd have done it long ago.'

'Who said anything about sleeping with him? You're still seeing him, aren't you? And I know you loved him.'

She put down the bag and clasped his cheeks between her hands. 'It's you I've always loved, as I've told you many, many times. This is about something different. This is work.'

'What kind of work requires you to cosy up to an old lover?'

Kate tried not to let her irritation show. 'The kind I do.'

'And what if I said I really don't want you to see him, even if it catapults us to the brink of the Third World War?'

'I'd say that would be fine, after tonight.'

'And why is tonight so important?'

'For all the reasons I shouldn't already have told you.' She held his look. 'This isn't some secret assignation. I'm going to see him very briefly in the middle of a party of about five hundred people.'

'What are you going to see him about?'

'I'm under direct orders from Sir Alan. I *really* can't discuss it. And I *really* have to go.' She blew him a kiss and pulled the door shut behind her.

The ambassador's residence was a comfortable red-brick building, set in its own grounds just north of Regent's Park. The previous incumbent had been a great fan of vinyl and guests had been encouraged to put a favourite LP from his voluminous collection on the turntable in the spacious entrance hall. But it had been all-change since then, and guests were ushered through the hallway now to a marquee in the garden.

Despite the rain, it was still warm enough for the flaps to be furled and some of the guests to have drifted out beyond its confines to smoke or take in the damp evening air. Kate circulated. Several of her US-leaning colleagues were present. Adrian Sandalwood, a direct contemporary and now the main liaison with the CIA, introduced her to a striking, enviably ageless blonde, who turned out to be his opposite number in London. 'You've met Cindy, of course.'

'I don't believe I have.'

'Kate runs our Russia Desk, so she has her hands quite full at the moment.'

'Jeez,' Cindy said. 'Welcome to our world.' She shook her great mane of hair. 'Our politicos are so weak and venal it's a job to find one they couldn't corrupt.' She touched Kate's sleeve with a hand that seemed a little older than her face. 'The first ballot must be around now, right?'

Kate glanced at her watch. 'Yes.'

'His Excellency has left the TV on in the main reception room, so I guess we'll hear as soon as it's out.'

'The result isn't in much doubt,' Kate said.

'You don't think the *Guardian* story will make any difference?'

'Not as much as it would once have done. In our world

of fake news, the truth is a matter of opinion. In the meantime, in every other respect, particularly on the charisma front, James Ryan and Imogen Conrad are streets ahead of anyone else. I don't think Meg Simpson has much of a following. I suspect a lot of MPs will waver, but not many will change their vote. Then we'll have to see what happens as they go out to the party members.'

'What about the sex tape? She fucks like a trooper, but that ain't what most folks want in a leader – at least, not when she's a woman.'

'Maybe. But times have changed here, too. No one is shocked by porn any more, not even when it turns out to involve our hitherto superficially blameless political elite.'

'It was an unbelievable piece of work,' Cindy said. 'More of a turn-on than any porn movie I've ever seen. But that might decide it – she has a body most women would kill for, so they definitely won't vote for her.'

Adrian had barely taken his eyes off Cindy during the entire conversation, but they swivelled now in the direction of the terrace, where the ambassador had made an appearance. 'Result imminent,' he announced, in a booming voice.

Cindy and Adrian set off for the reception room, along with almost everyone else, but Kate hung back. She looked up at the trees, listened to the distant hum of the traffic. It was hard to believe they were still in the heart of the city.

'I hoped you might be here,' Sergei said.

She snapped around.

Sergei's smile was as beguilingly crooked as ever. He wore a sleek charcoal suit, white shirt and woven silk tie. His wavy dark hair – tinged with grey now – was swept back from his forehead and his eyes still sparkled with wry amusement.

'And here I am,' she said. 'So the magic still seems to work.'

'The lady in red. You look as lovely as ever.' He nodded towards the last of the guests jostling for a glimpse of the TV screen. 'Don't you want to know who is through to the next round?' He had to stoop slightly to speak to her, even though she was wearing stiletto heels.

'I have a pretty good idea already.'

'Ah, you mean it's rigged – like one of our elections?'

She arched an eyebrow. 'Rumour has it that this *is* one of your elections. But isn't that rather a dangerous thing to say for a man in your position?'

'Everything between us has always been dangerous.' His deep brown eyes shone with mischief, then burnt with the intensity that had always made her heart beat faster. 'In the end it is always about trust, no?'

'Of course.'

'And what else can you base that on but instinct?' He smiled again. 'Have you placed a bet?'

'No.'

'You should. Your judgement has always been excellent.'

'I've learnt that trying to predict the future is unwise these days. Especially when it comes to politics.'

'True enough.'

'Perhaps *you* should,' she said.

'Me? Who am I supposed to want to win?'

'Something tells me you know the answer to that.'

A big man with a white beard came out onto the terrace. 'Ryan and Conrad,' he shouted across to a colleague.

'So there we have it,' Sergei said. 'Santa Claus has spoken. I'm just puzzled that he isn't also wearing red.'

'It's not Christmas yet.' She bit her lower lip. 'I need help, Sergei. I wasn't going to ask, but I have to. Why did you send me that letter?'

He removed a carefully folded white linen handkerchief from his jacket pocket and wiped a smear of lipstick from her teeth. 'Because time may have moved on, but I haven't.'

She wondered what an onlooker might make of this scene. 'That leaves me none the wiser. Did you play me? Us?'

'Of course not. Did you listen carefully enough to what I just said? It is cold in Moscow. And I am not talking about the weather.'

'There are those at Vauxhall Cross who take the view that you're GRU, and that they've used you to set this in play. You and your colleagues don't think all this messing about in Western politics is in Mother Russia's interests, and you want Vasily and his cronies gone. Is that right?'

'If I was GRU, I wouldn't have known about the meeting they were due to have on Igor's yacht, or what they were there to discuss.'

'My bosses think it's too much of a coincidence—'

'And what about you? Do you think I would use you like that?'

She shook her head. 'I've asked myself that question over and over again, but I cannot believe you would. However, I'm relying on an instinct formed nearly half a lifetime ago. And yet . . .'

He waited. 'And yet . . . what?'

'Why was I prepared to accept it?'

'Why would you not?'

'I don't know who you work for, how senior you are and who you're really loyal to. There's no one else in the world I'd accept such incredibly sensitive information from, then act upon it without question.'

'I am not anyone else in the world,' he said. 'Has anything changed? Between us, I mean.'

'I don't know.' Kate stared at the grass, her mind swimming with the danger. 'Yes. No. Maybe. Everything has changed. I don't know you any more.'

'Of course you do. I told you, time has moved on, but I really haven't. It hardly qualifies as grand tragedy. And, of course, it is not your fault. I was trying to help you, that's all.'

'You've come close to ruining me. You must know what

you set in motion. It's make or break now. I need more – or they'll close this down. And maybe me too.' She hated herself for her beseeching look and tone. 'I need proof, Sergei. Proof.'

'I was trying to help you, Kate. One day you will understand.'

Adrian and Cindy's imminent return robbed her of the opportunity to press the point.

'Ryan and Conrad,' Adrian said, as he reached them. 'So now it gets interesting.'

Kate introduced Sergei and they engaged in uneasy small-talk for a moment, until he excused himself. 'You should come to the dacha again,' he whispered to her, before he slipped away. 'Everything is just as you remember it. And my parents still talk of you often.'

After a decent interval, she went looking for him, aware that her heart was beating much faster than it should.

He appeared to have been swallowed into the night. She wiped the sweat from her palms and closed her eyes to calm the electric current racing through her stomach. How ridiculous. She was a middle-aged happily married mother of two and he'd made her feel like a girl again in no more than a few crisp sentences.

A band had started playing on the terrace, but Kate's appetite for the event had evaporated. She made her way back towards the entrance hall. As she left, Sir Alan materialized at her shoulder.

'Good party?'

'Yes, sir. How about you?'

'It rarely disappoints. And how I wish one could say that more often.' His car was waiting on the front drive. 'Get in,' he said. 'I'll drop you home.'

They were scarcely through the gate when he said, 'I'm hoping you're about to tell me we have a breakthrough.'

'Not really, sir. No.'

'I saw you chatting. Did you not get the opportunity to discuss his motives?'

'I know what his motive was.'

'Love?'

'Something very like it.'

'That might be . . . complicated.'

'Not if I don't intend to make it so. And I don't.' Kate turned to him. 'I'm not sure he knows much more than he told me.'

'Of course he does. There is no conceivable way he would have tipped you off about that meeting without knowing its agenda. And that leaves only two possibilities: the reason you suggest, or to play you – and therefore us – as Ian likes to believe.'

'He's not playing me.'

C shook his head. 'Odd. You told me a few days ago that you didn't trust anyone. So how is it that you trust him?'

It was a question Kate couldn't – or perhaps wouldn't – answer. And Sir Alan's demeanour was considerably less amicable as a result. She stared out of the window at the passing traffic.

'Do you trust your husband?'

Kate turned back to him. 'That's an unacceptable question, if I may say so.'

'No, Kate, you may not. You know the rules.' His tone was even steelier than she had prepared herself for. 'Ian came to me to talk about Viper. He had Stuart's phone records. One or two of the calls take some explaining.'

Kate thought about that. 'I've seen them and I imagine Julie gave them to him,' she said. 'But the number of Ian's calls to *her* would take rather more explaining than my husband working late on a damage-limitation exercise when an official in his employer's department had just been arrested by the police as a suspected paedophile.'

'It's not a revelation to me that Ian's every action has an ulterior motive – and sometimes many of them.' Sir Alan glanced at the kaleidoscope of lights on the windscreen, conjured up by a fresh squall of rain on the glass. 'You don't need me to tell you that we're damned if we go on and damned if we turn back. If we can't stand this thing up, then I'm finished. And so are you.'

'We're trying to do the right thing. What other choice is there?'

'You think that's Ian's philosophy?'

'No.'

'Ian has been waiting for such a moment for a very long

time. You saw how he behaved at the meeting in King Charles Street this morning. And it was unquestionably him who leaked that information to the *Guardian*.'

'How can you be so sure?'

'Because I know him. The person it damages in the long run is me. And that is why Ian did it.'

'Surely your long-standing friendship with the foreign secretary will protect you.'

'James is great fun. He's irreverent, amusing – and the most ruthless man I've ever met. In a landscape where rebellion, inconsistency and unreliability are without meaningful consequence, he's a wonderful companion. And I have no doubt our friendship, or his version of it, will endure. He'll still want to invite me shooting or to share a glass from the back of his Range Rover on Twickenham match days. But if I stand in his way, he'll cut me down. And, right now, I'm what stands between him and the job he's always wanted. So . . .' he smiled bleakly '. . . either we find proof that the original intelligence was correct, or it's goodnight, Vienna.'

'We must have this kind of conversation more often,' Kate said. 'It's lifting my spirits no end.'

'There's always the private sector.'

'I'll dust off my CV in the morning.'

Sir Alan didn't speak again until they were coasting down the street to her home. 'I have the measure of Ian,' he said. 'And, in a way, I find that easier to deal with. It's the questions that keep gathering around you that trouble me more.'

'Which ones in particular?'

'I don't think you need me to tell you that.'

His driver had pulled open her door before she could respond. She opted for a polite farewell as she stepped out onto the pavement.

'Goodnight, Kate.'

To her surprise – and no little delight – Fiona, Gus and Jed were all hunched over Fiona's computer in her bedroom, watching something together.

'Hi,' Kate said. 'Everything all right?'

Fiona hit the stop button. 'We didn't burn the house down.'

'Well, I'll take that as a positive. Dad not back?'

'Not yet.'

'Okay. I've got some work to do, so I'll see you in the morning.' Kate kissed them both. She almost hugged Jed, then thought better of it. 'I have to go somewhere tomorrow, but I'll be back in a few days.'

She had reached the door when Fiona said, 'Is everything okay between you and Dad?'

She swung back into the room. 'Of course. Why?'

'Nothing. It's just . . .'

'Just?'

'You're hardly ever here together. And arguing a lot

when you are.' Both Fiona and Gus were looking at her now. Jed was doing his best to pretend he wasn't there.

Kate sat on the edge of the bed. 'I should have said something. There's absolutely nothing wrong between Dad and me, though I can understand why you might think there could be. We're just going through one of those infuriating periods when we're both overloaded at work by a whole heap of things that can't wait to be dealt with. I'm really sorry if we're distracted and tired and sometimes ratty with each other, and probably with you too. But if there's a problem, it's out there,' – she waved a hand at the window – 'rather than in here.'

'What do you mean?' Fiona asked.

'I can't really explain now. I wish I could, but I can't.'

'Is it to do with the Russians trying to undermine the leadership election?' Gus asked.

This was so far ahead of the perspective she expected of her rugby-mad son that Kate simply stared at him. 'How do you know about that?'

'Our history teacher was talking about it. She said it's the same as they've always done, only worse, because now they're trying to get our leading politicians to work for them. Secret service, she called it. She wrote it up on the board. She said it's how Russia and China will destroy the West.'

'Well . . .'

'Is that true?' Fiona asked.

'That's what I'm trying to find out,' Kate said. 'I mean, in a nutshell. And it's bloody difficult, because they're extremely good at sowing discord, and half the time – most of the time, actually – they're spewing out lies and misinformation, and for us, working out what's true and what isn't gets more complicated with each passing year.'

'Are they threatening you?' Fiona asked.

'No, love. No.'

Fiona was frowning at her.

'What is it?' Kate asked.

'It's probably nothing.' Fiona glanced at each of the boys.

'What is it? Tell me.'

'She doesn't want to worry you, Mrs Henderson. It's just that . . . earlier this evening, there was a knock on the door. And Fi knows very well that you've said never open it when we're here without you at night. So we came upstairs and looked out of the window. There were two men, but we couldn't see their faces. They knocked again. Hard. And then they waited and knocked again.'

'It was really loud,' Gus said.

'Jed went downstairs,' Fiona said, with pride.

'Did you open the door?' Kate asked.

'No. I didn't think that was a good idea. And I didn't say anything because I didn't want them to know for sure that we were here.'

'He got a knife from the kitchen, Mum, and waited inside the door.'

Jed looked embarrassed. 'I put on the security chain. They must have heard me, because they knocked even louder.'

'It was terrifying,' Fiona said. 'Jed was amazing.'

'I wasn't,' Gus said. 'I was shitting myself.'

'Don't worry,' Kate said. 'I won't say a word to the A team. And good for you, Jed.' She turned back to her daughter. 'What did they look like?'

'They were wearing black leather jackets and black beanie hats. I couldn't see their faces. I don't know if they spotted us at the window. They never looked up.'

'Why didn't you call me?'

'I . . . We . . .' She glanced at her brother. 'We didn't want to bother you.'

'We would have called you,' Gus said, 'but they suddenly legged it. There were four of them,' he added. Fiona and Jed stared at him, confused. 'There were only two at the door. But I saw two more on the other side of the street. And they all walked off together.'

'Also in black beanie hats and leather jackets?'

'Yes. It was like they were in a gang or something.'

Kate got up. 'I'll be back in a minute.'

'Were they part of a gang?' Gus asked.

'In a manner of speaking. They were delivering a message, meant for me.'

24

KATE MESSAGED STUART to come home as soon as possible. She called the night desk at the office and asked the duty officer to send a detail to the house immediately. She promised to get the necessary clearance in the morning.

Two women and a rather sallow young man arrived about an hour later. Kate showed them around the house and introduced them to Gus, Fiona and Jed. They checked the back garden and all the external locks and asked a lot of questions about the black-leather-jacket brigade.

Once she had finished briefing them, Kate went back upstairs.

'Who are they?' Gus asked.

'One of our security teams.' She saw the look on their faces. 'It's just a precaution.'

'Are we going to be . . . all right?'

'Yes. Absolutely. I'm just playing it safe.'

Gus and Fiona decided they wanted to share a room for the first time since they were toddlers. Before Kate could offer to drop Jed home, Fiona asked if he could stay as well. 'We'd feel safer,' she said.

Kate didn't have a good reason to object, so Fiona and Gus topped and tailed in Fiona's bed and Jed was assigned the sofa in the corner, which was slightly too short for him. He went to brush his teeth while Kate kissed Fiona and Gus goodnight, and she bumped into him again on the landing.

'Is there anything else I can do, Mrs Henderson?' he asked.

'We'll be fine now, Jed. Thank you.' He was on the way back to the bedroom when she stopped him. 'Jed . . . It's always . . . useful to be reminded one can get things wrong. I misjudged you. I'm sorry.'

He rewarded her with the kind of smile that would probably have melted her heart if she'd been Fiona's age. 'I might have misjudged you, too, Mrs Henderson.' He hesitated. 'And, by the way, that red dress really suits you.'

'Steady, Jed,' she said, hoping he wouldn't spot the pink in her cheeks. 'One step at a time.'

She called Rav's mobile again when she was safely back

in her own room. No answer. She tried his home number. No answer there either. By the time Stuart came back half an hour later, she'd tried both numbers more than a dozen times, without success.

She heard him bantering to the team in the kitchen, then his uneven footsteps on the stairs. 'Are you okay?' he asked. He was quite pissed. He always got drunk when he was angry or upset with her.

'Yes. Fine.'

'What's going on?'

'Probably nothing.' Kate was by the window. The Roland Mouret was back on its hanger, and she was in jeans and a dark pullover. 'There were some men outside the house earlier, before I got back. Hammering on the door. Fiona and Gus got a bit scared. Jed's here with them. He was a bit of a hero, actually – went down and put the chain on the door.'

Stuart was getting more sober by the second. 'Who the fuck were they?'

'I don't know.'

'You must have *some* idea.'

'I don't. I'm just playing it safe for now.' Kate picked up her raincoat. 'I need to go out for half an hour. Do you mind holding the fort?'

'Of course not. Whatever you need.'

'I said Jed could stay. Gus is sharing Fiona's bed. Jed's on the sofa.'

'Well, wonders will never cease.'

As she walked past him, he took her arm and pulled her towards him. She forgot sometimes how strong he was. He looked as directly into her eyes as his still slightly blurred vision would allow. 'Are you really okay?'

'Fine. Just being cautious.'

'I'm sorry I wasn't here. Anything you want me to do, just ask.'

She kissed him tenderly. 'It's not your problem, it's mine.'

'It's ours.'

'I won't be long.' Kate pulled on a pair of black trainers and busied herself with the laces. 'I'm sorry – how was tonight?'

'We're through. But God knows what happens next. The party appears to have given itself the rather surprising choice of an adulterer or a Russian spy. It's not politics as we know it, but what is, these days?'

'You can say that again. How is she?'

'Her mood changes about every ten seconds, and she has no idea what to think about anything. It's quite hard keeping her on the level, and I have no idea how she's going to cope with the next few weeks. But at least she's still in it.'

Rav's building was shrouded in darkness. She parked a little way down the road and called both his numbers again. There was still no answer. She tried Julie, who picked up straight away. 'Sorry to bother you so late,' Kate said, 'but do you have any idea where our talented but elusive colleague might be?'

'At home, I guess. I think he flew back in from Zürich at teatime.'

'Where are you?'

'Still at work.'

Kate wondered if Ian was with her. She felt more betrayed by their dalliance than she had a right to. Two lonely adults seeking solace in an unlikely relationship – what was new? 'Could you check the flight manifests, see if he actually got on a plane?'

'Of course.'

Julie rang off and Kate waited.

There was no sign of life inside Rav's top-floor flat. She scanned each vehicle, up and down the street. Nothing out of the ordinary.

Julie called back. 'He was on the BA flight that arrived at Heathrow at five p.m. I'm just checking the CCTV. I'll tell you when I've picked him up.'

Kate realized she'd been half hoping Rav might have decided to go AWOL for a night or two and sample the fleshpots of Zürich. If Zürich had fleshpots. He was addicted to his phone. It was unheard of for him to ignore her calls unless he was deliberately avoiding her. And the alternatives didn't bear thinking about. She pressed the

WhatsApp button. *If you're avoiding me because I was shitty with you, then stop it. I need to know you're okay. Call now.*

She switched on the radio, surfed the dial for a few moments and then turned it off. She messaged again. *Stop fucking around. Make contact.*

'Come on, Rav,' she muttered. 'This is *not* funny. Where are you?'

She glanced up and down the street again and got out of her car. There was no answer when she punched Rav's buzzer. She retreated and looked up. No sudden play of lights on curtained windows. Nothing. She got back into the car and pulled up Zac's number. She hesitated for a moment, then thumbed the call button. He answered immediately.

'Zac, it's Kate Henderson.'

There was a momentary silence. 'You've got a nerve,' he said.

'Have you heard from Rav?'

'You mean since the raging argument we had after what you told him?'

'Tonight, I mean.'

'No. He's in Switzerland.'

'He's not. He flew into London earlier this evening. Should be home by now, but I'm outside the flat and there's no sign. And he's not responding to my calls and messages, which is highly unlike him.'

'Perhaps he's as pissed off with you as I am.'

'I wouldn't blame him for that. But he's the most professional officer I know. He'd respond on a work issue, no matter what.'

'Maybe he's had enough of you and your "work".'

'Zac, I'm worried enough about him to call you, despite the abuse I knew I'd get. So, is there any chance you could come round here and let me in?'

There was another silence. 'I'll be there in five minutes,' he said.

In fact it was more like three, his state of mind made blindingly obvious by the speed at which he drove down the terraced street and the screech of brakes as he brought his SUV to a halt. He was a tall, rangy man with a big nose and a generous beard, which seemed intent on invading his flowery designer shirt as he stalked towards the entrance. 'You've got me worried,' he said.

He opened the shared front door and they charged upstairs. He put the key in the apartment lock and turned it until Kate put a hand on his arm and a finger to her lips. She went in first. It was dark, with no discernible movement in the air. She was powerfully reminded of the moment Rav had saved her life in the Andros hallway, and did not turn on the light.

She glided noiselessly down the corridor, turning right into a bedroom. The duvet had been pulled back on one side, as if someone had recently been sleeping there.

On the opposite side of the corridor, state-of-the-art

kitchen equipment gleamed in the ochre glow of a street lamp. An electronic clock flashed at her, as if it was waiting to be reset. The room was a testament to what Rav called his OCD, everything so neatly stored it made her wonder if it had ever been used.

Kate took a knife from the magnetic rack by the cooker. She glanced at a photograph of Rav with his arm around Zac on a beach somewhere, stuck to the stainless-steel fridge, and then at Zac himself, framed by the doorway, his face so pale and gaunt that his eyes appeared to have sunk into their sockets.

She moved back into the corridor. Waited. Stepped into the living room.

It was even darker in here, with the curtains drawn. As her eyes adjusted, she saw the silhouette of a naked figure hanging from the ceiling. She switched on the light.

Rav had a belt wrapped around his neck, taut as a razor strop, attached to a wrought-iron ring set into an oak beam that spanned the width of the ceiling. His eyes bulged accusingly at her and an orange had been stuffed into his mouth.

'*No!*' she cried. She grabbed a chair, dragged it across, climbed onto it and tried to lift him down. 'Zac – *Zac!*'

She wrenched the orange from Rav's mouth, wrapped one arm around his waist and struggled to unbuckle the belt. She caught sight of Zac, frozen to the spot, by the entrance to the room. 'Help me!'

But he still didn't move.

Kate slashed and slashed at the leather with the knife until Rav came free. She lowered him to the floor, in the recovery position, bent over him and touched a fingertip to the carotid artery in his neck. She knelt and put her cheek to his mouth, hoping to feel a hint of breath on her skin.

'Rav . . . Oh, Rav . . .'

She rolled him onto his back, placed both palms on his chest and rhythmically compressed his ribcage, counting to herself as she went. When she reached thirty, she pinched his nose between her thumb and forefinger, opened his lips and lowered her mouth to his, desperate to fill his lungs with life-giving air. Once. Twice.

'Rav . . .'

She shook her head.

'No, no, no . . . Ravindra, my dear friend, *please* . . .' She cupped his cheek and rocked back and forth, cradling his head to her breast. 'Don't *do* this to me. Not after everything we've been through. Not like this, not now . . .'

The silence was deafening. She looked up at Zac, still rooted to the spot, as pale as driven snow. He was staring at Rav's body, mouth moving, but failing to form any recognizable words.

Kate pushed past him into the bedroom, pulled the duvet off the bed and used it to cover Rav, as if helping him recover some dignity in this moment of agony would make the slightest difference to either of them.

She stood beside him and looked around the room. Save for the chair she'd moved, the room seemed undisturbed. She switched off the light, went to the window and fractionally eased back the curtain. The street appeared deserted, except for a woman taking her dog for a late-night constitutional on the opposite pavement.

She took out her phone, dialled the SIS night desk and asked them to alert Ian and C. Then she called the police. Then Stuart. She warned him it was likely to be a long night, and that she would also have to go away tomorrow. His voice vibrated with concern and he wanted to know what had happened, but she told him not to worry.

Zac was now seated in the corner, his head bowed. He looked up, still struggling. 'What happens now?'

'The police come, then a load of people from the office. There will be a lot of questions for both of us. And then we get to feel guilty for the rest of our lives.'

'It was me who killed him, not you.'

'Actually, Zac, it wasn't either of us. You don't know Rav very well if you think he would hang himself from a beam with a fucking orange in his mouth because you went back to your wife for a week. Apart from anything else, he'd have wanted something a lot more original.'

'You didn't hear him crying on the phone.'

'Perhaps, but I did know him. And we've seen each other through thick and thin. There's no way on earth he would have wanted it to end like this.'

'So?'

'He made the mistake of calling in what he found in Switzerland. And that call killed him.'

'I don't understand.'

'You don't need to. And perhaps you never will. All you need to know right now is that he was murdered.'

'Who by?'

'I can't tell you. But he wasn't the first and, sadly, he probably won't be the last.'

Kate worked her way carefully through the apartment, and found absolutely nothing of interest. Rav's laptop was missing. So were his phone and the leather satchel he always carried with him. She looked for hiding places, but unless he had thought of something or somewhere very unusual, there wasn't one. She tried to enlist Zac's help, but he had sunk into a state of shock so deep he was barely capable of breathing, let alone speaking.

The police arrived first. They insisted on detaining her and transporting her to Scotland Yard. She waited in a spartan interview room until Ian and Sir Alan arrived. They didn't look as if they'd formed a rescue party. Grim-faced, they took the seats opposite her. 'We've had to talk to Five,' Ian said. 'They've opened an investigation. They'll be in touch in due course.'

'It doesn't take a genius to work out who killed him.'

'They're not looking into who killed him.'

'So, what are—'

'Viper,' Sir Alan said. 'We couldn't put them off any longer.'

'If there's anything you wish to tell us,' Ian said, 'it would help to do so now.'

'Help who?'

'Don't get cute, Kate. It would help all of us.'

'If I had anything new to tell you, believe me, I would.'

Ian took a laptop and a file from his bag. He arranged them fussily on the table. 'We haven't been going behind your back, Kate, if that's what you're thinking.'

'Why would I think that?'

'I've never felt your story added up. Not for one minute. In many ways I wish I could have swallowed it whole. But it just doesn't make sense. And we all have an obligation to act upon any reasonably founded suspicion.'

'That's Orwellian double-think, Ian, if ever I heard it. Why don't you just spit it out?'

Ian stared at her. 'It's not credible that you don't know who Sergei Malinsky really is.'

'I do know who he is.'

'Then spell it out for us.'

'He's a friend from my time as a student in St Petersburg. I lost touch with him, but he must have joined the Russian Foreign Service, possibly the SVR. I agree it's odd we have no record of him, but he wouldn't be the first. You know as well as I do that they keep people hidden in the diplomatic service for so long that we can't be sure of their exact operational role. I met him again at the American ambassador's party, as I've said, and he gave me the tip-off that led to the recording on Igor's gin palace.'

'So this guy, with an unspecified role somewhere within the Russian state apparatus, gift-wrapped this golden intelligence egg out of pure friendship?'

'I don't know why he gave it to me. All I know is that it turned out to be true.'

'You might concede he could have been manipulating you?'

'Yes, I might. But we have been over this. In the end it doesn't matter what his motives were because the information we gleaned from the operation has so far proved to be accurate. Unless the PM is faking it, and cooked this whole thing up with Vasily and the boys for their own amusement. We wouldn't have acted upon any of it otherwise.'

'It's a beguiling theory,' Ian said, 'but just not credible.' He opened his laptop, maximized a file on the screen and hit play. They all watched. 'The Winter Olympics in Sochi,' Ian said, by way of commentary. 'The opening ceremony. Here we have the Russian president, watching his mistress. But who should be sitting alongside him?' He hit the stop bar.

Kate peered more closely. 'Alexander Gregorin. So what?'

'His old friend from their days as liaison officers with the Stasi in East Berlin, now head of the GRU.'

Kate glanced at Sir Alan, who was examining her with

such stillness and purpose that she felt like a laboratory specimen. 'How is that surprising? Gregorin is exactly who you'd expect the Russian president to have at his side.'

'You're right, of course,' Ian said. 'But watch this.' He hit play again. The Russian president murmured something in Gregorin's ear, and, as he leant over to do so, the shot widened to reveal a third man. They were all laughing now.

'My goodness,' Ian said, making no attempt now to conceal his enjoyment of her discomfort. 'Sergei Malinsky, as I live and breathe. Silly me. While we were toiling in the vineyards, trying and failing to work out who he really is, he's risen like a spectre and now sitteth at the right hand of Alexander Gregorin. Except he's one hell of a hidden asset, because we've never seen him in Gregorin's company before – or with anyone else in the GRU, for that matter.'

Kate stared at the frozen image of her friend laughing at the Russian president's joke. 'So the GRU hide people deep inside the diplomatic service as well. How does this change anything?'

Ian planted his elbows on the table. His cheeks were flushed and a lock of his curly blond hair tumbled across his forehead in its enthusiasm to join the celebration. 'Are you really going to tell us you had no idea who he is?'

'That's exactly what I'm going to try to tell you, yes.'

'Or you could admit you're working for him.'

'And what is your evidence for that?'

'This whole operation suits Alexander Gregorin and the GRU down to the ground. Or indeed the underground. They embarrass the SVR and us at the same time.'

'I thought you said I was being manipulated?'

'I did think that – before I knew who he fucking was! Why would you keep that a secret from us unless you were working for him?'

'You think *I*'m working for the GRU?'

'I'm saying that's one of the vanishingly small number of conclusions one can draw from the facts now in our possession.'

Sir Alan stood. 'All right. That's enough. Ian, give us a minute, please.'

'Alan, I really think—'

'I said, "Give us a minute." Not "Would you like to give us a minute?"'

Ian returned the laptop and file to his case and walked out, taking care to slam the door as he did so.

25

'I HAD TO let him have his head,' Sir Alan said. 'You can be sure he'll give all that to our friends in the Security Service, and I wanted to see how you'd react.'

He poured Kate a glass of water. She drank it gratefully.

'You look like you need something stronger,' he said.

'If you were a proper boss, you'd have a flask in your pocket.'

He smiled and reached into his jacket. But it wasn't for any kind of alcoholic sustenance. With a magician's flourish, he took out what looked, at first, like playing cards, and placed them face down on the table. Kate could see that they were SIS staff security passes. Six in all.

'The Russians knew that you were going to be on Andros very shortly after the decision to go was taken. Regardless of whether or not the foreign secretary is a Russian asset, we cannot avoid the fact that we have a traitor inside our organization. So, who is Viper?'

He looked at the cards.

'Six people had enough information to allow the Russians to act as they did.'

He turned over the first card. 'Sir Alan Brabazon, better known as C.'

Then the second. 'Ian Granger, director of Europe and Russia.'

And the third. 'Danny Simmonds, Operations.'

'Danny didn't know what we were intending to do there.'

'But he knew the location. He knew you were tracking the *Empress*. He would have assumed it was connected to what you had learnt in Istanbul.'

'True.'

He was behaving more like a croupier now, in a high-stakes poker game. 'Kate Henderson, Russia Desk. Julie Price, Russia Desk.' He glanced up at her again. 'And, finally, Ravindra Singh, Russia Desk.'

He removed Rav's card from the circle he had created. 'And then there were five. Why did they kill him?'

'He called me from Zürich. He said he had something on the transactions to the foreign secretary's offshore company. Proof of the Russian connection.'

'Was anyone else aware of it?'

'No.'

'Was *that* why he was killed?'

'Until we come up with a better explanation. And I don't include a gay-sex game gone wrong. I can't find his laptop, phone or briefcase.'

C stared at the cards before him, absorbed, as if trying to force them to give up their secrets. He reached forward. 'Julie is a recent graduate recruit from the most thoroughly vetted generation in our organization's history. So, while she *could* be an agent, it seems unlikely.'

'Unless there's more to her affair with Ian than meets the eye.'

'Hmm. An attempt to cover her back?' C toyed with Julie's card, sliding it in and out of the circle, and ended up leaving it in.

'Operations is a big unit,' Kate said. 'They don't assign themselves. How could the Russians have *known* Danny would be in a position to help? The description we overheard on the *Empress* doesn't fit him.'

'Correct.' C moved Danny's card to the side of the table. 'So that leaves four: Julie Price, Sir Alan Brabazon, Kate Henderson and Ian Granger. The fact that Julie chose to have an affair with Ian seems out of character and surprising. The way in which you claim to have been given twenty-four-carat information as a Valentine's gift is not credible. And Ian's desperation to heap suspicion upon you is in itself suspicious.'

He pointed at the picture of himself. 'But how much better than all of that it would be if the Russians had the officer who holds the ring as their man.'

'If you mean to unnerve me at this point, I'd like you to know you're doing a great job.'

He sat back. 'I've liberated you from the clutches of our friend there.' He gestured to the door Ian had just left through. 'But purely temporarily. I want you on that plane to Greece. I'd like to use the time we have left to work every angle within reach. I'll keep the security detail with your family – around the clock, if need be – and you'll have a close-protection team with you abroad.'

'I don't need—'

'After what happened to Ravindra, it's not something I'm willing to compromise on.'

'Are they protecting me or watching me?'

He gazed at her steadily. It was impossible to read what was going on behind those eyes. 'Don't push your luck, Kate.'

She stared at the newly painted cold grey wall behind his head. 'All right,' she said. 'We'll go ahead as planned. But we'll come up with a different story for Ian. That way, if we see the Russians respond, you can at least narrow it to a choice between him and me.'

'But it must be *your* story, Kate. And you must tell *only* him. Otherwise, *I*'d be able to point the finger of suspicion.'

'That doesn't lift my spirits much further.'

'You have to keep in mind the possibility that the person you seek might be me.'

'What I keep in mind is – if that's true, then I'm in the deepest trouble. To misquote that Blair-era civil servant whose name I forget, you're fucked, I'm fucked, we're all fucked. So I'm not sure it's worth thinking about.'

Kate emerged onto the Victoria Embankment and stood in the lightly drifting rain for a few moments. She looked skywards and let it fall upon her face. Then she caught a cab to her car, drove home and parked opposite the entrance to the house. She could see one of their minders lurking in the shadow of a tree a little further down the street. The light in her bedroom was off.

Inside, she spent a few minutes being briefed by the head of the security detail. Her close-protection team would arrive in the morning. The rest of them would divide themselves between Stuart and the children. Kate was free to crawl upstairs to bed.

Fiona and Gus had dragged a mattress into their parents' bedroom and were asleep head to toe, their faces ghoulish in the halogen glow of the street lamp. Jed lay between the mattress and the wall, but Kate was beyond even remarking on this strange development in their domestic arrangements.

She elected to undress in the bathroom, brushed her teeth, then crept into bed. She kept her distance from Stuart, so as not to wake him, but he snuggled up to her, and wrapped his arms around her waist.

'Are they asleep?' she whispered.

'Can't you hear them snoring?'

Kate listened to Gus's ragged wheezing. It reminded her of the nights they'd had him in their room when he was a baby.

'Remember when we used to go on holiday and all sleep in the same room?' Stuart whispered.

'Our most romantic phase.' She pressed herself back into him, so that his breath was on her neck.

'Where were you tonight?'

'We lost someone.'

'Christ.' He raised himself on an elbow and gently turned her over so that she was facing him. 'Who?'

She wiped away a tear, and realized she could barely speak. 'Rav.'

'Oh, my God, Kate.' The bedsprings squeaked as he rolled onto his knees. 'How? Where?'

'I found him . . . hanging in his flat.'

'Jesus!'

'Careful,' she breathed. 'You'll wake them.'

Unable to hold back the tears any longer, she swung away from him and curled into a ball.

He gathered her up in his arms. 'I'm *so* sorry, my love. I know how much he meant to you. Was it . . . suicide?'

'No.'

'What happened?'

'I don't really want to talk about it.'

'Of course. Just . . . rest.'

'Someone murdered him.'

'Why would anyone kill Rav?'

'He called me from Switzerland. He had evidence of James Ryan's Moscow link.'

She felt him shake his head. 'Jesus. Is that why the protection team is still here?'

'No. They're here to watch me. I think the men who came round to scare Fiona and Gus were a set-up.'

'A set-up?'

She extracted herself gently but firmly from his grasp and sat up in bed. He knelt opposite her. 'I told you we have a mole, someone at the top of the Service. I think he or she might be trying to make it look like it's me.'

'What? How?'

She turned away from him, wondering how much she should say. But she had to tell someone. 'Sergei has been feeding me information. It was he who first tipped me off that some of the most senior figures in the Russian Intelligence Service were meeting on a super-yacht in Istanbul.'

'How did he know that?'

She turned to face him. 'He's never come onto our radar

before. That's not unusual. Sometimes they keep agents in deep cover inside the diplomatic service for a long time without using or activating them. But then he started to get in contact – just with small titbits at first, but it gradually became more serious.'

'Shouldn't you have refused to accept anything from him?'

'Maybe, but the letters came in the post. It would have been hard not to read them.' Stuart was obviously bridling, so she turned towards the window. 'It turns out that he's in the GRU, which is fighting a bitter turf war with the main foreign intelligence service. And not only that, he appears to be at a high level within it, too, close in some way to its chief.'

'Why is that a problem?'

'Because Sir Alan and Ian think I knew that and failed to disclose it.'

'And why would you have done that?'

'Ian is trying to suggest that the only reason I could have kept it a secret is that I'm working for them.'

'That's absurd.'

'Yes, but right now it makes about as much sense as any other theory and Ian can be bloody clever when he sets his mind to it.'

'So is Ian the mole?'

'He might be. But he's also weak and paranoid, so it could just be that he's panicking and trying to make sure the finger of blame doesn't point at him, regardless of whether he's guilty or not.'

'You have to stop this, Kate. It's madness. You have to get out.'

'I can't stop.'

'You *have* to. What about Fiona and Gus and . . .'

She raised a hand to his cheek. 'I can't. Not now. If I don't finish this, who will?'

Stuart got up. He skirted the still sleeping children, tweaked the curtain and looked down into the street. 'It is *not* our fight.'

'Then whose is it?'

'How can you be *sure* you have a mole? How do you know they're not playing you?'

'Because it's my job to know.'

'How do you hunt him?'

'The same way we always hunt moles. We channel them towards the noose, then pull it tight.' Kate lay down. 'I'm sorry, I need to sleep. I know this is very hard for you, but it's what I signed up for. It's my responsibility, my . . . duty. And I don't have any choice but to go on.'

Kate turned away from him again. Stuart got back into bed and she pressed her back against him to make it clear this was not rejection. She took his hand and wrapped his arm around her waist.

'Is it a bit weak to admit that I'm frightened?' he said.

'No. I am too. But we'll come through it.'

'Could they come after the kids?'

'I . . . don't think so.'

'But they might come for you?'

'I can look after myself.'

'Like Rav could, you mean?'

Kate didn't answer. She could hear his breathing and sense his alertness. 'I have to go away in the morning, my love.'

She could feel his body tense. 'Where to?'

'I can't say. We're in lock-down. I'm sorry, but do you mind holding the fort?'

'For how long?'

'The honest truth is, I don't know. A few days. A week, maybe.'

'Of course, Kate.'

He only ever used her name when he was irritated or upset. She waited for the inevitable withdrawal and he duly rolled away. 'You knew it would be like this. I told you.'

'Perhaps you did. But I don't mind admitting I'm not as tough as you are.'

'We're all tougher than we think.'

He didn't answer.

'I may be gone before you wake up.'

'Okay. Good luck.'

'Thank you.'

He went silent again. But she could tell he was still wide awake.

'I love you,' he said.

'I love you, too.'

'Brilliant,' Fiona said, from the mattress on the floor. 'Can we all go to sleep now?'

26

THE EASYJET FLIGHT direct to Mykonos touched down in a howling wind. The descent had been bumpy as the plane twisted in over the windmills and the whitewashed houses of Chora, and the fishing boats in the bay.

The wind tugged at Kate's hair as she came down the steps to a few spits of rain on her cheeks.

Julie met her and they didn't exchange a word until they were in the taxi. Tears rolled down Julie's cheeks and Kate pulled her head to her chest. For a moment, they embraced.

Julie straightened. 'I didn't sleep a wink last night,' she said. 'I just couldn't believe it. What have they found?'

'The inquest will say he accidentally hanged himself

while taking part in a sex game. The Russians very carefully and deliberately made it look like Gareth Williams.'

'The guy they found zipped up in a bag?'

'Yes, sorry, before your time. He was a really bright guy working on how the Russian Mafia and oligarch class were laundering their money. We should have learnt our lesson.'

'Why Rav?'

'A similar reason. He had proof about the foreign secretary. He rang me to say so. That call must have signed his death warrant.'

'Have *we* found the proof?'

'C has our people in Zürich trying to locate the woman he met there, but I imagine she will have disappeared as well.'

'Was she for real, or a set-up?'

'I guess we'll never know.'

'Where is the close-protection team?'

'I stood them down at the airport this morning. It caused quite a stand-off, but I want us to handle our own security.'

With its brilliant white houses and churches, dark blue shutters, domes and narrow patchwork of alleys, Chora was every tourist's fantasy. Lost in thought, Julie didn't seem to notice any of it. Kate decided to save it for later, and closed her eyes. She'd been up and out of the house painfully early, had dozed fitfully on the flight and her neck ached.

She'd called Yusuf in Istanbul and asked him to take up residence in Athens airport security. She could have asked the local station chief, but didn't know anyone there well and, more than anything now, she needed someone in place whom she could trust. She'd then called Ian to tell him she'd received a tip-off from her source that Mikhail was aiming for Santorini – so their entrapment operation would be focused there.

'More misinformation, no doubt,' he'd said.

To which she'd replied, 'Perhaps. But what they then choose to disseminate will tell us something pretty revealing.'

In any event, the trap was set. There was no one more qualified to spot a Russian wet team than Yusuf and his family. If the Russian team hit Athens and went on to Mykonos, Ian was not the man she was looking for. If they boarded a vessel bound for Santorini, her noose would tighten. She didn't doubt that the Russians would want to be where she was.

Even as the last whispers of summer faded into winter on the island – such a climate reminded her that autumn was a quaint and peculiarly English notion – the streets remained busy. Jeeps and scooters and quad bikes wove and swerved and tooted their way through hordes of pedestrians.

Julie had rented their base through Airbnb. The apartment had a roof terrace with spectacular views of the town and the hills beyond it, which boasted no shortage of Chora's trademark windmills. Danny had set himself up on the roof, beneath a canvas awning, and the surveillance teams were all in place.

She could see the *Empress*, anchored offshore. As always, Igor's super-yacht was hard to miss. And Danny's screens were already fired up with the live feeds – eight in all – from cameras attached to the surveillance teams. Kate put her hand on his shoulder. 'Hello, my friend.'

He responded with a wistful smile.

'Coping?'

'Depressed about poor old Rav, like everyone. But we're going to nail these fuckers, right?'

'Yes, we are. Got anything?'

'Not a dicky-bird. We think he must still be on board, but have no evidence of it as yet.'

'What are your plans?'

'Everyone's out now, but we'll work a shift system overnight.'

Kate unpacked in the room she had been assigned, went to the bathroom and washed the grime from her face. By the time she returned to the roof, the red sun was sinking behind the windmills scattered across the neighbouring hillside, no doubt launching a thousand Instagram boasts as it went. Kate sat next to Julie, took off her shoes and pressed her feet against a warm stone pillar.

The roof terrace was sheltered by a glass wall, but the

wind worried away at the canvas awning above them, and the clatter of its metal fasteners reminded her of a yacht's lanyards beating against its mast on a stormy night. Julie lit a Marlboro, took a few puffs and passed it across.

'Stuart will bloody kill me if he finds out,' Kate said, after inhaling more deeply than she'd meant to.

'Something tells me that's going to be the least of our worries.' Julie took back the cigarette and dragged on it long and hard, then watched the smoke curl upwards until it was whipped away by the breeze. 'So,' she said eventually, 'what happened?'

'Do you really want to know?'

'Of course.'

'I found him hanging naked in his living room. Not a mark on him that I could see.'

They waited for a while, keeping track of the feeds. A light or two sparkled across the water from the *Empress*, but there was no sign of anyone arriving or leaving.

Kate took Julie out to a local supermarket. The alleys around their apartment were filled with tourist shops, selling locally crafted jewellery, accessories, T-shirts, dresses and beachwear. A small and well-stocked supermarket supplied them with lettuce and tomatoes, arborio rice, stock cubes, onions, chillies and mushrooms, which they cooked together in companionable silence.

'He's never going to disappear, though, and neither is

Lena,' Julie said at length, as she diced and fried the onion. 'Jason hasn't, and he died a long time ago.'

'Do you want them to?'

'Yes!' Julie grappled with Kate's question for a moment or two longer. 'No. Of course not. I just want them to be here.' She stared into the pan. 'Are you ever frightened, Kate?'

'Pretty much always, these days.'

'Of what exactly? The idea we might be next, or the implications of whatever the truth turns out to be?'

'Both. And more.'

'As I lay awake last night, I thought about how much worse it must be for you. You have children, a husband, so much more to lose.'

Kate stopped chopping the mushrooms and gave her a hug. 'I'm very lucky,' she said. 'And I'd rather die than have any harm come to them. But you have your whole life ahead of you, with the strength and talent to make it wonderful.'

'Some days I think that. Others I don't.' Julie gave the onions a stir. 'If I was a mother . . . I really don't know that I could do what you're doing. Would I be here, now, if Jason was still alive? I'm not sure. But you aren't stepping back or wilting under the pressure, are you? You're a formidable opponent, and they must know that. I don't know that I could be.'

'You're the most resolute young woman I've ever met.'

'That's only because I have nothing to lose.'

'You're twenty-seven. You have *everything* to lose.'

'Twenty-eight, actually. And I still can't afford my own place. I don't have any of my own time. I'm fucking a guy I don't give a shit about, and who doesn't give a shit about me . . .'

'Why?'

She shrugged. 'I've asked myself the same question. Then I realized I already have the answer. It's because I don't give a shit about him. And he doesn't give a shit about me.' She gave Kate a rueful smile. 'Weren't you in Russia when you were my age?'

'Younger, the first time. And that certainly had its moments. At the end of my tour they threw me into Counter-terror. That was where I met Rav. We shared rather a lot. Many, many nights in Lahore and Peshawar and Kabul – and a whole lot of other places – when we talked like this.

'I'd just had Fiona and Gus. They were tucked up safely in their cots while I was out there wondering whether I'd see another dawn. It didn't seem to make much sense, to be honest. I thought about quitting a hundred – no, a thousand – times. But Rav saw me through, which is one of the reasons I'm not going to throw in the towel now.'

'How did he see you through?'

Kate thought about the many answers she could give. 'Plain old-fashioned decency is high on the list. And, in the end, the simple fact that he believed somebody has to do this. It *must* be done. So, if we hang up our boots and go home, another poor soul will have to step up in our place.'

'That's the speech all front-line commanders have doled out since warfare was first invented.'

'Perhaps because it's true.'

'I've spent a lot of time in this job trying to push death to the back of my mind,' Julie said. 'For ages, I didn't care – or didn't think I did. Rav used to know my true feelings better than I knew them myself. He'd say it was all cool, because we could make sensible decisions that would minimize the risk. There was no reason to suppose this life was any more dangerous than crossing a busy street or being an accountant and cycling home every day in a world full of articulated lorries.'

'I always envied him that quiet conviction. When I was in my teens, I thought we'd all live for ever. I didn't have a brother who became a random target on a big red London bus. The first time I was forced to confront the fact that death didn't just happen to other people was when my dad died. But it didn't make me fear it. It made me fear not making the most of life.'

'Having children changes everything, doesn't it?'

'The biggest wake-up call ever. And a tightrope act without a safety net. When they were born, I felt the greatest need to help make the world a better place. But for every minute of every surveillance op, I was tortured by the thought that I should be standing outside their bedroom door to make sure they were still breathing. And the realization that I did fear death after all. Their death. I'm paralysed by fear of their death. And Stuart's, obviously.'

'I guess we can only do our best. I think that was what Rav was trying to tell me.'

Kate added the mushrooms to the onions, as Julie continued to stir. 'That's where my mother's been so helpful. She made me feel that my best is a long way from good enough.'

'Do you believe in God?' Julie asked.

'No. But I'm old enough to recognize that we simply have no idea what lies beyond the boundaries of our knowledge and to take some comfort from that ignorance.'

'I don't know what that means.'

'In my youth I looked for answers with a terrible urgency. I craved certainty. Then I started telling myself that, in the end, we have to accept there's a vast amount we just don't know.'

Julie's face creased into a grin, and then she began to giggle.

'Here I am, musing upon the infinite mysteries of the universe, and you're pissing yourself with laughter,' Kate said. 'What's that about?'

'It's about you talking bollocks. You still crave certainty. You still believe you can show your mum she's wrong.'

Kate poured in the rice. 'You're really going to mess up this risotto,' she said, 'if you don't keep a proper eye on it.'

'Mrs H, you're truly an inspiration to us all.' Julie turned down the flame, then draped both arms around Kate's neck and kissed her cheek. 'And while we're on the subject of truth, I know you know about Ian,' she said.

Kate pursed her lips.

'Do you think a lot worse of me?'

'Safe to say he wouldn't be my choice. And from the way you've always talked about him, I didn't think he'd be yours either.'

'I shouldn't have said those things. It was a childish attempt to convince you – and perhaps even me – that it wasn't happening.'

'You've been lonely. I know that.'

'It really is just sex. I don't have time to date, and he seems to want it badly. Even if that doesn't necessarily mean he wants *me*. It's an arrangement.' Her eyes sparkled. 'And I do find him weirdly attractive.'

'From everything else you've said tonight, I'm not sure I entirely believe that.'

They took a bowl of risotto and salad up to Danny and ate their home-cooked feast on the floor below, enjoying the candlelight, and the silence.

'This risotto is actually quite good,' Kate said, when she had almost finished.

After their gin and vodka experience on Andros, they'd agreed to limit themselves to a glass of wine each, and Julie took a last gulp of hers. 'He's a different man away from work, you know. He's almost schizophrenic. In the office, he can't contain his ambition. When he comes in, he thinks the world is against him. But he's—'

'Married.'

'Yes . . . There is that. But it's complicated.'

'It usually is.' Kate touched her wrist. 'If he's two different men, how do you know which is the real one? And how do you know there aren't more than two of him?'

'I didn't think you'd understand.'

'I'm not judging you, Julie.'

'But you are judging him.'

'Not yet.'

'I suppose you wonder if I'm Viper.'

'Why would I?'

'You might think fucking him is out of character and that it could be an attempt to cover my back.'

'Your . . . affair surprised me. But it shouldn't have.'

'Why?'

'Because, despite your fantastic strengths, you're bruised. And lonely. You've learnt to bury what you really feel beneath a coat of armour.'

'That's what spies do, isn't it?'

'You might have convinced yourself that this is a comfortable transaction. Just sex. But I'm not sure it's going to end like that. You don't think you've let him in. But I can't help seeing it differently.'

'Thanks, Mum.'

'Seriously. You've made yourself vulnerable in ways I don't think you want to admit. And I hope he doesn't treat you too badly. But he will hurt you.'

'And you won't trust me now?'

'I know you, Julie. You're my friend. You're not Viper – you could never be Viper.'

'How can you be so sure?'

'Because I've been in this business a long time. So let's make a simple pact: we won't talk about Ian, and you won't discuss our work with him. When he does hurt you, you have my shoulder to cry on. And in the meantime, we carry on as we always have.'

'Okay.' Julie smiled. 'It's a deal.'

'Apart from anything else, I now need you more than ever.'

They immediately disobeyed their own wine rule and took the rest of the bottle up to the roof, but Julie didn't say another word. There was an intensity to her that felt like a mirror to Kate's younger self, but there was a distance sometimes, too, as if the issues she was wrestling with were not the ones she'd articulated.

Kate handed Danny another bowl of risotto, which he attacked with a relish that reminded her inescapably of Gus.

'What's this?' She pointed at the TV debate unfolding on one of his screens.

'ITV. Our two candidates.' He turned up the volume.

James Ryan had clearly hit his stride. 'I think what they did to Imogen was *absolutely* disgusting. Needless to say, I myself have led a life of blameless virtue . . .' He waited for the ripple of laughter from the audience. Or perhaps he was looking around for a mirror so that he could admire himself.

'If we could keep this within the realm of the vaguely credible, Foreign Secretary . . .' the presenter said.

'My point, exactly! As I've often said, there but for the grace of God, and the rest of it. The fact is, none of us are expecting to be hailed as Vestal Virgins, but the Russians have done a genuinely disgusting – I mean *revolting* – thing. When did they record this tape? Why did they record it? Why have they released it?

'Well, I think we all know the answer to that. They wanted to throw this election, as they have so many others around the world, into complete chaos. And I have to say that, so far, assisted by some unduly obliging, so-called media pundits, they've succeeded. We cannot allow this to continue. We simply cannot go on like this. That is my contention. We must remove this cancer from the heart of our national politics, and the easiest way to do that is to ignore it.'

The presenter turned to Imogen, on the other side of the

podium. 'What do you think? The foreign secretary is trying to help you here, is he not?'

'No, he isn't. Ignorance is most emphatically *not* bliss. As ever, my not totally honourable friend's apparent generosity of spirit helps me a little but helps him a lot. And that's very much the way he likes it.'

'Come on, Imogen,' James Ryan blustered. 'For God's sake—'

'No,' she said, tight-lipped. 'I will not "come on". I'm accused of being an adulterer. I hate that charge more than almost anything else that could be thrown at me. I've hurt my family deeply. I cannot begin to put into words how much I regret that. But no one is accusing me of betraying my country. No one seems to doubt that the Russian Foreign Intelligence Service had me under observation and cruelly breached my privacy. I don't know why they did, but I'm pretty sure I know why they chose to release it at this particular moment.'

'Honestly, Imogen,' Ryan said, 'for Pete's sake, can't you see? They were hoping we'd be standing here having just such an argument. This is what they want.'

'No, James. They're hoping you'll win. And if you're happy to benefit from this piece of arrant chicanery, you're a lesser man than even I perceive you to be.'

'Go on, Imogen,' Julie whispered. 'You tell him.'

If Imogen had intended to tease out his mean streak, she was doing a grand job. His head dropped a little. He turned to the presenter. 'I'm afraid that my opponent here, to whom I've been trying to extend the hand of friendship tonight, as you have seen, is now using this business – quite bafflingly – against me. We all know this is how our enemies operate. We understand that igniting this kind of argument at the heart of our democratic process is exactly what they hoped to achieve. I can only regret that the Education secretary has now chosen to do their work for them.'

'The charge,' Imogen said, 'is that you are an agent of a foreign power. It is one that we know MI6 is currently investigating. And I certainly hope they conclude their work before this leadership election is over. We cannot afford to doubt the fundamental loyalty of our prime minister. I know politics has become unpredictable of late, and a dirty word, quite understandably, to many, but if we allow these people to triumph, we may as well all pack up and move to Moscow.'

'Utterly preposterous,' Ryan blustered. 'Like I said, she's doing their work for them! It's tragic. And disgraceful.'

'Any movement in the real world, Danny?' Kate asked.

Danny minimized the ITV feed and brought up the static picture of the *Empress*. The yacht was in almost total darkness. 'Are we sure he's still there?'

'Unless he's shape-shifted and become James Ryan.'

Danny insisted he was happy to stay up all night, but Kate said she was tired. She would turn in and wake at four to relieve him. She went downstairs and WhatsApped Stuart: *Watched some of it. Good on her.*

Double or quits. And he doesn't fight fair, so why should we?

Kate lay back on her bed: *All okay at home?*

Yup. All good. Fi and Gus with me now. We'll go home as soon as we wrap this up.

Please tell me they haven't seen the video.

Everyone has seen the video, he replied.

Kate must have fallen asleep almost immediately, because the next thing she heard was the sound of the alarm drilling itself into her head. The wind had got up again too, rattling the windows and whistling across the rooftops.

She straightened her clothes, ran a brush through her hair and went up to the roof. The clank of the awning fixtures was intrusive and threatening. By the light of the moon, she could see the white horses whipping across the water.

'Morning,' she said to Danny.

He smiled. 'If you say so, boss, but it probably still qualifies as night, don't you think?'

'Go and get your head down.'

Danny remained reluctant, but she insisted they needed to pace themselves. Julie had left her cigarettes out, so Kate took one and smoked it. By the time the first fingers of light felt their way over the horizon, the pack was almost empty.

Danny reappeared.

'Not what I'd call an epic sleep,' she said.

'I tried.' He looked at the detritus in the ashtray. 'I see devoting yourself to a long and healthy life is going well.'

They sat in easy silence for a while.

'Tell me something,' Kate said. 'If you were working for the Russians—'

'Purely hypothetically speaking, I imagine.'

'Purely hypothetically speaking, yes. Picture this: a desk officer has identified someone who is willing to work for you, in a first-world country with a highly competent internal and external intelligence service – in other words, the kind you'd need to treat with more than a little . . . respect. How would you advise the agent and desk officer to communicate securely?'

'Assuming they could be listened to and overlooked at any time, you mean?'

'Yes,' Kate said. 'Assuming the imminent possibility of close surveillance.'

'Some kind of app buried within an app, probably buried within another app.'

'In English?'

'Oh, I don't know. I'd probably use WhatsApp. Everyone has it – there's no reason not to. It's end-to-end encrypted, so I'd hide something in there – a folder that would be bloody hard to find unless you really knew what you were looking for.'

Kate thought about this. 'Okay. But *we* have to hand in our phones, laptops and so on for random vetting. And it's no different elsewhere in Whitehall. So . . . let me ask you a slightly different question. If I had something of the kind you suggest on my iPhone, would our people find it when I handed it in?'

'Probably.'

'Why? You said you could hide it well.'

'I could. But they're good at finding stuff. The best.'

'So, how would that be a sensible way to communicate?'

Danny sucked his teeth. 'There's no totally foolproof way. Not in this day and age. There are just clever dodges and tricks that might work for a while. All I'm saying is, if you were asking me to set this up, that's the bit of the jungle I'd explore.'

'But then I'd repeat to you what you've just said to me – I need to be able to communicate quickly and easily, but I also need it to be a hundred per cent safe.'

'Impossible.'

'Think about it.'

Danny took the last of Julie's cigarettes. He never smoked. Almost never. 'Maybe a second device,' he said. 'Something like that.'

'What do you mean?'

'The point of maximum threat is when you're asked to hand in your device. So the problem is less in the everyday. I'd focus on how to beat the call-in.'

'Go on.' Kate had a terrible feeling she knew what he was going to say.

'Two identical devices, synced up and running all of the same programs. You could pick up one and then another – they'd look and feel exactly the same and have the same information on them, except one is clean, the other has the app buried in the app, or whatever you're using to exchange information.'

Kate stared at the *Empress*, out there in the darkness.

'You don't look very happy about it,' Danny said. 'But I think that's quite a clever idea.'

'It is, Danny. Thank you. Go to the top of the class.'

'You want me to talk to anyone about it?'

'No. Thank you.'

Julie came up to join them. 'It's the wind,' Julie replied. 'It's so loud.'

'Welcome to Insomniacs Anonymous,' Danny said. 'You may now begin our twelve-step programme. Just one entry requirement: bring more cigarettes.'

'There's a carton in my bag,' Julie said. 'You fucking get them.'

Kate kindly volunteered, and went to make coffee. She did that a lot, for the rest of the day. It seemed that no matter how hard they glared at the floating palace in the cove, they couldn't will it, or anyone on it, to swing into action.

Time crawled by.

Kate and Julie shopped for food again, and allowed

themselves to be distracted by one or two clothes shops. Julie bought a striped beach dress. 'I only got it because you liked it,' she said, as they wandered back to the apartment.

Kate put an arm around her shoulders. 'Yes, darling, I know. And I do. Though it's a bit on the revealing side, and I'm worried that the boys might like it a little *too* much . . .'

They made prawn linguine together.

'Danny wants to cook tomorrow night,' Julie said. 'I hope the office bean counters recognize how many euros we're saving them.'

'On past experience, I'd say their gratitude is likely to be underwhelming.' Kate started putting together a salad. The ingredients weren't the freshest she'd ever worked with. 'Have you spoken to your dad since you got here?'

'I talk to him every day.'

'What about?'

'Everything.' She grinned. 'Er, no. Not everything. My fears, my hopes. I spend quite a lot of time wishing aloud that I was less emotional, and he unsettles me by saying that I'm very like my mother.'

'From your description of her, you're nothing like your mother.'

'Hmm. Maybe I am, maybe I'm not. The older I get, the more I realize that you basically *are* your parents. Or become them, anyway. I mean, you have all the same characteristics, though it takes you time to spot which bit comes from where. Most importantly you inherit their value system, wholesale.

'Your teenage years are just a long period of radical delusion. Once you get beyond them, you start to see the reality and choose which of those values you wish to reject or replace. The rest rolls on from one generation to the next.'

'I'll tell my kids that. They'll be over the moon.'

'They're lucky. You know they are. And I bet they do, too.'

'They might say different.'

'Not if *I* asked them.'

They plated up the pasta and loaded a tray.

'Do you think you should have another go with your mother?' Kate asked. 'On the grounds that it's a relationship one should probably never give up on.'

'Do you still try?'

'Yes and no. I do, but usually end up wishing I hadn't.'

A Greek flag flapped above the balcony of the neighbouring hotel. Given what a mess the country was in, Kate rather admired the determination of the locals to remain proud of it.

'There's something terrible about the fact that the one seal of approval I still seek is the one that will never be granted,' she said. 'I've spent my whole life trying not to *be* her, but I still want her to celebrate me as *me*. Even if it's only once. So when I go round there I don't know whether it's an act of kindness – of the type my father admired and exemplified – or just another exercise in self-harm that I should have grown out of long ago.'

'What does Stuart say?'

'He's trying to ban me from going. If he thought he could get away with it, he'd put arsenic in her tea. He's quite practical like that.'

'I love your husband.'

'You're welcome to him.'

'Ha!' Julie grabbed the tray and headed upstairs. 'You don't mean that. You're lucky, and if you don't know it, you're a fool.'

'Actually,' Kate said, as they stepped on to the roof, 'I do know it.' Then, mostly to herself, 'But I am a fool.'

They ate while staring at the *Empress* on Danny's central screen. There were two lights on now, and zero movement.

'We should make a TV series of this,' Julie said. 'Kind of like *Gogglebox*, but marginally less compelling. The real work of SIS: watching paint dry.'

At around eleven, Kate went to bed. She was halfway through getting changed when Yusuf sent a WhatsApp message: *Still no sign of anyone.*

Kate thanked him. She thought for a moment, then sent a WhatsApp to C: *No sign of anyone rerouting to Santorini. So either too smart, or not Viper.*

His response was immediate: *It must be you, then. Or me.*

Must have left my sense of humour somewhere else, she replied.

You should never leave home without it.

There was a rap on the door. 'Something's happening,' Julie said.

27

KATE FOLLOWED HER onto the roof. The *Empress* was ablaze with light. Half a dozen crew milled around on deck.

'Moving on?' Kate asked. 'Or coming ashore?'

Moments later, Mikhail climbed down into the launch and headed towards the shore. The closest surveillance officer picked him up on the quay and his camera treated them to the full benefit of Mikhail's white skinny jeans, patent-leather shoes and brightly coloured shirt, open almost to the navel.

'Are those flamingos, or just pink splodges?' Julie said. 'Whatever, that's what I call dressing for a night out. I think we're in business.'

The first camera remained static as he walked into a beach bar called Neptune. Danny switched to the second surveillance officer's feed as he followed Mikhail inside. The place was heaving, the music loud and the lights on low. It didn't take long to spot that the men were mostly talking to the men and the women to the women. 'Bingo,' Julie said.

The surveillance officer was clearly going to have difficulty keeping his camera on target in there without drawing attention to himself, so the Russian swam in and out of focus. He cut a lonely figure at the bar, not yet in conversation with anyone, but clearly hoping to be.

'Let's go,' Kate said.

'Where to?'

'We're not going to catch him sitting here.'

Julie struggled to keep up with her as she threaded her way through the busy streets. 'What's the plan?'

'I don't have one,' Kate said. 'We're going to have to make it up as we go along.'

'What are we doing in a gay bar?'

'What do we usually do? We're a couple, looking to swing.' She turned towards Julie. 'You put your arms around my neck last night. In about ten minutes, you're going to have to kiss me on the lips.'

The Neptune was even noisier and more claustrophobic in reality than it had seemed through the surveillance lens. Kate made her way to the bar. 'I must be the oldest woman in here by about a decade,' she said.

'Don't worry, Mum,' Julie yelled. 'I don't think you'll be alone for long.'

'Very funny,' Kate said. 'What do you want to drink?'

'Oh, shit, I don't know. Mojito? But don't make the mistake of thinking it's just one and I'm yours.'

Kate ordered two and they huddled up close to the bar, since there wasn't much choice to do otherwise. Out of the corner of her eye, Kate could see that Mikhail still hadn't hooked up with anyone.

She and Julie exchanged small-talk and pretended to sip their drinks. A trio beside them moved away and created some space. It was quickly filled by a tall and very pretty blonde girl with a dragon tattoo that was creeping out of her crop top and trying to give her a love bite. 'Hi,' she said. 'You spoken for?'

Kate didn't know quite how to react.

'No,' Julie said firmly, and smiled.

The girl offered her hand. 'I'm Stacey, and, as you can probably tell, I'm from the Land of the Free.'

They shook.

'Whereabouts?' Julie asked.

'Michigan originally, LA more recently. But I mostly talk about Beverly Hills because no one ever wants to hear about Michigan and I don't blame them. I don't either. Where are you from?'

'London.'

'Are you a couple?'

Kate concentrated very hard indeed on sipping her cocktail.

'Yes,' Julie said. 'She's old enough to be my mother, but we try to gloss over that.'

'And you like to play sometimes?'

Even Julie looked a little nonplussed.

'Sometimes,' Kate said. 'Depends who with.'

Stacey moved closer. 'I'm good with three, but happy to go with more if you'd like.' She shook out her hair.

Kate could see now that her irises were fully dilated, and not just because of the intimate lighting. The girl was as high as a kite.

Stacey leant in and somehow managed to nibble Kate's ear. 'So how did you guys hook up?' she breathed.

'Oldest story in the world,' Kate said, taking half a step back. 'We worked together and . . .' she ran her fingertips down Julie's bare arm '. . . things kind of went from there.'

'Where's work?'

'A very boring department of our government. The passport division. So if you ever need to get into the UK, you know who to call.'

'I *love* London. I had a blast there. Do you ever go to Daphne's?'

'We don't go out much in the city. You know how it is.' Mikhail was talking to a toned twenty-something guy who looked like he'd come to a fancy-dress party as

Michelangelo's *David*. If Michelangelo's *David* ever bothered to get dressed. 'What brings you to Mykonos?'

'Oh, just living the dream, I guess. I was in TV production in LA, but they were a bunch of sleazeballs, so I had to get outta there. I saved my nickels and dimes and decided to keep travelling until they ran out. So you might need to buy me a drink . . .'

Kate waved at the waiter. As she ordered another mojito, she noticed that Mikhail and his new best friend were getting along very nicely. So nicely that he was caressing the guy's shirt pocket. It was time for them to move. She handed Stacey her cocktail when it arrived. 'Sorry,' Kate said, taking Julie's hand. 'Nature calls. If you know what I mean.'

'Jeez,' Stacey gasped. 'Was it something I said?'

'It's not you,' Kate said. 'It's us.'

Julie followed Kate as she slalomed through the throng. They reached the decking that led onto the beach. The DJ was now playing George Michael. 'It's not you, it's us,' Julie said. 'Nice one. And you know how I love it when nature calls, but can you let go of my hand now?'

Kate released her. 'Time for an argument. Keep it going through the bar. Your hands are younger than mine, so I'll bump and you search.'

'What am I looking for?'

'Room key card. I'm betting it's in the guy's shirt pocket. Mikhail isn't about to fuck him on his dad's super-yacht, is he?'

'You never know with these Russians. What are we arguing about?'

'My decision to dodge a threesome.'

'You're bloody enjoying this, aren't you?'

'Hello, Kettle, Pot calling . . .'

Kate leant forward to kiss her on the lips, and got a slap on the cheek in return. Aghast, she put her hand to her face, then turned and strode away. She didn't get far. Julie grabbed her arm and spun her around. 'She might not have been your type,' she screeched, 'but she is mine.'

'Grow up, Julie, for fuck's sake.'

'You're just a jealous bitch. You're *always* spoiling my fun.'

If there hadn't been so much at stake, they'd have struggled to get through it without dissolving into laughter, but Julie made a convincingly vicious young lover and the argument had all the conviction of a real one as Kate thumped into Mikhail and his statuesque young friend.

'Hey,' Mikhail said. 'C'mon . . .'

Kate feigned surprise. 'C'mon what?' she snapped.

Julie gave her a drunken shove, then fell back and breathed mojito fumes over Mikhail's companion's chest.

She must have been successful, because she then stormed off. Kate followed her. They kept walking until they were out on the beach. 'Result,' Julie whispered. Her cheeks were flushed with excitement. She held up two cards in the darkness – a room key and a driving licence.

'You're a clever girl. If I was gay, I'd definitely want to sleep with you.'

'In your dreams, Grandma.'

Kate turned and gazed out to sea. 'Are you hearing all this, Danny? We've got the key. He's staying at the Chora Beach Club. His name is Yorgos Mistolis.'

'You bet I'm hearing it,' Danny said. 'I love it when you girls talk dirty.'

A surveillance team was in place by the time they got to the beach club. Danny had located Yorgos Mistolis via its billing system. Room 1101 was right on the beach, simple to locate and equally simple to break into. They had it wired in less than five minutes, then hightailed it back to the roof of their apartment. The feed was high definition.

'Let the circus begin,' Julie said.

'That might be in rather poor taste,' Kate replied.

'After your performance this evening, I'm not sure you're in a position to cast the first stone.'

Kate and Danny both helped themselves to Julie's cigarettes. 'Just to be clear,' Kate said, 'I don't actually want to watch this. I'm just going to wait up until we're sure we've got them.'

'I find gay porn quite a turn-on,' Julie said.

'Men only or women too?' Danny asked.

'Both.'

'What are you doing after the show?'

They didn't have long to wait. And there wasn't much in the way of foreplay. The two men were barely in through the door before they were going at each other.

'I'm leaving before the interval,' Kate said. In fact, she stayed long enough only to note that they both looked as if they'd spent a lifetime in the gym.

'Good call,' Danny said. 'I think this'll go on for a while. And the dialogue is shit.'

'Call me when it's over.'

Kate tried to sleep but her mind wouldn't let go of the conversation she needed to have in a few hours' time. Was he really scared of his father? Was it credible that Igor did not know of his activities? And was it possible that, like so much of what had happened since Istanbul – in fact, since that first conversation with Sergei – all this could be interpreted as another attempt to set her up?

She must have dozed off because sunlight was creeping through the shutters as Julie gently shook her awake. 'You're on, boss,' she said. 'He's getting dressed.'

Mikhail was riding a scooter back into town, weaving to and fro across Danny's screen, his shirt half open.

'Looks happy,' Danny said.

'So would I be, if I'd just had that much sex,' Julie said.

Kate handed Danny her phone. 'Can you load up last night's stuff?'

'You'll be pleased to know I've put together some edited highlights.'

'How lovely. How long did it go on?'

'About three hours.'

'Jesus Christ.'

Kate watched Mikhail pull up in front of a café. Danny switched to the next camera. The operative wearing it followed Mikhail inside and took a seat far enough away from him to avoid invading his personal space.

'Perfect,' Julie said.

'I've learnt to worry about perfect,' Kate said.

'But we've been thick on the ground, and haven't seen a hint of anyone else.'

'I know, but we didn't on Andros either, until Rav and I were mugged by the wet team. And Lena still paid the price.' Kate stood. 'Come on, we haven't got the luxury of introspection.'

Julie delivered Kate to the café on the back of her scooter. Its layout was almost identical to that of the bar they had been in last night, with a spacious deck leading to the beach, but Kate was spared the pulsating bodies and the pounding beat. It was empty except for their surveillance guy studying the menu in one corner and Mikhail in another. Kate smiled at the waiter, steeled herself, then took a seat opposite her target.

'Good morning,' she said.

He looked up at her impassively. 'Oh, it's you again . . . let me guess. Your name is Jane or Susan and you're from the British Secret Intelligence Service.'

'How did you work it out?'

'Call me a fucking genius.'

'I could be an old friend of Katya's from Downe House or—'

'I know who my friends are. And you didn't go to Downe House.'

'Would you mind if I ordered coffee?'

'I don't mind if you shove a lacrosse stick up your arse, Jane. Or Alice. As long as you very quickly fuck off.'

Kate waved at the waiter. 'A cappuccino, please.'

She looked at Mikhail.

'I've ordered,' he said. 'Though I shan't be staying long.'

'You shouldn't rush. After what I've just seen, I'd say you need to replenish your strength.'

Mikhail stared at her. 'So, let me guess again. Some of your rather sad and voyeuristic operatives installed cameras in my new friend's bedroom. You've just enjoyed several hours watching two well-endowed and not unattractive men have vigorous sex. And you were so turned on by it, that you've come to ask me for my autograph.'

'That is not correct in every particular.'

'You're thinking that your duty as a woman is to tell my wife.'

'I've certainly admired your wife from a distance.'

Mikhail shook his head. 'It's so late, it's early. And as

you clearly don't need me to tell you, I didn't get much sleep. So I'm even less interested than usual in playing your stupid games.'

'I wouldn't call this a game.'

'So where do we go from here? You're going to send the footage to my father. You think I care?'

'No, Mikhail. We're not going to do that. And since you are neither naive nor stupid, I'm not going to pretend our hand is stronger than it is. But what we want isn't very substantial either.'

She paused long enough for her cappuccino to be delivered, then brought out her phone and played him thirty seconds of Danny's edited highlights.

'If we sent this footage to your father, I think it would be painful. But since I suspect he isn't in awe of your machismo anyway, it's not going to change the course of your life, or his, all that much. So we wouldn't do that. What we *would* do is send it to his opponents or, at least, one of their choicer websites. That would humiliate, embarrass and possibly damage him. I think you *would* pay a heavy price for that.'

'Or he could find out I've been talking to you, in which case he'd kill me.'

'Now I hope you're exaggerating. He's bad, but he's not mad, your father, as you must know better than anyone.'

'So what do you want?'

'We have a problem. As you must be aware, we recorded

your father and some of his former SVR colleagues in the boardroom of the *Empress*. So we know you have at least one agent at the heart of our political establishment, and a well-placed informant, codename Viper. I need to know who they are.'

Mikhail smiled. 'This is amusing. And you think they would tell *me* who these people are?' He stared at her. 'You know I work on the Polish Desk, right? I mean, if you really want to trade one of your second-rate operatives in Warsaw so I can maintain the illusion that I'm the Kremlin's answer to James Bond for a little longer, we might be in business. But . . .' He raised both palms. 'Seriously, *this* is why you came?'

'You're saying you weren't party to any of those conversations?'

'I have *no* idea what you're talking about. Or, at least, I didn't until I read about the foreign secretary in *The Times*.'

Kate leant forward, elbows on the table. 'Perhaps your father didn't share this with you. And I doubt he educated you at Eton so you could spend your life in Russian intelligence, so I guess this phase is designed to familiarize you with your system. But you were aboard the *Empress* when Lena was killed, and I'm afraid I refuse to believe you didn't know about that.'

Mikhail's eyelids flickered. He wasn't the ruthless bastard his father was.

'So how did you find out Lena was working for us?'

He gazed over her shoulder, out to sea.

'Let me make this clear. Given how much time you've spent in the UK, I think you know I can be relied upon to be as good as my word. We're interested in one trade. Give me something that might allow me to track down your agents and I'll let you go. Withhold what you know, and I'll make sure that not only is your father gravely embarrassed by this footage, but you're on every sanctions list circulated by every country any old Etonian is ever going to want to spend any time in. And, believe me, however tough you think you are, I can see very clearly you're not cut out to spend the rest of your life in a Moscow apartment block.'

'I have nothing to trade,' Mikhail said. 'Honestly.'

'How did you know Lena was working for us?'

'A message from Moscow, saying someone on board was passing information to the British and we needed to eliminate him or her.'

'Who's *we*?'

'My father and me.'

'When did you receive this information?'

'I can't remember.'

'How did you receive it?'

'We use WhatsApp, like everyone else.'

'May I see it?'

He almost handed over his phone, then thought better of it. 'This is all you're going to get. It's all I have. So do I have a deal?'

'Yes.' She held out her hand. 'Now give it to me before I change my mind.'

Mikhail scrolled through his phone and pushed it across to her. 'That message only.'

Kate took a shot of the screen and stood up. 'Good luck, Mikhail. I hope, for your sake, that we don't meet again.'

'I can assure you we won't.'

Kate slipped her phone back into her pocket. She had less than she'd hoped for, but more than he thought he'd given.

28

KATE TOOK JULIE and Danny back to London with her. The surveillance teams would de-rig and return in their own time. She got back to the office in the late afternoon and went directly to the basement, a long, dimly lit room with a dirty grey carpet, a low ceiling over walls with faded paint peeling in the corners and a bank of more than two dozen screens covering every aspect of and approach to the building, both inside and out. The hidden cameras were located as far away as Vauxhall Bridge Road and the Embankment to the north of the river, and those on the roof gave a full 360-degree view of the surrounding area.

Internal Security was run by a man called Jim, who had

spiky dark hair and large round glasses. The internal CCTV footage was stored digitally, and it took Jim a while to locate the feed that covered the Russia Desk's lifts. Kate and Julie stood either side of him as he fast-forwarded through the afternoon she had pinpointed with a little help from Mikhail.

'There,' Kate said. She checked the time. 'Five eighteen.'

'Jesus,' Julie whispered.

'Play on,' Kate instructed.

Jim hit the space bar again and they watched as Kate turned left to her office and Ian right to his. Their eyes followed Ian until he exited the frame.

'Freeze there,' she said.

They peered closer at the shot of Ian taking his phone from his pocket.

They thanked Jim and didn't speak again until they were in their own office with the door closed.

'It doesn't prove anything,' Julie said.

'The timing fits.'

'Yes. There is some circumstantial evidence. Your meeting with C is over by a quarter past five, yet Mikhail has his warning half an hour later. But it doesn't narrow things down conclusively and the fact that Ian is in a hurry to whip out his phone doesn't prove anything at all. In theory, it could still be you, or C himself.'

'Or you.'

'I thought you'd ruled me out.'

'Technically, we're all in the frame. But neither of us can claim that you're truly objective.'

Julie looked through the internal window, towards Ian's office. 'What should we do?'

Kate picked up her bag and slung it over her shoulder. 'I'll think of something. If either Ian or C asks, say I wasn't feeling well and had to go home. We'll speak in the morning.'

'Novichok poisoning?'

Kate smiled. 'A mild tummy bug should suffice.'

'Are you sure you're going to be all right?'

'I'll be fine.'

'You think I'll tell him?'

'Perhaps.'

'And that's why you made sure I saw the footage.'

'If it's Ian, no one can save him. Not even you. And you shouldn't want to. If we lose battles like this, our country doesn't belong to us any more. And it never will again.'

Kate strode home. The strap of her bag dug into her shoulder enough to give her a sore back by the time she arrived at her front door. The sole remaining member of the security detail told her the family had gone for a walk in the park.

He withdrew discreetly to the living room and left Kate in peace in the kitchen. She made herself a cup of tea and checked the mail. There was no mistaking the handwriting on the third envelope down, and her heart thumped a little harder as she opened it.

I have the proof you need, Sergei had written. *Come to the dacha. Come alone.*

The envelope had been posted from Kotka in Finland, just over the border from Russia and only a short drive from Sergei's family dacha.

Kate burnt his note and the envelope in the sink, sluiced the ash down the plughole, then sat at the kitchen table in silence.

Eventually she retrieved her coat from the hall and went out. She half expected to bump into Stuart and the children as she skirted the park, but she reached her mother's building without seeing them. She looked up, hoping the light would be off on the eleventh floor and she might be able to turn away with her conscience clear. But she was disappointed.

Lucy sat alone, gazing out over the London skyline. 'Hi, Mum,' Kate said.

There was no answer, so she repeated her greeting, but Lucy didn't stir. 'It's Kate,' she said. 'Your daughter.'

'Perhaps I did make mistakes,' Lucy said.

Kate sat next to her by the window. 'We all make mistakes.'

'Your father said you wanted him to leave me. I thought that was very cruel.'

'I just wanted him to be happy.'

'He was happy with me.' There was a long silence. 'But perhaps I did make mistakes.' Lucy turned to her. 'Where have you been?'

'At work.'

'You're always working. That was one of your father's mistakes.'

Kate had steeled herself not to rise to the bait. 'Would you like a cup of tea?'

'No, thank you, dear. I have more tea in here than a Calcutta street trader. I don't know that it's doing me much good.'

'Can I get you anything else?'

'No. Why are you here? I only saw you at the weekend.'

'I came to say goodbye.'

'For ever?'

'I don't think so. Just for a little while.'

'Well, I know how important you are. "She's practically running the government," our friends used to say. You must be *so* proud.' Lucy turned back to the window. 'Ambitious Kate. Clever Kate. All those As in all those exams. Still, you've got what you wanted.'

Kate knew her mother well enough to be certain she should leave it there, but she couldn't resist ignoring her own advice. 'And what did I want?'

'To prove you weren't me. And now you can parade your virtue and your happy family for the world to see.'

'It never ceases to amaze me how such a benign-looking

woman can have such an acid tongue,' Kate said. 'But I might be gone for a while and who knows what will happen in the meantime? So, if you want our last words together to be harsh ones, then carry on as you are.'

Lucy made her wait so long for an answer that Kate wondered whether she had toppled back into the dementia pit. Eventually, without turning her head, she said, 'I don't. Have a good trip.'

Kate stayed there as the minutes ticked by and then, very quietly, got up and left, a new layer of loneliness wrapping itself around her heart.

At home, Stuart and the children's welcome was as immediate and warm as her previous encounter had been grudging and cold. They were relieved to have her back. She went through the motions of engaging with everything they said, but she was not in the moment. She didn't know why she'd said goodbye to her mother. She couldn't bear to do it to her children. She was going away again, early in the morning, she said. It would be the last work trip for a while and she hoped she would be away only for a day or two.

Fiona asked if anything was wrong, but the evening haze continued all the way up to the moment she joined Stuart in bed. The concern in his eyes was raw. 'Are you all right, my love?' he asked. 'You don't seem yourself.'

'Don't I?'

'No. Even the children noticed. What's happened?'

'I went to see my mother. It was worse than usual.'

'Yes. She called when you were on your way home. She said you'd come to say goodbye.'

Kate lay down, facing away from her husband. 'I don't want to see her any more.'

Stuart gently coaxed her towards him. 'Your mother is a gold-plated, diamond-encrusted bitch, but that's not the reason, is it? What's happened?'

'I can't talk about it, my love. The conclusion of something.'

'Of what?'

'Everything I've been working on for as long as I can remember.'

Kate turned away from him again, so Stuart swung out of bed, circled around it and sat beside her. 'Please tell me.'

'I have to go to Russia tomorrow.'

'I thought all members of staff were banned from travelling to Russia.'

'We are. I'll have to go in under cover.'

'That's an insane risk.'

'It may be, but I don't have a choice. Someone has agreed to give me evidence—'

'Sergei?'

She couldn't bring herself to lie to him. 'Someone has made contact to say he has evidence to prove who's been betraying us. That's all I can say, so please don't question me any more or attempt to dissuade me. I wouldn't go unless I absolutely had to. I'll be all right as soon as I'm back. It'll be over. One way or the other.'

He touched her cheek. 'You know I'm here for you, don't you? Right behind you. Always have been, always will be. But are you sure it's right to go? There must be another way.'

'Yes. It is right. So, please, if you'd like me to go and sleep in the spare room, that's fine. I have to be up really early . . .'

Stuart withdrew. He switched off the light, but in the darkness she could tell that sleep eluded him, too. It was a long time before he succumbed to it.

When she was sure he was finally asleep, Kate got up. She emptied the bag she'd taken to Mykonos, filled it with cold-weather gear, then went down to the kitchen. She opened her laptop and sent a message to Ian and Sir Alan, separately but identically: *My source says he has proof of who has betrayed us. Am on my way to Russia to collect. More to follow.*

She WhatsApped Julie and Danny, asking them to meet her at Heathrow, then crept back upstairs. Gus did not stir as she kissed him, but Fiona was awake as soon as her mother's lips brushed her forehead. 'What are you doing?'

'Just kissing you before I go.'

'You never do that.'

'I always do that.'

'Not in the middle of the night.'

Kate sat on the bed beside her daughter.

'What are you doing, Mum?'

'I have an impossible few days ahead, my darling. But I have to go, and I don't think I can do it without your support.'

'What do you mean?'

'I think you know what I mean. Those men outside our house? They're there for a very good reason. And I have to settle the matter now. I don't think it's going to be easy.'

'Will you be all right?'

'Yes, I believe so. Otherwise, I don't think I could say goodbye to you and your brother. But I don't know precisely how it's going to end.'

'What about Dad? Surely you couldn't say goodbye to him either . . .'

'Exactly.'

'Is everything okay?'

'In this room? Yes. In the country? No.'

'But *you*'ll be okay? You're not going to take any . . . risks?'

'There's just something I need to do, and then it will all be over.' She smiled at her daughter. 'How is my new friend?'

'He likes you.'

'I apologized for misjudging him.'

'I know.'

'I should have apologized to you, too. I should have trusted your judgement.'

'You don't have to apologize to me. I deserve all the shit I get.'

'Well . . . some shit, perhaps. But not all of it.'

Fiona wrapped her arms around her mother's neck. Her tears were damp on Kate's cheeks. 'I love you, Mum,' she said.

It was the warmest hug she'd had for years and it made the walk out into the chill night the bleakest she had endured.

Kate called an Uber. She wanted her movements to be traced. And as she got into it, she looked back to see that her bedroom light had been switched on.

Kate spent half an hour with Danny in Carluccio's at Heathrow as he passed her the equipment and explained how she could rig it. Then they all boarded the flight to Helsinki.

29

THEY HIRED A car at Helsinki airport and didn't stop until they reached Kotka, where Sergei's letter had been posted. Kate had first come here with him on a day trip from the dacha to the Finnish capital. It had changed considerably for the better – and worse – since then. A major port in the Gulf of Finland, it had once thrived on its paper mills and other light industrial output, but globalization had taken its toll and the evidence was clearly visible in the ill-kept apartment blocks in the outer districts, gloomy now as the grey afternoon crept towards dusk. But the harbour had been spruced up and the coffee shop they stopped at, overlooking a tall ship by the quay, was a temple to Scandinavian minimalism.

They didn't talk much. They had agreed to part there. Kate would go on alone. 'Are you ready?' she asked, after they had sat in silence sipping coffee.

They nodded.

She hugged them both. 'I wish I was coming with you,' Julie said.

'No, you don't.'

'I'll happily come.'

'I need you here.'

Julie gazed at her. 'It's reckless to go alone, Kate.'

'It's reckless to go at all. Taking you would be even more so.'

Kate got into the car to forestall any further discussion and drove away without looking back. She only glanced in her rear-view mirror as she swung right at the end of the quay and saw that Julie and Danny were both still standing on the pavement, watching her.

It began to rain, the dull drizzle in flat grey, almost winter light, which made life in England feel like a ray of sunshine. And as she drove on with the pine forests to her left and the Gulf of Finland stretching away to the horizon on her right, she was so absorbed in a cascade of endlessly repeating thoughts and theories that it felt like only minutes later that she began the approach to the Vaalimaa border crossing. European and Finnish flags tugged violently in the breeze as she joined the queue.

Kate tapped her fingers on the wheel in the way Rav used to.

The rain strengthened. She inched forwards, listening to the steady beat of the windscreen wipers. The control booths were a blaze of light in the gathering gloom.

She reached the front of the queue and presented her passport, which said she was Ebba Johansson from Stockholm. Every MI6 officer at grade three or above had at least five, under assumed names, to allow them free movement. If pushed, Kate could speak fluent enough Swedish to convince anyone other than a native. But that didn't stop her chest tightening and her breath quickening as she drove across the tarmac to the Russian side.

There was a short queue there, too. She breathed deeply, and tried to prevent her heart thumping its way out of her ribcage.

As she wound down her window again, the Russian guard, a great bear of a man with a thick black beard and ruddy cheeks, grunted and stretched out a hand.

'*Dobry den*,' she said, as she gave him her passport.

He opened it without a reply, and entered her details into his computer. Kate kept her gaze away from the armed guards sheltering from the rain.

Time crawled by. She closed her eyes. If they had broken her alias and arrested her now, it would change everything.

The guard stamped her visa page violently and handed it back, still without a word. She drove on, relief flooding through her.

The rain strengthened again, billowing across her path, so that the journey onward was painfully slow. But as she turned off the main road to Vyborg and headed towards Sokolinskoye, a shaft of bright evening sunshine suddenly danced across a windscreen soon speckled with grit from the road surface.

As she bumped along the pot-holed track that finally wound through the pine forest to Sergei's parents' dacha, Kate felt suddenly, exuberantly, at home. She hadn't realized how much she had missed this place, which had remained unchanged since the Tsarist era. The track emerged beside the water, which glowed a rich orange in the sunset.

She could see a few brightly coloured dachas scattered through the woods, until the light faded and the sea merged with the sky. And at last she was on the gentle slope down towards the beach. A final turn to the right, and there it was in the sweep of her headlamps, its once neat green wooden cladding, shutters, balcony and white-framed windows faded by neglect.

Kate got out of the car. The night was eerily still. She knocked once, but no lights flickered on, so she opened the door and slipped inside. The interior was damp and chilly. A moonbeam fell across the crowded bookshelves on the far wall.

'Sergei?'

There was no answer. She slid open the box of matches that lay beside the candle on the table and lit it. The dacha had never had electricity and nothing had changed.

She glanced about her. All along one wall there were pictures of Sergei in various ice-hockey teams, beside those of the St Petersburg squad; his father had looked after their stadium. The gramophone still had pride of place on a wooden bench, with the family's vinyl records stacked neatly on the windowsill.

The room was dominated by an enormous stone fireplace, which faced a worn leather sofa and two tattered chairs. Someone had laid a fire and left a box of matches there too. Kate lit it and drew the rudimentary curtains to shut out the night.

The fire here burnt better than any she'd encountered before. She lit more candles and it wasn't long before the interior of the cabin was as cosy as she remembered it. She put on *Passion for the Russian Revolution 1917* performed by the St Petersburg Philharmonic and conducted by Yuri Temirkanov, whom Sergei had taken Kate to see on many occasions during that long winter in his city.

She went upstairs, candle in hand. There were two rooms, both with small double beds covered in furs. One was where Kate had normally slept, the other where she had longed all night to join him.

She had taken the precaution of stealing some cigarettes

from Julie, and back downstairs, she sat and smoked one by the fire. But the growing warmth of the ancient building, and of her nostalgia, still failed to put her mind completely at rest. Perhaps, she thought, that was his intention.

After a few hours of listening to the crackle of the flames and the rustling of the trees, Kate felt hungry enough to venture into the tiny back kitchen. It was damp, like the rest of the cabin, and looked as if it had recently been cleaned. There was no fridge, but the cool-box contained some borscht in a bowl covered with clingfilm and a bottle of red wine from the Crimea with a corkscrew taped to the side. There was little doubt it had been left for her. There were no curtains at the window, nothing to shelter her there from the looming menace of the forest.

Kate ate gratefully and drank some wine by the fire. And still the night delivered nothing but the occasional plaintive cry of the wind. Once or twice she moved to the front window and pulled back the curtain, but all she could see was the moonlight on the water.

Eventually Kate screwed up her courage and stepped out into the darkness. Though she was certain she hadn't left it open, her car door was banging against a naked trunk. She circled in front of the vehicle and pushed it shut.

She snapped around.

'Sergei?' she yelled, but his name was immediately smothered by the forest.

The shadows were making a fool of her. She walked

away from the house along the sand. In the days she'd come here with him, she'd loved the cabin's splendid isolation, but her surroundings were now closing in on her.

She started to see shapes and faces in the darkness. She turned back. The door to the dacha was open and yet she was certain she had closed that too. This time she locked it behind her.

'Sergei?' she called again, but there was no answer.

She picked up the wine bottle as a crude weapon and crept back into the kitchen. Once she was convinced it was empty, she swapped the bottle for a knife and climbed the stairs. There was no one in the bedrooms either.

She took the furs from the beds and carried them down to the fire, curling up in front of it, trying to console herself with the memory of having done so, often, with him. She had cast the die. Now she could do no more than wait.

Not for the first time, Kate found that intense fatigue could overcome even acute fear, and she awoke as the first hints of morning slipped in beneath the simple cotton drapes. She stood. The fire had burnt out. The air in the dacha was damp and cold again. She drew the curtains, to be greeted by autumn sunlight shimmering on a flat, calm sea. The wind had blown through, taking her fears with it.

She stepped out of the dacha and walked past the car

onto the beach. There, in the sand, she saw her footsteps from the night before.

And then another set, beside her own, which very clearly belonged to a man.

Kate looked about her. In this still, quiet place, there was no sign of life. She adjusted her clothes and walked on, her eyes fixed upon the path at the end of the beach, which led up a small incline to a clump of trees.

The sand was damp, her footfall heavy, but she could still hear her own breathing. She stopped again and looked back towards the dacha, then checked her pocket to be sure she still had her car keys.

She continued towards the trees, and there he was.

She found she could no longer move as he walked slowly towards her.

'Hello, my love,' Stuart said.

Her reply caught in her throat. But the strangest part of it was the feeling of relief that swept over her. She had come here to confront a fear that had been eating her alive. The truth was some kind of release.

'It had to be you,' she said. 'Ever since the appearance of that magically crack-free iPad. And the way you looked at Imogen. I've been such a fool.'

'The sins of the flesh can make fools of us all.'

'To betray me is one thing, but to betray your country, as you've been so clearly doing, is of a different order of magnitude, don't you think?' She slowly shook her head. 'Did the condom wrapper I found in the rubbish belong to you, after all?'

'No. My . . . liaison with Imogen . . . was very brief, and a long time ago.'

'I guess you owe it to me to explain how you could have been so stupid.'

'They start in such a small way, Kate. You know how they work. I guess it's what you do, too. And you convince yourself it won't really matter. What was I? Just a civil servant in the Department of Education. Who the fuck cared if, once in a while, I lunched at a good restaurant and shared the Whitehall gossip? They must have heard it from a million different places. But then they have you. And they start turning the screw.'

'I hope at least you're going to tell me that Imogen Conrad was the fuck of your life. That the betrayal and misery you've unleashed was, on some level, worth it.'

He took a step closer. 'You're so inflexible, Kate, so unyielding, so . . . certain. I—'

'Stay where you are and just tell me *why*.'

'Because I'm human. Because I made a mistake. Because I knew you would never accept or forgive it. Because I didn't want to hurt you. And because the price I was being asked to pay by the Russian Embassy seemed—'

'You mean the SVR.'

'Yes, yes . . . of course. I didn't understand at first who I was dealing with, or maybe didn't want to. But what they were asking for . . . it seemed a much smaller price to pay than the alternative, which would have been to destroy our love and wreck our family.'

'How long have you been fucking her?'

He shook his head. 'I said, it was only ever once – well, a few times, on foreign trips a long time ago. But they had a recording.' He looked as if he was about to cry. 'And I couldn't bring myself to break your heart.'

'*My* heart.'

'All right, my own. The children's. But what was the alternative? To confess and destroy our family? I just—'

'To confess and let me make my choice.'

'But I knew what choice you'd make. You would never have forgiven me, Kate. You know that. And what the Russians were asking for didn't seem so . . . serious, so terrible by comparison. I'm sorry, I know I should never have done it. I know you'll despise me, but—'

'Don't whine at me, Stuart. I don't want to hear that you're the victim in all of this.'

He closed in on her again, but she raised her hand silently and stepped back. She felt, suddenly, as if the ground was opening beneath her feet.

'I'm *so* sorry, Kate. I've been a fool. Worse than a fool. Much, much worse. I know the pain it will cause you. But it doesn't have to be the end of everything we've built.'

He couldn't keep the desperation from his voice now. And it only made it worse. She couldn't believe that the man she saw and heard was the one she had loved for so long, reduced to a pathetic, whining traitor and adulterer by the brief promise of Imogen Conrad's loins.

'There is a way out of this, Kate. It doesn't have to destroy everything, our family, Fiona and Gus's health and happiness—'

'A way out?' She couldn't keep the contempt from her voice.

'Please, Kate. Will you at least listen?'

'Where's Sergei?'

'They said he would come to no harm.'

'Where is he?'

'St Petersburg.'

'The SVR detained him?'

'Yes . . . yes.'

'And they faked the last letter, inviting me here to the dacha?'

'No, I think the letter was real. They've had him under surveillance.'

'So this is their fight back against the GRU and its influence on the president?'

'I don't know. I asked them not to hurt him.'

'But only if you can get me to agree to what you're about to propose?'

'Neither of us has a choice, Kate.'

'Don't we? How convenient.'

'If you agree, life can go on. I know it will be difficult

and there will of course be . . . adjustments. And I'll have to win your forgiveness. I don't doubt how tough that will be. But I forgave you your time with Sergei here—'

'You had nothing to forgive. I was *never* unfaithful to you.'

He stared at her. 'If you agree to let me be, we'll both go home to the life we love. If you don't, our children will be orphans.'

'I presume you asked Rose to step in and look after them? Or did you get on a plane and leave them to fend for themselves?'

'Of course I didn't. I dropped them at her house in London after you'd left.'

'What did you tell them?'

'That I had to do something to help you.'

'And as Viper, it's been your job,' she said, 'and I guess will now be mine – if I fall in with your plan – to support the foreign secretary once he walks into Number Ten.'

He didn't answer her.

'I assume he *is* the Russian spy we're really looking for?'

Stuart just stared at her, the colour rising in his cheeks. It was a question she knew he would have been instructed not to answer.

Kate breathed in deeply. She thought of Lena's naked body on the slab in Athens. 'You bastard,' she whispered. 'You weak, pathetic bastard. Lena is dead. Rav is dead.

And now you have the gall to stand here and ask *me* to betray my country as the price of *your* sins.'

'Kate . . .' He took another step closer.

'Stay where you are.'

'Come on, Kate. This is our life. The whole world is a cesspit. They want very little of us. Just to help, once in a while. To give their interests a hearing. Is that *so* bad?'

Kate stepped back. She wiped a tear from the corner of her eye and tried to clear her mind. 'I'm wired. And your masters must have known I would be, which is why you were instructed not to answer my question on the foreign secretary. Even now they're too smart to give me the proof I need.' She looked out across the water. 'Danny is over there, the other side of the Gulf, recording it all.' She turned back to him. 'So what now, Stuart? My husband, my love? Are you going to shoot me – and orphan our children, as you said? Are you really going to do that, with the world still listening? No,' she said. 'Of course not. Even you're not that much of a bastard. You came to say goodbye. And as for your people listening and mine recording over the water, we're at check, and checkmate will elude us both. For now, at least.'

She turned and walked away.

'Kate!'

She climbed into the car, turned the ignition and drove away. She saw a lonely figure stranded on the sand in her rear-view mirror, but she didn't turn back.

She remained staunchly upright all the way into the forest. Then she stopped, bent over the steering-wheel and cried until her stomach hurt.

She took a T-shirt from the bag she had never unpacked and wiped her eyes, then pulled the car back into the centre of the track and began the long journey home.

Epilogue

AS SCHOOL PLAYS go, it had been tolerable. Kate and Fiona chatted politely to some of the parents over warm white wine afterwards. Despite the presence of many of her own friends, Fiona had not strayed much from Kate's side all evening as they waited for Gus to emerge.

By and large, both children had responded to the events of the last few weeks as well as Kate could have hoped. She had told them the truth – what other choice did she realistically have? – and had tried her level best to make Stuart sound like any middle-aged man having a rush of blood to the head, a spin that she thought neither of them bought, but which had perhaps allowed them to lock away the darker elements of his behaviour in a place where they could deal with it another day.

Or, at least, she hoped so.

Kate had consulted a child psychologist about it, and a bereavement counsellor. They'd done their best, but neither of them could claim any experience of a man who betrays his family *and* his country.

That said, they'd already progressed quite substantially on the practical arrangements. Kate had stressed that Stuart's decisions did not change his love for them (how she'd hated having to give that speech) and she knew, despite her inner rage, that she had to do something about it. So, at some point in the future, she would facilitate the children flying to see Stuart at a neutral, pre-agreed location far from his new life in Moscow.

In the meantime, she'd had to tell them both that their father would never be able to set foot in the United Kingdom for as long as he lived, which they had found extremely hard to take.

'So he'll never be able to come to another rugby match?' Gus had asked.

Fiona had enquired, later, if he'd be able one day to walk her down the aisle.

'Only if you get married somewhere outside this country,' Kate had said. The bereavement counsellor had advised her never to lie to the children, difficult as that would undoubtedly be.

It was in the nature of her work, perhaps, that small-talk about school runs and the inadequacies of various teachers or individual school policies frequently seemed like tales from a different planet, but today Kate found it especially difficult to concentrate. She sipped the wine and nodded a lot. Gus came running in to say he'd like to go home with Pete Markell and she said that would be fine.

She noticed Fiona's gaze continually flicking back to her and took it as a sign she wanted to leave. She picked up her coat and came to retrieve her daughter. As they walked down the endless hallway, Fiona slipped her hand into her mother's.

They continued in companionable silence until they reached the entrance lobby. There, above the coat pegs, was a widescreen television, sometimes tuned to a school policy notice but otherwise defaulting to Sky News. As they passed, they saw the new prime minister, James Ryan, sweeping into Downing Street.

Kate and Fiona stopped to listen. For a man with the undoubted gift of the gab, it was a pretty uninspiring speech. 'I intend,' he said, 'to govern for all the people of this country, which is going to require some bold and visionary thinking.' It was a version of governing for the many not the few that they all trotted out. For all she knew, they might even have meant it.

Another woman had come to stand alongside them. Maggie, or perhaps Marjorie – Kate's memory failed her – a fussy mother of one of the many academic geniuses in Fiona's class, a woman whose horizons had never stretched far beyond Fulham. 'Didn't the press say he was a Russian spy?' she said. 'Honestly, what nonsense they do come up with!'

'What nonsense indeed,' Kate said.

As the woman bustled off, Kate glanced at her daughter and they smiled at each other, then walked out into the rain, hand in hand.

Acknowledgements

My wife Claudia has been a partner in the writing of all my novels and screenplays ever since we started work together on *Shadow Dancer* twenty-five years ago, so my primary and heartfelt thanks go to her. And we would not have got anywhere without Mark Lucas as our agent, who is simply a genius. But don't tell him that. We'd also like to offer heartfelt thanks to Bill Scott-Kerr, a brilliant editor, publisher and friend.

Double Agent

Tom Bradby

CORGI BOOKS

To Claudia, Jack, Louisa and Sam

Prologue

KATE COULD NOT decide whether the woman before her had a keen sense of humour, a deep-seated social autism or both. 'Why do you think *you*'d be a good fit?' she'd asked, after a long explanation of the critical role her former deputy and friend, Rav, had played in the day-to-day work of MI6's Russia desk.

'Like for like diversity replacement,' Suzy had replied, without the slightest hint of a smile.

Suzy Spencer was slim, pretty, northern, state-educated and half Vietnamese. 'The smart half,' as she'd put it. She didn't take prisoners, but that was perhaps no bad thing. 'I'm keen to spread my wings,' she said, 'I really am. The

Security Service has been good to me and I love working there, but I've always had half an eye on a life across the river here – the chance to expand my horizons, play on a wider field. I'm sure you understand.'

Kate supposed she did, though it was harder to recall, these days, as that wider playing field seemed ever more threatening.

'I'd be grateful, though,' Suzy went on, tucking a half-curl of neat black hair tidily behind her ear, 'if you could tell me a little more of what really happened to your deputy, Rav.'

'That case is closed, I'm afraid.'

'But I would need to know the background, would I not?'

'I don't believe so, no.'

'But if my life is also to be at risk—'

'It won't be.'

'Given what happened, I don't see—'

'The file is sealed. That's all I can say.'

'But these allegations that the prime minister is a Russian spy—'

'Unproven, which is why the file is sealed.'

Suzy didn't flinch, or back down. 'If I'm to take this role, Mrs Henderson, I'd appreciate knowing the background. That's all.'

Kate was tempted to wonder aloud why she was under so much pressure from her superior, Ian, to take this woman as her new deputy. Good for interdepartmental relations, he'd said airily, though he'd been fiercely territorial at even the hint of an incursion from MI5 across the river until his ambition to be the next chief had got the better of him. He'd been turning himself into the ultimate Whitehall warrior.

She leant back in her chair and stared out of the window at the morning commuters hurrying through the rain outside Vauxhall station – the unchanging backdrop to her working life. She'd ideally love to send this woman back across the river where she belonged, but she recognized that, given the questions over her own recent past, she'd probably lost the ability to determine this aspect of her future – and many others. 'It was called Operation Sigma,' she said. 'We received intelligence that a group of senior Russian intelligence officers used to meet regularly on a super-yacht owned by Igor Borodin, a former head of the Russian Foreign Intelligence Service, the SVR.'

'Of course I know who he is.'

'We – I – recruited a young au pair to take a job as nanny to Igor's grandson onboard. We persuaded her to plant a bug in his study. Shortly afterwards, we recorded him and his colleagues discussing the fact that the former prime minister had cancer and was about to resign. It was clear that one of the candidates to replace him was working for Moscow.'

'Which one?'

'Well, you'll have seen the leaks in the press—'

'The current prime minister, yes, but was it correct?'

'In the end, there was no way of proving it either way, which is why the case was sealed.'

'Did you agree with that decision?'

Kate hesitated. 'We cannot afford to see a democratically elected leader's mandate undermined without hard evidence.'

'Do you think he was guilty?'

'My view is immaterial. We need to be an evidence-based organization, particularly in this world of disinformation and lies.'

'What happened to Rav?'

'He was murdered.'

'But the coroner's verdict was suicide?'

'Look—'

'And as I understand it, he – indeed all of the work of Operation Sigma – was betrayed by an agent in your midst, planted here to assist the current prime minister's rise to office.'

Kate gazed at her icily. Bloody Ian, she thought. This woman was far too well-informed. So much for the file being sealed. 'That matter is also closed.'

'The agent – Viper – was your husband?'

'If you already know the answer, there is no need to pose the question.'

'I'm sorry, that must have been extremely hard.'

'I'm looking for a deputy, not a therapist.'

'And you won't regret hiring me. I'm very thorough.'

Kate watched the rain hammer the glass. She stood, determined to draw this audience to a close. She offered her hand. 'Thank you for coming in, Miss Spencer.'

'Was that all right?' Suzy asked, a sudden and rather startling hint of humility in her gaze. 'Did I get the job?'

'I'll let you know.'

Kate sat again and watched as Suzy retrieved her coat, then headed down the corridor. She couldn't really have had graver reservations about the woman, but that was beside the point. On this, she accepted, Ian would have his way.

But the much bigger question was simple enough: why was he so determined to inflict this outsider on them? It wasn't his idea, of that much she was certain.

1

Three weeks later

SAVE FOR A thin skein of mist that curled its way around the dome of the Basilica di Santa Maria della Salute on the far side of the Grand Canal, it was a bright, crisp, clear morning in Venice. The kind of day, in fact, that Kate Henderson might have been enjoying in any other circumstances. Sometimes being away with your family was murder.

'Why do you keep drumming your fingers on the table?' Gus asked. 'You hate it when people do that.'

Kate forced herself to stop. She smiled at Julie, who was sitting opposite. 'Your mum's a bit nervous,' Julie said.

'Under the circumstances, I think that's understandable, don't you?'

They lapsed back into silence and watched a gondolier paddle slowly past. The tables on the breakfast terrace were full of Chinese tourists, mostly glued to their phones. They didn't seem to be eating much either.

Kate couldn't resist returning to a study of her daughter's plate. 'Please eat up, love,' she said. Fiona had ordered a poached egg, Kate had insisted on toast, but neither was going anywhere near her daughter's stomach as yet.

'Just eat it, for fuck's sake,' Gus said. Remnants of his hearty breakfast were visible across a wide arc of the once pristine tablecloth.

'Gus, please!' Kate admonished. 'Don't talk to your sister like that. And don't swear.'

'Like *you* don't.'

'Not long to go now,' Julie said. 'And then we'll all be a lot happier.'

No one returned her cheerful smile. Normally, Julie's tumbling auburn hair, startling green eyes and full-figured beauty were enough to keep Kate's son mesmerized, but not that morning. 'Does Dad have a new girlfriend?' Gus asked his mother.

'For God's sake, Gus!' Fiona glared at him, her piercing blue eyes radiating fury. She'd applied make-up for the first time in months and pulled her hair back into a neat bun, which served to highlight her increasingly gaunt cheeks. There was no question that her conflict with food was on the cusp of robbing her of her looks. She got up from the table and stormed off.

'You haven't eaten,' Kate called after her. But Fiona was already halfway across the terrace. 'We're leaving in five minutes!'

'Well, *does* he?' Gus asked, once his sister had gone. In contrast to Fiona, his cheeks were becoming chubbier by the day and the pudding-bowl haircut he'd instructed her to carry out wasn't helping matters.

'Not so far as we know,' Julie said.

Gus glanced at her, then returned his gaze to his mother. 'But you said you can't ever get back together with him, so why would it be a big deal?'

Neither Kate nor Julie answered that. What could you say? Gus pushed himself to his feet. 'I'm going for a dump,' he announced.

'It's just the way you tell 'em,' Kate said, as he departed. 'I hope time spent with my children is proving a useful contraceptive,' she told Julie.

'Don't be so hard on yourselves. You've all got every reason to be tense.' Julie absent-mindedly tucked into a second croissant. She ate as she drank, as she lived, really: with an easy nonchalance.

'Have you got a cigarette?' Kate asked.

'I thought you said not in front of the children?'

'Well, they're not here, are they?'

Julie retrieved a packet of Winston's from her bag and threw them across the table. Kate took one, lit it and waved at the waiter, who reluctantly changed course and swung towards her. 'Yes,' he said abruptly. The Venice Charm School had worked a treat. She ordered another coffee.

'Because that will definitely help,' Julie said.

Kate inhaled deeply and leant back to face the Grand Canal. A half-empty vaporetto glided past in the direction of the Rialto bridge. The mist had reached the dome of Santa Maria della Salute and was now curling up into a clear blue sky. 'How are you feeling?' Julie asked.

'I'm not entirely sure. Nervous. Angry. Raw. Upset. Take your pick.'

'Do you have any idea what he *has* been up to in Moscow?'

Kate shrugged. Since she had discovered that her husband had betrayed not just their marriage but his country, she'd had no direct contact with him. After his defection, all communication had been routed through a consular official at the British Embassy in Moscow.

'*Does* he have a girlfriend?'

'I should think so, knowing him.'

'What will you say to him?'

'Nothing. What is there to say?'

'"You fucking bastard."' Julie smiled. 'That would be a start.'

'I said that already.' Kate took another quick puff and

stubbed out the rest of the cigarette. 'Come on. We can't put this off any longer.'

Kate went to brush her hair and touch up her face. She studied herself in the mirror, concluding she'd aged at least a decade in considerably less than a year. She sat on the bed, stared at the ornate ceiling and closed her eyes. This hotel had seen better days and she knew that feeling. The knot of tension in her stomach had been steadily tightening ever since she'd boarded the plane at Gatwick.

Fiona and Gus were on time for the brief stroll through to St Mark's Square. And once they were there, Julie distracted them from the slowly marching hands of time on the clock tower by reading aloud from the guidebook. 'Okay. This area by the water's edge is known as the Molo and these columns were carried home from Tyre by the Doge Michieli in 1125.' She turned the page. 'In fact, he brought back three, but one fell into the sea as it was being unloaded here. Huh. How about that?'

No one was listening to her. Kate glanced at her watch, as if it were a more reliable mark of time than the clock above them. She returned to surveying the groups of tourists across the square.

'Relax, Kate,' Julie whispered.

Kate didn't answer. She felt foolish for agreeing to meet here now. Venice was a hostile intelligence service's dream location. 'Why would they try anything?' Julie said, reading her mind. 'Stuart would never let them.'

Kate tore her eyes away from the survey of the square and glanced at her watch one more time. 'All right.' She looked at Julie. 'Just give me ten minutes, okay?'

'Yes, as we agreed.'

'What are you going to say to him?' Fiona asked. Her voice was softer now.

'I don't know, love.'

'It would help if you told us.' She glanced at her brother, who looked uncomfortable in a way he usually reserved for encounters with members of the opposite sex.

'I'm just going to talk about the arrangements for this visit and how we might work things in the future. If there's somewhere you'd be able to stay with him and so on.'

'Are you going to talk to him about what happened?'

'I don't think so. I'm not sure how that would serve any of us.' She rubbed her daughter's shoulder affectionately, but got no response.

Kate set off across St Mark's Square, weaving her way through the shoals of slow-moving tourists, then turning into Ala Napoleonica. Once she was out of view of Julie and the children, she paused by a shop and pretended to browse the jewellery display in the window as she glanced back the way she had come.

Nothing was amiss. Perhaps Julie was right. Why would anyone be watching her?

Kate walked on and paid her entry fee for the Correr Museum further down the street. She went into the cool, quiet interior and browsed through the costume section, with its fine collection of ancient fashions and silk banners.

'Hello, love.'

She swung around. Stuart was dressed in black jeans and a blue T-shirt, with a stylish leather jacket and trainers. He had shorter hair and designer stubble. He'd lost some weight, half a stone, perhaps more. He looked much more like the funny, irreverent young man she'd fallen so heavily in love with all those years before.

The one she'd known instantly she wanted to build a life with.

'You look well,' he said.

'I don't.' The sense of contentment she'd convinced herself she'd embraced appeared to have deserted her. She felt like a teenager again, giddy, uncertain, embarrassed.

'Where are the kids?'

'They're with Julie. They'll be here in a minute. I thought it was best to have a few minutes together first, just to . . . discuss practical things.' But even as she said it, she knew that wasn't true. Did it show?

'Of course. How are they?'

'They were all right for the first few months, but things have got a lot more complicated since then. You'll . . . see. Gus is taciturn, even by his standards, and Fi has got very weird around her food.' She felt on surer ground discussing their children.

'Is she seeing a therapist?'

'They both are. She's perilously close to anorexia, but we're monitoring it closely.'

Stuart nodded. It had always been so easy to talk to him. And it was, strangely, still. 'I'm sorry,' he said. 'How are you?'

'I'm fine.' She looked up at him and suddenly, through her disorientation, anger burst through. What did he expect her to say? That after seventeen years of marriage, more than twenty together, she had felt cleaved in two by his departure? 'I'm fucking fantastic, Stuart. What do you think?'

'I'm sorry.'

'And stop saying that.'

'What else would you like me to say?'

Kate bit her lip. She breathed out slowly, her head spinning, her stomach churning. It was like their first evening together, but without the giddy sense of possibility. 'How's life in Moscow?'

'Not much fun. I get a paltry pension for my betrayal, which is hard to live on. I'm trying to find work, but they have little interest in helping. They treat me as if I'm a vaguely infectious disease.' He smiled bitterly. 'Which perhaps I am. The British Embassy does a good job of killing off my chances with any company that checks in with them, so I'm a bit screwed, to be honest. But no more than I deserve.'

'Do you get a flat?'

'Yes. And a car. But both are pretty decrepit.'

They were silent for a moment. Kate stared at the floor, which seemed the safest place to look. 'I just wanted to discuss how things are going to work with the children in the future,' she said. 'I'm sure we'd both agree that their interests are paramount.'

'Of course.'

'I don't know what you were thinking, but—'

'I'll fall in with whatever you want to do. I'm sitting in Moscow, doing nothing. So . . .' he shrugged '. . . this will be all I'm living for. And they don't seem to care what I do or where I go.'

'Of course they care. They'll be watching.'

'I doubt it. I think my days of usefulness, or at least relevance, are at an end. The only issue is cash. I don't have much spare money, so I don't know how frequently I'll be able to travel around Europe.'

'You're surely not expecting me to—'

'I'm not expecting anything, Kate. I deserve everything that's coming to me.'

Tears crept from the corners of Kate's eyes and rolled down her cheeks. She wiped them abruptly away. 'My love . . .' Stuart stepped forward. Kate raised her hand and took a pace back. 'You know I'd do anything for a shot at redemption, right?'

'That's never going to happen, Stuart, and I'll stop bringing the children to see you if you go down that road.' She was surprised at how definitive that sounded.

'I'm sorry,' he said again.

The pain in him cut her like a knife. 'I need to go,' she

said. 'I'll be in touch about how you see the children.' She turned away.

'Why did you come, love?' he asked.

She faced him. 'What do you mean?'

'You could have sent the children up here on their own or with Julie. So why did you come?'

'I . . . I don't know.'

'Did you want to see my pain, to see if it looked anything like yours?'

'Perhaps.'

'Well, if you hoped to see a ruined man, I trust you weren't disappointed.'

'This is perhaps going to come across more harshly than I really mean it to – since I'm still too confused to know what I think about anything – but I would say that it's that kind of self-absorption and, indeed, self-pity that got you into this mess in the first place.'

She turned away and walked out. Julie and the children were waiting just outside the entrance. 'He looks well,' Kate said to Fiona and Gus. 'You go on up.'

Kate watched them disappear inside. Despite herself, the tears began to roll down her cheeks again. Without a word, Julie linked arms and led her friend slowly back towards St Mark's Square. They walked past the Doge's Palace and sat by the water's edge. Julie waited while Kate composed herself. 'So,' she said eventually. 'How was he?'

'Let's not talk about it.'

It was a glorious spring day now, the lagoon busy with the morning traffic. They watched a glistening white cruise liner heave into view. It seemed vast, a giant from another world entering a Toytown harbour. 'You want me to fetch you an ice cream?' Julie asked.

'Getting even fatter is the last thing I need.'

'Somehow that seems to be the least of your worries.'

'Perhaps you could explain one day how you eat so much and stay so trim.'

'I don't think about it.'

'That can't be true.'

'It is.' Julie was watching a shifty-looking man standing by the waterfront. He was theoretically selling leather bracelets. 'Perhaps we should just lie in the sun and smoke something medicinal.'

Given their employer's strictures in relation to illegal drugs – and the questions on the subject in routine positive vetting – there were many things Kate could have said to this, but she'd decided long ago that Julie's weekend penchant for dope and possibly more had better remain off-limits. She was the most loyal friend and colleague you could wish for. 'Could you at least pretend that you understand the rules of our employment?'

'You think anyone cares?'

'Yes.'

'It would do you good.' Julie waited. 'All right, so what do you want to do?'

'Drown myself.'

Julie stood. 'Come on. That isn't your style. It's a beautiful day. Let's go for a walk.'

Kate had agreed that Stuart would have Fiona and Gus for three hours, so she and Julie had plenty of time to fill. They headed for the Rialto bridge, then the Ponte degli Scalzi by the station and then to the Campo Santa Margherita, finally coming back across the Ponte dell'Accademia. 'You sure as hell do like to walk,' Julie observed, once they had returned to the tourist hordes in St Mark's Square. They had intended to catch a boat across to San Giorgio Maggiore, but they were out of time and patience and opted to go for a drink in Harry's Bar instead, which was a mistake. 'It would have been cheaper to be mugged,' she concluded.

Stuart had agreed he would WhatsApp Kate with a place to meet in the vicinity of St Mark's, but at two o'clock she still hadn't heard from him. She sent him a message, but there was no reply. 'What's he playing at?'

'Did you definitely say two?'

'Definitely.'

They left the bar and went to wait in the square. Two fifteen came and went and then the clock tower crept past the half-hour. Kate messaged again: *We can't do this if you won't keep to your word.*

At two forty-five Kate started to worry in earnest. 'Do you think we should call the office?' she asked Julie. Kate's bosses at MI6 in Vauxhall had concluded a meeting between a traitor and his children was not a matter for them to worry themselves with but had agreed to allow Julie to accompany her superior 'just in case'.

'Not yet. Give him another fifteen minutes before we start to panic.'

They watched the clock in silence, but a few minutes later, Kate's phone buzzed. *So sorry, didn't see the time. Just finishing pizza. Could we meet in the Chiesa San Giuliano – a couple of minutes from St Mark's?*

All right, she shot back.

It was a short walk to the church and Kate asked Julie to wait outside. The interior was chilly and her breath hung in the air as she glanced around at the church's baroque splendour. She could see no sign of Stuart or the children, so she walked up to the front of the nave and looked up at the giant oil painting of the Crucifixion on the wall beside her, a brooding, even foreboding window to a different, more spiritual age. She turned back to face the entrance. 'Stuart?'

As she started to retrace her steps, she swung around to confront a shadow shifting in the corner of her eye. A man in a dark raincoat was pointing a Browning at her stomach.

2

HE HAD A lean, angular face, with severely acne-scarred skin. Two colleagues emerged from the darkness to join him, pistols hanging loosely at their sides. 'What do you want?' Kate asked.

'Your children are safe. Come with us and they will not be harmed.' The men spoke Russian, of course. She cursed her complacency.

'Come where?'

'Do as you are told.'

'I need to tell—'

'No! Don't be foolish,' the man told her. 'It is not worth the risk.'

They ushered her out of the side door of the church and hurried her along the smooth cobblestones of Campo de la Guerra. It was a relatively wide street that led down to the canal, lined with pastel-coloured houses, shops and cafés. It was quiet by the standards of central Venice, but there were enough people for her to make a scene if she wished to. Kate glanced over her shoulder. The men had slipped their Brownings into their pockets.

At the end, she was forced into a launch. She turned to face them. 'Where are you taking me?'

'Save your voice,' the acne-scarred man told her.

'My children will wonder what's happened to me.'

'They're safe with your husband.'

'Is this his doing?'

The man motioned for her to sit. She refused. The launch set off gently, motoring deeper into the heart of the city in all its rambling, faded glory, the buildings around her a patchwork of peeling paint, plasterwork and exposed brick. As they crossed under the first wrought-iron footbridge, a group of Chinese children watched her pass.

The canal swung to the right, opening out to the baroque splendour of the church of Santa Maria della Fava, with its ochre bridge and peaceful square, full now of tourists sheltering from the city's busier thoroughfares.

Just beyond the church, the launch swung right again and immediately glided to a halt by a villa, with stone steps that stretched down to the water's edge. A young man in a smart white uniform was waiting for her. He offered his hand. She did not take it. 'Please follow me, Mrs Henderson.'

He led her through a cool, damp, spartan lobby, which looked as if it flooded when the tide was high, and up another set of stone steps to a richly furnished hall. A chaise longue upholstered in burgundy velvet lined one wall beneath what looked like a Picasso. A coffee-table stood alongside what looked like a solid gold Buddha the size of a small horse.

She followed the man up to a sitting room on the floor above, where the furnishings were lighter, to fit with the sun streaming in from full-length windows opened to the balcony. 'Please wait here,' the man said.

Kate stepped outside. It was very bright now, the sun warm on her face, the palms and bougainvillaea in pots curling over the lip of the iron railings. She returned to the room and walked around it, assessing the art that graced its expensive walls: a Monet certainly, another Picasso probably – no, for sure, now she looked closer – a Cézanne, Van Gogh's self-portrait with a bandaged ear.

'You have an eye for a master?'

Kate swung around. Mikhail Borodin stood in the doorway, six feet two of tanned, lean muscle. 'I have an eye for value. The paintings in this room must be worth two hundred million or more.'

'More, I think. But this is my home, my true home. And

it is my indulgence. As my father says, you cannot take it with you.'

'The art, or the money?'

'Both. Can I get you something to drink?'

'What have you done with my children?'

'Nothing. They are with Stuart, as Alexei should have told you. They are quite safe and I will return you to them within the hour, however this conversation progresses. I give you my word.'

'Your word's not worth a great deal.' Mikhail Borodin was the son of Russia's former intelligence chief, Igor. They had history from Operation Sigma, and not of the good kind.

'Well, let's see. I am sorry for the guns and the strong-arm tactics, but I didn't think you would come otherwise. Now, can I get you a drink?'

'Just get on with it.'

He gestured at the sofa. 'Please, sit . . .'

'I'd rather stand.'

'Come on, Kate, please . . . I am not going to hurt you.'

Kate did as she was instructed. Mikhail poured a glass of water from a jug filled with ice and fruit on the table. 'Cigarette?' He offered her a silver case.

'I'm trying to give up.'

'Wise. How have you been?' Perhaps it was Kate's imagination, but he seemed nervous suddenly.

'You've just kidnapped me in the heart of a European

city. You're on very thin ice. So get on with it – and whatever you have to say had better be good.'

'Oh, so it is like the time you filmed me having sex with a man I had met in a bar and then tried to blackmail me?'

Kate didn't answer.

Mikhail swirled the water in his glass. 'As you can probably tell, I am here on my own. My wife, my son and my father are all in Moscow.'

'So what?'

'Well, there is a reason for that. They are being prevented from leaving.' He leant forward. 'I'll cut straight to it. There has been a coup in Moscow. The GRU has finally seduced the president and got what it has always wanted. Control.'

Kate kept her eyes locked on him. The rivalry between Russia's Foreign Intelligence Service, the SVR – successor to the notorious KGB – and the GRU, the country's military intelligence organization, was legendary.

'Durov has been suspended,' Mikhail said.

'When?' Vasily Durov had been hand-picked by Mikhail's father, Igor, to succeed him as head of the SVR.

'Last week. He is being interrogated at an old KGB summer camp outside Moscow. Yesterday my father was supposed to join me here with my wife and son. They were all prevented from boarding the aircraft in Moscow.'

'Why?'

'No reason has been given. They were allowed to go home,

but they are under house arrest and are being watched around the clock.'

Kate kept her eyes on Mikhail, who was sweating now. His father was a long-standing friend of the Russian president, so she didn't think it likely he had been suddenly cast out from his inner circle. So unlikely, in fact, was it that it might just be true, however. 'How did Vasily and your father fall out with the president?'

'I don't know and neither do they. But . . . he's an unpredictable man. Normally it has to do with money, or loyalty, the only things he cares about. You understand that. No one can ever consider themselves truly a friend, and the closer you get, the more in danger you may be.'

'What does this have to do with me?'

'My father has been around long enough to know that the wind has changed. They will interrogate Durov until they have squeezed everything possible out of him. They will then put him on trial for corruption. In a week, or two at the most, they will arrest my father and take him to the same place. They are not going to bother with a trial for him.'

'My heart bleeds for you both.'

Mikhail ignored the remark. Having finished the first cigarette, he took another and pushed the case across to her. She accepted this time and leant closer so he could light one for her.

'My father has an offer. But we would need to move very quickly. In return for residency, the guarantee of a passport, freedom of movement in America and Europe, assurance that he will be able to keep his wealth, and security protection for life, he is prepared to bring you evidence that your prime minister is a spy working for Moscow.'

'Oh, yes?' Kate could feel the knot tightening in her stomach. The threat, even the likelihood, that this had long been true was unsettling enough, but hard evidence would be like a nuclear device exploding at the heart of British democracy. She shuddered at the thought she might be the one to detonate it.

'You should not make light of this.'

'What kind of evidence?'

Mikhail leant back, dragging deeply on his cigarette, as if to allow time for his offer to sink in. 'Payments, very large ones,' he said. 'Made to your prime minister, James Ryan, over many years.'

'The evidence my friend Rav managed to find before you killed him?'

'That had nothing to do with me – or my father.'

'We're not interested.'

'Oh? And what if I said we have even more than that on offer?'

'Such as?'

'Kompromat.'

'Our prime minister's lax personal morals are legendary. There can hardly be anyone in the country who doesn't know of his many affairs.'

'He would not survive this.'

'Oh, Christ, don't tell me – animals?'

'Your flippancy does you no credit. Underage girls.'

Kate felt the ground being cut from under her. Mikhail's gaze was locked on her. 'How young?'

'Fifteen – fourteen in one instance. He can be heard asking their ages *before* he has sex with them.'

Kate tried to compose herself. 'Where? He can't have been stupid enough to do it in Moscow?'

'Kosovo, during the war there.'

It made sense. The prime minister had once been an army officer and he had certainly served in Kosovo. Before he died, Rav had identified Ryan's female interpreter at the time as a probable Russian agent.

'If you always had this kind of kompromat on our new prime minister, why did you need to pay him?'

'As well as being profoundly immoral, your prime minister is extremely greedy. At the time, we were not certain even the kompromat was enough.'

'How do we know the video isn't fake?'

'Because when you see it you will know it is not.'

'Let me watch it now.'

'No. Only when they have accepted our offer.'

Kate finished her cigarette, stood up and went to the window. She watched the shifting eddies in the water below. 'You have a nerve, I'll give you that. Why should I trust you at all? I recruited Lena Sabic. She was a blameless young girl who'd had life stacked against her. I bullied and blackmailed her to come and work for you. And you murdered her. You cut her throat and left her for me to find in Greece.'

'I didn't do anything.'

Kate wasn't listening. 'And then, when my beloved friend Rav had managed to unearth some evidence of those payments you made to our prime minister, you murdered him, too, and tried to make it look like suicide by hanging the poor bastard from the light flex in his flat.'

'Not my decision, either.'

Kate turned to him. 'So, just to be really clear about this, hell will freeze over before I do anything to facilitate your very kind offer.'

'Is that so? We ask for nothing but a passport and protection in return for the greatest gift any intelligence agency has ever been offered and you turn me down flat? What would your superiors make of that?'

'Right now, I don't care.'

'I don't believe you. You want to know how your file in Moscow Centre concludes? The most conscientious – and *ambitious* – officer currently working for MI6 in London, tipped to be the first female head of the Secret Intelligence Service. A woman who regularly drives herself well above and beyond the call of duty, an officer who always appears to be trying to prove herself to someone or something, whose life has been dominated by the single-minded pursuit of exceptionality.' He looked at her steadily, daring her to deny it. 'And yet you want me to believe that this same officer is going to turn down an offer of such gravity without even passing it on to her superiors?' Mikhail shook his head. He held himself with the poised self-confidence common to all old Etonians. And, unlike his father and many others in Moscow, he had a sophisticated understanding of Western institutions and social mores, gained while he was educated in Britain, which had been Igor's intention.

'If I'm as ambitious as you say, I'd keep it to myself. You think my bosses want to know that you have cast-iron evidence their new prime minister is a Russian spy? They had a heart attack at the idea he *might* be. Certainty would kill them.'

'Come on, Kate.'

'You can call me Mrs Henderson.'

'Well, whatever you want me to call you, we both know one thing is true beyond doubt. Right now, our agent in Downing Street is passing the details of every file that crosses his desk – which, since he is the prime minister, means *every* file of any note, secret or otherwise – straight through to Moscow Centre and the office of our president. And I am offering you the chance to stop this calamitous threat to everything you hold dear.' Despite his polished air, a note of panic had crept into Mikhail's voice. But, then, fifty years with hard labour in a modern Russian gulag was probably an even less enticing prospect than the KGB hellholes of old. Even Eton wasn't preparation for that.

'You're a murderer.'

'We both know I am nothing of the kind.'

'Lena and Rav would say different if they were here.'

'I understand how upset you have been. We will offer something in good faith: the next step in the war on the West.'

'Which is?'

'A revolution in Estonia. The Night Wolves have bought a farm, just over the border, close to Narva.'

'Where?'

'We don't know precisely. It is a GRU operation. There will be unrest, the Wolves will burst from their lair and come to the aid of the Russian minority . . . so you will have something like war, as in Georgia and Crimea, but this time in a NATO ally. What will your prime minister do then? Will he consider himself to be bound by the famous Article Five? Is an assault on one really an attack on all?'

'When is this going to happen?'

'Soon. That is all I can tell you. But we will want to know you accept our offer by tomorrow night at the latest.'

'That's impossible, as you well know.'

'Then make it possible, Mrs Henderson. That is your job and everyone agrees you are good at it.'

'Show me the video.'

'Not here, not now. First, we need to know you accept our

offer in principle. Then we can agree to meet again. But we have very little time. I have been summoned back to Russia and I can hold them off only for so long.' He shook his head. 'We have our backs to the wall, Kate. If you won't accept what I propose, we will go to the Americans or the Germans. And once the deal is done, your superiors in London will inevitably learn that you rejected our offer.' Mikhail came towards her with a small scrap of paper. On it was written a number. 'That's how to contact me. But I ask you to be quick. I don't think we have more than a few days at best and, whatever you might think of me or indeed my father, you may have many years to regret this opportunity being lost.'

Kate slipped the paper into her pocket. 'Don't ever use my children like this again,' she warned, as she moved to the door.

'It was not your husband's doing. You should know that.' Kate stopped, turned back to face Mikhail. 'He cuts a somewhat pathetic figure in Moscow. For what it is worth, I think you are the love of his life.'

'Goodbye, Mikhail.'

'I think you mean *"au revoir"*. We'll meet again.'

Kate walked down to the ground-floor lobby and out on to the launch. 'Take me back to my children, please,' she instructed the man with the pockmarked face. Her chest had constricted so violently that she felt as if she was about to have a heart attack, the anxiety that had been her constant companion for months now threatening to consume her.

3

KATE WAS MET back at the church by the implacable set of her fifteen-year-old daughter's jaw. 'Where the hell were you?'

'I—'

'You promised you weren't going to work while you were here.'

'How did you—'

'Dad said you had to take a work call.'

'Yes . . . yes. I'm really sorry.' Kate knew better than to choose this moment to get into an argument with her daughter. She could see the hurt in her eyes. There were also scratch marks on her arm, a recent worrying indication of her tendency to self-harm. Gus, meanwhile, stared resolutely at the floor. Whatever had happened in the meeting with their father had evidently shaken them both. 'Let's go,' she said. 'Maybe we can find an ice cream.'

As the children turned away, Julie whispered, 'What the hell happened?'

'Pas devant les enfants.'

'I do speak French, you know,' Fiona threw over her shoulder, 'and in six days' time, I'll basically be an adult anyway.'

That sounded like a threat rather than an abstract statement of fact, but Kate let it ride. They did get ice creams on the way back, and sat on a wall by the canal in front of their hotel, eating them in silence.

Once inside, Kate left her children in their room to simmer down, and tackled Julie first. 'Mikhail and Igor's thugs,' she explained. 'They took me at gunpoint to Mikhail's fancy palazzo.'

'What did they want?'

'To defect.'

Julie looked at her as if she had just gone mad, her vivid green eyes clouded by confusion.

'They are offering us the video they claim to have been using as kompromat against the prime minister. It shows him having sex with underage girls.'

'Did you see it?'

'No. Only if we accept their offer in principle.'

'What if it's a fake?'

'He claims we'll know it isn't.'

'I thought they could fake anything, these days . . . But why would they want to defect?' Julie couldn't keep the incredulity from her voice. She sat down on her bed.

'Mikhail says his father and Vasily Durov have fallen out with the Kremlin and been ousted in a coup orchestrated by the GRU. He says Durov is under arrest, which likely means bound for Siberia at best, execution at worst. He and his father are desperate to flee to the West before the net closes on them.'

'Did you believe him?'

'It doesn't matter whether I believe him or not. If the video exists, if it's real – and he promised evidence of the payments they've made to the prime minister, too – then we have no choice. There was more. As a gesture of goodwill, he said we should know the Kremlin is planning some kind of coup in Estonia.'

'What?'

'There will be a "threat" to the local Russian population in Narva – protests or riots or civil disorder. The Night Wolves have bought a farm just outside, stacked it with enough weaponry to start a war. They will come to the aid of their "countrymen".'

'Why the Night Wolves?'

'Plausible deniability. A bunch of old army vet bikers. How would we prove they took their orders from the Kremlin?'

Julie contemplated that in silence. Neither of them needed to articulate the fact that this was the kind of confrontation that could spark a third world war. 'Are you going to call London?' she asked.

'No. I was thinking about driving to Rome to file from the embassy, but we don't have time. Let's go straight to the flight. I'll have to drop the kids off at home, but I'll text Danny now and see what he can find out. The CIA is bound to have good coverage on the border.'

'I've never actually seen the Night Wolves in action, so what—'

'Just volume at this stage. Any farm with a lot of outbuildings or barns, any sign of lorries moving or parked on a significant scale. Motorbikes, obviously. Any recent transactions recorded in the Estonian Land Registry, otherwise a list of all properties owned by ethnic Russians.'

'Should I talk to Karen in Tallinn?' Karen White was their station chief in the Estonian capital.

'No. And don't do anything to alert the Estonians either. As soon as I've dropped the kids I'll tackle Ian and the chief and we'll go from there.'

Kate went next door to speak to her children. Fiona was in the loo. Gus was on his bed, playing Angry Birds on his iPad. Kate came to sit next to him. 'Was it all right?' she asked, caressing the back of his head. He pulled away. 'What happened?' she asked.

'Nothing happened.'

'You both seem . . . upset.'

'I'm fine.'

'Was it nice to see Dad?'

The bathroom door opened and Fiona stepped out. 'Dad burst into tears. He said he was miserable in Moscow. He has no friends, no money and no life. He told us he had made one terrible mistake and he would pay for it for the rest of his life.'

Kate shook her head slowly. 'He shouldn't have said that.'

'Why not? It's true.'

'Because it loads the burden of his mistakes on to you.'

'He only made one.'

'Well, that's not quite true, is it?'

'It's absolutely true.'

Kate could see her daughter was spoiling for a fight. Fiona took off her hairband and shook her hair free. It was never a good sign. Kate knew she should walk away. 'He betrayed us and chose to betray his country,' she said quietly.

'He didn't betray Gus and me.'

Kate stood up. 'I'll meet you in Reception in twenty minutes. We're a long way past the check-out time I agreed, so don't be late.'

'Why won't you accept his apology?' Fiona asked. She looked as if she was about to smash something or burst into tears, or both.

'Let's talk about this calmly when we get home.'

'That's just an excuse not to talk about it at all.'

'I'll see you in Reception in twenty minutes.'

Kate went to her own room and sat on her bed. She noticed that her hands were shaking, got to her feet and went into the bathroom. She stared at herself in the mirror. Her face was white, her eyes bloodshot. She looked exhausted, which was no surprise. The acute stomach and back pain that had been plaguing her had returned with a vengeance. It was as if someone had wrapped a belt around her chest and was slowly tightening it.

She felt physically terrible. She walked to her bed, lay down and tried to concentrate on the breathing exercises the psychologist she had been seeing had recommended. They seemed to make no bloody difference at all.

She forced herself upright, packed the last of her belongings and walked down the grand staircase to Reception.

They caught the four o'clock flight home, the entire journey conducted in more or less total silence. Julie had made a concerted effort to jolly the children along before they boarded the plane until she received a text at Passport Control. After that she'd retreated rapidly into herself. Kate made no headway in winkling out of her what the trouble was.

She left Fiona in theoretical charge of her brother at home in Battersea and reached MI6's Vauxhall Cross headquarters just after eight. She stopped off at the ops room on the second floor, where she found Julie sitting next to Danny in front of a bank of computer screens. 'I think we've found it,' Julie said.

'Grab a seat,' Danny instructed. He had long dark hair, piercing blue eyes and pretty much always wore a black T-shirt, blue jeans and threadbare sneakers. He had a Chinese dragon tattooed around the side and back of his neck and the kind of easy smile that could stop grown women in their tracks. Or perhaps it was just Kate. She suspected he and Julie had once been an item but, if so, it was a rare outbreak of common sense on her friend's behalf: her taste in men was usually abysmal.

Kate did as she had been told. The floor was covered with styrofoam coffee cups and takeaway food cartons that had yet to make it to the bin in the corner. In his eating habits, and the curious absence of any visible impact on his waistline, Danny provided another painful reminder of her former deputy, Rav, who'd had a similar penchant for chaining himself to his desk in a tunnel of intense concentration. It was what made Danny – and had made Rav – so good at his job.

The images streamed from the CIA satellite covering this section of Estonia were so clear you could have seen a pebble in the grass. They were looking at a collection of outbuildings, but the screen next to them had a wider view of a village. 'Puhlova,' Kate said.

'You know it?' Julie asked.

Kate had met a Russian Army colonel there about a

decade previously. He'd promised information on the state of Russia's nuclear arsenal in return for very large cash payments, but she'd not believed a word he'd said and had turned down his offer flat.

'It changed hands two months ago,' Julie said. 'The new owner is a business registered in Helsinki.'

Danny closed in on the tyre tracks in the mud. Kate could see exactly what he was thinking: a lot of tracks, too narrow for a tractor, much too wide for a car. 'Hard to be sure until we see some movement,' he said. He zoomed in on a patch of grass just outside one of the buildings. Cigarette butts lay everywhere. 'A lot of workers for a small farm.'

'You find anything on the firm?'

Julie shook her head. 'A holding company in Geneva, another in Bern, then to Belize and finally Panama. If it's not the Russians, it's someone else with a lot of cash to spend covering their tracks.'

'How far back can you go?'

Kate's question was to Danny and he pulled up another screen and started to rewind the footage on it rapidly. 'Only a week, but that's what's weird. I checked the Met Office records. It rained really heavily nine days ago, so these tracks would have been obliterated if they'd been there before then. They must have been made after the deluge. But there's been no movement in or out of these barns in the past week.' He stopped rewinding and minimized the screen, pulling up another. 'We started casting around. We looked closer to the border . . . but neither of us could find anything. So then we went further away.' He froze the footage and closed in on a building by the Baltic. 'This is a hotel in Silamae on the beach. A congenial place to plan a coup.'

Beneath a lean-to beside the hotel, the rear wheels of several motorbikes were clearly visible. 'Not an army, exactly,' Danny concluded, 'but maybe the vanguard.'

'That's great,' Kate said. 'What's that on?'

'PCR2.'

'See what else you can find on both sides of the border.'

Kate left them to their work, then thought better of it and doubled back. She sat again, so that she was close to Danny: the people at the other end of the ops room would be out of earshot. 'Talk me through faking a video.'

'What kind?'

'If someone wanted to create a fake kompromat video, is it possible to do it convincingly enough to fool us?'

'I guess that really depends. What kind of video are we talking about exactly?'

'A sex tape.'

'It's hard to know without seeing it. I guess it would depend on the quality of the lighting, the camera angles . . .'

'But, in theory, is it possible that we could be completely convinced by a fake?'

Danny glanced over his shoulder to check no one was listening. 'In theory, yes. Who you are talking about?'

'The prime minister, say, or the US president.'

Danny nodded. 'You could fake footage of either of them giving a speech they never gave saying things they never said – and people have.'

'How?'

'Well, they've given thousands of speeches, so you feed all those into a powerful piece of software called a neural network. You direct the software to learn the visual associations between particular words and their mouths as they say them. And if you want the final version to be particularly convincing, you'd get the software to compete with a copy of itself, one generating the imagery, the other trying to spot the fakes. They call them generative adversarial networks and it's very effective. The computer goes on improving its work until it finds a way to beat the competing network that is trying to weed out the fakes, so you get pure computational hallucinations.'

'What about a sex video?'

'Same principle, though probably easier in reality. You just need to make the statistical connections between the individual you want to focus on and the aspect of his behaviour you wish to fake – in this case movement.'

'Could you spot a fake?'

'Probably. The GAN images have a creepy edge, though the software is improving all the time. The Russians might be ahead of us on this.'

'Could I spot a fake?'

'It all depends on the clarity of the image. If there is plenty of light and the visual and audio quality are good, you'd probably have a good sense of whether it's real or not. But the lower the quality, the easier it might be to pass off as a fake.'

Kate touched Danny's arm. 'Thanks.' She made a brief phone call to their liaison officer at GCHQ in Cheltenham to check whether they had any information on the claims Mikhail had made of a coup inside Moscow Centre against his father and Vasily Durov. She said they had heard nothing of the kind.

Kate walked up to the chief's office on the fifth floor. C, otherwise known as Sir Alan Brabazon, was waiting for her, looking out at the lights of the House of Commons twinkling on the far side of the river. As he turned to face her, she thought how much he had aged these past six months, his thick curly hair now flecked with grey and his hooded eyelids locked under a permanent frown. His wife, Alice, had seen her cancer return – this time to the liver – and her life was now almost certainly measured in weeks rather than months. He walked to his desk and picked up the phone. 'I'll get Ian up here.' He dialled and waited. 'She's here,' he said, and replaced the receiver.

He went to the sofa and chairs in the corner and motioned Kate to sit. He tapped his tortoiseshell reading glasses against his knee, his hands weathered from the hours he spent in the garden at his country home just north of Winchester. 'How was Stuart?' he asked.

'He burst into tears when he was alone with the kids.'

'I'm not surprised. A lifetime in Moscow probably wasn't what he had in mind.'

'He says they're treating him like a pariah.'

'Perhaps, but I doubt it.'

Kate had only a moment to consider this before Ian Granger burst in, as was his habit these days. He'd always liked to stage an entrance. *'Aghamo mshvidobisa,'* he said. Even by the standards of the service, he had a gift for languages and liked to remind everyone of this by peppering routine conversations with different greetings – in this case, Georgian.

'I fear this is not going to be good news.' He crossed his legs to reveal a brand new pair of suede Chelsea boots that matched the designer black jeans he had recently taken to wearing to the office. He now eschewed Savile Row tailoring, the qualities of which had once been one of his standard dinner-party riffs, and rarely seemed to bother with a haircut either, his long blond curls tumbling over the collars of his Ted Baker shirts. Sir Alan was much too aloof to notice Ian's cry for mid-life attention.

'Coffee, tea?' Sir Alan asked.

'Not at this hour,' Ian said. He'd discovered 'wellness' lately and told anyone who would listen it was 'dangerous' to drink caffeine past noon.

'Something stronger?'

Ian was about to decline, but then had second thoughts. 'Well, if you're offering.'

Sir Alan went to a cupboard in the corner, took out a bottle of Glenfiddich and poured three glasses. He didn't ask Kate whether she wanted ice or water.

Ian didn't wait for Sir Alan to take his seat before turning to Kate. 'Give us your worst,' he said, with what he considered his megawatt smile.

Kate tried not to let her irritation show. 'Mikhail Borodin and his father, Igor, want to defect. Mikhail says that Igor and Vasily Durov have been the victims of a coup in Moscow Centre, orchestrated by the GRU. He says that both men are under house arrest already. He's offering the video he says was used as kompromat to force the prime minister to work for them, along with evidence of the cash payments made to him over the years.'

'Do I dare ask what the video shows?' Ian said.

'He claims it's of James Ryan having sex with underage girls while he was an army officer in Kosovo. I asked to see it, but he said he would only show it to us once we accept his offer in principle.'

'What do they want?' Sir Alan asked.

'Residence here, passports – and a guarantee they'll be able to use the assets they have stored in the West. They also want to ensure freedom of movement throughout Europe and America. I said that wasn't in our gift.'

'And, no doubt, they're in a hurry.'

'Yes. There was one other thing. He offered what he called a parting gift. He says the GRU has been planning a coup in Estonia, which is now imminent. The Night Wolves have bought a farm just outside Narva and stored enough weapons there to start a small war. The Kremlin will create some kind of crisis involving the Russian minority and the Night Wolves will come to their aid.'

'And the Center Party will call for Moscow to intervene,' Sir Alan said, tapping his glasses against his leg again. Kate noticed some dark stubble beneath both sides of his chin, missed with careless shaving. It was most unlike him.

'We think we've probably found the farm. It's on PCR2.'

Sir Alan got up and went to his desk. Ian and Kate stood behind him as he put on his glasses and looked at the satellite feeds. 'The place by the beach on the right is where we think some of them are staying. If you close in, you can see the rear wheels of a line of motorbikes.'

'How long have the CIA got?' Sir Alan asked.

'Only a week. No movement in or out in that time. But it rained heavily nine days ago, so those tyre tracks outside the barn have been made since then.'

Sir Alan closed the feed and led them back to sit in the corner. He took a sip of his whisky and swirled the ice around in his glass.

Ian jumped into the silence, as was also his style. 'I'm suspicious,' he said. 'That's my first reaction, I'm afraid.'

Kate resisted the temptation to point out that he was always suspicious of anything he hadn't originated. Sir Alan continued to stare into his glass.

'I don't think this needs to take all night,' Ian went on, which invariably meant he had a dinner to attend, or an assignation, or both. 'We can monitor the situation in Estonia to see how it develops, but we shouldn't – *couldn't* – accept their offer to defect.' He looked at his superior. 'I'm sure you agree, Alan.' It wasn't a question.

'And why would you think that?'

Ian made a show of appearing incredulous. 'Because it smacks of a well-organized disinformation plot designed to take us for fools. They know Kate is in a vulnerable state—'

'Come on, Ian,' Kate said. She had not expected his assault on her to be quite so obvious.

'Withdraw that,' Sir Alan instructed him. 'And apologize, please.'

'All right, I'm sorry,' Ian said easily, without bothering to look at her or sound as if he meant it. He ran his hand languorously through his hair. 'But the stakes are damned high here. Just imagine if the PM gets wind of the fact that we're taking this seriously. He *is* the prime minister, after all, and likely to remain so, unless I'm missing something. The damage that could be done – the havoc he could wreak – on our organization might be terminal.'

'So you'd rather have a Russian spy running our country?' Kate asked.

Ian faced her. 'Well, first, we should be careful in our language. If we accept your theory, he isn't a Russian spy but an agent of influence. Compromised, yes, if it were true, but unlikely to be doing much more than simply giving their arguments a fair hearing. And, much more importantly, there is absolutely not a shred of hard evidence that he *is* working for the Russians.'

'That's what they're offering us,' Kate said.

Sir Alan was sitting back in his chair, watching the pair of them fight this out.

'It's a trap, Kate. Surely you can see that. They've offered us some tasty bait again. We'll be drawn in again. And then they'll seek to embarrass and confuse us. Again. They hardly need to bother with any serious operations, these days, because we do all their work for them.' Ian looked at them, waiting for a response, and, when he didn't get one, simply ploughed on. 'It's too damned *neat*. Last time, they drop in the intelligence that our prime minister has prostate cancer. We don't know this, so we discount it. Then, hey presto, he suddenly walks out into Downing Street to announce both his illness and resignation within twenty-four hours. We take this as clear evidence that the original operation was a stroke of genius and the intelligence it gleaned thus one hundred per cent genuine and correct. And the rest is history. Weeks of total chaos and confusion not just inside these four walls but in our country at large.' Ian paused to draw breath. If his frustration was confected, it was very convincing. 'And now here we go again. They offer us another juicy morsel. *Proof*, this time, in the form of some disgusting video of our new prime minister – and who can argue with that? It couldn't *possibly* be faked – that the original intelligence was correct. They know Kate will be inclined to believe—'

'Do not personalize this, Ian,' Sir Alan said. 'And that's an order, not a request.'

'But we're going around the same mountain.'

'Perhaps we are,' Sir Alan said, 'but if there is a video and a chance it proves that our prime minister is a liar, a traitor and a cheat, then we would be neglecting our duty if we failed to mount even a cursory investigation into its credibility. I have enough faith in our organization to believe us capable of determining whether a piece of video is faked or not.'

'But that's exactly the point. No one can ever determine that with one hundred per cent accuracy. So they've just put this fly out on the water, waiting for us to come up and swallow it whole, like a lazy trout.' Fly-fishing was another of the new hobbies Ian liked to show off about, along with skiing, shooting and an apparently endless succession of Ironman competitions. He glanced at his watch. 'Time is money' was another of his favourite phrases. 'I have to go or I'll be late.'

'For what?' Sir Alan turned his gaze towards him.

Ian was briefly flustered. 'I just promised not to be late for dinner.'

'I understand that your reputation for good timekeeping can't be held hostage by important matters of state, but all the same . . .'

Ian bridled. Only a short time ago, his brazen insubordination, even rudeness, would have been unthinkable, but his insolence was a testament to Sir Alan's fading power. He had been in the job for seven years now, his standard five-year term extended twice, but it was unlikely to be amended for a third time, and Ian's attempt to woo the prime minister to appoint him Sir Alan's successor was Whitehall's worst-kept secret.

'We really can't take this any further now, Alan.' Ian was addressing him as if Kate wasn't present. 'I'm happy to stay all night, if need be, *as always*.' He shook his head. 'But nothing is going to be said, I fear, that will persuade me to change my mind. I propose a keen watching brief on Estonia, but as for the rest . . .' he shrugged '. . . we should let it go.'

As Kate watched the two men squaring up to each other, like stags long past their prime, she was reminded of Stuart's succinct summary of Ian Granger. 'He's just a bit of a cunt,' he would say. 'Everyone has a boss like that once in a while.'

If thinking of Stuart wasn't in itself so painful, it might have made her smile.

Ian departed. Sir Alan peered at the whisky in his glass, then drank it straight. 'If he ends up as your replacement, I'm going to kill myself,' Kate said.

Sir Alan went to refill his glass. 'You'll have to excuse his manners. Ella has just filed for a divorce.'

'Christ. Why?' Ella was Ian's long-suffering wife. The pair had met at Oxford and he liked to boast of her incredible success in building an online retail empire selling sleepwear. 'I mean, I always assumed she must know about his affairs.'

'Suspecting is one thing, but it turns out knowing is another. She found the phone he'd been using to arrange his assignations.'

'With Julie?'

'He wasn't in a mood to be specific. It only happened this afternoon.'

'Oh, shit. That would explain it. She got a text while we were travelling back from Venice.'

'He tells me he's in love and fully intends to marry her.'

'Julie? He thinks he's going to marry Julie?' Kate was aghast. If the two of them having an affair was puzzling enough, marriage would be incomprehensible. 'She thinks it's just sex. Expedient, because she can't be bothered to date properly. I feel sorry for him.'

'I doubt that. I don't. Somewhere in there, beneath the vaulting ambition and the deep-seated insecurities, is a man whose heart is basically in the right place, but I'm afraid I lost sight of that individual a long time ago.'

'Subtlety has never been his strong point.'

'Or loyalty.' Sir Alan turned to her. 'How are you?'

'I don't know.' She thought about it. 'I just don't know.'

'Try not to take this the wrong way, but you don't look on top of the world.'

'Thanks. How are you?'

'As you would imagine. Alice decided in the end that she would go through another round of chemo, but the oncologist was fairly clear that he thought it unlikely to have much effect. If it doesn't, we're to be transferred to palliative care.'

'I'm sorry, Alan.' She watched him in silence.

He was as still as a statue. Then he shook his head, as if to dismiss a morbid train of thought. 'Tell Karen to go down to Narva tonight. I'll send out someone to help her and speak to the Estonians. We'll need a Cobra in the morning. I'd like them to know we were ahead of the curve if Mikhail is right and it does kick off.'

'What do you want to do about their offer?'

'Ian's objections are understandable enough. In the end, the only thing all that grief brought us six months ago was the knowledge that your husband was Agent Viper. So . . . I need to buy some cover. I'd like us both to brief the foreign secretary after Cobra. I think, for once, I'll conspire to leave Ian behind.'

'Is that wise? Briefing the foreign secretary, I mean.' The prime minister had sent one of his early leadership rivals, Meg Simpson, to the grandiose office overlooking Whitehall that had once ruled an empire. The press generally considered it a dull, uninspiring choice, designed to make sure he had no rival anywhere near him. Imogen Conrad, the dynamic younger woman who had given him a run for his money in the final round of the leadership contest, had remained where she was at Education.

'I think so,' Sir Alan said. 'Meg may not be as dazzling as either the prime minister or Imogen Conrad, but she's a hell of a lot more reliable than either. Did you check with Cheltenham for any traffic to support the idea of a coup in Moscow Centre?'

'Yes, and they've heard nothing of the kind either.' Kate stood. 'I'd better go. The children are looking after themselves, which is not ideal.'

She went downstairs and put her head around the door of her department. Only Suzy was there, which was far from untypical as Kate had quickly learnt. Suzy shared her predecessor Rav's work ethic but, sadly, not his charm. 'Julie briefed me,' Suzy said, with clipped Mancunian vowels, in such a way as to indicate Kate should really have done so.

'I'm sorry. Do you mind if I fill you in properly tomorrow? I have to run for the kids.'

'I understood the situation in Estonia was potentially critical.'

'We're watching it closely. Karen is going to Narva tonight. She'll report back in the morning.'

'Do you want me to do some work on anything?'

'No, don't worry. And don't stay late . . .' Kate got a few paces down the corridor before she had second thoughts and went back. If Suzy was determined to staple herself to her desk, they might as well make it count. 'Actually, it would be useful if you could do a briefing note on the Night Wolves for the foreign secretary and the PM, their links with the Kremlin and the GRU, their role in Ukraine, that sort of thing.'

Suzy looked pleased. 'Thanks,' she said. 'I really appreciate that.'

'There's a Cobra meeting first thing. I'll give it to the PM and the foreign secretary there.'

Suzy's smile broadened. Kate had already worked out that nothing pleased her new deputy quite as much as the prospect of catching the eye of their superiors.

4

KATE CHANGED INTO her trainers by the lift and walked out into the chill night. The wind was biting, so she took a cashmere beanie from her coat and pulled it down tight over her ears. Normally, this daily walk helped bring some order to her thoughts, but tonight, the rhythmic pace of the journey seemed to accelerate the rising tide of her anxiety. Now that Stuart had gone, the only person she shared her true state of mind with was her aunt Rose, who combined the role of mentor at work – as the long-time head of the Finance Department, it had been she who'd first encouraged Kate to apply for the Service from Cambridge – and surrogate mother at home. Kate's real mother was in a home nearby with Alzheimer's, which was a relief to everyone who knew her.

But even Rose was not aware of the long sleepless nights and the sense of a world closing in so fast that it was almost suffocating her niece.

As had been so often the case, it was a sense of duty that came to Kate's aid as she walked into the light and warmth at 17 Khyber Road. The single driving force of her life now was to try to limit the damage of her husband's departure on Gus and Fiona.

Not that she had any sense they appreciated it. Her thirteen-year-old son was hunched over his iPad on the sofa in the corner of the kitchen. Kate gently removed the headphones from his ears (which, she could not help noticing, were full of wax). 'What are you watching?'

'*Mission Impossible.*'

'Sounds like my life.'

He didn't smile. 'Is that a joke?'

She tutted in despair. 'Where's your sister?'

'She went out.'

'Where? I told her—'

'That *is* a joke. She's upstairs. With Jed.'

'Oh. What time did he come around?'

'About ten minutes ago.'

Kate went to put on the kettle. 'What did you have for supper?'

'Salmon, like you suggested.'

'Did she eat her—'

'I'm not going to be your snitch, Mum.'

Kate came to sit next to her son. 'You know this is serious, right? They say anorexia is the hardest mental illness to treat.'

'She isn't anorexic.'

'With respect, you're not a doctor.'

'And neither are you. If it's so serious, why haven't you taken her to see one?'

For all his detachment, Gus sometimes had a knack for putting his finger on the key question and she winced inwardly. She'd been asking herself the same question for some weeks. 'Right now,' she said, 'what with everything else, I worry that it might actually make it worse, not better. I'm hoping if we can just keep her on the straight and narrow for a little longer, the pressure will ease off.'

'You know that's not how it works, right?' Gus said.

'What?'

'Psychiatrists don't make you worse. That's not the point of them.'

Kate had no comeback to that. She kissed him thoughtfully, made a cup of tea and opened the bin to throw in the teabag. As she did so, she noticed the remains of what looked like an untouched piece of salmon fillet.

With a heavy heart, she went upstairs to knock on Fiona's bedroom door. 'We're fully clothed,' her daughter replied. Kate pushed back the door to see Fiona and her tall, rangy boyfriend lying in front of what appeared to be homework on Fiona's bed. Jed leapt to his feet and came to kiss Kate on both cheeks. Despite his tattoos and piercings, Kate had come to be very fond of him over the past few months. She wondered sometimes what they would have done without him. It was almost as if he was the glue holding their family – or sanity – together.

'Hi, love,' Kate said.

'Hi.' Fiona didn't move.

'Did you manage to cook supper okay?'

'Uh-huh.'

'Have you eaten, Jed?'

'Yes, thank you, Mrs Henderson. I had supper at home. How was the rest of your day at work?'

'Er, complicated, if I'm honest.'

Fiona's demeanour suggested there was every chance she would continue to ignore her mother, so Kate retreated to her bedroom. She ran a bath and soaked in it, then contemplated once more how lonely she felt in the middle of the night – or at any time, for that matter.

She had one more task, so she reached for the house phone and dialled the number for Rose's London home. It was a gorgeous four-bedroom townhouse just off the King's Road, in a row characterized by many shades of pastel.

'Is that you, Kate?'

'How did you know?'

'No one else calls this late.'

'I'm sorry.'

'How was your trip?'

'Oh . . .' Kate realized she hadn't had time to reflect upon the impact of seeing Stuart. 'I don't really know.'

'How was he?'

'Sad. A bit pathetic. He burst into tears on the children and told them both how much he hated his life in Moscow.'

'Oh, God, how selfish. And bloody unhelpful.'

'Yes . . . yes. I guess so.'

'Was that all?'

'Yes. Other than that, it went smoothly.' Kate had learnt to her cost over the last six months that, in the house of secrets, it was better to keep knowledge to herself, even if Rose was the reason she had joined the Service in the first place. 'Look, I'm so sorry to do this to you, but something's come up that's going to keep me in London this weekend, I think, so we'll have to cry off the trip to Cornwall.'

'That's a shame. We were so looking forward to seeing the children.'

'I know. I'm really sorry.' Rose and her husband Simon had a newly built holiday home – a temple to oak and glass – between the beaches of Polzeath and Daymer Bay, one of Kate's favourite places. As she thought of it, she realized she was disappointed too.

'Why don't you let us take them?' Rose asked. 'If you're going to have to work, it doesn't sound as if they'll have much of a weekend. And, of course, there's your mother. She'll never let us forget it and I'm not sure I feel saintly enough to take her on our own.'

Kate thought about this.

'It's settled, then,' Rose said. 'I'll drop by your office in the morning to work out the arrangements.'

'I don't know what I'd do without you.'

'You'd be fine. But . . . have you seen Dr Wiseman yet?'

'No.'

'Kate—'

'I actually have an appointment tomorrow lunchtime.' Kate had clean forgotten about it until then. And she had fully intended to cancel.

'Well, go. Whatever else is happening, make sure you go. Please. Or I really won't forgive you.'

'All right, all right . . . Oh, one more thing.' Kate bit her lip. 'Any news on Lena's sister?'

'I'm still waiting for the report from Belgrade.'

'What's taking them so long?' Kate had recruited Lena Sabic to work for the Service with the clear promise that they would free her young sister Maja from terrible circumstances in Serbia and bring her to England. Kate naturally felt Lena's death reinforced this promise rather than freed them from its implications, but it was not a universal view, with the cost and complications of an extraction in danger of triggering a major row at the top of the Service. As head of Finance, Rose was overseeing the operation, at Kate's behest. At least she would have one ally when it came to the crunch.

'It's complicated, Kate, you know that. I'll chase it up in the morning. In the meantime, get some sleep – and make sure you see Dr Wiseman.'

Kate replaced the receiver. Although she had been seeing a counsellor for months, sometimes singly, sometimes with the children, Rose had insisted the change to a psychiatrist was what she needed now.

Kate's phone buzzed and she picked it up to see a message from Suzy, sent via the secure in-house service they used amongst colleagues: *Julie just told me about the potential video. Jesus, what a fucking sleaze bucket. Am sorry, but you are absolutely right. You have to follow it up.*

Kate put her phone face down and switched off her bedside light. She stared at the ceiling, thinking of the phone call with Rose. There was no way she'd see Dr Wiseman tomorrow. It felt too much like opening Pandora's Box.

5

KATE WAS AWOKEN the next morning by another message, this time from Julie. *Switch on the TV.*

She glanced at her watch. It was 6.24 a.m. She pushed herself upright, reached for the remote and turned on the television.

The banner running along the bottom of Sky News read: 'Estonia: Kremlin calls attacks a "provocation".' It was emblazoned over footage from late last night of a mob wielding sticks and attacking a group of protesters in the centre of the Estonian border town of Narva.

The presenter, a slim woman with riotous blonde hair and the cadaverous air of someone who hasn't eaten properly for a decade, was talking to her political editor, a slim young man who looked like he was filling in between school and Cambridge. 'Well, the temperature seems to be rising rapidly,' the young man said. 'As you know, this all started when a group of men tried to pull down a statue of Lenin in the Estonian border town of Narva. Some of the local ethnic Russian population protested and were then attacked. Now, in the last few minutes, we've seen the Center Party in Tallinn, which principally represents Estonia's quite substantial Russian minority, issue a highly provocative invitation to the Kremlin to formally intervene – militarily, if necessary. Russian people are simply not safe in Estonia, it says. No word from the Kremlin in response, yet, but Estonia is of course a NATO ally and, under its Article Five, an attack – or a threat – on one is an assault on all.'

'So what has been Downing Street's response?'

'It's early in the day, of course, and I understand there is to be a Cobra meeting within the next few hours, but the briefing I received a short time ago suggests that the prime minister's overwhelming mood is likely to be one of caution. In the words of one source in Downing Street, it's not worth risking World War Three over a few punches being thrown in Estonia. But the Germans and the French are taking a much more robust line and I guess we'll wait to see exactly what emanates from the White House in the course of the day.'

'Would it be overly cynical,' the presenter asked, sitting

back in her chair with a sly smile, 'to cast our minds back to those allegations in the leadership election six months ago that the prime minister might in some way have been . . . how shall I put it? . . . compromised by the Russians – and to worry that this could be a factor?'

The political editor permitted himself an equally sly smile back. 'I think it's a thought you would whisper very quietly, unless you wanted to earn the PM's undying enmity. "Trash of the social-media age" is what they call all that in Downing Street. But opposition MPs will, no doubt, level the charge at him once again that he is in some way Moscow's stooge.'

Kate switched off the television and went to shower. By the time she was out, she had a message from Sir Alan warning that the Cobra meeting had been brought forward to 8 a.m., so she left an apologetic note for Fiona, asking her to make sure she got her brother on to the bus with her for school, and caught a cab direct to Whitehall.

She walked through the entrance just next to Downing Street and swung right to go down the stairs past the carefully preserved Tudor remnants of the palace that had stood there in Henry VIII's time. She handed her phone in to the guard sitting by the security portals at the bottom. Her pass didn't give her automatic clearance, so she waited for him to check her details against the names on the list, then open the door for her. She glanced through to the anteroom, where the more junior aides sat, sifting any last-minute intelligence coming in.

The prime minister, James Ryan, was already seated in the Cabinet Office Briefing Room, the setting for all Cobra meetings, waiting for everyone else to arrive, a very different approach from his predecessor, who had always liked to arrive last, preferably having kept his audience waiting. The PM was fifty-five, the same age as C, of whom he had been an exact contemporary at public school. He had the carefully cultivated crumpled air of the truly vain. His shirt did not appear to have been ironed and his thick, wavy dark hair seemed not to have seen a brush for days, giving him the appearance of a student who'd just crawled out of bed. He'd put on weight since crossing the threshold to Downing Street, his once handsome features now puffed and jowly. But he still liked to share his legendary charisma with anyone in his orbit.

'Kate Henderson, as I live and breathe. What a pleasure to see you.' He gave her a beaming smile.

'Good morning, Prime Minister.'

'Is it? I've been up for hours. It feels like lunchtime.' He glanced at the cabinet secretary, who sat beside him. She was a tall, grey-haired, mostly serious woman called Shirley Grove, who, it was said, occasionally exhibited a flash of supremely dry and rather cutting humour. She didn't find her boss funny in the least. 'Must be why I'm getting so fat,' the prime minister went on. 'I keep inventing extra meals.' He leant forward on the table and fixed Kate with a steely, half-amused gaze that was another of his stocks in trade, as if life was one long P. G. Wodehouse story. 'How *are* you, Kate?'

'I'm well, Prime Minister.'

'Sorry to hear about your husband. Sounds like a wretched fellow. Better luck next time. That's my motto.' He smiled again. His latest girlfriend had just departed Downing Street after what was said to have been another tempestuous row. 'I'm on the market,' he had quipped at a recent dinner.

Kate coloured. She couldn't think of anyone else tactless enough to make a joke of the breakdown of her marriage. But she was saved further embarrassment by Sir Alan's arrival, which chilled the air by several degrees. He nodded at the prime minister and sat at the far end of the table from him, as if deliberately trying to keep his distance. The two men were said by contemporaries to have been close friends at school, but, if so, Kate had yet to identify the cause of the current hostility between them. He was followed by the defence secretary as the room quickly filled. The foreign secretary, Meg Simpson, and her senior team were the last to arrive.

Simpson was smaller and broader in the flesh than she appeared on television and looked quite a few years older, too, with thick-rimmed reading glasses on a chain around her neck and a tight bob of grey hair. She wore barely any make-up and betrayed few signs of vanity. She looked flustered to have arrived last.

'Let's begin,' the prime minister said, as if they were about to have a party.

Sir Alan stood up. He sure as hell wasn't the entertainment. 'As you know, we scheduled this meeting yesterday evening, before the events in Narva. We had received a tip-off from a reliable source that the Russians were about to roll the dice again. Our working assumption is that the GRU is the agency responsible and they appear to be following the playbook that worked so well for them in Crimea: create unrest, claim the local Russian minority is under threat, and intervene.'

Sir Alan had the remote control for one of the screens at the end of the table and he flicked it on. It was showing the feed from PCR2 on SIS's internal server, which Danny must have switched out to line. 'This is a farm in a small village called Puhlova, which was bought from a local man by a firm registered in Helsinki some months ago. The true owner is hidden behind so many holding companies that it will take us some time to get to the bottom of it, but I think we can safely assume we will find it's one or other agency of the Russian state.'

Sir Alan zoomed in on the muddy ground and moved to point at the screen. 'It's hard to make out unless you look very closely, but you can see here the tyre tracks of lorries or heavy trucks. Our understanding is that the Night Wolves – which is a Russian paramilitary group mainly made up of veterans from the war in Chechnya and closely allied with the Kremlin – have stored enough weapons here to mount a serious challenge to the Estonian state.'

'Looks like any other farm,' the prime minister said. 'What have they got hidden in there? Pitchforks?' He was smiling, as if this was still some kind of joke.

'We don't know yet.' Sir Alan closed down the feed and clicked on another. 'Kate here and her team found this hotel nearby on the Baltic, which we think at least some of the Night Wolves are staying in.'

'Looks tempting,' the prime minister said. Kate glanced from one man to the other. It was hard to imagine that these two had once been school friends. If they were faking their disdain for each other, they were great actors.

Sir Alan flicked on Sky News, which was still showing pictures of last night's violence. 'We have no doubt that the original attempt to pull down the statue of Lenin, which of course triggered the protests and then the counter-violence, will have been orchestrated from Moscow. Indeed, the entire event, from beginning to end, appears to have been their work.'

'Why?' The prime minister leant forward on to the table again, his demeanour more serious now.

'To expand their sphere of influence, as they have in so many other places that used to be part of the Soviet Empire. That has to be our working assumption. The Night Wolves will come to the protesters' aid, possibly tonight. They will clash with Estonian security forces. The tension will ratchet up. The local Russian population will increase their demands for Moscow to intervene, possibly for the entire region to secede, as we saw in Crimea.'

'It's possible the whole thing is just a feint,' Ian said, desperate to be in on the act. Sir Alan didn't deign to look at him.

'A *what*?' the prime minister asked.

'A feint, Prime Minister, a manoeuvre, just designed to test us out.'

'I should say it's obviously designed to test us,' the prime minister said, turning to Kate. 'What do you think?'

She was acutely conscious of all eyes in the room being upon her and of the fury in Ian's flushed cheeks. He'd forgotten that a stilted formality was the hallmark of all Cobra meetings – at least, all those she'd attended – and his easy insouciance jarred, even if the sentiments were designed to appeal to the man at the head of the table. He looked under-dressed for the occasion, too. He was the only man in the room without a jacket.

'Ian may be right,' she said, throwing him a lifeline, on instinct. 'Perhaps they just want to see how we react. But then we have only to look at what happened in Crimea and even in Montenegro, with that attempted coup. So it might be wiser to assume they mean business again.'

'We've got about a thousand troops there?' the prime minister asked the defence secretary.

'That's right, Prime Minister,' he said. 'Nine hundred men

and women, principally from the Queen's Royal Hussars and the Rifles, armed with Warriors and Challenger II tanks.' He was a relatively young man for such a post, with a dramatically receding hairline and flawless skin. Like so many politicians, these days, he had been a special adviser before becoming an MP and always carried with him the air of a teenager pretending to be a grown-up. 'Of course, NATO can quickly move reinforcements in from neighbouring countries.' He pushed a sheet down the table. 'That is the list of deployments in the region. We can also look to reinforce swiftly from here—'

'It's too soon for that.' The prime minister glanced around the room, deliberately making eye contact with his audience. 'Ian here may be right. Perhaps it is a feint. We need to be careful not to overreact. And, in any case, I'm not sure the public is ready for us to go to war over a country few have heard of.'

There was a stunned silence in the room, its occupants carefully avoiding catching anyone's eye. Meg Simpson broke the spell. 'Prime Minister, I've spoken to the French and the Germans already this morning. We're talking about a fundamental tenet here of the most important and longest-lasting security alliance our nation has ever known. They want NATO to send reinforcements to Estonia today. We must—'

'I'm aware of all that, thank you, but not yet.' The PM was looking at the list of deployments in Lithuania, Latvia and Poland on the table in front of him. He had a reputation across Whitehall for chronic indecision, but there was no sign of it this morning. 'I have a call scheduled with the White House as soon as the president is awake. I imagine he will share my caution. For the moment, we remain as we were. I will circulate a draft press statement.' He stood abruptly and walked out, taking the list of deployments with him.

For a moment, nobody moved or spoke. There were a few coughs. Then the politicians and their staff stood and filed out in silence. Only Shirley Grove, the cabinet secretary, held back. 'Good work, Mrs Henderson,' she said, then headed for the door.

It was a strange aside, since Kate had never before met the woman, but perhaps she was just making up for her superior's bad manners.

6

KATE, SIR ALAN and Ian were the last to leave and they stood together for a moment in the morning sunshine on Whitehall. 'One can't blame his caution.'

Ian must have been aware that Sir Alan was intending to brief the foreign secretary on Mikhail's offer to defect, but the chief skilfully deflected him with a request that he return to monitor the unfolding situation in Narva and inform Downing Street directly if there were developments. It was a role Sir Alan knew he would be unable to resist.

Ian jumped into a taxi. Sir Alan and Kate walked the long way around to the front entrance of the Foreign Office in King Charles Street, perhaps to give them time to talk. 'If we needed anything to focus our minds,' Sir Alan muttered, 'it couldn't have been planned any better.'

'Exactly.'

'You're not convinced?'

'It feels a bit too neat, I suppose.'

'Which part?'

'This crisis blows up just as we need convincing that Mikhail's offer to defect is serious.'

'You think we should share that thought with the foreign secretary?'

'No. You?'

'Agreed. We need to see if this video exists and appears genuine. We can then take a sober view. But if they potentially have evidence, we have to see it.'

Sir Alan appeared lost in thought as they walked across the courtyard, up the grandiose staircase, and were ushered into the foreign secretary's enormous office, with its magnificent array of leather-bound books and treasures from the days when the UK had bestrode the globe. Meg Simpson sat behind her mahogany desk, looking out over Horse Guards Parade and St James's Park.

Normally, the foreign secretary received guests in the spacious red leather seating at the other end of the office, but perhaps she wanted to keep the great bulwark of the desk between her and the secrets they were about to impart. There was a single-page briefing note Sir Alan had evidently prepared on the desk before her and she plunged straight into its contents, without any reference to the strange Cobra meeting they'd all just sat through.

'I'd like to walk back a few paces,' the foreign secretary said. 'I obviously understand that the allegations about the prime minister's Russian connections first surfaced in the leadership election and have been a thorn in his side ever since, but I seem to recall that when I asked you about them in our first meeting here, you said that there was nothing to the charges and the case was closed.'

Sir Alan leant forward in his chair. In Kate's experience, he liked to dominate politicians and clearly felt uncomfortable at the expanse of wood between them. On reflection, perhaps that had been Meg Simpson's thinking. Kate's respect for her crept up a notch. 'In the end, the evidence we had was not conclusive.'

'Walk me through it from the beginning.'

'Kate recruited a young nanny called Lena Sabic to help us plant a bug on a super-yacht owned by Igor Borodin, who used to be the head of Russia's Foreign Intelligence Service and is – or was – a close friend of the Russian president. We planned the operation because we knew that Igor likes to keep in touch with what his successors are up to and has been in the habit of inviting them to join him on his yacht. The operation was Kate's idea and it was one of the most successful of the past decade. We managed to record a meeting of Russia's most senior intelligence officials, who were discussing our former prime minister's prostate cancer before it was known to anyone back here, including us. The way in which they were discussing the leadership election that would ensue from his resignation suggested to us that one of the candidates to replace him was working for the Kremlin.'

'I have not received a transcript of that conversation?'

'We closed the file.'

'Not to me.'

'I'll send it across later.'

Meg rewarded him with a thin smile. 'In any event, I assume that once the prime minister had declared his prostate cancer and resigned, that reinforced your notion that the conversation you recorded was genuine.'

'Yes.'

'So how did you proceed?'

'We began an investigation into the candidates.'

'All of us?' There was a twinkle in her eye. 'Even me?'

'Once the contest narrowed to Imogen Conrad and the prime minister, we focused our attentions there.'

'Perhaps it was me the Russians were referring to all along and I just didn't make the final cut.'

Sir Alan didn't smile back at her. 'Perhaps.'

'And what did you find?'

'Nothing conclusive, but a great deal of circumstantial evidence that James Ryan was recruited by the Russians as an agent many years ago, probably while he was an army officer in Kosovo. Kate's deputy, Ravindra, followed a lead to Geneva and may have uncovered details of the payments the PM has received over the years, but he was found hanging from the ceiling of his flat after his return. We later discovered that the woman he had gone to see in Switzerland – a former secretary to one of the Russian president's lawyers – had been killed and dumped in a wood.'

The foreign secretary turned to gaze out over St James's Park again. They watched the prime minister's convoy turn out of the back of Downing Street and speed away down Horse Guards Parade.

'As you will see from the file when I send it across,' Sir Alan continued, 'the original operation also pointed to a spy named Viper working somewhere in Whitehall, who had been helping their agent of influence.'

Meg Simpson turned back to face them. 'I don't recall you mentioning an agent in Whitehall.'

'It was my husband,' Kate said. 'The Service has kept the matter top secret at my request.'

Simpson's dark green eyes flicked from Sir Alan to Kate and back again. 'It sounds to me as if the decision to close this file was rather too hasty.'

'I don't think we had any choice but to pursue the original intelligence to see where it led,' Sir Alan said. 'But, equally, given that we could find no proof of anything, I felt it was our duty to let the matter rest once the prime minister had taken office.'

'I don't understand. You just told me the operation to bug the yacht was a great success.'

Sir Alan could see immediately where this was going. He edged forward still further in his seat. 'It yielded exactly the kind of intelligence we hoped it might.'

'That the prime minister was working for the Russians?'

'That our country's security might have been compromised at the highest level.'

'Might have been?'

'That's correct, yes.'

'So you think the intelligence was accurate and that the man or woman they were originally referring to in the bugged conversation was our current prime minister?'

'Yes.'

'But you closed the file?'

Sir Alan wasn't enjoying this. 'Froze the file would be a better way of putting it. We pursued every available lead, but came to a series of dead ends. We had to take a view. He is our democratically elected leader. To put it simply, I felt we had to put up and shut up.'

'So it doesn't matter to you if our leader is working with – or for – the Russians? Given what is happening today and, if I'm going to be frank with you, his tendency to inaction on the subject, I should have thought it was all pretty relevant.'

'Perhaps we should have done more to keep the investigation alive.'

'It would seem so.'

'But there was no proof and we had to bear in mind that the Russians might have been attempting to deliberately mislead us.'

'Which would make the original operation less a success and more a catastrophic failure, I should have thought.'

Kate glanced at her superior, who seemed suddenly to be tying himself in intellectual knots in a very uncharacteristic manner. But, then, he looked dead tired.

'And what do you think, Mrs Henderson?'

'About which aspect in particular?'

'Is the prime minister a Russian spy?'

'Yes.' Meg Simpson gazed at her steadily. 'I mean, I can add caveats about what exactly we mean by that term. But if you're asking me whether he has been compromised in some way by the Russians, then, yes, I think he has.'

'What did you make of his behaviour in the Cobra meeting?'

'It confirmed my suspicions.'

'Not everyone in your organization agrees with you, I believe.'

Kate glanced at Sir Alan, whose flinty gaze gave not a hint of anger. Fucking Ian, she thought. 'Not everyone agrees with me, no.'

'Then what makes you so sure?'

'I believe the original operation was well set up, so there is very little chance the intelligence was planted. I don't know how they could possibly have known the PM had prostate cancer—'

'Unless Viper told them,' the foreign secretary shot back.

'My husband was not aware of the PM's illness.'

'Are you sure?'

'Yes.'

'What about some other source? Perhaps you have another traitor in your organization who picked up the information from somewhere?'

'Perhaps, but the knowledge of the PM's illness was kept to such a tight circle around him.' Kate shrugged, tired of the interrogation suddenly. 'If you're asking me, I think the original intelligence was correct and the prime minister is very lucky we were unable to produce any direct evidence of his treachery.'

'And yet here it now is, popped into our laps by the hands of a potential defector.' Simpson was looking directly at her now.

'Potentially.'

'Do you believe it to be credible?'

'We'll have no idea until we see the video,' Sir Alan said.

'So what is it you need from me?'

Sir Alan glanced at Kate, as if he was unsure quite how to answer this.

'Cover,' Simpson replied for him.

'If this video were to prove genuine and the allegations surrounding the prime minister true, the controversy and potential damage to our democracy would be incalculable,' Sir Alan said.

'And if it were to prove a fake, you might end up with egg all over your face, which you would much rather was *our* face.'

'I don't think you'd thank us if this blew up without warning,' Sir Alan said.

'I doubt I'm going to thank you either way.' She flipped the file containing his single-page briefing note shut. 'You should know that I'm a patriot more than a politician and I came into politics motivated more by love of country than party. And if that sounds unbearably pompous, you may yet live to be glad of it.' She stood. 'I recognize from your note that time is pressing, not least because the events in Estonia make it so, but I would nevertheless like the weekend to think about it. There is a lot at stake here, as I hardly need tell the pair of you.' She nodded at them. 'Thank you for coming over.'

They walked unescorted to the door and let themselves out. 'She's a lot more impressive than she looks,' Kate said, as they descended the stairs.

'She's a ball-breaker.'

'That's a bit sexist.'

'Why?'

'You wouldn't call a man a ball-breaker, would you?'

'I might.'

'No, you wouldn't.'

'I'd call Ian a parasite. Does that count?'

Kate smiled. 'No, I don't think it does.'

They discussed Ian's evident deceit in the car on the way back to Vauxhall, exactly how and when he had communicated his reservations about the Russians' intentions to the foreign secretary.

They parted company at the lifts and Kate went first to the operations room, where Danny and Julie were seated in front of the screens in the corner, surrounded by empty coffee cups. It had clearly been a long night. Julie glanced up at her. 'You're going to want to see this.'

Kate bent closer to the screen. The video feed was of the farmhouse in Puhlova. It showed an enormous lorry, which had backed up into one of the barns. 'I don't know what they're doing, but . . .' Danny clicked a button in the corner and brought up another stream of video, which showed a group of bikers – perhaps a hundred or more – driving along a highway. 'They left their hotel about ten minutes after your Cobra meeting ended. They drove straight to the border, which they crossed about ten minutes ago. It looks like they're headed home to St Petersburg.'

Kate stared at the screen. This made absolutely no sense at all.

'There's more,' Danny said. 'I traced the lorry back. It took me a while.' He was now rewinding some footage. He hit play. 'It left this army base just outside St Petersburg at nine last night. I guess we can't say for sure it's a pull-out unless we can get sight of what the hell they're loading into that lorry, but it sure looks like one.'

'They knew we were on to them,' Julie said, her big green eyes fixed on Kate. She didn't need to add that, at nine last night, the circle of knowledge within MI6 had been very small indeed. Kate picked up the phone and dialled C's extension. He answered immediately. 'It's Kate,' she said.

'I know.'

'There's good and bad news. So far as we can tell, the Night Wolves are pulling out, with all their kit. I'll get Danny to put the feed back on PCR2 if you want to take a look.'

She waited while he got the correct screen up. 'Split the screen on PCR2,' she told Danny, and he did as instructed so Sir Alan could see the lorry being loaded up and the bikers on the St Petersburg highway. 'What's the bad news?' Sir Alan asked.

'Danny tracked the lorry back to its point of origin. It left a military base just outside St Petersburg at nine last night.' There was a long silence, as he absorbed the implications of this. 'What time did you inform Downing Street you wanted a Cobra meeting?' she asked.

'I called the cabinet secretary at midnight. I wanted to reduce the risk they would leak it to the morning papers. So . . . to state the obvious, to save you the trouble, the circle of knowledge was still very small at nine p.m., and restricted entirely to people inside this building.'

'You think Ian could have tipped off the PM, or someone close to him?'

'I'm starting to think Ian is capable of almost anything.'

Kate bit her lip as she turned this over in her mind. Blaming Ian was reasonable – his appetite for promotion was voracious – but also, perhaps, too easy. 'It doesn't make any sense, though. If they were really trying to stage a coup, why back off now?'

'Because they know we're on to them,' Sir Alan said. 'Because they've lost the element of surprise. Because, after the car crash that was the attempted coup in Montenegro, they don't want to look clumsy and amateur again.'

Kate glanced at Julie and Danny. Both were transfixed by the screens in front of them. 'Or because the whole episode was designed to convince us of Mikhail's good intentions,' she said. 'They stage an effective but brief theatrical show, which they know very well will be marked down as a quick win for us.'

'A train of thought that leads us to a still darker and more confusing place, because, if they're in a position to do that, it hardly suggests that Igor and his son have one foot in a Siberian gulag already.'

Kate didn't know what to say to that. It felt as if, every day, her work became a more complex and confusing mental jigsaw. If the question in Operation Sigma had been simple enough – was the original bugged conversation on Igor's super-yacht genuine or faked for their benefit? – the same could be said of this latest twist: was Igor and Mikhail's story true and their offer real?

But how to be sure of the answer? If what everyone sought was incontrovertible proof, all they ever had to fall back on was instinct – and primarily *her* instinct at that.

But it didn't waver. Not truly. She knew politicians were always going to want the comfort of proof, but intelligence rarely worked like that. Sometimes rock-solid instinct was all you were going to get. Thank God for Sir Alan. He, at least, understood this implicitly.

'I'd better call Downing Street,' he said. 'I'll place a small bet they'll spin this as evidence of the wisdom of caution – which is, of course, another aspect we should think about carefully.' He ended the call.

'You look like you've seen a ghost,' Julie said.

Kate mumbled a vague reply. She turned away and walked up to her office. Suzy was waiting for her. She had a way of addressing people – both hands on hips, her angular body tilted slightly forward – that they certainly didn't teach in Charm School. 'The original Operation Sigma case file is still locked,' she said.

Kate was tempted to reply, *Of course it bloody is*, but her brain was clouded by the conversation she'd just had with the chief, and its implications. 'Yes,' she said.

'Why?'

'Because we couldn't prove the prime minister was

working for the Russians, we had exhausted all potential leads, and, under the circumstances, it felt like locking away the allegations was the responsible thing to do.' Kate almost added that it had not been her choice, but decided against it. She sensed that, with Suzy, every word was likely to be taken down and used in evidence against her.

'But I need to read it.'

'I thought we went through this before you joined.'

'The allegations are still part of the political conversation. I don't think we can just bury our heads in the sand and prevent—'

'I can tell you what you need to know.' Kate dropped her bag beside her desk and sat down. Suddenly she felt shattered.

'I need the file, Kate.' Suzy was in the doorway. She seemed to fill it, despite her narrow frame, but perhaps that was just her demeanour. She tucked a strand of jet-black hair neatly behind her right ear. 'I don't want you to think I'm a stooge for the Security Service during my time here, but I'm really surprised they – we – were not called in to have a look at this. The director general would have a coronary if he knew the scale of the intelligence you'd kept from him. I mean, the prime minister potentially working for the Russians . . .'

'Well, to be clear, that is exactly what I will think if you take that kind of tone.'

Suzy stood her ground. 'I'm part of this team now, Kate.

I've been around long enough now to know what that involves.'

Kate got up, went to the filing cabinet in the corner, unlocked it with the key she kept in her pocket, took out the file marked *Operation Sigma* and handed it to her colleague. Suzy looked pleased, as if she had expected the conversation to reach a different conclusion.

Kate logged on to her computer. She'd barely had a chance to glance through her emails when their team assistant, Maddy, put her head around the door. She had an unerring ability to gauge instantly Kate's state of mind. 'You all right?'

'Why wouldn't I be?'

'O-kay.' She pulled a face. 'Glad I asked. Your aunt Rose called.'

'What did she want?'

'There's a problem with your expenses.'

'What?'

'All right, bad joke. She said she'd spoken to Fiona and would pick her and Gus up at four. She's sorted your mother with the nursing home. She'll pick her up just afterwards and they'll all head down to Cornwall together. You're welcome to join them at any point if you can get away.'

'Did she hear back from Belgrade?'

'Not so far as I know.'

'Will you check?'

'Of course.'

Maddy didn't retreat. There was clearly more. 'And?' Kate asked.

'She said I was to make sure you kept your appointment with Dr Wiseman – and walk you there myself if necessary.'

'All right, thank you.'

'What time is your appointment?'

'Two.'

'Are you going?'

'No.'

'Why not?'

'Maddy . . .' Kate faced her assistant, whose concern for her welfare sometimes felt intrusive.

'You have to go, Kate.'

'Last time I looked I was a grown woman. So I don't *have* to do anything.'

'You're not well.'

Kate frowned. 'What do you mean?'

'We all know what you've been through and you're not yourself. Surely you can see that.'

Having dropped her bombshell, Maddy withdrew. Kate was caught between irritation and despair. Was it that obvious? She'd barely had time to fashion an answer when Julie came in with questions of her own. 'What was their answer on Mikhail's offer?' she asked, as she sat on the desk beside Kate.

'The foreign secretary wants the weekend to think about it.'

'Lucky there are no time pressures, then. Do you think she'll go for it?'

'Sir Alan didn't leave her much choice. He was there buying top cover and she was smart enough to grasp that. She seems pretty thorough. I didn't realize he'd basically kept the original file from her, so I think she just wanted the time to go through it carefully. Ian had been there before us.'

'What do you make of the Night Wolves pulling out?'

'It's confusing.'

'Convenient, though. I mean, a quick win for us. It makes Mikhail look good.'

Kate was staring out of the window as she sifted the various different explanations for what had just happened in Estonia. None entirely made sense.

Julie stood and went to the glass wall overlooking the rest of the office. 'I guess you know that Ian's wife has booted him out,' she said.

'I do. I was a bit surprised, to be honest.'

'Not half as bloody surprised as I was.'

'What's your reaction?'

'I'm horrified. It was just casual sex, and now he's suddenly saying he wants to marry me.'

'What will you do?'

'I'll have to break it off.' Julie's voice betrayed no hint of emotion. She could sometimes, Kate thought, be a cold fish. Her hair was greasy, her T-shirt stained with a coffee spillage, but it did nothing to diminish a radiant, vibrant beauty. 'I see you gave Suzy the Sigma file,' Julie said. She was staring at their colleague, who was hunched over it on her desk.

'I didn't feel I had a choice. She'd have gone running back to her friends the other side of the river and they'd have made trouble.'

'Who do you think she's really working for?'

'The correct answer is that we're all on the same team. Isn't it?'

Julie rolled her eyes and walked out. Kate watched Suzy for a moment. So what if MI5 ended up knowing everything? Perhaps it didn't matter.

Kate picked up her bag. The foreign secretary's desire to have the weekend to think about it left open the possibility she could join her children and aunt in Cornwall and she couldn't think of a good reason to stay behind. But Rose would kill her if she missed her appointment with Dr Wiseman.

Before she went, Kate took the number Mikhail had given her from her pocket and sent him a WhatsApp message. *The foreign secretary has asked for the weekend, but I anticipate a positive response. Will keep you posted. K.*

Kate thought the mention of the foreign secretary would probably be enough to convince Mikhail they were taking his offer seriously and prevent him from approaching anyone else with his secrets, at least for a couple of days. The idea of the CIA, or indeed any other foreign intelligence service, having cast-iron proof of the prime minister's treachery – with all the leverage, complication and even humiliation that that would involve – didn't really bear thinking about, especially as it would come with the knowledge the British had deliberately chosen not to take up the offer.

He replied in a couple of seconds. *I am in Berlin. See you at 10 a.m. on Monday. Head for Alexanderplatz. Do not be late.*

Kate sent back: *Monday too soon. I can't make the wheels turn faster. Let's say Tuesday at 10 a.m.*

It was a long wait before she finally received a reply: *All right. No later, or the deal is off. And you're welcome, re Estonia.*

Maddy was at the door of her office again. 'The PM's just about to make a statement.' Kate joined the rest of her team in front of the big TV screen in the centre of the office, which was switched to Sky News. The prime minister swept up to a makeshift podium in Downing Street. 'I will make a full statement on the events in Estonia to the House this afternoon . . . but it is our understanding that if the Russians did intend to provoke unrest on the border, as some have alleged, then that threat is now receding. The protests have petered out and we do not believe there is a meaningful threat to Estonia's integrity and security. I have spoken to the Russian president directly this morning and he assured me that this is indeed the case, though he did ask that the Russian minority in Narva and in eastern Estonia be adequately protected, which is a perfectly reasonable request.' There was a pause as he looked up from his script and directly into the camera. 'I take this as further evidence of the advantage of a cautious, nuanced and balanced attitude to international relations. Nobody wants to rush into a war over a country few have heard of. That's the rub of it, like it or not. Thank you. Good day to you!'

He turned and walked back in through the door of Number Ten. 'That's going to make the Estonians feel good,' Julie said. 'He's a lot more bloody Neville Chamberlain than Winston Churchill.'

Kate didn't reply. She picked up her bag and went to the lifts, trying to shake the sense that she had just been manipulated in a way she couldn't yet quite articulate.

7

DR WISEMAN WAS a man of angular leanness, with a pair of square reading glasses that he took on and off as he alternated between asking questions and writing down her answers long-hand in a huge exercise book in the centre of his wood and chrome desk. He had a wide forehead, curly dark hair and a steady, level gaze. He reminded Kate of her first tutor at Cambridge, and her faltering attempts to explain herself were an uncomfortable echo of those encounters.

'It's really hard to describe,' she said. 'I usually feel all right when I first get up in the morning. I think. When I've slept. But then, as I said, I'm not sleeping well, and sometimes barely at all. In any event, once I get into the flow of the day, it's as if someone has crept up and injected some kind of diabolical chemical into my bloodstream, adrenalin or cortisol – or whatever. And then I just feel . . . *awful.*'

'In what way?'

'Just this nameless sense of dread, of being permanently on guard and anxious, as if someone is about to come around the corner and shoot me at any moment or, worse, the children.'

'And you say you felt like this before the events of six months ago, your husband's betrayal and the deaths of the young woman you recruited as an agent, then your deputy, Ravindra?'

Kate hesitated. Unburdening herself was painful. She felt as if she was standing on the edge of a precipice and all she could see was how far there was to fall. 'Yes, I suppose so.'

'When would you say it started?' He was looking at her over his glasses.

'I don't know.'

'Did you feel anxious as a child?'

'No. I was pretty confident.'

'One can be confident and anxious.'

There was a long silence. Kate stared at the floor as she racked her brains. And suddenly it was as if a window opened to allow a chink of light into the darkness. 'I guess I was, yes. Anxious, I mean.'

'About what?'

'Not the usual things, like exams. I was pretty cool about all that. I didn't mind very much what other people thought of me, either. I wasn't anxious about friendships, or whether anyone did or didn't like me or approve of what I was doing. But . . . I suppose loss . . . death.'

'Loss of what? Or whom?'

Kate thought hard about that, too. It was bloody difficult casting her mind back across the years and trying to unravel the complex weave of thought and emotion. 'Death, generally. The loss of someone or some people I loved, or of letting them down in some way. My own death, too, I suppose. Just the vagaries and impermanence of human existence. There were times when that uncertainty, the unpredictability of life, was paralysing.'

'Did you fear you would lose your mother?'

'No. I never had a relationship with her. I wasn't close to her as a young child, and after I learnt of her infidelity – she had a long-running affair with my best friend's father, a guy called David – I would say I came actively to hate her. I was brought up by my father. I understood from an early age that my mother was unreliable and often quite undermining, even poisonous.'

'Did your father challenge that?'

'No. That was the only issue I ever really had with him. I could never understand how he could love my mother. And, particularly, how he could go on loving her after she had treated him so badly. But he just quietly took me out of her orbit, which wasn't difficult because she is the most self-absorbed and, indeed, selfish woman I have ever met.'

'You were worried about losing your father, then?'

Kate had never thought about it like that. 'Yes, I suppose I was.' She stared at her hands. 'I definitely was. I had no siblings, so I guess my father was all I had. I was petrified something would happen to him.'

'Or that he would leave, that your mother would drive him away? Is that what lay beneath your resentment of her?'

'I knew he would never leave me.'

'Do you think you were the reason he stayed?'

Kate had never thought about it like that, either. It was an uncomfortable idea. 'I suppose so.'

Dr Wiseman continued writing. Kate glanced at the clock on the wall beside her. They had only ten minutes left and she was starting to panic it would not be long enough. Reluctant as she had been to start this process, now that it had begun she didn't want it to end. When was she going to get an answer? 'Was your father anxious?' he asked.

'About what?'

'Anything. You, your mother, life in general.'

'No.' She looked through the blind at the blurred figures hurrying by in the rain outside. 'Actually . . . yes, perhaps he was. I . . .' She sat up straight. Memories were crowding in on her. 'When I was about eight, or maybe nine, a friend of mine at school died very suddenly of meningitis. She sat at the desk next to me and she said she had a headache. I told her to go and see the nurse. The following day, the teacher came into the class to say that Jane had died in the night. I didn't know what to think or how to react. It was incredibly sad, but I didn't know what death meant. And in an awful way, life went on as normal.'

'But not for your father.'

'Exactly. Not for him. You see, Jane was also an only child. I think I understood then that my father was terrified of losing me. I remember him being quite strange around me for a while. I'd always been a bit of a tomboy, into climbing trees and fighting with the boys, and he had been very relaxed about that. But after Jane died, he was much more tense around me for a long time.'

'In what way?'

'Every way, I suppose. If I was going out into the garden, he wouldn't forbid me to climb the trees, but he'd come out and watch me, just to check I came to no harm.'

'How long did that last?'

'I don't know. A year, maybe.' Kate thought about it. 'But I suppose, in another way, a lifetime. I mean, he really worried about me a lot. I knew that. If I came home for the weekend, he would always say, "Drive carefully," at the gate when I was leaving.'

'Doesn't every parent say that?'

'I suppose so. But there was an intensity to it that I haven't really thought about until now.'

Dr Wiseman nodded. 'Given everything you've said, what do you make of the profession you've chosen?'

Kate took a long time to answer. It was a good question. 'I suppose there is a disconnect, as with many people, I should imagine, between what drives my intellectual curiosity and what ideally suits my psychological temperament.'

'Except that cannot be true. I imagine your job requires high degrees of natural empathy. How else would you have persuaded the girl you lost to work for you?'

Blackmail, Kate thought. Bullying. But she decided not to share that. 'I think I feel more in control the closer I am to the things I fear. I always worried about someone hurting someone I love, but this way I can seek out threats and defend myself and those I care for against them.'

'In order to keep your home life pure?'

'In what way?'

'To avoid the hurt your mother's betrayal caused?'

'I . . . don't know. Perhaps. But there is no perfect spy. We're as flawed as everyone else.'

Dr Wiseman glanced at the clock. He shuffled his notes. 'All right, I suggest we continue in a week or two. Please call Sarah to make another appointment.'

'How do we proceed? I mean, what's happening to me?'

He stapled his notes together. 'I'm going to refer you to Cognitive Analysis. That should take around twenty sessions—'

'Twenty?'

He didn't blink. 'We'll explore issues relating to your work, your past and your family of origin. I'll continue to see you at the same time. We'll need to consider pharmacology—'

'I really don't want to take drugs.'

He looked up at her sharply. 'Medicines,' he said. 'We call them medicines.' He smiled. 'And how interesting. You would take penicillin without a moment's hesitation, I have no doubt, so why would you not take a medicine that might help you recover from the highly anxious state you find yourself in?'

Kate felt pretty stupid. She didn't argue. 'What is wrong with me?' she asked.

Dr Wiseman closed the file. He took off his glasses, placed them carefully in the centre of the folder and looked up at her. 'I suspect that some genetics is involved and some imprinting. You may have a natural predisposition to anxiety, as it seems your father had, and in turn his behaviour, his fears over your safety, may have helped further imprint that natural tendency into you.' He wiped his forehead and began to clean his glasses. 'You spoke earlier of the impact of your father's death. Up until that point, you had looked to him to soothe your fears. After his departure, there was no one left to do that for you, save your husband, whom, as you also said, you clung to with too great a force.'

'But what can I do about it?'

'You will need to learn to self-soothe. To care for yourself, rather than rely on others to provide comfort. In short you must leave the anxious child behind you and learn to be comfortable in the adult and capable Kate, who is a mother to two children and a senior executive officer in one of our nation's most demanding professions.' He put his glasses back on the folder. 'It would help, I think, to begin that conversation quite consciously.'

'Between?'

'Your adult self and the frightened child within. The adult Kate Henderson is an incredibly accomplished and confident woman, making decisions of enormous importance for the nation at large. She is surely the person you need to soothe the scared child. If you can open up that conversation within you, it would help.'

That made a lot of sense. She stood. 'Thank you . . . thank you, Dr Wiseman.'

She left his consulting room and hurried out into the light drizzle. She turned her face to the sky and let the cool drops fall upon her cheeks, then roll over her chin and down her neck. The relief was immense. Someone understood.

Dr Wiseman's room was in Ealing Broadway, so she caught a cab all the way back to Vauxhall Cross and returned to her office with a spring in her step. She had barely got back to her desk before her new deputy was slipping through the door behind her. 'Kate . . .'

'Hi.'

Suzy closed the door. 'I read the file. Operation Sigma.'

'Good.' Kate waited, but nothing further was forthcoming. 'So now you're up to date.' She turned to her computer.

'Are you sure your analysis on Viper was correct?' Suzy asked. Kate turned back to her. 'I'm not trying to be difficult,' Suzy went on. 'It's just that, over at Five, I did quite a lot of mole hunts. You might even call it my speciality. And I'm not sure it makes sense that your husband was Viper.'

Kate tried to contain her irritation. This was about the last thing on the planet she wanted reopened. 'My husband admitted his betrayal.'

'I'm not disputing that, only the conclusion that he was actually Viper. We know how much effort the Russians have put into seducing and corrupting people across Whitehall. It makes sense that they have more than one – perhaps multiple – corrupted agent of influence. Stuart was expendable.'

'Not to me.'

'I'm sorry, bad choice of language.'

'Indeed.'

'I just mean . . . if you go back to the beginning of the operation on Igor's yacht, he's overheard saying, "Viper can help." If you consider the stakes, does it really make sense that Igor would be referring to a relatively tangential player in those terms?'

'Stuart worked for the prime minister's principal rival. He was married to me. I am not sure he was tangential.'

'I get that. Stuart was betraying you. In the heat of an operation, I totally understand that, as you began to appreciate his treachery, you would naturally conclude he was Viper.'

'But I was wrong?'

'I'm not saying that. It's just, to me, as an outsider, looking at this afresh, it doesn't make sense of Igor's comment. "Viper can help" implies someone more important in the food chain than your husband.'

'Perhaps, perhaps not.'

'And yet how could they possibly have known what Rav was up to in Geneva? According to the file, your husband had no idea of that.'

'They must have been monitoring his phone.'

'Rav was surely much too experienced and capable to have communicated with anyone in a manner that was less than secure.'

'He called the *Guardian* journalist.'

'True. I saw that. But he was unlikely to have told him what he was really up to.'

Kate thought about this. On Rav – perhaps – Suzy might have a point. And now that she had brought it up, Kate wasn't sure this doubt hadn't been nagging at her ever since Rav's murder. 'Okay,' she said. 'Thanks.' She debated telling her of the way in which someone in the Russian hierarchy had started the Night Wolves retreat from Estonia at nine the previous evening, but thought better of it.

The circle of knowledge had been the same small group: C, Ian, Julie, Danny and Kate. The betrayal of one or another was unthinkable.

'I'm not trying to be difficult, Kate.'

'I understand that.' She nodded. 'I do. You make valid points. I don't know how profitable it's likely to be to reopen this right now, but I will give it some thought.'

Suzy slipped out and Kate closed her eyes. 'Fucking hell,' she whispered to herself.

8

KATE TOOK THE opportunity to leave Vauxhall early that afternoon. She chose one of the six aliases common to officers at her level and asked Travel to book her on to the first flight to Berlin on Monday morning. She warned Operations to put Danny, her favoured team leader, on standby to manage the surveillance on the ground in the city, pending the foreign secretary's approval. And then she walked up to Victoria to catch the Circle line to Paddington.

The train journey to Bodmin Parkway should theoretically have been a time of relative peace and relaxation, but the temporary relief she had felt after her appointment with Dr Wiseman was overtaken by a tidal wave of further anxiety. If she had heard 'We have a solution' as she left his office, all she could hear now was 'You have a problem.' The questions crowded in: was she going to have to take drugs? Would she become addicted? Would they affect her ability to do her job? Why did she think like this anyway? When was she going to feel better? *How* would she feel better? What would happen if she got worse, if she lost control, if things began to spiral? Would she lose her job, her children? Who would look after them then?

The questions clattered in her mind. And that was before she had even got around to turning over whether she might really have been wrong about Stuart being Viper. Suzy had a point. But if not Stuart, then who?

She hoped to see Rose at the station, but instead she got only the cheery face of her husband, Simon. Perhaps it was a relief. She just about managed to make small-talk on the short journey up to the coast. Simon looked as if he had been in Cornwall for a month already, dressed in a T-shirt and shorts despite the season, his curly white hair as wild as the wind, which was blowing in hard from the west.

Rose knew something was wrong as soon as Kate walked through the door. 'Are you all right, my love?'

'I just need a few moments.'

'Well, you know where you are.'

Kate went straight upstairs to the main spare bedroom on the first floor, without saying hello to her children or her mother. She closed the door, drew back the curtains and looked out at the moonlight shimmering on the flat, calm water. She started to cry and, before she could contain herself, she was sobbing uncontrollably.

Her chest constricted again, as if she were having some kind of heart attack. She lay down on the sofa by the window and put her legs into the air. She tried to slow her breathing and bring some control to her quickening pulse.

There was a soft knock on the door and Rose crept in. She came closer. She'd bought a new pair of oval glasses, which somehow served to exaggerate the kindly expression that was her default demeanour. Her long dark hair was shot through with more grey now, though she seemed disinclined to do anything to hold back the march of time. 'Anxiety attack?'

'I don't know. I—'

'They are horrible things.'

'What the hell is happening to me?'

'You mean physiologically? You've been driving yourself too hard for too long. Too much stress. Too much trauma. The release of adrenalin and cortisol has become your body's learnt reaction and now your mind and your body are winding each other up, collectively panicking that things appear to be spinning out of control.'

'Have you ever had it?'

'Yes.'

'When?'

'It's a long story. It was in the period we were trying to

have children. I was very busy at work and I invested too much hope in . . . and . . .' Rose shook her head, clearly reluctant to go back there. 'The main thing you need to know is that it will pass. You will get better. As long as you take action now.'

'Did Dad suffer from anxiety?' Kate's father had been Rose's much-loved younger brother.

'Not that I was aware of, but . . . perhaps. He certainly wasn't himself after he found out about your mother's affair with David Johnson.'

'David Underpants.' Rose permitted herself the ghost of a smile. 'You know,' Kate went on, 'he used to wear these really tight swimming trunks that stretched high above his waist. Even as a child, even when he was supposed to be still our friend, I could see he was a ridiculous figure.'

'I'm not sure that helped your father.'

'I can still remember the call to Helen like it was yesterday. I was sitting on the stairs. I could tell from the moment she answered the phone something terrible had happened. She said she couldn't see me any more and when I asked why, she said my dad could explain.'

'Did he?'

'Not really. He said there had been some difficulty with Helen's father. I thought maybe he'd gone bankrupt, or they'd lost their house or . . .' Kate's voice trailed off. 'But then I couldn't understand why that was causing so much tension in our home.'

'Did he ever talk to you about it?'

Kate shook her head. 'You know how he liked to avoid confrontation. But I don't entirely blame him. What would he have said? "Your mother is poisonous, deeply selfish, dishonest and unreliable"? I already knew that.'

'I assume you have seen Dr Wiseman.'

'Yes.'

'How did it go?'

'When I walked out of his office, I felt as if a huge weight had been lifted from my shoulders. But as I came down on the train, I lost sight of the potential for a solution and all I could focus on was the certainty that I have a problem.'

'Well, you're in a very volatile state of mind. And you will be for a while. But the first step to recovery is to admit you're not well. Did you talk about work?'

'What do you mean?'

'Taking some time off.'

'I can't do that.'

'Kate—'

'I can't, Rose.' Kate sat up. The pain in her chest was still searing. 'Please don't push it. I just absolutely cannot take any time off now and that is all there is to say on the subject.'

Rose nodded in a way that made it crystal clear she was far from convinced and the matter was certainly not closed. 'All right. Just stay here for a while. I'll bring you up a cup of tea and tell the children you had to rest.'

'Did you hear from Belgrade?'

Kate's aunt hesitated a moment too long. 'Let's talk about it at work on Monday.'

'What happened?'

Rose was now staring at the floor. 'It's complicated.'

'How?'

'You know it is. We have to find a couple willing to adopt Maja there. Then we have to go to court to force the state to remove her from her mother, see through the legal adoption, then bring the entire new family over here. It's long-winded, extremely expensive, and success is far from certain.'

The anxiety in Kate's chest was exploding again now. 'We don't have a choice.'

'Ian thinks we do.'

'No . . . No. We made a promise!'

'Calm down, Kate. That's why I suggested we deal with it on Monday or whenever you're in a fit state to have a rational discussion about it.'

'We'll do it outside the law!'

'We can't, and you know we can't.' Rose's gaze was steely. 'Look, I'm on your side. I think Sir Alan will be, too, so I suggest in the strongest possible terms that you let it go for now.'

Once Rose had gone, Kate closed her eyes and started to cry again. She had never felt so hopeless and ashamed.

Rose came back with a cup of tea. 'Take your time,' she said. 'And if you can't make it down to supper, that's fine.'

'Can I help?'

'No. Absolutely not.' Rose pointed to the huge rolltop bath in the bay window. 'Run yourself a hot bath, look up at the moonlight, drink your tea and relax for a few minutes. I'll bring you something stronger in a while.'

'Thank you,' Kate said, as Rose reached the door. 'I don't know what I'd do without you.'

'With any luck, you won't find out for a while, because I intend to hang around for as long as I possibly can.'

'You'd better.'

Rose slipped out again. Kate ran a deep bath and tried to relax into it. But neither the hot water, nor the tea, nor the moonlight did much to alter the basic physiology of her body, which felt as if it was vibrating constantly.

Rose returned with a gin and tonic. 'You probably shouldn't,' she said. 'But I'm not sure it'll do any harm.'

Kate took a sip. 'Christ! What did you put in it?'

'Five parts gin.'

Rose went back to her cooking and Kate came down twenty minutes later as supper was being served. She felt quite drunk and consequently played little part in the conversation, which, in any event, didn't cover much of substance. They mostly talked about what they would do tomorrow.

It was at this point that Kate's mother chose, incomprehensibly, to pipe up. 'Where is Stuart?' she asked.

There was a stunned silence. The children stared at their food. 'Stuart went away,' Rose said quietly. 'You know that.'

'Where to?'

'Russia.'

'*Russia?* Why on earth did he want to go there?' She turned slowly to her daughter. 'Was he running away from you?'

'That's enough, Lucy,' Rose said. 'Would you like some more chicken?'

'I don't understand. Why did he leave?'

Kate nodded at Rose to indicate that she could and would handle it. Her mother always had the ability to rile her, if nothing else. 'Stuart is still my husband and the children's father, Mum, so I'd be grateful if you'd drop the subject.'

'Well, I did warn you.'

'About what?' Fiona asked.

'Leave it, love,' Kate said.

'I just want to know what Granny warned you about.'

'Oh, you know what. Your mother is awfully difficult.' Lucy looked from Fiona to Gus and back again. 'You both know that. She drove him away. I knew she would. I told her she'd never be able to hold on to a man.'

Even by her mother's standards, this attack was so vicious and brazen as to take Kate's breath away. But that didn't stop the rage exploding inside her head.

'I think you should go to bed, Lucy,' Simon said. 'No good is going to come of you sitting here with us at supper in this mood.'

They all turned to him. Simon was normally emollient, generous, munificent, steady. None of them had ever heard him talk like that before. Even Lucy was a bit taken aback. 'That wasn't a request,' he added, smiling.

Lucy put down her knife and fork, thrust her plate away and left the room. Rose waited a few moments, then pushed back her chair. 'I'd better go and see if she's all right.'

'Thank you,' Kate said to Simon.

'It's my pleasure.'

'Sometimes, I think the Alzheimer's is actually just a front to allow her an old age full of the pleasure of dispensing poison as and when the mood takes her.'

'Don't say that,' Fiona said. 'She's ill.'

Kate didn't fancy an argument with her daughter, so the rest of the meal passed off in small-talk.

Rose insisted Kate leave the washing-up and go straight to bed, but her fevered state of mind seemed to accelerate with the night. She climbed beneath the huge duvet ready to pass out, but something in her brain prevented her from drifting off. And the more she thought and worried about it, the more awake she felt. Worry became fear, then panic.

She didn't know whether it was better to lie there and hope that sleep crept over her or get up and distract herself, so she ended up doing both in turn. She switched on the bedside light and tried to read the new William Boyd novel she'd brought with her.

Then she switched off the light and lay still.

She got up, drew back the curtains and gazed at the moonlight, which shimmered on the still waters of the bay.

But as the hours of the night crawled slowly by, she had to acknowledge to herself that sleep would not come. As a consequence, the dawn was a kind of relief. The sun came up over the estuary with a crisp amber hue. Kate watched the light creep across the landscape, freeing her inch by inch from the terrors of the night.

She let herself out and walked around the headland towards the small town of Rock, crossed the golden sands of Daymer Bay and climbed to the top of Brae Hill, where the view took in a contrasting patchwork of green and blue all the way down to Padstow on the far side of the inlet.

Rose and Simon were already at the breakfast table by the time she returned, but there was no sign of her mother or either of the children. Rose poured her a cup of coffee. 'Did you sleep?'

'No.'

'Not much or not at all?'

'Not at all.' Kate shook her head. 'It's weird. It's a long time since I managed to go all night without any sleep.'

'It's not weird at all,' Rose said. 'You've been under the most incredible pressure. Something has to give.'

'I guess so.'

Kate pulled the newspaper across. 'NATO in Crisis' was the headline on *The Times*. 'The Germans say they still want to send more troops to Estonia, even if NATO refuses to do so officially,' Rose said. 'The French will follow suit.'

'Any word from Downing Street?'

'Still the same line, that the crisis is receding. It's a time to cool tempers, especially as the British public wouldn't wear being drawn into a conflict over a country like Estonia. Or words to that effect.' Simon put down his copy of the *Financial Times* and poured himself more coffee. 'Makes you proud to be British, doesn't it?'

Kate's phone buzzed. There was a message from C. *The foreign secretary has asked to see us at Chevening tonight. I hear you're with Rose in Cornwall, so will send a car to Paddington to bring you down there.*

'They want you back,' Rose said. Kate nodded, wondering how Sir Alan had known where she was spending the weekend. 'One of the advantages of not actually being your mother,' Rose went on, 'is that I don't feel obliged to nag. So just take this as a statement of obvious fact. I don't think you're in any fit state to be at work and I'm sure Sir Alan will understand if you explain it to him. And if you don't want to, I'm quite happy to do so.'

'I'll be fine. I'll catch the afternoon train back. I'll sleep tonight.'

Rose didn't make any attempt to hide her disquiet. 'All right, but let me know when you're ready to acknowledge that things are stacking up against you. There's no shame in admitting you've reached your limits.'

Kate buried herself in the paper. She had absolutely no intention of admitting she had reached her limits. She wasn't even entirely sure what that meant.

She woke the children at nine, so that they would have time to eat before their scheduled surf lesson. It took three attempts to get Gus out of bed, but once he was awake, he ate his breakfast with the speed of a gulag prisoner finally offered a square meal. Fiona had coffee, black, no sugar. Her once dappled cheeks looked gaunt, her greasy blonde hair tied back in a tight knot. Her vivid blue eyes were in danger of being the only trace of the beauty she'd once been.

Normally, she would pretend to eat something – usually cereal, which she would then push around her bowl until it looked as if she'd had some. But this morning, she didn't even do that.

Kate tried to get her daughter on her own on the way down to the beach, but Fiona wedged herself alongside Jed the entire way, as if she knew what her mother was trying to do.

Simon and Rose went back to the house, so Kate watched the surf instruction alone on the beach. Despite the sunshine, it was cold, and she kept her hands thrust deep into her pockets. Polzeath was a small community that swelled in the summer months. Drab in the rain, it could pass itself off as quaint when the sun was shining, as it was that morning.

All three of the children got up easily on their surfboards at the second or third attempt. Jed was by far the best and Fiona consequently lost his company to her brother on the walk back to the house. Kate thought her son's admiration for Jed bordered on adulation these days, but perhaps there was no harm in that.

Kate saw her chance and accelerated to fall into step naturally with her daughter. 'I knew you were waiting to pounce,' Fiona said.

'That's not kind.'

'I had breakfast.'

'Did you? I only saw coffee.'

'I wasn't hungry. I *am* eating.'

At least she hadn't said, *It's none of your business.* 'How are you feeling?' she asked, changing tack.

'About what?'

'I don't know. Life. School. Jed. We don't seem to discuss things as much as we used to.'

'Jed's lovely. I don't deserve him.'

'That's a bit harsh. He really loves you. And he's right to.'

'I don't need a pep talk, Mum.'

'I'm not—'

'What is it you want? Why don't you just spit it out?'

Kate felt unconscionably like bursting into tears. Was her daughter turning into her mother? 'We haven't really talked about how things were with your dad.'

'We have.'

'Not in any meaningful detail.'

'All right. What do you want to know? It was a bit shit. It was *obviously* a bit shit.'

'Was it nice to see him?'

'Of course. We still love him, even if you don't.'

'What did you chat about?'

'School. Friends. Jed. How he was doing in Moscow. When we might see him again. Whether it would be possible to live with him . . .'

Fiona had speeded up now, so that Kate had to jog a few steps to come back alongside her daughter. She could feel her throat constricting. 'I'm sorry, *what* did you just say?'

Fiona didn't slacken her pace. Kate was forced to take hold of her arm and spin her around. She was confronted by five feet seven of pure teenage fury: a young woman who seemed unsure as to whether to spit at her mother or burst into tears. Or both. Kate knew exactly how she felt. 'What do you mean, whether you could live with him?'

'Exactly what I said.'

Kate stared at her. She knew when Fiona was trying to provoke her and that she should not take the bait. 'I'm going to forget you said that.'

'Why? I meant it.'

'I don't think you did.' Kate couldn't keep the anger from her voice. 'Not just because it's grievously insulting, but because we both know it would be impossible.'

'Why? I'm sixteen in two weeks' time. Old enough to

have sex. Officially. An adult. If I want to go and live with Dad in Russia, I don't believe there's anything you can legally do to stop me.'

'That's not true, as you should know. Anyway, what about your brother?'

'He wants to come too. And he can, as soon as he's old enough.'

'And what about Jed?'

Fiona's face clouded. She didn't have an answer to that one. Kate was tempted to press her advantage, but she held her tongue. You really didn't need to be a psychiatrist to discern what was going on here. It was her job, as a mother, simply to suck it all up.

Fiona hurried to join her boyfriend. When they returned to Simon and Rose's house, Kate went upstairs to her bedroom and burst into tears. Again. Never in all her life had she felt so alone.

9

IF, FOR A contented mind, time is peace, then for a fevered one it's precisely the opposite. The nearly five or so hours it took for Kate to return to London were close to torture. The worse she felt, the more she wondered what was wrong with her.

C had promised a car would be waiting for her at Paddington. Kate got into it and closed her eyes for much of the journey down to Chevening, the foreign secretary's country residence. She was only interrupted by a text from the education secretary, Imogen Conrad. *Crazy times again, hon. You about?*

Kate had once enjoyed an artificial friendship with

Imogen of the only kind one can with a husband's boss. But the education secretary did not appear to think that being filmed having sex with Stuart and breaking up their marriage should be any kind of barrier to her future relationship with Kate. Using the pretext of having been appointed a governor at the children's school, she had bombarded Kate with texts ever since the scandal broke.

Kate mostly ignored her in what she hoped was a dignified way, but Imogen was insanely persistent and had a skin as thick as that of a rhinoceros. *Can we chat?* Imogen messaged, when she did not immediately reply. About bloody what? Kate was tempted to ask, but so far she'd held her tongue and was determined to continue to do so. Her dignity demanded she treat Imogen with the amoral vacuity she deserved.

Hun? Imogen texted again. She had once been so annoyed with one of Stuart's deputies in the Department of Education that she had suggested it would be easier to send around a message in a bottle. When he had been slow to respond to a subsequent text, Imogen had actually sent a message in a bottle. Stuart had thought that clever, sassy and really quite funny. Perhaps it was.

Kate stared at her phone. *Am in Cornwall with Rose and the kids*, she lied.

Assume you'll be home tonight for school tomorrow. So can I pop around at 10 p.m., say?

Kate didn't answer. What was the point?

She stared out of the window for the rest of the journey, trying to think about how she would manage the next two or three days. Rose could step in and look after the kids. She herself would take a sleeping pill tonight to make sure she finally got some rest. It was manageable. Of course it was.

Before long, the car crunched across the smooth gravel and swept past a tinkling fountain to the front of the red-brick Palladian Inigo Jones mansion that was the weekend home of serving foreign secretaries.

A uniformed member of staff ushered her into the grand hallway and showed her through to a small anteroom. She was surprised to find her new deputy waiting for her. 'Suzy?' she said.

'The foreign secretary asked me to come along.'

Kate was tempted to enquire as to how Meg Simpson had even known of Suzy's existence, but she made a mental note instead to keep an even closer eye on her deputy. 'Where is Sir Alan?'

'I believe he's in a meeting here already.'

Kate sat down on a stiff-backed cream chair by the door. The Sunday newspapers were carefully laid out on a coffee-table in front of an empty fireplace. She picked up *The Sunday Times* and glanced over the front-page story. She'd intended to catch up on the train, but the tiny shop on Bodmin Parkway station had not yet stretched to newspapers. 'Any read-out on the NATO summit beyond the headlines?' she asked Suzy.

'I only had a chance to speak to Sir Alan briefly on the way down here.' Kate noted they had not offered to share a car with her and that Suzy appeared keen to underline the fact. 'The read-out from the room is worse than the headlines. We're looking at a total split in NATO. Germany, France, the Benelux countries, everyone on Europe's eastern flank – in fact, pretty much everyone else – is keen to send reinforcements to Estonia, even if the crisis is receding. Washington and London insist that would be provocative.'

Kate wondered if this fissure in NATO had been the true purpose of the entire episode. If the Russian president's primary foreign-policy aim was to fatally divide his enemies, he was doing an exceptional job. He'd regained control in Syria, was busy attempting to hold the whip hand in Libya. Who knew where his ambitions really ended? 'What does the foreign secretary have to say about it?' she asked.

'I don't know, but I guess we're about to find out.'

The butler – if that was what he was – put his head around the door. 'Mrs Henderson?'

Suzy got up with Kate. The butler raised a hand and an eyebrow at her. 'Just Mrs Henderson, please.' He led Kate along the hallway to one of the drawing rooms, where the windows were open to the expansive gardens and a lake in the distance, illuminated now by a bright moon. Despite the chill breeze, there was a hint of spring in the smell of newly mown grass.

Meg Simpson and Sir Alan sat opposite each other in

stiff-backed chairs. There were gloomy old masters on the walls, an ornate white fireplace in front of them and a rich Afghani rug on the floor. As an image, Kate thought, it was every conspiracy theorist's fantasy of how a British foreign secretary and the head of SIS might conduct their business.

The foreign secretary, in particular, looked tired, as if the last few days had aged her considerably. 'I've reviewed the files,' she said, without introduction or small-talk. 'And it's my view that we should proceed to the next stage of this operation. You have the offer to meet Mr Borodin's son in Berlin?'

'That's right, ma'am. I've suggested Tuesday at ten a.m.'

'What would it involve?'

'In terms of resources?'

'If you could just give me an outline . . . I'm not familiar with how such operations work.'

Kate glanced at Sir Alan as she tried to assess what was really being requested here. No minister she'd dealt with before had wanted to know the nuts and bolts of such a relatively simple operation. 'I would go with one or both of my deputies as back-up. Then we'd have a team on the ground to conduct the requisite covert surveillance, just to ensure that neither side was being watched or followed and that the meeting would be able to take place in relative security and secrecy.'

'Will you be in a position to assess . . . to see the material?'

'You mean the kompromat video, ma'am?'

'The alleged kompromat, yes.'

'That is essentially the purpose of the meeting. As I'm sure Sir Alan has outlined, the potential defection of the former head of one of Russia's main intelligence agencies is highly unusual, not to say unheard-of, and down the line will require enormous effort, expenditure and a great many resources on our part. They will come to the meeting with the material. I'm sure of it.'

'It's the unusual-bordering-on-unheard-of bit that bothers me.'

'But that is why it's important I see the material first-hand. Once we've assessed it, we'll be in a position to say whether the defection is a risk worth running. But if they're prepared to bring us evidence that the Russians have been blackmailing our prime minister, I think it's a chance we must take.'

Simpson stared at the empty fireplace. The decisive air she'd cultivated at the start of the meeting seemed to have dissipated in Kate's discussion of the detail. 'You have my permission to go to the next stage,' she said finally. 'But no further. Assess the material, then let us speak again immediately.'

Kate realized she was expected to answer. 'Of course, ma'am. I'll come in to brief you as soon as I'm off the plane, although . . .'

'Yes?'

'Mikhail will want to know for sure whether we're prepared to offer his father and family sanctuary.'

'That's what we'll decide once you've assessed it.'

'He will almost certainly want an answer on the spot. And we may lose them if I can't give him that assurance.'

'Lose them to whom?'

'Another foreign intelligence service. The French, the Germans. Perhaps even the Americans. And they will know we turned Mikhail and his father down.'

The foreign secretary evidently didn't like the sound of that. 'Very well. Say what you need to say. We can always change our minds at a later date.'

'That isn't how we do business.'

Simpson looked up sharply. 'These people are sharks. I won't be lectured on morality by them, thank you very much.' That wasn't what Kate meant and both women knew it, but she let it go. 'If the material is legitimate, we will almost certainly go ahead with the exchange, repugnant as it may be. But we will take one step at a time.' She rang the bell and waited for the butler. Rather like the Queen, Kate thought, but didn't say. 'Could you bring Suzy in?' Simpson asked.

Suzy, Kate noted. Not Miss Spencer, or even Suzy Spencer. Just Suzy. They were clearly better acquainted than she'd imagined, but the question was how and why? Kate tried to catch Sir Alan's eye, but he was staring out of the window at the moonlight.

Suzy walked crisply in. 'Foreign Secretary, Sir Alan,' she said, nodding at each in turn. She sat. She was dressed in a tailored dark suit and a white shirt: a model of cool professionalism. Kate glanced down at her weathered trousers and scuffed brown suede flats. Perhaps she should have made more of an effort.

Suzy took a folder from her shoulder bag and placed it on the walnut coffee-table. It sat there like an unspoken accusation.

'Tea, coffee, a drink?' Simpson asked.

'No, thank you, Foreign Secretary.'

They waited. Suzy was enjoying her moment in the ministerial limelight. 'Get on with it, Miss Spencer,' Sir Alan said.

Suzy glanced at Kate nervously. Whatever she was doing, perhaps she was having second thoughts. 'I've been looking at the Operation Sigma file. It was extraordinarily well conceived and carried through, so none of this is meant to be a criticism in any way, but rather a reflection of the fact that we all know some things are bound to be overlooked in the heat of the moment.' Kate kept her eyes on her new deputy. 'I agree with Kate's analysis that many of the facts do fit the idea that her husband, Stuart, was Viper. While he did not know the details of the original operation in Istanbul, he was aware that it was a significant success and he clearly had some general idea of what it was about.'

Kate could feel her face reddening. In reality, Suzy was

protecting her here, since she had clearly worked out her boss had been somewhat economical in the file as to how much she had shared with Stuart.

'So, assuming Stuart passed on to his controllers the fact that Kate was returning to Greece to continue with the operation, that might well have been enough for Moscow to swing into action and put a team on her tail. Until this point, Stuart as Viper adds up.'

She flipped open the file and handed around some sheets stapled together. 'I've run a precise spot check on Rav's phone for the last twenty-four hours of his life, including the time he was in Geneva investigating the lawyer with close links to the Kremlin. As you can see from this timeline, there was virtually no activity. He was entirely off the grid. There is the call to the *Guardian* journalist, which Kate reported. I have spoken to the journalist in question directly. He seems a pretty straight guy and insists Rav just wanted the lawyer's name and told him nothing of what he was up to. He insists he spoke to no one about it and I'm inclined to believe him. Then there is the incoming call from Kate while Rav was in Geneva. After that, there are no calls and no spikes in any kind of electronic activity, save for here, at around six p.m. I think that's the message that Kate also logged in the file.'

Kate handed her sheets back to Suzy. The others followed suit, as they contemplated their contents in silence.

'I'd also say Rav strikes me as much too experienced

and talented an officer to have breached operational security in any significant way,' Suzy added.

'Perhaps he was followed,' Simpson said.

Kate glanced at Suzy, who waited for her to answer. 'That kind of surveillance requires a great deal of manpower, ma'am. And, as Suzy says, Rav was experienced enough to have taken anti-surveillance measures and to have reported any activity back to us in London.'

'So someone knew what he was up to in Geneva and tipped off the Russians?' Simpson said. She was looking directly at Kate.

'It looks that way, yes.'

'And it could not have been your husband?'

'That's correct, ma'am.'

'To be honest, I'm surprised these questions were not asked before,' Suzy said. They all turned towards her. Even Simpson was frowning at what felt like a gratuitous twist of the knife. 'I didn't mean . . .' Now it was her turn to redden.

'Who knew enough of what Rav was doing to tip off the Russians?' Simpson asked.

'Chiefly me,' Kate said.

'I knew,' Sir Alan added. 'So did Ian and Julie.'

'Just the four of you?'

'I would say so.'

Kate stared at the floor. My God, she wished Operation Sigma had never darkened her door. Nothing good had come of it, nothing at all. Kate wondered if Sir Alan would mention that the Russians seemed to have been tipped off about Estonia as well, but he must have decided that discretion was the better part of valour and she was not about to argue with him.

'Well, we can't pretend this is anything but uncomfortable,' Simpson said.

'My colleagues in Five will certainly want to know why these questions weren't asked before,' Suzy said.

Sir Alan looked at her. 'You are a very clever and ambitious woman, Miss Spencer, but you are in danger of overplaying your hand here, if I may say so.' Sir Alan's voice was at its most acid. 'We did not involve our colleagues at Five because we wanted to protect our operational integrity and the security of its ultimate source, Lena Sabic, the au pair we recruited to bug Igor's super-yacht. Once the operation was complete, we had no reason to believe anyone other than Stuart was Viper.' He glanced at Meg Simpson, before turning to Suzy and leaning forward to emphasize his point. 'Your logic makes several fairly enormous leaps. We have never determined who killed Rav or why. Perhaps it was the Russians, but it may have been someone else entirely, for motives we have not yet uncovered.'

'The file makes it clear you thought it was the Russians,' Suzy said tartly. She did not look as if she was enjoying her ticking off.

'Supposition and fact are two entirely different things. We don't know what Rav was up to. He was off the grid and not following orders from anyone here. Perhaps he met someone we are not aware of, or made a call using a landline. Or it may just be that the Russians had the lawyer or his assistant under surveillance.'

'I acknowledge all those possibilities, but I still think we should—'

'Close this down now.' Sir Alan smiled at her again. 'We have bigger fish to fry. We are potentially being offered evidence that our prime minister is a traitor, who seeks to undermine our response to Russian aggression. Nothing is more serious than that, and we cannot allow anyone to stand in the way of pursuing this matter to its logical conclusion in Berlin over the next few days.'

'But if I'm right, we'll be putting Kate and her team in danger if we allow them to proceed. Their entire operation could be compromised before it has even begun.' Suzy sounded almost plaintive.

All three looked at Kate. She shrugged. 'You raise an interesting question over Rav's murder, Suzy. We shouldn't and won't sweep it aside lightly. But I'm ultimately confident my husband was Viper. And I agree with Sir Alan: nothing can be allowed to stand in the way of this operation.' Kate was aware of the formality of her language. It almost sounded like she and the chief were in a police interview, but perhaps that was what having a member of Five around did to you.

The foreign secretary nodded. 'All right, we'll leave it

there for now. Kate, you and your team will go to Berlin and we'll assess where we stand on your return. But, I repeat, I want to take this step by step.'

It was clear their audience was over. Kate and Suzy both stood, though Sir Alan did not move. Kate turned back at the door. 'Would you like us to wait for you, sir?'

'No, thank you. We have other matters to deal with.' He smiled again at Kate.

She wished them both goodnight and walked out to the car waiting by the fountain in the driveway. Suzy got in with her. Neither spoke for some time, though even the driver must have sensed the tension in the back. Eventually, Kate could contain her curiosity no longer. 'How come you know the foreign secretary so well?'

'I don't.'

'Then why did she call you "Suzy"?'

'I don't know. I only met her earlier this afternoon.'

Suzy was staring out of the window to avoid Kate's gaze, but she was plainly lying. 'I think you tried to go a bit far in there, if I may say so,' Kate suggested.

'I wasn't trying to do anything except my job.'

'You could have fooled me.'

'I was asking a question you should perhaps have asked. And I think you know that.'

Her sanctimony stung Kate into a response. 'Don't they throw a spell at Charm School into the training programme for the Security Service?'

Suzy was visibly upset. 'I'm really sorry, Kate. I know my manner can be tactless. My last boss at the Security Service said as much and couldn't wait to approve my transfer.'

If the vulnerability in Suzy's eyes was not genuine, then she was a damned good actress. 'Look, forget it. You're right on both counts. I should have asked the question and I do know it.' Suzy smiled at her. 'Let's talk about it when I get back from Berlin.'

'I really think I should accompany you to—'

'I need you here.'

'I have to be there. I mean, I want to be. This is exactly why I asked for the transfer from across the river. Please.'

Suzy's transition from snake in the grass to vulnerable young woman and back again was bewildering, but Kate no longer had the energy to fight it. 'All right,' she said, but it didn't stop her train of thought. If Suzy knew the foreign secretary much better than she was letting on, then the question was how? And was she Simpson's eyes and ears inside the Service? Was that why she had been foisted upon them? Kate resolved to treat her with still more caution.

'Thank you,' Suzy said. 'Thank you very much.'

10

KATE WAS RELIEVED that the house was still empty when she got home, the children having not yet returned from Cornwall with Rose and Simon. The respite she'd felt during the meeting at Chevening receded with the onset of fatigue, and the energy drained from her once more. She put on the kettle to make a cup of tea, then thought better of it and poured herself an enormous glass of white wine instead.

She sat at the table to drink it, wondering if this was what being an alcoholic felt like. She looked at Nelson, quite possibly the laziest beagle she had ever come across, gazing up at her without much enthusiasm from his basket in the corner. She got down on her hands and knees to rub his head and scratch his tummy, then lay flat so that she could put her head alongside his in the basket. He didn't much like to travel, these days, so she relied on a neighbour to look after him when she and the children were away.

Good God, his breath smelt. Perhaps that was what old age did to you. She shifted position so that her head was resting on his back instead and closed her eyes. It wasn't exactly comfortable on the tiled floor, but she was as likely to get to sleep there as anywhere else.

She lay there until the smell of him got too much, then stood and walked through to the living room. She switched on the TV and channel-surfed for a few minutes.

She'd managed an entire vacuous half-hour watching *Game of Thrones* before the doorbell rang. She glanced through the keyhole to check that it was Fiona and Gus, no doubt having forgotten their keys, only to see Imogen Conrad standing there.

Damn, Kate thought. The very last thing she needed. Was the woman stark, staring mad? She waited, pretending no one was in and hoping her unwanted guest would get the message and turn away.

Fat chance. The bell rang again. Kate gritted her teeth, opened the door and smiled. She was determined not to give her former friend the satisfaction of seeing just how much hurt she'd caused.

When she was talking politics, Imogen rarely drew breath, and Kate could tell tonight was going to be no exception. 'What do you think?' she asked, as she marched through the kitchen to the living room beyond. 'Oh, God, wine on a Sunday night. I shouldn't . . .'

Kate hadn't been intending to offer, but she filled a glass more or less to the top, since she'd long ago learnt that Imogen really *did* like to drink, and returned to the living room. '*Game of Thrones*?' Imogen said, looking at the screen, paused on a dragon in flight.

'Better late than never.'

'I couldn't watch. Too much violence and all the energetic sex just reminded me of what I miss with Harry.' Imogen took a large sip of her wine. 'Too much information?'

'I should say so.'

'I'm sorry. I suppose you're single again.'

'I suppose I am.'

The silence that followed this reference to the fallout of Stuart's betrayal was awkward enough to have both of them avoiding each other's eye. In the immediate aftermath of Stuart's admission of his affair with Imogen – or, rather, their episodic trysts, since both denied it had ever been more than that – she had bombarded Kate with phone messages containing ever more profuse and abject apologies. They had been followed by letters, then unannounced visits.

Kate knew then as she did now that she should have

been angrier with her erstwhile friend, but she couldn't quite summon the bitterness the circumstances seemed to demand. Imogen was every clichéd politician writ large: engaging and entertaining, but unfaithful and untrustworthy. Kate had never laboured under any illusions regarding her, but Stuart was the rock she herself had built her life on. She reserved her rage, therefore, for him and allowed herself to be bludgeoned into submission by his former boss, knowing that Imogen's desperate attempts to preserve some vestige of their friendship were nothing more than an attempt to salve her own conscience. 'So, what do you think?' Imogen asked, still staring at the TV screen. Kate quickly turned it off.

'About dragons?'

'No! What's going on in Estonia.'

'Oh, that.'

'What do you mean, "Oh, that"? What else would I be talking about? I'm surprised you're not stuck at your desk.'

'I've just come back from seeing Meg Simpson.'

'What did she have to say?'

'About what?'

'The prime minister's response, of course! I mean everything we said – *you* said – during the leadership election looks like it must have been true. He's a Russian spy, isn't he? How else do you explain his utterly bizarre reaction unless he really is working for the Russians?'

'Innate caution?'

'But he isn't a cautious man, is he? In fact, we'd probably agree he's reckless by nature – and pretty bellicose when it suits him.'

'I suppose so.' Kate wanted to get out of this conversation. She was relieved to see the wine disappearing at a rate of knots.

'What are you going to do?'

Not refill the glass, she thought. 'About Estonia?'

'The suggestion that he's a Russian spy!'

Kate sat down on the arm of the sofa. She suddenly needed to. 'There's nothing we can do. We have no evidence. The case is closed. He's the prime minister, after all.'

'Have you spoken to Meg about it?'

'No.' Kate avoided Imogen's penetrating gaze.

'Are you all right?' Imogen asked. 'You don't look well.'

'Just tired.'

'I'm sorry. I know the past six months have been . . . very difficult.'

Kate smiled weakly. She had forgotten: Imogen also had a gift for understatement. 'I should probably get some rest. I understand what you're saying, but I honestly don't think there's very much we can do about it.'

Imogen drained her wine and stared at the floor, deep in thought. She started waving the glass in a circle, and Kate worried that she would ask for a refill. But she placed it decidedly on a side table. 'I'm going to have a word with Meg myself. I won't mention you – don't worry – but I think I should at least raise it with her. And perhaps the home secretary as well.'

'Why?'

'Because we can't let him get away with it.'

'As you wish.' Kate didn't doubt her former friend's political skills. She was one of the great survivors, after all. But she wasn't about to launch a leadership challenge so soon after losing her battle against James Ryan for the premiership.

Imogen hovered. 'I'm sorry, Kate. I really don't like to see you this way and I know I . . .' She smiled again and made her exit. What else, Kate supposed, was there to say?

Kate drained her own glass and went up to lie on her bed while she waited for the children to come in. It was strange to feel dog-tired, but not at all like sleeping, as if she were being hollowed out from within.

It was a shade after eleven when she heard the door go. Neither Fiona nor Gus bothered to come and say good-night, so she had to haul herself off her bed to do so. She went to Gus first. He'd flopped face down on to his mat-tress. 'How was today?'

'Fine.'

'Long journey back?'

'It was fine.'

'How was Fiona?'

'Fine.'

'You all okay for tomorrow?'

'Yeah.'

'I have to go away for a couple of days, so Rose said she'd be here.'

'I know.'

'Will you be fine?'

'Yeah.'

Kate allowed herself a smile as she kissed his head. She moved on to her daughter's room. Fiona was lying in bed, staring at her phone. 'You'd sleep better if you didn't look at that all night, you know.'

'Because you're the expert.'

Kate smiled again. Perhaps it was despair. 'I have to go away for a few days—'

'I know. Rose said. I'm staying with Jed this week.'

Kate recognized the incendiary device for what it was, but trod on it anyway. 'You can't do that, love.'

'Er, actually, I can.'

'This is your home. You can't just leave.'

'I'm going to Jed's house. Not Moscow or Beijing, or the moon. His parents are both doctors. I'm fairly sure I'll come to no harm. I'll be back by the time you finally get home anyway, so you'll hardly notice the difference.'

'But it isn't really fair to leave Gus here on his—'

'He won't notice either. Whenever he crawls out of whatever gaming hole he chooses to occupy this week, Rose will be there to spoil him. He'll be like a pig in shit.'

Kate was tempted to go on, but, for once, discretion got

the better of her. Fiona was right: Jed's parents were responsible people and she was unlikely to come to any harm.

She retreated, without kissing her daughter goodnight, took Nelson down the road for a night-time pee – he didn't bother – then came back to bed. She took 15mg of her sleeping drug of choice, zopiclone – double her normal dose – and lay down to stare at the ceiling until chemistry finally overwhelmed her worried mind and gave her at least a few hours of fretful sleep.

11

WHEN THEY ARRIVED, it was a flat, grey, cold March day in Berlin, a city that had been comfortably in the mid-teens for most of the weekend. Suzy revealed an unlikely eye for luxury in the choice of a hotel overlooking the Tiergarten, with a giant wooden sculpture of a crocodile's jaws in Reception, a nod to the proximity of Berlin's zoo and perhaps the situation in which they were about to place themselves.

It was called Das Stue, meaning 'living room' in Danish, and beneath the grand split staircase in the entrance lobby, the reception area had been designed to capture the warmth and intimacy implicit in the hotel's name. It was very

Berlinerisch, from the doorman dressed in bowler hat and Dr. Martens to the inverted art-deco lights arranged in the shape of a grand piano hanging from the ceiling.

Kate was shown to her room on the fifth floor, which had a long balcony overlooking the treetops of the Tiergarten. She ordered tea and sat outside in her winter coat drinking it, then took herself across the road for a walk in the park as the light was beginning to fade. Berliners were hurrying home with hands thrust deep in pockets and hats pulled low to ward off the chill. And yet, the signs of spring were all around: the daffodils were coming into bloom, the lime blossom drifting on the evening wind.

There were joggers and cyclists, dog-walkers and lovers out for an evening stroll. And it was so *quiet*. Berlin was the only capital in Europe that could pass for a town or even a village, and Kate had always had a particular affection for it.

She walked as far as the Brandenburg Gate, where shoals of tourists were still being talked through the days when this monument to a nation's bellicose past had stood just beyond the wall that had divided a city, a country and a continent. It occurred to Kate to wonder if it hadn't all been a touch easier for her predecessors when the threat from the East could at least be contained in part *behind* that wall: the days before they could come and go at will in all places at all times, whether it be to murder former spies in Salisbury or attempt to rig elections across the democratic world.

It took longer than she'd anticipated to complete the circle back to the hotel, so she skipped a shower in favour of touching up her make-up, then headed down to join her colleagues in the bar.

Julie was curled up with her feet tucked beneath her on a long aubergine-coloured sofa, opposite doors open to an internal courtyard. It was cosy in there too, with a low ceiling and black-and-white photos on all the walls.

A girl was singing slow jazz to the accompaniment of a keyboard player. A couple at the next table seemed grateful for the excuse to avoid conversation, the woman deep in her phone. Beyond them, two young parents also watched the singer in silence, apparently oblivious to their young son playing a game on his iPad between them. In the courtyard, two girls chatted, feet beneath thick rugs and an empty champagne bottle upside down in the ice bucket beside them. Kate joined Suzy at the bar and asked her for a gin and light tonic, then returned to sit next to Julie. 'Where is Danny?' she asked.

'Don't know.' It was standard practice for the covert surveillance teams to stay somewhere different for an operation such as this and to avoid communicating, except via the agreed method.

Suzy returned with their drinks. They listened to the singer for a while and Kate glanced about her once more. With its pastel rugs, parquet floor, the glass and chrome bar, this salon felt like a temple to modern Berlin: slick, stylish and low key, as if the city's violent, tumultuous past had belonged to a different world entirely.

Half an hour later, they caught a cab to a restaurant called Borchardt, which Suzy insisted was a 'Berlin institution'. It was a German twist on a French brasserie, with high ceilings, grand pillars, waiters dressed in black waistcoats and white shirts, and French café chairs and tables packed in close together, save for the upholstered maroon velvet booths along the far wall.

The waiter brought the menus and Kate glanced around her. It was the kind of place where people spend the evening watching everyone else – and eating *Wiener Schnitzel,* which seemed the main course of choice for every second table.

They ordered. Kate decided on *Schnitzel* – when in Rome – and gazed around the room again, as Suzy and Julie appeared to be getting along like a house on fire, until Suzy turned the conversation to the internal politics of their own organization and brought up Ian's ill-disguised ambition to succeed Sir Alan as C. 'Do you think he'll get it?' The question was directed at Julie.

'I have no idea.'

'But he wants it badly, right?'

'I should think so. Wouldn't you if you were in his shoes?'

'What's he like?'

'He's okay. A bit chippy sometimes.'

'I heard he's a bit of a player. On the romantic front, I mean.' Kate watched Suzy's expression. Either she was spectacularly ill-informed – since Julie's affair with Ian was now pretty much common knowledge inside the building and probably beyond – or she was being provocative, malicious, or both.

Julie shrugged to indicate she had no idea, or did not want to be drawn. 'I just need to go the Ladies,' Suzy said.

Julie waited until she was out of earshot before she exploded. 'What is she – fucking autistic?'

'I don't think she can possibly know. Even she isn't that stupid.'

'Everyone knows.' It was said with a disconsolate shrug.

'I'm not going to say I told you so.'

'Good!' Julie said. 'What a mess. I should have listened to you. He proposed to me last night.'

'What did you say?'

'No! Of course! I told him I was not the marrying kind and never would be. He burst into tears and said he was heartbroken and he would now be on his own for the rest of his life and . . . Oh, my God, I thought he was never going to leave. He just cried and cried like a baby.'

'That doesn't really strike me as a normal kind of reaction.'

'Well, I'm not normal, am I? Maybe I pushed him to it.'

'Is that what he said?'

'No. He was pathetic, rather than angry. But that always

makes it worse.' Julie nodded towards the Ladies in the corner. 'What's the deal with her? One minute she's really engaging and good fun and the next she's a monster.'

'That might be a bit of an exaggeration.'

'She told me she was investigating you.' Kate frowned. 'Yeah, exactly,' Julie went on. 'There's nothing like actually announcing you're the snake in the grass. She said she didn't think Stuart was Viper and that she'd been given permission to open the investigation. She said she'd narrowed it down to a choice between you, me, Ian and Sir Alan. I replied that as career strategies went, I thought she was on to a guaranteed winner – all three of her bosses and one of her juniors. That should see her floating in the River Thames fairly soon.'

'I think she might be getting carried away.'

'She can really get in the way, that's for sure.'

Suzy came back. They sat in awkward silence for a moment. 'Have you been talking about me?'

'Of course not,' Julie said.

'Is it true you're having an affair with Ian Granger?' Suzy asked.

Julie looked as if she'd been punched in the face.

Kate gasped. 'I really don't think—'

'Given the work I need to do,' Suzy said, 'it would be better for me to know.'

'This would be the investigation you've just been told to park by the leader of our organization?' Kate asked.

'It's just that I heard he'd left his wife and was having a relationship with someone else in the organization. One of my colleagues thought it was Julie. I really feel that's something I should be made aware of.'

'Well, if you're really desperate to know,' Julie said, recovering some of her poise, if not shedding her anger, 'then, yes, we had a brief affair. It was just sex. His marriage was breaking down anyway. He has now left his wife. We are not going to be together. Our relationship is over. Would you like to know what sexual positions we preferred?' Suzy's face was reddening. 'Isn't that the kind of information you find important at the Security Service?'

'There's no need to talk like that. It was a legitimate question.'

The food arrived, just in the nick of time, and conversation really flew along after that.

Kate was grateful to get back to her room. She brushed her teeth, took another double dose of zopiclone and crawled beneath the sheets. The last thing she recalled of that night was a message from Julie that said simply, *What a bitch.*

12

THE FOLLOWING MORNING, Kate was awake early after a short, disturbed and not very restful sleep. She made herself a cup of tea from the kettle in the corner of the room and sat on the balcony outside with a thick oversized coat on her lap.

She glanced at her phone. She opened and closed WhatsApp, flicked through Instagram, then depressed herself with a few minutes on Twitter. She mostly followed politicians and political journalists, and the rage these days was disheartening. It felt like the place everyone went to shout at each other.

She forced herself to put her phone in her pocket and

leave it there, which was always surprisingly hard when she was on her own. The sky over the Tiergarten was a brooding, portentous grey, with only the faintest lick of dawn light. The silence felt oppressive. Once upon a time, trips abroad had been accompanied with the regular buzz of the phone in her pocket relaying messages from Stuart, just the everyday frustrations – and sometimes pleasures – of a man left alone to look after his children. And of love. For the first time since his departure, she was aware of truly missing him: his laugh, his smile, his episodic thoughtfulness and concern for her, not to mention the physical affection and warmth.

She wondered when she would next have sex. Before she died? When she was eighty?

Kate finished her tea and was about to get up when her phone buzzed. It was a WhatsApp message from Sergei. *How are you?*

She stared at it. Was he telepathic? She messaged back, *Am good. Are you in London?* Her heart raced with the same kind of force as it had in the days when they had almost become lovers as students in St Petersburg, a world and half a lifetime away.

No, at home in St Petersburg. Be great to see you sometime.

Kate looked at that for a long while. What was he up to? What was it about? She couldn't think straight. She hadn't seen him since a meeting at the US ambassador's party in London at the height of Operation Sigma. And she hadn't heard from him since she'd travelled to his family's dacha in the Gulf of Finland, north of St Petersburg, expecting to have everything explained – his role in the GRU, the reason for tipping her off about the meeting of the Russian intelligence elite on Igor's super-yacht, the identity of the secret mole, Viper, in MI6 – along with confirmation that the prime minister really was working for the Russians.

Instead, she'd found Stuart waiting on the beach, with confirmation that he was Viper, and it was all over.

Except nothing was over. In her more troubled moments, she thought the game the Russians were playing might only just have begun.

She put the phone into her pocket and immediately took it out again. *How?* she typed. *Where?*

But there was no reply. She opened the photograph attached to his feed. It was of him smiling against the backdrop of a long beach and the Gulf of Finland, his family's dacha just visible in the distance. She waited and waited – and then could contain herself no longer. *Are you there?* she asked.

He didn't answer.

Eventually Kate forced herself from the chair and went to shower. She had to resist the temptation to look at her phone while she dressed, but when she could stave it off no longer, there was still no reply from Sergei.

The sense of anxiety, of dread, even, wrapped itself around her, but she forced herself through it, as if in a fog, and found herself the first at the breakfast buffet. She filled her plate and went to a remote corner table. She ordered coffee and drank it too fast. She didn't feel like eating. She wondered how Fiona and Gus were getting on at home. She called Rose's mobile, but got no reply there either.

Neither Julie nor Suzy made it to breakfast, so they met at eight forty-five in the lobby as agreed. Kate had her earpiece in and she set off on the route they had all arranged in advance with Danny.

She walked through the centre of the Tiergarten, skirting the Rose Garden, and then under the Brandenburg Gate to allow Danny and his team time to assess whether she was being watched and followed by members of any foreign intelligence service, most notably, of course, the Russians.

The idea was to move from crowded areas to open ones and back again, while officers on the streets worked behind her to get a sense of what they might or might not be up against. Danny, meanwhile, monitored the electronic activity in the immediate vicinity of her progress to check for any spikes that might suggest hostile officers communicating with each other while in pursuit.

Kate was halfway down Unter den Linden when the tiny microphone in her ear came to life with Danny's calm, steady voice. 'Take a turn into Bebelplatz.'

She did so, ambling slowly to the centre of the famous square, in which the Nazis had burnt books, to look through the glass window in the cobbles at its centre, which afforded a view of the library built in memorial beneath.

She returned to Unter den Linden and continued on past Museum Island to Alexanderplatz, which still had the bleak air of the square in east Berlin it had once been.

Despite her leisurely pace, Kate reached the corner of the square early and Danny instructed her to carry on beyond it. 'Need a bit more to be sure,' he said.

She walked on under the S-Bahn and swung left into Münzstrasse. Halfway down it, she turned into a vintage shop, where 'The Eton Rifles' by The Jam was playing on an old turntable. It was a pick-and-weigh store, where your choices were measured by the kilo, full of ripped jeans, denim shorts, leather belts, bags and jackets, sunglasses and every kind of hat that might have been fashionable in the sixties, seventies or eighties.

As she stepped back on to Münzstrasse, Danny's voice rang in her ear: 'Clear. Go back to the meet point.'

Kate retraced her steps, past the homeless people sleeping beneath the underpass, until she was standing by the bus stop in the corner of Alexanderplatz.

She waited. Julie had slipped a packet of cigarettes into the pocket of her jacket before she'd left the hotel and she lit one now to pass the time.

It started to spit with rain, so she joined the bus queue beneath the shelter. An old woman in front of her waved away the smoke.

A phone rang in her pocket. It was not her own. She took out an old-fashioned Nokia and answered it. She had not felt anyone place it there. 'I said come alone,' Mikhail said.

'We're not at the stage yet where I'm prepared to take that risk.'

'Go to the S-Bahn station. Head for Westkreuz. Keep the phone with you.'

Kate put the Nokia back into her pocket and crossed the road. 'He's asked me to get on an S-Bahn train to Westkreuz,' she whispered quietly into the microphone hidden inside the lapel of her jacket. 'How the hell did someone get a phone into my pocket?'

'Sorry, Kate,' Danny replied. 'We didn't see anything.'

Kate bought a ticket and walked up the stairs to the platform on the floor above, which was shielded from the elements by a grand semicircular metal and glass roof. The station was crowded for this time of day, a large group of French schoolchildren moving slowly along it. Kate walked on beyond them to where a young man was circling on a battered scooter.

A train pulled in and she got on to it. The students boarded with her and she listened idly to the meaningless chatter of someone else's children. The train pulled out. Grey buildings slid by beyond a rain-splattered window. The burner phone buzzed in her pocket. She answered it. 'Get off at the next stop. Don't end the call.'

The train rattled slowly into the station at Hackescher Markt. As the doors slid open, Kate did as she had been instructed. The voice at the other end of the line was silent. She waited. 'Get back on. End the call.'

She did, just as the doors closed. The train pulled out. 'I don't know if I like this,' she whispered into her lapel.

'Let's stay with it.' It was Suzy, who must have been assigned to the makeshift control room. 'We're sticking with you, not far behind.'

'Easy for you to say,' Kate muttered. The train rolled on, past Museum Island and across the canal. The phone rang. 'Get off at Friedrichstrasse. There is a coffee shop on the platform called Cuccis. Buy a coffee and wait.'

Kate was on the cusp of telling the voice at the other end of the line where he could stick his meeting, but he ended the call before she had the chance.

In the coffee shop, she ordered a black coffee and stood drinking it as the platform emptied, then slowly filled again.

The minute hand on the station clock crawled around the dial. Five minutes became ten, then turned into fifteen and finally twenty. 'I'm crying off,' Kate said.

'It's your call, boss,' Suzy said, to which Kate very nearly replied, *Of course it's my bloody call.* But with the same uncanny sense of timing, the phone rang again. 'Go down the stairs, cross Friedrichstrasse and head east.'

'Is this leading anywhere? I'm close to calling it off.'

'You were followed.'

The call was ended. Kate gritted her teeth. She did as she'd been told, emerging again into the spitting rain on the cobbled street the far side of Friedrichstrasse. She followed its passage east, past a series of down-at-heel cafés and restaurants.

She stopped to drop money into a busker's hat. 'Talk to me, Danny,' she said. 'He says I've been followed.'

'We don't know what he's on about, Kate. We think you're still clean.'

Kate walked on. She reached the end of the road, where the S-Bahn bridge crossed the canal. She lit another cigarette and turned around. There was nowhere she could sensibly proceed to without further instructions, so she paced and smoked with choking unease. 'Fucking hell,' she muttered. 'This isn't right.'

The phone rang. 'Get out of there,' Mikhail said. 'We've been compromised. Get out of there now.'

Kate threw away her cigarette. Two men emerged from the shadow of the S-Bahn bridge. One blocked the road she had come down, the second a potential escape route to her left. She instinctively turned right, only to be confronted by a car that screeched into view and swung around in the middle of the street. Kate was cornered, with her back to the canal, both men armed with thick steel bars. 'I've got trouble,' she whispered. 'Big bloody trouble.'

Kate glanced behind her. To swim or try to run?

She faced the men again. One was short, stocky and bald,

with tattoos that climbed from his neck up either side of his shaved skull. The other was surprisingly slight, with a thin moustache and the kind of wispy half-beard you'd normally see on a teenager. He was the more dangerous.

The short guy got out of line, came on too quickly and swung with too much force. Kate stepped aside, tripped him and smashed his skull on to the top railing of the fence by the canal. He collapsed with a low grunt.

Two more men had got out of the car and were advancing towards her. One had a knife, but her immediate concern was the guy who looked like an overgrown adolescent. He advanced with stealth. They circled each other for a moment.

He feinted one way, then brought the bar down in a vicious arc towards her skull. She swerved, but only just in time – she felt the tremor in the air as it passed her cheek.

He tried again too swiftly and this time she caught his arm, blocked his leg and used his momentum to send him tipping over the rail and straight into the canal.

But the other two men had split up, blocking any realistic chance of escape. Besides, one was now armed with a pistol. Kate edged along the fence as they closed in. The man she'd sent into the canal was yelling at his colleagues in Russian.

There was no way out of here. Kate wondered how Rose would cope with the children and whether Fiona's fragile state of mind would deal with the death of her mother as well as the loss of her father.

There was nowhere to run and no place to hide. And even if by some miracle she could disarm the man with a knife – a hundred times more difficult in real life than they ever made it look in films – a single bullet from the other advancing thug would end this encounter in a heartbeat.

She had all but given up and resigned herself to her fate when she heard a single cry: 'Kate!'

The man with the pistol turned, but he was not quick enough. Suzy pushed his arm up so that a shot pinged harmlessly off the metal strut of the bridge above, then slammed the heel of her palm into the brachial nerve on the side of his neck.

Danny and his colleagues were only half a pace behind her, so that the thug with a knife, who had seemed so menacing only seconds before, now found himself surrounded by four men and a female officer with a pistol trained at his chest. He didn't need any further warning: he ran for his life.

They all watched him go. Kate leant back against the rail. Suddenly she felt very faint. 'Thank you,' she muttered. No one seemed to have heard her. 'Thank you, Suzy,' she said. 'All of you.'

13

KATE TOOK THE decision to make a swift exit from the scene to avoid any operational fallout with the German police and their intelligence colleagues, whom they had deliberately chosen not to inform of their plans.

She went straight to her room once they had got back to the hotel, washed her face and sat on her bed. She noticed her hands were shaking violently. Her phone rang: C. She didn't answer it, but as soon as it rang off, he called again. 'Yes, boss?'

'What happened?'

'I don't really know. We stuck to the plan. Danny and his team allowed plenty of time for the covert surveillance and he was confident I was clear. Somehow Mikhail got a burner phone into my pocket. I don't know where or how – I didn't spot that and neither did the ops team. He called and said I'd been followed. He instructed me to get on to the S-Bahn and off again at Friedrichstrasse. He directed me to a spot under the S-Bahn bridge that did feel as if it had been deliberately designed for an ambush and then . . .' Kate gathered herself. 'I thought I was done for, to be honest. Suzy came out of the darkness at them like a wild cat. I wouldn't be here without her.'

'Who betrayed you?'

'I don't know.'

'Get back here and we'll work it out.' Sir Alan ended the call. Within a few seconds, her phone lit up again. This time it was Ian. But hearing his reproachful analysis was the last thing she needed, so she ignored him entirely.

She lay on her bed, but that didn't help. She made herself a cup of tea, but that had no positive impact either. Eventually, she used the in-house service to send a message to Julie and Suzy, instructing them to book everyone on to an evening flight, the operational teams included.

She went back out into the Tiergarten and walked fast, the events of the morning and all their possible implications churning in her mind. As she passed the Rose Garden for the second time, she pulled out her phone and sent Sergei another message. *You there?*

She still did not get an answer.

Kate continued on autopilot until she emerged from the Tiergarten just opposite the Holocaust Memorial. She made a point of visiting it on every trip to Berlin, and perhaps its unconscious allure today was a connection with something bigger, of greater importance.

At first sight, it seemed an inconspicuous, underwhelming memorial to the many millions of Jews killed by the Nazis, but as you moved from the low tomb-like slabs of smooth grey concrete on the periphery and into those of monstrous scale in the interior, a sense of the awesome nature of this, the greatest crime ever perpetrated against humanity, became at first unnerving and finally overwhelming.

It was two o'clock in the afternoon by the time she returned to her hotel room. Ian had called three more times, but she decided on a visit to the spa and sauna over responding to any of his messages. She sat next to a very fat, determinedly manspreading German in the sauna and kept her towel tightly wrapped around her. She swam afterwards and felt, in the round, a tiny bit calmer.

She returned to her room, only to find it much colder than she had expected. She came around the corner and saw the window was open, a man sitting in a deckchair outside with his back to her. It was Mikhail. He had a bottle of beer in his hand. 'I hope you don't mind. I helped myself from the mini-bar.'

'What the hell are you doing here?'

'You were followed.'

'Our ops team was confident—'

'Then they need a kick up the arse. We have been watching you ever since you landed at Tegel. And so have my former colleagues in the SVR. I am sorry you ran into trouble, but it was not of my doing.'

Kate felt acutely vulnerable standing opposite him in her dressing-gown. 'This is incredibly unprofessional.'

'Relax. You're safe with me, as I think you know.'

'What do you want?'

'Asylum. As we discussed.' He picked up a bag on the floor beside him and came into the room. He closed the doors to the balcony, took out a laptop and placed it on the desk.

'Take a seat.'

She did so. Mikhail opened the computer and logged on with touch ID. 'You'll recall that your prime minister was once an army officer in Kosovo back in the late nineties, attached to army intelligence. As you have guessed, his interpreter was working for us. He had an affair with her, which provided plenty of useful information, but the most important revelation was the sheer scale of his greed and sexual appetite. The latter included a penchant for young girls.'

Mikhail pulled up some video and hit play. It was evident straight away that the room had been rigged with more than one camera of the highest possible quality – and lit to ensure maximum visibility. There seemed absolutely no doubt that the man entering the room was James Ryan, now Prime Minister of the United Kingdom and First Lord of the Treasury. There was an old woman with him, who pointed at three girls rapidly getting to their feet by the coffee-table in the corner. 'Two virgin, but third also very young.'

The girls looked thirteen or fourteen – fifteen at most – and were dressed in high leather boots and short miniskirts. Their faces were caked with make-up, which failed to conceal their ages or their anxiety. The old woman departed. Ryan took a packet of white powder from his pocket, poured a thin line of it on to the table, rolled up a US twenty-dollar bill and encouraged the girls to partake. He was the last to bend over and snort cocaine, before the orgy – if you could call it that – began in earnest.

One thing was quickly evident: this was not his first time in such company. He knew exactly what he wanted for his money and directed the girls with all the confidence of a man who had done this countless times before. Initially, he only watched, but eventually he rose from a seat in the corner, unbuckled his belt and dropped his trousers and boxer shorts. He didn't bother to take off his shirt or socks. 'You don't have to watch the whole thing,' Mikhail said.

'Given what is at stake, I'm afraid I do.'

'It doesn't get any better.'

To begin with, Ryan was content to let the girls pleasure him, but he then insisted on having intercourse with each in turn – in the missionary position, while the others waited. All three of the girls cried as he entered them. 'Just fast forward to the end.'

'The end is the worst bit,' Mikhail said, but he did as he was instructed. When he reached the part where James Ryan was putting his trousers on, he hit play again. One of the girls was still crying. 'Tell her to shut up,' Ryan instructed the others. 'At least you will eat well tonight.'

He put on his jacket and left the room. Mikhail stopped the video. 'That's it,' he said. 'Not pleasant, but you can see there is no doubt it is him.'

'How can we be sure you haven't faked it?'

'Don't be absurd.'

'We both know it's possible.'

'Not with that kind of quality. Ask your experts.'

Kate nodded. 'You look like you've seen a ghost,' Mikhail said.

She glanced up at him. 'It's a lot worse than that, isn't it?'

'No, it is not. It is really very simple. I am offering you a quick and easy solution. No one can doubt that he is the man in this footage, or that its contents don't amount to a resigning matter, so all you have to do is get myself, my family and my father into Britain with this computer intact and then you can release the pictures and it will all be over.'

'You honestly think it's going to be that straightforward?'

'Why not? They say the foreign secretary is an honest woman. As long as you don't make the mistake of consulting anyone else, I don't see why it should be complicated.'

'How do you want to proceed?'

'Do we have your promise of asylum?'

Kate hesitated a moment too long. 'Yes.'

'Signed off by the foreign secretary, and with the stipulations we made, we are afforded your meaningful protection and are allowed to keep all our assets in the West?'

'Yes.'

'Where is the letter?'

'I'll have to get it. We—'

'We can take this shit anywhere!' The tension Mikhail had been doing his best to hide was starting to show. 'And embarrass the hell out of you in the process.'

'I said yes.'

'I need a letter from the foreign secretary.'

'I'll get it.'

'You should have brought it with you!'

'Come on, Mikhail. She was never going to authorize that until she knew the material was genuine.'

He slammed the computer shut and put it back into his bag. 'Well, now you have seen it.'

Kate stood. She walked to the window. She went to her jacket for a cigarette and offered the packet to Mikhail, who waved her away airily. She lit up, if only to give herself a few moments to think. 'We have a deal,' she said. 'I want to know how to proceed.'

He watched her, hands thrust deep into his pockets. 'I don't know if we should trust you.'

'Yes, you do. That's why you came to me in the first place.'

'Don't be so sure of yourself.'

'We have to lay our hands on this material. You know we do. So let's get on with it.'

He watched her smoking, his gaze unblinking. She wished she wasn't standing before him in a dressing-gown, hair unkempt, but perhaps that had been part of his calculation.

'My father's family was originally from Georgia, as I am sure you know. We still have a home in Tbilisi and another in Kazbegi, just over the border. He thinks he can get himself, my wife and son there. So that is where we will meet. The Russians have the commercial airport covered, so you will need a private plane on standby to come in and pick us up – or, better still, to remain on the ground until we are ready.'

'When?'

'This week. You can send me the letter from your foreign secretary tonight – tomorrow at the latest. I will find a way to show it to my father. You will need to unfreeze the assets you have seized in the UK, including the house in Knightsbridge, where we will have to live. The letter will need to confirm we are free to move around as we please in both Europe and America.'

'As you know, that's not in our gift.'

'You can deliver it. We will come with this video and incontrovertible evidence of the money we have paid to your prime minister over the course of the time he has worked for us – more than thirty million pounds in all – along with a global paper trail, which will allow you to seize the cash and arrest those who have helped launder it.'

They looked at each other. 'All right,' Kate said. 'You very much have a deal.'

Mikhail forced a smile. 'And hang the consequences.'

He picked up his bag and slung it over his shoulder. 'You'll be the most famous British MI6 officer since Kim Philby.'

'Just what I always wanted.'

He walked to the door. 'Sorry to have caught you off guard.'

'There is one other thing.'

He turned back to face her. 'You're getting more than enough for your money.'

'This concerns both of us. Is it true that my husband Stuart was the agent codenamed Viper?'

A flicker of alarm crossed Mikhail's handsome face, all the more noticeable for the speed with which he tried to hide it. 'What do you mean?'

'Are you sure Stuart was Viper?'

'Yes. Why?' He was looking her in the eye now. Perhaps with a little too much intensity, as if he was determined to hide the momentary flash of alarm she'd witnessed a few seconds earlier.

Kate leant back against the desk. 'Well, since you murdered my old deputy I was forced to acquire a new one, and she has some questions about our original operation that I'm having to admit I struggle to answer.'

'Such as?'

'Stuart didn't know anything about Rav's trip to Geneva.'

'So . . .'

'And Rav was much too smart to have drawn attention to himself while he was there.'

Mikhail shrugged. 'If I recall correctly, he went to see the lawyer François Binot. Maybe one of my colleagues had him under surveillance.'

'Why? Binot worked for you.'

'Exactly. Perhaps it was Binot who alerted us.'

'Rav wouldn't go anywhere near a man like Binot. And, besides, he would have called us straight away if he had sensed he was being watched.'

'I don't know . . .' Mikhail looked exasperated. 'Why does it matter?'

'Was Stuart Viper?'

'Yes.'

'Are you sure?'

'Yes. It was my father who recruited him.'

There was something about Mikhail's expression that unsettled Kate, not so much that he might be telling a lie – which he would likely pull off with consummate ease – so much as the sense that she, in turn, had unnerved him. But why?

'How did Moscow Centre know what Rav was up to? Because Stuart could not have told them.'

'Who says we killed Rav?'

'You did.'

'*If* we did, it was done without my father's knowledge.'

Kate thought about that. She had kept her gaze fixed on Mikhail's face. 'What do you mean *if*? You must know.'

'You are starting at shadows, Kate. It was not our work. That is what I am saying.'

'What if there is someone else?' she asked.

'Where?'

'In SIS, working for Moscow Centre.'

'You mean someone whom my father, the head of our foreign intelligence service until two years ago, was unaware of?'

'Perhaps he or she does not work for the SVR.' Kate moved to the window and looked out at the grey clouds illuminated by the dying rays of the sun. 'What about someone recruited and run by the GRU?' She turned back to him. 'A man or woman in a position to tell his or her masters in Moscow that Rav was circling close to Binot, a lawyer with intimate connections to the Russian president.'

She waited. 'A man – or a woman – in a position to warn his masters that we had come to Berlin with the aim of persuading you to defect.'

'You think anyone in the GRU gives a fuck what happens to us?'

'I imagine, if they succeed in removing you, your father and his successor from power in the SVR, they would be rather interested in inheriting the British prime minister as an agent of influence.'

'Stuart was Viper,' Mikhail said, with finality. 'The rest is just conjecture. I shouldn't let it keep you awake at night.'

But as he left, she knew with utmost certainty that this particular piece of conjecture would be keeping them both awake for many nights to come.

14

C WANTED TO see them once they had landed back at Heathrow, but there was a complication: his wife Alice was dying. Kate called him directly to reassure him it could wait and they would deal with the foreign secretary directly if need be. He would not hear of it, so the car delivered them in driving rain to the Lister Hospital, just down from Sloane Square. They had to cross no more than twenty yards of open ground, but they were dripping when they arrived in the Lister's hallway.

Kate had been instructed to go directly to room 307, but she asked Julie and Suzy to wait in the third-floor reception area.

The door to 307 was wedged ajar and she could see her superior in a chair with his back to her, reading quietly to his wife. Alice's eyes were closed, her pearly white face turned towards the window, classical music playing softly on a portable CD player in the corner. Kate watched for a moment, feeling like a voyeur. Middle age had written a few lines on Alice's elegant features, but illness had not robbed her of her beauty.

Sir Alan sensed Kate's presence and turned slowly, without breaking the rhythm of his reading. He nodded at her to indicate he would be with her shortly and returned to his wife.

Kate re-joined her colleagues. 'How is she?' Julie asked. Kate shrugged. She felt incredibly uncomfortable just being there.

'What does she have?' Suzy asked.

'Cancer,' Kate replied.

'What kind?'

'Originally breast, but now secondary in the liver.'

'That's bad.'

'Yes. But, for God's sake, don't say anything about it.' Kate didn't have a great deal of confidence in Suzy's ability to adhere to social norms.

'My mother had liver cancer,' Suzy added, cutting the feet from under her. 'The doctor said she would die in three weeks and he was right – to the day.'

Kate went to get herself a cup of coffee from a machine

opposite. 'You want anything?' she asked the others. They shook their heads.

'That should definitely help you sleep,' Julie said, as Kate returned with a plastic cup of dirty brown liquid.

A few minutes later Sir Alan emerged. He'd arranged for them to talk in an empty room at the other end of the corridor. Kate sat in a chair in one corner, Sir Alan stood by the window, while Julie and Suzy perched on the empty bed, like children visiting their parents.

'How is she?' Kate asked.

'She has a throat infection and a fever. She can't swallow and is in a lot of pain. The doctors think she has a few weeks left, so I'm keen to get her home again, but for the moment we're stranded here.'

'Sir, I'm sure we can deal with the foreign secretary directly.'

'Let's just get on with it. Talk me through the video.'

Kate couldn't think of a worse time or place to be discussing this. 'I'm not an expert, but, to me, there's no doubt that it's him. The entire thing is shot with very high-quality hidden cameras. He enters the room. Three very young-looking girls dressed in high leather boots and short skirts get up from a sofa in the corner. An old woman, who is clearly the madam, promises him that two of the girls are virgins and the other still very young. He takes a packet of what looks like cocaine from his pocket and encourages them to snort it first, before doing so himself with a rolled-up twenty-dollar bill. He asks them to undress and to . . . well, to pleasure each other, which they do not very convincingly. He is clearly no newcomer to this kind of scenario and he directs them to do a series of specific things to each other.

'Then he stands, unbuckles his belt and comes to the bed. He has removed his underwear, but keeps his shirt and socks on. The girls then pleasure him, before he has intercourse with each of them in turn – in the missionary position. All three girls appear to be crying as he enters them. Afterwards, one is still shedding tears and he instructs the others to "tell her to shut up". He adds that all three will "eat well tonight", then dresses and departs.'

There was a long silence. Sir Alan had his back to them. He was staring out across the rooftops, which were just shapes in the darkness. 'You watched the whole thing?'

'Yes, sir. It was unbearably sordid.'

'And you are absolutely one hundred per cent certain it was him?'

'Yes. It was the way he talked, the way he moved . . .'

'It could not have been faked?'

Kate hesitated. Had she been too quick to believe what had appeared to be the evidence of her own eyes? 'It's real – it has to be,' she said. 'And it is definitely him.'

Sir Alan looked like a man trying to hide frustration, anger or both. 'What arrangements did you make?'

'He and his father want a letter from the foreign secretary

guaranteeing protection, free travel in Europe and America, and the ability to enjoy their assets in the West unhindered, which I promised they would have tomorrow. They will assemble in Tbilisi, where Igor's family were originally from, or a home they have in Kazbegi, close to the border, by the end of the week. They want a private plane to fly them direct to London, so that they do not have to pass through the main airport terminal, which he said was watched by the Russians. They also promised to bring with them evidence of the cash they have paid to Ryan – more than thirty million pounds in all.'

'The foreign secretary wants to see us tomorrow morning at her London house,' Julie said. 'Just Kate and me.'

Suzy looked as if she might object, but thought better of it after catching sight of the expression on Sir Alan's face. Ice radiated more warmth. 'Talk me through the operation,' he said. He was still addressing Kate, as if the others were not there.

Kate shook her head. 'I'm still confused by it. Danny and his team were convinced I was clean by the time I arrived in Alexanderplatz. I don't know how Mikhail got a burner phone into my pocket. And I have no idea how they managed to ambush me at that point in Friedrichstrasse.'

'Did you raise it with Mikhail?'

'I asked him whether Stuart was Viper.'

'What was his answer?'

'He said Stuart was definitely Viper, but he seemed less

sure about the possibility of another mole. I suggested that a second source was working for the GRU.'

Sir Alan fixed each of them with a steady gaze in turn, his pale blue eyes tinged with a melancholy Kate had never witnessed before. 'Who knew about the meeting in Alexanderplatz?'

Suzy stood up, as if this had been her cue. 'The same group. You, Kate, Julie, Danny.'

'And you,' Kate told Suzy.

'And me, yes, though I can be ruled out since this mole, if he or she does exist, was part of the original Operation Sigma.'

'That's merely your conjecture,' Kate said. Suzy flushed. For a woman so tactless, she appeared to have a strange aversion to confrontation.

'What about Ian?' Julie asked.

'I informed him,' Sir Alan said. Kate tried to conceal her surprise. Ian had not bothered to ask her the details of the operation in Berlin – which, now she came to reflect on it, was odd in itself – and it would have been all too easy for Sir Alan to keep them from him. If there was a potential leak, then the need-to-know principle ought to have been paramount.

The thought came to her unbidden that Sir Alan's actions could be interpreted as a deliberate attempt to widen the circle of knowledge.

'What about the foreign secretary?' Julie asked.

Sir Alan shook his head. 'She didn't know the time or the place of the meeting.'

'She was aware of the time,' Kate said quietly. 'And she knew it was in Berlin.'

'All right,' Sir Alan said, moving towards the door. 'We're going around in circles. It's quite possible they've been monitoring Mikhail. Kate and I will pick this up with the foreign secretary in the morning. Suzy, I want you and Julie to start preparing the ground in Tbilisi. Work on the assumption that we'll get approval for the extraction and permission to hire some kind of private jet. And whatever security detail you think we might need, double it.'

'Should we inform the Georgians?' Suzy asked.

Sir Alan looked incredulous. 'Of course not,' he said, and Kate could see Suzy privately cursing her inexperience.

As they moved towards the door, Sir Alan put his hand on Kate's shoulder to stop her. 'One moment,' he said. The others hesitated, but he gestured at them to continue. 'I'll see you in the office in the morning,' he told them, 'and very well done. For all the issues, we got what we went to Berlin for and that is a feather in all of your caps.' That seemed intended more for Suzy than the rest of them and she smiled for the first time since they had left Berlin.

He waited until the door was closed, then sat on the bed.

'Are you all right, sir? As I said, I'm very happy to—'

'I'm as all right as you are,' he said, 'which is not very bloody okay at all. But neither of us has any choice but to plough on, do we? Anyway, that's not why I asked you to stay behind. We may have a problem with the foreign secretary.'

'In what way?'

'She's getting cold feet.'

'Why?' Kate couldn't quite believe this.

'Because it's a very big call and she simply isn't used to making them. She's about to authorize an operation to oversee a major defection – which, for all that we're recommending it, is still a significant step for someone new to this kind of decision-making. The controversy it will bring with it would likely test the bravest of politicians and Meg Simpson is not one of them.'

'You think she'll refuse to send the letter?'

'I don't know. But all I am saying is that it's not a given she'll agree to this tomorrow and we may have to work hard to persuade her.' He stood again. 'I'd better go back to Alice. Get some sleep, Kate. You look like you need it.'

By the time Kate passed the room further down the corridor, Sir Alan was seated at his wife's bedside again, head bent as he read to her. Kate watched him for a moment, envious of his devotion and loyalty. It made her feel lonelier still.

She walked home, despite the rain, which had slowed to a drizzle. She found herself wishing Sir Alan had not left her with that departing instruction about sleep, which loomed larger with every step she took homewards. She recalled the days when the house in Battersea had represented only comfort, love and rest. Now it served as the instrument of her torture, and that alone made her feel guilty. What kind of mother doesn't want to return home to her children?

She passed her own mother's nursing home and felt the familiar pull of filial duty. She overrode it and had almost reached her front door before guilt got the better of her and she doubled back. Why did she feel any loyalty to the woman who had spent a lifetime traducing and belittling her? It made no sense at all.

But Lucy was a shadow of her normal self today. She sat in an armchair, facing the window, gazing out into the darkness. 'Hi, Mum,' Kate said, as she installed herself in a corner of the window seat beside her.

'Hello, my love.' Her smile was full of quiet warmth. 'I was just thinking about you.'

'Glad I stopped by, then. Can I get you a cup of tea?'

'No, thank you. And I'm pleased you came. I'm so sorry for the things I said in Cornwall. I don't know what got into me.'

Kate stared at the floor. Her mother had resolutely refused to seek any psychiatric or psychological help over the years, determined to view even the suggestion she might as a sign – or, rather, an accusation – of weakness. It was impossible to be certain whether she was a depressive, or bipolar, or was dragging around some other psychological disorder, but the speed with which she oscillated between two entirely opposing personalities still took Kate's breath away. And even now, after all these years, she couldn't help the rush of warmth she felt at even the slightest expression of love or affection.

'I know I've made it hard for you and I'm sorry.'

'That's all right, Mum.' It wasn't, of course, not by the longest shot. But what else could she say?

'I think your aunt Rose brings out the worst in me.'

That wasn't true: her mother was capable of being equally poisonous at all other times, but she let that ride as well. 'I don't know why,' Kate said.

'She's always wanted to think of you as her own child.'

'She does her best to look after me.' If there was an accusation in that, it was designed to stop her mother in her tracks.

Lucy nodded, as if to acknowledge this. 'All right. I don't want to pick a fight. I know she's the mother you never had. But she's more competitive than she lets on and I'm never certain she's as generous – or perhaps I mean as straightforward – as she appears.'

It was said without rancour, or bitterness, or the twinkle in the eye with which Lucy usually delivered her malicious barbs, so if it was an impression she took issue with, Kate didn't doubt it represented, for once, her mother's genuinely held view. Lucy was looking at the picture of her former lover on the side table. 'I think you'd better put that away now. Perhaps you could retrieve the photograph of your father from the drawer.' Kate did so and they both sat in silence for a while, as if determined to enjoy this momentary contentment. Kate could hardly take her eyes off her father's kind, smiling face.

They retreated into safer subjects after that: the weather, Fiona's dress sense and Gus's gaming habits. Kate waited for the wheel to turn, for the malice to creep back in, but her mother retained her equanimity throughout and they parted, much later than Kate had intended, with a hug. 'You do look tired, love,' Lucy said, as she released her.

'I am.'

'It must be hard without Stuart.'

'Yes.' Kate couldn't help bridling. 'Nothing I didn't bring upon myself, I'm sure.'

'I didn't mean it like that and you know it. I understand that trying to have it all – and do it all – on your own must be impossibly difficult. But you must sleep. And if you need help, please ask for it – from whomever. Rose. Even me.'

Kate didn't pick that up immediately, but neither did she walk away.

'I know we've had our differences over the years, but I've never shown the children anything but love, and I'm not so gaga that I can't look after them now and again.'

'I understand, Mum. Thank you.'

'You can't look after them if you're not well yourself.'

'I'm fine.'

'I don't think you are, but I'll leave it there.'

Kate walked home slowly, as if to make the feeling of relative warmth last. She wished she had stayed longer. Why hadn't she lingered awhile?

It wasn't until she turned the key in the door that her rational mind reasserted itself. It said everything, surely, about her upbringing that twenty-five minutes of relative normality could have elicited such a response.

Rose had cleaned the kitchen so that it was immaculate. She sat at the table, reading an old copy of *Vogue* and drinking herbal tea. She stood to hug Kate. 'What can I get you?'

'Valium.'

'As bad as that?'

'Basically. It's been a long day. Is Gus still awake?'

'He might be.'

Kate threw her coat on to the sofa. 'I could murder a glass of white wine, if I'm completely honest.' She went up to find Gus face down on the bed with Nelson beside him. For once, she didn't feel inclined to move their ancient dog.

'Don't take him,' he said, as she sat gently on the bed.

'I don't know how you can bear the smell.'

'You don't notice it after a bit, though Rose gave him fish skin for dinner.'

'Yuck.'

Gus turned on to his back and looked at her. 'How was your trip?'

Kate couldn't remember the last time he'd asked a question like that. It was the night all her ships were coming in. 'Complicated.'

'Why?'

She smiled. 'State secret.'

'Did you see Dad?'

'No. I'll arrange another meeting with him very soon.' Kate couldn't miss the longing in her son's eyes. 'You miss him?'

'Sometimes.'

'Me too.'

'Will you ever get back together?'

'I don't see how. Quite apart from all the emotional damage, it's a practical impossibility.'

'Will you get another boyfriend?'

'I sincerely doubt it.' She squeezed his leg under the duvet. 'You are my priority and always will be. Have you spoken to Fi?'

'No.' There was a long pause as Gus stroked Nelson's ear. Kate sensed he had more to say. 'It feels a bit strange here without her.'

'It's only for a few days.'

'Maybe. She's behaving very weirdly.'

'How was Rose?'

'She's great. She's so kind. I guess she's how Granny should be.'

'Granny has her own issues.' Kate bent down to kiss her

newly articulate son and ruffled his hair. For the first time in a very long while, he held her tight. She stood and moved to the door. 'I'll see you in the morning,' she said.

'Will you leave Nelson?'

'Of course.' She paused. 'Things might be a bit busy for the next week or two at work, but it will calm down after that.'

'Like it did last time?'

'Fair point. I'm going to consider asking for a period of absence so I can spend more time with you.'

'Okay.'

'Would that be a good idea?'

'It's up to you.' She took that as a massive endorsement. 'Why is work busy?' he asked. 'Matters of life and death?'

'Political life and death, perhaps.'

'Fiona told Jed you're basically James Bond.'

Kate had to stop herself laughing. This was turning into a very surprising conversation. 'My work is *supposed* to be secret,' she said.

'Not to family. And I guess Jed is family now.'

'I guess he is.'

'Is it true?' Gus persisted.

'No one is James Bond. He's a bit ludicrous, really.'

'Jane Bond, then. That's kind of cool.'

'Sleep well,' Kate said. She was still smiling as she walked into the kitchen. 'I don't know what you've done to him,' she told her aunt. 'I just had an articulate, affectionate conversation with my teenage son.' She glanced at the wine. 'You'd better make that a double.'

'He's a lovely boy. So funny.'

Kate sat opposite her aunt. 'He seems to be missing his sister, which is an even greater wonder. Is she all right? I texted her earlier and got no reply.' Kate took a large slug of wine.

'She's fine. I imagine she'll be home in a day or two. I sense the Jed exile might be wearing a bit thin for both of them . . . I'm not going to preach,' Rose continued, 'which would be incredibly tedious, but, my God, you look tired.' Kate glanced at her aunt, whose gaze radiated concern. 'Are you still on the sleeping pills?'

'Yes.'

'Zopiclone?' Kate nodded. 'Be careful,' Rose went on, 'they're highly addictive.'

'I know, I know. I'll be fine. I won't need one tonight. I'm dead beat.' She took another slug of Pinot Grigio. 'Did you have anxiety or depression?'

'The one tends to lead to the other.'

'Yes, I guess so.'

'But mainly the former.'

'About what exactly?'

'I came to define my self-worth by my ability to become a mother. The more times I failed, the more anxious I got about never succeeding. But, as Dr Wiseman will already have told you, I'm sure, it's rarely just one thing.'

Kate nodded. 'You said you were very busy at work?' The question was genuine: the Finance Department had always seemed to be a pretty sedate place.

'It was in the period I was attached to Operations.' Kate looked at her aunt, gobsmacked. Rose permitted herself a wry smile. 'I know, I probably should have told you about it long ago.'

'When – I mean, how long ago? Where? Doing what?'

'I joined as a Finance trainee straight from university. But in those days you could opt to transfer to Operations for an attachment. The idea was to give those of us who were going to spend our lives bean-counting a sense of life at the sharp end. I guess it would have been 'ninety-two to 'ninety-six. Something like that. I was mostly working in Bosnia.'

'With Sir Alan?'

'Yes. And Ian at the tail end.'

Rose was staring into her wine as she swirled it in her glass, as if to conjure old memories.

'How come you never told me about it? I feel embarrassed not to have known—'

'I had my breakdown straight after that and had to take four months off work.'

'Do you know what tipped you over the edge?'

'Everything. Alan was mostly focused on Mladic and his Bosnian Serb friends. Ian took over from him. I came in and out, trying desperately to get pregnant in between and repeatedly miscarrying. I pushed myself far too far and was very stupid about it. I'm anxious you don't do the same.'

'So what did you do when you returned to work?'

'Transferred back to Finance, prioritized my marriage and my mental health and tried to wipe the period from my memory.' Kate could see that her aunt was now determined to change the subject. 'How was Berlin?'

'It went to plan, mostly. The foreign secretary has a very big decision to make, which Sir Alan predicts she is not going to enjoy.'

Rose knew better than to ask any more. She got up and went to wash up her mug. While she did so, her phone buzzed. Kate glanced at the screen. It was a message from Sir Alan. *Call you later,* it said.

Rose turned, noticed the message, picked up her phone and slipped it into her pocket, without meeting Kate's eye. She kissed her niece tenderly on the head and headed for the stairs. 'Sleep well,' she said.

Kate finished her wine in melancholy silence. *Call you later . . .* What was that about?

Almost certainly none of her business.

In fact, definitively none of her business.

But still . . .

She washed up and followed Rose up the stairs. She removed her make-up, brushed her teeth and collapsed into bed, convinced she would go straight to sleep.

But the more she circled closer to it, the more her mind began to torture her again. For a long time, her patience held. Just rest, she told herself. Sleep is close. It will happen. But it didn't. Not quite.

Her pulse quickened. She recognized the signs and got out of bed. The digital alarm clock told her it was just after two in the morning: four hours until she needed to be up.

She went down to the kitchen, switched on a side lamp and sat in the chair in the corner reading *Vogue*. After twenty minutes, she didn't know if she was tired or not. Was sleep creeping up on her? It didn't feel like it, but the clock on the wall was closing in on half past two, which meant her window to sleep was closing fast.

She returned to bed. Her self-discipline held for what seemed like an age, but as the minutes marched past the panic crept back in. She tried some yoga, slowed her breathing right down. She felt better and attempted again to drift off. But it was ultimately always the same threshold she couldn't cross. She realized she was sweating it too much and tried to roam far and wide with her thoughts. They returned, like a dog with a bone, to her inability to sleep.

The dawn was once again a relief, the sun inching along the painted terraced houses opposite. She had a shower, dressed and put on her make-up. She faced the day, momentarily uplifted by the fact that, for now at least, she was roughly able to function.

15

IF IAN GENUINELY saw himself as the next C, Kate thought he was going a strange way about getting there. Even by his own standards, his outfit for the breakfast meeting at the foreign secretary's grand stucco residence on Carlton House Terrace was eccentric. He'd grown his hair long so that his blond curls tumbled over the collar of a shirt that might have been appropriate for an evening in the Caribbean. His black jeans were ripped above the knee, his ubiquitous suede Chelsea boots scuffed and dirty, as if he had walked there across a field. He wore a black cardigan, half done up to lend his cry for attention – or possibly help – an air of vague respectability.

Perhaps *he* thought he was James Bond. This certainly appeared to be the message he was conveying to the foreign secretary, of a man too busy, important and, frankly, dangerous to bother with the conventional Whitehall dress code.

What was more surprising was the way Suzy was watching him. Even while he warmed them up, as they waited for the foreign secretary, with the story of his last Ironman event – he had done many and could talk about them at vast length – she barely took her eyes off him. My God, Kate thought, there really is no accounting for taste.

Sir Alan stood with his back to them, looking out over the Mall. Kate thought he held his emotional pain in his upper body as if it were a physical affliction, which she supposed in the end it was. She tried to think of something that might comfort or distract him, but he seemed far removed from everything around him, as if he was preparing to make the journey to the other side with his wife.

As a superior, she reflected, he had always been broadly supportive: encouraging when she got it right, steely when she screwed up. She was far from beyond wanting to please him. For a moment, she thought of how it would be if Ian managed to claw his way into Sir Alan's chair. Intolerable, really. Unimaginable. She'd have to quit. But now that her family was supported by her salary alone, what, exactly, would she do?

Their 'breakfast', which consisted of croissants and other

pastries, fruit salad, orange juice and two large pots of coffee, lay untouched in the centre of the table and as Ian droned on and wretchedly on about his training regime – 'You have to cycle for two hours before dawn or you never get enough in' – Kate had to restrain herself from getting stuck in. It was hardly a scientific revelation that chronic sleep deprivation left one absolutely *ravenous*.

Meg Simpson stormed in like a thundercloud. She didn't bother to wish any of them good morning. And more pressingly, from Kate's point of view, she did not show any inclination to reach for the pastries or even the coffee. Kate weighed the social acceptability of opening the score.

C hadn't bothered to join them at the table. 'Would you care to join us, Sir Alan?' Simpson asked, with more edge than the situation appeared to demand. Kate wondered if she knew of his wife's illness. He did as he was asked, looked at Kate and, as if reading her mind, reached for the coffee and a pastry. She mouthed her thanks and he allowed himself a smile.

'Sir Alan has briefed me,' Simpson said.

'It was an excellent operation, conducted with the utmost professionalism,' Ian offered, 'but I hold to my initial view that—'

'I am well aware of your views,' Simpson shot back. Ian's face reddened. It occurred to Kate that if Ian was Viper, or some other agent working for the SVR or the GRU or any other arm of the Russian state, he was not subtle in covering his tracks. Simpson shuffled uncomfortably in her seat. She stared at the coffee pot in front of her. 'I do not find myself willing as yet to write the letter you say you need, or to set in train the actions it would instigate, or deal with the consequences that might arise.'

They waited for her to elaborate.

'You may be inclined to view that as political cowardice. I would prefer to see it as caution.'

'The difference is academic,' Sir Alan said. 'We are not interested in motive, only conclusion.'

Now it was her turn to look stung. 'I am aware that this is not what you wanted to hear.'

'We have a bounden duty here that is not, I think, in question.'

'I disagree. Our greatest duty is to preserve the integrity of our democracy, which, I am afraid, includes an essential belief in it.'

'It's hard to think of anything that would erode it more swiftly than the idea that we all sat here knowing the prime minister was working for our mortal enemy, not to mention his past actions, and resolved to do nothing about it.'

'But that is where all this falls down for me. Upon reflection, and taking into account what you've told me, I don't think I do yet believe that.'

'Kate has watched the video, in full, revolting detail, an act of conscientious duty in itself. She is not in any doubt that it is genuine.'

'I understand that. I have always found our prime minister's personal morals repellent, though even I did not believe he would sink this low. But the fact that he is a profligate adulterer – even in this repellent way – does not *de facto* prove he is a Russian spy. And if we were to go ahead and accept this defection, we would be destroying him.'

'We have a former head of the SVR – or at least his son – categorically stating that they recruited James Ryan to work for the Russian government while he was serving in Kosovo and that they used this video and enormous cash payments, the details of which they will bring with them, to blackmail and induce him.'

It occurred to Kate that she had never asked Mikhail if the video had been sufficient of itself to turn James Ryan, but the conversation was moving too fast now. 'This is my point,' Ian said. 'What if the Russians are just using this to destroy the prime minister and cause maximum possible chaos and disruption to our political system?'

Normally a master of self-control, Sir Alan visibly struggled to maintain it. He stared at Ian with barely concealed disdain. Kate glanced at Suzy, who had the good sense to remain silent. She wasn't looking at Ian with quite the same admiration now.

'I'll be honest,' Simpson said. 'What really troubles me here is the context. In the very first briefing note to me on this matter, you made very clear that you were not aware of any putsch within the SVR, the GRU, or at the apex of any other part of the Russian political system. This news has come out of nowhere.'

'That is because we very rarely get a break at this level. We're being offered an unprecedented opportunity that we cannot in all conscience turn down.'

'But isn't it just a bit *too* convenient?' Ian asked, all innocence once again.

'We lose nothing by proceeding. We have to give two people, who mean nothing to the public at large, asylum. Once they are here, we can all assess the video and the evidence of bank payments for ourselves. If we do not believe them to be genuine, we argue they came here under false pretences and act as we see fit.'

'Except they will have a letter with my name on it. What would be our explanation for why I wrote it if we decided this offer was not genuine? I'd look naïve at best, downright stupid at worst. The prime minister would be livid that I had even entertained the idea and I wouldn't blame him.'

Sir Alan shook his head curtly. 'You have no choice, ma'am, I am afraid.'

It was Meg Simpson's turn to redden. She didn't like to be lectured by anyone, but she was on shaky ground and she knew it. 'I'm not saying I won't write the letter and authorize this operation, just that I need more. If you can find further detail on the context, on what is really going on in Moscow, then I would feel a great deal more confident. Has there really been a putsch? If you can confirm there has, without equivocation, then I guarantee I will sign that letter.'

To Kate, this information seemed theoretical at best, irrelevant at worst, and she could see Sir Alan felt the same, though he chose to internalize his anger, in front of the group at least. He stayed behind as she, Suzy and Ian filed out.

They didn't speak until they were on the Mall. Suzy ordered a taxi and Ian let her climb in before he turned to Kate. 'Do you fancy walking back?'

Her head was so paralysed now with sleep deprivation, coffee and the strange tension of that meeting that she had already decided as much. Not that she would normally have welcomed Ian's company.

It was a lot warmer that morning, the daffodils blooming in St James's Park, which was more or less deserted. They were level with the great expanse of Horse Guards Parade before Ian finally blurted out what was on his mind. 'Have you spoken to her?' he asked.

'Who?'

'Julie, of course!'

'About what?'

'Don't be obtuse, Kate.'

She tried to think of any subject she less wanted to discuss with him. 'What was that all about?' she asked, gesturing back to the foreign secretary's residence behind them.

'You know what it was about,' he said. 'The Russians

love playing games and sooner or later we need to stop responding. I just don't agree with you and Alan on that, but it's an honest difference of opinion and I'm perfectly entitled to express my views, convenient or not. Isn't that his mantra? "We are not here to agree"?'

'This is different and you know it.'

'You both think it is. But I'm less certain. I don't blame her for her caution. You'll probably get your letter, whether it's a good idea or not, but she's just covering her arse. I don't see any harm in making us go through the hoops.'

'We have a week at most until the offer disappears – perhaps to a rival, who may be in a position to embarrass us.'

'Everyone else will have exactly the same reservations, Kate. All Alan has to do is write a moderately convincing brief and you'll have your letter. And she's right to question it – even you can't deny this has all come out of the blue. Have we heard a single other source talk about a coup in Moscow Centre? Don't you think we would have seen *some* other reporting of it?'

'Not necessarily. You know how long it takes for news of any change at the top in Moscow to leak. Besides, I have seen the video.'

'If it's real.'

Kate could see further argument was pointless. She turned her attention to a group of Japanese tourists feeding the ducks. The enthusiasm of their children, their joy, was briefly distracting.

'Besides,' Ian continued, 'don't change the subject. Have you talked to her?'

'About what exactly?'

'Us, of course! Jesus, Kate, you can be wilfully dense sometimes.'

'What aspect of "us" would you like to discuss?'

'She won't return my calls.' Ian stopped and faced her. Kate noticed that the chest hair that poked out from his open-necked shirt in tufts was grey now. He suddenly looked older, too. Not that she could talk. 'This is serious, Kate.'

'What is?'

'I'm in love with her, goddamn it.'

Kate did not know whether to laugh or cry. She felt as if she was being hollowed out from the inside with exhaustion and nervous tension, and here was this absurd man-child pouring out his heart – and to her, of all people. 'You'll have to talk to her, Ian. I really can't help you.'

'But you're her friend. She trusts you.'

'I'm also her boss and you're mine, so this conversation feels inappropriate on any number of levels.'

'Oh, for God's sake! Don't be a prig. I just told you I loved her. This isn't some wretched office fling. I care—'

'But that is exactly how she sees it. I'm fairly sure it was just sex for her. She's told me that often enough.' Ian looked as if she had slapped him across the face. 'Don't look so surprised. Isn't that what most extra-marital affairs are supposed to be about?'

'No! Jesus . . .' Ian was clearly bewildered. 'What do you mean, just sex?'

'Oh, come on, Ian. This is like talking to one of my teenagers.' Much too like, Kate wanted to add. 'Julie is a very tough and, if we're being honest, somewhat damaged young woman. She has many demons to slay, which I'm sure she'll manage to do in her own good time. She was having an affair with you because it came without baggage. Your declaration of undying love is the last thing she wants to hear.'

'Damaged?'

'Her mother! You must know that her mother abandoned them when she was still a child?' He seemed mystified. 'And her brother?' Kate added.

'He was killed, yes . . .'

'On that bus on 7/7. They'd had an argument. She was more or less a mother to him and she blames herself because he skipped school that day.'

'But that's why I love her. She's complicated . . . interesting.'

'You have a wife, Ian.'

'Had! I must be the only man in the country whose calls are rejected by both wife and mistress. It's absurd!'

Kate thought that probably took them to the nub of the matter. Only Ian could mistake a bruised ego for a broken heart. 'I have to get back,' she said.

'I'll see you there. I'm just going to drown myself in the pond.'

'You'll have a job,' Kate said. She walked on through St James's Park, enjoying the feel of the sun on her face. It was still early. Civil servants were arriving for work in a steady stream at the front entrance of the Treasury building. She skirted Parliament Square and walked on down towards Millbank, past a group of Kurdish protesters demonstrating against the depredations of the Turkish state outside the House of Commons.

She joined the morning rush through the space-age security pods at the front entrance to the SIS building and exchanged small-talk in the lifts until she reached her floor. Julie was waiting for her, and no sooner had Kate run through the essentials of the meeting with Meg Simpson than Julie was bringing her back to her least favourite subject of the moment. 'What is wrong with him?' Julie asked.

'I assume you mean our boss?'

'He keeps pestering me, day and night. I'm going to have to report him to HR if this goes on. And I really don't want to do that – for either of our sakes.'

'He just declared to me his undying love for you in St James's Park.'

'To *you*?'

'Try not to make that sound like an insult.'

'Don't be ridiculous, Kate. You can't stand the man.'

'True. I can think of people he would more logically choose to confide in.'

Julie left with a departing shot at her former lover: 'He's a total idiot.' Kate almost replied that she could have told her friend that, and had, but she managed to swallow her words. She closed the door and watched Julie walk across to her station on the other side of the office. Kate closed the blind, sat at her desk and logged on to her computer. She shut her eyes, fatigue overwhelming her.

Her phone buzzed and, for a surprising moment, her heart skipped at the thought it might be Stuart. Ian's declaration of love for Julie had reminded her of the early days of Stuart's courtship at Cambridge, when he had refused to take no for an answer. But it was C: *One p.m. at Grumbles restaurant, Pimlico.*

It wasn't a request, much less an invitation. He could be Olympian in his detachment, though as he nursed his wife in her death throes he had more than excuse enough.

Kate slipped the phone into her pocket. Why had she thought it might be Stuart? And why had her heart skipped a beat at the prospect?

Comfortable, comforting Stuart: she was conscious again of missing him and the steady to and fro of everyday domestic interaction. But it left a bitter taste in her mouth. Why had he thrown all that away for a few nights in bed with Imogen Conrad? For the rest of her days that would make her feel about two feet tall.

16

IT WAS THE kind of instinct born of long experience, but it took Kate some time to be sure.

She walked on up Belgrave Road as planned and turned into Churton Street. She passed the blue awning of Grumbles and carried on towards C's house in Churton Place. It was bright now, the sky a clear and vivid blue. The customers of a café called the Roasting were sitting at small metal tables outside, their faces turned towards the sun.

Kate stopped at a flower shop just beyond it and lost herself in there for a moment or two, as if killing time.

She emerged again and, without looking back, walked on beyond Churton Place and turned left into the street market in the pedestrian section. The vendors mostly sold food and she drifted past their stalls, picking up some vegetables and fruit to test their quality and bending closer to smell some of the cheese on the trestle at the end.

She quickened her pace, heading towards Victoria, but it took her until she was on the other side of the station to be absolutely sure she was right. She had come up the escalator to the small shopping mall on the first floor and now doubled back. Almost immediately – coming up on the opposite escalator – she saw the young Indian man in a grey T-shirt and leather jacket she had first spotted as she had turned from Lupus Street into Belgrave Road.

Kate went into WHSmith and bought a copy of *The Times*.

She walked across the station concourse, then swung quickly right on to Wilton Road. As she passed Rosa's Thai Café – inexplicably another of C's favourite local restaurants – she saw the girl with the green chinos and brown pumps.

Kate didn't break her stride. She went to a café called Pimlico Fresh at the end of Wilton Road and ordered a latte. She took it to a vacant seat outside and looked up and down the street to see if she could make out any more of her watchers.

She wasn't in much doubt as to who they were or what they were doing, but she wanted a few moments to think about it. She had toyed with the idea that the men and women following her might be Russians, but she had dismissed it. Unless Moscow's operational teams had made epic strides in their ability to assimilate convincingly into a London scene, it was not conceivable. Besides, why on earth would the Russians want to follow her to lunch?

Kate took out her phone and called Suzy. Her deputy answered straight away. 'When were you thinking of telling me you've put a tail on me?'

'I haven't done anything, Kate.'

'All right, let me rephrase the question. When were you thinking of telling me that your friends at the Security Service have put a tail on me?'

'I think I made clear they are not really my friends.'

'Could you at least deny it?'

'I told you they'd opened an investigation. The plain fact is you almost certainly have a mole. It's their job to find him or her.'

'I thought C had expressly forbidden this?'

'The DG made a courtesy call. C tried to claim that, if there was a problem, it was an internal matter and any investigation would breach operational security, but the integrity of all government agencies is MI5's business, as you well know. I did inform them of my questions about Viper, but it's out of my hands now. It's out of all of our hands, to be honest.'

'Did they put their most incompetent team on me, just so I would know they were watching?'

'I doubt it. They don't really think like that.'

'What do they hope to achieve by trailing me to lunch?'

Suzy sighed. 'This isn't really going anywhere. I'll see you when you get back.' She ended the call and Kate nursed the rest of her coffee in cold fury. Her mood hadn't lifted by the time she arrived at lunch with Sir Alan.

He was in the corner booth, which she knew to be his regular, opposite a sign for 'Rue Mozart'. It was a cosy place, with wood-panelling on the walls and an eclectic mix of street signs and photographs from around Europe.

Kate was so used to the air of authority that her boss always carried with him, consciously but also effortlessly, that the sight of him shorn of it seemed more shocking than it should have been. He looked tired, his shoulders hunched uncomfortably and eyes hooded. 'I'm sorry,' he said, gesturing at their surroundings. 'I've just managed to get Alice home, so this is about as far as I want to stray from her at the moment.'

'We can go and have a coffee at your house, if that would be easier.'

'No, it's actually a relief to be out of it for half an hour.' He glanced at his watch, as if to double-check that that was all it was likely to be. 'There is only so much of the impending tragedy any man can cope with.' He shook his head. 'It's funny, I suppose others might say we're more acquainted than most with the tenuous and temporary nature of human existence, but even that doesn't stop you being holed below the waterline.'

'I'm sorry.'

'Everyone is. And it doesn't make a damned bit of difference.' Sir Alan gestured at the waiter, who had just arrived at a table opposite. 'Part of the trouble is that she doesn't want to go. Neither of us has ever felt much need to consider the possibility of a life hereafter, but now she's so close to the threshold that seems a bit of an oversight.'

The waiter came. Sir Alan ordered salmon, Kate cod. He asked for a glass of red wine. 'I can't remember the last time I drank at lunch,' he said.

'I'd order a bottle if I were you.' Kate looked at him seriously. It had never occurred to her before in how much affection she held him. If he were to step down, she would certainly miss his phlegmatic wisdom and easy temperament, but also the kindness he had displayed after Stuart's departure for Moscow. She wished there was more she could say or do. 'If it's not an impertinent question, how much longer?'

'Less than two weeks. Our youngest son, John, is coming back from South Africa, so she's determined to hold on until he makes it.'

'How heartbreaking.'

'In all those years together, you never really contemplate what it will be like to say your final farewell. And I can't quite decide whether this slow, steady route – in which, at least, everyone gets to say goodbye in the way they see fit – is better than an abrupt exit.'

Kate found herself wishing that Stuart was dead rather than divorcing her. But she kept that thought to herself.

'Were you followed here?' he asked.

'Yes. I called Suzy and she didn't deny it.'

'She's got some ambition, that girl, not to say a fair degree of brass bloody neck.' The waiter brought his red wine and he took a healthy swig. 'Well, you may be encouraged to hear that they've been following me also.'

'You?'

'Don't look so surprised. If you are a suspect, then I must be, too. They appear to have assigned me their least experienced team. I spotted them as soon as we left the hospital and I assured them that my wife was dying and I would be unlikely to stray far from home until she had departed to the other side.' He took another sip of his wine.

'I could murder a smoke,' Kate said. 'I'm not sure what's happening to me.'

'You look how I feel, so I'm not surprised.' He glanced at his watch once more. 'I spoke to Andrew Blaine in Moscow this morning and I had a long conversation with Ian. None of our sources have picked up the rumours of Vasily Durov's demise inside Moscow Centre, though those we have managed to contact acknowledge they've not personally seen him for some time.'

'That's hardly news, given how reclusive he is.'

'Exactly. I've spoken to the foreign secretary again. She's digging her heels in, adamant she's not going to write that letter unless we can give her greater reassurance that what Mikhail says about the changing of the guard in Moscow is true.'

'That'll take time we don't have.'

'Have you heard from your friend Sergei?'

Sir Alan's blue eyes were on her now. She thought about lying to him, but rapidly changed her mind: this was neither the time nor the place. 'Yes and no,' she said.

'Meaning?'

'He did contact me. Just something very innocent.' She got out her phone and found the texts. '"How are you?" I replied I was good and was he in London? He answered, "No, at home in St Petersburg. Be good to see you sometime." I sent a message back and never got an answer.'

Sir Alan was looking out of the window. 'I'm guessing you received the message in Berlin?'

'Yes.'

'Have you had any contact with him since then?'

'I tried a couple more times and gave up when I didn't get an answer. I have enough on my plate without wondering about someone I used to like.' Kate realized that was more information than she'd needed to share.

'Would you still say his motives for that first tip-off about the meeting on the *Empress* in Istanbul were personal?'

Kate stared at her hands. How often had she asked herself this question? So much seemed to hang on it – and more with each passing day. 'I think so, but it's impossible to be sure without spending a little time with him. I'm going on a friendship of half a lifetime ago and the man I knew then. But people change. So . . . I don't know.'

'Has he been in touch with you since Stuart's defection?'

'Not until that exchange in Berlin.' The waiter came with their food. Sir Alan tucked into his as if he hadn't eaten for a week. 'I could try to make contact again,' Kate said.

'I thought you said he wasn't replying?'

'I know where his parents live in St Petersburg.'

'We could ask Andrew to send someone up. But it seems a long shot.'

'I meant I'd go myself.'

He looked up at her sharply, his lunch forgotten. 'I'll pretend you didn't suggest that, Kate.'

'Just hear me out.'

'No. It would be a ridiculous risk, which I couldn't countenance and nor should you.'

'It has to be me,' she said. 'They grew up in the old Soviet Union. They wouldn't dream of talking to someone about their son unless they knew him or her.'

'I'll have a word with Andrew, see what he thinks.'

It was said with finality, but Kate couldn't let go of the idea. It was against every conceivable current procedure and protocol for a senior serving officer to travel undercover into Russia alone. But C was right: everything that had happened had begun with Sergei and they would make no real headway until she could see him and get a sense of what his motive truly was. Meg Simpson had said she needed certainty, and Kate could see only one way to get it.

She pushed the food around her plate. Sir Alan stared out of the window. 'There was one other thing,' she said.

He faced her again. 'Go on.' Kate finished the last of her cod, though she wasn't in the least hungry. 'The suspense is killing me,' he said.

'I know what you're going to say, but I do feel really strongly about it.'

'The wrong sort of preamble for a successful negotiation, but never mind.'

'When I recruited Lena Sabic to go and plant that bug on Igor's yacht, I looked her in the eye and swore that, if she kept her side of the bargain, I would make sure we rescued her sister, Maja, from Belgrade, and brought her to this country.'

Sir Alan didn't blink. 'And we assuredly would have done so if Lena had survived.'

'But that's just it. Lena paid for this deal with her life, which, from my – from *our* – point of view, writes it in blood.'

'Interesting use of terminology, which I don't know that I accept.'

'I made a promise. I can't break it.'

'Meaning?'

'Well, for a start, I'd have to resign with immediate effect if we refuse to implement it.'

'The implication being that you would be unable to oversee this current defection, which would make it unlikely to happen?'

'I didn't say that.'

'I should hope not,' he said, 'because that would be blackmail, which I do not respond to well, as I hope you know.'

'I'm not blackmailing you or anyone else. I'm just trying to tell you I feel very strongly about it, to the extent that I'm prepared to sacrifice my career, if need be.'

Kate had expected this to be difficult, but the depth of his annoyance took her aback. 'I admire the true nature of your moral compass, Kate, but we have to separate dream from reality here. Of course we would all like to make good on that promise to Lena, myself more than most. But "saving" Maja, as you might see it, cannot be more than a fantasy. Leave aside the epic expense of a protracted legal process and her resettlement here, who is she going to end up with now Lena is dead?'

'Me.' The shock on Sir Alan's face was genuine. 'I'll adopt her.'

'Have you lost your mind?'

Kate had not given this outcome any thought before it emerged from her mouth, but she moved from instinct to certainty in a heartbeat. 'I feel more in possession of it than I have for quite some time.'

'What would Gus and Fiona think?'

'I have a hunch they'd wholeheartedly support it.'

'They lose a father and gain a deeply damaged refugee sister? Are you sure?'

'If that is the only way it can happen, then so be it.'

He leant back and, finally, smiled. 'I'd braced myself for a fight on this subject, but even I didn't expect you to go this far.'

'You talked about it with Rose last night?'

There was a hint of something in his eyes for the most fleeting of moments – surprise, perhaps, or was it guilt? – before he recovered his composure. 'I asked her to prepare the report so, yes, we have been conferring, if that is what you mean.' He shook his head. 'Look, I'll promise to give it some thought. That's all I can do.'

'You can promise you'll do everything in your power to make it happen. And that is the price of me remaining in the Service.'

His gaze was steady, remorseless even. 'You're a tough woman, Kate. That's why I admire you. But this is a test of leadership. I understand the promise you made to Lena, but circumstances move on. This is a financial and legal minefield and it would be foolhardy for all of us to embark on it.'

'Nevertheless, it is the price I've set.'

'I've always seen you as a potential successor, one day. I think we should view this as a test of whether you have the necessary emotional and analytical clarity for such responsibilities.'

'If it is, I fail it. Willingly.'

He smiled, as if impressed, despite himself. 'Fair enough.' He picked up his coat. 'I'd better get back. I have a tab here, so no need to wait for the bill. Thank you for taking the time to see me.'

Kate stepped out with him and watched him all the way to the turn into Churton Place. He didn't look back.

She walked on towards Vauxhall Bridge, trailed by her MI5 watchers, her resolve stiffening both in relation to adopting Maja – what else could she honestly do? – and the idea of going to find Sergei in St Petersburg. Although it occurred to her the latter might be an attempt to escape the consequences of the former. She told herself going to St Petersburg had nothing to do with the loneliness that was becoming an aching chasm within her.

Back in the office, she closed her door. Sir Alan would fire her. Of course he would. Julie would advise against it. Ian would dance cheerfully on her grave. Suzy would probably take it as clear evidence she really had been working for Moscow all along.

She'd crossed the border from Finland before. What was the chance that the guards there would be on the lookout for a lone intelligence officer from London travelling under an alias she had never before used? She looked at the picture of Rav on the edge of her desk. He would have told her she was mad. And that, more than anything, decided it.

She had to go. Were it not for the prime minister's rank treachery, her former deputy and friend would be sitting here, she was sure. If she had to walk through hell to prove it, so be it. There was a knock and Kate swung around. It was Julie. 'I can tell you have a plan,' she said. 'It's the way you hold your shoulders.'

'Close the door.'

Julie did as instructed. 'Go on then. Hit me with it.'

'I'm going to St Petersburg.'

'What? Do you have a death wish?'

'Meg Simpson is not going to write that letter. Not unless we can find some corroboration of what Mikhail told us. We have to know that Vasily is definitely out. I have someone who will know and might tell me.'

'The same guy who tipped you off about the original meeting on the super-yacht, you mean? The one you have never quite admitted to?'

'Yes.'

'The one Ian claims was once your lover?'

'He was never my lover.'

'That's not the story doing the rounds.'

'I'm not interested in what story is doing the rounds.'

'Is C aware of this? Or Ian?'

'Neither of them. I floated the idea to Sir Alan and he expressly forbade it.'

'You'll get fired, whether you succeed or not.'

'Probably. But I'm doing this for Rav and I can live with the consequences. If I don't, there's the very real chance that our prime minister will get away with murder.'

'I'll come with you.'

'No. I go alone. It's the only chance I have of getting what I need.'

'Well, I'll travel with you at least as far as Finland, like last time.'

'They'll fire you, too.'

'No, they won't. I'll threaten to sue Ian for sexual harassment. And, anyway, I couldn't care less.'

'I'm going to book myself on the morning BA flight to Helsinki. Do not tell another soul, Julie.'

'You are stark, staring mad, but perhaps that's why I like you.'

Suzy had arrived back in the office during the tail end of that conversation and was looking at them quizzically. Kate debated what they should tell her and decided that nothing was the only sensible answer.

Eventually, Suzy could restrain herself no longer. She knocked and came in. 'Anything I can help with?' she asked.

'I had lunch with C,' Kate said. 'We were just talking about it. He says Meg Simpson is not inclined to write that letter. So this will have to go back into the long grass.'

Suzy looked personally affronted. 'Surely she has to write it.'

'Politicians don't have to do anything.'

'What are her reasons?'

'The risk that we're being played. She wants more evidence that what Mikhail says about the changing of the guard in Moscow Centre is true. Without it, she won't take the risk.'

'So how do we get that?'

'C is talking directly to Andrew in Moscow. We'll have to see what he can find out, but time is not on our side.'

Perhaps it was the effects of lunch, but Kate felt overwhelmed by fatigue. She sat down at her desk and faced her computer, which was intended as a clear signal to Julie and Suzy that this audience was over. They took the hint.

Kate struggled to think clearly about what she needed to do. Her mind seemed shrouded in fog. She closed her eyes, but that didn't improve matters. All she could think of was her overwhelming desire to lie down in the corner of her office.

She stood again and went along to the Ladies at the end of her floor. She glanced at herself in the mirror. She looked about sixty.

The only private space in the entire building was the shower in the corner. She went in, locked the door and sat on the bench where she used to change on the days when she ran into the office. Her heart was thumping again, getting faster as fear and anxiety threatened to overwhelm her. She lay down in the basin of the shower cubicle, with her feet up against the bench, trying to slow her breathing. She felt as if she were having a heart attack.

Eventually, the panic subsided, but the feeling of total

depletion did not. She curled up in the bottom of the shower tray, like a dog in a basket, and closed her eyes. She could feel the damp beneath her, but didn't care. All she wanted was some kind of release. It didn't come, but as she began to plan how she would make it to Russia she could at least begin to focus on something else.

Eventually, Kate stood up. She left the cubicle and ran a basin of cold water. She splashed some on her face and looked at herself in the mirror again. She texted Dr Wiseman's secretary and asked if there was any possibility of speaking to him – urgently.

She returned to her desk. She took two of the passports with fresh identities, neither of which she had used before, from the drawer and waited until Suzy left the office, then collected a thick wad of dollars, euros and roubles from the safe in the corner. She emailed Julie to say she would meet her at Heathrow in the morning, put on her trainers and started to walk home.

It was a relief to be in the house alone, but that didn't last long. She had only been home for ten minutes – just enough time for her to be seated at the table with a cup of herbal tea – before her mother called. Kate had an instinct, based on years of experience, that today she shouldn't answer, that everything would be different. She let the first few calls ring out, but picked up on the fifth. 'Yes, Mum,' she said.

'They're trying to poison me.'

Kate took a deep breath. A tear crept on to her cheek at the prospect of the familiar downward spiral. 'Who is?' she asked quietly.

'The fat black one.'

'You mean Lisa?'

'I don't know her name!'

'Because why would you?' Kate whispered.

'What was that?'

'Nothing. I don't know how many times we've been through this, Mum. Or how many more times we're going to have to. I've met every single one of the nurses in the home and they are, without exception, nice and caring individuals. No one is trying to poison you.'

'Perhaps you put them up to it!'

'I'm going to end this call now.'

'Telephone the police! I want to report the black bitch.'

'Mum! Do not speak about Lisa like that. It is grotesquely racist and frankly unforgivable.'

'If only David was here. He was the only one who ever cared for me.' Kate bit her tongue. She didn't doubt that the photograph of David Bloody Underpants on the beach in his absurdly tight swimming trunks pulled high above the waist had by now been swapped back to pride of place on her mother's side table.

Kate ended the call. The phone immediately started buzzing again. She pressed call reject repeatedly, and they engaged in this terrible game until, somehow, a call from the home itself managed to slip between her mother's frantic redialling.

It was from the long-suffering care manager, Jessica. She said she felt she needed to inform Kate that her mother had punched Lisa that afternoon. Lisa had been so upset she had gone home sick. The home could not, Jessica said, tolerate this behaviour much longer and they would soon be asking her mother to move elsewhere unless matters improved rapidly.

There was nothing Kate could say in her mother's defence. She promised to come round and speak to her. She wondered if she would one day be forced to care for her here at home, on the grounds that nowhere else would take her.

Kate rang off and immediately broke her promise. There was no way she could face her mother or her issues. She went to the sitting room and lay down on the sofa. Rose kept an immaculate house and the place was spotless.

She closed her eyes and put a cushion over her face. She had given up trying to sleep. The phone rang again and she saw that it was Dr Wiseman's surgery. She picked up. 'Dr Wiseman.'

'I'm sorry it's taken me some time to return your call.'

'No problem at all. Thank you for taking the trouble to ring.' Kate waited for him to open the dialogue, but she had recognized already that he used silence to draw his patients out. 'I don't know what to do,' she said eventually.

'When I left your clinic, I felt a degree of relief, elation even, as if someone finally understood me, as if I might even understand myself. I took it that, yes, I had issues, but I could see the possibility of resolution and that brought great hope.

'But whereas I saw a potential solution in the light of day, in the dead of night all I could think of was that I had a problem. And my mind just wouldn't – couldn't – switch off. I took sleeping pills one night, then worried I'd get addicted to them, so last night I was determined to doze off without them—'

'Why were you determined to do that?'

'Because I know they're addictive.'

'Who told you that?'

'A friend. Well, my aunt, actually. So I didn't sleep a wink on Friday – or maybe Saturday night. Then I took a zopiclone and did sleep, before I didn't take one and didn't, if you see what I mean . . . So I was wondering what I should do.'

'Take the medication. Do you have a decent supply?'

'Yes, yes. So I should just take them every night?'

'Yes.'

'Every night?'

'Yes.'

'But I don't sleep well with them. I only get three or four hours and I still feel terrible. I think they stop me sleeping properly.'

'You're not sleeping well because your mind and body are in a highly agitated state.'

'I see. So. Every night?'

'Until you next come to see me, yes. Then we can talk about moving you to a different medication.'

'What kind?'

'There are various options. Mostly likely, one of a group that are known as SSRIs – serotonin reuptake inhibitors.'

'Antidepressants?'

'Are you going to google this?' It was said with just a trace of bite.

'I might.'

'They are medicines that will help with your anxiety, but also have a strong sedative quality to help you sleep at night. They are not physically addictive in the longer term and there is no reason to think they will be required for a lengthy period in any event.'

'But if there is a strong sedative quality, I won't be able to work properly, surely.'

'You take them at night to help you sleep. In the morning, you'll be fine. Perhaps a little groggy, but otherwise you'll carry on as normal. However, regarding that "normal", I would strongly suggest you consider taking an extended leave of absence from your work.'

'I can't do that.' There was a long silence. 'I'm sorry, Dr Wiseman, but I just can't. I have some very important operations running.'

'To which you are indispensable?'

Kate thought long and hard before answering. She could

sense already there was no beating this man. Not in the logic stakes. 'I know this will seem egotistical and, most of the time, you'd be right to question me, but in this particular instance, it's undeniable that I must remain involved.'

'I see. And is it worth your health?'

'In this case I would have to say yes.'

'Even if, in putting your own well-being at risk, you might also threaten the health of your children?'

Kate hadn't thought of it like that. She never thought of it like that.

'Is this what you're thinking about at night when you cannot sleep?'

'No. I mean, yes, sometimes. But mainly it's just that nameless fear. That something will happen to one of them.' Kate got up and stared out of a gap in the curtains into the dark night beyond. A mortal enemy about to storm the room. 'And, I suppose, yes, fear of abandonment, I guess you might say, so much worse since my husband left.'

'Understandably so.'

'Yes.' Kate watched the slow progress of a man with a selection of small dogs on leads. 'It's made worse every time I see my mother. In the last twenty-four hours alone, she has shifted from being kind, considered and thoughtful to spiteful and utterly poisonous, with a healthy dose of racism thrown in.'

'Your mother is, by the sound of it, a very damaged woman.'

'Yes, I see that.'

'She cannot care for you because she is too busy wrestling with her own demons. That is the cycle you must break. As I said to you the other day, you must learn to reassure yourself.'

'But if I know how toxic it is to see her – and, believe me, I do – then why do I always go? I can't resist it.'

'Your mother has always been a critical voice, when what you wanted – what any child needs – is reassurance and support. That is the paradigm. The more she denied you praise, love and assistance, the more you craved it. This is the essence of all emotional abuse. But this is the cycle we must break.'

'Why don't I just stop seeing her?'

'It would make sense to restrict your visits for a while, but as your mother is unlikely to change, it is your psychology we must focus on, so that you see your mother for the sad and damaged woman she actually is, not the instrument of your torture.'

'The thing is, I *know* that,' Kate said, 'but I haven't been able to change the way I think and feel about it.'

'That is the purpose of this process. I would like you to think about the serenity prayer – whether it's a faith you follow or not is beside the point. *O Lord, give me the serenity to accept what I cannot change, the courage to change what I can and the wisdom to know the difference.* You cannot change your mother, or her behaviour, so you have no choice but to accept it. However, you can change the way you think and feel about it – and in so doing you will liberate yourself from the mental prison that the abuse has created for you.'

Kate sat down again. 'I do understand,' she said. 'I've been trying to visualize the conversation you talked of and it does make sense. And about the time off work, I will think about it.'

'Do. Or it may be taken out of your hands.'

Kate didn't like the sound of that. 'Will I get better?'

'I'm afraid I can't answer that. All I can say to you is that many people do. But you must commit to the process – to recovery – with the same determination you have approached your working life. Then, I think, there is a high chance of success. But no one else can do that work for you.'

'Yes . . . Thank you.'

'I'll check with Sarah when your next appointment is and I'll see you then.'

Kate ended the call. She put her phone down, placed her face on her knees and closed her eyes.

17

GUS BLEW IN through the door with rare loquacity. 'I've been made captain of the As,' he said.

Kate sat up, feeling dazed. If she hadn't slept, she had nevertheless been lying on the sofa in a kind of trance. Perhaps that was where you ended up: perpetually caught between wakefulness and sleep. 'The what?'

'The As. Mr Jenkyns just told me. Next term.' He took in her confusion. 'Cricket, Mum!'

'Oh, of course. Yes, sorry. Congratulations.'

'Do you mind if I call Dad?'

'Ermmm . . .'

'I'd really love to tell him. He'll be so pleased.'

Kate couldn't see a reason to refuse. Gus dialled from his own phone and it was a revelation to her that he had Stuart's new number in Moscow. 'I've been made captain of the As,' Gus said, without introduction.

She watched her son listen for a moment, his face aglow with his own and his father's pleasure. 'Mr Jenkyns said it was between me and Horsington and that I had shown a much greater degree of maturity. I'm still going to open.'

Gus laughed at something his father said. 'It's cool,' he said. 'Thanks, Dad. I wish you could come and watch. Maybe we can do a tour to Venice!'

Kate felt like she was intruding, but she couldn't drag herself away. She watched her son revel in the news with his father in the full knowledge they would never share in the game. For the first time, she wondered if she had been right to insist so resolutely that she and Stuart could have no future together. Gus looked up at her and handed her his phone. 'Dad wants to talk to you.'

With that, Gus discreetly disappeared into the kitchen. 'Hello . . . Stuart?'

'Kate . . .'

'Yes, what is it?'

'Isn't it great about Gus? He'd never have admitted it to either of us, but he's been holding out for that. It'll mean the world to him.'

'The pleasure on his face was something to behold.'

'He needs a bit of a boost. They both do.' Kate didn't

know what to say to that. 'All I have to do now is persuade the school to televise all under-fourteen A games and we'll be away.'

'Is there something I can do for you, Stuart?' There was a coldness to her tone that did not, she thought, reflect the way she felt.

'I just wanted to hear your voice.'

Kate closed her eyes. 'Please don't do this.'

'I'm not doing anything, love. I'm just lonelier than I've ever been in my life and hearing you or the kids on the phone is all I live for.'

'I'm sure there are many women in Moscow who would be only too pleased to console you.'

'That's a bit beneath you, if I may say so. I'm not here wallowing in self-pity, just telling you the truth. Do you have any idea when I might be able to see the kids again?'

'You mean after the last time went so well?'

'That was hardly my fault. And, from what I could gather, it might have been the making of your career.'

It was said with some edge to it. Stuart had always accused Kate of putting her work before their family. 'I have to go,' she said.

'How is Fiona?'

'She's fine. She's staying with Jed.'

'Blimey. I'm surprised you're allowing that.'

'You might be surprised at a lot of things. But it all changed the day you left.'

'All right, fair enough. I suppose I deserved that.'

'Goodbye, Stuart.'

'Goodbye, love. I miss you, though I know you don't want to hear that.'

'I don't. And if you keep saying it, I won't take your calls.'

Kate pressed the end button and walked through to the kitchen to give Gus back his phone.

'How was he?'

'He's missing you,' Kate said.

'You mean all of us?'

Kate looked at her son, who occasionally exhibited a maturity that surprised her. 'He's very lonely there. But . . .'

'He made his bed, so he has to lie in it?'

'I don't think I'd put it quite like that.'

Gus held up his phone. 'Anyway, thanks for letting me speak to him.' He headed for the door.

'Do you talk to him often?' Kate asked.

He turned back, looking shifty. He was certainly not a good liar. 'I guess so.'

'Every day?'

'Most.'

Kate forced herself to smile. 'That's good. I'm glad. It's exactly as it should be.'

Gus smiled back at her, his face flooded with relief and warmth. 'Thanks, Mum. You're the best.'

He disappeared up the stairs. Kate fed Nelson, who picked at his food with disdain, and started to think about supper. She put on some music and gradually felt the tension ease in her shoulders, losing herself sufficiently in the therapeutic process of cooking to miss Rose's key in the front door. 'Sorry I'm late,' her aunt said, as she placed her bag on the side and hung up her coat.

Kate swung around. 'You gave me a shock . . . You're not. Late, I mean.'

'Good day?'

'Er . . .' Kate thought about what she could say without giving away her true intentions. 'I had lunch with Sir Alan, who's just managed to get Alice home. He didn't seem in great shape, as you'd expect.'

'I know. Poor man. Did he take you to Grumbles?'

'Yes.'

'Must have been important to spare the time in a week like this.'

Kate recognized this as her aunt's subtle way of asking a question. 'Yes, but I suppose I'd better not go into it.' She thought of raising the matter of Maja's extraction from Belgrade, but decided to avoid that as well.

'Have you heard the news?'

Kate shook her head.

'The Germans have already dispatched an expeditionary force to Estonia. The French say they'll follow suit. The foreign secretary described it as sensible, the prime minister as rash. Cabinet discipline seems to have entirely broken down in this country.'

'It's all just signalling now the Russians have backed off,' Kate said. She turned to face her aunt. 'I'm sorry to have to ask another favour,' she said, 'but I have to go to Finland for a few days. Could you bear to hold the fort one more time?'

'Finland?' Rose exclaimed. 'I guess I shouldn't ask.' She smiled. 'At some point, I'd better reacquaint myself with my husband or Simon will divorce me. Are you sure you're up to it?'

'Yes. I'm fine. Really.'

'Have you been sleeping?'

'Yes,' Kate lied. She carried on cooking. Rose poured two very large glasses of white wine.

At supper, Gus was garrulousness itself, regaling Rose with his plans for the Compton House under-fourteen A cricket XI. They meant nothing to Kate and not, she suspected, much more to Rose, but neither said so.

Kate had texted Fiona repeatedly over the course of the evening and received no reply, so she set out after dinner for the brief walk to Jed's house. She was surprised to spot a car on her tail. Surely her watchers at the Security Service didn't think she was stupid enough to meet a Russian agent handler when she knew she was under surveillance. But that was their business.

Jed's parents were a charming couple in their late fifties, who lived in a spacious top-floor apartment overlooking Battersea Park on Prince of Wales Drive. They offered her a glass of wine and politely avoided displaying any sense of puzzlement at the way Kate's daughter had taken up residence in their home.

Fiona and Jed were both allegedly absorbed in homework and didn't appear for half an hour – and then only, Kate suspected, at Jed's insistence. His diffident, kind manner hid a touch of steel in the soul, which she was coming to be very fond of.

Fiona kissed her mother and sat in a corner while the rest of them made polite small-talk. They discussed the NHS, the fracturing of politics and the collapse in governmental discipline. Kate told Fiona her brother had been made captain of the Compton House As, in which she showed no interest whatsoever.

Eventually, Jed's parents politely withdrew, followed a few moments later by their son. Kate couldn't help but notice how thin her daughter looked. Clearly, living temporarily with two doctors had not convinced her of the health benefits of eating. 'What do you want?' Fiona asked.

'Nothing,' Kate said. 'I just have to go away in the morning for a few days, so I wanted to check you were okay.'

'I'm fine. Where are you going?'

'Finland.'

'What are you going to do? Invade Russia?'

Kate tried to smile. Sometimes she had to admit to finding her daughter's humour baffling. But perhaps she should be grateful Fiona knew enough geography to be aware the two countries were neighbours. 'No. Just a routine thing. I shouldn't be away long.'

'I'll be home at the weekend,' Fiona said, offering an olive branch.

'Great. I'll really look forward to it. Shall we do some cooking together?'

'Okay.'

'Anything you'd particularly choose?'

'I like that new Indian book Rose gave you.'

Kate smiled again. Her daughter was a born-again vegetarian. She couldn't help recalling the days when their conversation had routinely flowed with such ease. What had become of them? 'Do you speak to Dad much?' she asked.

'Why?'

'It's just Gus said tonight that he and Dad talked most days and I thought that was . . . well, very good. I hoped you did, too.'

Fiona sensed a trap. 'I do speak to him, yes.'

'Then that has to be a good thing, doesn't it?'

'Of course.'

Kate could see she wasn't going to get much further tonight. She stood, happy to bank such incremental gains. She wanted to tell her daughter how much she loved her, how she missed the easy familiarity they had once known. But the kitchen of her boyfriend's parents' home hardly seemed the place. She hugged Fiona and was pleased that she got at least a half-hearted hug back. 'Night, my love,' she said.

'Night.'

'I'll really look forward to the weekend.'

'Me too. Enjoy Finland.'

Kate walked back down to the street outside, some spitting rain and her ever-present watchers. She spent the journey home working out how she was going to lose her tail in the morning without her pursuers discovering her escape so that they put out an alert on all aliases she had on file, which would certainly prevent her passing through Heathrow. It was not going to be easy.

18

KATE WOKE EARLY and sat at the kitchen table, drinking tea and going over the provisional plan she had come up with the night before with the aid of an old London *A–Z* she'd located on Stuart's bookshelf. It still seemed the most viable option in the cold dawn light.

She assumed that, if MI5 was tailing not only her but the head of the Service, they would have secured the legal permission to deploy a range of measures from the home secretary, including electronic interception – which was why she'd needed the *A–Z*, rather than Google Maps. But this gave her the chance to lull them into a false sense of security, too, particularly if they felt she was heading somewhere expected and routine.

So, she began the day with an early call to Dr Wiseman's secretary, asking for an urgent appointment. She left a message, explaining she'd had another night without sleep and would be coming up to Ealing now, in the hope he could fit her in.

Then she left the house on foot, with a gym bag over her shoulder. The last impression she wanted to leave her watchers was of a woman off on a lengthy journey.

She walked north, skirting Battersea Park, crossing the river, then heading east with the flow of commuter traffic. She wove through Pimlico and finally disappeared underground and into the tube at Victoria. She'd estimated a team of at least four, but probably no more – resources were always tighter than anyone might imagine, even in the search for traitors – and she spotted the first man in the surveillance team as she swerved away from what seemed a full carriage at the last minute and ducked into the next one along. He was bald and wore blue jeans and a green Patagonia fleece, but he mistimed his lunge and only just made it through the doors. One or two commuters looked at him in surprise as he stared at the floor. Kate smiled. Amateur.

She picked out the second in the next carriage along once she had changed trains to the Central line at Oxford

Circus. He was leaning against the side, reading a copy of *The Times*. He was wearing brown walking shoes, a grey outdoor shirt and a Gore-Tex jacket. But who goes to work in rush-hour dressed like that?

She'd noticed in the transfer between lines at Oxford Circus that the bald-headed man had disappeared from view. Clearly he'd sensed he'd been spotted. She moved closer to the man in the Gore-Tex jacket now, as if to let him know that she'd sussed him out, too. He paid no attention.

Part of the reason why using Dr Wiseman had appealed to her was that Ealing Broadway lay at the end of the line. And, since she had also picked the very last carriage in the change at Oxford Circus, the numbers began to thin out beyond White City. The man in the Gore-Tex jacket got off at West Acton. She saw him muttering into his lapel mic as he walked away down the platform.

Kate sat down to survey the rest of the passengers. There was an art, of course, in doing so without being seen to do it, which made it a slow process.

As the train rattled towards its final destination, she had mentally given the remaining passengers the all-clear, but she changed her mind at the last moment about the couple at the far end of the carriage. They'd been chatting amicably, a passable imitation of lovers going to work, but what were the chances of two people in their twenties heading to work at the same tube station at the same time?

A workplace romance, perhaps. But somehow she doubted it. Their conversation had been too intense, too consistent. Couples who were that garrulous were also physically all over each other, in the first flush of love. She made a mental note to check that the pair did not appear anywhere on the journey beyond Dr Wiseman's office.

She left the train at Ealing Broadway and walked down the platform towards the barriers. She kept her gait easy and relaxed – it had long been a part of surveillance training to learn instinctively to spot changes in how a suspect held him- or herself – and, ten minutes later, hurried through Dr Wiseman's reception without so much as a sideways glance.

The doctor's secretary was on the phone, so, without greeting or explanation, Kate walked on to the bathroom at the back. She closed the door, opened the window, climbed through and dropped noiselessly into the suburban garden beyond. It was tougher to get over the fence on the other side without incident – she ended up having to commandeer a wheelbarrow – but she calculated she was into the street beyond in less than thirty seconds.

She allowed herself to look back, then carried on briskly along the route she'd memorized from the *A–Z*. Her phone, now switched off – as you would expect of a woman in an appointment with her psychiatrist – was no longer able to give away her progress.

The only part of the operation she had not been able to

plan was how exactly she would get from there to Heathrow, but in the end her luck was in and she hailed a taxi shortly after she re-joined Madeley Road in search of a bus.

Kate waited for Julie as agreed at Pret A Manger on the other side of security at Heathrow. She had booked her own ticket for the next flight to Helsinki as soon as she'd arrived, having checked that there was another seat available for Julie. Her heart still thumped hard after the adrenalin rush of beating the surveillance team. The coffee did little to calm its rhythm. She'd resorted to a double dose of zopiclone the night before and the four hours' sleep it had afforded her barely touched the sides of her fatigue. She still felt like death, and for a few brief moments she considered calling off the trip to St Petersburg – then immediately thought better of it.

Julie arrived, flustered, with a copy of *The Times* tucked under her arm. 'Sorry, it took me ages to shake off the Security Service guys.'

'I think they've changed their teams.'

'Makes sense. Suzy must have advised them to. That girl is an absolute snake.'

'She's needy and insecure, which is not a great combination. You sure you lost them all?'

'Yes. You?'

Kate nodded. 'There was a couple I only spotted at the very end, but I've been watching carefully. They've not reappeared. Did you book your ticket okay?'

'Yes, the flight's nearly empty by the looks of it. You want another coffee?'

Kate shook her head and Julie returned with a double espresso. She flipped over *The Times* so that it was headline up. It referred to the split in the NATO alliance between the boldness of the Germans and French and the caution of the British prime minister. 'I accept we both have our doubts about the wisdom of this trip, but you're right. We don't have a choice.' Julie gestured at the headline. 'I've been thinking about the sacrifices all our forefathers made in the last war. And for this, a world in which our leader is an immoral traitor in league with our enemy? We're growing uncomfortably accustomed to things being fucked up, but we shouldn't.'

Kate shrugged. What else was there to say?

'Are you sure you don't want me to come all the way with you?'

'I'll need some back-up here.'

Julie nodded and left it there. It was true enough and they both knew it.

Julie finished her coffee and they made their way towards Passport Control and security. They glanced at each other as they approached the border checks, but they passed through without incident and breathed a sigh of relief. By the time MI5 realized its mistake and caught up with them, they would, with any luck, be well on their way to the Russian border.

*

The flight landed at Helsinki in a hailstorm, the plane buffeted so violently on the approach that Julie's knuckles went white as she gripped the armrests. But the sun had broken through dark clouds by the time they had hired the car. Leaving the airport, they drove east beneath a spectacular rainbow. 'It's a sign,' Julie said, smiling.

But the risks inherent in what Kate was about to do weighed heavily on them and they passed most of the rest of the journey in silence.

They stopped at the coffee shop in Kotka where they had parted company when Kate had made her fateful journey to Sergei's dacha on the Gulf of Finland six months before. It was not a place with comfortable associations. They ordered sandwiches and coffee and looked out at the tall ship still berthed on the quay. The clouds had almost cleared now and the sun glinted off the water. 'I can't shake the feeling that this journey does not lead to happy outcomes,' Julie said.

'Me neither.'

'You think we should turn back?'

'I can't.'

'I'd still rather come with you.'

'I know you would and I love you for it.' Kate smiled at her friend. 'What are you going to do about Ian?'

'Does it matter?'

'I'm trying to take my mind off what lies in wait the other side of that border.'

'Well, I'll definitely report him to HR if he even thinks about firing me for this, or you.'

Kate smiled. She swirled the milky remains of her coffee in the bottom of the cup. 'How about a last fag?' They stepped outside, where a chill wind was blowing in off the water. Julie took a packet of Marlboro from her pocket and offered it to Kate. 'How's your sleep?'

'Chemically induced and not at all restful.'

'You're really not in a fit state to go. You know that? In fact, you look like you should be checking into a health farm for the rest of the year.'

'I tell myself I'm doing it for Rav and that makes me feel better.'

Julie drew deeply on her cigarette and turned away to blow the smoke up towards the clear blue sky. 'You ever think Suzy might have a point about Stuart not being Viper?' she asked.

'Stuart was Viper, I'm sure of that. She might have a point that he's not the only person who's been betraying us.'

'You, me, C, Danny or Ian: it's not the most encouraging collection of fucking suspects, is it?'

'It's also possible, as C says, that there is no one else and the questions are no more than conjecture, coincidence and paranoia.'

'Does it ever bother you that he and the prime minister were close friends at school?' Julie took another drag. 'I mean, I forget about that inconvenient fact for long periods and then I suddenly remember and think, Fucking hell, that is *weird*.'

'Why?'

'I don't know. It's just, if they were friends, I mean really *friends*, and James Ryan had been recruited by the Russians, wouldn't it be a natural next step to bring his old mucker in on the action?'

'You seem to forget that Sir Alan has been right behind us in everything we're trying to do. It's Ian who's taken a stance one might suggest is helpful to Moscow.'

'Ian's not a Russian spy, I can tell you that much.'

'What makes you so sure?'

'He's far too weak. He wouldn't dare and the consequences of being caught would terrify him so much he wouldn't be able to get out of bed in the morning.'

'What if he was blackmailed or bribed?'

'How? His wife is rich, so he doesn't need the money. I can tell you he's straightforwardly and vigorously heterosexual, and I don't think he has any particular kinks beyond the average – and I'm not sure even evidence of an affair, or several, would have been enough to push him to take the risk of working for Moscow. He's basically just a child.'

'Although that, in itself, might be a good cover.'

Julie thought about it. 'Maybe. But still . . .'

Kate threw away her cigarette. She smiled. 'Thanks for this last conversation. It's encouraged me no end.' She hugged

Julie. 'Wait only two days,' she said, as she walked to the car. 'If I'm not back then, return to London and confess. What will you do?'

'Try to go off grid and see if I can avoid our pursuers from the Security Service once they catch up with us – for my own amusement, if nothing else.'

'Trailing us here would involve a lot of manpower and expense,' Kate mused. 'They might just sit tight and wait until our return.'

'You think Ian, or even C, will be so relaxed?'

'You should call them. Give Ian a holding statement. A lead came up. We had to preserve operational security so—'

'They're never going to buy that.'

'Agreed, but they'll know damned well what I've gone off to do and they won't want to do anything to jeopardize my safety.'

'Showing a lot of faith in them both,' Julie said, 'but suit yourself.'

Kate found herself glued to the rear-view mirror until Julie had dwindled into the sinking sunlight. A farewell to security, for the immediate future, at least.

The journey through the endless pine forests passed swiftly, as she turned over the last conversation in her mind. It was better, perhaps, not to chase one's tail in a state of doubt and confusion, always seeking yet more agents of the enemy: it had undone so much good work in intelligence agencies all over the world, from the days of the CIA's James Jesus Angleton onwards. But Julie had had a point when she'd raised the schoolboy friendship between Sir Alan and the prime minister. On some level, it bothered her too.

It was dark by the time she reached the Vaalimaa border crossing, the European and national flags cracking crisply above it in the breeze on the Finnish side as she waited behind a long line of lorries. The wind blew in from the Baltic in great gusts, buffeting the hire car and unsettling her. It was half an hour or more before she was presenting an Irish passport in the name of Kate McGillis to the stony-faced young man in the glass booth on the Russian side of the crossing. '*Dobrý den*,' she said.

He didn't look up. He swiped the passport through the computer and glanced over the accompanying paperwork. All her passports – she had six at any given time – had in-date tourist visas for Russia.

The young man, his skin as flawless as his expression was impassive, stared at his screen for what felt like an age. 'Drive your car in to the right here and step out,' he instructed her in English. 'My colleague wishes to speak to you.'

Kate did as she was told, her heart thumping. By the time she had parked, a woman was waiting for her. She was young too, with blonde hair pulled back tightly and bright blue eyes. 'Please come this way.'

She ushered Kate into a room with a table and two

chairs on either side of it. The woman sat, the passport and accompanying entry form in front of her. She might have been pretty, but for the angular set of her chin and skin marked by childhood acne. 'What is the purpose of your visit to Russia?'

'I have always wanted to visit St Petersburg. I'll only be here for a few days.'

'Where are you staying?'

'At a hotel on Admiralty Embankment.' Kate pointed at the form she had actually filled out in the office in London before she'd left. Then she took out the Expedia booking confirmation and pushed it across to her.

'Do you have friends in St Petersburg?'

'No.'

'You travel alone?'

'Yes.'

'When did you arrive in Finland?'

'This lunchtime.'

'Why did you not fly direct to St Petersburg?'

'I had a friend in Helsinki I wanted to see. We had lunch together.'

'Where?'

That caught Kate off guard, but she didn't blink. 'Well, she actually lives between the capital and Kotka, so we had lunch there, in a café on the quay. I can't remember the name of it.'

The woman stared at the passport and the piece of paper

beside it, as if both were a mystery, the truth of which would soon be revealed. 'What is your occupation?'

Kate pointed at the piece of paper again. 'I work for Oxfam.'

'In Dublin?'

'In London.'

'You do not sound Irish.'

'My mother is English and I was brought up in London. But my father is still alive and lives in Dublin.'

'What is his name?'

'Dermot.'

Another silence. This time, it took on a more threatening air.

It's just routine, Kate told herself. How could they know anything? SIS's passports and back stories were legendarily efficient. They had to be. There was even a man called Dermot McGillis in Dublin who would agree he was her father if asked, and she had his number in her phone.

'Is something wrong?' Kate said. She allowed a trace of irritation in her voice. A real tourist would be annoyed at the delay by now.

'Wait here,' the woman said. She left the room, closing the door carefully behind her.

Kate looked up at the clock on the wall. It was seven and the night had long since closed in, the wind rattling the windows and rushing beneath the door. She was cold and longed for a cigarette.

She waited. The deadpan, slow, deliberate obfuscation of Russian officials was designed to unsettle the guilty and she could see no logical reason yet for concern.

Time dragged. Five minutes crawled past, then ten.

Until the woman stood before her again. 'You may go,' she said abruptly.

Kate resisted the temptation to ask what that had been about and got back into her car. 'Thank you,' she said, smiling at the woman. She headed off into the night.

The journey on to St Petersburg was long, featureless and sodden from the rain that had recently doused the perpetually potholed roads. But as she closed in on the old Russian capital, the temperature dropped and the episodic bursts of spitting rain became steadily drifting snow. At first, it melted on the damp tarmac, but by the time she had made her way through the industrial outskirts to the city's grand European centre, it had blanketed its streets in the magical winter coat Kate remembered so well.

She parked outside the front entrance of the hotel, which was right on Admiralty Embankment, and checked into the sleek modern reception area. She asked the valet to take care of parking the car and made her way to her room on the fifth floor.

The décor was a temple to modern Russia's celebratory absence of taste: a riot of purple, with an expensive television and a cream sofa from which to watch it. Kate pulled back the net curtain and gazed out at the River Neva, almost lost in the blizzard. She glanced up and down the embankment.

She took a small bottle of whisky from the minibar and swallowed two zopiclone with its contents.

All she was aware of, as she turned out the light, was the rapid beating of her heart.

19

KATE DIDN'T BOTHER with breakfast. She put on her coat and the beanie she had stuffed into its pocket and walked out into the Arctic winter chill. She'd been up since dawn had broken and had remained at the window ever since, watching the sun creep steadily across the Neva and the grandiose buildings of Vasilyevsky Island opposite.

Kate walked across Palace Bridge, stopping to lean over the side at its centre. The spire of the Peter and Paul Cathedral glistened in the bright sun, the river flowing steadily beneath her, not yet frozen despite the biting cold. Palace Square was almost deserted, the tourists not yet having emerged from their expensive hotels. She lit a cigarette and sucked in the smoke with the fumes of the morning traffic. It made her feel resolutely wretched, but she worked her way through half of it before finally flicking the remains into the river below.

She started walking and immediately stopped. What was she doing here? The carefully constructed operational arguments folded in the face of the loneliness that gnawed away at her. She knew damned well why she was really here and it made her feel foolish, nervous and naïve by turns. She was back to being a fourteen-year-old girl preparing for her first date with Pete Carter, the trainee anarchist.

She glanced at her watch. She walked on past the Rostral Columns – once primitive lighthouses for river traffic on the Neva – the great massif of the former Stock Exchange, the honey-coloured buildings of the university and the severe grey beauty of the Academy of Sciences. At this end, close to the Strelka, the island still bore the hallmarks of the grand administrative centre the city's founder, Peter the Great, had once intended. But the further you walked from the Neva, the greater sense you got of the mercantile past that had been its true destiny. Sergei had liked to summon an image of its Tsarist heyday, when the summer air was filled with the whistling of winches, the cries of seagulls and the shouts of the ships' crews as an avalanche of varied cargoes was unloaded from all over the Russian Empire and well beyond. The days of a great Russia, he'd said, how different things might have been but for the Revolution.

It was why she'd always called him a dreamer.

The island had been laid out in lines, and from Kadetzskaya down to the fifth line, it maintained a fairly well-bred air. From there to the fourteenth had been the middle class and commercial district, and beyond, the tenement houses of the poor – and each part of the island still bore the mark of its history, in spite of, or perhaps because of, the brutal decades of Soviet rule. Kate skirted St Andrew's Cathedral and browsed through the rudimentary food on offer in a morning market, killing time.

She slipped into a café that had existed since Tsarist times and ordered coffee. On the walls, there were pictures of the last of the Romanovs at Livadia, their estate in Crimea. Alongside them, in pride of place close to the door, hung a framed portrait of the current Russian president, as if his connection to the former royal family was perfectly obvious.

When she could contain her patience no longer, Kate walked on to eighth line and the still grubby tenement building that housed the apartment that had once belonged to Sergei's grandfather, an important Communist Party official and officer in the city's maritime section, who'd somehow managed to keep his head and position throughout Stalin's reign of terror.

She climbed to the top floor and knocked. She could see her breath on the air. She pushed her hands deep into her pockets.

The door opened just a fraction.

Either Kate's memory wildly deceived her or Sergei's mother, Olga, had shrunk dramatically. If never exactly overweight, she had been a well-built, handsome woman far removed from the bent, shuffling figure that peered at Kate now through the mists of time. 'Yes?' she asked, with the strong Kiev accent that betrayed her familial origins. 'Can I help you?'

'Olga, it's Kate.' She spoke in Russian, and stepped backwards into the light from the landing window. 'Sergei's student friend from England.'

The old woman's face lit up. She opened the door wide. 'Kate?' The smile had all of its old welcoming warmth. 'Can it really be you? After all this time? Come in, come in.' Kate stepped into the gloom. Olga gripped her arms. 'Let me look at you.' There was light in those old eyes now. 'How well you are,' Olga said. 'What are you doing here?'

'Just passing through . . . on business.'

'But after so long!' Olga shook her head in confusion. 'Come in,' she said again, beckoning her further into the flat.

Kate followed her down the hallway to the living room. 'What can I get you?' Olga asked.

'Whatever you have.'

Olga took her coat, placed it on a chair in the corner and disappeared into the kitchen to put on the kettle. Kate took a seat by the old gas fire. This room was like a step back into Soviet time, the curtains and chairs grey and dark red with an old-fashioned wireless in a Bakelite case. Kate glanced at the walls around her, still filled with pictures of the St Petersburg ice-hockey team, whose stadium Olga's husband Pietr had managed, and photographs of Sergei, the couple's only child.

Olga returned with two cups of black tea and a plate of homemade *pryanik,* a kind of flat honey bread that Kate had developed rather too much of a taste for in her time as a student. She smiled as Olga offered her the plate. 'You remembered.'

'Of course.'

Olga spooned sugar into Kate's tea without question, then leant forward to take her hand again, eyes bright. 'Tell me everything! Sergei says you are married.'

'Was.'

'Ah, I'm sorry. But these things happen.' Olga and Pietr's devotion to each other had been legendary. 'Children?'

'Two. Fiona is nearly sixteen and Gus – short for Angus – thirteen.'

'You have pictures?' Kate fumbled for her phone and flicked through it until she found a photograph of Gus and Fiona. It had been taken on the terrace of the hotel in Venice. Olga nodded approvingly. 'Such a pretty girl. Like you.'

'Ha, I'm not so sure.'

'Do you work in Russia?'

'No.' Kate realized she had lied too quickly. 'Very rarely.'

Olga's beady eyes gazed at her steadily. A former teacher, she was a hard woman to fool. She could and did switch from Russian to English and back again, but Kate continued to speak to her in Russian. 'If only he had won your heart,' Olga said heavily.

Kate stared at the floor. 'I'm not so sure he didn't.'

'I mean truly.'

'Perhaps if I had not been already committed to someone else . . .'

'And now, it seems, you are free.'

'Yes, I suppose I am.'

'Is that why you have come?'

The directness of the question had Kate suddenly lost for words. 'No . . . I don't think so. Not specifically, but in the hope of seeing him perhaps. He was always a great friend to me.' Kate looked at the photograph of Olga's husband on the dark dresser beside her. It was from his days as a soldier in the Soviet army. 'How is Pietr?'

'Only the dead can know.'

'Oh . . . I'm so sorry.' Kate could feel her face reddening. 'When did . . .'

'A few months ago.'

'I'm sorry, Olga. I know how close you always were.'

'Sergei is devastated. I think somehow it is even worse for him. He worshipped his father.'

Olga retreated into her thoughts. Kate turned to the

window. It seemed indelicate to intrude further. 'Is Sergei here in St Petersburg?' she asked, as innocently as she could manage.

'He came to visit me yesterday. It is difficult now he has to spend so much time in Moscow.'

'Do you know where I can find him? It would be great to share a cup of tea at least, for old times' sake.'

Olga's expression was inscrutable. Kate had the disconcerting sense this kindly old woman was in some way laughing at her. 'Where are you staying?' she asked. 'I will let him know you are here.'

'At a hotel on Admiralty Embankment,' Kate said. 'But please do tell him. He has my number. It would be great to see him if he has time before going back to Moscow.' The words didn't sound like her own. She stood, too hastily, tipping her tea on to the floor. 'Olga, I'm so sorry.'

The old woman waved away her concern, and as Kate set off to get a cloth from the kitchen, Olga gripped her wrist with surprising strength. 'It is all right,' she said quietly, looking directly into Kate's eyes. 'It is all right.'

Kate stood, but Olga did not let go of her. 'Why are you really here, my dear?'

'Some business. I . . .'

'After all this time?'

'After all this time, yes.'

'You look . . . alone.'

'I am.'

'We have one life.'

'And I have made a mess of mine.'

'It is not too late. It is never too late.' Olga released her. 'I will tell him. What he makes of it I cannot say.'

Kate retrieved her coat. Olga accompanied her to the front door. 'Be careful, my dear, won't you?'

'Of course.' Kate had no wish to enquire in what way the caution had been intended.

The wind was still biting outside and Kate huddled in a tenement doorway to smoke a cigarette. She glanced at her watch. It was not even ten o'clock.

She started walking again, back to the bridge and the Admiralty Embankment. She headed for Nevsky Prospekt, on the grounds that at least there would be life there at this time in the morning. Shoppers seemed thin on the ground – the Russian economy was all hard grind unless you happened to have an oligarch's bank account – so she installed herself in the Literary Café, once the Wolf and Beranger, the restaurant from which Pushkin departed for his fatal duel in the 1830s. She ordered coffee and some smoked-salmon blinis, which came with sour cream, gherkins and onions. She pushed them around her plate without much enthusiasm, thinking she was turning into her daughter.

She switched on her phone for the first time since she'd left London. The only messages were from Suzy – a successive string of texts asking where she was and what she was doing, presumably sent at the behest of her friends in MI5. The silence from colleagues in Kate's own organization was ominous. Sir Alan and Ian must, she surmised, have guessed her intentions. There would be hell to pay when she got back.

She'd not had a single message from anyone else and she couldn't help drawing a contrast again with the days when Stuart had held the home front, her days and nights punctuated by the steady ping of messages, the sentiments of which ranged from amused to exasperated. No one prepared you for how lonely parenting became with divorce.

She killed as much time as she could in the café, then continued her promenade down St Petersburg's main shopping street. She was aware that fatigue was making her sloppy, so although she had seen and sensed nothing to rouse her suspicion since she'd crossed the border, she attempted some basic dry cleaning. The Russians were good at surveillance on home turf, and she had to acknowledge they might well have outfoxed her.

She passed the Stroganov Palace and moved at leisure through the Lutheran church. She crossed the road and wandered through the grandiose Corinthian columns of the Cathedral of Our Lady of Kazan, then walked on over the Griboyedov Canal and turned into the striking arcade of Gostiny Dvor, St Petersburg's main bazaar since the mid-eighteenth century. The shops and stalls here were more sophisticated than she remembered. She bought some retro

Soviet-era T-shirts for Gus, Fiona and Jed, and then crossed Nevsky Prospekt again to the beautiful Style Moderne building that housed the delicatessen Yeliseev's.

She took her time there, then emerged again to cross the Fontanka river. She walked through the Moscow railway station before returning to Gostiny Dvor and installing herself in one of its corner cafés. She was just resisting the temptation to look at her phone when it finally pinged.

It was a WhatsApp message from Sergei. *Hey, hear you are in St Petersburg. Great news. A bit pressed today and have to catch the night train to Moscow tonight. You want to come with me?*

Kate stared at it until her vision started to blur. *Why not?* she replied, before she'd had time to consider the implications.

Great, he pinged back. *See you on the station's central concourse at 11 p.m.*

20

ST PETERSBURG'S MOSCOW station had changed markedly since Kate's last visit; the triangular Soviet-era ceiling that had once seemed so gloomy was leavened now by modern lighting. But the map of the rail network of the old Soviet Empire still had pride of place, and Kate was gazing up at it when she heard the familiar voice behind her: 'Look who it is . . .'

She spun around. He stood before her, every inch the student she remembered. He wore black jeans, a dark blue T-shirt and a black leather jacket, with expensive-looking suede loafers on his feet. He hadn't shaved, the stubble along his handsome jaw the same lustrous black as the thick, wavy hair on his head. He was wearing glasses for the first time, with a tortoiseshell frame. 'Nice shoes,' she said, looking down at his feet. His love of expensive footwear had been a private joke between them as students, since he'd once admitted to stealing more than a few pairs on his trips to the West.

'Tod's,' he said, smiling at her. 'And what is more, I paid for them myself.' He glanced at a bar in the corner. 'Come on, let's celebrate.' He moved to a steel table, dropped his bag on the floor and leant over the bar to order a bottle of vodka.

'What are we celebrating?' Kate asked.

'Our reunion. Here in Russia. After all this time.' He smiled again. 'You must be mad to come here.'

'Or desperate,' she said.

'For what?'

'Let's not go there.'

He poured two glasses. They toasted each other. '*Nostrovia*,' they said together, downing the shots in one.

'You look well,' he said.

'I look knackered, clapped out and old, but nice try.'

'You haven't changed.'

'Liar.'

'Same smile, same angular cheekbones, same delicate nose.'

'More lines, more bags and a hell of a lot more baggage.'

'That makes two of us.'

'Oh, yeah? Do you have an ex-husband?'

'No, you have something on me there.' He refilled her glass. They drank again.

'Are we going to carry on like this all night?' she asked.

'Why not? Moscow always looks better with a hangover.'

Kate glanced up at the board above her. 'Why are you taking the train?'

'Have you flown Aeroflot? Besides, I love the night sleeper. It reminds me of childhood holidays in Yalta. The romance of the long journey, the sense of freedom in time suspended . . .'

'Ah, yes,' she said. 'I remember you invited me.'

'Balmy nights, ethereal light, the magic of old Russia. I was convinced you would finally succumb.'

'Perhaps I would have done.'

'So close and yet so far.'

This time it was Kate who refilled the glasses. She suddenly had an overpowering urge to get wildly, blindly drunk. 'Do you ever think of what might have been?' she asked.

'Not as often as I used to. I mean, not more than once a month.'

'I'm sorry,' she said.

'For what?'

'Leading you on. You would have had every reason to hate me.'

'But I loved you. And I still do.' His megawatt grin – its

evident sincerity, the way it seemed to transform his face – still had the ability to floor her. 'But it has been so long. I'm not saying I have been waiting for you. There have been other women. Just none who matched up.'

Kate stared into her glass. 'Damn,' she said.

'Is that what you came all this way to hear?'

'I don't know why I came.' She looked up at him. His gaze was locked on to her. She dived for safer territory. 'It was good to see your mother,' she said.

'She was overjoyed. She always thought I should have proposed to you and gone to live in the West.'

'I'm sorry about your father. He was an incredibly kind man.'

'He could be. Especially to strangers, who might think well of him.' Sergei's relationship with his father had always been complicated, a consequence, Sergei had once said, of the old man's thwarted ambition. But he had been only kind and charming to Kate.

She glanced at the clock on the wall. It had just gone a quarter past eleven. 'Come,' he said. 'We'd better board.' He took the bottle of vodka and the glasses with him.

Sergei led her out of the station concourse to the platform. The Red Arrow train bound for Moscow was a long, sleek machine in red and grey livery to match its name. Women in red coats with black felt and fur hats stood on the platform waiting to welcome their passengers to first class, and Sergei seemed to know where they were heading.

He presented their tickets, climbed aboard and led her down the narrow corridor. 'Don't take this the wrong way,' he said, 'but I booked us into the same cabin. I figured after all this time we would spend most of the night talking anyway.'

Kate didn't risk an answer.

The first-class cabins were a resplendent rich red, from the bunks to the curtains to the velvet seat backs. Sergei stored his case and Kate her slender gym bag, careful not to bump into each other, and then they sat on opposite bunks. Sergei poured two more glasses of vodka. 'All right,' he said. 'Now we really begin. *Nostrovia*.'

'*Nostrovia*,' she replied, and they drank again. Her head was starting to spin.

The train shunted a few times, forwards and back. And then it began to move slowly away from the platform, the urban grime beyond it softened by a thin dusting of fresh snow. 'I was sorry to hear about Stuart,' he said.

'Were you?'

'Yes. I know how important your family is to you.'

'Have you seen him?'

'In Moscow?' He shook his head. 'By all accounts, he cuts a sad figure. The officers of the SVR don't have a great reputation for looking after their agents and defectors.'

In the long silence that followed, she held his gaze. 'Who do you work for, Sergei?'

'You know the answer.'

'But that's the thing. I'm not sure I do.'

'I work for the Russian government.'

'The GRU?'

He didn't reply, but in this case she took his silence to indicate consent.

'Why did you tip me off that Igor, Vasily and the others would be on that yacht in Istanbul?'

'Does it matter?'

'Yes.'

'To help you.'

'Why?'

'Because in all this time I have not been able to get you out of my head.'

'My colleagues think you told me what was to happen on that yacht in an attempt to discredit your rivals in the SVR.'

'And you? What do *you* think?'

'I . . . don't know.' And as she said it, she was aware that she really didn't. Not honestly. 'I don't believe you would cynically mislead me.'

'What else do we have to rely on in life but our instincts?'

Now Kate was wishing she'd gone a lot slower on the vodka. 'All the same, that leaves the possibility that you told me the truth, which also happened to be in your interests and those of your organization. There would be nothing dishonourable in that.' He was looking out of the window, at the snow falling across a ghostly landscape. 'I need to ask you something else,' she said. 'Is it true that Vasily Durov has been deposed as head of the SVR and is under house arrest?'

'He's not under house arrest. Not yet.'

'But the Kremlin has turned against him?'

'There is a battle. It is not clear who will come out on top.'

Kate searched those big dark eyes. She was not sure how much longer she could keep up the pretence of professional detachment. 'We have been offered evidence of our prime minister's treachery.'

'What kind of "evidence"?'

'The details of how and when payments were made and a copy of the sex video used to entrap him, filmed with underage girls while he was an army officer serving in Kosovo.'

Sergei nodded, as if entirely unsurprised. 'Who has offered it? Durov?'

'Igor and his son. They also feel under threat as a result of their alliance with Durov and are convinced the net is closing in on them here. They are prepared to give it to us in return for asylum in the West. So is the video real or fake?'

'I don't know. But you need to be careful, Kate.'

'Of what?'

'You think, after all these years, that your husband was the Russian state's only asset at the heart of British intelligence?'

'Who else?'

'There are secrets even I do not know. But you took a huge risk coming here. It was brave, but also foolish. What if they have been following you?' Sergei took another sip of his vodka and came to sit beside her, half twisted on the couchette seat so that his knee was touching her thigh. Then, quietly, 'If you pursue this, it may cost you more than your career. You must know that. A reason to live for tonight, though, if ever I heard of one.' He took the glass from her hand and placed it on the table. He reached behind him and flicked the lock on the door.

He faced her. Kate's head swam, her heart thumping as it had when she had been a student in that dacha aching for this moment. He touched her hair, her cheek, the white, freckled skin at her neck.

And then he kissed her.

The smell of him, the taste and warmth of his lips . . .

She'd not thought of sex beyond an academic curiosity since she'd learnt of Stuart's betrayal, but now desire exploded inside her. They moved with the urgency of the condemned, his firm, sure touch on her leg, beneath her skirt, pushing up her thigh until her blue polka-dot dress was rucked up at her waist to reveal long slim legs above blue socks and scuffed sneakers.

He unclasped the back of her bra with practised skill and kissed her stomach, working steadily downwards. She arched her back, aching for him, and he gently freed her until all she saw was her white underwear wrapped around one leg, before losing herself completely in him.

It had never been like that before, was all Kate could think as she lay lazily in his arms afterwards. Never with Stuart – not in all honesty – loving and marvellous and fun as that had so often been. And certainly not the first time with Pete Carter, which had been painful and mortifying by turns, or with the young boys who'd followed him episodically before she'd met Stuart.

It was as if, in some strange way, this secret had been revealed at the time of life when she needed it most.

She was so lost in her reverie that it was many minutes before her total failure to reach for any kind of contraception struck her. She rolled off the bunk in a hurry, retrieved her underwear and rearranged her dress and bra into crumpled respectability.

'What is it?' he asked.

'I just need the loo.'

'You're an incurable romantic.'

'Back in a second. Don't go away.' She reached the door, glanced back at him. 'It was worth the wait. That's all I'll say.'

He smiled at her. 'It was a pleasure to discover you like to make love with your pumps still on.'

'I always knew you were a pervert.'

Kate skipped down the corridor and didn't think about

the possibility she might be pregnant again until she had been sitting on the toilet for quite some time. What was she trying to do – shake it out?

She cast her mind back. Her last period had been . . . Shit, how long ago? Maybe a month. No, two. Perhaps even three. She'd always been irregular at times of stress and it had taken a long time to get pregnant with both Fiona and then Gus.

She couldn't be pregnant. She probably wasn't even still ovulating.

But what if she was? She couldn't even begin to imagine explaining the circumstances to the children. What would she say? That she'd had a one-night stand with an old flame on a trip to Russia?

There was no way she could have an abortion. Ever. Not after the joy both children had brought her. And probably not even before that, either, if she was honest. My God, what had she been thinking? She stared at her underwear on the floor and at her offending blue sneakers. She'd have to get a morning-after pill. From a chemist in Moscow.

Yes, why not? It made sense. She'd ask Sergei to take her to one. And, anyway, the extra time together might even prove useful: it would give her the chance to tease out of him more information as to what was really going on in Moscow Centre.

She pulled herself together both physically and metaphorically, washed her hands and walked back down the corridor with the pleasant certainty that, conception or not, this was unlikely to be the last time she had intercourse with Sergei that night.

'You ready for dessert, sir?' she asked, as she pulled back the door. But the sight that awaited her smashed every last sentiment from her except instinctive, animal panic.

Sergei lay naked on his back, his lean body covered with blood, his throat sliced from one side across to the other.

21

KATE SAT DOWN on the bunk opposite him. The walls were splattered with blood from Sergei's severed artery, which had been sprayed across a wide arc in his violent death throes. There was blood on the window, even on the vodka bottle, as he had evidently scrambled to get hold of some kind of weapon with which to fight back.

Who had killed him? Where were they?

She stood again, yanked the door shut and locked it. She sat down, trying to think straight against the tide of far too much vodka. Her heart thumped like a jackhammer in her chest.

Where was the killer?

Gone. He must have been waiting for Kate to leave before attacking. If he'd wanted to kill her, then . . .

He would have. He'd have murdered them both. Surely. No, definitely. But who was behind it. The GRU? Sergei's colleagues, infuriated he might spill their secrets? In which case, why not kill her, too?

The SVR? Its supposedly departing head, Vasily Durov? Igor Borodin and his son Mikhail?

The Russian Mafia?

But why *not* kill her, too? Why wait for her to leave and kill only him?

Somebody passed outside. Christ, what about the guards? What would they do when they discovered this? She'd be arrested, tried, sent to prison for more than a lifetime . . .

She had to get out of here. Now. Her DNA was everywhere – all over every inch of him and the carriage. No attempt at a clean-up was likely to do any more than deepen a state of suspicion as to her true intent. She took her bag from the rack, opened the door and looked up and down the corridor. It was dark, save for the night-lights and the moonlight reflected off the snowy landscape beyond.

She pulled the door firmly shut behind her and walked away down the carriage. She went through the connecting door to the next. It was quiet, but for the rattle and hum of the wheels on the tracks below. At the end of the corridor, she heard two attendants chatting quietly in their galley, but she flitted past them into another carriage. And then another, until she could progress no further. She put her bag down by the door and simply waited.

She pulled down the window a fraction and lit a cigarette. She smoked it as she looked out at the endless succession of snow-covered pines, fields and houses.

Kate waited for the consequences of the terrible scene she had witnessed to take their natural turn, but the strangest part of it all was that nothing whatsoever happened. The train did not stop suddenly at a small station in the middle of nowhere. No police stepped on board. No guards came running.

After an hour, or perhaps two, a guard came to his galley at the far end of the train. He caught sight of her and put his head around the side to ask if she was all right. She shrugged, pretending not to understand the language, and he left her in peace.

In the dead of night, nothing stirred. She smoked cigarette after cigarette, then closed the window and sat on the floor, resting her head uncomfortably on the wall of the carriage.

Dawn broke. The train clattered on through the grubby outskirts of the Russian capital and eventually glided to a halt inside Leningradsky station.

Kate was the first off. She did not look over her shoulder, because they knew where to find her if that was their intention, though she did have the clarity of mind to reflect on how little idea she really had of who 'they' were. Tired, distraught, shocked as she might be, nothing made any sense at all.

She almost ran through the bright concourse to the pedestrian section of Komsomolskaya Square beyond. She stopped by the line of yellow taxis and looked back over her shoulder at the clock tower above the station. It was eight thirty. She glanced about her. If they were watching, she certainly wasn't in a fit state to pick them out from the huge thronging crowd of early-morning commuters. She briefly considered getting into a taxi or heading straight back to catch a return train to St Petersburg.

She brought up Google Maps. She needed somewhere to sit, to think. She found Sokolniki Park was only a short distance away and walked there fast, oblivious to the people around her.

There was an Orthodox church adjacent to the park, so she installed herself in a pew at the back and closed her eyes. The moment she did so, she conjured an image of Sergei's face, his eyes bulging with the pain and shock of his sudden death. She hadn't seen any particular sign of a struggle: had it been someone he knew, expected even?

Who could have killed him? And why?

She wasn't on the passenger manifest but they must have watched them get on the train. If so, why had she been spared? Kate tried to pull herself together. She looked around the empty church.

She walked to the entrance and peered out. Two women in long trench coats leant against an iron fence by the road, as if waiting for her. She retreated again.

On an instinct that she later spent a great deal of time trying to analyse, Kate decided to call Stuart. He answered on the third ring, as if he had somehow been expecting her call. That was almost enough to prompt her to ring off straight away, but not quite: she was desperate. 'Hi, love,' he said, 'how nice to hear you.'

'Where are you?'

'Er, at home. Well, if you can call it that. In my apartment in Moscow.'

'I need your help.'

There was a momentary pause. 'Of course. How?'

'I'm in Sokolniki Park. There's an Orthodox church. I'm sitting at the back of it. Please come and get me.'

'In Moscow?'

'Yes.'

'Jesus, Kate, what are you doing here?' If he had truly expected this call, then his surprise was well faked.

'I just need your help urgently. I don't know if it will cause trouble for you and, well, I'll understand if you want to turn me down.'

'Of course I'll help you. I'll leave now. Just keep your phone on.'

Kate went back to the entrance and peered through the doorway. The two women had moved off. She stepped out and looked up and down the street, but there was no sign of either of them.

It took Stuart almost an hour to reach her and her first thought was again how incredibly well he looked. He was wearing a dark green T-shirt, but the same black jeans and leather jacket as when he had met her in Venice only a few weeks – or was it days? – ago. 'I'm sorry,' he said. 'The traffic is horrendous at this time of the morning.'

It was all Kate could do to prevent herself throwing her arms around him. He looked so . . . safe. Just like he always had: her Stuart. For a moment, they didn't know whether to kiss or hug. Kate eventually put him out of his misery by brushing his cheek. 'Can you take me to your apartment?' she said. 'I just need some time . . .'

'To what?'

'Please don't ask any questions.'

'Of course.'

He led her to his car, a battered old white Fiat. A man in a dark North Face raincoat, jeans and trainers stood just beyond it, smoking, as if waiting for something or someone. Her, she assumed.

They got into the car and pulled out into the morning traffic. Kate glanced in the side mirror. She watched a black BMW 5 Series saloon turn out behind them. 'Everything all right?' Stuart asked.

'Fine,' she lied.

Their progress was slow. The capital's roads might be

filled with many more shiny new cars since her first visit as a student in the early nineties, but they didn't move any faster. Kate kept a nervous, watchful eye on the side mirror. The BMW dropped back, but never out of sight. She bit her nails.

'Everything all right?' Stuart asked again.

'Yes,' she said. 'Fine.'

Stuart's apartment was out in Taganka, on the twenty-third floor of a concrete block that looked forbidding against a dark grey Moscow sky. The landing smelt of urine, and the wind had gathered rubbish into its corners. Kate glanced over the railing to see that the BMW had parked outside the block opposite. She averted her gaze before Stuart could remark upon it.

He let her into a small flat that had all the antiseptic appeal of a serviced apartment. It was clean and newly painted, but spartan and infinitely depressing. There was a small kitchen, with cheap Formica cupboards and a tiny table pressed up against the window, a single bedroom and a small sitting room at the end, with a cream leather sofa and two chairs in front of a large widescreen TV. 'It's not much,' he said, 'I know.'

Kate felt like bursting into tears, for him, for them, for the mess she was in. But the warmth of his smile stalled her. 'I can stretch to tea, though,' he said. 'English Breakfast or Earl Grey?'

'English Breakfast would be great,' she said. She was

looking at the wooden dresser, which was full of photographs of the children, but also of the four of them as a family and of Kate. The one at the end was his favourite, taken on the day of their graduation, overlooking the river. She'd been drunk and happy, carefree in a way she could scarcely remember. 'I told you,' he said, following the direction of her gaze. 'Memories are all I have.'

He withdrew to make tea. Kate tried to divorce herself from her emotionally loaded surroundings in order to make sense of what had just happened.

Who had been watching Sergei? Why had they let her live?

What in the hell was she going to do now? She moved to the window and looked out. The BMW was still there.

Stuart returned with two mugs of steaming tea and a plate of biscuits. He'd made it strong for her, as she liked. 'How are the kids?' he asked, as he sat on the sofa opposite her.

'They're well. Gus was very thrilled about being made captain of cricket.'

'I know. It's going to break my heart, not being able to watch. You'll have to send me some video.' He smiled again, clearly keeping up a cheery façade at some cost. Kate was thinking about the men in the BMW downstairs. Were they waiting for back-up, for others to join them? Was the idea now to kill both her and Stuart here in this flat? Would that be a double problem solved? 'How about Fi?' Stuart asked.

Kate tried to concentrate on the conversation. There was no point in alarming Stuart. 'She's difficult to reach still. She spends a lot of time with Jed, but I'm not sure that's a bad thing. He's a very nice young man.'

'Despite the tattoos and piercings?' He was smiling again. She gave him a weak grin in return. 'I don't mean to pry, but I assume you're in some kind of trouble.'

'I need to sleep,' she said. 'Then I'll work out what to do.'

'Of course. Just finish your tea. I'm afraid I only have one bedroom, but if you don't mind, you can sleep next door . . .'

'I'm grateful for anywhere to put my head down right now.'

They sipped their tea during another long and surreal silence. 'Just so I know . . . I mean, I don't mind, but forewarned is forearmed and all that. Am I going to be in trouble?' he asked.

'I doubt it. Something just happened. I don't know how, still less why. I need time and space to think before I work out what to do next.'

'Of course. I understand. What are you doing here in the first place?'

'I was meeting someone.'

Stuart couldn't hide his hurt at that. 'I think I can guess who. What happened?'

'I'm really sorry, I just need to rest.' She put down her tea.

He leapt to his feet. 'Of course,' he said. 'Of course. I understand.'

He showed her through to his bedroom next door, which had a small en-suite bathroom with a loo and shower. There were more photographs of the family on a bookshelf, and by the bed there was one of Kate alone, taken only a few years ago in the Italian Dolomites. Kate didn't know what to say. This was not how she had imagined him living here. 'Do you mind if I take a shower?' she asked.

'Of course. I'll leave you to it . . . Anything else you want, just shout.'

'If you need to go to work or—'

'I don't have a job to go to. I'll be reading a book next door. I'll leave you to sleep for as long as you want.'

He retreated. Kate undressed, stepped into the shower and tried to shake off the sense of guilt she felt as she washed away the legacy of another man with her husband's favourite mint shower gel and Australian shampoo.

She dried herself and cleaned her teeth with his brush. She took the top off the Acqua di Parma aftershave and sniffed it. She'd given him his first bottle in a Christmas stocking almost a decade before and he'd stuck to it religiously ever since. That was Stuart, loyal to a fault. Except, as it turned out, in the one way that really mattered. Kate dried herself, put on a clean pair of knickers and a T-shirt, and sat on his bed. She took half a dose of zopiclone this time, since she wasn't sure how long she should sleep.

She pulled back the curtain and checked the street outside once more. The BMW was parked there, still, but the men inside did not appear to have been joined by anyone else. Who in hell were they?

She lay down and tried to ignore the light streaming in through the thin yellow curtains and the sight of her own cheery face gazing down at her from the table beside the bed. Was it conceivable Stuart had put these pictures out after her phone call or did he really have this beside his bed all the time?

Her thoughts led inexorably back to Sergei. She could think of no reason why they would kill him and let her live. What had he planned to tell her? What would she have found out? She thought of his final few words: *If you pursue this, it may cost you more than your career. You must know that.*

There could be only two candidates for his murder, surely: either it was the GRU shutting down a renegade officer who'd had no motive but to assist the woman he'd always loved. (What was it he had told her? *You think, after all these years, that your husband was the Russian state's only asset at the heart of British Intelligence?*) Or it was Mikhail, Igor and those close to them trying to protect their exit strategy.

She turned it over and over in her mind. Was it Sergei they had been watching, or had they been tipped off that she was on her way and followed her from the moment she'd crossed the border?

Kate flopped over, so that she was face down; the way

she traditionally slept. She could smell her husband in the sheets and the sensation was comforting.

They'd known she was coming. That was what she kept returning to. And they'd killed Sergei before he could give her a full account of Moscow's men – or women – in London.

But he might already have done so, in which case why not kill her, too?

Because to murder her would cause them problems. There would be an international outcry: a British civil servant killed on a Russian train. Too much trouble, perhaps. Better to send her back confused and disoriented.

They were protecting someone. They'd been tipped off she was coming and they'd closed down her source.

That much seemed clear to her. Concentrate, she told herself, on the pieces you can see and understand, not the many parts of the jigsaw you can't know and may never know.

Kate shut her eyes. She tried to think of something else. She breathed in hard again and attempted to transport herself back to the carefree days of her life with Stuart. She turned from one image of him to the next: walking along Constantine Bay in Cornwall the summer before last; Stuart laughing his head off, roaring drunk, on the night the picture beside her had been taken in the Dolomites.

After a while, she noticed the sheet beneath her was damp with tears.

She pressed her face down harder, trying to clear her mind, as she waited and waited for sleep to come.

In the end, the chemicals did the trick, but, as ever these days, not for long. When she awoke, the clock on the table beside her told her it was just after midday. Kate got up and pulled back the curtain to reveal shards of sunlight glinting off the rows of concrete tower blocks. It was bright. The BMW had disappeared. There was a white van further along, parked with its engine running. Perhaps they planned to kidnap her.

She sat on the bed. She felt grim, but was gripped now with at least one clear thought: she had to get out of here, right away, by any means possible.

She pulled on a pair of jeans and packed her dress into her bag. She brushed her teeth again and emerged to find Stuart reading his book next door. 'Did you sleep?' he asked.

'A bit. Thank you.'

'You looked like you needed it.'

'I did.'

'Cup of tea?'

'Why not? I might actually drink it this time.'

He went to the kitchen and returned with a sandwich as well as tea. 'I figured you'd probably need to eat.'

She was ravenous, so she didn't argue with him. He watched her eat in silence. She finished, and sipped her tea. She was aware his eyes had yet to leave her face. There was a hunger in them she'd not seen since the first days of their courtship. She tried to suppress the wave of pleasure it brought. And in that moment, she knew he would do absolutely anything she asked. 'I understand if you don't want to do this and I wouldn't blame you. But could you drive me to the border?'

'Where?'

'Finland. In fact, St Petersburg, because I need to pick up my hire car.'

'Wouldn't it be quicker or easier to fly or catch the train? I can come with you to help allay suspicion if that's the issue, but it's a very long—'

'I'd rather go by road and I'm in no fit state to make the drive alone, as you can probably tell.'

He looked at her for what felt like an age, his mind evidently turning over this strange twist of fate. 'I'd do anything for you,' he said. 'Anything at all.'

Kate went to the window and looked out once more. The van had moved off. She scanned the street outside carefully, sweeping one way, then the other. If they were still watching her – and they must be – she could not see how. 'All right, then,' she said. 'Let's go.'

'Now?'

'Yes.'

22

BEFORE THEY LEFT Moscow, Kate said she needed to go to a chemist. Stuart was resistant: if she really was in trouble, shouldn't they leave straight away? But Kate was adamant and would not give a reason. In the end, he took it in mute silence and she half suspected he guessed why it was a matter of such urgency. She bought a bottle of water and swallowed the morning-after pill before she got back to the car. The only thing that worried her was that the last time she'd relied on this last resort against an unwanted pregnancy – ironically on that skiing holiday to the Dolomites when they'd supposedly been using condoms until they'd both got too drunk on the last night – she had bled profusely and for a long time. She'd also bought two large packets of sanitary towels.

If Stuart had guessed at the truth, or something like it, it might have explained the long period of silence. It was as if he was nursing a hurt and trying to find a way to broach the subject. 'It must have been quite some reason to take the risk of coming here,' he said eventually.

'I can't really talk about it,' she said. She glanced into the side mirror once more. The Volkswagen Golf she'd thought was tailing them had turned away at the last traffic lights and her suspicion had landed instead on a dark Volvo that appeared to be hanging back at a steady distance. 'Tell me about your life in Moscow,' she said.

'That's going to be a very short conversation.' They'd reached the outskirts of the capital now and were driving north towards a portentous, brooding sky. 'What do you want to know?'

'Are you still hunting for a job?'

'Yeah.' He shrugged. 'I met my "handler" – if that's what you'd call him – last week and I complained to him about my lot. He seemed quite sympathetic and promised to see what he could do. They've said they're going to ask me to lecture new recruits on how Western bureaucracies work. I think it would be different if I was you. Then, I guess, they'd be looking to put me to use, but an awful lot of what a civil servant does is well known to them. My guy did seem quite interested in my read on the PM and Imogen and the current state of British politics, so maybe something will come of that.'

'Do you have friends here?'

'You mean a girlfriend?'

'No. I was just—'

'Well, the answer is no and no. I've mostly been feeling sorry for myself, I'll admit. It's been very depressing. I spend a lot of time in the local gym and that's about the only thing that's keeping me sane.'

'You look fit,' she said. It was true. She'd found it hard not to admire his bulging arm muscles when he'd been sitting in his T-shirt in the flat. 'So what do you do all day?'

'I get up. I have breakfast. I read the British newspapers online and congratulate myself on escaping the crazy crock of shit that is our politics before feeling unbearably homesick. I go to the gym for a couple of hours. I'm tight for money, so I come home for lunch . . . I watch TV in the evening, but I try to spend the afternoons reading a book. Otherwise . . .'

'Haven't they helped you at all? I mean socially or . . .'

'Not really.' He forced a smile. 'It's like I've fallen off the end of the earth. I'm not complaining. I've made my bed, so I have to lie in it. Those couple of nights I spent with Imogen are turning out to be just about the most expensive in history.' He shook his head ruefully. 'I know there's no way back. Somehow I have to make it work here. I need to find a life, friends, whatever. I've asked if there's an SVR football team I can join. If not, there are a few other expat organizations I can maybe fall in with. It's just . . . there's a lot to let go of and I'm not there yet.'

It started to rain, first with a few drops and then in great thumping balls of water. The Panda's windscreen wipers struggled to keep up. Kate's gaze was drawn relentlessly back to the side mirror, but the Volvo had disappeared from view and she could no longer be sure they actually had a tail. If anything, it confused her still further.

'Was it worth waiting for,' Stuart said, his gaze resolutely dead ahead, 'your night with Sergei?'

'Were your trysts with Imogen?'

'No,' he said emphatically. 'Not that it will make any difference, but she wanted more. It was me who cut it off. I felt unbearably guilty, of course, but it was also just . . . second rate, mechanical, by comparison.'

'Just for the record, it doesn't make any difference.'

He peered closer to the windscreen. It was misting up now so he put the fan on full. 'You didn't answer my question,' he said.

'I don't need to, do I?'

'And yet you're here in my car. I guess I'm taking quite a risk driving you wherever it is you're really headed. So it would be polite at least to try to indulge me with an honest—'

'Sergei is dead.'

She watched the colour drain from Stuart's face. He

tugged at the stubble on his chin, a sure sign he was nervous. 'Christ,' he said. 'Jesus Christ, Kate.'

'I didn't come here to have sex with him. I came to ask him a question that only he would conceivably be able to give me an answer to. This morning, I found him with his throat cut.'

'After you'd . . .'

What was it with men? Kate thought. Why were they so obsessed with the act of sexual intercourse? 'You mean after we'd had sex?' He didn't answer. 'Yes, if you want to torture yourself with the truth, after we'd had sex. I didn't intend it to happen. I didn't especially want it to. But I'm lonely, too, and strung out, and bereft and confused. In the maelstrom of all that, I finished what I shouldn't perhaps have started all those years ago. And, yes, also, the earth did move for me, not better or worse than making love to you, just different.'

She saw the hurt in his eyes and wished instantly she'd held her tongue. 'Is that what you wanted to hear?' she asked.

'Of course not.'

'Then don't ask a question if you don't really want to know the answer.'

There was another long silence. 'I did want to know,' he said. 'Thank you for telling me the truth.'

'So that you can torture yourself with it?'

'Perhaps it will release me.' He turned to her. 'That

picture of you by my bed wasn't for show, Kate. I've never stopped loving you, not for a single second.'

Regret flooded her now: for his betrayal, for their estrangement, for the life they'd had and the future that might have been, for the brutal honesty of her tongue. 'I'm sorry,' she said again. 'I should have kept all that to myself.'

'I think I had it coming.'

'That doesn't make it any better.' She thought of the flat they'd just left and the window it had offered into his life here as it was and as it might be. The barren, hopeless bleakness of it chilled her.

'Won't they come after you once they've found the body?' he asked. 'Why haven't they come already?'

'It depends who you mean by "they".'

'Well . . . I don't know – the police, the Mafia, the SVR, whoever was involved.'

'The police certainly, I'd guess.'

'Does that make me an accessory to murder?'

She didn't answer that. Sitting there now, Stuart's crimes, which appeared to amount to a couple of nights of careless sex with Imogen Conrad, didn't seem to match the punishment Kate was putting him through. Regardless of whether she made it out of the country or not, there was a reasonable chance he might be made to pay a very heavy price.

Bleak as his current life in Moscow might be, it barely held a candle to the prospect of a long stretch in a Russian prison. 'I'm sorry,' she said again. 'I shouldn't have dragged you into this.'

'Stop saying you're sorry. I knew exactly the risk I was taking getting into this car with you. And I'd do it again, a hundred times over.' He forced another smile. 'Besides, I trust you. Aren't you James Bond?'

Kate tried to grin back at him, but doubted she managed more than an awkward grimace. They lapsed into silence after that, but they were only about three hours north of Moscow before the onset of heavy bleeding forced her to ask him to stop at a truck-stop diner.

She disappeared into the filthy toilet, and by the time she emerged, he was sitting at a metal table by the window with two mugs of coffee and a sandwich each. 'It's going to be a long night,' he said. 'I thought we could use this.'

Kate slipped on to the tattered red plastic bench opposite him. The chrome and steel décor was supposed to conjure the image of an American roadside diner, but, like many imitations in modern Russia, it was way off. Kate sipped her coffee and stared out at the traffic thundering past. It was still raining heavily, the light gloomy and visibility limited.

'You had to take the morning-after pill,' he said, gesturing at the packet of sanitary towels on the seat beside her. 'I remember you travelling home from the Dolomites with a bagful of them after that last night in the hotel.'

'You have a good memory.'

'For all the best moments. And there were a hell of a lot of them.' He swirled the coffee in his mug. Kate was suddenly desperate for a cigarette, but they'd given up together at least a decade ago, and she was too proud to admit she'd fallen off the wagon.

'Tell me honestly,' he said, still staring into his drink. 'Is there even the slightest chance you might one day forgive me, that we might . . . I don't know, be friends, or . . .' He trailed off, though she knew well enough what he was asking.

'If you want to know if we can ever be a couple again, as we were, then the answer is no. You betrayed me and you know who I am, how I am. You understand why it matters so much to me, however black and white you might find it. But you'll always mean something to me. Just in a different way now.' It wasn't the answer he'd hoped for, she knew, and he gazed disconsolately at the table, brushing his fingertips to and fro. 'I can't give you what you want. I can't take back time, or change the passage of events. But I can see how bleak your life here is and I'd like to do something to ease it.'

'Oh, yeah? And how are you going to manage that?'

'I don't know yet. The Service is quite happy to have you in Moscow. The last thing they would have wanted was to put you on trial. In time, when the way ahead is clearer, I think we can use that to our advantage.'

'How?'

'I can make it an argument about the children's welfare. They'll never let you come back to the UK, but it is just about possible I could persuade them to turn a blind eye to you living somewhere else in Europe – in France, perhaps, or Spain, somewhere you can build a proper new life for yourself and the children can visit regularly.'

There were tears in Stuart's eyes now. He wiped them away brusquely. 'I don't deserve you, that's for sure,' he said.

She reached out and put a hand over his. He slowly turned over the palm until their fingers were interlocked. 'I can't help, though, if you keep wanting to take it beyond friendship,' she said, but she was aware as she did so that the finality of her words were at odds with the emotion coursing through her. She removed her hand.

He wiped the tears from his cheeks. 'Thank you,' he said. 'Thank you. I'm never going to forgive myself for what I did to you. Sometimes I think it would be easier to stay here and punish myself. I just don't know what I was thinking. I must have been out of my mind.'

They finished their coffee and sandwiches and hit the road again. Kate half expected Stuart to ask her to drive, but he seemed to expect to soldier on. The rain stopped and, once in a while, a few rays of evening sunshine glinted off the pooled water on the tarmac.

And when they were finally swallowed by the night, Kate felt fatigue creep up on her until her head was lolling uncomfortably between the side of the seat and the cool glass of the window. At one point, Stuart reached over and put his sweater beneath her cheek. 'Where are we?' she asked.

'Just beyond Tver,' he replied, and then she drifted off again, a bleak, dreamless sleep, so that every time she was shaken awake, she felt more tired than she had been before.

Kate was dimly aware of a petrol stop somewhere, but it was two in the morning when Stuart shook her properly awake again. 'I'm sorry,' he said. 'I can't keep my eyes open and it's getting a bit dangerous. I'm just going to grab a coffee and something more to eat. You want to stay here, or come in?'

His arm rested easily on her shoulders. 'I'll come in,' she said.

The long, dark building was a no-frills café without the pretences of the previous diner. It had metal chairs and tables and a battered linoleum floor. A pretty, dark-haired girl leant against the counter and indicated they should take a seat. A much older man – perhaps her father – was asleep against the wall behind the bar.

'What can I get you?' she asked in English. Kate asked for coffee and something to eat in Russian. The girl gestured lazily at a counter along the far wall and Kate understood well enough: at this time in the morning, they weren't going to get anyone to cook for them. Perhaps not at any time in the morning.

Kate went to take a look. The breakfast spread ran to a selection of cold meats, cheeses and gherkins that looked as if they had been sitting there for ever. 'Rather you than me,' she reported back. But Stuart was made of sterner stuff. He returned with a plateful. She watched as he worked his way through it.

'What have you been thinking about?' he asked.

'Nothing.' She certainly didn't feel like admitting she'd been unable to get out of her mind the feel of his fingers locked in her own.

'You've got something you want to get off your chest.' He piled meat and cheese on to a slice of bread and took an enormous bite. He had never been an elegant eater. 'That's the advantage of having been married to someone for half a lifetime.'

Kate weighed what she had been proposing to say. She wouldn't have imagined it even an hour ago.

'We're almost there, so . . .' he smiled at her '. . . speak now or forever hold your peace.'

Intuitive as he was, he was not about to guess this. 'What if I said there was a chance – a very, very slim one, but the glimmer of something at least – that I might be able to find my way back to how I felt before?'

The colour drained from his face. The shock was palpable. 'I'd do anything,' he said, 'absolutely anything you asked of me.'

'It would require you to be honest about something.

Completely honest. And I'd have to be certain you were telling the truth.'

'Of course.'

'Even then, I'm not offering any guarantees. The road would be long and hard and we might not get there, but . . . it might open the door.' He waited, spellbound by this unexpected turn of events. He scratched nervously at the stubble on his chin. His yearning for a second start was not in doubt. 'I need to know what you told your handlers in Moscow.'

'About what?'

'Everything.'

For a moment, she watched something – a flash of resentment, a warning, a moment of doubt – slip through his conscious mind before he faced her again with unalloyed eagerness, but whatever it was, it triggered a counterbalancing reaction in her own mind: was her offer real? Did she mean it? Was it even possible? Or was she just using him? Even she didn't know the answer to that one.

Kate took the plunge nevertheless. She nodded. He downed a last swig of his coffee and answered her. 'I know it may not seem much, but I mostly talked to them about Imogen and British politics. They were interested in her ambitions, particularly in my take on whether she was ever going to realize them and, if so, how, when and why that might happen.'

'Did you get the impression they wanted her to be promoted?'

'They were careful never to ask leading questions. They just seemed genuinely interested in my views on the political scene.'

'Did they ask for papers?'

'Sometimes, yes. If I was on the circulation list for anything that was unusual or interesting, I'd hand it over. I was trying to keep them happy, you know . . .'

'What did you tell them about the Service?'

'Nothing.' He was clearly aghast. 'For God's sake, Kate, I'd never have betrayed you like that.' Kate was almost tempted to say that fucking their friend was a rather bigger betrayal, but this time she held her tongue.

'They must have asked.'

'They did, but I just said you never, ever talked about your work at home – which was true, most of the time.'

'Did they ask you to access my phone or computer?'

'Yes, but they're all password-protected and I told them that. To be completely honest, they didn't seem *that* incredibly interested.'

'What do you mean?'

'Well, they asked about you, definitely, but I didn't feel that I *had* to deliver any of the detail they requested or they'd expose me. When I said I didn't know or couldn't find out, they didn't press me.'

Kate thought about this. It was certainly not what she'd expected to hear. 'Did you tell them about the operation in Istanbul?'

'What operation?' If his confusion wasn't genuine, Stuart had turned into an amazingly competent actor.

'"How did it go in Italy?" you asked me. "Istanbul," I answered.'

'I don't know what you're talking about, Kate. I can't remember that at all.'

'What about when I went to Greece a few days later?'

'What about it?'

'Did you tell them about that?'

'No! Why would I have done?'

'Did they ask about it?'

'No.'

'Did you tell them the former PM had prostate cancer?'

'I didn't even know he had it until he made that announcement in Downing Street.'

He was obviously confused now. But not half as disoriented as Kate was. Even as he spoke, her mind was spinning. If Stuart hadn't told Moscow about Operation Sigma, who the hell had?

'To be completely honest with you,' he went on, 'I sometimes wondered why they wanted to recruit me at all.'

She looked up at him again. 'Why do you say that?'

'When they cornered me – blackmailed me – it all seemed incredibly urgent and elemental. They were brutal. They said they'd show you the video of Imogen and me and destroy our love and marriage. I absolutely believed them. They seemed ruthless, determined. But almost as soon as they'd got what they wanted, it was as if their interest waned. I mean, we'd meet up – about once a month, on average, I suppose – but even then they'd quite regularly postpone one or other rendezvous. Every time I was so relieved and started to convince myself they'd lost interest.

'And even when we did meet, they didn't seem that interested in what I had to say. It was like going to lunch with a benevolent but distant relation, who was trying to feign interest in everything you do.'

Kate shook her head. 'I don't understand.'

'It was almost as if the purpose of recruiting me was to tick a box, or meet a target. As I said, we talked about politics and Imogen, who was up and who was down. I discussed policy in some of the areas I was working on, but they weren't at all interested in that. They asked about you or the Service only rarely and when I said I didn't know anything, they didn't pressure me to try to find out more. I didn't tell them anything they couldn't otherwise have picked up from watching the news.'

Kate was looking out of the window. A lorry had pulled up and an enormously fat driver stepped down and waddled towards the diner. She was pretty sure now that they were not being tailed, but she couldn't make sense of why not. Did they intend to pick her up closer to the border? Perhaps they had a tracking device on Stuart's car.

'Did I say the wrong thing?' he asked.

'In what way?'

'For a shot at redemption.'

'It isn't about that,' she said, though in a way it was: a test of whether she thought he was capable of telling her the truth. 'What you say is . . . surprising.'

'Why?'

'Their disinterest.'

'I know. Sometimes I think it would have been easier if I had been passing vital state secrets. At least that would have felt important. They ruined my – our – life for nothing.'

Every time Stuart veered into self-pity or self-justification, she felt her hackles start to rise. She could have pointed out, and very nearly did, that it was his decision to screw Imogen Conrad rather than their exploitation of it that had ruined their lives, but what was the point? It made her sound and feel shrewish and embittered, and it was a train of thought and emotion she was trying to choke off.

Instead, she tried to make sense of what he had said. It occurred to her that Stuart might indeed have been a box-ticking exercise or, more worryingly, a red herring to disguise a much more important agent somewhere in Whitehall or perhaps even MI6. So perhaps Stuart had really not been Viper, after all.

Which meant, of course, that Viper was still active.

How easy it was for Moscow to throw Stuart to the wolves when suspicions started to sink in that there was a mole somewhere in the system.

But even this train of thought rested on a basic premise: that Stuart was telling the truth.

'Did you mean what you said,' he asked, 'or was it just a trick to get more information out of me? I wouldn't blame you if that was the case. I deserve it. But it would help to know.'

There was a long silence. Kate had to suppress another deep craving for a cigarette as she watched the young girl behind the counter light one and suck the smoke deep into her lungs before blowing it towards the blackened ceiling. The lorry driver had disappeared, apparently to the toilet. 'I did mean it. In a curious way, despite the awful circumstances, these few hours we've spent together have been the greatest peace I've known since the day you left.'

'For me, too.'

'But I can't change the fact that you wounded me deeply. The trust we had, the unique bond, is broken. For ever. We can't repair that. So, in truth, I don't know what I want. I miss you. I miss what we had.'

'My sparkling wit.' He was smiling at her.

'Everything but that. So I . . . don't know. I'm opening the door. Partly for the kids' sake. I'm not certain that I'll ever be able to walk through it. I can't give you any promises. Perhaps we can find a way back to friendship. I'd hope that was possible. I don't want to hate you. I don't want the children to have that bitterness and rancour in their lives.

But as to whether something more than that ever develops, I really can't—'

'That's enough for now. I don't want to push it.' He put his palm over hers. 'I know it's going to take a long time.'

Kate withdrew her hand. If his touch had thrilled her earlier, she now couldn't bear it. 'I'm sorry,' he said. 'What did I say?'

'It's not what you said, but what you did. I . . .'

He nodded. 'I understand. I'm sorry.' He stared at his hands. She couldn't help noticing how fine they were, always one of the most attractive things about him. 'I'm here for you,' he said. 'Always. If ever and whenever you need me. That's all you should know. I have nothing else in my life, and if I never have anything else but your occasional friendship, that's enough for me.' He smiled at her, and the genuine love and warmth in his gaze brought tears to her eyes. She brushed them impatiently away.

'How would it work?' he asked. 'This friendship, this new life, just to give me some hope to live for.'

'I don't know. I'd have to do some thinking about it. I'd need to persuade the Service to turn a blind eye to you moving permanently to take up residence in France or Spain or Italy, perhaps.'

'France. It's closer.'

'Okay. You'd have to work out where you wanted to go. Then we could try to make a plan so the kids could come over once or twice a month. Maybe sometimes I could come along.'

'Sounds great.' His smile was broad. She found herself smiling back, the warmth spreading through her. 'Come on,' she said. 'We'd better get going.'

Back in the car, most things were the same: the intermittent rain, snow and hail, the poor visibility, the condensation on the windscreen and the gloom of the drab Russian night.

But something was different. Hope had transformed their demeanour. Kate could hear it in Stuart – he was mentally far away, but humming old songs from the eighties – and feel it in herself. She found her mind roaming through the possibilities she had just outlined. Where would he go? What would he do? She found herself excited already at the prospect of getting on a plane with the kids to spend a weekend with their father in the South of France. Not for love, much less for sex. But the prospect that a true and decent friendship held, well, that was something to hold out for.

She thought about sex. She'd changed her sanitary towel in the disgusting toilet in the last diner and, while there was certainly some bleeding, it was nothing like as profound as the last time she'd taken the morning-after pill. She allowed her mind to roam worriedly over the possibility that it might not have worked. Christ, what if she really was pregnant?

All of which led her back to the thought of Sergei's slaughtered body in that carriage. The momentary sense of well-being that had enveloped her evaporated in an instant.

They barely spoke for the last leg of the journey, as Kate wrestled with what she would tell her superiors back home.

What did all this change?

They reached Kate's hotel on Admiralty Embankment. The weather had closed in to the point where Vasilyevsky Island was barely visible through the driving snow. They got out of the car and, for a moment, neither of them spoke. 'I'll follow you up to the border,' Stuart said.

'Why?'

'Just in case there are any issues. I have a Russian passport, after all. I'm officially a citizen. Maybe that might help.'

'It's fine.'

'I'd like to, just to see that you're okay.'

She nodded. 'Thank you for your help.'

'It's been the best twenty-four hours I've had since I left. I'll be high on it for days. I'll go home and start researching places to live in France. That's exciting. I mean, really thrilling. It gives me something to live for and I'm grateful.'

'Let's not get too ahead of ourselves. As I said—'

'I know what you said, love. But this is going to save my

life. What happens after that is in the lap of the gods. I understand that.'

'You may have some trouble when you go back.'

'I may, but I don't care.'

'Will you tell me if they come looking for you?'

'Probably not. They've already robbed me of everything I care for, so I don't mind what else they do to me and they know that.'

A gust of wind whipped the snow into Kate's face and she brushed it from her cheeks before she leant in to kiss him. 'Bye, then,' she said. Stuart gripped her, wrapping his great arms around her and pressing her to his chest. It brought tears to her cheeks again and, as soon as she was free of him, she brushed them away.

'I'll be thinking about this journey for weeks,' he said. 'A pretty strange turn of events.'

Kate tried to smile at him. Without another word, she walked to her own car, got in and drove away. She did not look back. And, within minutes, she was crying so hard she had to pull over to the side of the road and press her aching forehead to the steering wheel. She cursed softly, took out a face-cleaning cloth from her bag and wiped her eyes. She glanced at herself in the wing mirror and attempted to apply some lipstick and mascara. But no amount of touching up was going to magic away the impression of complete exhaustion.

She pulled herself together and drove off before Stuart

could come along and ask her what was wrong. She was grateful for the comforting sight of his headlamps behind her. She could still see no sign of any other tail.

There was only a short queue at the border crossing, but as she edged towards the barrier, Kate had only one thought: if they had put out an alert for her after discovering Sergei's body, then her image would already be plastered up on the wall in every exit point all over Russia. Tail or no tail, was there really any chance they would let her leave?

23

THE BORDER GUARD either had a keen wit or no sense of irony at all. 'Why do you want to leave Russia?' he asked.

'I'm sure I'll be back,' Kate said, though she doubted it.

'They say it rains in Ireland all the time.' He was a lugubrious man, in his forties or fifties, with large spectacles and cheeks like a bloodhound's. He stared at her passport and scanned it into his computer. Kate watched the snow twist and turn in tight eddies just the other side of the barrier.

She wondered what would happen if she had to hit the accelerator and drive for her freedom. She turned around to see if Stuart was still behind her, but he had disappeared.

'Irish?' the guard asked, as if genuinely challenging the evidence in front of him.

'Yes.'

'I went to Dublin once, and Belfast.' His English was remarkably good. 'I don't remember much about it.'

'That's often the way.'

He stared at the screen beside him. 'What have you been doing in Russia?'

'I was just in St Petersburg, seeing the sights.'

'Did you go on to Moscow?'

Kate hesitated a moment too long. 'No.'

There was a long silence. He was evidently waiting for some instruction from his computer. Kate leant closer to the windscreen and peered ahead into the gloom. They'd open fire on her if she drove for it, that's for sure, but it was only a hundred yards at most. She looked at the guard by the barrier, his assault rifle idling at his hip.

'You are free to go.' The guard smiled at her. 'Come back soon.'

'I will,' Kate said. The barrier went up and she drove on with a heavy sigh of relief and still more questions. It had felt as though the guard was waiting for a specific instruction but, if so, why would it have been to let her go?

Julie was waiting for her in a beaten-up old Volvo saloon just beyond the barrier. Kate didn't get a chance to ask how long she'd been there before Julie threw her arms around her. 'Fucking hell, Kate.' She released her, held up her phone.

'I had literally just decided to give you ten more minutes before I pressed the nuclear button.'

'I'm sorry. It took a lot longer than I thought.'

'There's been hell to pay from London. Ian guessed the truth immediately, as did Sir Alan.'

'It's all right. I've got enough to make it worth it.'

'What the hell happened?'

'I'll tell you in the warm.'

Kate glanced at Julie's car. 'I hired it for cash from a guy I met in a bar in Kotka. It's quite the place, as it turns out. I have to drop it back so I'll see you in the café by the quay.'

Kate followed her and, by the time a few rays of sun finally burst through the morning clouds, they were both slipping into a corner table for breakfast. 'You want caffeine or nicotine first?' Julie asked.

'Nicotine.'

They stepped back on to the quay and watched a long line of students walking up the gangplank to the tall ship. The sun shimmered through its rigging. Julie lit up and gave the cigarette to Kate before producing another for herself. Kate sucked the smoke deep into her lungs and exhaled into the sky above. 'Shit, that feels good.'

Julie watched her. 'You going to explain, or am I going to have to wheedle it out of you?'

'What happened in London?'

'Ian claims to have kept the dogs in MI5 at bay by

quoting operational security. But he says he's going to enjoy firing you when you get back. Now, spill the beans. Did you meet Sergei?'

'Yes.'

'Where?'

'He was travelling to Moscow, so I went with him on the night train. It was the only way I was going to be able to see him.'

'And?'

'We talked. I told him the truth about what we'd been offered and why, and asked him whether he thought what Mikhail had said to us about his father was true.'

'How did he respond?'

'That it was.' Kate took a last drag of her cigarette and stubbed it out beneath her shoe. She'd thought of little else but what she would say to Julie since they'd left St Petersburg, and at no point on the journey had she come to a firm conclusion to tell this exaggerated version of what Sergei had really said, but what purpose would the truth serve?

Either the video and the accompanying financial evidence that Mikhail and Igor offered was real or it was an incredibly convincing fake. They would never know until they got it to London and ran all the appropriate tests.

Sergei had, in truth, offered her nothing *conclusive* on the political ups and downs of Moscow's intelligence elite, only that some kind of internal civil war was under way. So why burden Julie, Sir Alan or still less the foreign secretary with further doubts? What they wanted was certainty. So she had resolved, on instinct, in this moment, to give it to them.

'Christ,' Julie said. 'So it's all on the level. For sure?'

'Nothing is for sure. I told him what Mikhail had said, and he agreed that it was in line with the rumours he'd heard. That is as good as we're going to get.'

'What will you tell London?'

'Exactly what we agreed. I came here to Kotka to meet Sergei. It took him a few days to get across the border and I stayed out of communication because I didn't wish to compromise his security. But he made it over, I met him here for an hour – and he told us what we needed to know. We don't have to admit that I went into Russia.'

'You think it will be enough?'

'As I understand it, from Sir Alan, the issue now is mainly about removing the foreign secretary's excuses. We need to line it all up for her so she has no choice. This is the last piece of the jigsaw.'

Julie threw away her cigarette and they went inside to warm cold hands with hot coffee. 'What are you not telling me?' Julie asked.

'About what?'

'I don't know. You're holding something back. To do with Sergei, I would guess. Did what I think happened finally take place?'

Kate didn't answer. She hadn't liked lying to Julie in the first place and had no wish to compound it with further evasions, half-truths or outright falsehoods.

'You've waited long enough,' Julie went on. 'So I guess you slept with him.'

'I was followed after I got off the train,' Kate said, changing the subject. 'I managed to lose the tail in the subway, but it spooked me. Moscow is a long way from home. I weighed my options and decided my best bet was to call Stuart and ask him to drive me straight to the border.'

'And he agreed.'

'Guilt goes a long way.'

Julie shrugged. 'I'm not sure I entirely believe you, but it's your business so I'll let it go.' She looked directly into Kate's eyes. 'Just so long as you're absolutely on the level about what Sergei told you.'

'Of course I am.'

'Then why are you not meeting my gaze?'

Kate looked up into her friend's eyes. She could feel her cheeks colouring. 'There are things you don't know and don't need to. In fact, for your own sake, it's much better that you don't. It was my decision to go in there and mine alone. I knew the risks. So if there is any fallout, I'll face it alone. All you do need to be sure of is that we have little choice but to accept this defection and face the consequences. I cannot go the rest of my life knowing we allowed a cowardly set of politicians to wriggle out of the implications. If we're going to do that, we might as well all pack it in and work in the City.'

'If that speech was meant to reassure me, I should probably tell you it was a total failure.'

'I got what I needed. That's all you have to know.'

'Well, maybe,' Julie said. 'Whatever happened in there, you're an absolute fool to keep it to yourself.'

'We go back to London with one clear message, as I have outlined. Agreed?'

Julie gazed right back at her, those big green eyes full of doubt, fear, possibly even suspicion. But, eventually, she nodded. 'Agreed, boss. For better or for worse.'

They spoke little for the rest of the journey to Helsinki airport. After turning in the hire car, Kate suggested Julie contact Sir Alan and Ian to give them the basic agreed outline of what had happened and to arrange the necessary meeting with the foreign secretary so she could sneak home on their return to London.

She found Fi and Gus eating dinner with Rose at the kitchen table. They all seemed very pleased to see her.

They chatted idly for a few moments before Rose said she needed to get back to Simon and quietly slipped out. 'We missed you,' Fiona said, as soon as she'd gone. 'I mean, Rose is lovely, but we've been really looking forward to you coming home.'

It was enough to have Kate reflecting once again on the strange shifting currents of teenage emotions, but the warmth of her own response perhaps explained her spontaneous decision to share more than she'd intended. 'I saw Dad,' she said.

'My God, where?' Fiona asked.

Kate had her son's rapt attention now, too, and their evident devotion to their father touched another chord within her. 'In Moscow.'

'What were you doing there?' Gus asked.

'I had to go into Russia for work. Things didn't go quite the way I'd planned, so I had some time on my hands. I called Dad and we agreed to meet up.'

'Where?' Fi asked.

'I went to his flat in Moscow, which is, in all honesty, a very depressing place. It's tiny, cramped, soulless and on the umpteenth floor of a grim Soviet apartment block.'

Gus was staring at the table, as if he was about to burst into tears. But Fiona could sense her mother had more to impart.

'I don't want you to get your hopes up unduly, but it was clear to me that this was not a reasonable way to go on for any of us.'

'What do you mean?' Gus asked.

'You miss him. If I'm completely honest, I miss him, too. And he's miserable.'

There was a stunned silence as the pair absorbed the

implications of this. 'So what are you saying?' Fiona asked eventually.

'That, in the first instance, I want to get him out of that terrible place to somewhere he can be much happier and you – *we* – can visit him.'

'Like where?'

'He suggested France.'

There was another silence as they registered what she'd said. Kate got up and went to get a glass of wine. There was half of an open bottle of rosé in the fridge, so she helped herself and returned to the table.

'Where in France?' Fiona asked.

'That's up to him. Somewhere he can get a job and make a life for himself – and that's easy to reach from London.'

'So we could visit him, like, every weekend?' Gus said.

'I think every weekend would be stretching our resources a bit thin now. He doesn't have a job and may struggle to find one. He doesn't speak much French, so far as I know. But every other weekend, perhaps.'

'You said "we",' Fiona chipped in.

'Like I said, I miss him, too.'

Fiona and Gus looked at each other, bewildered, their hopes and fears fighting for traction. 'Are you going to get back together?' Gus asked.

Kate worried that she had gone too far – much too far. But seeing the hope in his eyes – and perhaps it was, after all, only a reflection of her own – she didn't quite have the courage, or will, to row back. 'I'd rather not say that, because the truth is I don't know. I think it's unlikely. His betrayal hurt terribly and I'm not sure I can ever feel the way I did before.' She gulped some wine. 'But I miss him. I'd like to see him – not as a wife, or partner in the first instance, but certainly as your mother. I think we can find our way back to friendship. I don't know yet whether more than that is possible.'

'But the door is open?' Fiona asked.

Kate hesitated. Was it? Was that really true? 'Yes,' she said. 'It might be.'

As soon as she uttered the words, Fiona burst into tears and left the room. 'Yes,' Gus said, standing and punching the air. 'Yes! I fucking knew it.'

'Language,' Kate said, though she was struggling to wipe the smile from her face.

She followed Fiona upstairs and knocked softly on her bedroom door. 'Not now,' her daughter replied, but Kate thought that, for once, she could probably get away with ignoring her. She slipped in quietly and sat beside Fiona on the bed. 'It's all right, Mum.'

Kate put a hand on her shoulder. 'I'm sorry, my love,' Kate said.

'For what? There's nothing to be sorry for.' Fiona straightened, wiped her eyes with the sleeve of her baggy sweater. 'You have no idea how much Gus and I have prayed to hear those words.' She looked at her mother. 'I hope you meant it. Neither of us could take being let down again.'

'I told you how I felt. That's not the same as promising any kind of outcome. I can't say that we'll be together again as a couple, much less that we can recreate what we had before. But I think we can, with enough goodwill, be friends, and that would greatly improve all our lives, wouldn't it?'

Clearly, it wasn't what Fiona wanted to hear. Like her brother, she yearned for what they'd once possessed. 'It's enough,' she said. 'For now. But how will it work? I thought Dad wasn't able to stay in Europe except for very brief visits.'

Kate stood and moved towards the door. 'Dad is guilty of treason. If he ever sets foot in this country again, they'll put him on trial and he'll go to prison for a very long time. But that would also come with an avalanche of bad publicity for the Service that it would be keen to avoid. I negotiated them turning a blind eye for that trip to Venice. It's possible I could do the same for a longer period – perhaps indefinitely – so long as he agreed never to return to the UK.'

'So he can't ever come home?'

'Never.'

Fiona's gloom seemed to return at being reminded of this fundamental truth and she took to staring at her hands.

'I have to go to the office briefly,' Kate said. 'Would you mind holding the fort here with Gus?'

Fiona looked up and gave her a broad smile. 'Of course not.' And, as she walked down the stairs, Kate tried to recall the last time she had seen her daughter smile like that. A long while ago, that was for sure.

24

IT WAS JUST past eight by the time Kate reached SIS headquarters in Vauxhall, and the third floor was deserted. She walked through to her office in the corner, switched on the desk lamp but not the overhead light and fired up her computer. She logged on, pulled up the electronic version of the Operation Sigma file and punched in the passcode.

She read through it slowly, methodically, trying to view it through fresh eyes. If Stuart was telling the truth about the relative paucity of the material he'd passed on to his handlers, that left two possibilities: either the Russians had stumbled upon Lena's presence on the yacht through luck rather than judgement, or Sergei was right and they had a much more important source than Stuart in or close to London Centre.

Kate checked through the timeline carefully once more. It was possible that someone in Athens had spotted her coming through the airport and alerted the Russians. But why would they have immediately scrambled a wet team from Moscow?

She went backwards again to the original operation to get Lena and the electronic bug on to the yacht in Istanbul. She stared at the screen. It had long troubled her that the *Empress* had departed her buoy close to the Kempinski Hotel in the middle of the night. Why would the captain have done that, unless they had been alerted to something amiss?

She pulled up the phone logs, which Suzy had attached, and tracked her own movements. After returning from Istanbul, she had entered the SIS building that day at 15.58. She had gone straight to the meeting with Ian and Sir Alan. There had been plenty of time in the course of the evening for someone to have alerted Moscow.

Kate stared out of the window into the darkness. Did she *actually* believe Stuart, or did she just *want* to believe him?

She went back to the file and continued scrolling through it. She read the coroner's report on Rav's death. Verdict: suicide.

There was no sign of foul play and no indication anyone had entered his apartment on the night he'd died.

It was a conclusion that had appeared to suit everyone, including his partner, Zac, who seemed determined to blame himself. And although Kate did not believe the verdict for a single second, she had the uncomfortable sense it might have suited her, too, as she wrestled with the collapse of her marriage.

She opened the account of Rav's movements, such as they could be determined, in Geneva in the twenty-four hours before his death. Suzy had also attached the CCTV log from a newsagent opposite the entrance to the offices of the lawyer Rav had said he was going to see. It confirmed that, whomever he had met, he had not been there.

She read Suzy's report of the events in Berlin. It ended with a simple conclusion: *On the balance of probabilities, it seems likely the Russian state security apparatus had been tipped off to expect us.*

Kate thought about the last chapter in this file, which she had no intention of writing: that somehow they'd known she was crossing into Russia to meet Sergei.

'You could say they've been expecting us at every turn,' Suzy said.

Kate spun violently around. 'Jesus, you gave me a shock.'

Suzy stood by the door, arms crossed, eyes fixed upon the file open on the computer. Her petite, slender face was much less pretty when she was angry. 'Julie said you were in Finland meeting a contact.' Kate didn't confirm or deny it. 'I don't appreciate being kept in the dark, Kate.'

'Incredibly, not everything is about you.' Kate turned back to her computer. The questions the files seemed consistently to ask were preferable to those from her subordinate.

'It would have been courteous at least to let me know you'd be gone for a few days. I've looked a total idiot.'

Kate didn't bother to answer that. She had many problems. Suzy's bruised ego wasn't one of them.

'At any rate,' Suzy said, 'it doesn't change the question those files keep on asking.'

There was a long silence. 'I just need a bit of time to think,' Kate said.

But it was going to take more than that to force Suzy to withdraw: she leant back against the filing cabinet, as if settling in for the long haul. 'Either someone is tipping them off as to your every move,' she said, 'or they're actually tracking you.'

'Perhaps they found a way to inject a microchip into me.'

'Stranger things have happened.'

Kate glanced at her. 'This is real life, Suzy, not the movies.'

'You ever consider the possibility that this has been a set-up from the very first moment?'

'Of course.'

'No, I mean, really, that they've planned every stage of it methodically: the original tip-off about the meeting on that yacht, the news that the former PM had cancer, conveniently true, the idea that the leading candidate to replace him was working for them and now, suddenly, the "proof" that it must be true in the form of a sex video.'

'You've spent too much time listening to Ian.'

'I mean, I know you have this great source and—'

'How do you know that?'

'Ian told me.'

Ah, so that was it. It shouldn't have surprised Kate that Suzy had chosen to throw in her lot with Ian. That much had surely been inevitable.

'Don't you think it feels like a classic Moscow long play?' Suzy asked. Now she was using some of Ian's favourite language as well.

'I'm tired, Suzy. Do you mind if we discuss this another time?'

'I'm just trying to help.'

No, you are not, Kate thought. 'I know,' she said. 'Thank you.'

'What did the source you went to see tell you? I'm assuming he or she was the person who tipped you off in the first place.'

'Our agent told me Mikhail's account of what has happened to his father is accurate. I'll be briefing the foreign secretary to that effect in the morning.'

Suzy gave her a thin smile. 'I guess it's your call.'

She slipped away into the darkness. And it was all Kate could do to stop herself punching her computer. But she couldn't quite persuade herself to log off and go home. She stared at those pictures of the *Empress* leaving the quay in Istanbul in the middle of the night. Who had known enough to warn them? Sir Alan, Ian, Julie, Danny. That was it.

But only Julie could conceivably have tipped off the Russians about her trip to see Sergei.

Unless Sir Alan had guessed what she was intending to do.

Kate got up and went down to Operations, where Danny was on the night watch. He had his feet on the desk, a cup of tea resting on his chest. 'Here comes trouble,' he said easily.

'You here on your own?'

'No, I have someone from GCHQ on attachment. I sent him to get us a takeaway. From north London.'

Danny was idly flicking a pound coin with his thumb and forefinger. Kate sat and watched him. 'Did you and Rav always cheat at Spoof?' she asked.

Danny flipped the coin once more. 'Of course.' It was something of a field tradition that operational staff always played Spoof – a game in which you have to guess the number of coins people have in their hands – for the dinner bill. The first time she, Danny and Rav had worked together, on a trip to Turkey, northern Syria and then Mosul, Kate had lost almost every time. 'Why do you ask?'

'I was just thinking about it the other day. How did you do it?'

'Secrets of the subordinates, Kate. I'm not telling you that.'

'Whose idea was the laundry trolley?'

He smiled at the memory. 'Rav's.'

On the last night of what had been a long, arduous and dangerous trip, Kate had accused them of cheating at Spoof and left them to pay the bill in an Istanbul restaurant. They'd blocked the exit of the restaurant until the owner got angry and then they'd bombarded her with calls when she got back to her room. When she finally switched off her mobile and unplugged the hotel phone from the wall, they'd persuaded the porter to open her door, then bundled her into a laundry basket and wheeled her around the hotel. 'God, I miss him,' she said.

'Me too.'

'You were a nightmare together.'

Danny flicked the coin one last time, caught it in his palm and bunched his fist. He sighed heavily. He'd frequently called Rav a blood-brother and claimed him as the family he'd never had.

'Could I ask you a favour?' Kate said.

'Depends what it is.'

'I need some internal phone logs.' Kate gave him the date and then a piece of paper with the names she wanted checked. He almost spat out his tea. 'You're joking?'

'Not exactly, no.'

The laughter lines around his eyes had disappeared. 'I can't start rooting around in the chief's phone records.'

'I just need to rule him out of something.'

'You know we're all officially suspects, right? A team from Five came to my apartment last night.'

'Yes, I do know.'

Danny stared at the sheet before him for a long time, as if it would make the problem miraculously disappear. With a frustrated grunt, he logged on to the computer beside him and went hunting for what she had requested. She watched as the electronic dots darted around the screen before him. 'In the office until eight p.m. Then at home in Pimlico.' He closed in on the screen. 'No activity at all there until the phone goes off at eleven p.m.'

'How about Julie?'

'Are you really going to do this, Kate?'

'I have to.'

He checked Julie next. The screen remained blank all night. 'Phone off.' Kate nodded. 'Who next?'

'Ian.' He pulled up the log. 'Busy between five and six,' he said, 'something going on.' The dot on the screen clearly located Ian in his office.

'Then . . .' The dot moved across London now and Danny closed in on its final destination. 'Chelsea . . . That's home, right?'

'Frith Street, yes.'

'Okay, yeah, so home. One more burst of communication

at nine p.m., then phone off.' Danny turned to her. 'You haven't asked for my phone log.' There was a strange glint in his eye. He was smiling knowingly at someone over Kate's shoulder.

She whipped around to see Julie's departing wisps of auburn hair. She turned back. 'Another complication.'

'What kind?'

'Anything going on between you and Julie? I know that look.'

'No!'

'Are you sure?'

'I think I'm entitled to say it's none of your business.'

'She's only just broken off with Ian.'

'Nothing's going on.'

'I'm not going to ask if you know what you're doing.' She smiled at him and stood. 'Thanks for your help.'

'Remember me when I've been sacked,' he said.

She'd got almost to the door before she had a final thought. She turned back. 'Could you just do one other thing? How about the logs of Rav's phone for the weekend before his death?'

Danny pulled them up. Rav's phone was consistently located at his home on Sunday, but it was switched off all day on Saturday. 'That's . . . odd,' Kate said.

Danny nodded. 'I guess so.'

'Why would he have his phone switched off all day?' she asked.

He shrugged. 'Maybe he just wanted some peace. Maybe he had another phone.'

Kate thanked him again and went to get her bag from the office. She ran out into the rain and caught a taxi to the Fulham townhouse that Rav's former partner, Zac, shared with his wife. They and their children were gathered around the kitchen table, a picture of familial warmth in a pool of light on this dreary night. She almost lost her nerve, but she rang the bell before she could change her mind. Zac came to answer and the expression on his handsome, youthful, slender face moved from neutral curiosity to visceral hate. 'You,' he said.

'I'm so sorry to trouble you, Zac.'

'I have nothing to say to you.'

'I don't blame you. But there's just something I really need to ask.'

She had expected him to slam the door in her face, but he held his temper. 'What?' he asked.

'Would you mind if I came in?'

He stepped back to allow her inside. He ducked his head into the kitchen to explain to his family that he would be a few moments and led her through to his study at the back of the house.

It was a wood and glass addition, which stretched out into the garden. It might have been bleak and dark on that gloomy, rainy night, but it had been decorated with the same refined but austere flair as the rest of the house. Kate took in the photographs of their ideal family, which appeared to cover every tiny scrap of available space. There were no photographs of his dead boyfriend.

Zac closed the door and sat opposite. A picture of his wife in a swimsuit in what looked like the South of France loomed over his shoulder. He did not seem to be conscious of the incongruity. 'What do you want?' He had long, feminine eyelashes and brooding dark brown eyes. But petulance didn't suit him.

'I'm really sorry,' she said again.

'You can't ever be sorry enough.'

There were so many things Kate could have replied to this, not least that no one had forced Zac to return to his wife and shatter her old friend. But what was the point? 'I'll make this quick,' she said.

'Good.'

'We're still looking into various issues relating to Rav's death.'

'Like what?'

Kate was trying not to be put off her stride by his hostility. 'He was murdered, as you know.'

'The coroner found no evidence of that.'

'The fact that there was no evidence doesn't change the reality that it is the most likely explanation for his death.' Zac breathed in deeply. 'He may have been upset with you,' she went on, 'and me, for that matter, since I should never have told him you'd been staying back here with your wife. But that wasn't why he died. He did not kill himself. Rav would never have done that.'

Zac shook his head. 'I've been through this with the police, with MI5, with your people. And I'm sick of it. He's dead. He's still dead. And the hows and the whys just don't matter to me any more. I'm trying to move on.'

'I understand that. I have only one question. What was he doing on the Saturday before he died? His phone was off all day.'

'I told the police that.'

'Would you mind explaining it to me, too, and then I can leave you in peace?'

Zac stared at the floor. Kate glanced around the room again. Rav's absence here was quietly devastating, as if he had been airbrushed from existence. Zac looked up and seemed to divine the direction of her thoughts. 'I can't,' he said. 'I just can't. She'd kill me.'

'I understand.'

'I used to have a picture of him on my desk, but it upset my eldest son and . . .' He stared at his hands. 'I'm sorry . . . My God . . .'

He started, very quietly, to sob. Kate didn't know what to do. She stood and moved to comfort him but he raised a hand to prevent her. She watched as he brusquely wiped the tears from his cheeks. 'I'm sorry,' she whispered.

'There's nothing to be sorry about. Look, there isn't much to say. I did see him. He was very angry with me when I got back to the apartment on that Friday night, as he had every right to be. We argued. I came here. The next morning he was waiting when I went out to get a newspaper. He was regretful, tearful. He begged me to have a coffee with him. We went to a café just up there on Fulham Broadway.'

'What did you discuss?'

'He said he understood that I was conflicted, uncertain. I told him I didn't know what to think. I was confused. I loved him. I told him I always would, but I didn't want to abandon and let down my family, not just Emily but the kids . . . I was all over the place. He was actually incredibly thoughtful and kind, as you would expect. He kept saying he understood and would support me – be my friend – whatever I decided . . .'

Zac was still wrestling to hold back the tears. Kate waited until he had regained control of himself. 'Do you know what he did for the rest of the day?'

He seemed confused. 'No. We hugged in the door of the café. I said I needed some time, space. He said he'd always love me and then he was gone. That was the last I saw or heard of him.'

'He didn't say what he was planning to do?'

'He said he was driving to the West Country. He'd been trying to track down a former school master there.'

'At Sherborne?'

'I don't know. It was the place the prime minister went to school.'

'He was still investigating him?'

'Not him. The other one, your boss, Sir Alan whatever his name is.' Kate gasped. 'Are you all right?' he asked.

'I don't understand.'

'What?'

'It's just . . . How can you be so sure that it was Sir Alan he was investigating?'

'He was a bit obsessed with him. I told him it wasn't a very good career-development strategy.'

'What do you mean he was obsessed with him?'

'He was always asking me about public-school friendship.'

'In what way?'

'He had this conviction that there was no way you could become best friends in an experience as prolonged and intense as boarding school – based on my descriptions of it, though Eton is a bit different in various ways – and suddenly not be friends years later. He kept on referring to it as an unbreakable bond. He had tracked down the housemaster and said he was going to talk to him about Sir Alan and his friendship with the prime minister . . . Are you all right? You really don't look well.'

Kate insisted she was absolutely fine. She thanked him and left. She caught an Uber and asked it to stop about half a mile from home. She needed to clear her head.

It had started to drizzle. She stood for a moment in the darkness and let the cool water land on her cheeks, then run in tiny rivulets down her neck.

The same thoughts circled in her head until she felt dizzy.

Was Stuart telling the truth?

What had prompted Rav to become fixated on investigating Sir Alan's past?

She walked for a while, then stopped beneath the shelter of a beech as the rain thickened. She watched it thump on to the pavement beside her. It reminded her of all those childhood days when she had sat in the kitchen with her father, waiting for the rain to cease so she could go out and climb the beech at the end of the garden.

How she yearned now for the comforting and warm certainty of his love, for his ability to magnify her hopes and banish her fears. She closed her eyes and could almost feel his arms around her, the roughness of his bristles on her cheek and the comforting smell of his aftershave.

God, she felt alone. Why had she told the children she could be friends with Stuart again, that it might work, implied that she would even consider welcoming him into the marital bed as her lover? She must have taken leave of her senses. 'Get a grip, girl,' she muttered, under her breath.

She straightened, heading home to what was left of the bottle of rosé – or perhaps open a second – and another hefty dose of sleeping pills.

She would have downed both at the double, but Fiona was waiting for her at the kitchen table, her bright face shining with newly found contentment. 'I spoke to Dad!'

'Great!' Kate said, without thinking, as she headed for the fridge. She found she'd all but finished the half-drunk bottle earlier and fetched another from the cupboard. She filled a glass with ice and sat opposite Fiona.

'Are you all right, Mum?'

'I'm fine.'

'You're drinking a lot and you don't look well.'

'Work is complicated,' she said. But not nearly as difficult as life, she felt like adding.

'We got out a map and everything. He's keen on the Dordogne in France. Far enough south to be a bit warmer – which would be great – but near enough to make it possible to drive, if we wanted to. We looked up flights and Gus and I reckon we can easily get to Bergerac, or maybe Bordeaux.'

'That's good news.'

'He's not sure what he's going to do for work. He said he reckons he'll have to think outside the box about that.'

'Would it not be easier to go to Paris? Dad is very bright and I am fairly certain he'd find work there.'

'He likes the idea of somewhere warmer. So do we. He said there's a lot of English people in the Dordogne and they even play cricket there, so Gus was super-excited about that.'

Kate washed down two sleeping pills with a slug of wine. 'Roll on the future,' she said, with as much sincerity as she could muster.

'Do you take those every night?' Fiona asked.

'Erm . . . not every night, no.'

'Honestly?'

'All right, too often, yes.'

'I know you're worried about me, but it's yourself you need to be paying attention to.'

Sometimes Fiona was capable of wisdom well beyond her years, Kate thought. 'You're right,' she said. 'But I can't think about it right now.'

She finished her wine, kissed her daughter and left her nursing a cup of tea at the kitchen table as she went up to bed. For once, she was asleep almost the moment her head hit the pillow.

25

AS ALMOST EVERYONE who has ever had even mild insomnia will attest, four hours' pill-induced sleep is not enough. Watching the dawn light creep through the shutters and across the kitchen table several hours after she had risen, Kate had quietly promised herself that, as soon as Mikhail and his father were safely brought into the UK, she would request time off work and make a concerted attempt to sort herself out. She had grasped that her job was breaking her. And that, in turn, might have influenced her decision to keep the morning's rendezvous with the foreign secretary simple.

With Sir Alan's wife now hovering between life and

death, the meeting took place in the kitchen of his Pimlico home, one floor beneath the bedroom in which Alice was being nursed night and day. That lent the proceedings a surreal and distinctly uncomfortable air, which, it was clear, none of them was immune to. The foreign secretary, Meg Simpson, arrived last and didn't bother to take off her long, fawn raincoat, as if she were going to run at the first hint of news she didn't want to hear. She took a seat opposite her permanent secretary, a strikingly young-looking man with wavy blond hair and a bright tie. He must have been forty, but looked twenty-five at most.

Opposite him sat Ian and Kate. Sir Alan was at the end of the table, beneath an enormous watercolour of a Cairo street market. Kate recognized, but could not quite recall, the artist. As in so much of the rest of his life, Sir Alan had exquisite taste in art.

'I'm very sorry to force you to meet like this,' Meg Simpson said. 'Kate, you take the floor.' Like the rest of them, Sir Alan had no wish to extend the meeting a second longer than was necessary.

'You asked for more evidence,' Kate said, facing the foreign secretary, 'so I activated a source whom I believe to be completely reliable. At considerable personal risk, he agreed to travel out of Russia to meet me near Helsinki in Finland. We talked for about an hour and he confirmed, in essence, what Mikhail, Igor's son, told me in both Venice and Berlin.'

'What do you mean, "in essence"?' Simpson asked.

'He was honest about what he didn't know. He couldn't be certain of exactly what had happened in terms of the internal dynamics of the very top tier of individuals close to the Kremlin. But he confirmed that Vasily Durov and Igor Borodin were under house arrest and that the widely held view was that the Kremlin had concluded both they and the SVR in general were becoming too arrogant and over-mighty.' Kate stared at the spotless oak table before her.

'So he confirmed the GRU had been engaged in some kind of coup against its rivals in the SVR?' Simpson asked.

'Yes.' This lie was coming harder than she'd imagined. Kate studied her hands. There was a long silence. She finally looked up and watched the faces around her. A grim group they assuredly were. Surprisingly – or maybe not, given the relentless nature of his ambition – Ian was the first to break ranks. 'This really leaves us with no choice, Foreign Secretary. I've had my reservations. You know that. But this is crystal clear: a reliable agent, talking to one of our most experienced and able officers. We have no choice but to pursue this to its logical conclusion now.'

Simpson gave him a withering stare, but he didn't back down. If this was to go ahead and ruin a prime minister, he wanted to own it. 'My advice is that we must proceed with all due speed.' *My* advice. He made it sound like the most weighty and significant thing in the world. Meanwhile, Sir Alan gazed out of the window.

'It doesn't assuage any of my doubts,' Simpson said. She was visibly squirming now. She'd taken her glasses from around her neck and was tapping them nervously against her knee.

They waited her out. 'If the video is fake, the ramifications are horrific. Your source can't verify it, can he?'

Ian had rolled up his sleeves. He leant forward, elbows on the table, intent on taking control of the meeting now. 'The truth is we have done all we can, Foreign Secretary.' He gestured towards Kate. 'Kate has done a frankly amazing job, which we should all acknowledge. If there is an inquiry . . .' He let that hang. It was his standard way of cornering politicians. '. . . then we will be required to show that we acted at every turn in good faith. This looks like due diligence to me.'

'I am fully cognizant of the possibility of an inquiry into all aspects of my work at any point, now or in the future,' Simpson said acidly.

'I understand that, Foreign Secretary, but this is surely about the balance of risk. Because of Kate's good work . . .' My God, she thought, he's laying this on thick. He was making sure the blame game was well advanced if subsequently it all went wrong. '. . . we can characterize with confidence the worst that can happen.'

'Which is?'

'You are completely right about the video. As we have discussed before, there is the real possibility that it is a "deep" fake and that the financial information they say they are going to provide will prove to be a long and misleading trail to nowhere. But if we conclude they are misleading us, we have a choice: simply to let them be and ignore them or throw them out.'

'Except they will have hired the most expensive lawyers in the country to make that impossible,' the permanent secretary said. He had a very deep, steely voice.

'All right. The worst that can happen is they get an unwarranted passage to freedom and security in the West. Not ideal, but they're hardly public figures. Who is ever going to know?'

'Are you familiar with British politics and our press?' the permanent secretary shot back.

That seemed to silence the room. Simpson had taken to staring out of the window too. 'This is so fraught with risk and complication,' she said, 'that every political instinct I have rebels against giving the go-ahead.'

'Perhaps you should pay attention to them,' her permanent secretary muttered to her.

'But you leave me no choice.' She looked at Ian. 'As you have so helpfully pointed out, any subsequent inquiry will make inaction look like cover-up, or worse.'

'Are you sure?' the permanent secretary asked.

'Sadly, yes.' She stood, looking squarely at Kate. 'I hope to God you know what you're doing.'

Simpson and her permanent secretary walked out,

leaving Kate with Ian and the chief. Sir Alan hadn't said a word. 'You want coffee?' he asked eventually.

'I'm fine,' Kate said.

Ian declined. 'How much longer?' he asked Sir Alan softly.

'A day. Two. Three. Soon, in any event.'

'I am so sorry.' It was said with quiet sincerity.

'I'm going to have to leave it to you both,' Sir Alan said. 'I know it's a lot to ask, and in normal circumstances I'd be with you in the trench, but I can no longer pretend that we're in anything but the very final chapter.'

'We can handle it,' Ian said confidently. 'There's no reason to think it will be anything but straightforward.'

'Nothing like this is ever straightforward.'

'I understand that. But we'll do our best.'

They left him to the gloom of his thoughts and circumstances. Kate found herself dwelling on how she would feel if she were told Stuart had terminal cancer and only weeks to live. It was hard to keep conversation with Ian going as he started to try to discuss every aspect of the operation. He had a spring in his step and she found it difficult to work out exactly why. Was it his chance to prove himself to Meg Simpson, or had he some other outcome in mind?

Suzy and Julie were waiting in the office and Kate briefed them on the decision that had been taken. Suzy appeared thrilled until Kate told her that she would have to remain in London. She argued about it until Kate put her foot down, at which she retreated into a barely disguised sulk.

Julie slipped out with her. Kate closed her door and sat with her back to it, eyes shut as she tried to still her thumping heart. The pain in her stomach and central back had grown in intensity again. She felt about a hundred years old.

Ian had made clear he was going to run the operation and had already insisted on deploying himself to Tbilisi with her, but Mikhail was her contact, so there was plenty for her to work through. She took out her phone and sent him a message, using Signal this time, as all staff were advised to do from time to time: *Green light. We will arrive in Tbilisi tomorrow.*

She got a reply in seconds. *Good.*

Kate logged on to her computer. She started researching Kazbegi, deep in the Caucasian mountains, where Mikhail had indicated his father would cross the border. She had lost herself in the task when Julie burst in. 'Have you seen?'

'What now?'

'Go to the ITV website. Someone's leaked it.'

'Leaked what?' Kate asked, in exasperation, but Julie didn't dare answer and, as soon as she pulled up the site, Kate could see why. She stared at the headline, as if it belonged to a different world entirely: *Russian Defector Offers MI6 Sex Video Evidence PM Is Moscow Spy.*

Kate stood, physically backing away from the screen. 'I'm counting down to your phone erupting,' Julie said.

Kate was hardly able to grasp what had happened. How long ago had she left the meeting? Half an hour? Forty minutes, at most. Who could possibly have picked up the phone to the media? The foreign secretary? No, surely not: this seemed destined to end her career within minutes. Her permanent secretary? But what could conceivably be his motive? 'Who in the hell . . .' Her voice trailed off.

'Ian.'

'What?'

'Of course. Every which way he wins. He tips off the PM. He tips off the press. Then he tells the PM's people the leak came from the foreign secretary's office. She is screwed, Sir Alan is embarrassed, the PM is grateful.'

Kate shook her head. 'Even he isn't that brazen.'

'Of course he bloody is! Can you think of anyone else with the sheer brass neck to do something like this within an hour of your meeting?'

Kate didn't have time to give this a lot of thought. Her phone rang. It turned out to be the Downing Street switchboard. 'Mrs Henderson, I have the prime minister for you.' Kate waited, her heart thumping.

'Good afternoon, Mrs Henderson,' he said. 'May I politely ask what the fucking hell is going on down there in Vauxhall?'

'Prime Minister—'

'I'm not going to trouble your chief. I'm aware his wife is dying and I've known him long enough to be sure this isn't his doing. With my next call, I intend to unceremoniously fire the foreign secretary for gross incompetence, not to say disgraceful disloyalty. So I'm going to need someone to offer me an explanation. And I have a hunch that person is you.'

'Prime Minister—'

'Get your pretty little backside in here right now. I'm in my office at the Commons. I'll expect you within ten minutes.' He ended the phone call. If you could slam down a mobile phone, it had sounded as though he had certainly done so. 'Who was that?' Julie asked.

'The PM.'

'Holy shit.'

Kate sat down. She closed her eyes, tried to gather herself. 'I have to go,' she said. Julie didn't dispute it. 'I have to go,' she repeated.

'I know!'

Kate got up, pulled on her coat, slung her bag over her shoulder and walked through the outer office. Suzy was nowhere to be seen, but Maddy stood in front of the TV screen, transfixed. It was tuned to Sky News and the strap at the bottom read: 'Foreign Secretary Fired Over Fake Sex Video'. News moved so fast these days.

26

KATE WAS GRATEFUL for the fresh air and decided to walk up to the House of Commons. Streaks of morning sunlight cut through the bank of dark cloud and gave the Mother of Parliaments a golden hue. She crossed Lambeth Bridge, slipped across Victoria Gardens and went through security like any other visitor before making her way to Central Lobby.

A taciturn but pretty young woman with straight black hair came to meet her and escorted her to the prime minister's office behind the Speaker's chair. 'I don't know what the hell you people are playing at down there,' she muttered. Kate wondered again at the supreme – and annoying – self-confidence young special advisers attached to Downing Street were wont to exude, as if they had just inherited the earth.

The prime minister rose from behind his desk as she entered and guided her to a seat in the deep green chair by the door. He didn't bother to offer her tea or coffee. 'Well?' He sank on to the wide sofa opposite.

He ran a hand through his dishevelled hair as his special adviser curled up on the sofa opposite, long legs and short enough skirt just revealing the tops of lace stockings. She hadn't offered her name. 'You asked to see me, Prime Minister,' Kate said, glancing at all the weighty tomes lining the bookshelves in the old-fashioned wood-panelled room. Kate thought of the much greater men and women who had occupied the office before him. How had it come to this?

'Of course I asked to bloody see you.'

Kate wasn't going to make this easy for him. If her career was to expire, as seemed likely, if not frankly inevitable, it was only reasonable to derive some enjoyment from its dying embers. She waited. So did he, but not for long. He could barely contain his rage and it was the first time she had ever really witnessed it. His temper was legendary. 'Well, are you going to offer me an explanation or not?'

'Of what, Prime Minister?'

'Are you totally deranged?' the PM said, as his special adviser glared at Kate, shifting in her seat, so that her skirt rode up another notch. He surely couldn't be having an affair with her as well, she wondered idly.

Kate thought of that terrible video. Real or fake, true or false? So much seemed to ride on her judgement, her instincts. Had she believed in its credibility because she thought the character of the man she'd seen in it matched exactly that of the one before her? 'We've been trying to do our duty,' she said quietly.

'Don't be absurd,' the special adviser spat at her.

The PM leant forward, elbows on knees, so his eyes seemed hooded and brooding as he awaited an answer. Kate thought he was ageing rapidly. 'The former leader of the Russian SVR, Moscow's equivalent to SIS—'

'Yes, yes, I know what the bloody SVR is by now, for God's sake. That's something you have achieved in your determination to give yourself a starring role in my life story.'

'He offered to defect.'

The PM just stared at her. *'And?'*

'There appears to have been some kind of coup at the heart of the Kremlin. It is incredibly unusual – not to say unheard-of – for such a senior official to offer himself to us. He'd bring with him a treasure trove of material on all aspects of their operations in the UK and everywhere else in the world. It was our judgement, and that of the foreign secretary, that it was an offer we had to explore.'

'What does this fellow want?'

'Asylum.'

'So, do you want to explain to me how ITV has this story today and what it is about?'

'The man in question, Igor Borodin, has been one of the most influential intelligence figures in Russia for the last decade or more. I have been dealing with his son. It was he who first approached me to explain what had happened in Moscow and to offer his father's services in return for asylum for his immediate family.'

'And?' The PM still looked as if he was about to explode, puffing out his cheeks nervously.

'Among other things, they said that you had been recruited into their service many years ago while you were serving as an army officer in Kosovo. The son, Mikhail, played me a video that purported to show you having sex with three underage girls.'

The PM looked as if he was ready to leap up from his seat and throttle her. 'And you believed this disgusting codswallop?' The special adviser had uncurled herself and sat upright on the sofa, the colour drained from her face.

'The video was incredibly convincing. Now, it's possible that it's what we would call a "deep fake". Because motion-capture technology and AI are so advanced, it's possible, for example, to have a public figure say and do things that never actually happened. But there is no way of assessing that until we can get the video back into our labs to test it in the most thorough possible way.'

'You're talking, Mrs Henderson, as if I'm not here. Unless I'm mistaken, this grotesque fake is of *me*.'

She looked at him steadily. 'I understand why you're so upset and angry, Prime Minister—'

'Angry? I'm bloody livid!'

'I understand that. And, in your shoes, I would feel the same. I am merely trying to explain the reality of the situation we found ourselves in as dispassionately as I can.'

'And you and your colleagues, in your wisdom, decided to take this seriously?'

'There are many factors here. We could possibly have chosen to ignore the video—'

'God's blood, it's not of me!'

'—purporting to be of you, and all the other evidence, which they suggest they would bring with them, including detail of the many financial payments made over the years.' He was shaking his head now. 'But, ultimately, none of these things was material. The crucial fact is that an offer to defect of this kind is a priceless intelligence jewel. We had to pursue it.'

'Without my knowledge?'

'The foreign secretary was fully informed.'

His eyes bored into her. 'In all honesty, that is not the kind of mealy-mouthed crap I expected of you.'

'I'm sorry to disappoint you, Prime Minister.'

'And neither is that! For God's sake, Kate. I thought you were a good egg. Is this your friend Imogen Conrad's doing?'

'She's not my friend.'

'You could have fooled me.'

'You may recall she had an affair with my husband.'

He shrugged. 'Fair enough.' He got up and paced behind his desk. He picked up a squidgy stress ball and pumped it hard in his fingers.

His special adviser had curled herself up again. 'No one will believe it,' she purred soothingly. 'You've wanted to get rid of Meg for an age.'

'She's never coming back. Never! Bloody bitch.'

Kate's experience of government at the highest level had been of such exaggerated formality that the Prime Minister's relentless foul mouth was a shock, if not necessarily a surprise. It made her reflect on just how well he hid his true nature behind that easy-going affable exterior. 'You know what the worst of it is?' He was looking at Kate, waiting for an answer.

'There are quite a few aspects of this that would qualify as "the worst of it", Prime Minister.'

'All right, drop the "Prime Minister" crap. It's not very authentic.' He leant back against his desk, tossing the stress ball into the air and catching it. 'The worst of it is that I sense you believed it. You thought it was true.' He picked up two more balls from his desk and started to juggle. He was rather good at it.

'Believing what you see is a basic human instinct. But I'd like to think I'm smarter than that. It wasn't my job to form a view either way on the video.' Kate reflected as she spoke that she had, which had perhaps been a mistake. 'In the end, for us, it was simple: we couldn't turn down this kind of offer. Everything else is incidental.'

'Not for me it isn't.'

'Look, I'm extremely sorry about this leak. I don't know what happened. It occurred within an hour of our meeting with the foreign secretary this morning and the fact that it happened is absolutely inexplicable to me.'

'I doubt that. And, if so, you don't spend enough time around politicians.'

'I don't see how Meg Simpson benefits—'

'A safe pair of hands if I fall.' He put down the stress balls. 'Surely even you can see that.'

'I don't think Meg Simpson leaked this.'

'Really? She's not as cosy as she looks.'

He came to sit opposite her again, landing with a thump. 'All right, Mrs Henderson, let me tell you this. We're going ahead with your operation. We'll accept Igor Whatever-His-Bloody-Name-Is into this country with open arms. And we'll expose exactly what our friends in the Kremlin have been up to.'

Kate stared at him. If he had a reputation for being unpredictable, she sure as hell had not expected that.

'You look shocked,' he said.

'It wasn't entirely the outcome I expected.'

'Exactly. Because your world view is unfortunately

limited enough to conflate those men who enjoy the company of women too much with those who seek to abuse them.'

Kate could feel her cheeks reddening. In his case, that was indeed exactly what she had done.

'I hereby authorize you to do whatever you see fit to expedite this defection. But do it quickly. I intend to brief the press in full as soon as this man is in the country and we have established to your satisfaction that what he has to offer is as fake as the Hitler diaries.' He returned to his desk and took a seat beyond it. 'You are dismissed!'

Kate got up and walked out. The special adviser led her down the long corridor beside the Commons chamber. 'You didn't expect that, did you?' she said. 'You people aren't nearly as smart as you think. I love the way he outmanoeuvres you.'

It was all Kate could do to refrain from punching her. 'I can find my way from here,' she said icily.

'I need to see you out.'

'I can manage, thank you.'

The woman turned away in irritation and Kate marched on towards Central Lobby. But there was one more surprise in store for her on a day that had already held too many. Imogen Conrad stood waiting. 'They said you were here,' she said, without any other form of greeting.

Kate didn't break her stride and Imogen fell into step with her as she swung right towards the entrance.

'I've just had a text from the PM, asking me in. What the hell is going on?'

'I really can't talk about it.'

'Come on, Kate, for God's sake . . .'

'If he's texted you, perhaps it would be an idea to go and see him.'

Imogen took Kate's arm and brought her up abruptly. They were close together. And, not for the first time, Imogen's olive skin, full lips and wide eyes annoyed her: she was too damned pretty for her own – or anyone else's – good. 'Is he going to offer me the job?'

'How on earth would I know?'

'Did he talk about it?'

'No.'

'But you were in seeing him, right?'

'I can't talk about it.'

'Well, if I'm about to become your boss, I can instruct you to do so.'

'Once you do become my boss, you can call the chief, or one of his deputies, and request a formal briefing on any subject you like. But in the meantime the answer is no comment.' Kate started to walk away.

'You are absolutely infuriating,' Imogen threw after her, but without much conviction, and it occurred to Kate that one of her friend's – if you could call her that – more redeeming features was her utter imperviousness to all criticism or insult.

She burst out of the House of Commons, wove through the tourists outside and marched away down Millbank with grim purpose. She had no idea what to think. The operation had been green-lit and Imogen was about to be made her direct boss. You simply couldn't make it up. She took out her phone and glanced at a news alert. Below the item about the 'so-called sex video' and of the foreign secretary's departure there was a report that the US president had cancelled a state visit to Denmark because it wouldn't sell him Greenland.

The world was laughing at her.

Imogen Conrad had been formally appointed foreign secretary by the time Kate returned to the office and she had already given up being shocked: one politician mired in scandal over a sex video appointing another formerly mired in scandal over a sex video. Perhaps they would make one together.

Kate gathered together Julie and Suzy. She called Ian, who practically ran down the corridor. '*What* is going on?' he said, as he burst in, which more or less confirmed her – or, at least, Julie's – suspicion that he must have been the cause of the leak.

'I've just been summoned to see the prime minister.'

Ian looked put out. 'Kate, it really isn't your place to—'

'He wasn't handing out gold stars, Ian.' Kate was enjoying the sense of being at the end of her tether and felt better than she had for a long time. At some point on the walk back, she realized, she had taken the decision to resign from the Service in search of a quieter life once this was over. The relief made her feel light-headed. 'He has authorized the operation.'

There was a stunned silence. 'He did *what*?' Julie asked.

'He said the sex video is a fake and he now has to prove it.'

Ian was ahead of the others. He had a superhuman ability to sniff out the political ramifications in all things. 'He'll say it's fake anyway.'

'What do you mean?' Suzy asked.

'If we bring Igor in, the PM will insist the video is examined by experts he appoints and they will conclude it's a fake. He'll come out looking like the victim of a wicked plot, not the wretched traitor he may very well be.'

This was injudicious, for Ian, and Kate saw the surprise in Julie's eyes in particular.

'It's a trap,' Suzy said.

'Of course it is,' Ian said. 'But we still have all the cards. We'll have Igor. We'll have the video and evidence of the payments he's been receiving. If Downing Street wants to play games with this, they've chosen the wrong people. Game on.' He nodded at them with schoolboy enthusiasm and strode away down the corridor. Suzy went after him. Julie and Kate watched them go.

'What's got into him?' Julie asked.

'I don't know,' Kate said. And it was true. Ian's conversion to their cause was perhaps the most worrying turn of all.

27

THE AIR FRANCE flight banked smoothly and straightened as it followed the course of the Mtkvari River on its way into Tbilisi, the ancient Georgian capital that had served for so many centuries as the crossroads between East and West and gateway to the Caucasus and Central Asia.

By the time they disembarked, the sky was a rich dark red beyond an old Russian Tupolev plane silhouetted on the far side of the runway. There was a newer Boeing 747, too, painted white, with 'Cargo' emblazoned in bright orange on its side. It looked like some kind of rendition flight. Perhaps, Kate thought, that was appropriate under the circumstances, though the Service certainly didn't run to hiring a Boeing to fly out a defector.

The old Soviet terminal was banished behind a barbed-wire fence across the apron, so they were bussed to the shiny new gateway to Georgia, which looked like a couple of stacked pancakes. There was nothing but gambling ads for casinos in the baggage waiting area, but immigration was painless – a country that actually welcomes visitors, Kate reflected – and their bags arrived swiftly enough to have them in the car Suzy had organized from the hotel within minutes.

Their driver was a big, burly man, probably younger than he looked. Ian immediately engaged him in fluent Georgian, which he insisted on answering in English, to Ian's visible irritation. He launched into an unstoppable tirade on the greatness of his nation, its friendly people, its varied landscape – 'Visitors say Georgia has everything, why would you ever leave?' – and its courage: 'We are very, very old country,' he said. 'We protect our lands against Turkish people, Iranian people. Many times. Many times.'

They were packed into a new minivan, but he insisted on trying to drive it like a Ferrari, so Kate attempted to distract him by asking where he was from. 'Kakheti,' he said. 'Georgia best wine-growing region.' It turned out he had been brought up and schooled in the dying days of the old Soviet Union and, like many men and women of his generation, he had mixed feelings about their former Russian overlords. On one level, he was irritated by their continued interference in Georgian affairs, but on another he recognized the value of Russian tourists and was fighting a losing battle to persuade his children to learn the language. 'French, German, Spanish, English, of course. They would rather learn anything but Russian.'

After that, he couldn't be stopped. He talked about his love of rugby, but mostly seemed to want to curse his government – all governments, in fact – as well as Turks and Iranians. As they roared towards the centre of town, he had to swerve to avoid a couple crossing the road. The woman was wearing the *niqab*, which elicited another muttered insult. 'I'm sorry,' he said. 'I just don't like them.'

They were speeding past Tbilisi old town and Kate looked out at the brightly painted houses with their striking exterior balconies, many of which appeared to hang in mid-air. This gave Ian a chance to play the role he'd adopted as Suzy's caring and thoughtful tour guide, holding her hand through 'her first major foreign assignment', as he put it, though it wasn't and she didn't need her hand held. Berlin had proved that. 'They really are quite something,' he said, pointing out a particularly spectacular example of the local architecture. 'I had a house just up here with the most incredible courtyard.'

As a transparent and not especially subtle attempt to make Julie jealous, this flirtation was surely doomed to failure – 'He's a moron,' she'd whispered to Kate on the flight from Paris. 'I can't imagine what I saw in him' – but Suzy appeared to be lapping it up.

'Tbilisi was destroyed by the Persians in 1795,' Ian told her, 'so it turned to Imperial Russia for protection. They reneged on everything they'd agreed, but made it a place to be reckoned with, a true crossroads between East and West. Most of the old houses you see are essentially a mixture of cultures and styles.' He was warming to this theme. 'You get these amazing exterior staircases that literally cascade down the hill, following the natural contours of the slope.'

'Tbilisi very old, very beautiful,' the driver chimed in, not to be displaced as tour guide. They were racing away from Freedom Square down Rustaveli Avenue. 'Here is Parliament building. Heroes butchered in 1989.'

'So was Georgia always part of the Russian Empire?' Suzy asked Ian. Perhaps it was her imagination, but Kate had the sense she already knew the answer to this perfectly well. If she was playing him, he took the bait.

'No, it declared independence at the end of the First World War, after the Tsar had stood down. But it only lasted about a year before Lenin ordered the troops in to take it back. It was why it was one of the first Soviet republics to declare independence when *glasnost* got going.'

'I thought the Georgians had a pretty good run of the Soviet Empire?'

'They did, if you can ignore the deportations, mass shootings and trips to the gulag. Stalin was their man, too, of course, so they have rather mixed feelings about him now. They maintained a pretty strong sense of national identity throughout, so maybe it was no surprise they were among the first to want out.'

They arrived at the hotel. Suzy had booked it through the Travel Department and Kate thought she must spend much of her life on the Mr & Mrs Smith website, since Rooms Hotel Tbilisi bore a striking resemblance to Das Stue in Berlin, and was another study in low-key luxury. The central lobby had floor-to-ceiling bookcases on both sides, though all of the books appeared to be in English – a sign of the direction the hotel, and perhaps the country, was facing. They walked over polished red and cream tiles, past a curved green velvet and wood sofa and renaissance chandeliers until a bellboy in red hat and jacket, with a gold tassel on the shoulder, leapt at Kate's small shoulder bag and insisted on escorting her to her room.

She rummaged in her pocket and produced a twenty-lari tip.

It was a big room with a free-standing iron-clawed bath, sumptuous green velvet curtains and bold black and tangerine wallpaper. The lighting was low, the atmosphere moody. It was comfortable, luxurious even, and so clearly designed for couples in the first flush of lust as to be the last place on earth Kate felt like being. She thought painfully of the night on the train with Sergei and found it hard to push the image of his distorted face from her mind.

She washed her face and went downstairs to wait for Julie in the bar. She ordered some kind of lavender cocktail – made with gin and coconut – and sat beneath a giant painting of a woman seated backwards on a zebra. It was that kind of hotel.

Kate's cocktail arrived, shortly followed by Julie. 'What is *that*?' she asked.

Kate sipped it. 'Too sweet for you.'

Julie waved at the waiter. 'Gin and tonic, please. Hendrick's, if there's a choice.' As he disappeared again, Julie took in their surroundings. 'A stoner's paradise,' she said. 'Have you spoken to Mikhail?'

Kate took out her phone, checked the Wi-Fi hadn't hooked up to the hotel's system, then sent him a Signal message. *We're here.*

She got a reply straight away. *Good. Will let you know where to meet tomorrow 10 a.m. Be ready.*

Kate answered: *Would rather we set venue.*

But Mikhail was obdurate: *No, this is our backyard. Do as we ask.*

'I bet you a hundred quid he shags her on this trip,' Julie said.

'He's just trying to make you jealous.'

'That may have been his original intention, but he's loving the attention. He won't be able to resist. You know what it's like, the excitement of your first big foreign gig. She'll be all over him like a rash.'

'He's not that stupid.'

'He absolutely is and you of all people know it.'

Kate thought about having a word with Suzy and warning her off. But she actually felt a little sorry for both of them. Their loneliness was so transparent. 'Would you be upset?' she asked Julie.

'Not in the slightest.'

'Are you sure about that?'

'One hundred per cent certain. Every time I look at him, I feel a bit sick at what happened between us. I can't imagine what I was thinking.' She could see the scepticism in her friend's face. 'Genuinely, honestly.'

Kate was struck by her colleague's ability to cleave off a set of unwanted emotions. No wonder Ian was so shaken by it.

Ian and Suzy arrived together. Perhaps he'd continued his tour of Georgian history all the way to her room. Suzy had booked a restaurant a short walk from the hotel, and since it was still a balmy evening, they took a table just beyond the rose-covered pergola on the terrace. Ian demanded a menu in Georgian, rather than English, and ordered for all of them. The food – tender green beans with soft walnut paste, beetroot quenelle and lightly fried corn bread, a Georgian speciality – was better than the conversation. Ian marched on with his history lesson, gesturing wildly at the twinkling lights of the city beneath them. He'd arrived in 1990, the Service's first man in – 'an incredible opportunity for an ambitious young officer' – and he gave Suzy a blow-by-blow account of that era, from Gamsakhurdia's departure for Armenia and Chechnya to the long rule of Eduard Shevardnadze, Gorbachev's foreign minister, of whom Ian was an unreconstructed fan.

But just when Kate's thoughts had wandered inexorably back to Sergei's stricken face, Ian turned to her. 'Have you been in touch with our man?' He glanced around them to check they were not overheard.

'Yes. He's here.'

'What about his father?'

'I assume so, but I didn't ask.'

'Where are we going to meet?'

'He said he would set the venue, but to be ready to move at ten a.m.'

'No. I'm not having that. We'll set the meet point.'

'I tried to insist, but he said it was his backyard and they would pick the venue.'

'Then tell him different. We have the whip hand.'

Kate could tell Ian was trying to show off to Suzy, but she wasn't in a mood to indulge him. 'We have to be careful. We don't know what their agenda is, we don't know what they're dealing with from their side, and we don't know who else they have been talking to—'

'What do you mean?'

'If you were them, wouldn't you have cast the net wider than just us? If we delay, or prevaricate, or muck them about in any way, there's a chance they'll bolt and pull the lever somewhere else.'

'Doesn't that sound a lot like the operation that went so badly wrong in Berlin?'

'Yes, but we don't have a choice.'

'We're not the ones trying to escape a lifetime in a Russian prison, or worse. I'd feel a lot more comfortable if we were setting the parameters.' Ian shook his head to underline his disapproval. 'Have you discussed this with Danny?'

'Not yet. I was going to talk to him when we get back to the hotel.' Danny and his team were staying at the Marriott, just a short walk down Rustaveli Avenue. They'd come in via Istanbul earlier in the day.

'All right. Julie will go with you.' He was pointing at Kate. 'I want both surveillance teams deployed. I'll play quarterback.' Ian rolled up his sleeves. 'What about the plane?' It was directed at Suzy.

'It arrives the day after tomorrow. We've told the Tbilisi authorities we're picking up a film location crew. We've filed a flight plan direct to London for eight p.m., but we can change that. We can push back by about twenty-four hours, but after that we start to have issues with the pilot.'

'What have you told Sarah?'

This was directed at Julie, who had been instructed to liaise with Sarah Creaven, SIS's Tbilisi station chief. She left her reply just long enough to make her insolence felt. 'That we need to extract someone and it's conceivable there may be issues, but we didn't want to inform the Georgians and hoped it would pass off smoothly.'

'Did she guess?'

'I don't know. I didn't ask her.' Kate nudged Julie under the table.

'Does Mikhail know there's a time constraint on the plane?' Ian asked Kate.

'Not yet.'

'You should tell him.'

Kate wasn't enjoying being given direct instructions on what had been her show from start to finish. 'They're in a hurry to get to London. I don't think they need to be told that we're keen to get it over and done with too.'

Ian nodded. 'We're in good shape,' he said, then ordered more wine and embarked on a long soliloquy about how Georgians made theirs differently.

Kate took another double dose of zopiclone when she got back to her room in the hotel and undressed quickly. She asked herself when she would next dare to attempt to sleep without chemical assistance, but knew that this was neither the time nor the place.

Her head had been down barely five minutes when an argument broke out down the corridor. She heard Julie's voice and hauled herself out of bed to intervene.

Julie was in the doorway of her room, leaning against the frame in a black, see-through nightgown. Ian stood before her still fully clothed, part supplicant, part bull in a china shop. 'Ian!' Julie shouted.

He had his foot in the door. 'I just want to talk,' he pleaded.

'Hey,' Kate said. 'Come on . . .' It was like her friend to answer the door without bothering to put on a dressing-gown just to provoke him. She felt a flash of resentment at having to be the grown-up in this equation.

'I've told him a hundred times,' Julie said. 'He just won't listen.'

'We owe it to each other to talk,' Ian said, ignoring Kate entirely.

But Julie kept her eyes on her friend. 'You tell him!'

'Keep your voices down, both of you,' Kate said. 'This is not the time or the place—'

'Why does she answer the door like that, if not to make a point?'

'Ian,' Kate said. 'No woman is required to dress in one way or another when you bang on her door in the middle of the night.'

'It's only just past ten.'

'Go to your room.'

'After everything that has passed between us, it's just bizarre she won't agree to sit down and talk things through for a few—'

'What do you mean, "everything that has passed between us"?' Julie asked. 'You mean sex, normally in the missionary position, which is about as far as your imagination ever seems to stretch.'

'For God's sake . . .'

'Stop it, Julie.' There was steel in Kate's voice now. 'I mean it.'

'I'm going straight to HR when I get back from this trip. I've told him a hundred times I do not wish to talk to him about this ever again. I don't know what part of his tiny brain can't grasp—'

'You think I give a damn if you report me? You can stick a copy of your complaint in the post to King Charles Street and Downing Street as well for all I care! All I am asking for is a bit of respect. Like it or not, we have been in a relationship for more than a year and—'

'It was just fucking sex, Ian, and lousy sex at that.'

Ian looked as if he was about to explode. Or cry. Or both. But they were saved by Suzy's appearance. She'd taken off her make-up erratically and her cheeks were stained with mascara. 'Is everything all right?' she asked.

There was a brief silence, before Ian pulled himself together with lightning speed. Perhaps it was the potential loss of professional respect from the newcomer, or that he'd already identified her as his next conquest, but he managed a very quick turnaround. 'All fine. Still debating who sets the meet point tomorrow. I was uncomfortable with the way we left things, as you know, but . . . I can see we have no choice. Goodnight.'

He walked away, down the corridor. Suzy retreated in the opposite direction. 'He's a cunt and she's welcome to him,' Julie hissed, so that both of them could hear, before she closed the door without ceremony.

28

KATE AND JULIE sat on the plush velvet sofa in the Rooms Hotel reception area. 'You nervous?' Julie asked her.

'A bit.' And she was, too. But then, when had the stakes ever been higher?

Mikhail's text came in bang on time. Kate showed it to Julie and they left the hotel. 'The Peace Bridge,' she said quietly, into her lapel microphone. 'We'll walk.'

'Get a cab,' Ian barked. But she ignored him. She got a greater feel for things on foot. She offered Julie some chewing gum and they strolled down Rustaveli Avenue easily, past the buskers and the beggars, the restaurants open on to the street and the market stalls selling quite sophisticated tourist memorabilia. They took the underpass beneath Freedom Square, where Julie pointed out, with a smile, a shop selling handguns, and came up at the corner of the old town.

Julie had been in charge of mastering the topography, so Kate let her lead the way down towards the river. It was hard not to be impressed by the crumbling splendour of the centuries-old city that Ian had been so enthusiastically lecturing Suzy on. This section was like a microcosm of the country, with pockets of sophistication, style and wealth cheek by jowl with evidence of the neglect and decay of the Soviet years. Painted balconies on old houses, with delicate Moorish latticework, or Ottoman yoke arches, stood side by side with crumbling bricks and ugly Russian iron staircases.

It had started to rain, and as they reached the incongruous glass and metal Peace Bridge, they took shelter under a tumbling vine in a street full of boutique hotels, stores and restaurants aimed at Tbilisi's ever-expanding tourist trade. Julie lit a cigarette and shared it with Kate. They didn't need to tell their watchers where they were, or that the waiting was dragging out. Kate's phone buzzed. She glanced at it. *Walk away down Erekle II Street. Keep going.* She showed the message to Julie, who nodded. 'You need to look it up?' Kate asked. Julie shook her head.

They started moving again, walking across a car park, then beneath a line of cypress trees as they passed a section of the old city wall. This was the heart of the tourist old town, the houses newly painted and the restaurant tables sheltered beneath plants overhanging from shady terraces. They passed a church and found themselves in a square with Tbilisi's famous clock tower. Kate's phone throbbed again: *Go down to the river, get a taxi to the Dry Bridge.*

Kate called him via Signal. He answered immediately. 'I'm not doing this again,' she said.

'The Georgians have been watching me here in Tbilisi. I have to make sure they are not following you.'

Kate ended the call. 'Moving to the Dry Bridge,' she said quietly. Julie was still checking this on her phone as Kate was relaying the instruction to a taxi driver on the quay. He seemed to understand.

It was only a short journey and the taxi disgorged them into what looked like a flea market that stretched along the riverbank. Kate and Julie browsed the stalls in the morning sunshine. It was as if every citizen of the capital had assembled every piece of junk that had ever been in their possession to sell to tourists. There was a stall offering plugs, adaptors and every kind of electrical accessory, another selling old tools. An old man had a huge selection of knives laid out on a long table, a woman next to him a ten- or fifteen-feet-wide section selling old crockery. Behind them both was an old Lada so full of debris there was no possibility of even a cat squeezing inside it.

Kate and Julie kept walking. They found an old man

selling Soviet film posters, another offering medals and Soviet badges. Julie lingered on the posters. 'I love these,' she said.

A new black four-wheel-drive Toyota Land Cruiser roared up. Mikhail was in the passenger seat. 'Get in,' he said. 'Both of you.' They did as they were told. He leant behind him. 'Turn off your packs,' he said. 'They're going off grid, whoever is listening. We know where you are and we'll contact you when we are ready to leave.'

'We can't go off grid,' Kate said.

'It wasn't a suggestion. My father's order. I think you will concede he knows this part of the world better than any of you are ever going to.'

'Do *not* agree to go off grid,' Ian instructed in their earpieces.

'Now,' Mikhail said.

Kate glanced at Julie. She nodded and they both switched off their packs. 'And your phones.' They took them out and powered them off. Mikhail nodded with satisfaction and Kate couldn't quite suppress a moment's pleasure at the thought of Ian's reaction. 'Where are we going?' she asked Mikhail.

'Out of town. My father will cross the border tonight. We have a house nearby. You will meet him. In the morning, we will make the run for the airport.'

'How far out of town?'

'Not far.'

Mikhail nodded at the driver and he roared off again. They lapsed into silence as they spun past the hard evidence that this ancient city had not escaped the depredations of the Brezhnev-era central planners, with concrete housing, block after block, leavened only by the occasional splash of colour.

If the Soviet Union had succeeded only in making every one of its citizens poor, independence had clearly made a tiny number of Georgians rich. They passed a Porsche garage and one for Jaguar Land Rover, as well as a smart-looking shopping mall, with the French supermarket Carrefour advertising its wares with a giant sign on the roof, but the overall impression was of poverty and neglect.

Eventually the housing blocks petered out, to be replaced by shabby single-storey dwellings, and then they were out of the city altogether, following the foaming waters of the River Terek. 'How far are we going?' Kate asked.

'A few hours. Three, perhaps. It depends.'

'Where are we going?'

'Relax.' He turned and smiled at her. 'Have you ever been to the Caucasus?'

'We're not here to take in the sights.'

'I told you, these are our lands. We are safer here.'

But safer seemed a distant prospect. They were following the Georgian Military Highway, the long single-track road that had allowed the Russians to dominate this southern republic for two centuries. It was full of potholes and packed with lorries, all of which made glacial progress, so the driver felt compelled to dice with death at every turn in the long and winding road.

By the time they reached the Jvari Pass, the weather had closed in, reducing visibility to only forty or fifty yards in the sleeting rain. That didn't deter the driver from overtaking at will, so they were frequently forced to duck back in to avoid a lorry or truck coming the other way with only inches to spare. 'Does he always drive like this?' Kate muttered, but Mikhail did not answer and neither did Julie, who was gazing out of the window.

They passed the Gudauri ski resort, which looked like a drab construction site lost in the mist, and then the Russian-Georgian friendship mural at the highest point in the path, which had been made in 1983 to celebrate the long relationship between the two countries, and ignored by every Georgian since.

They started to descend again and it wasn't long before they broke through the dense cloud into a wide, lush valley. This was the landscape that had so inspired Russian writers from Lermontov and Tolstoy to Pushkin and Gorky: rich green valleys linking rugged mountains that reached for a dramatic cobalt sky.

The sun danced off a reservoir nearby, bringing an even greater majesty and grandeur to the landscape. Kate and Julie stared out in silence all the way down to the village of

Kazbegi, or Stepantsminda, as it had been renamed, which had the air of a modern-day Klondike, mining the new gold rush that was international tourism.

They swung off the main road, past guesthouses, cafés and tin-roofed shacks with market gardens, and roared on up the hill to a long wooden building that appeared to have been newly restored. 'Check in here,' Mikhail said, as they came to a halt at its entrance. 'I will pick you up later. Do not switch your phones on. I will find you.'

Kate and Julie got out and walked into one of the strangest places Kate had ever seen. It turned out to be the sister establishment to the Tbilisi hotel they'd stayed in, a former Intourist site that had been the subject of a dramatic makeover to turn it into a kind of Soho House in the Caucasus. Only the Intourist poster by the lift – *Welcome to the Soviet Union* – had survived its past, as the interior was an open, stylish expanse of wood and leather all the way up to the bar at the far end of the room. Large brass binoculars on stands by the floor-to-ceiling windows gave guests the chance to gaze up at the wonders of Mount Kazbegi, which towered high above its surroundings on the far side of the valley.

Kate and Julie agreed to share a room, but went straight out to order coffee on the wide wooden deck in front of the hotel. They sat in silence for a while, watching the clientele, who seemed to represent a rainbow coalition of different nationalities, from the blond Norwegian family sitting next to them to a large group of Chinese tourists and two Iranian women in the *niqab*. If Georgia had always been a melting pot, it seemed determined to turn that heritage into the widest possible flow of visitors and tourist dollars.

'Is it too early for cocktails?' Julie asked.

'Yes.'

They ordered Diet Coke and sat soaking up the sun. A crisp wind whipped away the last remnants of cloud to reveal the summit of Mount Kazbegi, the legendary heart of the Caucasus, to whose flanks Prometheus had allegedly been chained.

Gergeti Trinity Church, which sat atop the hill directly opposite, was bathed in sunlight, the landscape a riot of brilliant green meadow. 'This may very well be the most beautiful place I have ever been,' Julie said.

'It is awe-inspiring,' Kate agreed. They ordered food, which appeared promptly. 'You shouldn't provoke Ian,' she said.

'You're not my mother.' Julie was eating an enormous slice of traditional Georgian cheese bread, as if it was set to be her last meal on earth.

'No, but I am your boss.'

'I didn't ask him to come to my room in the middle of the night.'

'And you definitely shouldn't be answering your door in a see-through nightie.'

'If he's going to shag Suzy, I might as well remind him of what he's missing.'

'I thought you didn't care.'

'I don't.'

'Well, you sound as though you do.'

'No, I'm just being mean. Given what a twat he is, I'm entitled to punish him.'

'It's beneath you.'

'It so bloody isn't and you know it. Besides, wouldn't you relish the chance to rub Stuart's nose in it?'

Kate thought about this. The complexity of Julie's emotional landscape was a challenge much too far for Ian's schoolboy simplicity, though perhaps that had been why he'd fallen for her so hard. She could be quite cruel when she wanted to be, and Kate wondered if Danny knew what he was getting into.

She watched Julie finish off the last of the cheese bread. 'I need some pudding,' she said.

She ordered Soviet cake and Kate sat back, stared at the mountain and thought about what her friend had just said of Stuart. With the benefit of some distance – geographic and with the passage of time – she had started to regret her recent commitment to Stuart and the children. She was by no means convinced she wanted to give her marriage another try or would be able to. She thought of Ian's childish petulance last night, the plaintive cocktail of wounded ego and bruised pride. How was it so many men seemed not to have progressed beyond the emotional maturity of small boys? Were they just spoilt, mollycoddled, smothered?

She wondered if that was what she was doing to her own son. It was hard to imagine, since he rarely let her close enough to love, let alone smother him.

The Soviet cake came. It was a grey sponge made from condensed milk, so sweet Kate almost gagged. 'How can you possibly eat that?'

'It's delicious.' Julie wolfed it down.

After that Kate lay back in her chair, her face turned up to the sun. She was told to take her feet off the table by a waiter, who ignored the rowdy Georgian kids nearby, playing their music loudly on a portable speaker. 'Dick,' Julie said, as he departed.

Julie stared at the kids next to them with growing irritation. They looked like they were stoned or high, dancing around the table self-consciously. Kate made a mental guess as to how long her friend would last and had it right at about three minutes.

Julie marched over to them. 'You want to turn that off?'

They were startled to have been challenged so abruptly and they instantly complied, as meek as lambs. Julie was a formidable presence.

Kate sunbathed for about an hour. Julie grew bored and wandered off down to the town. Kate borrowed a swimming costume from the hotel and did some lengths in the basement pool. It had floor-to-ceiling windows, as if the hotel's designer had been determined that at no point should you be deprived of the magic of that view.

They met for drinks before dinner and Kate insisted they stick to Diet Coke. After dinner, they went back outside and wrapped themselves in rugs left out for the purpose. They gazed up at the stellar night sky, the snowy peak of Mount Kazbegi majestic, even luminous, in the crystal-clear air.

They had both dozed off when Mikhail shook them gently awake. 'Sorry, sleeping beauties,' he whispered softly. 'Time to go.'

29

AS FAR AS Kate could tell, there was no one behind them. But the driver gunned through the village of Stepantsminda, as if the entire Russian intelligence community was in hot pursuit.

They roared up the hill past Gergeti Trinity Church and on into the valley behind.

There was only one house here, a set of twinkling lights high up above Gergeti, in the lee of Mount Kazbegi. They pulled through a set of security gates that seemed spectacularly incongruous in the middle of nowhere and then Mikhail led them up the stairs to the terrace above.

The house was done up in a similar style to the hotel

opposite – a temple of oak, fur and glass – with a roaring fire on a giant raised hearth. A woman in a black skirt and white shirt hurried forward to offer them a drink in fluent English. They both declined. Mikhail warmed his backside against the fire. 'How was your day?' he asked Kate.

'Pleasant. It's quite a spot.'

'We used to come here a lot when I was a child.'

'When did you build the house?'

'Six years ago.'

They lapsed into silence. Mikhail appeared uncharacteristically nervous. Kate went out to the wooden deck and looked back towards the rear of Gergeti Trinity Church. Julie appeared beside her and offered her a cigarette. Kate couldn't resist. 'I'm definitely giving up when we get back.'

'Me too.'

'Mrs Henderson.' Kate spun around to see a bull of a man striding across the lounge towards her. He wore blue jeans, cowboy boots and a scuffed leather jacket. He looked like a tougher, fatter George W. Bush, his hair greying at the temples. He exuded purpose, confidence, as men in his position often did. 'Thank you for coming all this way.'

Igor Borodin had been such a remote and legendary figure in the shadowy world of espionage for so long that Kate was momentarily lost for words. Bright blue eyes scrutinized her with barely concealed curiosity. 'You'll need a drink,' he said.

'No, thank you.'

'It wasn't a suggestion.' He went to the table, poured four glasses of vodka and brought them on a tray towards them. They all dutifully toasted and drank. 'Welcome to the land of my forefathers,' he said. He returned to the fire. 'Sit,' he said. That wasn't a suggestion either. 'What happened in London?' he asked. It was directed at Kate. When she didn't answer immediately, he put a booted foot on the sofa next to him and leant on his knee. 'We are capable of reading the news.'

'The foreign secretary authorized this operation. Then someone leaked it.'

'Who?'

'We don't know yet.'

'And then?'

'The prime minister personally authorized that it should go ahead.'

Igor seemed surprised by that. He dropped down into the sofa, put his boot on to the long oak coffee-table and gazed into the fire. 'Why?'

'He'll find a way to take control of the authentication of the video and make sure it's pronounced a fake.'

'And what does that mean for my son and me?'

'Nothing. Your defection is an enormous coup for SIS in any event, so you will be safe. None of us can really be sure how the politics will play out in the end, but it won't make any difference to you.'

'If it is pronounced a fake, the pressure to send us back where we came from will be irresistible.'

Kate shook her head. Sometimes, even the most sophisticated of opponents were wont to underestimate the strictures of the Western democratic system, in which no amount of politics was permitted to overwhelm the law. 'You'll have the most expensive lawyers money can buy, which is saying something, and our courts will never send you back to Moscow.' She glanced at Mikhail. 'You know that.'

'The leak compromises the operation.'

'Strangely, it forces the prime minister into a position where he has to accept your defection.'

Igor turned to her. 'You were very foolish to seek out your friend Sergei Malinsky. The GRU has its own spies in London. They knew you were coming.'

'Who are their spies?'

'If I knew the GRU's secrets, I would not be sitting here.'

'How do you know I came to meet Sergei?'

'Everyone in Moscow is aware of it.'

'Why did they not kill me as well?'

'Because we protected you, for long enough to get you out of the country.' He gave her an icy smile. 'You are our passport to the West. We just did not expect you to do something so foolish.'

Kate avoided Julie's gaze. She stood, placed her glass carefully on the table. 'The plane will be ready to go at five p.m. tomorrow. I think we should leave here in the morning, so that we are ready just in case it comes in early. We have a secure room at the airport.'

Igor nodded. Now she came to think about it, he had all the warmth of a reptile. 'Mikhail will show you to your rooms,' he said.

Mikhail did so and bade them goodnight. Kate hadn't had time to sit on her bed before Julie burst through the door. 'When were you going to tell me about Sergei?'

Kate put her fingers to her lips, to indicate there was every chance the room was bugged, but Julie just shook her head in incredulity. 'You think it matters?'

'I didn't tell you because it would have served no purpose.'

Julie was genuinely furious. 'What happened?'

'I told you. I took the train with him to Moscow.'

'Yes, but you left a mildly important bit of the story out.'

'About halfway through the night, I went to the loo. When I came back, he was dead. They'd cut his throat. There wasn't much sign of a struggle, so I think it was someone he knew.'

'You think . . .' Julie pointed to indicate Igor.

'I don't know.' Kate sat on the bed, fatigue overwhelming her. 'That was why I called Stuart. I had to get out of there. But I have no idea who killed Sergei, or why they spared me and let me escape.'

'Maybe it was like he said. They were protecting you.'

'Who knows? Perhaps they saw me coming, just as they apparently did in Andros and Berlin. I've been over it a thousand times. I've looked through the files. Suzy is not wrong: the unanswered questions are legion. But that is in the nature of our business. What we don't understand will always be greater than what we do. There are many things we can't see and may never get to find out about. So, I've decided to concentrate only on the fundamentals before us.'

She stood up. 'This offer of defection is unrivalled. Why would Igor want to come to the West unless the story he tells is real and his offer of cooperation genuine? I've seen the video. They have promised evidence of the many payments. We have no choice but to proceed.'

'What do you mean – they saw you coming?'

Kate shook her head. 'I don't know if Stuart was Viper or not, or if he was, whether someone bigger and more important was left behind. He swore to me on our drive to St Petersburg that he never passed on any important operational details about my work.'

'And you believed him?'

Kate went to the window, pulled back the curtains and gazed up at the snowy peak of Mount Kazbegi. 'I don't know. I wanted to.'

'But he's lied to you and cheated on you before.'

'True, but he's desperate for reconciliation.'

'He says he is.'

'He's not a good actor.' Kate turned to face her friend again. 'Perhaps they've just found a way to track my movements that I have yet to work out. I don't know. We may never know. If you're asking me, I suspect Igor or some of his people were alerted to my presence in Russia, perhaps by someone at the border, and resolved to eliminate Sergei lest he undermine their story or spoil their plan to defect in any way. Nothing else makes sense to me.

'So, I return always to the same point. I think this offer to come over to us is real. The video looked credible. The politics of what happens after this may prove very complicated and, the way I feel, I might not want to be around to witness it. But that's a battle for another day.'

'What do you mean, you might not be around to witness it?'

'I have to sleep.'

'If you're resigning, so am I.'

Kate was already reaching for the zopiclone in her bag. Julie took the hint and withdrew.

Perhaps it was the purity of the mountain air, but Kate slept until about eight the following morning. There was no sign of Igor and Mikhail, so she helped herself to coffee and a croissant from the lavish breakfast laid out on the dining table and ate it on the terrace. After that, she left by a side gate and walked down to the Gergeti Trinity Church, which was thronged with tourists even at that time of the morning, the monks fussing around the under-dressed women, demanding they cover their legs and heads.

By the time she returned, Igor and Mikhail stood by the SUV, with Mikhail's wife and young son. Another was just pulling up behind it. 'We need to go,' Mikhail said.

'What's the rush?'

But he waved away the need for an answer. Julie came out, still eating her croissant, and they got into the back of the second SUV. 'What's going on?' Julie asked Kate, as the doors were closed on them. Kate shrugged.

They reversed out on to the gravel track beyond the gate, then followed Igor and Mikhail's lead towards the valley floor. The weather was better, but the return journey was no less terrifying. Soon enough, though, they were back on the course of the River Terek as it found its way down towards the capital, the dramatic mountain scenery replaced by dilapidated houses hidden behind the ash, poplar and sycamore trees that lined much of the road. It was just after midday as they passed through the city centre and, not long after that, pulled into the old Soviet-era terminal building that served as the waiting area for private flights. Ian and Suzy were already there and the former's smile at his capture of this huge intelligence fish, and the credit he would no doubt claim for it, could on its own have powered the plane.

After the introductions had been made, Igor retreated with his family to the far side of the room, pointedly indicating he had no desire to engage in small-talk.

Ian strode over to Kate. 'I told you not to go off grid.' She didn't bother to answer and she didn't need to, his excitement overriding any temptation for further recrimination. 'This is coming off like a dream,' he said. 'Any sign of problems?'

'Not yet.'

'Anyone on your tail?'

'He wanted to move earlier than we expected this morning, but I wouldn't read too much into that.'

'Excellent.' He looked at his prized catch. 'What a bloody coup,' he said softly to himself, barely hiding a note of self-congratulation. 'The plane is coming in early,' he said. 'Should be here any moment now.'

And so it was, landing in the distance and pulling up within fifty yards of the terminal entrance. There was no security, of course, their only brush with officialdom a tame Customs official, whom Sarah Creaven had brought to check their passports, including the fakes that had been supplied to Igor and his family.

Kate gossiped with Sarah, whom she'd worked with in Lahore for a while, and then they were all walking towards the plane. They climbed aboard, Ian dropping into the battered leather seat beside her. He glanced at their surroundings. 'Only the finest on Her Majesty's Secret Service,' he muttered, then peered out of the window to check that no one was steaming in to intercept them. 'Like bloody clockwork,' he said again.

Kate's phone buzzed. It was a WhatsApp message from Fiona. She opened it with a smile to find a video of her daughter. She put in her headphones, attached them to her phone and pressed play. Fiona was tied to a chair, with her brother, in some kind of warehouse, both stripped to their underwear. They looked terrified.

'Mum,' Fiona said, crying. 'They kidnapped us, blindfolded us, took us somewhere miles away . . .' Fiona glanced nervously off camera. 'They say they know what you're doing and if that plane takes off with the defeater . . .' another terrified glance '. . . the defectors aboard, then they'll behead us both. Please, Mum . . .' She and Gus started to weep. 'They'll let us go if you leave the defectors there in Georgia . . .'

The screen went black.

30

A MINUTE LATER, Kate stood opposite Ian on the tarmac, an afternoon breeze tugging at her hair. The engines were already running, so they'd had to walk away from the steps to be able to converse. And Ian was shaking his head. 'We can't,' he said.

The panic in Kate's chest was so intense she felt as if she were about to have a heart attack. Ian forestalled a tirade with a raised hand. 'We'll find them,' he said. 'We'll throw everything at it, but this operation is a matter of national security.'

'They have my children!' she shouted.

'And we'll stop at nothing to track them down.'

She gestured at the plane. 'We have to leave them here.'

'Kate—'

'For God's sake, Ian. The operation is compromised. Someone has told Moscow when, where and how we were intending to extract them. They are threatening to kill—'

'And we'll stop them before they have a chance even to think about doing that, but we have absolutely no indication your children will be any safer if we abandon this operation. In fact, the reverse may be true. We will immediately have lost any leverage.'

'We have to leave them!'

'Kate, just think about this for a moment. If we depart without them, whoever has your children will have no incentive whatsoever to keep them alive.'

'I'm calling Sir Alan.'

'No! Do *not* do that. I am in operational charge here and I expressly forbid—'

She walked away from him.

'Kate! I'm warning you!'

She pulled up Sir Alan's number and dialled. Ian tried to take her phone away and she rammed her shoulder into his chest. 'For God's sake!' he yelled.

Sir Alan answered. 'I'm making the assumption this is a matter of life and death.'

'They have Fiona and Gus. They've just sent me a video of them both stripped to their underwear and tied to chairs in what looks like a warehouse. Fiona says they'll be beheaded if we take off with Igor and Mikhail onboard.'

Sir Alan was silent for a moment. 'Is there any possibility the video they sent you was faked? Have you tried to get hold of either of them?'

Kate had not even considered this possibility. Her heart skipped a beat. 'No, I—'

'Have you told Ian?'

'Yes, he's here. He's trying to insist the operation goes ahead.'

'Establish your children are missing. If they are, you'll have to call the operation off. Tell Igor and Mikhail we'll come back for them. I'll call the ops room and press the emergency button.'

He rang off. Another call came in, this time from Fiona and Gus's school. 'Hello, Mrs Henderson. I do hope everything is all right. We're just checking why Fiona and Gus were both absent from school today.'

Kate didn't wait to hear what else she had to say. She called Rose. Her phone went straight to its message service. She tried the Finance Department.

'Celine Jones,' a woman said.

'Celine, it's Kate Henderson from the Russia desk here. Is Rose there?'

'No, Mrs Henderson, she is not. I was about to call you, actually, because I know she's been staying at your house this week. She hasn't come to work today and her mobile phone goes straight to answering machine. I was wondering if everything was all right.'

Kate ended the call. She turned to find Igor Borodin striding towards her. Ian tried to interrupt his progress, but Igor swatted him away as if he were an irritating distraction. 'What is going on, Mrs Henderson?'

'They have taken my children. They're threatening to behead them if we take off with you onboard.'

'My former colleagues will have subcontracted the work to Serbian or Albanian gangsters. As soon as they know in Moscow they have thwarted this defection, the gangsters will cover their tracks. The only chance your children have is to take us on that plane with you.'

'We'll come straight back for you.'

He glared at her. For the first time she thought that what she saw in those eyes was fear. 'If that plane takes off without us,' he said, 'we are dead. And so are your children.'

'I've told her the same thing,' Ian said, but Igor Borodin continued to ignore him, his gaze locked on Kate.

'I've spoken to the chief,' she said, as much to Ian as to Igor. 'I have the authority to make a decision. I can't take off with you onboard. If you can wait here in Tbilisi or close to the border, I give you my word we will return for you as soon as I know my children are safe.'

Igor took her arm, led her roughly away. Ian followed. 'Stay there!' Igor bellowed at him. He dragged Kate to the corner of the terminal building, so that they were out of earshot. 'Your children are safer with us onboard,' he said. 'Believe me.'

'I can't take that risk.'

'You have no choice.'

'I'm sorry. It's my call. You would do the same.'

Igor's gaze never left her face. 'Your prime minister works for us,' he said. 'I recruited him myself in Kosovo. If I don't get on that plane, you will never prove it and the truth will die with me here in the Caucasus.'

'I understand that.'

'You have a duty to your country to take us with you.'

Kate shook her head. 'Let me talk to Ian for—'

'No!' Igor gripped her arm furiously again. 'That joker. You want to know how we have been aware of your every move? The operation in Andros? Your deputy Rav on a plane to Geneva?' He gestured contemptuously at Ian, who was dancing from one foot to the other in a bid to contain himself. 'Because that useful idiot is so desperate to be C, he tells your prime minister everything and always has, even when he was foreign secretary. And what Ian told him, James Ryan passed on to us.' He shook his head. 'There was no other source, as you have been wondering, but just your superior's relentless ambition and loose tongue.'

Kate felt dazed. 'But I never told Ian I was coming to St Petersburg and—'

'Come on, Kate. Wake up! The GRU has known for a long time your Russian lover Sergei was leaking material.

It was all we could do to get you off that train in one piece. I saved your life. Now you must do the same for me and my family.'

Kate looked back at Ian. Of course. It explained so much. How could she not have imagined he would do anything – anything at all – to make it into Sir Alan's chair? 'I can't.'

Igor leant closer. His cheeks were bright red now. 'This is your last chance, or the truth dies with me.'

'I'm sorry. I can't.'

'You're a fool!' Igor spun away from her.

'Mr Borodin,' Ian pleaded, as he stormed off. 'I will call the prime minister . . .'

But Igor paid him no more attention. He stalked towards the plane and, moments later, he, Mikhail and the rest of their group hurried back towards the terminal. 'For God's sake, Kate,' Ian said. 'I need to speak to the PM. This is a catastrophe.'

Kate called Danny. 'I need you,' she said. 'We're in the private terminal.'

Kate climbed back onboard. She ignored Ian, who was in a state of advanced panic, swinging wildly between fury at her, feigned concern for her children and fear as to the impact of this debacle on his career.

Danny arrived and, from then on, Kate entered a narrow tunnel, the intense terror that gripped her giving everything she said and did vivid focus. They started by pulling up the CCTV all around her house in Battersea as the plane took off.

Danny broke into the closed-circuit system of the news-agent on the corner and they all watched as Rose, Fiona and Gus were bundled into a grey van. Julie and Ian – who had given up flapping around and was now sitting on the floor beside them, his own laptop open – started tracking its progress through the road and traffic cameras all over the country. Suzy spoke to the Metropolitan Police to enlist their support and kept an open line between their ops room and SIS headquarters in Vauxhall.

They called out its progress. 'Wood Green,' Julie said.

'Enfield,' Ian added. 'Now Harlow.'

'Stevenage,' Julie called back. 'Where the hell are they going?'

'Luton,' Ian answered. 'They're in Luton.'

Kate had her eyes fixed on Danny's laptop. He'd closed in on the men marching her children to the van in the dawn light. One had a snake tattooed on the back of his right hand.

So Danny was now working through all the databases at his disposal, from those at SIS to those kept by the Met, MI5 and the National Crime Agency. Only in the last did he get a match, and the file it connected them to made Kate want to throw up.

Arlind Sadiku, the man with the snake tattoo, was an Albanian gangster renowned for his control of the London cocaine trade and a penchant for extreme violence.

The last road camera the van had passed was on the way into Luton. The process of tracking it beyond that grew more complicated as Danny was forced to hop from one private CCTV system to another. Julie, Ian and Suzy joined him in the work and they eventually located the van in a car park outside a nondescript warehouse.

By now, the entire machinery and power of the British state were hurtling towards this small group of Albanian thugs. Sir Alan had been as good as his word and they were told that a team from Hereford was on standby.

Ian, who had picked up the role of point man inside the plane, wanted to know that he had Kate's authorization for the SAS to go in. She nodded. What choice did they have?

They waited. Ian and Danny tracked the progress of the rescue through the SIS ops room, which was taking a video feed from SAS headquarters in Hereford. 'Helicopters airborne,' Ian said.

'Three minutes,' Danny said.

And then they counted down. Two. One. Thirty seconds. Twenty. Ten.

'Roping down,' Ian said.

'Blowing doors,' Danny added, a few seconds later.

'Dogs in.'

There was silence. How long did it last? Ten seconds, twenty, a minute?

It felt as if it would never end.

And then, from Ian: 'No one there. Damn. They've flown. They've gone. Jesus. How did they get away?'

There was no time for recriminations or doubt. They returned to leapfrogging the CCTV systems. Somewhere, somehow, they'd missed something.

The plane eventually landed at Northolt. Danny and Kate were still gazing at his laptop as they boarded a helicopter on the tarmac, bound for a Cobra meeting in London.

It was MI5 who eventually found the missing link: CCTV footage from a dry cleaner revealed that, just by a roundabout, the gangsters had pulled over for a few seconds to perform a very slick changeover, switching their cargo – now prostrate in body bags – into the back of a lorry. 'They're dead,' Kate shouted, against the noise of the helicopter.

'Unconscious,' Danny said. 'They wouldn't move them any other way.'

They began the process of tracking them again, this time to an industrial park on the outskirts of Luton. It was Danny who got there first, just before they ran from the helicopter to a waiting car at Battersea heliport.

Danny got into the back beside Kate. Julie was in the front, Ian in a car behind with Suzy. 'We can't risk a rescue,' Danny whispered to Kate, as the car roared away.

She looked at him, confused.

'The moment they hear the rotors, they'll kill them.'

Kate's phone buzzed. She opened a video from Fiona's

WhatsApp account. It showed her daughter's terrified gaze for only a moment, before her face was pushed down. Someone held up a huge blade and began the process of beheading her.

Kate screamed, dropped the phone.

Danny picked it up. 'It's fake,' he yelled, above the sound of the rotors. He gripped Kate's shoulders, looked her in the eye. 'They're screwing with us. It's fake!'

'No . . . No . . .'

'Look at it. Look at the quality of the pictures. I told you! There's a weird sheen to those images.'

Kate could not bring herself to examine the footage. Julie turned. 'What about the sewers?' She put her computer on Danny's lap. On it was a planning application that detailed the sewage arrangements for a huge industrial park.

Danny nodded. 'They'll expect another airborne rescue. They probably left someone behind to see what happened at the place the other van went to.'

'I'll text Ian.'

Kate was too paralysed to think straight. 'I don't know . . .'

'It's the best way, Kate.' Julie turned to her again, vivid green eyes staring into Kate's own: firm, friendly, certain. She radiated steel and confidence. 'We have your back.'

They reached Whitehall and were whisked down the stairs towards the Cobra room in the Cabinet Office. But as they reached the last security barrier, Ian turned to her. 'You can't come in, Kate.'

'What do you mean?'

'They are your children. We can't allow you to be in the meeting.' His manner was kindly, reassuring. 'We'll do everything we can. Julie's idea is a good one. The director of Special Forces is looking into it right now.'

'No, I have to be in there—'

'You can't be. You know that.'

'But—'

'Please trust us.' Kate had never seen Ian like this before. There was a calm sincerity to his demeanour that was entirely surprising.

But still she rebelled against it. 'I can't just sit here.'

'We'll get the car to take you back to the office. Julie can go with you.'

'No, no—'

'Or we can drive you up to nearer the scene.'

'I'll stay here.' She nodded. 'Tell me as soon as you hear anything – anything at all.'

Ian squeezed her arm once more and handed his phone to the security guard, who checked his name against the list and allowed him through.

Kate leant against the wall and sank to the floor. She placed her head in her hands.

A few minutes later, she looked up to see the prime minister standing over her. 'Are you all right, Kate?'

She started to get up. 'Stay where you are,' he insisted, but she stood anyway. 'I'm so sorry,' he said. 'This is a bloody awful business. I just wanted to say we're doing everything we possibly can.'

'Thank you.'

'I know how terrifying it must be.'

'Yes.'

'Sir Alan, the Special Forces chaps, everyone is very confident, so I don't think there's anything to worry about. You know how good they all are.'

'Of course.'

There was an awkward silence. 'Look,' he said eventually. 'Why don't you come in? I know it's against all protocol, but, as prime minister, I can probably overrule that.'

The PM nodded at the guard, who let them both through the barrier.

Everyone was in the anteroom, grouped around a screen that carried the video feed from Hereford.

The lead soldier was charging the rear of a building. A man alongside him blew out the lock with a Hatton round, and then they were inside a cavernous warehouse, full of pallets stacked with cement and other building materials. Agitated warnings in Albanian bounced off the tin roof and echoed around the building. A man rounded the corner with an Uzi and was instantly silenced with two rounds from a Sig 556 high-velocity rifle.

They were into a corridor. Kate held her breath as the

lead soldier – with the camera on his head – passed one open door, then another.

They reached the last room. The soldier moved forward as he and the man next to him 'sliced the pie', covering the room in an arc with their weapons as they moved through the doorway.

Gus and Rose lay on the floor, bound and gagged but conscious, their faces frozen in a grimace of pure terror. But between Kate and her children stood a nervous young Albanian gangster, tattoos all over his arms, who was using Fiona as a human shield. The lead Special Forces soldier did not hesitate, delivering an instant double tap – two shots – through the lower jaw to the part of the brain that controls the spinal cord. The gangster dropped immediately.

And there, in the middle of the screen, was the face of her bound, gagged daughter, whose mouth was wide open in a silent scream.

Epilogue

IN OTHER CIRCUMSTANCES, Kate might have cracked a smile at the sheer irony of it.

How many weeks had it been since she had sat in that same corner office interviewing Suzy Spencer for the role as her deputy? Four? Five? And yet here she was being questioned in return, their roles – even their seats – neatly reversed.

Alongside Suzy loomed the tall, angular, lugubrious Shirley Grove, the cabinet secretary, a woman so devoid of charisma she might have merged with the wallpaper. Kate was learning too late that these were the most dangerous mandarins of all.

'So, if we could recap,' Grove said. 'In the beginning, you thought Sergei tipped you off about the original meeting on Igor's super-yacht out of . . . friendship?'

'Yes.'

'Though you considered it possible he was also acting on behalf of his bosses in the GRU?'

'That's correct.'

'As a result of a power-tussle at the heart of the Kremlin, as they tried to gain the upper hand on their rivals in the Foreign Service, the SVR?'

'Yes.'

'In other words, a win-win for Sergei. He pleased his bosses and the woman he loved?'

'Something like that.'

'You therefore thought the conversation you recorded on Igor's super-yacht genuine?'

'Yes, of course.'

'And that James Ryan was the Russian spy or agent of influence?'

'Yes.'

'So when you were later told that the GRU were coming out on top in this power struggle and that Igor wanted to defect, in return for bringing you hard evidence of the prime minister's treachery, that seemed perfectly credible?'

'Yes.' Kate wondered how long this history lesson was going to last.

'You were further convinced that Stuart was Viper, the agent mentioned in that original overheard conversation?'

'I don't think there's much doubt that Stuart was working for the Russians.'

Grove nodded. She turned the page, moving on. The issue of whether there was another Russian mole at the heart of Whitehall was a much more open question, of course, but Kate wasn't going to raise that now. Her priority was to get out of there fast, with the minimum chance of any recall.

'The foreign secretary was reluctant to accept Igor Borodin's defection at face value,' Grove went on. 'She wanted more evidence. That was why you went to St Petersburg and then Moscow in search of Sergei?'

'Yes.'

'He confirmed your supposition at the time, that Igor was losing the power struggle and needed to get out of Russia?'

'Yes.'

'And you believed Igor Borodin killed Sergei to prevent any potential interference with his planned defection?'

'Not immediately, but I came to that conclusion shortly after it went wrong.'

'Why?'

'It was the only explanation that made sense to me.'

'At the time.'

'At the time, yes.' Kate would dearly have loved to find a

way to make Igor pay for Sergei's murder. But it was too late for that.

Grove turned another page. 'When Mr Borodin told you on the tarmac at Tbilisi airport that the prime minister was definitely working for Moscow and that Ian had unwittingly passed on information to our enemies by keeping him informed at every turn, you believed that too *at the time*?'

'I did, yes.'

'So, in short, when you took off from Tbilisi, you were firmly of the view that the PM was a traitor and that Ian Granger was, at best, an indiscreet and ambitious fool who had unwittingly assisted him.'

Kate glanced out of the window at Ian, who was pacing the corridor. 'Yes.'

'You have not heard anything from Igor Borodin *since* that conversation on the tarmac?'

'No one has. Not us, not GCHQ. He and his family have vanished off the face of the earth.'

'Where *did* you think they had gone?'

'I assumed that, if the GRU had won the power struggle and he was caught in the act of defecting, he and his family were probably in a Siberian gulag or dead already.'

'I see,' Shirley Grove said, without emotion. She turned over another page and cleared her throat as she approached the climax of this charade. 'And yet you *now* say that everything you once believed in relation to this case was *wrong*?'

'That's correct.' Kate met her deputy's flinty glaze. How

slow she had been to realize that Suzy's true purpose – as instructed by Grove and her master, the prime minister, no doubt, and, of course, aided and abetted by Ian – had not in fact been to open up the Operation Sigma file but to find the means and the method to ensure it remained closed. *For ever.*

'So to be clear,' Grove went on, 'you are now saying it was a set-up, right from the start. A great big Fabergé egg of a fake. Far from being rivals, the GRU worked *with* the SVR to sell us – to sell *you* – the mother and father of all intelligence dummies. The prime minister was never working for the Russians, the sex video was a fake, Stuart was the only agent working in Whitehall – and he was easily expendable in the cause of creating terrible chaos, confusion and mistrust at the heart of our democratic system?'

It was a moment before Kate realized Grove was expecting an answer. She certainly was exacting her pound of flesh. 'Yes,' Kate said. 'Absolutely.'

If the price of escaping all this was to flip everything she really believed on its head, she might as well do it with conviction.

'Sergei was killed just in case he blurted out the real truth to you on the train – that you had been deceived and manipulated *right from the start*?'

'Yes,' Kate said again, with excessive conviction. 'That *is* correct.'

Grove tapped her pen on the file. 'A cynic might note, Mrs Henderson, that you have announced you wish to leave the service with immediate effect. This way, the case is conveniently closed. There will be no committee of inquiry, no torturous, complicated, draining search for the truth. Just closure. The prime minister recovers his reputation, the Service can move on and you . . . well, you walk away, with your reputation and references intact. Free as a bird, one might say.'

'I'm not a cynic,' Kate said. And when she realized that Grove had truly no sense of humour, she went on: 'Ian was right all along. It's not easy to admit that, but it's true.'

If nothing else, she thought, she was becoming a much better bloody liar.

'We shouldn't blame Kate in any way,' Suzy chipped in. 'It was all so plausible. Who wouldn't have jumped at such a sensational story? If true, it would have been the most amazing intelligence coup of the modern era, enough to make anyone's career.'

Kate didn't dignify this with an answer.

Grove leant forward, her reading glasses brushing against her clipboard. There were a lot of ticks on her checklist now. 'After all this,' she said, 'you suddenly wake up one day and decide that Ian Granger was right all along and that you *were* duped?'

'Yes.'

'You didn't meet anyone, see anyone, receive any new information before experiencing this Damascene conversion?'

'No, but when I had time to reflect, it was the only explanation that made sense.' She forced another smile. Given they all knew that Grove's sole aim here was to bury this file in the darkest recess of the Service's vaults, her show of probity was beginning to grate. 'You know as well as I do, Mrs Grove, that in our world we never get hard and fast answers. There is no black and white. When you have ruled out all other potential explanations, what remains is the truth, however unlikely. Upon reflection, I decided Ian had been right. I feel no shame in admitting it.'

'So you accept this matter is closed?'

'Absolutely.'

'Good. Good.' Grove nodded sagely. 'We appreciate your cooperation, Mrs Henderson. I know this has been a tough time for you.'

'And the prime minister.' Grove looked confused. 'I mean, to have been falsely accused in this way,' Kate said. She was laying it on really thick now, but why not? She might as well enjoy it.

She glanced up at the light above her, in which she suspected a microphone was hidden. Whoever was listening – MI5, certainly, perhaps even the prime minister himself – she hoped they appreciated the effort she was putting into her show of contrition.

'Yes, yes. Monstrous. Very difficult.' Grove stood. 'Thank you, Mrs Henderson.' She offered her hand. 'A relief to all of us, I'm sure, to have this matter finally resolved.'

Kate took the proffered hand. She even kissed Suzy, though she didn't grace Ian with an answer when he asked her in the corridor outside how it had gone. Let his ambition sweat a moment longer.

'Kate,' he said, as she turned her back on him. 'Thank you for your contribution.'

She faced him. 'To what?'

'This inquiry. And the Service, of course.'

'Is that some kind of joke?'

'No, no. I wanted to thank you for all you have done.'

Kate retrieved her bag and walked away, without bothering to offer him a reply.

She found Julie waiting for her by the lift. 'Don't,' Kate said, raising a hand to forestall any show of emotion, for which she no longer had the stomach.

'I'm not going to cry,' Julie replied. 'Not now, anyway.'

'One day soon we're going to meet up and get very, very pissed. And we're never going to talk about any of it again.'

'You did the right thing, Kate.'

'You don't think that. And I'm not convinced I do, either. So I need to get out of here before I change my mind.'

'I do think it, actually.'

Julie launched herself into Kate's arms. They held each other until Kate released herself and belted for the stairs before the emotion welling inside her could find expression. She was damned if she was going to be seen leaving the building for the last time in tears.

Sir Alan was at the last security barrier, readying himself to leave to get back to the hospital. Rose was beside him, her arm still in a sling from the kidnap. The doctors had made clear to all of them that the mental scars would take much longer to heal.

Rose touched Kate's shoulder in support. Sir Alan did not appear to know what he should do. 'I thought I'd better pipe you out,' he said.

'Off, I think.' He looked confused. 'Don't you pipe someone off? It's a naval term.'

'Yes, yes, perhaps so.' He stared at the floor. 'I'm sorry it had to end like this, Kate.'

'I'm not. I should have made this decision a long time ago.'

'Are you certain you're doing the right thing? I'm sure my successor—'

'Your *successor*?'

He glanced at Rose, as if it was a decision they had reached jointly. Not for the first time, Kate wondered just how far the friendship between her aunt and their superior extended. But she choked off the train of thought. Not her business. 'I've taken the decision to stand down,' Sir Alan said. 'The search for my replacement has already begun.'

For a moment, Kate was less sure of her own decision. Perhaps it was the old competitive spirit or, as she would have preferred to see it, her conscience. 'So Ian got what he wanted.'

Sir Alan glanced at Rose again. 'We can make sure there's a future for you here, Kate.'

She wavered for only a moment more. 'No,' she said firmly. 'To answer a question Stuart once asked of me, I don't think in the end it *is* possible to be a warrior for truth and the mother I'd like to be. And if I must choose, then I know what it has to be.'

Kate could have told Sir Alan – and, indeed, Rose – that an agreement to allow Stuart to come and go unhindered in continental Europe had been the explicit quid pro quo with Shirley Grove for lying through her teeth a few minutes ago or, as Grove herself had put it, 'telling the complete truth of the entire affair'. But they would, no doubt, have guessed as much.

Kate kissed Sir Alan. 'Bloody good luck, my friend,' he said.

She hugged her aunt, who whispered only, 'See you at home.'

She nodded at the security guard, who let her out of the building for the last time.

She swung right and headed westwards towards Battersea in the drizzle.

It was a gloomy night, but warmer than it looked, a close humidity wrapping the capital in its suffocating embrace. Kate shrugged off her coat, slipped it over her arm and glanced back at the organization to which she had devoted most of her adult life.

She walked on, faster and with greater purpose. Tonight, she had her own version of truth or, rather, of her role in this universe.

She was going home.

Where she belonged.

She picked up the pace and burst through the front door of the house to find Fiona and Gus waiting in the kitchen.

Kate took them in her arms, their warm hands wrapped tight around her. 'It's over,' she whispered. 'It's all over now.'

Acknowledgements

My primary thanks, as always, to my incredible wife, Claudia, my partner in life and work. I'd also like to thank my brilliant agent, Mark Lucas, and wonderful editor, Bill Scott-Kerr – and indeed Eloisa Clegg and all the fantastic team at Transworld. Thanks also to Rayhan Demytrie for her help in Tbilisi. And thanks to those in the Security Services who assisted but would prefer to remain 'in the background'.

Read on for an extract of the next book in the series

TRIPLE CROSS

Prologue

KATE HENDERSON WAS now certain.

She'd seen the clean-shaven man with faded jeans, olive T-shirt and fawn trainers whilst she waited in line at the butcher's shop on the square. And the woman with dark glasses, a lime sundress and what looked like a blue Chloé handbag had been paying for parking just in front of them when they arrived in the centre of town an hour ago.

Kate put down the giant aubergines she had been about to buy, nodded regretfully at the wizened Frenchman behind the trestle table and wandered nonchalantly back along the market stalls until she was standing beneath the entrance to the Grand Cathedral, the Église

Notre-Dame de Bergerac. She glanced up at the clock and weaved her way across the road and into the pedestrian zone beyond.

It was the kind of day the south of France was invented for, perhaps 23 or 24 degrees in the sun, and she was grateful for the patches of shade as she turned left and wandered along a side street, gazing unhurriedly into the shop windows. She went into a store selling the most expensive stationery she'd ever seen in her life and spent a few minutes trying out fountain pens at the counter.

When she emerged again, she did not look back and was careful to move with the same relaxed gait and rhythm. She walked on through a covered market, stopping to buy some pastries, finally returning to find her husband and children still at the table in the little square, lingering over the dregs of their coffee.

'Success?' Stuart asked, noticing that his wife was not carrying much in the way of groceries.

'Yes. We need to go.'

'Take a seat. I'll order you a café au lait.'

'We need to go now. Don't make a fuss. Don't argue. Don't look surprised or shocked. Just get up, go in and pay, and then we'll leave.'

They all looked at her, dumbfounded. 'What's going on, love?' Stuart asked.

She gave him a broad smile, turning her back to the cathedral, so that there was no chance any of her watchers could read her lips. 'Just do as I ask, Stuart. And please don't ask any more questions.'

All three of them looked like they wanted to argue with her, to fight against this intrusion of the past into their fragile idyll, but they knew better than to try. Fiona and Gus stood on either side of their mother as they waited for their father to pay.

'It's getting hot,' Kate said.

Neither answered.

'Even I might have a swim later,' Kate went on.

Stuart returned. 'Most expensive coffee in history,' he said easily. 'Almost as bad as bloody Venice.'

Kate smiled at him and they turned down the cobbled street in the direction of the quay and the river.

And now Kate spotted a third shadow; she'd seen the young woman with a nose piercing and Crocs at the fig stall at the market around the cathedral.

Or was she imagining things?

Kate moved faster. She took Fiona and Gus's hands and they held on to her willingly. 'Come on,' she said. She wanted to run, and started to pull both her children along.

'What is it?' Stuart whispered. 'What's spooked you?'

Kate shepherded them across the road that ran alongside the Dordogne River, sparkling now in the midday sun. The quay doubled as a car park. 'Get in,' she said, as they reached their rented Renault Clio. She took the keys from Stuart.

'You're not insured, love,' he said, but she ignored him. She slid in behind the wheel, pulled the driver's seat forward, glanced in the rear-view and side mirrors.

The man in the olive T-shirt was forty or fifty yards behind her, but moving fast.

'What the hell is going on?' Fiona's voice was shrill with fear.

Kate reversed steadily, ignoring her daughter. As she turned on to the road, she watched the man get into a black Volkswagen Golf with the girl with the pierced nose. 'Damn,' she said.

'What is it, Kate?' Stuart asked again as she spun around the corner, accelerated to the top of the slope and swung right on to the narrow old bridge that led away from the town.

'I don't know yet.'

'Are we being followed?'

'I think so.' She glanced in the rear-view mirror at the Golf on their tail. 'Yes, we are.'

'Why?' Fiona asked, trying to keep the fear from her voice now – and failing.

'Please, just give me a minute. I need to work out what's going on here.'

Kate weaved her way through the tiny hamlet across the bridge and then accelerated up towards the cemetery. She barely touched the brakes at the crossroads, prompting Fiona to squeal in terror, and then hammered up the hill towards the vineyards that criss-crossed the slopes beneath the grand château of Monbazillac.

She was touching 120 kilometres an hour on the straight section of the narrow road, and was still at sixty or more in the tight chicane beneath the village, but the Golf stayed with her. As they passed the château, Gus turned and looked back down the hill. 'They're still behind us, Mum!'

'It's all right,' Stuart said calmly. 'Your mother knows what she's doing.'

Does she? Kate thought. *It's starting to feel like a really long time since I knew what I was doing.*

She slowed to a crawl through the next village, past the pretty church, the elaborate new town hall and what looked like a wine-shop-cum-restaurant. And then she floored the pedal on the long, gentle slope beyond it.

Halfway down through the vineyards, the speedometer nudged 140. She hit the next set of tight turns a shade more slowly, but it was all she could do to keep the Clio on the road. Fiona screamed. Gus's knuckles whitened as he clutched the grab handle just below the roof. Even Stuart's face was starting to drain of colour.

As she rounded the final corner, Kate yanked the wheel left. The Renault shot up a gravel track and flew off the crest of the hill. Kate hit the brakes as it landed and skidded to a halt beneath a copse of trees.

The Renault's dust cloud drifted away into the wood as they waited. Kate's heart hammered in her chest.

They listened.

The Golf had roared into sight on the road below them, slowed for the curves and then accelerated again as it emerged into the valley.

Kate finally exhaled.

'Fucking hell,' Fiona said. 'You nearly killed us.'

'Jesus, Mum,' Gus added. 'You are the man.'

'Woman, I think you mean,' Stuart corrected. 'And yes, your Mum does know how to look after us.'

Kate had closed her eyes. She would not, could not, go through all this again.

Chapter One

KATE KNEW SHE was in trouble from the expressions of delight she was currently witnessing on her children's faces. No matter how often she'd repeated on the plane on their way to Bergerac that this trip did not imply any kind of formal rapprochement with their father, they were now listening spellbound to his endless reminiscences about happy times in their past.

'You totally owned him!' Gus said.

'The look on his face!' Fiona added.

The story in question concerned an argument at a ski lift in Les Arcs a few years previously, triggered by Gus's irrepressible determination to jump the queue. Stuart had faced up to an aggrieved middle-aged Frenchman with such force that the man had immediately backed down. Kate hadn't much cared for the incident in the first place, and the story didn't improve with the telling.

But she didn't interrupt. The meal had already proved to be a minor miracle and she saw no good reason to burst its fragile bubble. Fiona had eaten everything put in front of her without even being prompted. Gus was more garrulous than she'd seen him for some time. He'd taken the opposite route to his sister – his pallid cheeks were fleshy from too much comfort eating, the impression of teenage puppy fat accentuated by the terrible helmet haircut he'd allowed his sister to inflict upon him. But his face was currently transformed by laughter. So too was Fiona's. For a moment, Kate was able to forget the stark angularity of her daughter's cheeks, which betrayed the seriousness of her growing mental disorder.

After the car chase that morning, they had seen no further sign of their pursuers. Aside from a brief conversation back at the rented farmhouse, when Kate had said she couldn't think of any reason why anyone should be following them, they'd all appeared to push it to the back of their minds, perhaps because the fear of slipping back into the past was too much for any of them to deal with.

But Kate remained firmly on guard.

She tried to relax as she witnessed the pleasure her family took in each other's company. She didn't like Stuart's goatee beard, nor his attempt to relive his youth in tight T-shirt and jeans – he had clearly been working out, if nothing else, while exiled in Moscow – but even she had found herself laughing at some of his appallingly unfunny jokes, and his determination to be on good form was infectious. She realized she felt better than she had done in months.

She could see, though, that both Fiona and Gus saw this day as a curtain raiser on a longed-for reunion between their parents that must surely now be imminent. And Kate already dreaded the journey home, when she would have to explain once again that their father's betrayal of his family and his country still made the chance of any kind of reconciliation remote.

Kate reached for the bill. Stuart, once so quick to take responsibility for paying for everything – their marriage had been curiously old-fashioned in that respect – looked sheepish. They both knew he didn't have the means to pay for anything at all, these days. Kate was coughing up for the farmhouse, too.

'Thanks so much, love,' he murmured.

'It's a pleasure,' she said, with as much sincerity as she could muster.

They piled out of the restaurant and into the car. Kate let Gus sit in front beside his father, who shouldn't really have been in the driver's seat. But drink-driving was perhaps the least of their problems. She tried to keep her quick scan of the car park discreet. There was no sign of the black Golf – or any other vehicle that might reasonably be ready to follow them.

'Cool place,' Gus said.

'Nice food,' Fiona added, without catching her mother's eye.

'Would we be able to go to school here?' Gus asked.

'Depends if you want to start speaking French,' Stuart said. 'Though I guess it would help in the next lift queue bust-up.'

'They have international schools, don't they?' Fiona asked.

'I think they possibly do in Bordeaux. I haven't looked into it yet, but I will.'

Stuart glanced over his shoulder. Perhaps he was looking for some sign of approval from his wife. Kate kept her counsel. She was very far from ready to contemplate moving here to begin life again with her former husband. Conversation dwindled inside the car, until it was drowned out entirely by the steady hum of cicadas through the open windows.

They turned right past the sandstone church and wound their way through the village to a bumpy track that led through a coppice to the farmhouse, hidden away in the fold of the valley and surrounded by its own vineyard.

Kate had stepped out of the car and was halfway to the

front door when she noticed the dark Range Rover parked in the corner of the drive next to the swimming pool. 'Get into the house,' she said to the others.

'Love, I'll check—'

'Take the children inside, Stuart.'

As Kate walked towards the car, two of its occupants climbed out of the rear. She was momentarily dumbfounded to be confronted by the Prime Minister of the United Kingdom, James Ryan, and his Cabinet Secretary, Shirley Grove.

'Kate Henderson, as I live and breathe,' the PM said. He'd put on weight again and looked older. His cheeks were puffed and saggy. He had his hands thrust deep in his pockets and a curious half smirk, like a schoolboy caught stealing from the local sweet shop. It was his political stock in trade.

'Good evening, Mrs Henderson,' Grove added.

'What are you doing here?'

'Good question,' the PM said. 'On the money, as always. Can we talk somewhere? Can't be overheard by your husband, I'm afraid.'

Kate barely hesitated. 'No. We can't. I'd be grateful if you could leave.'

'We've come a long way, Kate.'

'I don't care how far you've come. I've retired. Mrs Grove here made me a promise to that effect.'

'Indeed she did, and she meant it, I'm sure. But events

have a habit of upsetting the best-laid plans, as you very well know.'

'That's not my problem any more.'

'I'm afraid what we have to tell you may encourage you to change your mind.'

'I don't want to hear it.' Kate began to turn away, in no doubt that she really, really didn't. Not this time.

'You don't have a choice, Kate, because *not* listening to what we came here to say could prove injurious to both you and your family.' The Prime Minister gave a barely discernible nod towards the house.

'Is that a threat?'

'A fact, I'm sorry to say.'

'Was it your people following me this lunchtime?'

'An Army surveillance team. We just needed to be sure you didn't have any troublesome company.'

'Why the Army?'

'It'll make sense if you let me explain.'

'Just hear us out, Mrs Henderson,' Grove said. A thumb scratching at the edge of her woollen cardigan belied her calm, even impassive demeanour.

'Wait a minute,' Kate said. She went into the house, where Stuart and the children were sitting anxiously around the kitchen table. 'It's the Prime Minister.'

'What? What is it?' Stuart asked. 'What do they want?' He wasn't doing a good job of hiding his nerves.

'I've got to hear him out. Probably just something from

the old days they need help or advice on. I'll be back in half an hour. Don't wait up for me.'

'You said you wouldn't do this any more, that it was over,' Fiona said. She stood up and backed towards the cooker, as if preparing for a confrontation.

'And I have no intention of breaking that promise.'

'Who was following us this morning?'

'That's what I intend to find out.'

Kate left before they could ask any more questions.

'There's a bar in the village,' she told the Prime Minister, before squeezing awkwardly on to the back seat between him and Grove. The PM's personal protection officers were in the front.

They took a corner table in the empty bar, where the bearded, world-weary patron looked irritated to have business at this late hour. They ordered a bottle of rosé and the PM waited until the patron was out of earshot before he began. 'Look, I know what you'll be thinking.'

'It's not a classic opening gambit.'

He smiled grimly. 'I read your extracts in the inquiry report completed before you left MI6, and I know you didn't believe a word you were saying.'

Kate frowned. What the hell was this? 'So you've come all this way to accuse me of lying to exonerate you?'

'Just hold your horses a minute and hear me out.'

The anxiety that Kate had spent the months since she'd left MI6 carefully suppressing tightened her chest and stomach again; the pit of dread, as she had come to know it during her time in government service. 'I don't want to go over this again. And I don't have to. I am no longer in your employment.'

'The man who started this great intelligence juggernaut rolling was a friend from your time studying in St Petersburg.'

Kate stared at him for a moment, then got up. 'I'm really not doing this again. Enjoy your wine.'

'Wait!' He leapt to his feet, his face creased with worry, a far cry from the public-school smooth-talker she'd found so easy to dismiss. 'Please, Kate . . .'

If he was faking his own concern, he was doing it unbelievably well. She sat down again slowly. 'You have five minutes.'

'We've been left with no choice but to go over old ground with new eyes.'

Kate did not answer.

He took her silence as leave to continue. 'All right. This chap Sergei was a friend from your time as a student in St Petersburg, correct?'

'It's in the file.'

'He ended up in London and it was clear to you that he was working for one of the Russian intelligence agencies?'

'Yes.'

'Who knew of your prior friendship with him? I mean, within MI6?'

Kate shook her head. She couldn't see the relevance of the question. 'Anyone on the top floor would have had access to my vetting files. It's in there somewhere. We have to declare any significant friendships prior to joining the Service, and I did so.'

The Prime Minister glanced at Shirley Grove, who had aged visibly since Kate had last seen her. The lines around her eyes were thick with accumulated fatigue of the kind Kate had once known all too well. She gripped her reading glasses in her right fist, as if about to use them as a weapon.

'The original tip-off that Russia's intelligence elite was in the habit of meeting on this super-yacht in the Med in the summer came only from this chap Sergei, your friend?'

'Correct.'

'So you set up the operation to bug it. And you immediately struck intelligence gold. You overheard them discussing the fact that the last poor bloody PM had prostate cancer and was about to resign and that a candidate to replace him was obviously working for Moscow. Since I was the front-runner, you assumed it must be me?' He scratched his rangy, unkempt mane of thick, dark hair. How she longed to set about him with a brush. 'Bingo, I can see that,' he went on. 'But did it ever occur to you that it was all a bit convenient, and that it might be a set-up to cause chaos in the West?'

'Oh my God.' Kate was angry now. She pointed at Grove.

'I gave her all this. I gave you everything you wanted. I completely cleared you in that damned inquiry report before I left SIS. I said I admitted it was all a set-up from the start and I had been played by Sergei—'

'But you didn't mean a word of it.'

Kate stared at him. What *was* all this about?

'I'm not interested in some crap inquiry,' the Prime Minister went on. He leaned forward, his anger matching her own. Even in this low light, his eyes were a deep, vivid blue. She had the briefest sense of why so many women had lost their heads to him. 'I travelled all the way down here to find out what you *really* thought.'

She held his gaze for a moment more. Was this just another trap? 'Yes, it occurred to me that the tip-off was convenient, but I trusted Sergei. I'd known him a long time. I just didn't think he'd lie to me.'

'And, let's face it,' replied the PM, 'it doesn't take a huge leap of imagination to assume that any one of the skeletons in my closet could have been used to blackmail me into working for Moscow.'

'I never said that.'

'But you'd only have been human if you thought it. So when you're told that a Russian defector has all the hard evidence to prove your theory, of course you jump at it. And, as I understand, the video of me apparently having sex with under-aged girls in Kosovo looked entirely authentic and convincing.'

'I was certain it was you in the footage, yes.'

The PM didn't flinch, his gaze still locked upon her. 'I'll tell you something, Kate. I may be many things – and part of my peculiar appeal appears to stem from my ability to admit to them, more or less – but I am *not* a paedophile. Nor have I ever paid a woman of any age for sex.' The hint of a smirk as he reached for his wine glass suggested that he still believed he didn't need to, but Kate didn't allow herself to react.

'Look,' she said, wanting to be away from here now. 'I have been through this over and over again. I gave Mrs Grove everything she needed to show it had been a set-up when I left MI6. You were completely cleared. I left in disgrace, effectively. And the quid pro quo was that I was going to be allowed to get on with my life.'

'And to meet up with your husband here in Europe,' Grove said tersely. 'An agreement we have adhered to, despite the fact that the one thing no one disputes in this whole sorry affair is that he was working for the Russians and should rightly be rotting in a British jail.'

Kate didn't dignify this with an answer. 'Just tell me what you came for.'

The PM glanced at Grove again. He took another sip of his wine and Kate joined him. She had the sense that she was going to need fortification tonight. He put his elbows on the table and leaned forward, as if to impart a confidence. 'There is a mid-ranking diplomat in our embassy in

Istanbul called Tessa Winkelman. She is not one of your former colleagues, as I understand it?'

Kate shook her head. 'Not as far as I know, but it's a big organization.'

'As part of her work, she is our representative on a body called International Women in Business, which is a Turkish government quango of some kind. One of the other members she has got to know is the Russian rep, who appears to be another mid-ranking diplomat called Natasha Demidov.'

'Demidova,' Grove corrected.

'Exactly,' he said. 'The women attended a conference up in Ankara and some drink was taken. In her cups, this girl told a very strange story. She said she was in fact a senior officer in the SVR and had originally been sent to Istanbul tasked with seducing an agent in the rival service, their military intelligence agency, the GRU. His name was Sergei Malinsky. And the purpose of the seduction was to feed him the information that would set up the greatest hoax in intelligence history – that the British Prime Minister was really a Russian spy. But it had all gone too far, she said. Sergei had died very suddenly on a train between St Petersburg and Moscow, apparently of a heart attack, though she said he had always been in extremely good health. Is this ringing any bells, Kate?'

Both the PM and Grove had their gaze fixed firmly on her now, but she didn't blink. If they were looking for a reaction, she was determined they weren't going to get one.

'The last thing Miss Demidov—'

'Demidova,' Grove corrected again.

The PM shot her an irritated glance before he continued. 'The last thing she said before disappearing into the Istanbul night was that Tessa needed to get this information directly to me. On no account could it go through MI6, she repeated. Tessa naturally asked why not. Because, Demidova said, there was an informant in Vauxhall. Agent Dante, the most senior traitor the Russian state apparatus had ever possessed in the UK, someone at the *very* top of the service, a man who all roads led through, a mastermind who had helped plan this entire operation with the former head of the SVR, Igor Borodin, and his successor, Vasily Durov. If this information went into MI6, she said, she would meet the same end as Sergei.'

The sound of cicadas through the open window was suddenly deafening.

'You appear to have gone very silent,' the PM said.

COMING 2021

SHADOW DANCER

Tom Bradby

Colette McVeigh: widow . . . mother . . . terrorist. A woman who has lived the Republican cause for all of her twenty-nine years. A woman whose brothers are both heavily involved at senior levels in the IRA, whose husband was killed by the British security forces. A woman who is now an informer for MI5.

Apprehended by the police in an aborted bombing attempt in London, Colette is given two choices: talk and see her children again or stay silent and spend the rest of her life watching them grow up from behind bars. But as Colette put herself in increasing danger to keep her side of the bargain, her handler at MI5 realizes his professional integrity has been fatally compromised . . .

'Taut, purposeful and above all else human . . . a compelling story of love and torn loyalties . . . Exceptional'
Daily Telegraph

'The best book on the northern conflict since *Harry's Game* . . . An excellent read on any level'
Irish Independent

THE SLEEP OF THE DEAD

Tom Bradby

The brutal murder of a local woman and the disappearance of her six-year-old daughter shattered the rural serenity of Julia Havilland's childhood. Soon followed by Julia's father sacrificing himself on a Falkland hillside in an act of characteristic yet baffling heroism, she has many childhood scars that resolutely refuse to heal. So when Julia returns home from China fifteen years later, it is to a place of ghosts.

Whilst she awaits the outcome of the enquiry that seems destined to end her short but spectacular career in military intelligence, Julia is drawn back across the landscape of the past, confronted by demons she has spent her life running from. Her very survival counts on it for there have been more deaths since she left, and the dead will not sleep . . .

'Confirms Bradby's considerable promise as a thriller writer'
Daily Mail

'Intriguing and emotive, this is a slow builder that proves to be well worth the wait'
The Mirror

THE MASTER OF RAIN

Tom Bradby

Shanghai. 1926. Exotic, sexually liberated and pulsing with life, it is a place and a time where anything seems possible. For policeman Richard Field, it represents a brave new world in which his past can be forgotten. His first moment of active duty is the brutal and sadistic murder of a young White Russian woman, Lena Orlov.

With the International police force crippled by rivalries, it is soon clear that Field must make his own way through the investigation. And in a city where reality is a dangerous luxury, Field is driven into the darkness beyond the dazzle of society, in to a world where everything has its price and the truth seems certain to be a fatal commodity . . .

'Nigh on impossible to put down . . .
[An] intelligent thriller'
Time Out

'Rich, dark, atmospheric, this fine novel captures time and place perfectly. A great crime story that ends up in a place you won't predict'
Lee Child

THE WHITE RUSSIAN

Tom Bradby

St Petersburg 1917. The capital of the glittering Empire of the Tsars and a city on the brink of revolution, where the jackals of the Secret Police intrigue for their own survival as their aristocratic masters indulge in one last, desperate round of hedonism.

For Sandro Ruzsky, Chief Investigator of the city police, even this decaying world provides the opportunity for a new beginning. Banished to Siberia for four years for pursuing a case his superiors would rather he'd quietly buried, Ruzsky finds himself investigating the murder of a young couple out on the ice of the frozen river Neva.

Pitted against a ruthless murderer who relishes taunting him, Ruzsky must face his own past as he fights to save everything he cares for, before the world around him goes up in flames . . .

'Unfailingly evocative . . . Reminiscent of *Gorky Park*'
The Times

'Intrigue of the highest order . . . sad, atmospheric and richly entertaining'
Washington Post

BLOOD MONEY

Tom Bradby

New York 1929. The Wall Street Crash.

Rookie cop Joe Quinn has been given a shot at the NYPD's main headquarters squad. His first case could put his name up in lights: a banker has taken a dive from a tall building onto Wall Street. Pretty soon, the dead man has company – a group of old buddies is being eliminated, one by one.

For the young detective a case that starts as an opportunity swiftly becomes a nightmare. An increasingly complex trail leads further and further into the upper echelons of the police force and towards his own father, once New York's foremost celebrity cop. And at the heart of the investigation lies a woman whose love he has fought to deny for many years.

'The smoky romantic notion of speakeasies and Irish beat cops . . . is captured beautifully'
News of the World

'This feisty, pacey thriller has it all – nervy gangsters, crooked politicians, gutsy cops . . . A top-notch piece of crime writing'
Press Association

THE GOD OF CHAOS

Tom Bradby

1942. The Nazi hammer is about to fall on the beleaguered city of Cairo. As tension mounts, a key British officer is found viciously murdered. Nobody can fathom the motives behind the killing, and it is certainly the wrong time to start asking questions.

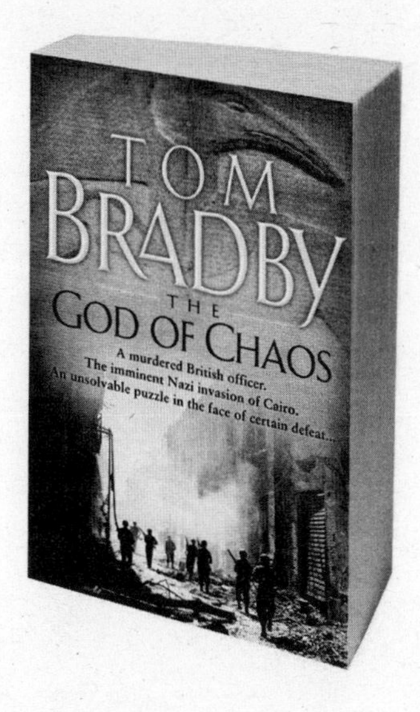

Former New York cop Joe Quinn is a maverick whose methods run against the grain of the British military police.

Tasked with uncovering the truth of the Cairo murder, despite the circumstances, Joe has a lot to prove and not much time to do it in. And it's clear that the closer he gets to the truth, the more danger he's in . . .

'Bradby has the talent of a reporter but the heart of a storyteller'
Daily Mail

'The kind of historical fiction that may send you back to the real history books to learn more'
Washington Post